"Dees brings readers into an action-packed world with superhuman operatives. . . . This is a book you can't put down." —*RT Book Reviews* on *Flash of Death*

"There's action and hot attraction galore in this addition to the Love in 60 Seconds series. Dees does a terrific job of advancing the overall series while lending her unique talent to her vibrant individual contribution."
—*RT Book Reviews* on *The 9-Month Bodyguard*

"Dees's exciting, action-packed story speeds along on all cylinders with a smoking-hot pair at the center of it all. Your fingers will get exercise as they rapidly turn the pages of this compulsively readable tale."
—*RT Book Reviews* on *Night Rescuer*

"A solid, suspenseful plot, tormented, vulnerable characters, and beautiful, compelling writing will keep you turning the pages."
—*RT Book Reviews* on *Deadly Sight*

"Dees blends action and intrigue in this character-driven romance with deft skill, keeping readers enthralled until the final secret is unveiled and the last chase winds down." —*RT Book Reviews* on *Close Pursuit*

THE
SLEEPING
KING

CINDY DEES
AND
BILL FLIPPIN

A TOM DOHERTY ASSOCIATES BOOK
NEW YORK

This is a work of fiction. All of the characters, organizations, and events portrayed in this novel are either products of the authors' imaginations or are used fictitiously.

THE SLEEPING KING

Copyright © 2015 by Cindy Dees and Bill Flippin

All rights reserved.

A Tor Book
Published by Tom Doherty Associates, LLC
175 Fifth Avenue
New York, NY 10010

www.tor-forge.com

Tor® is a registered trademark of Tom Doherty Associates, LLC.

ISBN 978-0-7653-7030-3

Our books may be purchased in bulk for promotional, educational, or business use. Please contact your local bookseller or the Macmillan Corporate and Premium Sales Department at 1-800-221-7945, extension 5442, or by e-mail at MacmillanSpecialMarkets@macmillan.com.

First Edition: September 2015
First Mass Market Edition: August 2016

Printed in the United States of America

0 9 8 7 6 5 4 3 2 1

This book is first and foremost a gift to our families, friends, the many players who helped create and populate the Dragon Crest Universe, and to three extraordinary women, without whom this project would never have happened: Pattie Steele-Perkins, Linda Quinton, and Claire Eddy. Thank you, and lay on!

ACKNOWLEDGMENTS

The Dragon Crest project is a collaboration of literally hundreds of creative minds over a thirty-year period. From epic battles to gypsy parties, the world of Urth would be a less-rich place by far without each and every player who has dressed up in period garb, ran around in the woods, believed in the vision, and woven their own thread into the great tapestry of the world. It is not possible to name each and every one of you here, but you know who you are. Pour us an ale, and find us a quest; we'll meet you in the fields and give it our best. Let the adventure continue. . . .

THE
SLEEPING
KING

Anton Horatio Constantine fidgeted anxiously in the solid gold doorway behind an Imperial secretary, who announced in the flat intonation of a deaf man, "Anton Constantine."

Insolent bastard didn't even announce his full name. As if he were a lowly servant himself.

"Bid him enter, already!" a male voice snapped.

Anton recognized the irritable tones of his mentor and sponsor at court, Archduke Ammertus, whose coattails he'd been shamelessly riding in the Imperial Seat. The archduke was not only an angry man, but also an ambitious one. The kind who would aggressively place his favored servitors in critical positions of power. Anton had parlayed his service in Ammertus's Dread legion into continued service at court in hopes of becoming one of those favored ones.

His own relentless lust for power flared and he quickly tamped it down. With downcast eyes, he glided into His Resplendent Majesty, Maximillian the Third, Emperor of the Eternal Empire of Koth's private receiving chamber. It was a much smaller version of the Great Golden Throne Room, but still fabulously opulent in its own right.

The floor was made of solid gold, as were the jewel-inlaid golden walls and ceilings. Even the line of servants off to the left were beautiful and perfect, as still as statues, deaf one and all.

The display of raw wealth was such that Anton felt faintly ill with envy. He could swear the green serpent tattoo on his forehead actually burned with jealousy.

"Come closer, Constantine." The resonant, terrifying voice of the Emperor emanated from the black throne at the far side of the room.

Shock slammed into Anton. Maximillian himself was present at this meeting? What could it mean? Terror and avid excitement warred like serpents knotted in his stomach. Hastily Anton knelt and made his obeisance at the foot of a magnificent gold dais leading up to the sinuous carved obsidian throne in the shape of a flame.

He held his forehead to the floor until Ammertus cleared his throat and intoned, "Rise and bask in the glory of Koth, Constantine."

Anton rose and assumed a ramrod-stiff position of attention before his ancient benefactor, an ageless warrior of a man with a thick, messy head of red hair. The archduke stood to the right and one step down from the Emperor in the position of the Emperor's champion. Ammertus's son and demiscion, High Lord Tyviden Starfire, stood at his father's right hand one more step down. Only slightly less violent and twisted than his sire, Starfire was possibly more ambitious even than Anton.

To the Emperor's left stood his chief advisor, High Perceptor Iolanthe, mother of Maximillian's daughter and heir, High Princess Endellian. One step below her stood High Marshal Korovo. Ammertus stood as representative of the Emperor's nine archdukes and duchesses, while Iolanthe and Korovo served as his personal advisors. What topic could possibly draw so many of such power to this council? And why on Urth did they summon him into their midst?

"You served me faithfully as an Imperial Army officer in the Changing Lands of Kentogen, Constantine, and you served me well in Haelos."

Ammertus's words twisted around him, living things, probing the edges of his mind, seeking chinks in his mental armor. Anton blinked them away, immediately regretting the display of lack of control.

He forced his mind back to the topic the Emperor and his council apparently discussed today. *Haelos? The northern continent? Why that?*

Images rolled unbidden through his mind. Or perhaps were called forth by the Emperor's will. Whether Anton wished it or no, the memories overtook him. A more uncivilized, uncouth place he'd never seen. The prisoners-turned-colonists who lived there, scraping a living from the untamed wilds, were little more than savages, criminals and malcontents banished from Koth to live or die as their will to work dictated. The continent's natives were no better—a motley assortment of races, many of them monstrous half-breeds born of unnatural unions.

"Haelos has not been restless in a while," Maximillian commented.

That was good. Right? Why then did he hear dissatisfaction in Ammertus's answering grunt? Was that a flash of avarice in Starfire's hooded gaze? Anton waited cautiously. He would not speak unless told to.

"His Resplendent Majesty has decided to grant the penal settlement of Dupree on Haelos the status of full colony. Which means its warden will need to be replaced with a governor."

Was *that* why they'd summoned him to this meeting? Were they considering *him* to be governor of the new colony? Exultation roared through him before he managed to corral its rampage.

"You have served me *loyally* and well these many years hence, as well," Ammertus declared. Emphasis on "loyally."

He was widely known to be Ammertus's man, as faithful a dog as the archduke's own son. That the archduke saw fit to remind him of it in the context of this discussion was intriguing. A message to Maximillian that Anton was his man, mayhap?

Ammertus continued, "You are suited to Dupree as well as anyone. And of course, you safeguard the Emperor's interests tirelessly at all times, do you not?"

He opened his mouth to agree most fervently that he lived only to serve the Empire, but a movement off to his right startled him into glancing away from the Emperor for a second. Horrified, he slammed his gaze back to the throne. To look away from the Emperor uninvited was an egregious insult to His Resplendent Majesty. Abject relief turned his gut to water as he saw that Maximillian, too, had looked over at the opened golden door and failed to notice Anton's unpardonable breach of etiquette.

"What is it, Oretia?" Ammertus snapped.

Anton's eyes widened. *Oretia? The oracle of the Imperial Court?* It was said the powerful Child of Fate had never been wrong in centuries of prophecies. Supposedly, it was she who foretold the death of the first Emperor, she who predicted the mysterious disappearance of the second Maximillian. It was also rumored that she was a key power behind this Maximillian's throne for the thirty-two hundred years of his reign.

Given her age, Anton expected her to look old. He expected wrong. She was born of the extremely long-lived race of janns, her skin swirling with the colors of the elements to which janns aligned themselves. However, if the rumors of her age were accurate, the Emperor himself must have gifted her with exceptional longevity. At a glimpse—and that was all he dared allow himself out of the corner of his eye—she could pass for a woman of middle age, the sort who worked hard at preserving herself. Her bare arms were firm even if the mottled skin covering them looked somewhat leathery. Fine wrinkles crisscrossed what Anton could make out of her face, but as her scowl eased, her skin smoothed into a falsely young mask.

"A prophecy comes," she announced in a surprisingly lush and throaty voice.

Ammertus retorted, "Write it down and show it to His Majesty later. We are busy now!"

Anton gaped at her scornful gaze, locked in anger with Ammertus's. She dared defy one of the archdukes, only exceeded in power by the Emperor himself? Did she have a death wish? Belatedly, Anton remembered himself. He hurled his gaze back to Maximillian and missed the rest of the silent battle of wills raging around him. But the air fairly crackled with it, a faint, metallic smell of ozone abruptly permeating the golden room.

Oretia snarled, "Your petty politics can wait. The power building within me is unique. Olde magicks touch me this day!"

The Emperor's eyebrows twitched into a momentary frown—a mighty loss of control for him. *So. Olde magicks worried him, did they? Interesting.*

Maximillian leaned back casually on his throne, whereas Ammertus leaned forward aggressively. "Is this prophecy about His Resplendent Majesty?"

"Would I be here if it were not?"

Maximillian ordered in a bored tone, "Tell me, then."

"It comes an-o-n . . . ," her voice trailed off, taking on a singsong tone as she drew out the last syllable. "Ahh, the power of it. Perhaps I shall not share this after all. . . ."

Ammertus moved faster than Anton would have believed possible, launching himself off the dais and across the room to the oracle. The archduke embraced her head in his hands, shoving her up against a golden wall, staring into her eyes as if he would suck her brains from her skull. A visible field of energy built around the two of them, pulsing with almost sexual intensity.

"Sing for us, little Oretia," Ammertus crooned.

Anton shuddered at the depravity and power in that voice. Gads, and to think the Emperor surpassed that power by orders of magnitude.

The oracle moaned, her body arching into a taut, vibrating bow, only her head still, trapped between Ammertus's clutching hands.

"The end," she gasped. "I see the end."

"Of what?" The archduke was breathing heavily, something repulsive throbbing in his thick voice.

She spoke in bursts torn from her throat. "A nameless one . . . wakes in the wilds . . . shackles break—" Her voice broke on a hoarse cry and she sagged in Ammertus's grip, clawing ineffectually at his hands on either side of her head.

"What?" he shouted, shaking her violently. "Show me."

The force of that mindquake drove Anton to his knees, buffeting him nearly unconscious. His thoughts scattered, ripped asunder by that awful voice. Struggling to hang on to his fragmenting sanity, Anton stared up at the Emperor sitting at ease on his throne, completely unaffected by the massive mental energy flying through the air. His ageless face was devoid of expression, his eyes reflecting only bland disinterest.

Even Starfire seemed to be experiencing mental distress, and a look of concentration wreathed his features as he shielded himself from his father's psychic assault. Iolanthe and Korovo did not appear mentally overly distressed by Ammertus's outburst, but they did look mildly annoyed by it.

Of a sudden Oretia straightened in Ammertus's grasp and, to Anton's amazement, tore free entirely. She paced the width of the golden room, sparks flying from her hair as she whirled to stalk back. She paused before the throne, staring at it and the man on it, nodding to herself. The guards on either side of the Emperor tensed as she stalked up the stairs to stand directly in front of Maximillian, who might have been carved from the same obsidian as his throne for all that he reacted.

Her voice, preternaturally deep, resonated off the walls like a terrible storm. "Hear this, for I speak true. A nameless one comes. From the depths of the untamed lands to destroy us all. Olde magicks returned, change born of earth and stars. Greater than thee, Maximillian, Last Emperor of Koth. When Imperial gold is bathed in blood, your fate is written and cannot be undone. The end of Eternal Koth is nigh."

Profound silence enveloped the room. Everyone stared at the oracle standing defiantly before them, her head held high, the tips of her hair glowing in a bright nimbus around her.

The building fury upon Ammertus's thunderous features made Anton cringe in spite of himself. He knew that look. The archduke was dangerously close to snapping. Ammertus had never been known as a reasonable or particularly stable man when crossed.

Anton was stunned as the oracle raised an accusing finger and pointed it at the enraged Kothite noble. "And as for you,

Ammertus, Archduke of the Colonies. Your line shall end in the Cradle of Dragons."

Ammertus and Starfire both jolted at this. Anton noticed Ammertus's hand drifting to the long red braid tucked in his belt. It was said to be the hair of his permanently deceased—and favorite—daughter, Avilla. But it was Ammertus who drew in a long breath of outrage and fury, all the more frightening for how long it took him to fill his lungs. And then he screamed. "You *lie*!"

The mind blast accompanying the accusation knocked Oretia off her feet, flinging her backward violently. She must have hit her head, for she collapsed in a rag doll heap, spilling blood over the golden dais. She rolled bonelessly down the steps and came to a halt at Anton's feet, a disheveled tangle of limbs and hair.

Terror for his own fate exploded within Anton. It was a cowardly impulse to think of himself first before the broken oracle dying before him, but he'd never claimed to be a hero. And he had seen just how insane Ammertus could be in the midst of one of his rages. Anton dived to the floor beside Oretia, not to aid her, but to hide behind her.

"She *lies*!"

This mind blast rippled through the air in visible waves, spreading outward faster than the eye could track to slam into everyone else in the room. From his vantage point on the floor, Anton watched the worst of the wave pass overhead. He grabbed Oretia's elbows and yanked her body across him. Just in time, too, for the mind blast ricocheted like a living thing, now bouncing crazily throughout the space, smashing into any and all soft living thing, sundering flesh and blood more easily than the sharpest sword. Even Starfire hit the floor, arms thrown over his head and face buried against the steps.

Blood erupted throughout the hall as the servants fell like ninepins, sliced neatly—and not so neatly—into ribbons of meat and bone. Oretia took the brunt of the blast above him, bathing him in hot blood.

Her head turned slightly and he nearly gagged at the sight of her eyeball dangling out of its socket by slimy strands of nerve and vein. Her remaining eye locked on his, unfocused, glazing over with encroaching Death. She moved feebly, struggling to gather herself for one last effort.

Her flayed facial muscles twitched uselessly. Whether she managed to speak it aloud or merely projected it into his brain, Anton registered only a single croaked word.

"Awaken."

And then her bloody and broken body went limp across his.

Ammertus ranted and raved for several minutes, storming around the room, destroying anything and anyone who dared cross his path. Finally, he devolved into mad, childlike laughter. Anton lay frozen on the floor, unashamedly pretending to be dead.

"Enough, Ammertus," Maximillian said with quiet authority, all the more sinister for its lack of emphasis. "I know your grief is great, but do not let it get the best of you. "Steel your resolve. You lost much in Haelos, but we are in Koth now. And henceforth, please refrain from slaughtering Children of Fate. Prophets of their power do not grow on vines, and I have use for them."

Anton risked peeking up. The Emperor had not moved from his casually seated position. Starfire pushed cautiously to his feet, looking around at the carnage with disdain.

Anton stared at the destruction. The entire room was covered in blood. Floors, walls, ceiling—where there once was gold, now there was only obscenely red blood, flowing, dripping, clinging to every surface. *When Imperial gold is bathed in blood . . .*

Had the prophecy already begun to come true? *What was the last bit? Oh yes.* When Imperial gold is bathed in blood, your fate is written and cannot be undone—

"Get up."

Anton lurched as Ammertus snarled from directly above him. The archduke's fury had transformed to something bitterly cold and a hundred times more vicious than the screaming rage of the past few minutes.

"I have a job for you, Constantine. . . ."

CHAPTER

2

A distant cicada buzzed in the noontide heat, the harsh
note rising until it broke, leaving behind only a lazy
breath of breeze. Raina, second daughter of the House
of Tyrel, lay on a carpet of fine, soft grass, gazing up idly at
the trees overhead.

As far as anyone could tell, a land as large as or larger than
Koth stretched away to the west and south of the lone inhabited
corner of this great continent, as yet unexplored. Dangerous.
Unknown. The colony of Dupree clung to its little
corner of the continent tenaciously, carving a place for itself
in the great forests and untamed wilds of a new land. Tyrel
lay at the very edge of that inland expansion, not entirely safe,
but not entirely uncivilized, either.

The day's warmth, its stillness and somnolence, called for
a nap. Even the swarm of gnats flitting in and out of the
dappled sunlight like tiny sparks of faerie dust moved more
drowsily than usual. Only the little brook at her feet was in a
hurry, rushing from rock to rock on its busy way to wherever
it eventually went.

"I know a secret."

Raina turned her head indolently to gaze at her companion and the source of the words. Her surrogate big brother and best friend in the whole world, Justin Morland.

Lanky and lean, he was two years her senior and showing signs of becoming a man. He ought to be training with the men-at-arms this warm afternoon. But instead, he'd invited her to go fishing. Just like the old days when they were carefree children. A rare treat, this, what with his duties around the castle and her studies occupying so much time.

She retorted, "Of course you know a secret. Today is my sixteenth birthday, and my mother tasked you with getting me out from underfoot so my surprise feast can be laid!"

He grinned, flashing devastating dimples. "Well, there is that. Promise to act shocked so she doesn't have me caned."

Raina plucked a blade of new grass and commenced chewing the stem. "She's strict, but she'd never flog you. You're like one of her own sons. Still, I vow to act positively stunned."

They both chewed on grass stems for a time, extracting the sweet green tang within. Then Justin drawled, "I know another secret. A big one."

That roused her to a more alert state. "Do you know what my birthday gift is?"

"No. But I know where it comes from."

"Where?"

He didn't answer.

She sat up. "Tell me!"

"I'm not sure I should."

"You can't tell me you've got a secret and then not share it!"

"But I like tormenting you."

"Tell!" Raina pounced on him, pummeling his chest with her fists. They were probably too old to be cavorting thus, but they'd grown up together scrapping like a pair of puppies and it was simply what they did. Their mothers would be appalled—after all, he and Raina were no longer children. Awareness of his maturing masculinity and her budding femininity hovered at the edge of her consciousness, but she pushed it away. This was her Justin.

"Your mother told my mum you're getting a visitor. He's bringing your surprise."

"Who?" Raina demanded. She ought to play coy if she wanted Justin to tell her anytime soon, for he was a terrible tease. But she was too curious about all the heavily charged secrecy surrounding her birthday gift this year to restrain herself.

He sat up abruptly, dumping her on her backside. She laughed up at him, and without warning she attacked again. They wrestled like the old days, except he was careful with her now. They both knew he was stronger and a more skilled fighter than she. Still, he let her win.

Panting, her face hot and her hair flying akimbo out of its braid, she straddled his chest, her skirts tangled around them both. The necklace she never took off dangled between them, its silver medallion embossed with a tiny tri-petaled blue flower nestled among three leaves, winking in the sunlight. "Do you yield?" she demanded.

He grinned up at her. "To you, my lady, I shall always yield."

"Then spill. Who brings my gift?"

"I don't know."

"Where does he come from?"

His voice pitched low as befitted the telling of something forbidden, Justin murmured direly, "Alchizzadon."

Alchizzadon.

The word whispered through her mind like a dark incantation, thick with threat. The sun slid behind a cloud just then, and a chill shivered across her skin. Or was it the single uttered word itself, shrouded in mystery and menace, that sent foreboding chattering down her spine?

What little she knew of Alchizzadon was stolen knowledge, overheard in tiny bits gathered over many years. The word made her father's jaw go rigid with fury. But in the privacy of Lady Charlotte's solar, the word made Raina's mother's eyes wistful, filled with regret and . . . if Raina wasn't mistaken . . . longing.

What was this place, Alchizzadon?

She'd pored over every map in her family's magnificent— secret—library and never once found it. No village or city bore the name, no castle or keep. She'd asked her older sister, Arianna, once if she knew what or where it was and had gotten slapped for her troubles, along with a hissed warning never to utter the word again. And the mystery around Alchizzadon had only deepened.

She was to have a present from that very place? She climbed off Justin and plunked down in the grass, hugging her knees to her chest. The laughter suddenly sucked out of the day, she asked on a sigh, "How long are you supposed to keep me out here?"

He squinted up at the sky. "At least another turn of the hourglass." Then he grinned up at her. "I bet I can catch a bigger fish than you."

"Hah! Do you have line and hooks?"

"Of course," he replied scornfully.

He always had them stashed in a pocket or pouch somewhere on his person. She rose to her feet and reached down to help him up. His hand swallowed hers nowadays, new calluses on his palms abrading her tender flesh. He rose to his full height, a hand span taller than she, even though she was somewhat tall for a human female. He was growing up. They both were.

But they had today.

"I'll race you to the willow grove," she challenged.

He laughed. "With those skirts? Hah. You'll eat my dust."

Laughing, she darted off through the trees. He didn't let her win this time and was casually trimming a long, supple sapling when she finally arrived, breathing hard. She held her side until the pain in it abated and then picked out a likely fishing pole. Using the dagger from her healing pouch, she sawed at the young willow.

"Let me do that. We'll be here all day waiting for you to cut it through, muckling."

She scowled. He'd called her muckling after the manor's squealing piglets for as long as she could remember. "You're still a pest!" she retorted.

He lifted the dagger from her hand. "You adore me and you know it."

"Hah."

Grinning, he made short work of cutting down the tree. "You need to keep this dagger sharper. You never know when a keen blade will save your life."

"You sound like my father."

"He's a fine swordsman. He knows whereof he speaks."

"I care not for such things."

"Of course not. You're a girl. Not to mention you stink with swords."

She stuck her tongue out at him, but he was right. As talented as she was with magic and healing, she was equally untalented with anything that had to do with weapons.

The two of them made their way to the stream and got down to the serious business of fishing, arguing good-naturedly over whose fish was bigger. The largest on her string was a finger width longer than any of Justin's, but his biggest catch was the heaviest of all, a fat female with a belly full of roe.

Regret tugged at Raina as the sun inevitably began its descent toward the horizon. As excited as she was for her birthday feast and her mysterious visitor bearing gifts, she didn't want this day to end. A perfect day.

Finally, reluctantly, they declared the fishing contest a draw. Justin picked up both strings of fish and threw them over his shoulder. She captured his free hand and swung it back and forth jauntily as they hiked out of the woods. As the trees thinned and the low, gray outline of the keep came into sight, he gently disentangled their fingers.

"It is not meet for us to be seen skipping along holding hands."

"Why not? We've done so our whole lives."

His face went closed. Serious. "Times change. People change."

Sudden dread coursed through her. Call it premonition or silly, girlish superstition, but her chest clenched so tight she could hardly breathe. She stopped, dragging at his hand to swing him around to face her, and forced words past the heavy lump in her throat. "Promise me you'll never change."

He frowned at her. "Why do you say that?"

"Just promise." She added earnestly, "Please?"

"All right. Fine. I promise." A pause. "And you're still a silly muckling."

Her throat relaxed of a sudden, and all was right with the world once more. He would always be her Justin. They continued on, walking toward the long shadow of the walls looming ahead. Her family's keep was neither fancy nor large, a lump of rock designed for practicality and defense. But it was home.

"What do you suppose the visitor is bringing for my birthday?"

"A bucket of spiders."

She punched his upper arm. Ever since he'd dropped a giant hairy black spider down her dress when she was six she'd been terrified of the creatures.

He snorted. "You hit like a girl."

A new, arch voice intruded from nearby. "She shouldn't hit at all. It isn't ladylike."

Arianna.

Raina rolled her eyes at Justin. As usual, her older sister was perfectly turned out, every glossy lock of brunette hair in place, her gown impeccable, her manicure flawless. Raina abruptly became painfully aware of the dirt caked under her own broken fingernails from digging in the riverbank for worms. She glanced down furtively. As she feared. Her dress was covered in grass stains and dried mud. Wisps of hair straggled in her face, as fair and golden as her sister's was dark and sable. Raina pushed her disheveled locks back defiantly.

"At least we did something productive today. Justin and I caught your breakfast for the morrow while you sat around being pretty and useless."

Arianna drew herself up and said huffily, "I shall be the bride of—" She broke off.

"Of whom?" Raina challenged. To her knowledge, no match had been arranged for her or her sister. Tradition held that the elder daughter got to travel the wide world and seek a husband far away for herself while the younger daughter stayed home and managed the family's lands and holdings. It wasn't fair in the least, not that anyone had bothered to ask *her* about it.

"You'll find out soon enough. Sooner than you know," her sister replied smugly.

Raina didn't have the slightest idea what Arianna was talking about and, furthermore, couldn't care less. Such matters were still a lifetime away for her. She shrugged and continued walking toward the keep.

"Who's that?" Justin asked suddenly.

She followed his pointing finger and spied movement on the rise where the Tyrel Road topped it. A cluster of robed men walked this way at a steady, traveler's pace. "Probably guests arriving for my party."

"I don't recognize them. Nor the blazons and symbols on their robes," Justin muttered.

Raina frowned. The only strangers who came to this remote little corner of the colony were tax collectors. But it was far too early in the year for that. She squinted at the two tall figures leading the little party. Justin was right. The dark green cloaks and angular silver runes upon them were foreign to her.

"Let's go greet them," she declared.

"It would not be wise until we know who they are . . . ," Justin started.

Impatient of his caution, she burst into a run. Of course, he was obliged to keep pace beside her. "You're an idiot," he grunted.

"You forgot to add 'reckless and impulsive,'" she panted as his stride lengthened, forcing her to work at keeping up with him.

The travelers stopped sharply, seemingly startled at the sight of locals racing at them pell-mell. Justin slowed, and Raina was grateful to pull up. The stupid corset her mother had recently taken to making her wear was giving her an awful pain in her side.

"Greetings, gentlemen," Justin said formally. "Welcome to Tyrel."

One of the new arrivals was of an age with her father; the other was perhaps two dozen summers in age. The three men behind the pair in dark blue were obviously servants and each carried a bulky pack.

Raina eyed the two in front. Their cloaks were made of rich wool, the clasps at their throats finely worked silver with triangular symbols on them. Their blazons were intricately worked silver badges with an ancient-looking and stylized triple-leaf design highlighted in green enamel. Even at a glance, she saw the craftsmanship in the baubles was superior. And yet, for all their finery, a disturbing air clung to the men. Sinister. She frowned, failing to put her finger on the source of her disquiet.

"Well met, young sir. And who might you be?" the older one replied formally.

"I am Justin Morland, a servant of the manor. And this is Lady Raina, second daughter of the house."

Both travelers' gazes snapped to her with avid interest . . . and something else. Something that sent a ripple of unease climbing her spine. It was as if they measured her. But for what? The younger one's mouth curved up in a self-satisfied smile that made her skin positively crawl.

The older one asked, "Is Lady Charlotte in the manor?"

His tongue wrapped all too familiarly around her mother's name for Raina's liking. She replied stiffly, "Aye."

Arianna, who had not deigned to run like a hoyden, caught up with them just then, not a hair out of place and not the least bit out of breath. "Greetings. Welcome and well met, I am Arianna of Tyrel. To whom do I have the honor of speaking?"

Raina gritted her teeth at her sister's smooth courtesy. How come she could never manage to sound so calm and collected?

"Greetings, my lady," the younger one murmured as he bowed deeply. "It is an honor, indeed, to meet *ane lu kagiri*."

Raina started. She'd heard rumors of dead languages actually existing, but had never found any real evidence to support the rumors. Where did these men gain access to knowledge of any tongue other than the one spoken by everyone, everywhere? The syllables the young man spoke barely tickled at the edges of her understanding as if they were some incredibly ancient form of Common. She took a stab at its meaning. *She who waits?* Why would the fellow call her sister that?

The older one spoke hastily, as if to distract from his young companion's slip. "Our journey has been long and the road dusty. Perhaps a drink to wet our parched throats is to be had?"

Arianna went into full hostess mode, then, bustling about and calling for servants to come relieve the travelers of their loads and bring water and wine right away.

Raina trailed along behind the party, Justin faithfully at her side. She muttered to one of the mud-spattered load bearers, "From whence come you?"

He looked startled to be addressed, and answered in a bare mumble, "We be Jena men. But them two's"—he jerked his chin toward the men in green and his voice dropped into a bare whisper—"said to be Mages of Alchizzadon." He made a hand sign to ward off evil magics.

Although Raina wasn't generally superstitious, she understood the man's fear. There was something ominous about the pair. What on Urth could her mother have obtained from such men for her birthday present? Frankly, she wasn't sure she wanted to receive such a gift.

The parade passed under the sturdy portcullis and gained the outer bailey of the keep, which was paved more in muck than cobbled stones at the moment. The visitors were ushered into the manor proper, and abrupt quiet fell in the yard. Justin made to leave her side and head for the kitchens with the fish, but Raina touched his arm. He halted questioningly.

"Thanks be to you for today," she said softly. "It was the best gift ever."

He smiled down fondly at her. "You are most welcome."

The moment froze itself in her memory, imprinting indelibly upon her mind, never to be forgotten, the pungent scent of lye from the recently cleaned stables and the crusty smell of hot bread, fresh from the brick beehive oven beside the kitchen; the red glow of the sunset highlighting one side of Justin's face and casting the other in shadow; the coolness of coming evening upon her bare arms.

He spoke quietly. "Go get ready for your party, muckling."

"You will be there, will you not?" she asked anxiously. The new guests gave her a bad feeling, and a corresponding compulsion for him to be near surged within her.

"I would not miss your party for all the world."

Impulsively she stretched up on tiptoe and dropped a quick kiss on his cheek. It wasn't the sort of thing they did between them, and her face heated up. She whirled and ran for the keep.

THE SOUTHERNMOST MARGIN OF
THE COLONY OF DUPREE

Will jumped carefully from boulder to boulder at the bottom of Hickory Knot, the big hill just beyond the village of Hickory Hollow, balancing his precious cargo in one hand and trying to remain silent all the while. It was his favorite moment of the day, taking the evening meal to the watch. The sun slipped below the horizon and long shadows hid his movement as he climbed.

Adrick was on duty this eve. Will always tried to sneak up on the seasoned barbarian hunter, and Adrick always spotted Will first. Once the pot of stew was delivered, as often as not the older man invited Will to sit with him for a while. He'd regale Will with stories of his latest hunt or show him a thing or two with whatever weapon he happened to be carrying that night: spear or bow, dagger or axe.

It galled Will that his own father steadfastly refused to teach him even the most basic weapon skills, muttering instead about the danger of being discovered carrying such knowledge in his head. As if the Empire would ever bother investigating the thoughts of a cobbler's son living on the very farthest edge of the civilized world. Oh, Ty taught Will plenty about sweeping floors and stoking forge fires and threshing grain, and even about controlling his emotions, silencing his mind, and marshaling his thoughts. But his imagination ran to heroic adventures and glory in battle.

Into thick brush, now, Will crept more slowly, easing through the brambles cautiously. The slope grew steeper, and he had to use both hands to steady the ceramic pot, which made the climb all the trickier. He'd never approached the clearing atop the knot from this direction before. If he could be quiet enough about it, he would finally win the ongoing contest with Adrick for certes.

He reached the ring of stones crowning the Knot and crouched low, crawling with three limbs while he cradled the stew pot in his left arm. In the gathering dusk, he spied a corner of Adrick's fur-trimmed cloak on the far side of the giant old hickory that gave this spot its name. Will grinned. He eased upright, stepped carefully over the low stacked stones, and charged the tree on light, quick feet.

"Got you this time, Adrick!" He gave the cloak a victorious yank—

—and the rough wool fell to the ground, slithering off the butt of the lone spear planted in the dirt. He started to whirl, to seek his tricky prey, when cold steel bit at the joining of his chin and neck.

"Not bad, boy. Not bad at all." The steel pulled away.

Will huffed in disgust. "I'll never be as good as you, Adrick."

"It is nae true. Ye'll make a fine hunter fer sure, if yer father ever lets ye off the leash and out of yon hovel." The older man swept the pot from Will's hand and held it to his nose, taking a long, appreciative sniff. "Ahh, yer ma's squirrel stew. Best cook in the Ring, she be."

Adrick made his living traveling the ring of settlements surrounding the margins of the Wylde Wood, hunting and trapping as he went. The woodsman sat down on a flat-topped boulder that made for a decent bench and gestured Will to sit beside him.

Will looked down at the hollow, a muddy village straddling the intersection of two footpaths in the middle of nowhere. While some might call it a fine enough place to live, far from the prying eyes of the Empire, he called it his prison. He desired nothing more than to leave home and see the world. To seek adventure. Honor. Glory.

"Truth be, boy, it is the stew that gave ye away. Smelled it afore ye set foot upon the slope. Good climbing, by the by. Watched yer whole ascent, I did. Clever to come by the most impassable route."

Will's spirits lifted at that. He rubbed idly at the sore spot under his chin where the razor-sharp dagger had pressed into his flesh. "Mayhap I should not have talked my father into making you that dagger, or at least not making it so sharp."

"Ty's blades take an' hold fine edges, they do," Adrick replied, running the pad of his thumb lightly along the gleaming blade. "Woodsman's best friend, a good blade. Yer sire should make ye a sword, and soon. It is time and more that ye've a long blade at yer hip."

Will snorted. As if he hadn't had that argument with his father a hundred times or more already.

"'Ave ye ever asked yer ole man where he learned to make such a weapon? It is a passing strange skill fer a cobbler in the Wylding."

Will shrugged. Ty had long refused to answer any and all questions about his past.

Silence fell as the woodsman dug into the pot of stew with gusto. Finally, Will's impatience was such that he had to blurt, "Will you show me a new trick tonight, Adrick?"

"Tell ye what, boy. If ye can run back to yer house, give yer ma this rabbit I snared, get yer folks' leave to come back to the Knot, and run back here afore I take my fill of this here stew, I'll let ye stand watch with me. And I might just be talked into showin' ye a thing or two."

Exultation leaped in Will's chest as he jumped to his feet. "I'll be back before you've finished half the stew!"

"I'm thinkin' gettin' permission from yer pa's goin' to be the real test!" Adrick called after Will as he took off running.

"You underestimate my skill with words!" Will shouted over his shoulder as he sprinted down the curving path to the vale below.

Will ran down the main street and skidded to a stop at the threshold of his family's freshly whitewashed cottage, last in the row, only a little ways from the encroaching woods. He wiped his muddy boots upon the rope mat before the door. His mother was nothing if not a stickler for cleanliness. He supposed it had something to do with her being an elf. None of the human women in the village worried nearly so much as she did about a little mud on their floors.

He ducked through the low door and into the homey warmth of the cottage. The interior glowed golden from the light of the fireplace and his mother's prized oil lamp. "Here's a rabbit for you, Mother. Adrick sends it with his regards and says thanks be to you for your delicious stew."

Serica smiled from the rocking chair where she was currently attending to some mending. "Hang it by the fire. Your father can skin it when he's finished with his work."

Will glanced over at his father, hunched on his cobbler's bench, sewing on an upside-down leather boot. Ty made the sturdiest, warmest, and most waterproof boots in the Ring and had steady work keeping the locals' feet shod. Often as not, payment came in the form of food or labor traded, which meant it was an annual struggle to raise enough coin to pay the Imperial taxes. But they got by better than most, Will supposed. Their house was warm and snug, and there was always enough to eat upon the table.

"Adrick says I may stand watch with him, tonight," Will started.

Serica looked up in alarm, and then gave a little cry as she pricked her finger with the needle. She sucked it as Ty answered without looking up from his boot, "No."

"Why not?" Will cried. "You never let me do anything. I am not a hothouse flower that will wilt at the first sign of frost!" He wasn't entirely sure what a hothouse flower was, but he'd heard his mother make the same complaint a while back when Ty didn't want her to go out visiting a friend a few villages over by herself.

One corner of Will's father's stern mouth twitched in amusement. Sensing an opening, Will pressed his point. "Adrick's the finest woodsman in these parts. If I am not safe with him, then there is no safety to be had in the Wylding. It is just for one night. And he promised to show me—" Will broke off. He'd almost slipped and mentioned their secret weapons lessons. "—woodcraft skills," he finished lamely.

Serica and Ty shared a long look.

"Every other boy in the Ring my age has been standing watch for years," Will pleaded. He added with more heat, "You have to let me grow up *sometime*."

Serica spoke in her gentle, modulated voice. "He has a point, my dear. Perhaps he could stay a few hours. . . ."

Will held his breath in agony as his father considered the idea.

Finally, Ty laid down needle and sinew and stood slowly, stretching the kinks out of his back. "A few hours, only," Ty said heavily. "I shall place a lamp in the window. Come home when I put it out."

Will whooped and swept his mother up in a hug, twirling her around in his joy. She protested in her gentle way and he set her down, laughing.

"You will need a blade, Son." Ty moved over to the big iron-banded trunk in the corner. The lid creaked open and he fished around within it. He emerged carrying a tangle of leather. He held out what Will saw was a belt and long sheath. The leather-wrapped handle of one of Ty's longer weapon-daggers stuck out of the sheath.

Will threw himself at Ty and wrapped him, belt and all, in a quick, hard hug. "Thank you, Father!"

His father rummaged in the chest again, and this time emerged with a leather coat with metal rings sewn onto it. Will recognized his father's armor and shrugged into it with a certain reverence. It was a little big on him, but would keep him warm and dry and stop a wolf bite.

As he put the armor on, his father pulled a spear out from

under the bed. Will was more comfortable with that weapon than with edged weapons. He took it and tested the balance. Like all of Ty's weapons, it was superb.

"Off with you, then," Ty said gruffly. "No sleeping on the job, eh?"

"No, sir!" And Will was out the door into the gathering dark with another whoop of joy. His mother's soft laughter carried on the firelight spilling out behind him.

Full dark was upon the vale, and a sliver of moon was just rising behind him as Will charged up the path to the Knot. The cry of a big cat split the night, startling Will. Cougars were not known to be native to this area. He burst into the clearing in hopes of seeing Adrick still seated with his stew pot, but the woodsman was standing, an odd expression on his face. *Blast it.* Adrick had won, yet again.

Will screeched to a halt. "I told you I'd talk them into letting me—" Why was Adrick looking down at his own belly like that? "Is aught amiss—" Will started. But then he spied the dark, wet . . . something . . . sticking out of Adrick's chest.

The woodsman looked up at him in blank surprise. Adrick's legs crumpled, and Will dropped his spear to leap forward and catch the woodsman as he collapsed like a puppet whose strings were let go all at once.

Behind Will's friend stood a huge monster with undershot tusks, crude leather armor over bumpy green skin, and massive muscles. A bloody spear dripped in the orc's left fist. A giant jagged-edged axe rested in his right hand.

Orc!

As that realization exploded across Will's mind, the beast leaped with shocking speed across the small clearing, putting himself between Will and the vale below. It took no great woodcraft to know the monster had just cut him off from the village and help.

The orc grunted something unintelligible and took an aggressive step forward, axe held high. Will took a stumbling step back and bumped into the giant hickory at his back. He fumbled for his father's long dagger clumsily and brandished it awkwardly. The short weapon was sure death against an opponent with much longer weapons, though.

The orc grunted and scooped up Ty's spear, then stunned Will by tossing it to him. He dropped the dagger and caught in midair the lighter, faster weapon with its metal-sheathed tip.

The orc settled into a fighting stance. Will seated the spear under his arm as well. The orc grunted approvingly and advanced, circling to Will's left. It was a fight the beast wanted, then. The orc stowed his own spear as Will stared. *Was he actually trying to even the odds?*

The orc used his now-free hand to thump his chest and grunt, "Du'shaak."

What on Urth does that mean? Not that Will had any time to ponder it, as the beast took a swipe at him with that gigantic axe. A weapon that large and heavy was, perforce, slow. Will jumped back out of its arc, and the fight was on.

Not that it was much of a fight. This creature was clearly an experienced warrior. And he was a boy from the hollow, untrained in the ways of war thanks to his stubborn father. He stabbed awkwardly at the orc with the spear as Adrick had shown him to do. Spears were thrusting weapons, after all.

Using one giant fist, the orc grabbed the spear just behind its metal head and lifted it up into the air, with Will clinging in panic to its hilt. His feet cleared the ground entirely and the orc swung the spear, slamming Will into the giant hickory, shoulder first. Dazed and in pain, he stubbornly refused to release the spear. The orc yanked it again, sending Will hard into the tree trunk and to his knees this time.

"Du'shaak!" the orc snarled as Will scrambled frantically

to his feet. Adrick ▮
go down. To do so i▮
through him, as the ▮
viously angry beast sh▮
a rag doll.

The orc swung his axe▮
metal head entirely off t▮
tossed the spearhead away▮

Realization broke over W▮
orc would pound him to de▮ ▮ ▮ ▮ ▮ the
monster didn't cleave him in ▮ ▮ ▮ ▮ ▮rsed axe. Already he felt beaten to a pulp a ▮ ▮ ▮ losing strength.

Without real thought, Will's desperation changed forms. Shifted from fear to thought, thought to intent, intent to action. Golden light crackled down the remaining length of the broken weapon, exploding off the jagged tip like chain lightning in a burst of force magic.

The spear nearly flew out of his hands as the magic discharged violently. His opponent was thrown backward even more violently, flying across the small clearing and slamming hard against a tree. The orc roared, his ugly face contorted in rage, and charged, seriously intent on killing Will now.

What was that?

It was one thing to dabble with his secret talent for magic alone in the woods. To push flexible limbs away from him and create tiny glowing points of light. But that massive bolt of damaging energy? Where did that come from? If anyone found out he could do something like that—

—the thought did not bear finishing. If someone from the village had spotted that distinctive flash of magic and reported him to the authorities, orcs would be the least of his problems. If he was lucky, he would be reported to the Mage's Guild as an unlicensed magic user. He could end up forcibly

drafted into the guild to serv▮
reported to Governo▮
be arrested ▮
pect to be until ▮
his master ▮
The orc ▮
conce▮
th▮

it. If he was unlucky, he would
Anton's men. Then Will could ex-
and sold into slavery to wield magic for
death.

scrambled to his feet with a roar of rage and Will
trated with all his power upon maintaining his grip on
broken spear. It was the only thing separating him from
death at the hands of the enraged beast.

Hastily he called more magic to himself, blasting it down
the length of the mangled weapon. The bolt of force damage
wasn't nearly as powerful as the last one, and the orc was
prepared for it this time. The beast absorbed the magic with
a painful grunt and only staggered back momentarily.

Will stumbled back as well, doubtful that he could throw
magic at his foe a third time. The spear was now effectively
a wooden staff. This was a weapon with which he was much
more familiar. He'd threshed more wheat than he cared to
think about with just such a stave over the years. Ty had
shown him a dozen different ways to swing a threshing pole
to prevent muscle fatigue, too. He waited for the orc grimly
as the beast gathered himself one more time in the scant
moonlight.

The orc charged with a wordless shout, axe high over his
head. Will ducked and dived left, sweeping the staff with all
his strength into the orc's shins. It wasn't an elegant move by
any means, but effective. The beast tripped awkwardly. Staggered. Fell. Almost as if something or someone pushed him.
And the momentum of his fall threw him headfirst into the
stacked rock wall.

Will stared as the orc lifted his head in a daze. A strange,
reddish, mark in the shape of a barbed seed was on the beast's
forehead. Adrick had spoken of orcs marked by irregular red
scars. *Boki*. The Lords of the Boar. The fabled orcs of the

Forest of Thorns who nearly laid Dupree to waste when Will was but a babe. What was one doing here so far from his home?

It dawned on Will belatedly that this was his chance to leap forward and drive the broken end of the spear through the beast's neck. But the idea of having to look that creature in the eye and kill him in cold blood froze Will in place. He was no murderer. Some might argue that yon orc was no better than a boar or a stag, but Will could not deny the orc was intelligent and had demonstrated a rough honor in giving him the spear to defend himself. He owed the orc no less respect. He would not cut the defenseless creature down in cold blood.

A faint smell, as of rotting meat, caught Will's attention. He lifted his head sharply, scanning the valley below. All was quiet. Too quiet. The entire wood around the hollow had gone dead silent. And creatures of the forest never lied. Furthermore, it made no sense for an orc to travel alone. This one must be a scout of some kind. Which meant—

Will fell to his knees beside Adrick's corpse and tore open the woodsman's belt pouch. He fished around frantically, fumbling through the bits and baubles jumbled within. His fingertips encountered a smooth, curving surface, and he grasped it firmly. In a single swift movement he pulled the ox horn forth and stared in dismay. Its entire small end, the blowing end, was smashed. *Useless.*

Swearing, he scrambled to find Adrick's whistling arrows and bows. The scream of one of them would warn at least some of the villagers. But the arrows, too, were broken into worthless matchsticks. The orc scout had done his work well.

Hoarse shouts—dozens of them—erupted behind Will, an unintelligible gibberish of harsh grunts and growls. *Great stars above.* That was no simple raiding party. It sounded like a small army erupting from the forest behind him. Tree branches splintered and leaves flew every which way as orcs, goblins, and even ogres burst out of the woods almost on top of him.

Great Lady, grant me speed, he whispered in his mind as he turned and ran as if the Lord of the North Wind himself blew Will forward. A roar went up behind him as the creatures spotted him and gave chase. He could only pray to reach the village and rouse its inhabitants before everyone was slaughtered in their beds.

He headed straight down the hill, leaping over fallen logs, dodging low-hanging boughs, and tearing recklessly through brambles that snatched at his clothes. He hoped his knowledge of the slope would lend him speed while the rough terrain slowed his pursuers.

His heart lodged in his throat and flailed there like a dying sparrow. His thighs pumped up and down, heavy with panic. Sweat popped out on his forehead. A stitch stabbed at his side. His lungs caught on fire. And still he ran as if a reaper from the Void were after him. Which wasn't so very far from the truth. An arrow schwinged past his ear.

As he burst into the valley from the north, he spotted a second wave of orcs and goblins charging the village from the west in a coordinated flanking attack.

He drew within shouting distance of the cluster of huts. "Orcs! Ogres! Goblins!" he shouted at the top of his lungs. "To arms! The hollow is under attack!"

Charlotte of Tyrel was as nervous as a maiden as she waited impatiently for her guests to freshen up, Pacing in agitation, she flung her hands up in disgust as it dawned on her she was wringing them. *Bah*. This would not do. She was the Lady of Tyrel, now. Not that sixteen-year-old girl from long ago.

She glanced at the paper-wrapped package sitting on her desk and wondered yet again at its contents. It had arrived the previous week with a note saying that it was for the elder of her two guests. What was Kadir up to, the sly old dog?

A knock on her office door had her whirling toward it. She forced herself to take a steadying breath, then called out imperiously, "Enter!"

She nodded formally at the older of her two guests. "Kadir. Welcome." Awareness of him shivered through her like the magic of his caresses all those seasons past.

"*Lady* Charlotte," he murmured, emphasizing her title with faint irony. He remembered, too, did he? "How do you fare?"

"Very well, thank you. And you? I trust your journey was pleasant."

Kadir grunted, "It was long. The roads between Jena and here are dismal." Jena, largest city in the Midlands, was at the exact opposite corner of the region from Tyrel.

They traded a few pleasantries before he brought up the reason he was here and the one subject she most dreaded discussing with him. Kadir asked soberly, "Does she know yet?"

Charlotte was taken aback at his directness. He had to know full well this was a subject she much preferred to talk circles around. She had hoped their old liaison would count for something, that he might find a gentler way of breaking the news to her daughter than he ultimately had to her all those years ago. But apparently not. Her back stiffened and she moved behind her desk to sit. If his desire was for this conversation to be purely business, so be it.

She moved around her desk and sat down. "I believe this package is for you."

"Ahh, yes. I was expecting that. I am relieved to see it arrived in a timely manner." He leaned forward to pick it up.

She watched curiously as Kadir unwrapped the package to reveal a rather ugly stick, no longer than her forearm and no thicker than her finger, covered with bumps. "What is that?"

"It's just a dousing rod."

She was scholar enough to know that it was not just any dousing rod. Rather, it was a magic-imbued rod and, given who was holding it, likely a powerful one. "Where does it come from?" she ventured to ask.

"The Council of Beasts. It is made from wood of the treant Whisper."

"The progeny of Spirit? That Whisper?" she blurted, startled.

Kadir shrugged disinterestedly. "I believe the council said something like that. I have no interest in their totems and nature mysticism. All that concerns me is that this rod aids in finding and transporting objects and people. If my companion and I had this a month ago, our journey to Tyrel would have taken a fraction of the time and misery."

She eyed the rod askance. So much power in such an unassuming little twig? It was hard to credit. Almost as hard to credit as the mythic Council of Beasts itself having touched an object that now rested in her study.

"And why do you have need of such a thing here?" Charlotte asked.

Kadir smiled, a false politician's smile over an inscrutable gaze, and she needed no further answer. It was a contingency in case her daughter gave him problems. Charlotte almost wished Raina would. Almost.

"With the accidental death of the young man you were planning to overtly pledge Raina to, we have had to move up the schedule for her," Kadir announced.

Charlotte stared, stunned. "I beg your pardon?"

"We cannot risk something happening to her before she can do her duty to us."

"And how do you plan to explain her offspring if she is not safely married off to some local boy?"

"That is not my problem."

"Well, it is mine!" she snapped. "The tradition is that the daughters of Tyrel become engaged in their sixteenth year. They marry soon thereafter, and then you get your babes on them. *After* they marry. By law, bastard daughters do not inherit landholdings, which would give both of us headaches in training the girls and trying to explain why they *do* get to become the Ladies of Tyrel."

Kadir shrugged. "The decision is made. How you explain Raina's sudden offspring is up to you. But this happens now."

Dismay poured through her. Kadir did not understand. The shame of it . . . the logistic problems . . . and then there was Raina herself. She would never agree to bear children outside of marriage—

Justin. He and Raina had been inseparable forever. He was common born, but educated enough and a good-looking lad. Charlotte's husband said he showed promise as a swordsman, and she herself had sensed a latent talent for magic in the youth. He was not ideal, but he was close at hand, and Raina would likely agree to a betrothal to him. Yes. Justin could work.

"It will take some time to arrange, but I think I can salvage the situation here," she said slowly, her mind racing.

"No," Kadir replied firmly. "Now."

Impossible! She opened her mouth to say so, but the younger mage of Alchizzadon, the one to whom she had yet to be introduced—an omission she was intrigued by from Kadir—spoke up first. "Does the girl know aught, yet?"

"The girl" was her daughter. And had a name. An

impertinent question, that. But then, she supposed he might be somewhat impatient to meet his future lover. A little resistance overcome by a love poison and, stars willing, Raina's experience would leave behind the same sorts of pleasant memories that it had for her.

Why then the sudden rage bubbling within her breast? It took her wholly by surprise. Memory came pouring back; she'd nearly revolted against this long tradition of her family's when she'd been Raina's age, and a remnant of that rebellion flared in her now.

Her adult reason took control once more. In spite of the wrinkle Kadir had thrown at them with his insistence on proceeding immediately, all would turn out right. Justin would cooperate. He was obviously sweet on Raina, and who would say no to marrying into a title and wealth? As for Raina, she would not fight a betrothal to Justin. Regarding the other part, the one involving the mages, she would be upset at first, stubborn even. But after the love elixir . . . yes, everything would be fine.

It had been Kadir's eyes that turned aside the crisis for Charlotte all those years ago. They'd had been dark and soulful, brimming with sympathy for her, and had softened her heart just enough that logic and cajolery—and a love draught—had won the day. Something similar, some tiny thing, would soften her own stubborn daughter's heart. Eyeing the young man speculatively, she allowed that he was handsome enough to capture her daughter's fancy.

"Your husband? Does he remember anything?" Kadir asked.

She pulled her attention back to the conversation at hand. "No. The spell of forgetting has held."

"Bring her to us, Char," Kadir said gently. "It is time

she knew the truth. Do you wish me to be with you for the telling?"

She gasped at the old endearment, her lingering doubts punctured by it. The moment of rebellion drained away, leaving her empty. Sad. "No. It will be best if I tell her in private."

Kadir nodded in understanding. "As you wish."

She rose from her desk to fetch Raina, personally. She needed the time to compose herself after Kadir's bombshell revelation that everything must happen right away. She had no doubt there was more to the decision than simple concern that Raina might have an unfortunate accident. Which alarmed her mightily. What information was he keeping secret? A prophecy of some kind? A vague notion of warning her daughter nagged at Charlotte. But how could any young girl truly prepare for the revelations to come? How was she supposed to prepare herself for it as a mother?

She had dreaded this moment her entire adult life. But, inevitably, sickeningly, it had arrived. The moment of betrayal was upon her.

Raina was surprised that her mother had yet to make an appearance at her birthday feast. Charlotte was nothing if not a fine hostess. Arianna had, of course, stepped in and taken over welcoming the guests and ordering the meal served. Raina suspected, though, that most here were more interested in the ale than the food.

The great hall had been transformed by streamers of white gauze and cascades of spring wildflowers into a magical bower for the night. As she looked out across the assemblage, warmth filled her at the collection of familiar faces. Neighbors and servitors alike, this was her family, and she felt safe and loved surrounded by them like this.

Interestingly enough, the visitors from Alchizzadon had not put in an appearance. It was almost as if they knew themselves to be intruders to this gathering.

The hour grew late and the assemblage was well into its cups, and still there was no sign of her mother. Raina spied Justin seated near the back of the hall with a brace of manor lads. He grinned and hoisted a brimming mug of ale at her. She smiled fondly as he broke into a bawdy song that was taken up immediately by the other feasters.

"Daughter." She started at her mother's voice behind her on the dais. She had not seen Charlotte arrive.

"Oh, Mother, my party is wonderful—" she began.

"Come." Charlotte cut her off; her voice was as hard and cold as diamond under the raucous singing.

Alarmed, but sensing the need not to make a fuss, Raina pasted on a false smile and slipped from her seat. As she stood, she happened to glance at the crowd. And caught Justin's concerned gaze upon her. He knew her too well. He'd marked that something was amiss. A question gleamed in his eyes, and she gave him a reassuring smile. He nodded slightly, but a promise remained in his gaze. If she had need of him, she had but to ask.

Her mother's agitation was such that Raina did not ask what was wrong, but merely followed, worried, to her mother's office. Charlotte held the door and Raina stepped past her into the chamber.

Raina ought not have been surprised that the Mages of Alchizzadon were behind her mother's disquiet, not to mention the untimely interruption of her birthday feast. She studied the men closely, not bothering to disguise her interest. Both were tall, the older one thick and powerful under his cloak. The younger one was leaner, enveloped in restless energy.

Her mother closed the door, then sat down stiffly behind her desk. This was to be a formal meeting, then. Her mother gestured her to a chair by the corner of the desk, and she perched on the edge of it obediently.

Raina glanced sidelong at the mages and then looked again. From this angle, with the lamplight striking him just so, faint tattoos had become visible all over the older man's face. The slashing lines and curlicues were reminiscent of the runes upon his cloak and had the effect of obscuring his face until all she really noticed was his eyes. They were black and penetrating, with power that stripped a spirit bare.

The older man's gaze thankfully slid away from hers and

locked with Charlotte's. They traded a long, intense look that Raina could not make heads or tails of. There was most certainly a history between the two of them, but she could not fathom its nature.

The younger man had a single runic mark on his neck, climbing the left side of his jaw. If she looked at him straight on, it was barely noticeable. He was handsome in a bland sort of way. In a crowd, her gaze would slide off of him without ever really lighting upon him. Although self-disciplined, he betrayed faint discomfort in the hunch of his shoulders. He met her gaze for the briefest moment. And in that instant she could swear she glimpsed pity.

Pity? Normally, she was acutely aware of and able to interpret the unspoken currents flowing through situations like this, but for once she was confounded.

"It is time," Kadir finally broke the silence by announcing.

Charlotte's mouth compressed into a thin, white line of displeasure. Raina's anxiety momentarily gave way to amusement at seeing her mother so discomfited.

"Give us a moment alone, if you please, gentlemen."

Without comment, both men stood and moved to the door. "We shall be directly outside," Kadir murmured gently. That almost sounded like words of support from him. Her mother's gaze softened for an instant at his turned back.

The door closed behind the two men, and in a moment a magical glow became visible between the wooden panels and the floor. *A wizard's lock?* The mages had locked her in here with her mother?

What in the world was afoot? Raina turned to Charlotte expectantly and was stunned to see the woman at an apparent loss for words. "What in stars' name is going on, Mother?"

"Perhaps I should have told you from the beginning that this day would come. But it seemed kinder to let you have your childhood in innocence."

The same dread that had overtaken her earlier when the mages arrived crept along Raina's spine once more, running its cold fingers insidiously up the back of her neck.

"As you know, our family has a long history of holding these lands. Since the time of a great king: a human named Hadrian who was also a great mage."

Raina blinked. The Kothites had always ruled Urth. This Hadrian must have been a king within the Kothite Empire, then. But here? In Haelos? A legend, then.

". . . and this man chose for himself a bride. A daughter of the House of Tyrel by the name of Arianna."

The dread fingers slid around her neck to clutch at Raina's throat. Her sister was named Arianna. The firstborn daughter of the house was always named Arianna. Tradition had it that, to every generation of the family, the first two children born were always girls. No one seemed to know why it was so. But so it incontrovertibly was. Maybe not entirely legend, this tale of her mother's.

Her mother continued, "The story has been handed down through the Mages of Alchizzadon since the time of its occurrence that, on their wedding day, a great attack happened. Hadrian took up sword and wand to defend his lands. He vanquished his foe, but at great personal cost. He called upon more magic than his body could withstand and burned himself out entirely. He would have died had not his court mages rushed in to stabilize his body and trap a small piece of his spirit within it. But without a massive infusion of great magic, his . . . husk . . . could not be revived. He has lain in stasis, neither alive nor dead, ever since, awaiting the day when the descendants of his court mages find a means of gathering enough of the raw, unchanneled magics of a bygone age to infuse them into his remains and revive him."

In spite of herself, Raina's mind raced, reviewing her training in the healing arts. A spirit balanced forever on the sword's edge between life and death was not natural. Spirits fell into one realm or the other, but they did not hover endlessly between the two. Such a state, defying the laws of life and death, would have to be caused by powerful ritual magic of some kind not to have worn off eventually. Surely high-magic cures had been tried to restore this king.

Charlotte was speaking again. "Time passed. Generations came and went. Yet, the Great Mage—as he became called—slept on. Meanwhile, the House of Tyrel waited."

How could a story like that have survived so long? Frankly, it sounded like an overblown hearth tale to Raina. She asked skeptically, "And you are certain these mages speak truth with this tale of theirs?"

Charlotte nodded firmly. "They have hidden and guarded the story from the Empire with great care. I am confident they speak the truth as they know it."

"Mayhap they use it to gain favors and gold from us," Raina retorted.

"They take nothing from the House of Tyrel. At least not in the way you think." Her mother paused, apparently searching for words. Charlotte's gaze drifted to the window and her eyes darkened with memory.

Raina waited so long she wondered if her mother had forgotten she was not alone. Finally, unable to contain her curiosity, Raina asked, "How do they seek to restore the Great Mage, Mother?"

Charlotte started. She seemed to gather her thoughts and then continued, "Our family made a promise to the king moments before he left to do battle for his kingdom. We vowed that when he returned, his bride would be waiting for him. Arianna of the House of Tyrel."

The dread tightened its hold on Raina's throat, digging its claws in so painfully she struggled to breathe. How would a bride restore this mage of theirs?

"For all these centuries, we have kept our promise. The firstborn daughter of each generation is given the name Arianna and is trained in all the arts and skills befitting a queen. And when the Great Mage finally rises, she will be ready and waiting."

It was as if a bright light exploded inside her head. So much suddenly made sense! All of her sister's years of training that seemed so useless out here on the edge of civilization. Etiquette and comportment, art, dance, and music. Training in managing great castles and estates. Endless study of history and politics and diplomacy. Arianna was being prepared to be a queen. Oh yes. It all made perfect sense.

Of course, as the little sister, Raina had been forced to tag along and endure the same education from the expensive tutors. In addition, her early talent for magic had secretly been nurtured outside the purview of the distant Imperial Mage's Guild, who, thankfully, had no chapter house or members for a hundred leagues around. It added yet more hours of study and practice to her days, for mastering the physics of magical energy was an arduous endeavor at best.

Charlotte remained silent, yet Raina sensed the real crux of the tale had yet to be told. "This is all well and good, Mother, but how does it affect me? So far, my sister is the point of your story."

"Ahh, but you are wrong. This story is about you as well. For you see, any bride of the Great Mage must remain unmarried. Pure."

"But I thought Arianna was supposed to travel. To find a husband abroad."

"That is the story we put forth to explain our tradition to outsiders."

It was all a lie? Her mother was speaking again.

"Another daughter must be born each generation to take the previous Arianna's place. And that task falls to the second daughter."

Raina felt like one of her brothers had just punched her in the belly. *She* was the second daughter. She took a steadying breath. Then said reasonably, "So I am destined to bear daughters as my first two offspring. And I shall be expected to raise one of them as a queen. I can do that."

Charlotte sighed. "Your duty extends beyond that, I am afraid."

Now Charlotte's eyes gleamed with pity, too. Grief, even. Raina glanced toward the door, a desire to bolt so strong she barely managed to keep her seat. The trap her mother had laid was near ready to spring.

"How so?" Raina asked cautiously.

"There is a problem in producing a bride fit for the Great Mage."

Here it comes. "What sort of problem?"

"He was born long ago. In a time when magics were more powerful than they are today. Much more powerful. And the king was an exceptional mage even for his time."

Charlotte hesitated.

"And?" Raina prompted in an agony of impatience and fear.

"And it has fallen to us to produce a bride of sufficient magical tolerance that lying with the Great Mage and bearing his children will not destroy her."

Destroy her? *Destroy her?* Her brain refused to make sense

of the words. By main force she managed to choke out, "Destroy her? How?"

"I speak of olde magick. Raw. Unchanneled. If magic today were the flame of a candle, by comparison this olde magick would be a wildfire roaring before a storm. Exposure to it would burn out the spirit of any person of normal constitution. Kill them permanently."

Raina frowned. Suspicion blossomed at the back of her consciousness. Her own extraordinary talent for magic. Her ability at an unheard-of age to harness and channel tricky ritual magics. Her capacity to produce huge amounts of magical energy—much beyond what most adult mages mastered with a lifetime of practice. "We've been bred to tolerate such magics, haven't we? The daughters of the House of Tyrel."

Charlotte nodded, looking mightily relieved that Raina comprehended. "You understand, then, why the father of your daughters must also be a powerful mage, carefully selected—"

"What?" Raina started to stand. She would've run from the room, but her heavy gown tangled around her legs and prevented it.

Charlotte's voice rang out, lashing Raina before she could escape, driving her back down into her seat. "It is your duty, Raina. Three hundred generations of women before you have done their duty, and so will you." Her voice softened. "A marriage will be arranged for you to a nice young man. When that has happened, the mages will . . . provide one of their own of sufficient magical power to strengthen the line. Your husband will be given poisons of forgetting. He will believe, along with everyone else, that your daughters are his. Once you have borne the required daughters, you will be free to have children with your husband and live out your days in peace."

Comprehension burst across her brain and she leaped to her feet. "I am not your husband's child?"

And then the rest of it hit.

The mages were here. Now. Did they expect this travesty to transpire soon, then? How soon? Was one of them supposed to be the father of the next generation of daughters? A total stranger? Would they marry her off and then have one of them force himself upon her until she bore a child? She stared at her mother in horror.

Charlotte held up an imperious hand. "Don't say it. Listen to me, Raina. They have elixirs. Magical drinks to make you deeply infatuated with the young man they have chosen, and him deeply infatuated with you. Trust me, it will be a special and wonderful experience. One you will never forget. A cherished memory."

"How," Raina demanded in a terrible voice born of rage and outrage, "can drug-induced rape to make a . . . a broodmare . . . out of me possibly be anything other than humiliating and appalling?"

Charlotte opened her mouth to speak, but Raina cut her off. "How can you ask this of me? You've been a victim of this degradation . . . this crime . . . and yet you would perpetrate it on me? Your own daughter?"

Her mother stared at her, stricken, and said soothingly, "I know it comes as a shock. But give it a little time. You will grow used to the idea."

Raina enunciated carefully, "I will never consent to be anybody's broodmare. I will choose the father of my children, and I will not cuckold my husband. If I happen to have a daughter, I will agree to raise her in the family tradition of preparing her to be a queen. If she chooses to do the same for her daughter someday, that will be her choice. Her choice, Mother."

Charlotte closed her eyes for a long, pained moment. "I understand you are shocked. I reacted the same way at first.

But it gets better. Who knows? You may even grow fond of the father after a fashion."

Raina reached for her neck and the blazon of House Tyrel hanging there from a silver chain. With a violent wrench, she broke the chain and slammed the pendant onto her mother's desk. The three-petaled white flower on its blue lapis field glinted up at her. She put her palms on her mother's desk and leaned forward, staring daggers into her mother's eyes. "Know this, Mother mine. I will never lie with a man of your choosing to satisfy those mages. Do I make myself clear?"

"Crystal." Placating Charlotte gave way to authoritarian Charlotte. Raina's mother glared back, matching dagger for dagger. "And know this, Daughter mine. You will do your duty if I have to tie you up and pour the poison down your throat with my own hands."

Raina whirled and yanked open the office door. She threw up her hands and blasted away the wizard's lock with so much violence that two mages waiting outside staggered back against the far wall. She raced past them, furious tears burning her eyes. The younger mage made a grab for her, but she ducked under his arm and darted for the stairs.

She heard the beginning of a confining spell incant behind her in Kadir's voice and then Charlotte interrupting him sharply, "No! Let her go. We do this my way."

An instant's gratitude for her intervention was swallowed up quickly by Raina's burgeoning sense of outrage and betrayal. She did not know how she would avoid the fate those monstrous mages and her mother had planned for her, but she would find a way.

CHAPTER

4

S omething slashed through Will's sleeve, plowing a
furrow across his upper arm. He ignored the searing
pain. A stray arrow was the least of his troubles at the
moment.

Frantic figures appeared in windows, yanking wooden
shutters inward and slamming them shut. *Thank the Lady.* At
least the villagers wouldn't be taken completely by surprise
and slaughtered in their beds. A few men emerged, half-
clothed in nightshirts, trousers, and assorted bits of armor,
awkwardly wielding rusty swords, cracked wooden shields,
and various farm implements. They formed up in a crooked
line. The local militia, such as it was.

He veered left for the tidy cottage at the far end of the lane.
Home. The front door cracked open, and Will was stunned
to see two dark-cloaked figures slip stealthily into the night.
He recognized the tall form of his father and the petite,
elegant silhouette of his mother.

What were they doing? A mob of monsters was attacking!
His parents needed to take cover inside!

A clash of steel and shouts of battle rang out behind him.
The first villagers had engaged the orcs just beyond the clustered huts.

"This way!" his father called out low and urgent, waving at Will to join them.

Not understanding, he nonetheless angled left as his parents sprinted for the woods.

Will caught up with them as they reached the first hedge-row. His father hurdled the wall easily. His mother paused to rip off her skirt, revealing hunter's leggings beneath. Shocked, Will watched her clear the fence in a single graceful leap. He followed suit.

All three of them flinched as a bright orange glare burst into the sky behind them, and a howl of enraged glee went up. Green-skinned goblins had just set Rand the lumberjack's roof afire. The dry thatch flared like an enormous torch against the night sky. Goblins danced around the hut in a frenzied orgy of bloodlust. A scream curled forth from within. Will stared in horror. Rand's wife and four young children were inside that cottage!

"Get down," Will's father bit out under his breath in a tone that brooked no disobedience. Will dropped to his knees beside his parents and peeked through a crack in the wall.

One of the largest of the orcs stepped forward, brandishing a long sword and shield. Slung across his back was a gnarled club made of wood a bloodred hue. He bellowed in guttural and barely intelligible syllables something to the effect of, "Cattle of Koth, bring me your bull!"

Will frowned. What did that mean? Apparently, the beast wanted the village's leader to step forward and fight. Except Hickory Hollow had no need of a leader. How were the villagers to answer the gruesome creature's challenge?

"Ki'Raiden," Will's father breathed. "Sixth Thane of the Boki."

They *were* Boki. What were they doing so far from their

traditional territory a hundred leagues and more to the north of here? And what in stars' name were they doing issuing challenges in a nothing little hamlet in this out-of-the-way corner of nowhere?

Will stared at the Boki leader, attempting to ascertain how his father was able to tell one orc from another. He spotted a long white scar passing vertically over Ki'Raiden's left eye . . . perhaps it was by that his father identified the Boki thane.

"Whey-uhh dra-gon? We see his fire."

One of the villagers stumbled forward as if he'd been elbowed unwillingly out of the ragged line of defenders. Lars. A lumberjack, and the strongest man in these parts, if not exactly the brightest. He was probably as good a fighter as the hollow had to offer this Ki'Raiden.

"Stan' an' figh'. Foh lif' ub yo' pee-puh!" the orc shouted.

Stand and fight for the lives of your people? That sounded like an honor challenge. What did a Boki army want with such things?

The goblins and ogres behind Ki'Raiden let out a chorus of ululating howls. The thane snapped something over his shoulder, and his mobbed troops fell mostly silent. The thane thumped his chest and grunted something too quietly to hear from here.

Lars and the Boki warrior commenced circling each other warily, each measuring his opponent and seeking an opening in which to attack. The combatants went in and out of sight between the powerful torsos of the orcs now forming a rough circle around them.

Into that suspended moment of violent anticipation, something disturbing occurred to Will. How did his father know the name and rank of a Boki thane? And, furthermore, recognize him on sight? Ty was a humble cobbler. A man turning old before his time and settling into the weary drudgery of advancing years, waiting to die.

But then Ki'Raiden leaped on the attack, and Will's horrified attention was riveted by the quick and brutal slaughter of Lars. Will had never seen a man gutted before. Blank surprise showed on Lars's face as his entrails slithered to the ground in a cascade of glistening silver for several seconds before his legs buckled. A woman wailed from inside a hut. Deb. Lars's wife.

The Boki thane threw his axe to the ground in disgust and bellowed, "Bah! Iz no honor kill peasan'!" Ki'Raiden stomped down the line of terrified villagers, sniffing each of them in turn. "Whey-uhh dra-gon?" he repeated. Why he no defen' yo ho-nor?"

Will frowned in surprise. Was the Boki insane? Dragons were the stuff of children's hearth tales and not real. And even if they were, what would a dragon have to do with this tiny hollow? The villagers stirred in consternation before the furious orc.

"Whey-uhh yel-low dra-gon? We see magic. Know he hee-uhh!" Ki'Raiden roared.

One of the men must have said something to the effect of the orc being mistaken, for Ki'Raiden backhanded the fellow viciously across the face. The villager dropped to the ground like a stone.

Will's stomach sank just as hard. He whispered to his father, "They saw me. I used magic to defend myself from their scout. They'll be looking for me." *Oh, stars. Lars is dead because of me*. His father stared at him, and something akin to fierce pride flared for just an instant in Ty's eyes.

The Boki continued his tirade, finally declaring the villagers no better than sheep and deserving of a sheep's life. Shame burned in Will's gut. He had to do something. He couldn't just sit here and watch them die, slaughtered like lowly beasts. His legs uncoiled and he drew breath to shout a challenge.

This was his fault. He had to fix it. As Will began to rise, a heavy hand landed on his shoulder, forcing him back down.

His father whispered sharply, "Do not be a fool. You would die for nothing. And there is more at stake here than you know."

"But—"

His father threw up an imperious hand, cutting his argument off before it found air. What? Didn't Ty think Will was good enough to fight for his friends and neighbors? Nothing he ever did was good enough for his father. Will hadn't even been allowed to join the local militia when other boys had long served in it. Ty had merely drilled Will in how to use a broom and a threshing pole. To paint and shovel and chop wood. He acted as if Will were a stripling lad who couldn't begin to handle himself in a real fight.

Mayhap Ty was ashamed of his human son. Had he wanted so badly for Will to be an elf like his mother? Of course, Will was disappointed that he hadn't inherited his mother's centuries-long life span. But it didn't mean he was flawed. He was simply human. And after all, Ty was human. Most people on the northern continent were.

Will hissed, "He's going to slaughter them all. We must do something!"

"No!" Ty hissed back. "We must not."

"Those are your friends. Neighbors. Have you no heart? How can you watch them be killed like sheep? Or are you truly the coward they whisper you to be, hiding from anyone who might recognize you and name you gutless?"

"Is that what they say of me?" his father muttered.

"Is it true?" Will demanded.

Ty scowled at that.

"Fight, Father. Be a man. Defend your home, curse you!"

"You do not understand what you ask . . . the time is not yet right . . . the cost—"

"To whom? You? To the next man that beast guts?" Will battered at his father's resistance, but words failed him as outrage clogged his throat. "Did you not teach me to do the right thing? To stand up for justice? For the weaker man who cannot defend himself? What do you stand for if you will not stand by your friends?"

To his credit, Ty looked intensely chafed.

Will's mother spoke up, adding, "If not now, my love, when will we make our stand? For all these years we have bided our time while memory of freedom slips away. The values you would pass on to your son are being forgotten, stripped away one by one by the Kothites. Perhaps this is the portent you have been waiting for." She glanced back at the village. "You can win this fight. You know you can."

Ty took a long, assessing look at the carnage behind them as if trying to decide if this was the moment he'd been waiting for. Will held his breath while his father measured the enemy and weighed the options. Finally, unable to hold his silence any longer, Will whispered raggedly, "We have to help them."

Ty exhaled hard, his face settling into steely determination. "All right. It is time. I will do as you ask." Will started to pump a fist in triumph until Ty's voice cut across his celebration low and hard. "But we do this my way."

Will glanced at his mother for support in resisting his father's condition. But as always, her solemn, wise eyes pierced his anger, making it seem impetuous and childish. Sobered, Will reluctantly muttered, "Your way."

Ty nodded briskly. "To the woods, then. And the emergency stash."

What emergency stash? Will's mother nodded as if she knew what Ty was talking about. *These two had made plans for a Boki invasion?*

"And bring along that spear. I'll see what I can do with it."

Will blinked as his father took off running low and fast into the woods.

Townspeople screamed and the seething mass of monsters howled behind them as his parents started for the woods. Will glanced back and caught sickening glimpses of the massacre unfolding—the invaders waving bloody axes and pikes in the hellish glow of the fires, orcs hacking through doors, dragging women and children out by the hair. He saw one of the men bearing a pitchfork face off against an orc. He was all but cut in half by the beast's axe.

Nauseated, Will turned away and crawled as fast as he could for the trees, envisioning the wholesale slaughter that accompanied the screams and groans and howls behind him. He risked another look back and swore he saw an ogre lift a severed arm and take a bite of its bloody meat. Gorge rose in Will's throat.

And somewhere in the midst of his anguished impatience for Ty to get on with saving the villagers, rage took root within him. The deep, implacable kind that grew and festered over time, that made a man hard and cold, that vowed—and delivered—violent reprisal. An eye for an eye. A limb for a limb. Blood for blood.

His mother reached the end of the stone fence and angled right, following the shadow of an alarmingly sparse line of gorse bushes. Will could barely make her out, so well did she blend in with the shadows and so fluidly did she creep along. He'd had no idea she could move with such stealth!

Will read her lips as much as he heard her whisper over her shoulder to him, "Stay low. We must reach the woods unseen. Whatever you do, do not look back."

Too late. Images of the nightmare behind him had burned themselves into Will's memory forever, nesting like serpents in his mind. Creeping on their bellies through the cold, wet weeds, he and his parents made for the shelter of the trees.

A few more screams split the night, but then those, too, faded away, leaving only the wailing and howling of the monsters and their orgy of death. The tangy smell of burning wood and the sharper smell of burning flesh filled Will's nostrils. His stomach heaved, and he arched his back, catlike, as the contents of his stomach poured out upon the earth.

Just shy of the tree line, Ty's voice floated out of the trees, surprising Will mightily. Ty ordered, "Stay here, Son. When your mother signals you, gain the attention of one or two orcs, then run for the woods. You know the pine-split boulder atop the first ridge?"

He knew the spot and nodded. It was a broken boulder, its halves pushed apart on either side of a mighty pine as if the towering tree had grown right up through the middle of it.

"Lead the orcs to me there."

"Then what?" Will whispered back, his heart already pounding at the prospect of being chased by orcs.

"Stay out of the way and do not get hurt. I will do the rest." Will gaped at his father's terse response as Ty continued, "We must make haste. The Boki will send out search parties, and we must be in place before then."

Who or what were the Boki looking for this far south, so far from the Forest of Thorns? What could they possibly care for a place like Hickory Hollow?

Will swiped the back of his hand across his mouth, which now tasted foully of bile, and crouched, readying himself to run. Those beasts had killed his friends. His neighbors. He would avenge their deaths. Every last one of them. He knew not how, but he vowed it would be so.

How long he waited for his mother's signal Will couldn't say, but it seemed a dozen eternities. Finally, blessedly, he spotted her just within the first tree line. She waved at him once, twice, three times.

He pushed to his feet and looked back at the village, which was fully ablaze now. The glare of the fires blinded him to the fate of his neighbors, for which he was grateful. A pair of huge shadows crossed between him and the flaming village. He started to shout, but then thought better of it.

Ty had said to draw out one or two orcs, not the entire war party. Will kicked a stone hard into another one, and as he'd hoped, the resulting clatter made both orcs' heads jerk up sharply.

He ducked and took off running then, bent low and dodging back and forth in case they thought to send spears or arrows his way. The trick was to be hard enough to spot that the pair of orcs would not be certain of what they'd seen and would not send up a general alarm. The orcs were shockingly fast, though, and gained on him much more rapidly than he had anticipated.

He was not hollow born for nothing, however. He knew these woods as well as he knew his own hand. As he reached the first trees, he dived flat on the cold ground and wiggled through a low gap in a stand of dead blackberry canes left over from last summer. The dried thorns should slow the orcs down enough to give him a greater margin before them.

He headed for the split boulder at a dead run. As he flew through the trees, he imagined an orc behind every one, a goblin lurking in every shadow, and his heart lurched at each and every one. But finally, he made out the silhouette of the mighty pine ahead. He put on a last burst of speed up the hill. Those cursed-fast orcs were closing in on him yet again. He dashed around the boulder and nearly bowled into his father.

"Stay here!" Ty hissed as he stepped out from behind the rock. "Have you still got your bracelet?"

Will frowned, startled. He never took the braided leather band with its greenish stone off. It had been a gift from Adrick. "On my wrist," he replied.

"Good. Keep it on."

Adrick had said that the bauble would protect Will from harm, but he'd thought the woodsman was just being superstitious. Was there some truth to the claim, or was his father just as superstitious as his old friend?

Ty thrust a staff into his hands as he moved past. Will examined the weapon quickly. It was his spear. Except the broken end had been cut off, the new end banded by a piece of metal. How had his father accomplished such a repair so quickly? There was no time to ask, though, as his father moved down the hill.

Will stared in disbelief. Where on Urth did his father get that shield? It was not a foot soldier's round, wooden implement. Rather, strapped to his father's left arm was a kite-shaped shield made of thin metal painted a rich shade of blue. The ease with which his father carried it announced its extraordinary lightness.

Ty assumed a fighter's stance, and a chain-mail shirt caught what little starlight filtered through the trees. Not the heavy, clumsy, hand-riveted mail manufactured in the colonies, this mail had impossibly tiny rings so tightly woven it looked almost like cloth. The beautifully crafted gambeson under the mail looked made of thin, supple leather. It was dyed the same blue as the shield and inlaid with gold wire in an intricate design. Will's father's leather gauntlets were similarly dyed and decorated. And then there were the rows of blazons on his chest, Mage's Guild, some sort of family crest, a yellow dragon that matched the one on his gambeson, what looked like combat campaign badges—a lot of them—and many other blazons that looked like favors granted for services rendered.

"Get down!" Ty snapped over his shoulder as he strode down the small slope.

Will rolled his eyes at his father's back and blatantly disobeyed. No way was he missing seeing Ty fight orcs. He eased around the boulder, keeping to the dark shadows under the heavy pine boughs.

The fight, if one could call it that, was so short and fast Will could hardly believe his eyes. Two bolts of bright golden light shot from Ty's right hand, one after another, striking each of the orcs squarely in the chest. The pair dropped like rocks. Ty leaped forward and with quick flashes of a dagger slit their throats from ear to ear.

What. Was. That. Light?

Oh, Will knew the answer well enough. He simply couldn't believe his eyes. His father possessed magic? Was that where he'd inherited his own gift for it? Why, in stars' name, hadn't Ty taught him how to use it, then?

And not only did his father have magic; he also could cast spells powerful enough to drop a full-grown orc like a rock! Battle mages were incredibly rare, and what few there were lived lives of luxury in Imperial guild houses in big cities. They were not humble cobblers struggling to scrape out a bare living on the edge of civilization.

His mother jogged up to him, then, and he was stunned to see that she had added a ranger's leather jerkin to her attire. It was covered with small, sewn-in pouches that looked stuffed with the tools of the trade. An elegant long bow and quiver were slung over her shoulder with the ease of long familiarity. Hanging from her belt was a short sash covered in blazons, none of which he recognized. One had a tree on it, another some sort of house crest. A third blazon appeared to be made of amber.

As shocked as he was by her tracker's attire, his first words were, "What *is* all of *that*?" He jerked a thumb over his shoulder toward his father methodically cleaning his blade on the loincloth of a dead orc.

"*That* is your legacy, my son."

He hated it when his mother went all cryptic and elven on him. "What's that supposed to mean?" he snapped.

"You have all the tools to become what your father is."

"A humble cobbler on the edge of civilization?" he retorted sarcastically. "No, thank you."

"This is not the time for childish attitudes!" she snapped back. "Listen to me, Will. You can be as great a battle mage as your father if you wish. He has given you all the building blocks you need to develop your abilities."

Of a sudden all the boring lectures about calming his mind, emptying his thoughts, and disciplining his emotions took on a whole new meaning. He'd always thought Ty merely taught him how to avoid the sorts of thoughts and words that would get him killed by the Empire.

His mother muttered, "It is time for you to become a man and take up the torch your father has passed to you."

Now she told him to grow up? After all those years of treating him like a helpless child?

"How am I supposed to master magic if he never taught me?" Will demanded.

"Because it is a simple and powerful truth that cannot be taught, cannot be proven, and cannot be measured. The most powerful magic is all around us. It is in the air we breathe, the earth we stand on, the water we drink, and the fire that warms us. It is always and forever, never waning, never fading. It is what you feel in your heart, what you know in the deepest part of our spirit, and what you believe in your wildest dreams. It is simple and pure like the scent of lady's breath."

Lady's breath was a beautiful plant that produced sweet-smelling white flowers. Its leaves were burned as incense and made healing poultices for wounds. It was said the last breath of the Green Lady upon the land had created the plant.

Something rustled in the bushes behind them and Will whirled. Without thinking, he channeled his magic through the broken spear he clutched and blasted the orc scout into an unconscious heap. Will watched in shock as his mother darted forward and efficiently finished off the beast by slitting its throat.

Ty, who'd raced up the hill, no doubt at the sight of Will's magic blast, reached them, sword drawn and hands glowing dangerously.

"It's handled," Will's mother murmured.

Ty turned an amazed stare on Will, who glared back, furious.

Serica interrupted the burgeoning confrontation sharply. "There is no time for this. Husband, the trail is laid."

Trail? Was she a trained tracker, too? What other secrets had his parents kept from him all these years? Will shot her a thunderstruck look, brimming with demands for answers. Her exotic uptilted eyes flashed him back one of those severe "not now" looks of hers that quelled all questions.

"Give me that." His father held out an expectant hand, and Will laid Adrick's broken spear in it. "Close your eyes, both of you," Ty ordered.

Will did as instructed. A bright flash shone beyond his

eyelids for an instant but was gone before his eyes could fly open and see the source.

His father held out Adrick's spear to Will, remade yet again. The entire end of the staff, a forearm's length of it, was now wrapped neatly in what looked like copper. "How—" Will started.

"An old spell I know," Ty interrupted impatiently. "Go back to the edge of the forest and draw another patrol to me."

"Are you mad?" Will demanded.

"You are the one who insisted I save your friends. Bring me another pair of orcs."

Will ran down the hill without giving voice to the myriad questions dancing upon his tongue and went in search of another Boki patrol. He did not need to leave the forest to find one. He darted across the path ahead of this duo and the chase was on. This time he had no way of slowing the orcs' pursuit and the creatures had drawn frighteningly close by the time he charged up the hill toward the split boulder.

He caught a flash of reflected light as his father leaped out of the brush on the attack. The weapon in Ty's hand looked like a long sword, but made of no material Will had ever seen before. It gleamed milky white in the shadowed glen. Will skidded to a halt underneath the pine tree and lurched as his mother materialized beside him.

"What is his sword?" Will whispered.

"Dragon's Tooth," his mother replied absently, her concentration entirely on the scene below.

Was that its name, or was she suggesting that was an actual . . . Dragons didn't even exist. Right? *Right?*

Will's jaw sagged as his father slipped his left arm free of his shield and thumped his chest with his left fist, uttering something in what sounded for all the world like guttural orcish. His foes bared their huge teeth in bloodthirsty grins as

Ty donned the shield once more and gestured the orcs forward with the tip of his sword. Both orcs pulled huge battle-axes off their backs and advanced.

Will started forward, but his mother grabbed his arm tightly. "Hold," she breathed. "He wishes to make enough battle noises to draw more orcs this direction."

"But he's outnumbered," he whispered back.

"It is only two orcs," she replied dismissively. "And it is not as if they are thanes."

He stared aghast at her unconcerned face. What was he supposed to say to that? Boki were known to be among the fiercest and most skilled fighters in the land. The last time they had poured out of their forest and attacked the humans, they had nearly annihilated Dupree. A clash of weapons captured his horrified attention, and he watched in shock as his father's gleaming white sword danced like chain lightning, darting in and out, leaving nicks and cuts behind everywhere it went.

If he didn't know better, he would say that Ty was toying with the orcs. Apparently, the orcs concluded the same, for they began to growl. The pair separated, attempting to flank Ty, concentration now grim upon their hideous visages. Will would have stepped forward again to help, but again his mother forestalled him.

Apparently tired of swordplay, Ty abandoned his light fencer's stance and settled into a deeper, bent-kneed stance Will recognized all too well from years upon years of beating wheat to knock the grains loose with staves. Which, now that he thought about it, had often been about the heft and length of an actual sword.

With casual efficiency, Ty went on the attack using a swift, turning move that Will had seen many times before on the threshing floor. His mother flinched as the left-most orc's decapitated head thudded to the ground a second before the body collapsed. Ty reversed the sweep to his right, smashing past the orc's defenses and burying his weapon in the creature's chest.

The orc bellowed as Ty yanked his blade free. Before the second orc had barely hit the ground, Ty grabbed the creature by the feet and commenced dragging it into the brush.

"Go help him," Will's mother urged. "That roar will bring more orcs than your father hoped for."

Will rushed down the hill and grabbed the roughly shod feet of the headless orc. The stench was unbelievable as he dragged the heavy corpse after the first one. His father kicked the orc's head into the bushes just as the sounds of more orcs approaching disturbed the woods.

"Get out of here," Ty ordered tersely. "Go cover your mother, and give her time to kill orcs as they come. And no more magic out of you unless you are going to die. I'll continue to use mine so they concentrate on me and not you."

Will nodded, taken aback at the terse tone of command ringing in his father's voice. It was unlike anything Will had ever heard from Ty. To Will's ear his father sounded just what he thought a Kothite general in charge of a great army would sound like.

Numb with shock, Will took the spare quiver of arrows his mother shoved into his hands as she strung her bow and assumed an archer's stance. His mother? A trained archer?

"Keep the quiver on my back full," she ordered, her gaze trained on the slope below.

He had a feeling that this time when the orcs came there would be many more. And this time there would be thanes among them.

CHAPTER

5

Princess Endellian did her best to look bored as she followed her father, Emperor Maximillian, down the long hallway to the most isolated corner of the Imperial palace where the Empire's most secret business was conducted. It was isolated for good reason. Even now, faint screams echoed down the ornately decorated hall toward her. With casual ease of long experience, she blocked from her mind the terror and desperation accompanying the noise.

The smaller "interrogation" chamber behind her father's throne was used mainly for oracles who had already been made to understand their need for utter cooperation with Maximillian. But the chamber to which they proceeded now was where that cooperation was learned.

Harder to block than the agony accompanying the echoing screams was the random and frequent mind probing her father projected in an all-encompassing net around him. Even his daughter was not exempt from his continuous scrutiny.

In fact, he particularly watched her. As his heir, she posed perhaps the greatest threat to his throne of all. Not to mention that of all their kind, she came closest to matching her mighty father in mental power. Even the nine archdukes who were Maximillian's contemporaries in origin were not as powerful as she.

And then there was her suspicion that he actually wanted her to intrigue against him. Not seriously enough to threaten his throne, of course, but enough to hone her skills in the art of manipulating the complex politics of the Imperial Court.

Even so, it was a delicate dance to shield her innermost thoughts from her father without him realizing she was doing so. Whether she succeeded or not was anyone's guess. Mostly, she made sure to couch all of her plotting in terms of how she was serving the best interests of the Empire with her machinations.

"You are unquiet, my princess."

She turned an innocent gaze upon her sire. "I confess I cannot abide the mewling of these oracles of yours. Please forgive me if I block their whining from my mind."

"These Children of Fate are a fragile lot to be sure but their gift for true prophesy cannot be denied. Their Mistress has imparted great power in them."

And yet it is an enduring mystery from whence came their extraordinarily accurate tellings of past and future, as if they see beyond the Wall of Time itself.

Maximillian commented, likely in direct response to her thought, "The Children have a taste of Fae magics about them. Such power allows them a certain freedom from the limitations of our world. While their powers of prophesy are enhanced, their forms lack any real protection from the rigors of that power."

Ahh, but the weakness of those bodies also gives you power over the Children of Fate.

Maximillian responded to her thought dryly, "True enough."

A pair of guards swept open the door before her father and she followed him into a torture chamber outfitted to take maximum effect upon the vulnerable flesh of the Children, who were becoming harder and harder to find throughout the Empire. It had been nearly a year since one had been brought in, and Laernan had reported secretly to her that the latest one was not particularly talented or the least bit cooperative. Apparently, this one had expected to be tortured for his visions and flatly refused to give them up shy of torture. Although it was not Laernan's preference to resort to such crude tactics, he was willing to get his hands bloody when necessary.

The uncooperative oracle turned out to be a shirtless man of middling age chained upon the left-most wall, wrists and ankles manacled in a sprawling X well above the floor. His gut was split open at the moment, Laernan's fist buried in his innards. The prisoner screamed hoarsely, his voice cracking and abruptly falling silent.

Of course, the prisoner did not die. The Lord High Inquisitor was of sufficient mental power to forcibly hold the man's spirit within his body, regardless of how broken it might be. The prisoner could be roused to full consciousness with little more than a thought by his torturer, and Laernan did so now. The screaming took up where it had left off.

"How are we doing today?" the Emperor asked his chief inquisitor pleasantly over the din.

Laernan extracted his hand from the prisoner's gut, wiped it upon a towel, and bowed deeply to his liege. "This one exerts much effort of will to die. He will fail, of course."

The oracle slumped in his shackles, sweat and blood streaming down his body. Endellian noted that this one had the distinctive hourglass-shaped infinity sign of his kind crudely carved into his right side. It looked as if the prisoner had marked himself thus.

The oracle was bold in his defiance of her father to display his symbol so aggressively. *Ahh, well.* Laernan would extract the defiance from the fellow soon enough.

"What details have you garnered?" her father asked a little less pleasantly.

"They continue to repeat essentially the same prophecy:

> "From the Dragon's Cradle the heroes came,
> Who break the hold upon the Black frame.
> Without a name or history stands bold
> Heir to a blood both wondrous and old.
> A true child of the roses will be born,
> With flames of the first city to mourn."

"Anything else?" Maximillian drawled in supreme boredom.

"The Children continue to be stubbornly silent on the subject of this nameless one who thinks to threaten you. Either they do not know, or else they guard the secret with particular tenacity."

"Get me a name."

"That's just it, Your Majesty. There is no name."

She noted with approval that Laernan had carefully avoided any mention of the end of Maximillian's reign. As unconcerned as her father had seemed that night sixteen years ago at hearing the prophecy, she had always suspected he'd been secretly alarmed by the oracle's death brought on by the prophecy of his own end.

"Get me a name before I am forced to take extreme measures," her father growled, openly displeased now. The waves of his ire rolled through Endellian's mind, and she was careful not to block them in any way. It would not do to show resistance to her father while he was in this mood. He was apt to mind blast first and get around to regretting the results later.

The only other person in the room, a woman leaning against a far wall well back in the shadows, commented wryly, "If Laernan's Taming does not constitute extreme measures, surely your . . . guest . . . must quake to think what actual extreme measures will entail."

Endellian glanced up and, out of the corner of her eye, spied a yellow tint and hint of vertical, slit irises in the woman's bland face. She looked more fully upon her father's ward, and the impression faded away, replaced by entirely unremarkable, brown human eyes.

Endellian's gaze narrowed. Miralana never let her human form slip with the Emperor. But then, he was probably the only being in Koth who could truly hurt her.

Irritated at her own inability thus far to cow her adopted little sister, Endellian glided over to the woman. "Miralana. I did not feel your presence," she purred as she rested a hand on the woman's impassive cheek. The faintest ridges of layered scales and the thinnest blush of blue appeared under her fingertips. "Clever girl. How did you sneak up on me without me sensing your presence?"

"Does my ward displease you?" Maximillian inquired lightly.

That made Miralana's eyelids flicker briefly, for even she feared the wrath of the Emperor.

Without breaking eye contact with her sister, Endellian answered, "Not at all, Father. My sister merely makes a joke." She murmured low, "You never can resist poking at me, can you?"

"No, Mistress," the woman replied emotionlessly.

Child. Endellian sifted through the human thoughts shifting upon the surface of Miralana's mind. Nothing to be concerned about. But as always, the deeper, alien portion of the woman's mind was impervious to her probing. Sensing no immediate malicious intent, however, she backed out of her sister's rather unpleasant-tasting consciousness.

"It took no great insight to guess what Maximillian's purpose was in raising Miralana at Court. She would be an incredibly useful tool one day. Although the power required to wield her in the way Maximillian planned to was mind-boggling to consider.

Greed for the kind of might her father wielded pulsed through her. The kind that stopped entire armies with a word. That killed with a mere thought. That shaped reality itself with casual, brutal efficiency. Someday, she would have such power, and it would make her impervious to the threat Miralana posed.

Oh, Miralana would never turn against her or Maximillian. She dared not, for the Emperor knew her son, Kane, and where to find him. Ironic how Kane, an accomplished killer in his own right, should be so very vulnerable at the end of the day.

The obvious lesson of Miralana's position in the Empire was never to fall in love and never, ever, to indulge in off-spring. If those things could bring such a being low, they were weaknesses a future Empress could ill afford.

The oracle was screaming again, this time in an even higher pitch and with greater intensity than before. Endellian recognized the sound of a mental invasion by her father. It was utter domination of the mind. Whereas Laernan tamed the will, Maximillian broke it. No one could resist him. She was told there was no more exquisite pain anywhere than when Maximillian stimulated every single nerve in the body to the most excruciating and unbearable agony. His victims were, of course, forced to remain fully conscious all the while, unable to faint, unable to die.

"Tell me!" Maximillian snarled at the hapless oracle twitching on the wall. "Who does this prophecy speak of? *Give me the name.*"

A liquid splat announced the moment when the oracle's body literally exploded.

"Revive him," Maximillian ordered in disgust.

This oracle was lucky. As often as not, Maximillian simply ordered another oracle brought in and strung up. Or perhaps her father sensed special vulnerability in this one. She eyed the mangled corpse of the seer speculatively.

Laernan stepped forward obediently and forced the oracle's spirit back into its broken body, which the inquisitor also used his mental powers to repair just enough to sustain life's functions. Whimpering announced that the oracle lived once more. Meaningless babbling announced, however, that the oracle was not in his right mind.

"Enough for now," Maximillian announced.

"Yes, Your Resplendent Majesty," Laernan answered. "So shall it be. If I might—"

The Emperor cut him off. "Come, my dear. I am hungered."

Personally, her appetite was ruined by the sight, smell, and general squishiness of the oracle's innards, and she made no secret of it as she took a mincing step over the mess on the floor and headed for the door. Maximillian swept out of the room with no further delay, for which she was grateful.

But as she nearly reached the exit, Laernan did something odd. He made direct eye contact with her, which was a blatant breach of protocol. She raised a questioning eyebrow. His urgent gaze darted to the broken oracle hanging limp upon the wall and back to her.

The inquisitor muttered low, "He has not given us the information we seek, but he has been speaking. Quite a bit, in fact."

Prophecies? "Interesting," she responded carefully.

He nodded significantly in the affirmative.

She cast a wary glance at the door through which her father had passed. "I will return. Speak of this to no one."

Laernan bowed in acknowledgment.

With a quick, resentful look over at Miralana watching passively in the corner, a suggestion of a scaled crest topping her skull and disappearing down her back, Endellian swept from the torture chamber, hurrying to catch up with her father before he noticed her delay. Miralana might tease her, but they shared the common bond of being their difficult father's children. The creature would not tell Maximillian of the brief exchange with Laernan.

Raina looked up and down the dim hallway, deserted for the moment. She had to escape *now*. Her mother would expect her to rant and wail for a few days against the whole idea of bearing babes for the Mages of Alchizzadon but eventually to bend to her will. No one stood against the will of Lady Charlotte for long; the woman always got her way. Therein lay her weakness. She would assume Raina would give in. And if she gave her mother time to employ the cajolery and bullying tactics she was so good at, Charlotte might very well be right.

She should go to her father for protection. He would never stand for what Charlotte and the mages had planned for her. Which made her frown. He would never stand for it. Her mother and the Mages of Alchizzadon must have altered his memory. Could they also alter his loyalties? If his mind had been tampered with, she could not trust him to aid her. He might turn her over to her captors instead.

Time. That was her greatest enemy. She must leave right away. Tonight, even. But where to go? How to escape the heavily fortified keep? She knew nothing of such things. Help. She needed help. Justin. As children, he and her brothers had forever been slipping out into the woods to play against the orders of their parents.

He should still be at the feast. She raced for the great hall, desperate to beat her mother there. Hopefully, Charlotte and her two henchmen would seek her first in her own chambers. Or mayhap the stables.

She slowed to a more moderate pace as she reached the kitchen. Grabbing a rough apron to cover the bright white velvet of her gown, she slipped into the hall behind a gaggle of servants bearing platters of bread. It was said to absorb the liquor in one's belly and reduce the effects of drunkenness. She looked around desperately. *There.* Justin was still at one of the long tables in the back, seated upon a wooden bench. She slipped onto the bench beside him, slouching low to avoid being seen.

Her father shouted a toast from the head table, and everyone around her hoisted a mug. Ale sloshed and the crowd grew even more boisterous as the mugs were emptied and refilled.

"Drink up, muckling." Justin shoved a tankard of ale into her fist. "What's brought you slumming with the common folk?"

Someone guffawed and made a coarse comment about the Ladies of Tyrel marrying young because they hankered to lie with a man. Any man.

Raina stilled abruptly. Why not? What was to stop her from dragging Justin outside this very minute and lying with him? Even if she didn't make a child with him, her mother and those cursed mages would have to wait some weeks to find out for sure that she was not with child before they proceeded with their plan. It might buy her enough time to come up with another idea.

She leaned close to him on the bale of straw and placed a shy hand upon his knee as if for balance.

"What the—" Justin brushed her hand aside quickly. "No more ale for you," he announced, alarm lurking at the back of his gaze.

She murmured under the din, "I need your help."

"With what?"

"I need you to lie with me, right away. Tonight."

His eyes popped wide open in shock. "What?"

"Surely you know what I speak of."

"Of course I know!" he retorted sharply. "I was hoping *you* did not know what you spoke of."

She spoke in an urgent whisper. "They want to feed me a love poison and let a stranger get a child on me."

He stared at her in blank incomprehension. "Who wants to do this?"

"My mother. And those men. The Mages of Alchizzadon."

Ever the quick one, he grasped immediately where she was going with this. "But if I am with you first, we might make a babe instead."

"Exactly."

"Raina, I can't. You're a daughter of Tyrel. And I'm—"

She cut him off. "—the one I would choose if I had to do this thing."

"—and I'm a commoner. Besides, it is not honorable. It is not worthy of either of us."

"You don't understand," she wailed in a whisper.

"I cannot believe they'd really do such a thing."

Panic erupted in her belly. He didn't believe her. The idea was too outrageous for him to accept. Had she not looked into Charlotte's eyes and seen her blind belief that she was doing the right thing, she would never have believed it herself. But she *had* glimpsed her mother's eyes. And she *did* know it to be true.

"Go back to the dais and your party, muckling. We'll talk on the morrow and sort out this misunderstanding. If it comes to being with you, we'll do it properly with your family's permission and our troths pledged." A short pause and then he added, "But I am sure it will not come to that."

Come to that? He said it as if being with her were a worse sentence than slavery aboard an Imperial galley. Not to mention that marriage apparently would not interfere with their cursed plan in the least. Far from it, in fact. Despair burned wetly in her eyes. If Justin wouldn't help her, then she was truly alone. As strong-willed as she was, she couldn't hold out against them all forever. Particularly if they planned to imprison her and poison her.

"I'm so sorry," she whispered.

He squeezed her hand briefly, then gave her a little shove. "Go. Before someone sees you down here and we both get in trouble."

Right. Go.

T y backed up the hill, joining Will and his mother under the pine boughs. His father muttered, "If he has any inkling that I am nearby, Ki'Raiden will send out most of his men looking for me."

"More likely he will come for you himself, my dear," Will's mother answered as unflappable as ever.

Will whispered into the ensuing pause, "What in the Lady's great, green forest is going on? First Boki attack the hollow, then you cast humongous battle magic, and now you say the Boki are looking for you?"

"It is a long story. Another time, boy."

Serica's whisper floated out of the dark. "No. Now, I think."

"What say you?" his father responded in surprise.

"Think, my dear. Will must leave us. Now. Before Ki'Raiden finds us. You know the thane will not stop until he succeeds. Our son must take the quest with him—"

Will cut her off with a wordless sound of fury and fear. "How can you be so blasted calm when that monster's coming for us?"

"Quiet!" she snapped back at Will. "Quickly, my love. It is time. You saw him channel that magic. He is ready."

"More than ready," Ty grunted. "I can name on one hand

the mages who can do that. And completely untrained, no less."

If one of them didn't explain what was going on soon, Will was going to explode.

Ty continued quickly, "There is much you do not know of me, Son. I have not always been a cobbler tucked away in a tiny village."

Will had to restrain a guffaw at that. This much he could figure out for himself after seeing that flash of deadly light from his father's fist. Not to mention the fancy armor and weapons. Will's parents huddled for a moment, whispering.

From the pine trunk at his back, a thread of . . . something . . . flowed. A faint energy. Awareness. Mayhap Mother Urth herself sensed and responded to his rage and disbelief. Living as he did so close to the land, he doubted not that the Green Lady lived and that her life's force flowed through all living things, binding them one to another in an endless cycle. So his elven mother had taught him, and so his own heart told him to be true.

But of a sudden he found himself wondering what was true and what false. Was everything his parents had taught him a lie? His world, so simple and orderly, had been turned to chaos in the span of a single hour, and nothing made sense anymore.

His father continued, "I have spent my life in search of truth, Son. A truth that will change the world. And now you must take up the search in my stead—"

His mother tensed beside him, interrupting, "Someone comes."

Ty whispered urgently, "What do you hear?"

Her words were mere breath, the sound traveling only a few feet. A tracker's skill, that. "Boki. Scouting party. Four, maybe five orcs spread out in a line."

Will gulped. If that many orcs found them, he and his parents were dead. Unless, of course, Ty's magic was sufficient to blow up an entire band of orcs.

Serica murmured, "They have acquired the countertrack I laid. They follow it now."

She could track *and* countertrack? Will's jaw sagged stupidly as he stared at her shadowed face.

"Quickly, Tiberius," his mother muttered. "We have two, maybe three minutes."

His father nodded and whispered urgently, "Will, you must get word of this attack to a man in Dupree right away."

"Have you lost your wits? There are Boki out there. Let us hide—together—until they leave, and then we all can take the message to this man."

"There is no time." Ty added heavily, "The Boki will not leave until they find me."

"We have mayhap one minute until they are close enough to hear us," his mother whispered.

"What do the Boki want with you, Father?"

Serica intervened smoothly. "Ahh. They have gone off the track again." She added in satisfaction, "They pursue my second countertrack."

She was a *master* tracker? The world had officially gone mad. She must have caught the thought in Will's eyes, for she muttered, "I was not always a cobbler's wife and your mother, you know. Quickly, Ty. Tell him. If you would send him to die, he has a right to know why."

Ty scowled, but did not argue with her.

Will looked back and forth between the two of them expectantly.

Ty took up his unspoken challenge. "I dared to search out a man whom the Boki are rumored to guard. A sleeping king.

An ancient and powerful elf who, when woken, prophecy says will lead us all to freedom."

The words rippled across Will's skin with a life of their own, their power making him shiver. *A sleeping king. Prophecy. Freedom.*

"Freedom from what?" Will whispered.

"The Kothites."

Will inhaled through his teeth on a hiss. Rebellion? To be caught thinking of it was suicide. To try it, even in small measure, was a death sentence for your family and all the people you'd ever known as well. Everybody knew rebellion was impossible.

Ty continued urgently, "The elven king ruled this continent before the coming of the Kothites. No one knows how or why, but he fell into an eternal sleep. The old legends say he waits until his people's moment of greatest need to wake again and lead them to safety. You must take up the quest, now."

"You want me to go into Boki-infested woods and risk dying for a children's hearth tale?"

"It is no hearth tale. I have seen the evidence of his existence myself. His crown. Made of eternally living, gold-edged leaves. A thing of great magic. Meant only for his brow. He's real, all right. You must find the Sleeping King. Wake him."

"Me?" Will's voice broke on the syllable in patent disbelief.

"They come this way," Serica muttered.

Ty glanced at her and continued in haste, "I was not alone in my search. Aurelius Lightstar. Selea Rouge. Leland Hyland. We were companions in the endeavor. But we failed. You must complete the quest in our stead. Seek them out. But trust no one else. *No one.*"

"He cannot do it alone!" Serica burst out.

Ty cut her off sharply. "He is all we have left. He must do it. We are old, tired men. This quest calls for fresh legs. The courage of youth."

"The rash recklessness of youth—" Serica started. She broke off abruptly, listening. "Ki'Raiden comes," she breathed. She turned fast and pressed something smooth and faintly warm into Will's hand. "By this token, Aurelius will know you and help you."

"Here. Put on this Boki tabard. And this belt and tooth necklace. They will make your silhouette look Boki from a distance." She helped him don the gear quickly.

Will jumped as his father's hard hand clamped down on his upper arm. Hot breath touched his ear. "Go now. Run like the wind. Your mother and I will occupy the Boki as long as we can. Go to Dupree. The Mage's Guild. Speak only to Aurelius. Tell him what happened here."

The hand loosed Will with a hard shove, and Ty took off running in the opposite direction, toward the approaching war party, gathering speed for a one-man charge.

"I will not leave—" Will started.

"Go!" his mother bit out with a ferocity he'd never heard from her before. Her bowstring twanged in the dark and then twanged again so quickly that the two sounds were barely distinguishable.

Ty crashed into the first of the orcs, his sword swinging like a thing possessed. Will stared in horror at the violence of it.

His mother muttered an apology and then something hit him in the chest. A faint, musical tinkling of glass breaking was audible over the din of orcish battle cries below. Was that a—

Raina hid in the darkest shadows at the back of the hall, lurking behind a wall hanging like she had as a little girl, frantically reviewing her options. She was half tempted to go back and beg Justin to run away with her. He would surely go with her rather than let her run away from home alone.

Except he might try to talk her out of it, too. He might even raise an alarm and hand her over to her mother. He'd become so bloody responsible of late; it was entirely possible he would betray her.

She knew practically everyone still drinking in the hall. Mayhap someone else here could be convinced to render aid to her. Scanning the rows of rapidly deteriorating revelers, her gaze lighted on a likely pair. Two elves who'd passed through now and again for years, traders rumored to be smugglers. Her mother had always been suspicious of them and considered them dodgy characters to be watched carefully. How they'd gained entrance to the feast tonight was anyone's guess. But mayhap they could help her slip out the same way they'd slipped in.

She waited impatiently for several servants to emerge from the kitchen, this time carrying the leftover desserts—fanciful confections made of spun sugar in the shapes of mythical creatures. Oooh, and red raspberries . . . her favorite. A pang of longing to stay and gorge herself on the pretty treats struck her. Except she was not so shallow as all that. She sidled in behind the line of servants and dropped quickly onto the bench beside the elves. One had the distinctive flame markings upon his skin of a pyresti—a fire elf. Natives of the nation of Pyrestan, they aligned themselves with the element of fire.

The other elf bore the stylized tattoos of a kindari—an untamed elf of the deep forests. His reminded her faintly of a spider's mandibles and fangs. She'd been taught that his kind had no homeland in particular. Rather, they aligned themselves with nature and the Green Court of the Fae historically. Their culture was clan based, and each clan apparently aligned itself with some specific animal. She would lay odds that his was a Spider clan.

"Good evening, gentlemen," she murmured.

They stared at her but, like most of their kind, revealed little emotion beyond mild curiosity. "Good evening, Lady Raina. To what happy circumstance do we owe this honor?" the pyresti replied.

"I haven't much time, and I need a favor."

That brought a hint of surprise into their eyes. "Of course. We are honored to serve the House of Tyrel," the pyresti murmured.

"This favor will greatly anger the House of Tyrel," she responded with reluctant honesty.

Definite interest sparked their gazes now. "Ask nonetheless," the kindari chimed in.

"I need to escape the keep, tonight. Immediately, in fact. I was hoping you could help me."

The elves exchanged quick glances that could have been anything from avid greed to deep skepticism. So hard to read, elves. All elegance and urbane sophistication on the outside, but who knew what went on between those pointed ears of theirs?

"And after you escape the keep?" the pyresti asked. "What then?"

She stared at him, flummoxed. She hadn't given a moment's thought to that. "I will keep on running, I suppose."

"It is an arduous path you propose to follow. Outlaws are not treated kindly in the Empire. They experience few comforts such as these"—the pyresti gestured at the hall around them—"and fewer safe havens."

The kindari objected, "It isn't as dire as all that, Moto."

"To a soft, coddled human from a noble house, it would be worse!" the pyresti retorted.

Desperate, she changed tactics. "What are your names?"

"I am called Moto," the pyresti replied. "And my talkative friend, here, goes by Cicero."

Called. Goes by. Those were not their real names, then. Which meant she had chosen well. These two must be the smugglers rumor said they were. "I do not jest, gentlemen. I must leave as quickly as possible. Even now, my mother and two powerful mages search for me to do me unspeakable ill. If you are to assist me, it must be now."

She looked furtively around the hall and lurched, bumping into Moto in her startlement. "There is one of my pursuers, now."

Kadir had just stepped into the great hall. Thankfully, he was at the far end of the large room and he was scanning the high table at the moment.

Cursing under her breath, she all but slid underneath the table in her panic not to be spotted.

Over her head, the two elves exchanged one last, long look between them before Moto grinned down at her. "You will require my cloak. Your garments practically glow in the dark. A small tip, my lady. White is the worst possible color for stealth. You would fare better to clothe yourself in gray or green, or even a dull brown like my forest friend, here, favors."

"If there were sufficient time for me to return to my chambers and change gowns, we would not be having this conversation," she muttered.

"Point taken. How are you at feigning drunkenness?" Moto murmured as he swept off his cloak and dropped it over her head. It smelled of pickled cabbage and the fiery hot sauce pyresti were known for dousing human food in. Quick, strong hands sorted the wool out around her, and in a moment she was able to see once more, albeit from behind the deep folds of a hood pulled well down over her face.

"This way, my lady," Cicero murmured.

"You mustn't call me that," she grumbled.

"Aye, true enough," the kindari laughed back. She realized with a start he was pretending to flirt as if she were a strumpet he was luring outside for a "midnight stroll."

Unable to see much beyond the flagstones beneath her feet, she stumbled along beside him, clinging to his arm with a certain credibility in her blindness. Her direction sense told her they headed for a rear exit from the hall.

"This way!" a low voice hissed. Moto.

Interesting that the pair had not brought up the topic of compensation for their help. Did they have a certain payment in mind? Although assault at their hands would be no worse than what the Mages of Alchizzadon had planned. Mayhap the satisfaction of thwarting her mother was payment enough for them. Or mayhap they were in the business of collecting favors owed. She'd heard something to that effect once about how bandits and outlaws operated.

The night had turned cold, the ground lightly frosted, and she was grateful for Moto's cloak. She pushed the hood back enough to see the main bailey of the keep, but was dismayed when Moto rejoined them and gestured toward the stables.

"They will look for me there," she whispered urgently.

"I just reconnoitered it," Moto whispered back. "Naught waits within but cows and goats. And the midden door is the speediest way out of the keep."

The midden door. Of course. It was a hinged section of the barn's exterior wall that swung outward to allow grooms to shovel manure through it. Dung rolled down the steep slope behind the keep, and local peasants hauled it away to spread upon their fields as fertilizer. It would make for a messy escape, but better than no escape at all. And it was Moto's cloak, after all. If he was willing to roll it in dung, who was she to argue?

They crept into the darkness of the barn, and the warm animal smell of it embraced Raina in familiar comfort. Her breath caught on a sob. She was going to miss home terribly.

Moto stumbled beside her and came to an abrupt halt, alarming her, and he grabbed her arm in a shockingly strong grip. His eyes burned like twin embers, glowing with an unholy light aimed at her. She recoiled, frightened.

"Cripes. Not now," Cicero whispered urgently.

Moto mumbled something in an odd accent that made her jolt. It was nearly the same ancient, vaguely elvish accent Kadir and his companion had used earlier! She frowned, concentrating on the elf's hoarse voice, and the sounds gradually sorted themselves into meaning.

". . . black is the name of the king, and green the heart of the slayer. Stars explode and ages turn before their battle ends. . . ." Moto grabbed her cloak, dragging her face close to his. His dark, unseeing gaze burned with madness. ". . . A sleeping king awaits thee, neither alive nor dead, fated to thee as thou art to him. You shall hold more power over him than you know. Wield it wisely, or the kingdom will crash down around us all. 'Twill be your fault. All your fault . . ." His voice trailed off.

She jerked away from his unnaturally powerful grasp. Staggered back. A sleeping king? Did he mean the Great Mage? How could he possibly know? A kingdom crashing down? Her fault? She looked up in dismay at Cicero and mumbled, "He's hallucinating."

The second elf shrugged. "He sees things on occasion. Professes that it comes from being dragon touched. He's surprisingly accurate, though."

In the name of the Lady, please let Moto be wrong this time. But the sick feeling in her gullet proclaimed her wish a lie. That was prophecy she'd just heard. And it bore the unmistakable ring of truth.

"We'd best be going now, my la—" Cicero broke off. "We'd best be going."

Moto roused beside her and shook his entire body like a dog emerging from a river. He snapped, "What are you standing around staring at? Let's go!"

"Someone comes," Cicero announced urgently. "Hide!"

Raina looked toward the door in alarm and recognized the broad-shouldered profile. Her father.

"What are you doing out here at this hour, Daughter?"

"I needed a moment alone to think." She glanced about surreptitiously, and the two elves seemed to have melted into the shadows.

"What could possibly weigh heavy upon the mind of my lovely daughter on her sixteenth birthday?" her father asked with humor in his voice.

Her heart wrenched at the word "daughter." *If only.* She

blurted, "Do you know what the Mages of Alchizzadon really do?"

He frowned. "They study rare magics. Now and again one passes through this way and is generous enough to share a bit of it with our family."

She snorted. That was one way of describing it. "Have you ever heard of a legend of an ancient mage who was supposed to marry one of our ancestors?"

"No." Her father looked genuinely ignorant of the legend. He was a man of deep honor; she could not imagine that he would lie to her.

"The mage fell into a stasis and could not be roused, and our family is supposed to keep a bride waiting for him in case he ever does wake?" she tried.

"That sounds like rather a waste of time and resources," he commented. "If the fellow did not wake fairly quickly after he went to sleep, he would have starved to death soon enough, would he not?"

"So you know nothing of a scheme by the Mages of Alchizzadon to breed a woman to be his wife and using our family as bloodstock?"

"We are not cattle, Raina. We are an established and noble family. What you speak of is ridiculous."

"Tell me this, Father. Have you any memory of taking a forgetting poison? Not long after you and Mother were married?"

He chuckled. "Well now. That would be the point of a forgetting poison, wouldn't it? No one remembers taking one. They forget doing so."

Frustration roiled through her. The mages had covered their tracks too well. Her father, like Justin, would flatly refuse to believe any accusations she made, on the grounds of their extreme absurdity.

"There you are!" a deep voice announced in satisfaction from behind them. "I knew you'd make a run for it, and sooner rather than later."

Raina and her father whirled to face the bulk of Kadir, effectively blocking the barn door.

"You're more like your mother than she will admit," Kadir continued. "Stubborn to a fault, both of you."

"I can attest to that," her father said, commiserating. As if he liked this monster in blue robes!

Raina considered the alleyway behind her. It was a long sprint to the midden door, but mayhap she could make it before Kadir struck her with that strange magical energy that clung to him.

"Don't try it," Kadir warned. "I had the midden door nailed shut a little while ago. Raina, why do you fight your mother on this? It is a great honor to be trained by my order."

Trained? *Trained?* "Is that the story you will put forth to cover kidnapping me?" she demanded angrily.

"What is this?" her father asked in confusion. "Raina is to be trained by you? Why do you call it kidnapping, Daughter? Do you not wish to study with the greatest mages in the land?"

"No," she answered forcefully. "I do not!"

Kadir intervened. "Your refusal to cooperate here compels me to remove you to Alchizzadon by force, if necessary."

A second shadow appeared in the doorway. It was the younger mage, who announced, "The rod, sir."

"Here now," her father said strongly. "No one is forcing her to go where she does not want to."

Kadir took the small stick held out to him and commenced incanting in that ancient tongue of theirs. Something about creating a link. A journey taking no time, beginning and end as one.

She didn't need to hear any more. He was opening a portal, no doubt back to Alchizzadon. The younger mage took a threatening step toward her, and the tableau exploded into violent action all at once. Her father's sword slithered out of its sheath. Two slim elven shapes charged out of the shadows at the younger mage. She bolted toward Kadir, or more accurately toward the exit at his back.

Her father shouted, "Nay! You shall not remove her from this place!"

The air around Kadir wavered as the portal started to form. The mage dived for Raina. She dived for the door. Her father dived for them both.

Magic flashed beside her and Moto cried out as the younger mage blasted him with some kind of spell that froze his entire body in place, paralyzed mid-swing of his sword.

A fast-moving object slammed into Kadir, knocking the large mage almost completely off his feet—her father, bellowing a war cry as he attacked.

Kadir staggered from the impact of her father smashing into him just as Raina drew abreast of him. The mage flung his arms toward her, seeking to snag her as she ducked low. Cicero yelled something incomprehensible—a warning, mayhap—and swung his sword forward over her shoulder to block the mage from grabbing her.

She snatched the rod out of Kadir's hand in hopes of disrupting the portal and dived for the floor, using her momentum to roll past the robed mage. A mighty explosion slammed into her, knocking her flat and sending a jolt of searing pain up her arm. The bolt of magic sank into her entire body, making her tingle painfully from head to foot. It threw Kadir and her father backward, slamming them into the open barn door. Something heavy landed on top of her and she hit her head on the ground hard enough to knock her a bit silly.

Everything went dark and silent.

A tangy smell of crushed leaves and bruised moss filled her nostrils. The weight rolled off of her abruptly, and she scrambled to her feet. She tensed to make a mad dash across the bailey for the portcullis—

But there was no bailey around her. No keep. No Kadir. No fight. She still gripped the rod in her hand, and it was warm. Pulsing slightly.

Just trees and more trees ringing a small, beautiful clearing bathed in cool moonlight. What was this passing strange place?

She turned to stare at Cicero, who half-crouched with his sword drawn, his gaze darting every which way in search of threats. He was real enough, apparently.

"Uhh, Raina? Where are we?"

She answered him slowly, "I have no idea."

A faint haze of gas, smelling of rotten eggs, floated in the air around Will for an instant. And then fear tore through his mind, ripping away all reason, all thought beyond one. *Flee this place.* The terror was incredible and irresistible. He spun and took off running with every ounce of strength in his being. *Must get away.*

Branches tore at him and he charged on heedlessly, the spurs of terror buried deep in his sides. He ran and ran, beyond pain, beyond breath, straining with his entire being to flee.

As suddenly as it started, the fear stopped. It drained away in the blink of an eye. And in the next blink, Will understood what had happened to him. His mother had struck him with fear gas poison. *Of course, she was an alchemist, too.* The sarcasm was sour in his mind.

He turned around with the intent to go back to his parents' aid. And they would be in . . . what direction? He was deep in a thicket, surrounded by heavy underbrush. He did not recognize this place at all. He scrambled clear of the bramble patch, clutching his now-shredded clothing closer. Pain began to register. On his face and hands. He was covered in bloody scratches.

As he tried to jog off in what he thought was the direction he'd come from, his limbs refused to cooperate. His legs trembled with exhaustion and his lungs burned like he'd breathed fire. He cursed his mother and her twice-cursed fear gas as he stumbled to a halt. His gut told him he wasn't going in the right direction anyway. He angled to his left and moved off again. No, that didn't feel right, either. He turned in a full circle and no direction at all felt right. Like it or not, he was well and truly lost.

Will paused to think. As he recalled, the effects of gas poisons generally lasted on the order of five minutes or so. By the time he ran back from whence he'd come, which was likely to take a fair bit longer than five minutes the way he felt now, the fight would be long over. Not to mention, he had not the slightest idea which direction to go. For all he knew, he would plunge even deeper into the forest.

The wise thing would be to hunker down until dawn, get his directional bearings, and make his way back to Hickory Hollow.

But then, when had he ever been wise?

Adrick always said to know his way before he moved. At the thought of his friend and mentor, grief and rage burned his eyes. Will swiped at his face and forced himself to concentrate. *Look first,* he could hear Adrick admonish. The trees were too thick in this spot to use the stars to navigate. *Listen second.* He went perfectly still, holding his breath as he closed his eyes and focused all his energy on his ears.

The forest creatures were still, no doubt as a result of his noisy charge through the wood. Off to his left, he thought he might just hear the sounds of battle. But it was at the very edge of his hearing. Ahh, to have his mother's ears—

Assuming she was not dead. Which both head and heart told him to be a foolish assumption. Grief welled up again, and yet again he forced it down. He must survive, now. Find his parents. Save them if possible.

He wandered toward the sounds until he lost track of time and began to believe he had imagined them. He kept expecting to come to some place or thing he recognized. A particular tree or stream or even a path. But he managed to miss every last landmark he might have used to orient himself.

He thought he heard a new noise. Froze. Turned his head side to side to ascertain the exact direction of the ever so faint sound. That way. Roots grabbed at his feet and stones hidden under dead leaves waited to turn his ankles as he raced forward.

He took note of a tree well ahead and one close behind. When he reached the tree ahead, he used the tree behind him to sight ahead once more as Adrick had shown him to do. It was how a woodsman kept to a course and did not end up wandering in circles.

He sighted forward twice more before he noted that the trees thinned ahead into a wide clearing. *Praise the Lady.* Finally, he could check the stars and know what direction he traveled. But a few more steps brought him to an abrupt halt. That was no clearing. It was the Southwatch Path, the forest cut well back from it.

This road was nearly two miles beyond Hickory Hollow! He'd run at least twice as far under the effects of the fear gas as he had guessed. No wonder he'd been lost. Did he dare step out of the tree cover and follow the road back to the hollow? It would be by far the fastest way back to his parents and the other villagers. But the open path would also expose him to any Boki patrols roaming the area. Would the Boki be so bold as to march right down this road? Indecision rooted his feet to the ground.

He could not stand here all night. He might as well check out the road. Crouching low, he crept forward to peer out at the path.

A destroyed wagon lay on its side, three cloth-covered lumps that could only be bodies scattered around it. He checked carefully up and down the road for movement. Nothing. If Boki had done this, they were no longer in sight.

But he did not trust the orcs not to use the wagon as bait to draw in more victims. He backed into the forest a bit and quickly plucked twigs from the trees, tucking them into his clothing randomly as Adrick had taught him. He scooped up handfuls of dead leaves and sprinkled them over himself liberally, too, the bits sticking to his leather jacket. Streaks of mud upon his already-dirtied face and a few handfuls of grass in his collar and he was ready.

He eased out of the tree line on his belly, slithering like a snake toward the wagon. Down into a swale and back up out of it, then the dirt path loomed inches from his nose. Still no movement from the forest. Carefully, he rose to a crouch in the shadow of the wagon. Still no attack.

He straightened cautiously and approached the first body, a human in leather armor and gauntlets—likely a guard of some kind. He nudged the man with his foot. No response. He nudged harder. Glassy, staring eyes looked up at him, and he recoiled. Poor sod looked dead.

Will moved on to the next body, another guard judging by his garb. He rolled the fellow onto his back. A gaping hole in the man's chest made it pretty clear this one was dead as well.

Will moved around the wagon and saw two more bodies on the ground. Both attired in white trimmed in red. *Members of the Heart?* He moved toward the first healer, and this fellow, too, was bloody and unresponsive. *Must be dead.*

Will turned to the last victim. A young girl of an age with him, pale and beautiful with long dark braids and still, exotic features. He touched her cheek. Warm. *Alive, thank the Lady—*

With a banshee scream, the girl lurched upright. He scrambled backward and landed on his behind as she leaped to her feet in panic. "Murderer!" she yelled, charging him. Her right hand glowed menacingly.

A blast of magic shot wide of his head and smashed randomly into the bottom of the overturned wagon. Another blast flew into the grass beyond the road.

"I'm not . . . I mean no harm . . . I but checked for survivors! . . . ," he cried out.

"To loot us? Thief!" She whipped a short sword out of her belt and swung furiously at him.

He plastered himself flat on the ground to avoid a beheading at the hands of this crazy girl. She all but knocked herself off her feet, overbalancing after the wild swipe at him. He rolled and jumped to his feet.

She shouted, "You dare take advantage of our misfortune? Attacking the Heart is an Imperial crime punishable by death!"

She must have thought he was a Boki. "Will you quit shouting at me?" he finally shouted back. "I am trying to help—"

The blast of magic hit him squarely in the chest with a burst of heat and a tingling across his skin. He looked down in horror expecting to see a bloody hole in his chest. But he was surprisingly intact. This girl was completely crazy!

He opened his mouth to declare that very thing—but no sound came out. Stunned, he tried again. Nothing. He tried to force a shout past whatever blocked his throat—

—The wench had *silenced* him.

Furious, he glared at her. He stripped off the Boki belt and tabard and threw the necklace of teeth and bones to the ground, and then pointed at his throat.

"Not a chance!" she retorted. "Came back to loot us and finish me off, did you? What is the matter? You didn't steal enough supplies the first time?" She swung the short sword in his direction, but he dodged the blade easily. His father was ten times that fast with a broomstick.

Still, Will had no desire to find out what other, more lethal magics she might have in her arsenal. He danced backward away from her clumsy attack, holding his hands well away from his sides to show her he was unarmed and meant her no harm.

She flew at him like an angry sparrow defending her nest from a hawk, wisps of dark hair flying across her furious, frightened face. He twisted and dodged her completely unskilled swordplay until the whole thing began to strike him as rather hilarious.

Perhaps it was the grin upon his face or maybe his failure to attack in kind, but one or both finally seemed to penetrate her panic. The sword wavered. Lowered to her side. The angry glow about her right hand dimmed somewhat. The wildness drained from her huge, dark, entirely mesmerizing eyes as she stared at him.

He pointed once more at his throat.

"Oh, it'll wear off soon enough," she groused. "It has been almost five minutes already."

Sure enough, the tightness around his throat began to ease, and in a few moments he was able to ask cautiously, "Did orcs attack you?"

She nodded at that, then added in a rush, "I could not believe it when they charged out of the forest. What on Urth are orcs doing in this area?"

"It's a long story and I do not know the half of it," he

replied grimly. "Do you have any healing for your companions?"

She shook her head miserably. "I know some healing spells, but I cannot renew a life, yet." She added defensively, "It's a difficult spell to master."

"What happened?"

"I was tired and the *prala*—the brother—told me to take a nap. I was sleeping when the orcs charged out of the woods. They knocked the wagon over. I must have hit my head and kind of panicked—"

From what Will had seen of her wild reaction to him there'd been no "kind of" about it. She'd completely gone to pieces.

"—I tried to help, but the orcs were so big and strong . . ." She began to cry as she spoke, her story interrupted by sobbing breaths. "So many of them . . . and not just orcs. Goblins and monsters . . . our guards were killed so fast . . . the *prala* tried to fight with magic, but he's a healer, not a combat caster . . . I didn't know what to do . . . then something hit me on the side of my head." She buried her face in her hands, unable to continue.

But he got the gist of it. Awkwardly, Will stepped forward and put his arms around her slender frame. She threw herself against him, wrapping her arms tightly around his waist. He stiffened in surprise and patted at her back ineffectually as she sobbed into his shirt. *How long was she going to be doing this?*

Clueless as to how to proceed—his mother had never devolved into emotional displays—he stood there for what seemed like a week of Sundays.

Eventually, the girl raised her head and stepped away from him. "Thank you," she murmured.

For what? He let her wet his shirt for a few minutes. He

mumbled something incoherent, and it seemed to satisfy the emotional girl. "What's your name?" he asked.

"Rosana. You?"

"Will." He frowned, not wishing to offend her, but there was something different about her, and the accent . . . "You're not . . . Are you . . ."

"Gypsy," she answered defiantly. "The great gaj—sorry, the high matriarch—in Dupree took me into the Kaer—gah! I did it again. The Heart—so it's all legal and aboveboard."

"Umm, okay." Will looked around the clearing cautiously. "We probably should get out of the middle of the road in case another Boki patrol comes back."

"Boki?" she repeated skeptically.

Curse it, curse it, curse it. He wasn't supposed to talk about it to anyone but that Aurelius fellow in Dupree. He back-tracked quickly, doing his best to play stupid. "Isn't that what all orcs are called?"

"Hardly," she answered scornfully. "Boki are legendary fighters. They're a particular tribe of orcs and live in Forest of Thorns in the far north of Dupree. They do not live anywhere near here."

"Oh." A pause. "We still should get out of the road."

She ignored him and instead took a long, critical look at the wagon. "The axle is broken. Not to mention the oxen are long gone. The orcs have probably eaten them by now," she added sadly.

"Liked the cows, did you?"

She threw him an annoyed look. *Bossy little thing.*

"We must walk. Which means we'll need portable supplies," she said briskly. "Find a sack while I gather food and gear."

Like he didn't know what equipment was important?

Irritated, he did as she said, nonetheless. She was the Heart member, after all.

Of all the Imperial guilds, the House of the Healing Heart was by far the most widely respected in the colonies. They were always willing to heal a commoner in return for whatever the person could afford to pay, even if the patient could afford to pay nothing. Without the Heart, and healers like this girl, willing to brave the dangers of a half-tamed land, a difficult life in the colonies would be nigh impossible.

In a few minutes he surveyed the small pile of supplies she'd collected. Rope, flint and steel, a long sword and two daggers from the guards, flatbread, dried meat, and several water skins. He added a waterproof tarp, a wool blanket, and a coil of snare wire to the pile, then commenced stuffing it all in the two large bags he'd found.

He passed her the smaller and lighter of the two sacks, and she lashed it to her back cleverly using a length of rope and a spare sword belt to distribute the weight comfortably on her hips.

Reluctantly, he muttered, "Can you show me how to do that?"

She smiled brilliantly at him. "A boy willing to ask a girl for help? Maybe you're not so dim-witted after all."

Dim-witted? Were he not so interested in how she tied his pack and the way her soft, quick hands flew across his shoulders and down his back, he might have taken offense at that.

"How did you and your friends come to be here, tonight?" he asked curiously.

"This afternoon, we threw a wheel. By the time we got it fixed, dark had fallen. We tried to reach Hickory Hollow to spend the night. But the orcs attacked us instead." She devolved into muttering under her breath that sounded suspiciously like she was taking the orcs' names in vain.

"I'm from Hickory Hollow. I need to go back and check on my family."

She spoke sorrowfully. "We saw the fire of your village burning just before we were attacked. Orcs never burn until after they're finished looting and killing."

She might as well have thrust a dagger through his heart. He sat down hard, right there in the middle of the road. His parents? His friends? All dead? It could not be. His mind went blank at the enormity of it.

"You were right before," Rosana said. "We need to go."

He looked up at her bleakly. They were all gone. Everyone he knew. Slaughtered like sheep. Ty had failed to save them. And his own insistence on his father making the attempt had gotten his parents killed, too. It was all his fault—

Rosana chided gently, "You are not the only person ever to lose friends and loved ones. This is the Kothite Empire. Tragedy and suffering are all around you."

Stung, he retorted, "I know the suffering the Empire causes!"

A pause. Then she announced, "You will not get anywhere planted on your bum in dust."

He clambered to his feet and muttered, "Has anybody ever told you that you can be a wee bit pushy?"

"Maybe once or twice." She smiled crookedly at him. "Northeast, to Dupree, then. That's where the nearest Heart chapter with a heartstone is. Spirits from here would go there to resurrect."

Hope fired in his breast. *Resurrection? Of course.* Maybe his parents—and the others from the hollow, of course— would resurrect in Dupree. It was an optimistic thought to latch on to, and at the moment he had need of such.

She started off down the road, and he followed, hurrying to catch up. "I think we should stay off the path—" He broke off, grabbing her arm in warning. He signaled for her to be silent and she nodded her understanding of the woodsman's signal.

There it was again. Twigs snapping, underbrush rustling, and leaves rattling underfoot. A big group. Headed this way. And totally unconcerned for stealth. Rosana looked at him frantically for confirmation and he nodded grimly. *Orcs.*

Stay close, he mouthed. And then he took off running as lightly as his exhausted legs would carry him, racing for cover with Rosana on his heels.

Wait here," Cicero ordered tersely.

Raina nodded, watching in amazement as he climbed the largest tree edging the clearing as easily as a squirrel.

He was back in a minute. "We appear to be at the southern margin of a line of forested hills. To the north and east stretches nothing but tree cover. To our west, the woods thin somewhat. If we are to find civilization, logic dictates that it will lie that way."

Logic dictates? That was awfully educated language from a bandit. It was a phrase she was known to use, in fact.

"Where are you from originally?" she asked him, trying to keep suspicion from creeping into her voice.

"The Sorrow Woods. North of Tyrel."

"Are there schools in the woods?"

"Not all bandits are ignorant louts," he observed. "Particularly not when they are bandits on account of the Kothite Empire."

She had no idea how to respond to such a statement.

He smiled sardonically at her. "We do not have a school, but my village has a sponsor. A woman whom outsiders call the Black Widow. She keeps the oral histories of my people and teaches the stories to my kin. She is knowledgable on many subjects and enjoys teaching the children of my village."

"Do you recognize this place, then?" Raina asked, looking around curiously. "Is it Alchizzadon?" Her gaze darted about seeking rune-marked mages wearing dark blue in the shadows.

"Not unless Alchizzadon is a clearing in a wood," Cicero replied dryly.

"The porters said the Mages of Alchizzadon came from Jena. If we are near there, we might be close to their home."

Her companion shook his head in the negative. "These are rowan trees, and the hills around us are old. Worn down. Jena is surrounded by oak forests with young, sharp mountains to the north. And rowans like a cooler climate than Jena's."

Still, a prickle of magic tingled across her scalp as she looked around the clearing. Mayhap it was just the moonlight kissing the carpet of woodland flowers, soft grass, and moss that made it seem so extraordinarily beautiful. Each massive tree ringing the clearing was nigh unto perfect in form and symmetry. Every leaf was green and lush and perfectly placed upon its respective branch. The rod still gripped in her fist was growing warmer, vibrating gently, almost as if it were a living thing.

"I do not ever recall seeing rowans so tall," she commented. The few specimen rowans she'd seen before were little more than stunted shrubs.

"These ones are unusually robust," Cicero agreed. "And amazingly well tended. Trees as ancient as these are rarely in such good health."

"Have you ever seen a wood so lovely?" she breathed.

He looked around, a frown taking root upon his brow. Of a sudden he took her by the elbow and hurried her toward the edge of the clearing. He muttered, "Let us be quit of this place, and quickly."

"Why?"

"Because this clearing is fae touched."

She turned eagerly to look at the clearing again. Might she see a pixie or a sprite if she looked carefully?

"Yon is a dryad grove," Cicero growled. "I've no desire to tangle with one of them. Evil, conniving wenches, one and all."

Raina swore she heard a faint tinkle of laughter on the cool night breeze. Cicero must have heard it, too, for he dragged her practically at a run toward the edge of the clearing.

He all but lifted her off her feet in his haste to be quit of the place. She did not fight him. They passed out of the grove and suddenly the night seemed darker and colder. Colorless. Cicero took off running, never letting go of her arm.

When her breath came in gasps, her legs were failing, and she felt faint, Raina begged, "May we please slow down and rest? I'm like to die of exhaustion if we go much further at this pace."

With one last worried look over his shoulder, Cicero did as she asked. She flopped onto the ground, grateful for the cool and damp of the moss beneath her. When she had re-covered enough breath to speak, she panted, "Who was laughing back there?"

"Dryads."

Dryads were fae tree spirits known for their powers of se-duction over males of all species. No wonder Cicero had been sweating grapes. She looked down at the rod in her hand, now cool and still. Just a stick. She stuffed it in her belt pouch.

"Are you planning to run me like that again?" she asked.

"Maybe. Why?"

"Then you're going to have to help me remove this blasted corset."

His eyes widened in alarm as she stood up and presented her back to him. She wasn't brave enough to look over her shoulder and see what Cicero thought of all that. She merely waited expectantly, as if it were perfectly normal to have a male elf, and a bandit at that, partially undress her.

Something cool swept down her spine, and all of a sudden her dress sagged, all but falling off of her. She snatched at it in shock, squawking, "Did you just cut all my laces?"

"It seemed the most expedient way to get it off."

"You not only cut my corset strings; you cut my dress strings, too. How will I hold my dress up, now? I cannot run around the countryside naked!"

"Oh. I confess I am not familiar with women's clothing."

"You think?" she snapped.

While she pulled the awful corset out from under her clothing and discarded it into the bushes with great satisfaction, the kindari rummaged in his pouch and came up with a ball of rough twine. She rolled her eyes, but let him lace her dress together after a fashion with the hemp. She expected it made her look like a cheap doxy, but there was nothing she could do about it, at present. Frustrated, she stomped after him in the dark.

Cicero commented apologetically over his shoulder, "You didn't run too badly for a girl, and a human to boot. Particularly wearing that corset contraption."

She retorted, "Next time you want me to run like that, just kill me and be done with it!"

He laughed under his breath as she drew Moto's cloak close around her. "Now what?" she asked Cicero.

"I was about to ask you the same. What are your wishes, my lady?"

"I think we can safely dispense with the title. This is definitely not Tyrel, and my circumstances make it a likely wager that I shall never return home. My title is meaningless now."

"If you do not object to my asking, what predicament made you flee from prosperity, safety, and a loving family?"

It was still too new a wound, too painful to speak of. She shook her head and answered merely, "Mayhap someday I shall speak of it. But please believe me that only the most dire of threats drove me away."

Thankfully, he let the subject drop. Idly, Cicero picked up a stick and pushed aside the pine needles to expose a square of black dirt completely foreign to Tyrel's red clay and white limestone. He commenced drawing random shapes in it.

"Have you any idea where we are?" she ventured to ask.

"How far is it possible for that ritual you interrupted to have projected us?" he countered.

She winced. "We could be anywhere on Urth. Literally. We may not even be on the same continent anymore. For all I know, this could be Koth." Although somehow, that did not feel right to her. This place was still . . . familiar.

He did not look happy at that prospect of landing in Koth.

"I suppose the first order of business is to figure out where we are," she offered. "We could make camp for the night, and on the morrow see if we can find someone who can tell us what place this is."

"It is my considered opinion that it would be better to travel now," Cicero replied.

"But it is dangerous at night. Bandits and outlaws are out and about."

"*We* are bandits and outlaws. You ran away from home and are a fugitive, are you not? And I . . . rendered aid to you."

Hah. He had been about to declare himself an outlaw in his own right.

He continued, "Imperial soldiers move during the day. Hence, we are prudent to move at night."

"Cicero, I have no right to ask it of you, but please do not leave me alone in these woods." She laid a beseeching hand upon his arm. Something of kindness, rough honor, seemed to emanate into her palm. She continued, "I have no coin to pay you, but I will find a way to—"

He interrupted sharply, offended. "I require no coin to lend my protection to a young girl who would otherwise be alone in a dangerous wood in a strange land. I will turn my sword and my skill to your protection as long as you have need of them." She must have looked fearful still, because he added more gently, "I give you my word."

Gratitude nearly brought her to her knees. "Just don't run me into the ground, please?"

That got a grin out of him. "Stick with me and I will make a fine outlaw of you."

She could do a lot worse than a kindari protector. The forest elves were renowned for their woodcraft and tracking skills, not to mention their skills as hunters and warriors. She supposed it came from surviving in the wilds and having to defend themselves from whatever threats came their way. Not to mention they were known for flying into incredible rages in battle that rendered them impervious to pain and fatigue. The trick was to avoid provoking such a rage when in the presence of kindari, however.

The night's hike took them through gradually thinning forest. At one point, the girth of the trees diminished sharply, and Cicero murmured that these woods had been harvested within the past decade or two by the Forester's Guild—a sure sign that the two of them neared human habitation.

The night grew chill and damp, and were it not for Moto's sturdy cloak she would be shivering with cold. Her dainty slippers did nothing to protect her feet from the cold and the rough ground, though, and she was miserable even with the cloak.

Cicero followed game trails that, although meandering, made his and Raina's progress through the forest easier. Deep in the darkest hour of night, they ran across a road. It was barely more than parallel wheel tracks half-smothered in grass, but a road nonetheless. They trudged along side by side in the tracks until she thought she was going to fall over from exhaustion.

They were at the base of a long slope and she had just taken a deep breath to gird herself for the climb when Cicero abruptly grabbed her arm and dragged her off the road into a thick stand of brush. He pressed a finger over his lips and she nodded her understanding. That was when she heard what had sent Cicero diving for cover. Men. Talking.

Three silhouettes topped the hill. Similar in height and nearly identical in dress, they all wore tabards with vertically halved heraldry. Some light color lay over their hearts and a dark shade lay on the right. All three wore boiled-leather armor under the colors, long swords on their hips, and mailed coifs on their heads. Soldiers, then.

The patrol drew parallel to their hiding place and she made out their colors. A black griffin in gold on the left, and black on the right. Her jaw dropped. *The Haelan legion?* If she was not mistaken, the badges on the men's chests identified them as members of a Dupree regiment.

Were they close to Dupree?

The city lay on the northeast coast of the continent, capital of the colonized lands in this corner of Haelos. Tyrel lay south and west nearly as far inland as it was possible to go and still be in civilized lands.

She reviewed what little she knew of Dupree. It was named

after Jobère Dupree, discoverer of this continent. As capital, the city was thick with Imperial presence. Apparently, colonized lands constituted only a tiny corner of the continent. The Emperor must be salivating at the notion of an entire, massive continent to settle and bring to heel. All those lovely resources to exploit for his own wealth and power . . .

She glanced at Cicero, and he looked nearly as thunderstruck as she. He must recognize the colors, too. The soldiers, jesting and laughing among themselves, passed out of sight over the next ridge.

Cicero gestured for her to follow him farther off the path. Crawling on their hands and knees for the last bit, he led her into the center of what appeared to be an impenetrable tangle of vines and brambles. He stomped the center flat, though, and cut out the worst of the thorny vines. "Rest, Raina. I shall stand watch through the night."

Rest? Surely he was not serious. But he eased his sword—which she noted was a finely made blade—free of its sheath and laid it across his lap. She drew Moto's cloak close as best she could and lay down, squirming until only a few thorns poked her.

What had she done by her rash decision to run? Just how much trouble were she and Cicero in? The specter of a disastrous ending to this misadventure loomed close, leering down at her in the night, coming for her.

Doubt began to set in. Was all of this worth it? Was she really so determined to avoid the fate of the women in her family? If it had been good enough for her ancestors for three hundred generations, why was it not all right for her? Was she merely being spoiled and rebellious? Was it so wrong to just do what her mother and the mages wanted and then get on with her life?

Arianna seemed pretty happy to go along with the

program. Of course, she was young and beautiful and got treated like a princess, and when Raina's daughter grew up to take her place—

Raina sat bolt upright in the dark, scratching her face on a thorn painfully.

"Is aught amiss?" Cicero whispered sharply.

"No. Sorry." She lay back down, appalled. When her daughter took Arianna's place, then what? What would happen to her sister? Raina's own sister had to have supplanted Charlotte's older sister as the resident bride-in-waiting . . . and then the full horror of the mages' scheme slammed into her.

Auntie Ari had left Tyrel a couple of years previously. There had been a big ceremony and feast to mark the occasion. It had taken place only days after Arianna turned sixteen. Raina remembered her aunt's departure vividly. It was the only time she'd ever seen her mother cry. She'd wondered at it at the time. But now it made perfect sense. Charlotte and Auntie Ari had known their farewells that day were forever.

Ironic how the locals had cheered at her aunt's departure. They'd all beamed with pride that yet another daughter of Tyrel was going forth into the world to find herself a rich and noble husband and spread the reputation of Tyrel as a cultured and civilized place far and wide. *Hah.*

Where had Ari gone? For that matter, where did all the Ariannas go? If a new one was born and trained every sixteen to eighteen years, there might realistically be three or even four generations of brides-in-waiting alive somewhere. Surely such educated and accomplished women would go forth and make significant marks upon the world. Yet in all her studies, Raina had never run into any reference to such women. How was it they all faded into obscurity?

Were they allowed to have their own families after they

were released from their obligation? The Ariannas were bred to be extremely gifted with magic. Surely their children would inherit some of that. If they were marrying and having children of their own, then after three hundred generations Tyrel should be crawling with extraordinarily talented magic users. And yet it was not. Which meant—

Her outrage was complete as the logical explanation smashed into her.

. . . Which meant the Mages of Alchizzadon captured or killed the Ariannas. Prevented them from living out their lives as they wished.

Raina frowned. She'd never seen a Mage of Alchizzadon in Tyrel, never heard of one passing through except for the two at the manor house now. Auntie Ari had muttered something as she left about walking into the rising sun until the road ended. That must be where the mages did the deed.

Had she been obliquely referring to walking out into the arid Nomad plains to die? Raina had read a few references to ritual suicide in such a manner being an old tradition in Tyrel. Horror rolled through her. It was *barbaric*.

"What do you know of the plains that lie to the west beyond Tyrel?" she asked Cicero abruptly.

"The Arianna Plains?" he asked, surprised.

"Is that what you call them?"

His voice held a frown as it floated out of the dark. "That appellation would be how they are known to everyone with whom I am acquainted."

Shocked, she demanded, "Why is that?"

"An old hearth tale speaks of a girl by that name being jilted by her lover and, in her grief, walking out into those plains to die."

Raina snorted. The hearth tale was not so far from true. Funny thing. She'd never heard the name Arianna Plains or seen the area marked thus on a map. But then, it would not do to let the current bride-in-waiting know what fate awaited her, now would it?

There was no way her sister knew she would be sent away to die when she was barely into her thirties. Arianna would not be so smug did she have any inkling of the brutal end awaiting her.

She and her sister had had their disagreements over the years, but Raina wished no ill upon Arianna. And Raina certainly had no wish to see her sister die. She bloody well wasn't passing on this cruel tradition to her own daughters, either!

A startling thought occurred to her. If she never had daughters, it would buy her sister more time to live. She would have to be kept around until her replacements could be bred, would she not? Charlotte and the Mages of Alchizzadon would have to come up with a replacement broodmare. Maybe wait for one of her younger brothers—the oldest one was barely twelve—to grow up, marry, and have daughters of his own before the family tradition could resume. The introduction of her father's blood into the line of daughters of Tyrel would likely be a major setback for the mages, but that was the price they paid for playing fast and loose with other people's lives.

She *had* to find a way to break the tradition once and for all. Not only for her own sake, but also for her sister's.

Curse the Great Mage anyway. Who cared about some old legend—

Her thoughts derailed abruptly. That was it. The Great Mage. If she found a way to gather the magics to restore him, her sister could marry the man and the House of Tyrel would no longer have to use its daughters so sorely.

"Cicero?"

"Hmm?"

"Do you know of any source of really old, really powerful magic?"

"For what purpose?"

"I need to . . . power up . . . something very old."

"Like an artifact?"

It wasn't a bad analogy. Certain powerful, and typically old, magic items could retain long-term magical charges upon them. If their energy ran out, they could be recharged. Usually artifacts were named, which acted as a signal of what they were. "Yes, something like that," she answered.

"How ancient a magic do you seek, and what quantity of power do you need?" he queried.

"I'll need ancient magic and potentially a lot of it," she answered reluctantly.

"The only source of ancient magic that I have ever heard of would be the Mythar," Cicero answered.

"What's a Mythar?"

"Who is a Mythar," he corrected. "The Mythar was lord of all the nature guardians. The Mythar was said to be an elf who went on to become a great king."

"How long ago was that?" she asked eagerly. "And was he by any chance a magic user?"

"How would I know how long ago it was? I am kindari; we keep our histories by word of mouth, not written documents. Details like time get lost in the passing down of the stories. "As for magic, I suppose he used it. Most nature guardians are masters of nature magic and, hence, magic casters."

That sounded promising. If this Mythar fellow still existed, he might be able to restore the Great Mage.

"Any idea where I might find the Mythar?" she asked.

"That knowledge rests far, *far* above my station in life to possess."

"Would your Black Widow know where to find him?"

"I sincerely doubt it. I've heard all of her stories, and none of them even hint at such a thing."

Raina was disappointed but not discouraged. She had a name. It was a start.

Will and Rosana crouched in the woods just beyond the crossroads. They'd been creeping through the brush and trees all night. He'd heard movement that was likely two-footed humanoids several times through the night, but never close by. Whoever had been out there had been moving fast and in force. Like an orcish war party.

To her credit, Rosana had not complained about the rough conditions or the all-night trek. And her woodcraft was not half-bad for a city girl. She moved lightly and quietly for the most part.

With the coming of daylight he expected the orc raiding party would go to ground and rest. It should be safe for him and Rosana to move along the roads through the day, "should" being the operative word. They would make much better time on a road than picking their way through brambles and bushes all day. He didn't know about Rosana, but he was too exhausted to do much more than stumble along a nice, smooth path at this point.

"Is it safe now?" Rosana whispered.

"I think so. Orcs are not known for traveling during the day."

She cast a worried look at the broad clearing ahead of them. "So it is a choice between fast, dangerous travel and slow, safe travel."

He shrugged. "If we take the road, we'll see the Boki coming in enough time to run for cover. Maybe they catch us and maybe they don't. Or we can stick to the woods, take three times as long to get clear of the Wylde Wood, and still maybe run into them."

"What do you think?" she asked.

Straight ahead was the Southwatch Fort. A small contingent of the Haelan legion of the Imperial Army was stationed there and should, by rights, be warned of the Boki invasion. But his father had been specific. Go to Dupree. Speak to no one of the orcs except some fellow in the Mage's Guild there. Aurelius. That path lay to the left.

And to the right . . . to the right lay Hickory Hollow, a burnt-out and deserted hull of a village according to Rosana.

He was the only survivor; he knew it as surely as he felt the ground beneath his feet. Maybe some in the hollow had spirits strong enough to make it all the way to Dupree to resurrect. But he doubted it. He remembered overhearing his parents discuss the capital city being right at the limit of how far a disembodied spirit might travel successfully from Hickory Hollow. He hadn't understood at the time what it meant and was only now comprehending it fully.

It meant that all the residents of the hollow were permanently dead. And his parents, too. Grief slammed down on Will like an avalanche, crushing his chest in agony too painful to breathe against. A choked sound escaped his throat before he could cut it off. Their deaths were not fair. The dead deserved justice. But stars knew, the Empire would not serve up any reckoning for the fallen of Hickory Hollow. This world only offered up noble ideals like justice and mercy to the rich and powerful. The rest of the populace lived and died in misery and poverty, virtual or actual slaves of the Empire and its nobles.

"Castlegate Falls is to the left, and Dupree lies beyond it," Rosana finally blurted. "I say we go there."

He'd learned overnight that she could be entirely single-minded in her focus. And at the moment all her energy was directed at reaching the Heart in Dupree as soon as possible. But his choice was not so simple. The logical thing to do was go straight on to the Southwatch Fort. Warn the villages of the Ring. Unless he believed his father, and unless something much bigger was afoot than a simple orc raid.

Did he believe his father about any of it? About some story of a sleeping elven king? About quests and crowns and rebellion?

How much did he really know of his father? The warrior-mage of last night, boldly challenging and crushing Boki fighters, bore no resemblance whatsoever to the simple cobbler Will had grown up with. Had everything he'd thought he'd known about his father been something else entirely? What if Ty's paranoia had good cause? What if he had been in hiding all along? Then his secrecy and insistence on never drawing attention to himself or his family would make sudden sense.

What about that suit of armor worth more than everyone in Hickory Hollow together could earn in years? The white sword his mother had called Dragon's Tooth? As far as Will knew, there was no such thing as dragons. If he was right, then that meant his father owned a *named* sword. An artifact of enough power to earn a name of its own could very well be the worth of a small kingdom. Then there was the way Ty had snapped orders as if born to command and handled a sword and shield like a seasoned knight. What of all that?

And the magic. Why on Urth had Ty never revealed his skill with it and garnered a life of wealth and ease for himself and his family, unless he truly had been secretly contemplating and planning rebellion? Did Will dare follow his parents down that path? No matter how much the notion might fire his blood, it would most assuredly lead to his destruction.

Had he not seen all he had last night, he would have accused his parents of losing themselves in wild fantasy. But he *had* seen. And he *had* heard of this Sleeping King fellow, now. It was not something he could unhear or unknow. Like it or not, his parents had transferred their illicit quest and its attendant risks to him. The only question left to answer was, what was he going to do about it?

"What are you waiting for?" Rosana demanded.

"Nothing," he answered in decision.

"Let us get going, then. We've far to go to reach our journey's end."

She was most certainly correct. A long journey lay before him no matter which path he chose. And a happy outcome was not likely at the end of any road he took. But he could honor his parents, at least.

He nodded with finality. So be it.

Rosana grabbed his hand, and he let her drag him down the left-hand turning of the path. Toward Dupree. In search of a man called Aurelius and whatever he might know of a quest to find a sleeping king.

Raina trudged along behind Cicero, tired and hungry and thirsty. But mostly tired. They had been walking all day, stopping only to hide when other travelers came close. She did not know what she would have done without the kindari. A sense of comfort clung to him. Mayhap it was because his presence made her feel slightly connected to home, still. Although taciturn for the most part, Cicero seemed generally at ease with her as well. But then, she had that effect on most people.

She chewed anxiously on a fingernail as she weighed her options. A perplexed farmer had paused long enough in plowing his field earlier to inform her and Cicero that they were in Hyland, a week's hard march west of the city of Dupree. The hills they had walked out of overnight were the Grimshaw Hills. Not, the farmer informed them, a place anyone who wished to live for long visited. He gave them directions to the main highway between Hyland and Dupree, somewhat south of their current location.

Her mother would search for Raina up to a point. But instinct told her that part of Charlotte secretly approved of her daughter's rebellion. Her mother would probably not give chase outside of Tyrel, which Raina most definitely was, now.

The Mages of Alchizzadon were another story, however. They would not give up the search for her anytime soon. They had years in which to find her and kidnap her for their purposes. She must do the unexpected. Keep the mages off balance and off her trail. Everyone would expect her to go back to Tyrel, or at least the Midlands, which lay just to the north of Tyrel. To places she was familiar with and where her name and rank held some weight. Dupree it was, then. They would find this main road and circle back to the east and the capital city. She'd be twice cursed before she'd go down to defeat cowering like a terrified mouse. After all, she was a daughter of Tyrel.

The outrage that had driven her from home last night had dwindled to a dull, steady ache of betrayal. Why had her mother gone along with the mages' plan? Raina trudged on, determination to foil the mages hardening in her heart. Or mayhap it was nothing more than pure, bullheaded stubbornness that kept her moving. It wasn't noble, but it was enough to shuffle her feet forward, one weary step after another. Away. Away from those who were supposed to love her and keep her safe. Away from those who'd failed her.

As sunset's pink faded to gray, Cicero veered off the path. She staggered after him, so exhausted she barely spotted the thin thread of smoke rising ahead of them until they were practically upon a low sod cottage.

"I believe it would be best that you call out a greeting rather than myself," Cicero muttered. "A female voice is eminently less threatening than an unknown male voice."

"If you got rid of that sword, you'd be a fair sight less threatening," she mumbled back.

Cicero's only answer was a snort of never-going-to-happen.

"Hullo!" she called out over the growling of her stomach.

In a moment the sagging door opened. A crofter peered out suspiciously. "'Oo goes?"

She dared not use her own name, but hadn't thought of a false name or cover story. She stammered, "Uh-h, travelers. Seeking board and bed for the night."

"Ye got coin?"

Her mother or a servant had always carried money for Raina. Alarmed, she glanced at Cicero, who shook his head in the negative as well. "Nay," she answered the peasant, "but we've skills to trade."

He looked her up and down in a way that made her skin crawl. Suddenly she was entirely grateful for that lethal sword on Cicero's hip.

A female voice floated out the door, "'Oo be ye flappin' at, Arv?"

"Summat travelers. Offerin' ta trade skills for sup and a piece o' floor."

"Wha' skills?" the woman asked.

The man looked back Raina's way. "Whadda ye do?"

Raina thought fast. She dared not offer Cicero's skills in smuggling, thievery, or swordplay. As for her, teaching court dances or classical lute tunes or poetry composition would be of no use here. Nor fine needlework, illuminating a manuscript, or translating between a dozen different languages. "I can cook and clean," she tried.

The farmer grunted, "Mag does 'at. Do ye make candles or soap or spin thread, mayhap?"

Oh, why hadn't she paid more attention when her tutors had tried to teach her the details of such things? Desperate, she offered, "I can make a magical light that will last throughout the night."

The man's jaw dropped. "Slip of a thing like ye can do magic?"

The woman exclaimed from inside, "Magic? Be she an 'ealer?"

Raina replied eagerly, calling out to be heard by the woman inside, "I can do some healing!" The Heart controlled the teaching and use of healing magics very closely, but she'd been allowed to learn a few simple healing spells outside the guild because of her noble rank.

"Praise be." The farmer was shouldered out of the way by a gap-toothed woman of indeterminate age with an enormous belly proclaiming an advanced state of pregnancy. "Me name's Mag. Whot's yourn?"

Cicero intervened smoothly, "I am known as Cicero and my traveling companion answers to Carin."

"Come wit' me, Carin. Me milch cow's ailin' and I canna lose her." Mag rubbed her round belly. "Not wit' a bun in the oven so close to cooked."

Raina frowned. What was this woman doing with that

bucket and broom in her hands? Didn't she know expectant mothers should not work? They were to rest and relax and concentrate on growing the babe. It was said to be bad for the babe to do aught else. But this woman appeared to have been in the midst of heavy housework to no ill effect.

Then the rest of the woman's words sank in. A cow? They wanted her to heal a *cow*? She had no idea if her healing magics would even work on an animal. Only one way to find out. And if it meant food, no matter how rude, she'd give it a try.

Raina asked in resignation, "Where's this beast?"

The woman led her to a low lean-to behind the hovel. Mag stomped heedlessly through the muck and manure, while Raina picked gingerly through it as best she could. Not that it mattered. Her slippers were already ruined.

"'Ere she be," Mag announced.

Raina spied a giant white-and-black bovine standing in a dark corner, her head hanging low. She made her way to the animal and laid a hand on her side. The animal jerked her head up, and Raina leaped back.

"She won' 'urt ye. She's 'bout to keel over dead. Ye came jus' in the nick o' time."

Raina reached out again and touched the beast's rough hide. The cow was hot to the touch. Feverish. And her breathing was raspy and labored. "Do you know what's wrong with her?" Raina asked Mag.

"Milk fever. Gots infection in 'er udder."

Raina leaned down to have a look. The normally pink bag was grotesquely swollen and a dark, angry red. A spell for curing disease, then. She knew how much magical energy a human required. Did a cow require more power in the delivery of the spell due to its size? Or perhaps multiple castings of the spell? Why had she never thought to ask such questions of her instructors?

It appeared she got to learn on the job. She laid her hands on the animal, cleared her mind, took a deep breath, and summoned power to her. She murmured an incant, and a cool, white glow built around her hands, dancing on the beast's hide. The cow lurched away weakly. Raina followed the animal's movements, maintaining her contact with the animal's rough coat, infusing the healing as slowly as she could into the creature so as not to panic her. Slowly, slowly, Raina felt vitality returning to the cow. As her flagging spirit grew stronger, Raina expended some extra energy just to be sure the cow would recover.

She lifted her hands away from the animal. "I think she'll be all right now."

"Orc's breath! Look 'ee there!"

Raina glanced down, and the cow's udder was already mostly returned to its proper size. It was still somewhat pinker than normal, but nowhere near like it had been before.

"I ain' seen no healin' like that afore. Ye be a mighty mage."

Gall roiled in her gut. Of course she was gifted. The females in her family were bred for magic. She was no different from yon cow.

"Come 'ee to the hut. We 'ave aught worthy to pay for what 'ee just done, but I'll share whot we've got."

Raina smiled. "A hot meal and a place to sleep for the night are all my companion and I ask."

"Roight fine-lookin' young man 'ee got there."

She stifled a giggle. Her and the bandit? He'd fly into one of the famous battle rages of the kindari if he heard Mag suggest such a thing.

The woman led Raina back to the sod hut as the last

vestiges of twilight faded into true night. She ducked under
the low door frame and stopped just inside, appalled. The
only piece of furniture in the room, a wide plank set on two
tied bundles of straw turned on end, was crowded round
with no fewer than six filthy children and Arv. They sat on
more tied bundles of straw.

Did such poverty exist in Tyrel, or had she been sheltered
from it? Was this how *all* peasants lived? It was hardly better
than an animal burrow.

Although a fire burned in the fireplace and the rough space
was warm. A kettle simmered over the fire, and the smell
emanating from it made Raina's mouth water profusely.

Several of the children slid over and made space for her at
the makeshift table while Mag dished up wooden bowls of
stew for everyone. Raina drank hers without the luxury of a
spoon. Apparently, travelers were expected to provide their
own. She must remember to pack one the next time she ran
away from home.

The stew desperately needed seasoning, but it was hot.
And filling. Casting the magic had made her even more
voracious than she already was, and hunger was the best
seasoning of all. She drank three bowls before she began to
feel guilty for hogging this humble family's limited fare.

"Arv, ye'll ne'er believe whot she did . . . why, the cow's
practically as good as new. Just like 'at. I ain' ne'er seen the
like. . . ."

Raina tuned out the woman's description of the feat she'd
just performed, concentrating instead on the sallow faces of
the children. She reached out with her mind and was distressed to sense the weakness of their spirits. When her
hostess finally wound down, Raina asked, "Mag, when you
dress out an animal carcass, what do you do with the liver?"

"Why, I toss it to the dog if 'e be about."

"You might want to cut it up small into a stew and let the essence cook out of it. 'Twill put color in your children's cheeks and give them more energy. And spinach. Do you grow spinach in your garden? It is good for children and new mothers."

The woman nodded, wide-eyed. "Where did ye say ye be from? We don' get no 'igh 'ealers through these parts."

Cicero inquired casually, "With what frequency do healers travel through this area?"

"Maybe every other harvest. But none so gifted as yer lady frien'."

Arv piped up, "Las' 'eart 'ealer ter pass through were 'at crazy White 'eart feller. Whot were 'is name, Mag?"

"Balthazar. On 'is way to 'eal them orcs up north las' year. Ain' seen 'im since. Them Boki mus've kilt 'im."

Aghast, Raina replied, "What do you do for healing in the meantime?"

Mag shrugged. "We make do wit' 'erbs and potions. No' the fancy magical kind, mind ye. Jus' teas or poultices ter ease a tooth ill or the like."

Raina frowned. She knew a fair bit about herbal remedies, and many of them were effective. But just as many that floated about the market squares were completely useless. Mag might have just solved the thorny problem of how to finance a journey to Dupree, though. She asked, "Are people generally willing to trade bed and board for healing magics and potions?"

Everyone at the table laughed as if she'd just asked the most ridiculous question they'd ever heard.

"Gor' yes! 'Tis 'ow mos' 'ealers make their way. They go village ter village an' farm ter farm tradin' they's services for a meal 'n' roof."

Raina nodded slowly. Indeed.

Arv interrupted her thoughts. "Be ye in a great 'urry ter reach yer destination, then?"

Yet again, Cicero intervened. "To what end do you ask such a question?"

"Mag's time be comin'. 'Twould be a great comfort to 'ave someone such as ye 'ere. If'n she passed on and lef' me wit' all these bairn, Oi'd be in a bad way, Oi would."

Raina looked at the little faces around her, fear glinting in their big-eyed gazes at the idea of losing their mother. She glanced up at Mag. "How long until the babe comes?"

"On the morrow, may'ap. Mebbe a few days 'ence."

Raina winced. She and Cicero probably shouldn't tarry so long in one place. But then he shocked her by shrugging and announcing, "We are in no particular hurry to reach any specific destination."

She stared at him, stunned by his declaration, before turning to Mag. "There you have it. We shall tarry until the babe comes."

Justin prowled the keep restlessly as he had ever since Raina blinked out of existence in the doorway of the barn two nights before. He'd failed her. She'd begged for his help and he'd refused her. By the Void, he'd all but thrown her at that ruffian who'd disappeared with her to the Lady knew where. *Where are you, muckling?*

Justin being consumed with worry for her safety, his feet carried him without conscious thought to the southeast tower, and more specifically to the landing before Lady Charlotte's solar. If anybody knew where Raina had gone, it would be her mother. Not that Charlotte was likely to tell. Even the dullest clod could see the thick tension between the mistress of the keep and her two unwelcome guests.

The door to Lady Charlotte's office was closed. No doubt

she was closeted with those cursed mages who'd scared Raina into bolting.

He glanced up and down the curving stairwell. The torches had already been lit, which meant the night watch was already posted. No one should come this way anytime soon. But just to be safe, he dipped the corner of his cloak in the bucket of water under the torch and used it to snuff the light. A faint odor of scorched wool filled the narrow landing.

He sidled up to the door and crouched at the keyhole. A key was in the lock and blocked his sight, but sound seeped out readily enough.

". . . portents are strong. Everything will reach a crisis soon."

That was Kadir. The older mage.

"Bah!" Charlotte exclaimed. "Dreams and visions. They're naught but fancies and wishful thinking. What is soon to a soothsayer, anyway? A turning of the moon? A year? A hundred years? I care not for such nonsense unless these charlatans can tell me where my daughter is."

Justin rocked back on his heels, disappointed. Charlotte didn't know where Raina was, then. Unless she lied to the mages.

Kadir was speaking again. ". . . not understand. Great cycles of time and history are coming together all at once. We are deeply alarmed. The prophets with whom I consult are emphatically not charlatans. Such a convergence has not been recorded in millennia."

Justin sucked back a hiss that threatened to escape his teeth.

Kadir added forcefully, "And our daughter is at the very center of it all."

Our—What? Why would Kadir refer to Raina thus?

Periodic swishes of fabric indicated that Charlotte paced

her office. A long silence unfolded, and Justin waited in agony to hear more. What mess had Raina landed in the middle of?

"Where is she, Kadir? Where did that blasted dousing rod take her?"

A deep sigh. "Would that I knew. We could not afford to lose that wand. My order was hoping to use Rowan's Wand to go in search of other artifacts associated with Rowan herself and with the Green Court."

Justin frowned. What court was this? The Imperial Seat was the only court he'd ever heard of.

Kadir continued, "Something strange happened when the girl touched the wand. A burst of magic—"

"Backlash," Charlotte said impatiently.

"Nay," Kadir said slowly. "She interrupted the casting of the ritual at the critical moment. Something more than backlash occurred. I worry for Raina's safety, wherever she might be."

Charlotte snorted. "She had no concern for the danger of a backlash. She was more interested in avoiding being transported to Alchizzadon as your prisoner."

"No need for drama, Char. You know it was for the best."

"Best? She's disappeared to stars know where. She could be in grave danger!"

Justin silently cheered Charlotte for expressing his sentiment exactly.

"She strikes me as the type to land on her feet," Kadir replied mildly.

Justin had to give the fellow that. Raina had a decent head on her shoulders and a fair helping of common sense. Most of the time. When she wasn't talking crazy about being forced to have a child with a stranger or blowing up magic rituals. But if Kadir had been planning to kidnap her after all—to which the whoreson had just admitted—could Raina's other wild claims also be true? Justin's eyes narrowed dangerously. If those mages thought to hurt her, they had a surprise coming in the form of his blade.

"She's a lot like you," Kadir commented quietly.

"I did not run from my duty when the time came!"

"Ahh, but you fought it."

"In the end I did the right thing."

Justin frowned. What they had asked of Raina was most certainly *not* the right thing.

Kadir was speaking again. ". . . girl makes a good point, you know. What we have demanded of the daughters of Tyrel is a travesty."

Charlotte's desk chair creaked sharply as if its owner had just dropped into it heavily, mayhap in shock.

Kadir continued, "We have foreseen a revolt like this for several generations. We thought you might be the one, but at the last minute, you relented. Raina, however—"

"What do you mean, you foresaw a revolt?" Charlotte exploded, cutting him off.

"Think about it. We have bred a line of arch-mages. Women more powerful than almost all other known wizards. The daughters of Tyrel are educated. You own land. You are the result of thousands of years of concerted effort to create extraordinary women. It was inevitable that eventually you would realize your own power and break free of us."

Break free? Justin's mind stumbled over the thought, paralyzed by the implications of it.

"But . . . but . . . the Great M-m-age . . . ," Charlotte stammered.

"Ahh, yes. The Great Mage. His time draws near. Very near, indeed, if the portents are true."

Charlotte jolted. "Then it is more important than ever that

we recover Raina! The House of Tyrel dares not fail in its duty after so long."

Kadir sighed. "We were not able to place a rune upon her before she bolted. We have no way of tracking her. She's smart, resourceful, and, if she's at all like her mother, stubborn."

"I have asked terrible things of both of my daughters. Tell me it was not in vain. That my girls will be the ones to end this."

"Raina has gone from us. Perhaps she will find a source of magical power strong enough to rouse the Great Mage. Perhaps it is fated that she will be the one to end our long wait."

Great Mage? Magic to rouse him? What was all this? Justin frowned, straining to hear more.

Kadir said quietly, "Our soothsayers think there's a possibility—slight, but possible nonetheless—that Raina may solve the problem of rousing the Great Mage."

Charlotte snorted. "The Mages of Alchizzadon have worked on that for thousands of years. What could a mere girl do that the greatest scholars of our age have failed to achieve?"

Kadir replied, "For several months, seers across the colony have been reporting similar visions and prophecies. Mind you, they live and work separately. And yet, they are seeing nearly identical signs. The stars are aligning."

"Toward what event?"

"I am not at liberty to go into the details of our seers' visions. We have our agents combing the Midlands and beyond in search of her. If she can be found, she will be."

An urge to bolt out the door in search of Raina himself nearly overcame Justin. Charlotte was speaking again. ". . . sure she's not dead?"

"Positive. The portal opened for just an instant. I saw Raina and that kindari fall through."

"To where?" Charlotte exclaimed in frustration.

"The Wand of Rowan could have taken them anywhere it has been in the past. Who knows where it chose to take them?"

It chose? Kadir spoke of this wand as if it were a living thing. Justin had picked up a few tidbits here and there over the years about magic—he had a habit of eavesdropping on the secret magic lessons that had been arranged for Raina over the years—but he'd never heard of a sentient magic item.

"Where would the wand take a stranger new to its use?"

Kadir spoke quietly enough that Justin had to press his ear to the door to hear the answer. "The grove of the rowan treant, Whisper, lies in Dupree. Guarded by dryads. Perhaps the wand went home to its maker."

"The wand bears fae magic? Bah!" Charlotte burst out in disgust. "A fae spirit could have thrown Raina anywhere!"

Every story Justin had ever heard of the fae painted the mythical creatures as sly, conniving tricksters with dark senses of humor and a wide mean streak. And one of them had taken Raina?

Kadir spoke soothingly. "The fae are bound by the rules of their courts. I do not believe they would harm an innocent young girl."

Justin scowled. Well, at least the man admitted that Raina was innocent in this entire affair.

"Where is this rowan grove?" Charlotte inquired.

"West of the city of Dupree."

"Why on Urth would Raina be cast all the way there?"

Kadir's answer was grim. "I would not presume to know the workings of any fae magic. The timeless ones do not see the world as we do, and work for their own mysterious purposes."

Justin leaned against the wall beside the door, cursing himself roundly. This was his fault. Raina'd asked for his help the night of her party and he'd ignored her. Sent her away from him. He'd known her all her life and never once had she given him cause to believe she was anything but honest and forthright. He should have believed her.

He'd heard enough. His next move was obvious. He snuck away from the solar on grimly silent feet. He'd helped make this mess; it was up to him to help fix it. If Raina was not in this rowan grove, mayhap the dryads there would know where the treant's rod had sent Raina.

He returned to his pallet in the dormer for the castle lads and quickly packed the gear he would need for a long journey. A stealthy trip to the kitchen to supply himself and he was on his way. Foreboding weighed heavy upon him. Raina was caught in the middle of something huge, and it was his duty to rescue her. The night was cold, but he did not feel it nipping at his nose as he set his feet to the north road at a steady jog.

The footpath to Dupree was a treeless slash through the Wylde Wood, its margins trimmed back a good thirty feet on each side. Keeping this end of the path open fell to the men of the hollow to do each year and was a source of much grumbling about wasted effort. But today Will was abjectly grateful for the broad avenue of short greensward on each side of the actual track. No Boki ambush could be set in such a wide space.

After he spent a few hours walking the path nervously, Will's exhausted mind began to play tricks on him, questioning if he really was fleeing from Boki, actually racing to report an invasion of the borderlands and the slaughter of dozens of innocents. The journey took on an unreal quality as he grew light-headed with fatigue. Maybe none of it had happened. Maybe he'd imagined it all.

He would wake up from this strange dream having dozed off under the spreading branches of the old hickory during an uneventful night's watch. He would shake his head at his morbid nightmare and walk down the hill to get breakfast. He'd eat the last of the winter fat sausage, fried crispy brown in his mother's big iron skillet, and have a mug of oatmeal thinned with cream still warm from the milch cow.

But as hunger turned to sharp pain in his gut and fatigue

turned to sharper pain in his thighs, his dream-like state also passed. And then the memories came. Wave upon wave in violent, excruciating detail that would not stop. The knot of vengeance unfulfilled grew in his gut and tightened into something akin to fury. He'd heard bleeding-heart greenskin lovers argue in the past that orcs and goblins and their kind were entitled to live and breed and die in peace. But the bleeding hearts were wrong. Orcs were vicious beasts with no respect for, nor right to, life.

He and Rosana walked on and on, and during that long march he learned to hate. He tasted rage, bitter and hot upon his tongue. He sipped of it. Then drank of it. Then gorged on it until he nigh drowned in its ichor, wrath suffusing the farthest reaches of his being. If he ever came across Ki'Raiden again, he would kill the Sixth Thane of Boki. Slowly. Painfully. By torturous degrees for each of the citizens of Hickory Hollow the thane had slaughtered.

The light brown strip of dirt before the two of them wended its inexorable way north, back toward the heart of the colony and more heavily populated areas. Will knew the path well, having walked it every spring since he was big enough to push a handcart loaded with boots his father had made over the winter.

It was nearly noon when the footpath widened out into a pair of wagon ruts and another hour before it widened again into an actual road. The forest gave way to fields dotted with cottages, and eventually Will spied the massive stone outcropping of Giant's Fist in the distance.

"What's that?" Rosana asked abruptly, breaking the long silence that had held between them for most of the morning.

"The Giant's Fist. Story goes that a giant was turned to stone here and buried." Will had always thought it a silly story, but if the hearth tale of the Sleeping King was real, who was to say that this one was not as well? His mother maintained that someone had merely embellished the natural shape of the rock, carving it a bit to look like fingers with rough nails and craggy knuckles. His father only shrugged when asked his opinion on the matter.

Perhaps Ty had known more on the subject than he was willing to say. Maybe he knew whether or not it was possible to turn a giant to stone in such a fashion. What else had he known about magic that he'd never shared with his only son? Will cursed his father anew for not deigning to teach him more of the ways of magic beyond a few simple spells.

Rosana's only response was a skeptical noise.

They walked on in silence, each immersed in their own loss and pain.

Several hours beyond the Fist lay Castlegate Falls, the largest market city in the region. It boasted an Imperial Army outpost and its population swelled to nearly a thousand people on a big market day. It was steady at about half that between times.

Ironically, this was what Will had always dreamed of as a boy: coming to the city on a hero's errand. Unfortunately, he'd failed to imagine the tugging grief and sickening loss that accompanied such an errand.

As he neared the town, his apprehension grew. The ravages of the Empire upon the countryside became more apparent in decimated forests and ugly pits where ore and precious gems had been crudely torn from the earth. The soothing presence of nature around him ebbed.

He and Rosana shuffled through the short line of people waiting outside the walls for a cursory search by the town guard prior to being allowed inside the walled city. After a small eternity, it was finally Will's turn. Rough hands patted down his ribs. "What's yer name, boy?"

"Will the cobbler's son."

"Where ye from?" Hands rudely grabbed his crotch and then slid down his legs.

"Hickory Hollow." He knew the next question—asking for his purpose in being here—so he went ahead and answered it. "I'm here as escort to yon healer." Normally, Will would have reported the Boki attack upon her caravan, but his father's instructions to speak to no one of the orcs but Aurelius rang in his ears.

The soldier replied scornfully, "Why'd ye be keepin' company with the likes of a gypsy?"

Will shrugged. It was never wise to rise to the baiting of the army. They had heavy fists and the law on their side.

Behind him, Rosana snapped to the guard rudely patting her down, "Orcs attacked a Heart caravan. They killed the guards and left me for dead. I must go to the Heart house immediately and make my report. Unhand me and let me pass!"

Will winced. Gypsies were not well liked in the best of times in these parts. He turned hastily to make an apology for her, but was startled to see the guard gesture for her to move along. Did the Heart colors carry so much weight, then, that even a snappish gypsy wearing them was shown a modicum of respect?

The first soldier muttered, "Straight on to the town square, then. The Heart's among the other guild halls."

"Thanks be," Will mumbled as he took Rosana by the arm and hustled her out of range of the guards. He half-whispered to her, "You should not be so high-handed with soldiers. Around here, they despise your kind for being thieves and cutthroats."

"My kind are despised everywhere!" she retorted. "I was lucky the *Kaer* took me in when I showed a talent for spiritual magic. It was they who protected me from slavers and bigots like those back there. I was barely three years old when the *Kaer* found me after the Boki insurrection."

He stared, shocked. "Do you remember your family?"

"No. The Heart is my family, in truth. That is why I call it the *Kaer*. That is an old word for family among my kind."

"And those other words you used? *Prala* and . . . and *gaj*?" His tongue stumbled over the unfamiliar syllables.

"*Prala* means brother. *Gaj* is mother. *Pena* is sister, and *daj* is father." She shrugged. "I do not even know what gypsy clan I come from. I think of the *Kaer* as my family, so why not call it that?"

He shrugged back.

She grabbed his hand and hurried forward. "Come."

He'd never gone into the town of Castlegate Falls proper. His father always veered left just inside the gate and headed for the open field of the farmer's market to sell his boots and shoes. This moment marked the end of the familiar in Will's journey. From here on out, all would be new. A burst of excitement momentarily overtook his fear.

The street was a morass of mud and dung at first, but as he approached what he estimated to be the middle of the town cobblestones replaced the mire. He gazed up at the marvel of three- and even four-story buildings. Normally, he would revel in the sheer noise of the place. But today it was an obscenity. Didn't they know a terrible tragedy had happened? That innocents had died and their murderers were on the loose, perhaps headed here to wreak their violence next upon these laughing, oblivious fools?

Shopkeepers gossiped and shouted, oxen bawled, chickens pecked and clucked underfoot, and everyone seemed in a great rush to get somewhere. But then, so was he. Moving as quickly as the heavy foot traffic would allow in the clogged street, he and Rosana made their way to the Heart.

The thoroughfare spilled into a square large enough to fit all of Hickory Hollow inside it. He gazed around in amazement at the gaudily decorated buildings ringing the plaza. The familiar green and brown of the Forester's Guild. The purple and black of the Merchant's Guild. The red-and-gold sunbeams around a red heart on a white field of the Heart. A couple more guilds he didn't recognize. That building with the gray-and-black door and stylized mountain shape must be the Miner's Guild. Next to it stood the red and black of the Slaver's Guild with its distinctive chain-link motif. And beyond that, the blue and gold of the Imperial Mage's Guild.

Even if he hadn't known the Mage's Guild's colors, he'd have spotted the building in an instant. It was surrounded by a faint shimmer of magic, visible from the corner of his eye when he didn't look directly at it. There must be some sort of magic shield around the entire building! Such a display of power awed him.

He angled out into the square to avoid walking directly past the Slaver's Guild. He was human, a citizen race not subject to enslavement on sight, but the place gave him the jitters anyway. Slavers were known for randomly grabbing locals and impressing them into slavery to fill their quotas— usually later in the summer, though, after the planting was done and well before the harvest. Still, there was no sense in taking any chances. After all, he was in excellent health and on his way to becoming a tall, strapping youth.

Rosana threw the Slaver's Guild hall a disgusted look but gave it as wide a berth as he did.

He murmured, "They cannot take you as long as you wear Heart colors, right?"

"They would not dare," she muttered back. "The Royal Order of Sun would annihilate them all. There would be many dead bodies before the Order stopped killing over such an outrage. And not many people would be inclined to heal dead slavers, would they?"

Good point. The Heart building was whitewashed, its trim painted in alternating red and yellow. It, too, was surrounded by a faint magical glow. When they approached the steps, however, a young fellow standing in the open doorway ducked inside for a second and the glow disappeared.

Rosana started up the steps confidently. "Well, what are you waiting for?" she demanded while Will stood rooted at the bottom of the stair.

"Is it safe? That magic shell won't harm us?"

She grinned down at him like he was the most uneducated bumpkin she'd ever seen. "It's only a wizard lock. The initiate has already let it down for us. Even if it's not down and you run into it, the magic will only repel you and not let you approach the building. Wizard locks won't hurt anyone."

Oh. Feeling stupid, and feeling irritated at feeling stupid, he tromped up the steps after her. The common room of the Heart house was shabby, albeit welcoming, with a cheerful air about it. An unfamiliar hint of magic tingled faintly in the air. It made him uncomfortable, but Rosana seemed to breathe it in like the smell of fresh bread warm on the hearth.

A tall woman with brown hair came out of the back room and introduced herself as Sister Denia. Rosana burst out, "Have any spirits come here in the past day looking for a field resurrection?"

The healer frowned. "Not in the past day. We had a farmer come in three days ago. Died of an ague. Resurrected successfully and went on his way back home."

"Nobody from Hickory Hollow?" Will demanded. "Nobody at all?"

"No. Has something happened out that way?" Denia asked.

Rosana answered before he could, "A Heart caravan was attacked on the Ring Road by orcs. Brother Angelo was killed. Both our guards were killed, too. The orcs left me for dead."

"Orcs?" Denia exclaimed. "They have not been active since the insurrection—what, fifteen years or more ago? The notion of an orc attack is absurd. And no, no Heart members have come in. Like I said. Just the farmer."

Rosana bristled. "It's not absurd. I saw the orcs with my own eyes."

"Well then. I suppose we must send word of this to Dupree right away. Oh, dear. I haven't the spare personnel, not to mention guards, right now to send a messenger. The brothers and guardians are out collecting donations so we can produce a batch of potions . . . ," the woman trailed off muttering to herself.

Rosana spoke up quickly. "We will take the news to the Heart in Dupree for you. Will, here, can be my guard."

Denia gave him an assessing look. "Can you fight?"

Startled, he replied, "I guess so. But—" But he was no professional soldier, and he certainly could not defend Rosana against another orc attack.

Rosana, predictably, cut him off before he could say all of that. "I cannot touch him with my blade when we spar, and I am an accomplished sword fighter."

No, she wasn't. He opened his mouth to say so, but the toe of her boot whipped out and connected sharply with his shin. Her long skirt mostly covered the blow from view, however.

He swallowed a yelp as Denia nodded. "Well then, that's settled. You two shall take word of this attack to Dupree. There is stew in the kitchen. I just made a fresh batch. Let me go into the office and write a note. . . ." She left the common room, muttering to herself about the contents of the letter.

"What was that for?" he complained, rubbing his shin.

"You need go to Dupree to see if your family and friends resurrected there, yes?"

"Well, yes."

"This way you can travel under a Heart writ, and maybe, just maybe, arrive in one piece."

Ahh. Clever, that.

"Stay here. I'm going to go insist that the *Kaer* pay for your service. Then you and I will collect food and water skins and leave for Dupree."

She left the common room, and he headed for the kitchen and a bowl of stew to ease his growling belly. By the time Rosana and the adept returned to the common room, he had filled both his pack and Rosana's with supplies for their journey from the cupboards in the kitchen.

While Rosana gulped down a bowl of stew and a hunk of bread, Denia instructed, "Head for the dock down by the river. That letter will gain you quick passage to Dupree. Look for a barge named the *Tough Knut*. The captain's a friend of the Heart, a Kelnor called Rhone Ironknot. By river is the quickest route from here to the capital. I counted out enough silver for your passages. Save the rest for food and lodging."

Rosana nodded and patted her belt, where a small leather pouch hung at her waist. Will recognized the chink of coins as it moved. He waited until they had been let out of the magic ward around the Heart building to mutter, "You should tuck that inside your skirt. Cutpurses will spot yon pouch a mile away."

Rosana's right hand moved in a blur and of a sudden something exceedingly sharp pricked at his ribs. "A cutpurse will find himself gutted fast if he tries for my purse,"

He took a careful step backward, away from her dagger.

She murmured, "Have you never heard it is bad for one's health to attempt to separate a gypsy from his gold?"

"I have not, but I see the wisdom in the words," he replied a bit grumpily. He rubbed the sore spot where her blade had poked him and headed for the town's postern gate and the docks beyond. She might be easy on the eye, but the gypsy was as prickly as a thornwood tree.

They spotted a big, vaguely military-looking barge near the end of the dock. It was worn, but looked relatively water worthy.

Rhone Ironknot was typical of the Kelnor dwarves found throughout the colony's hills; his long beard was twined with beads and this morn's breakfast. He waved off the letter Rosana held out to him and smiled widely at the pretty gypsy. "Yes, yes, welcome aboard, Healer. You, too, lad. You look like you could pull your weight in a pinch. Forest bred, are ye?"

Will was startled. "How did you know?"

"Yon dagger, of course. Style's straight out of the Wylde Wood. West end of the wood if me eyes don' mistake me. Been seein' those leather-wrapped grips a few years on, now. Like to meet me the bloke makin' them blades. Lay odds, I would, 'e's soldier trained. Them blades got fine balance fer a fightin' hand."

A lifetime of his father's paranoia stilled Will's tongue against announcing that his own father had made the blades. Particularly in light of the recent revelations regarding Ty and his hidden past.

Rosana leaped across the gap between the dock and barge as lightly as a fawn. Will made the jump a fair sight less gracefully. The vessel dipped a little under his weight and his stomach gave a heave as he stumbled in search of his balance.

Wondering if he would regret his decision to travel with

her, he followed Rosana aft on the roomy barge. They waited for an hour while the kelnor and his men finished loading barrels onto the vessel. Then Ironknot shouted at them to find a perch and stay out of the way of the pole men.

Will and Rosana settled atop short casks marked with crudely painted nails as dockhands cast off and threw the heavy lines over to their craft. The barge crawled away from the dock at first. But then the current caught its blunt prow and swung it downstream. Choppy, open water in the middle of the river sent them nodding and bobbing like a pheasant on the hunt for a mate.

Will groaned as the queasy sensation intensified in his gut, and Rosana laughed without a shred of pity. "Landlubber!"

He scowled at her balefully. He was already regretting his choice of traveling companion. Deeply.

Raina spent the next day helping Mag with the chores, collecting and drying medicinal herbs and teaching Mag their uses. And, to everyone's vast delight, Raina gathered cooking herbs and showed Mag how to make her stews savory and tasty. For her part, Mag showed Raina that pregnant women were by no means helpless creatures. Far from it. Although Mag tired easily and her back ached, she was still capable of plenty of vigorous activity and, in fact, seemed the healthier for it.

Raina had grown up assuming that, because they lived so close to the land, the spirits of the common peasants would somehow be strengthened by the link. But, she was surprised to discover that the exact opposite was apparently the case. It was not the land that drained them, but rather their families. It was as if a piece of both Arv's and Mag's spirits had left them and entered each of their surviving children. Raina wondered in between lifting, carrying, cooking, and cleaning if this phenomenon explained why common people so often failed to resurrect.

As interesting and exhausting as sampling the life of peasants was, Raina's thoughts were mostly elsewhere. Her initial fury had dimmed, leaving behind a vague sense of guilt. Her mother's rage at being disobeyed aside, Charlotte must be worried sick about her. And Raina had no doubt her father was furious. He was an intelligent man, and based on her comments to him just before Kadir had shown up at the barn, he would figure out that he'd been tricked by Charlotte and the mages. Her mother would have some explaining to do, and Raina wasn't the least bit sympathetic. Her mother deserved to answer for her actions.

Raina only felt bad that her father would be hurt and angry at being deceived. He would blame himself for her flight as well. He was responsible for the security of the castle and all those within it. Knowing his rigid knight's sense of honor, she realized he would deem himself to have failed her. And Justin, so much like her father in temperament, would react the exact same way.

Ahh, Justin. The mere thought of him was enough to bring tears to her eyes. They had been inseparable for nearly their entire lives. Although their duties had pulled them more apart in recent years, she'd always known he was close by, always ready to take care of her, to make her laugh or make her hurts go away. Being away from him like this felt as if part of her had been torn out, leaving a gaping wound that would not heal. When the fire had burned low and Mag, Arv, and the children lay snoring in their blankets, she had allowed herself to cry for him, sobbing silently into the crook of her elbow.

He would be distraught that he hadn't taken her seriously when she came to him for help. He would kick himself for not following her, for not stopping her from running away or at least making her take him with her. Reluctantly, she admitted to herself that maybe a tiny part of her feelings of anger and betrayal was aimed at him for those very reasons.

She tried through the next day to make suggestions here and there to ease her hosts' lot—a clever way to rig the well with pulleys to make hauling up buckets of water easier, a simple bellows to help start and stoke fires, hinging the hook in the side of the fireplace to swing heavy kettles of hot stew or boiling water more safely off the fire.

When he wasn't out hunting and bringing back a brace of rabbits or quail for supper, Cicero spent his time building furniture for the family. A real table and benches to go with it, and a clever rocking chair made of willow branches he soaked in water, bent into place, and then lashed into shape.

Raina figured out how much magic it took to heal a goat versus a cow, and how much to mend a child's cut finger. And she gained a deep respect for the dogged determination of these common people to simply survive. She'd had no idea how truly privileged a life she'd led before.

Grit lodged under her fingernails, she braided her hair to keep its greasy locks out of her sunburned face, and her white dress had faded to dull gray with ground-in dust and sweat. She was going to dream this night of a hot bath in a real bathtub.

But she got no chance. Only a few minutes after the household had settled down for the night, Cicero's low, charged voice came out of the hovel's darkness. "Someone approaches."

In the glow of the banked fire, Raina spied him gliding to the door, sword in hand. Arv joined him in a moment carrying a wicked-looking axe.

"Douse the fire," Cicero ordered.

Raina was the closest adult to the fireplace and she jumped up with alacrity to throw the bucket of water on the embers. A great, hissing cloud of steam rose up.

Mag gathered the children in a huddle in the corner and shushed their frightened whispers.

"They draw near," Cicero reported under his breath. "Ready yourself, Arv."

In the expectant silence, Raina finally heard what had alarmed her companion. Stomping feet, jingling armor, and the confident rattle of weapons. Lots of them. It sounded like a large party jogging in formation. A rhythmic grunting accompanied the pounding footsteps. "Huh . . . huh . . . huh . . . huh."

Those are not humans incoming. Covering her hands with her cloak, she drew magical energy to herself. She only knew healing spells, but she could keep Cicero and Arv alive in the doorway for a while, mayhap. She'd heard her father refer to the usefulness of backpack healers in combat before. A vague plan of standing at Cicero's and Arv's backs with a hand on each of them and pumping healing into them as they fought took shape in her head.

She crept in the blackness from her place by the fire over to join the men. She mostly felt Cicero's nod of acceptance of her unspoken offer to help.

The attackers were coming from the south moving fast to the north. It sounded as if they had just topped the rise a hundred yards or so beyond the hut. Not following a road then, but rather traveling like an arrow over whatever terrain presented itself.

"Huh . . . Huh . . . Huh . . . Huh." The grunts grew distinct enough she could almost smell the fetid heat coming out of inhuman throats.

"Orcs," Arv breathed.

Cicero spared the crofter a momentary, appalled stare and then went back to concentrating fiercely on the door and what his ears were telling him. "At least twenty of them," he whispered.

"Huh. Huh. Huh. Huh."

The sound became almost painful it was so loud and close. Cicero and Arv braced themselves for the assault, and in her terror Raina drew massive magical energy to herself, more than she'd ever pulled before. Much more. She even registered pulling spiritual energy to herself from each of the people in the hut, now.

"Huh . . . Huh . . . Huh . . . Huh." The grunts were not quite as loud as they had been a moment ago.

"Huh . . . huh . . . huh . . . huh." The orcs were definitely drawing away from the hut.

Arv and Cicero traded perplexed looks. Cicero murmured, "Do orcs often pass by crofters' huts without attacking?"

"Not as I've ever 'eard."

"Unbar the door. Let me out," Cicero bit out.

Arv wrestled the heavy bar from its iron sockets on either side of the door. Before the hefty oak had barely cleared the holders, Cicero had slipped outside and, as quiet and insubstantial as a shadow, disappeared into the night after the retreating orcs.

Raina helped Arv re-bar the door, and the family went to bed once more. This night they would risk no fire and sleep in a cold hut. She stretched out under Moto's cloak on a straw mat on the floor like everyone else. It made her hip bones and shoulders ache, but she didn't complain. These people had a hard life and teetered perpetually on the ragged edge of starvation or death. That reality was more starkly clear than ever to Raina after their near miss with the orcs. Sleep was slow in coming, and when she dreamed it was not of baths but of bloody battles.

A long, low moan drew her from her exhausted slumber some time later, however. The sound was unmistakable. *Mag's babe is coming.*

A deep chill hung in the air. Arv was already rolling off his and Mag's pallet. He moved to the fireplace and Raina heard him laying a fire by feel in the dark. He gave the new bellows

Cicero had fashioned a few pumps, and a tiny flame jumped among the tinder.

"When you've got that going, boil me a pot of water," Raina directed him. "Everything that touches Mag or the babe must be dipped in the boiling water to banish diseases upon it. Every towel. Every rag. Understood?"

Arv nodded.

The labor was quick, for Mag had already birthed many children. The babe, a fat boy, came feetfirst and squalled his way into the world lustily. But Raina worried about Mag. She'd felt the moment when a portion of Mag's flagging spirit passed into the child, and the women had not much more within her to give. A certain hopelessness passed from mother to child in that moment as well, linked spirit to spirit. It was a knowing sunk into the bones, planted firmly within their spirits, that aspiration for any more than this pitiful lot in life was futile.

The afterbirth did not pass quickly; and when it finally did, it was torn and incomplete. Mag continued to bleed as well.

Arv peered over Raina's shoulder at the seepage. "Ye oughter pack the birth canal wit' sawdust and mud. 'Twill set up hard like mortar and cork the bleeding."

Raina snorted. "And introduce infection and kill her."

Although she knew Arv's crude remedy wouldn't work, she worried that Mag was too weakened by the birth to withstand the stress of magical healing. It had been known to send certain people into shock and even death. Her teaching in birth magic was that women had to rest and recuperate for at least a full day before they could stand magical healing, Her instructors thought it had something to do with the mother giving a piece of her spirit to the babe at the time of birth. Until that portion of the mother's spirit recovered, magic was dangerous.

Over the next few hours, Mag weakened and grew pale. Before Raina's eyes, the woman was slipping away. And there wasn't a thing Raina could do about it. Helpless frustration burned in her gut. Mag smiled wanly and told her not to worry, but Raina knew better. She felt the woman's spirit slipping away inch by inch when it should be coming back.

With dawn's pale light came no sign of Cicero. Worry for his safety jarred against her confidence in his skill at avoiding detection.

Raina sent the children to a neighbor's croft to share the news of the passing orcs and the birth of their brother—and to get them out of the hut before their mother died in front of them. For Mag could not last much longer. Arv paced and drank the local rotgut until he was a blubbering mess. Raina finally tossed him out as well with orders to drink himself into a stupor in the barn.

By midmorning, Mag lost consciousness and her heartbeat became so faint that Raina could barely hear it, even when she pressed her ear directly on the woman's chest. Frantic with her inability to help, Raina crouched beside the woman, her fingers pressed against the life pulse in Mag's throat.

And then it stopped.

Raina felt about urgently. Checked the life point in Mag's wrist. Listened to her chest. Put her hand over Mag's mouth to feel for breath. Nothing.

Stars above! Mag had died. She couldn't let her slip away like this! Her children needed her! Mag's spirit could not possibly be strong enough to make the journey to Dupree, resurrect there, and come back. Her permanent death would be disastrous for this family, the very thing Arv was desperate to avoid by asking Raina to stay for this birth.

She had to do something!

There might be a way. . . .

A very high-level magic cast by powerful healers . . .

Did she dare try it?

She'd never cast the spell. . . .

But she'd studied a scroll describing it and she'd seen it cast. Had memorized the incant . . .

. . . and Mag was already dead.

She had nothing to lose by trying.

Queen Gabrielle of Haraland breathed a sigh of relief as she stepped outside. The Imperial gardens were as grandiose as the rest of the palace, but at least out here there were trees and blue sky and the freedom of crisp mountain air moving in and out of her lungs. An urge to cast off her confining clothes and dance barefoot upon the greensward surged through her.

The Garden of Nations—which contained a plot for each of the kingdoms of Koth with native plants and laid out in the fashion of that country's culture—called to her. Haraland's garden never failed to relax her with its grassy walkways between fragrant lilacs and magnificent rose beds. It was much like her home—refined, elegant, and lush. Haraland was often called one of the jewels of Koth. One of the largest and most prosperous of the hundred kingdoms of Koth, it was blessed with a mild climate, fertile valleys, ocean access, rich mines, and thick forests.

But today, her steps took her to a part of the Garden of Nations she'd never seen before.

Out here, away from the oppressive presence of the Emperor, she allowed the resentment she usually held at bay to surge forward. Most of her life had been spent navigating kings and courts and politics with grace and finesse. But nothing could have prepared her for the Emperor and the intrigue-laden morass with which he surrounded himself. It was almost as if he encouraged the maneuvering and backstabbing as a way of keeping his subjects occupied and distracted.

Her greatest blessing was her husband, King Regalo. He was kind and loyal and loving. He wanted more children, but she was loathe to bring any child into the world to grow into a pawn under the Emperor's heavy hand. Regalo told her she must have faith and take a chance on their children finding happiness. Mayhap if they went back to Haraland for another while . . . Then she might consider taking the risk of bearing another child.

In a tiny act of rebellion against the Empire, she did give in to her urge to dance in the emperor's garden. How long she cavorted like a young girl she could not say. Until she was out of breath and her hair was coming out of its pins.

She looked around, panting, and was startled to realize she had no idea where she was. It looked like a natural forest thick with trees and underbrush. Only thin streaks of sunlight wended through the greenery, creating a mysterious atmosphere. She thought she saw a large, cloaked figure retreating rapidly, bat-like, around a bend in the path, but it was no doubt just a trick of the shadows.

How did she come to be here? She looked around in distress. With her breathing problems, she dared not stray too far from the palace and its healers.

"Your Highness. How dost thee fare this fine day?"

She looked up sharply and saw another figure approaching quickly from the other direction. This one was not furtive and shadowed, however. Quite the opposite. He was dressed in a shining white shirt of satin that seemed to glow in the forest glade. He passed by her guard, who nodded in recognition and let the newcomer pass.

A shockingly handsome elf came to a halt and executed a short bow before her. He was kindari, with russet hair the color of oak leaves in autumn. His face was covered by a finely drawn scrollwork of red-brown lines reminiscent of a darvan. The stag's antler's swirled around his eyes and across his forehead. She had seen him at court before, and his blazon, embroidered over his heart, was of a magnificent stag. As always, when she looked at an elf she had seen long ago she got the impression of time standing still for him while she aged doubly fast.

"I'm sorry," she murmured courteously, "I do not believe we have been introduced."

"A grievous oversight on my part," the elf replied with a smile so dazzling she actually felt a bit befuddled. "I am Talissar."

Ahh. She knew the name. He was consort to the Queen of Quantaine. His good looks and charm were gossiped about frequently at court. Queen Lyssandra, a silvani—high elf— was said to keep him at home in Quantaine most of the time for fear that he would be stolen away from her at court. Now and again, rumor linked Talissar with Princess Endellian herself. Gabrielle could see why the heir to the throne might favor this one. He was exquisite.

Belatedly, she realized she was staring at the fellow. "I apologize for staring, good sir. You are as beautiful as the court gossips say. You must get tired of people ogling you."

His smile softened. Took on a genuine warmth. "My humble thanks. That is the kindest compliment I have heard in a long while."

"Well, you are in the Imperial Seat, after all," she replied dryly, the implication clear that kindness was not a sentiment oft practiced there.

He laughed, the sound of his humor as warm as a carillon of chiming bells. *My, my.* No wonder Queen Lyssandra had made him her official companion.

"Beist thee well, Your Highness?" he asked her in thinly disguised concern.

Startled, she replied, "Why, yes. I am fine. Thank you for asking." Was some rumor afoot that she was ill? It was a strange question for a stranger to ask. "Walk with me?" she invited politely.

He held out his left forearm formally to her. "My pleasure."

She laid her fingers lightly upon his embroidered shirtsleeve. The fabric was impossibly smooth under her fingertips. He surprised her by plunging deeper into the trees along a narrow path that did not look as if it had been tended in a while.

"What is this place?" she asked curiously.

"We wander a portion of the Quantainian garden. If such natural woods makest thee uncomfortable, we shall return forthwith to the rose gardens of Haraland," he declared.

She glanced over her shoulder at her bodyguard trailing along a few paces back. "This glade is pretty. I am merely surprised and not discomfited. I confess, I have never seen this part of the garden."

He asked cautiously, "Thee hast never strolled aimlessly and looked up to find thyself here before, then?"

Odd. That was exactly how it had happened today. "No, never."

"Camest thee here alone?"

"If you do not count my guard, that would be correct."

He frowned. "Hmm."

"What is amiss, Lord Talissar?"

He shook his head as if to clear an absurd notion from it. "Thee hadst about thyself the look of a person operating under . . ."—he hesitated and then plunged ahead, ". . . "a subliminal compulsion. Thee hast never been alone in the company of a Kothite High Lord, perchance?"

She would never put herself in such a compromising

situation! She was a married woman. A queen. Devoted to her husband. "I would never dally with anyone at court!" she exclaimed, offended.

He held up his hands in apology. "I in no way meant to offend nor to impugn thine honor, Your Highness. One hast but to spend but a few moments in the presence of thee and thy husband to know thee wouldst never betray him."

"Then why the questions?" she pressed. It was entirely incongruous of this sophisticated man to bring up such unpleasant innuendos randomly.

He answered reluctantly, "In the past, I have seen women in this particular place before with a particular look in their eye as if they knew not what brought them here. And they were generally here to meet . . . a particular person."

"Who?" she demanded.

With a hand over his heart, he made a short bow of apology. "It would be imprudent of me to name him."

So. This seducer was powerful. Prominent. And used his Kothite mental abilities to compel women to come to him, eh? That was despicable. "Why this place?" she speculated.

Talissar did not miss her meaning. Why would a Kothite lord mind-control women to come to this wild corner of the gardens for trysts with him? "Thee must admit this place is completely unlike any other in the gardens. Who knows? Perhaps his . . . conquests . . . did not know themselves still to be on the palace grounds."

She shivered and drew her light shawl closer about her shoulders.

"I confess I have seen thee before in this place . . ."—he paused and then added delicately, ". . . dancing."

Appalled, she stared about in dismay. "I must leave this glade and never return!"

He said gently, "Do not hate the forest because of how one man abuses its natural solitude."

She did not know what to say. She had been here before? Why did she have no recollection of it? And she had *danced*? What was wrong with her? They strolled in silence for a while as she tried and failed to come up with answers.

Talissar eventually commented, "Whenever I come here, I imagine that a kindari gardener secretly saved this spot from being trimmed, chopped, and contorted into some un-natural charade of nature."

Gabrielle laughed, grateful for the welcome distraction from her disturbing thoughts and delighted at the irrever-ence of the observation. "Have a care to whom you say such things, or you will find yourself the main course at a torturer's feast, sir."

Talissar stopped and half-turned to study her intently. His voice low and charged, he asked, "Wouldst thee betray me to the Emperor for my lack of proper respect?"

There was clearly more to the question than met the ear. But what? She answered carefully, "Never, sir." Her gaze strayed involuntarily to the guard now standing on the path several dozen yards away.

"Ahh, yes," Talissar murmured. "Thy knight, Krugar, did not fare well at the hands of the Emperor and his lackey, did he?"

She was startled at the mention of the name. Vague mem-ory of a servant of her husband's came to mind. The fellow had caused some sort of scandal a long time ago. She'd all but forgotten the incident. Why would the kindari bring up such an obscure event? She looked searchingly into his eyes. Was he sent here by Maximillian to test her loyalty?

His voice dropped ever lower. "I will say it if thee will not. Thy man did not deserve what he got. He merely protected his liege lady from attack. Perhaps the very attack that brought thee here today against thy will. He did his duty, and was punished terribly and, dare I say, unfairly for his loyalty and faithful service."

What on Urth did he speak of? "What game do you play at?" she murmured back. "Is this a trap?"

"No trap, Your Highness. Upon that thee hast my word."

Clearly, he had a purpose in approaching her. This was no chance meeting in the gardens. "What is your business with me?" she asked.

"The rumors of thy forthright nature are not exaggerated, I see," he commented. She frowned, not seeing his gambit, as he continued smoothly, "My queen hast asked me to broach a small trade matter with thee rather than bother thy busy husband with it directly."

"And what would that matter be, good sir?"

"Our two kingdoms are, as thee knowest, the primary sources of ironwood for the Empire."

Of course. The ironwood dispute. The rare and nearly indestructible wood was in great demand by the Empire. Regalo wanted to limit harvesting of the trees to ensure the survival and proper reseeding of the ironwood forests. Rumor had it that, because of Regalo's stubbornness on the matter, Queen Lyssandra was under enormous pressure from the Forester's Guild and Imperial weapon makers to increase her harvest to levels that would ultimately destroy the ironwood stands in Quantaine. The short-term profits Quantaine stood to gain would largely make up for last year's poor harvest there, however.

"What would you have me whisper in my husband's ear, sir?"

Talissar seemed taken aback at her blunt question. With a glance at her guard, he walked on with her and did not answer.

Instead, he led her all the way through the trees to the edge of the massive rampart marking the edge of the White Crown Plaza. Her guard stayed within the margin of the trees, several dozen yards away, guarding any approach from that direction as she and the kindari moved to the wall to take in the view.

She trailed her fingers across the smooth white granite, amazed anew at how it never aged or weathered. Although, like the Empire it housed, the granite was not truly white. If a person looked closely, specks of silver and black flecked the stone.

The Imperial Seat of Koth, located in the mountain range known as Thoris's Shield, was comprised of eight cantons perched on the leveled tops of eight mountains forming a rough octagon beside the Sea of Light. The various cantons were connected by the Sky Walks, a series of delicately arched white granite bridges said to have been built—grown, actually—by giants. The notion of such big, ungainly creatures creating structures of such lightness and grace, let alone *growing* stones, made her doubt the story, personally.

Running through the center of the mountain cluster was the Crystal River. Spanning it was a cluster of bridges that formed a circular, intricate, rose-like pattern in the very center of the octagonal mountain range. Atop this structure of flying buttresses sat the White Crown Plaza, a massive terrace sprawling over the broad river and well beyond both its banks. Upon the plaza sat the Imperial palace and its grounds.

She knew better than to look directly down over the edge of the wall. The drop to the glittering river below was dizzying to contemplate. She'd always thought that, from a distance, it looked as if the support bridges were the linked fingers of giant hands, offering up the palace and its black flame like a jeweled crown to the heavens themselves.

"Thee and me, we are in an interesting position," Talissar said thoughtfully.

"How is that?"

"We are close to thrones, trusted by our spouses, yet neither of us holds much sway in our own right. Our influence is indirect. Hidden."

Where was he going with this? It was as if he circled about some point he wished to make but could not find the courage to address directly.

Talissar planted his elbows upon the wall and stared out to sea. He let out a sigh and lost the rigidity she had not known was in his posture until it melted away. Throwing her a sidelong glance, he murmured, "I find thee a most interesting study."

"How is that?" This genuinely interested Gabrielle. It was not the sort of thing courtiers often discussed openly.

"Thee hast not entirely forgotten thy knight, even after all this time. The strength of thy mind is impressive."

"I have no idea what you speak of, sir." Gabrielle declared.

"I have been observing thee, Your Highness, for a very long time. Thy mental discipline is extraordinary. To have functioned so long at court and barely given away thy doubts about the Empire? Really. It is extraordinary."

"I beg your p-p-pardon?" she sputtered.

Talissar shrugged. "Is it possible that thy reluctance to bear more offspring might stem from thy . . . distaste . . . for the current regime?"

Gabrielle stared. People were speculating on her long-time childless state? And her dislike of Maximillian was common knowledge? Horror and cold, hard terror poured through her. She must leave the court. Immediately. Before the Emperor got wind of her treasonous leanings.

"Please, do not panic. I am most circumspect in my observations."

"How can I not panic?" Gabrielle exclaimed. "If you believe you see these things, anyone can claim to see the same!"

Talissar responded urgently, "I assure thee, I can hold my tongue and would never betray thee. Quite the opposite, in fact."

Gabrielle went still. *The opposite of betrayal? What on Urth does that mean?*

"Thine instincts beist exceptional," Talissar complimented quietly. "Even now thee sensest where I am going, although I have not yet led thee down that path of logic."

Confusion warred with fear. She dared not say any more until this elf showed the cards in his hand.

The kindari sighed. "Your Highness, I understand that thee darest not risk more until I have revealed myself entirely. Queen Lyssandra has no idea that I approach thee, but it is for her that I put my life in thy hands."

"Your life? What madness do you speak?" Gabrielle ventured to whisper when he did not continue.

With a glance at her guard, Talissar angled his back more fully to the fellow and spoke in an undertone that would not carry five feet, his lips never moving. "I share thy dislike of the Emperor. I also happen to believe this Empire is not necessarily as eternal as he would have us all think."

She sucked in a sharp breath. It hissed between her teeth and settled like a viper in her breast. He spoke outright treason. His words were death to think, let alone utter.

As if he read her thoughts, he muttered, "Why dost thee think I stay so far from court except when absolutely necessary? I cannot chance having my mind come under scrutiny."

"Does your queen know the direction of your thoughts?" Gabrielle demanded.

"Of course not. Maximillian watches his Council of Kings far too closely for that. She takes no part whatsoever in what I speak of. She has no idea who I approach, what actions I take, or what plans we make."

We? The word exploded across her brain like one of Maximillian's fireworks displays. It was *conspiracy* he spoke of. Her jaw fell open. The audacity it took to speak such words, on the very grounds of the Emperor's palace no less, astounded her.

"A select few of us, close to the Council of Kings, with indirect access to information and resources, have the capacity to . . . influence . . . certain events. Dost thou understand what I am saying?"

She nodded, too dumbfounded to speak. Intrigue was the main dish of daily fare at court. Guilds jockeyed among themselves for control of various natural resources. Kings jostled with one another in search of power, wealth, and expanding their borders. Alliances came and went at court like the ocean's tides.

But Maximillian stood above it all, the spider in the web, plucking and pulling at the strands, building new ones as needed. Cutting out the bad ones entirely, if need be. As long as none of the paeans threatened the stability of the overall web, he allowed them to play their little games among themselves.

But what Talissar hinted at . . . outright insurrection . . . was aimed at destroying not only the web, but also the spider.

He continued low, "We move slowly. Carefully. Our actions remain small. Nothing to draw undue attention. Now and again, we affect a minor trade decision. Perhaps assist a like-minded person in earning a position of influence. Divert Imperial attention away from an area or event for a moment."

She realized she was shaking her head back and forth in denial. It was not possible. No one could topple Maximillian from his throne. If it were possible, surely it would have been accomplished centuries ago.

"Observe the bridges beneath us," Talissar said. "Individually, they are each far too fragile to hold the massive weight of this palace. But linked together, they form a powerful and solid foundation. What would happen if one of the Flying Bridges should fail?"

He answered his own question with a shrug. "Probably nothing. But what if many of these perfectly polished surfaces hid invisible cracks and flaws? Over time, stresses upon the stones wouldst build. Eventually, one bridge would fail. And another, and another, faster and faster, until the entire network crumbled and fell, bringing down the Seat of Eternity and casting it into the waters below to be swept away."

She was, in a word, astonished.

"Slowly, slowly, we undermine the foundation of this empire. One bridge at a time. One stone at a time. It may be the work of many lifetimes, but one day . . ."—his voice was steely with determination—". . . one day, the Empire will fall."

"Why?" she whispered hoarsely. "Why do you speak of this to me?"

He answered simply. Lightly. "Because I have convinced the others at long last that thee canst be trusted. And we desire thee to join us, of course."

Raina closed her eyes and focused on erh talisman. Summoned all the magic she had within her. Reached out with her mind, seeking other spirits nearby. She reached out farther across the width and breadth of the land to all the people living here. When she'd successfully touched a great river of life energy, then she reached out delicately for Mag's spirit. It should hover near the woman's body for several minutes before it dissipated. If Raina could just find it before that happened . . .

There. A gentle prickling across her skin, as if an invisible ghost occupied the space nearby. It wasn't exactly a feeling of being watched. It was more like being breathed upon. Unmistakably a spirit fully separated from its body hovered close.

To focus her mind, Raina spoke the Life incant aloud, using the exercise to gather the magical energy infusing everyone around her. It had weight in her hands, slight, but tangible nonetheless. As she did not have to project the magic very far from herself, she could afford to gather a lot of it to her. Shaping it into strength, vitality, hope, and maybe just a touch of her own stubborn will, she laid her hands on Mag's still chest and blasted every bit of it into the dead woman.

The explosion slammed Raina backward against the wall of the hut. Clods of dirt showered down upon her, slipping down her shirt and landing in her hair as a great wave of the life energy she had shaped rushed outward, through the walls of the hut, over the hill, and beyond. She spit grit out of her mouth as she lurched forward and dropped to her knees beside Mag.

The woman was deathly pale and still. But then her chest rose fractionally. Breath rattled in her throat. Her chest fell and rose again.

Exultation roared through Raina. She'd done it. She'd restored Mag's spirit to her body. Raina sat back on her heels, profoundly relieved. The scrolls she'd read said life spells would cure mortal injuries enough to ensure the patient did not die from them again as part of the body's rejoining with its spirit, although the subject would be left very weak for days or weeks if not given additional healing. But the woman was alive. Alive!

Mag's eyelids fluttered. Opened. She looked up at Raina vaguely. "The babe . . . ," she mumbled.

"A healthy, strapping boy. And you're going to be fine, too."

Surprise registered in Mag's eyes. "How—"

Raina cut her off gently. "Rest now. You're on the mend. Everything's going to be all right."

But Mag was having none of that. She held out her arms expectantly, and Raina filled them with the woman's newborn son. Raina could almost see their spirits touch, recognize each other, and bind tightly one to the other. Mag hummed a quiet lullaby, its melody sweet and unbearably sad. And then she did the oddest thing. She began to cry. Raina lurched forward in alarm as tears rolled down the woman's cheeks and dripped off her chin and onto the babe's head.

"What is amiss, Mag? Do you have pain? Dizziness? Faintness?"

"Wha'? Gor' no, girl. I be fine."

"Then why do you cry? What's that song you're humming?"

"It is the Lament. Every mother sings it to 'er babe. Leastwise, common folk do."

"Does it have words?"

"If so, they's been lost to this land." Mag picked up the haunting tune again.

As she listened idly to the lullaby, exhaustion washed over Raina. Probably the aftereffect of the effort of collecting so much magic and then draining herself of it like that. She hated to think how illegal casting that life spell had been. If the Heart ever found out what she'd just done, she would be in serious trouble. Tampering with life and death was exclusively the province of the Imperial healer's guild. Like all guilds, the Heart took grave offense at any intrusion upon its purview.

As a general sense of defeat and hopelessness came over her, something within Raina rebelled. *No!* She would not give in to it! She reached for that spark of vitality and energy that had been present before and drew it to herself. Magnified it. Sent it back out from whence it came.

Mag's voice trailed off. Then, with renewed vigor, she announced, "Gor, enough of tha', now. Whot say we fetch the wee bairn's siblings to meet 'im?"

Raina brought the children home and prepared a batch of healing broth to help Mag regain her strength and ward off infection. It was evening before Arv emerged from the barn, shovel in hand, bleary-eyed, and obviously sporting a splitting head.

"Be ye 'ere to bury me?" Mag demanded merrily when he stumbled into the hovel.

He stopped cold in the doorway. "But ye were dyin'—"

"Do I look dead, ye ole drunk?"

Laughter filled the hut. Raina's heart swelled. She'd done a good thing here, Imperial law be cursed.

Arv turned to her in awe. "I have no words . . . nothing to repay ye—"

"I ask only your friendship. And perhaps a water skin for my journey. Oh, and maybe the spoon you carved for me."

The crofter outfitted her with not only a water skin and spoon but also fire-starting stones, a sturdy leather pack to carry the various herbs she'd collected, an oiled cloth for rainy weather, and he even forced her to take a precious glass bottle to use for mixing potions.

Raina lay awake listening for Cicero's return as long as her exhaustion would let her that night. But still he did not come. Where was he? Did he live after rushing out in pursuit of the orcs? Had he been injured? Should she go looking for him? But how would she proceed in orc-infested forests without getting caught herself? Did she dare continue her journey alone? Did she have a choice? The questions spun round and round in her head until she was fair dizzy from them.

But gradually one truth emerged. She must go on. She must go to the great city of Dupree and interview scholars and historians to find out more about this elven Mythar fellow. If she did not solve the puzzle of how to rouse the Great Mage, all would be lost.

F or pity's sake, give us a more cheerful tune!" Anton
Constantine snapped at the paxan slave strumming a
fat-bellied stringed instrument in the corner. She
was dour and not his type, but her music could make the stars
themselves smile. The dirge she strummed now, though, was
killing the party mood. Of course, knowing her, that was her
intent.

The paxan glanced up at him, the closed third eyelid in the
middle of her forehead lending her a baleful expression. But
she did shift into a lighter ditty. He tilted his head back and
opened his mouth. Another slave girl, a young human he was
nearly tired enough of to send away, stood behind him with
a wine skin. Gads, Delphi's vineyards produced fantastic
wines. Mayhap he should kill the landsgrave and take them
all for himself. The slave girl squirted a stream of deep ruby
liquid into his mouth.

Nothing like a good love potion to put a female into a cooperative and affectionate frame of mind. He'd perfected the
formula over the past decade and kept a good supply on hand
at all times.

He reclined lazily among the pillows as yet another slave
girl commenced massaging his neck and shoulders. He must
remember to feed her another potion on the morrow. It had

been nearly a full turning of the moon since he last fed the talented masseuse one of his special poi—

The chamber door flew open, interrupting his ruminations. A soldier marched in, full of himself, his uniform stiff and pristine. *Krugar.* Anton rolled his eyes. He almost preferred the lazy slobs the Haelan legion took in to these self-important, ambitious types who came along now and then.

"What do you want?" he snapped.

"I come from Southwatch Fort. Bearing a message for your ears only, Governor."

He never did tire of hearing that title directed at him. He'd had to wait a full decade for that old fool Volen to kick the bucket. He might have engineered the old geezer's demise at the hands of invading Boki, but he'd made certain that his hands were entirely clean of the murder. The first governor had been older than dirt and showing no signs of giving up on life.

If there had been any questions at court about the nature of Volen's final death, Archduke Ammertus must have diverted them. More than once in his first few years down here, his mentor at court had intervened to protect Anton and make sure his man had free reign in the colonies to do whatever he willed. Anton figured it was the archduke's way of taking petty revenge against the Emperor for banishing Ammertus's son, Starfire. Ammertus's spawn had gotten into an altercation with Krugar over some insult given to Krugar's queen, young Gabriel of Haraland. It had been very noble and tragic, with Krugar throwing himself on his proverbial sword over some slight to her honor. As punishment for striking Starfire—who outranked him considerably—Krugar had been banished to Haelos, never to return to Court. Served him right.

In the meantime, Anton was more than happy to run amok in Haelos and squeeze the land and people for every last copper they could choke up.

Krugar cleared his throat a touch impatiently. Impatient whoreson. Always had been. Effective officer though. His men were the best the bedraggled Haelan legion had to offer.

Anton rolled his eyes. What was that buffoon Mowery from Southwatch ranting about now? He'd stuck the sergeant in the farthest corner of Dupree he could so he didn't have to deal with the fellow's incompetence any more than absolutely necessary. "Let's hear it then," Anton drawled.

The soldier looked down pointedly at the slave girl now massaging Anton's calves. Krugar never had approved of his extracurricular activities. Pointedly, Anton pulled her into his lap, and she immediately reached for his shoulders.

He waved an indolent hand to encompass all the females in the room. "No need to worry about them. They're all wildly in love with me. Can't see past it to pay the slightest attention to my business."

On the off chance that Krugar was a spy for the emperor, Anton cultivated a persona of being a completely incompetent lush around him. For years, he'd sought a way to turn Krugar, to blackmail or coerce the soldier into serving him and him only. But to no avail. Krugar lived a pristine life.

But Anton Constantine was no dummy, by the stars. He'd turned Imperial spies before, and this one would be no exception. He could be patient until Krugar revealed a flaw in his personal armor. Anton had long believed the adage that the best place for one's enemy was clasped to one's breast.

"Well, what are you waiting for?" he snapped. "You have not delivered Mowery's dire tidings, yet."

"His troops report that orcs have attacked a village in the Wylde Wood. Several other sightings of an orc raiding party have been reported."

Orcs? He stared blankly at Krugar through the haze of the copious wine he'd been drinking. He sat up abruptly, dumping the slave girl on the floor. "Mowery's men are mistaken," he blurted.

"They are not. I have seen a destroyed wagon with two dead guards and a dead Heart healer upon the road with my own eyes. Orc sign was clear. Heavy axes were used to hack apart the bodies and the oxen were taken."

"That does not mean we have been invaded by orcs. It merely means bandits with axes attacked a caravan."

Krugar replied stubbornly, "It was orcs. I smelled their stench at the scene."

Anton snorted in disbelief. His secret treaty with the Boki had held for nearly fifteen years. The Boki, who generally controlled all the other orcish tribes in the region, had made no rumblings whatsoever of any plans to break the truce. And they would do well not to break it, either.

His gaze narrowed as he stared up at the soldier. Orcs on the move, eh? What were they about, those cursed greenskins?

"Krugar, I need you to go north. To the Forest of Thorns. Find out what the orcs are up to and report back to me."

"So shall it be, Governor." Krugar turned smartly on his booted heel and marched out of the room while Anton gaped at the soldier's retreating back. Anton hadn't heard that phrase since Koth.

Why in the devil had Krugar chosen those words? What deep game was this spy of Maximillian's about? Had Krugar just signaled a willingness to change his alliance from the Emperor to the governor of the colony? Or was it all an elaborate test of his loyalty by Maximillian? If the Emperor thought to trip him up, he was sadly mistaken. He could play at plots within plots with the best of Imperial courtiers.

Anton looked down at the slave girl hugging his calf adoringly. "Now where were we?"

"I was about to give you the best back rub of your life, my lord."

Laughing darkly, he turned his attention away from political intrigue. Krugar should remember that he was very far away indeed from the Imperial Court. This was Anton's turf. He pulled the strings in Dupree. Not Maximillian.

Arv told Raina that Imperial troops would be thick to the east. The wilds lay to the west, and those orcs had headed north. Castlegate Falls was the nearest settlement to the south, most of a day's walk away. She had but to follow the road until she came to it. He seemed to think that even she could not get lost en route. Without Cicero to lead her, though, Raina was less certain of that. But after the elf's failure to return from following that Boki squad north, she had no choice. Cicero could have headed back to Tyrel or be dead for all she knew. Arv needed to stay home and help Mag with the new babe, and he had a farm to tend.

It was high time and more that she grew up and learned to fend for herself. Justin would call her a 'fraidy muckling if she could not even follow a road to town by herself. With fond farewells all around and wishes of good speed on her journey, Raina set out.

It was the first time in her life she'd walked a road alone. She was struck by the pall that hung over the impoverished land, as if misery and suffering were the main crops grown and harvested in this place. Peasants waved a weary hullo now and again as she passed them toiling in their fields and vegetable patches. It was as if everyone had forgotten what happiness, or even hope, was.

Or mayhap the daily grind of simple survival was so overwhelming that no one had time or energy to think about aught but their next meal. Keeping a roof overhead. The next tax collection. An oppressive weight settled over her, and even Raina found herself having to fight off a sense of futility. What if she failed to find sufficient magicks of the olde kind to restore the Great Mage? Her chances of succeeding in her quest were extremely small. Why even try? Mayhap she should just give up and go home.

But then memory came to her of her sister laughing in delight over some bauble. Memory of her mother's tears as Raina's aunt left home and walked into the east. She reached forth with her spirit and found the spark from before. A tiny pinprick of vitality and energy within the dreariness. She drew it to herself carefully.

If she did not stand up for her future daughters, who would? The rightness of her cause filled Raina once more and she strode on, her step jauntier. It was a grand adventure, and she would relish the telling of it to an avid Justin someday.

Castlegate Falls turned out to be a decent-sized settlement with defensive fortifications around it. The guard at the gate directed her to the far side of town to find a riverboat headed toward Dupree. Arv and Mag had assured her she would be able to trade her healing skills for the cost of passage. She was in no rush, however, and took her time wandering past storefronts offering rich fabrics and jewelry and fine furnishings she had never seen the like of before.

A friendly shopkeeper apologized for the pitiful selection of wares, citing a poor harvest that had depressed the local economy something terrible. Apparently, the city of Dupree was doing much better, however, and the merchants there were thriving. To her country-raised eye, though, this place was a sultan's bazaar of exotic riches.

She might have had a top-notch education, but for the first time she comprehended just how isolated her life had been until now. A burgeoning sense of escape sent joy leaping through her. Who knew what wonders lay around the next corner?

She passed through the town square, agape at the imposing guild halls jostling among themselves for preeminence. From the sinister Slaver's Guild to the garishly colorful Entertainer's Guild, she was reluctantly enthralled by the display of wealth and power. Here was the mighty Kothite Empire at last, not a distant threat, but real and tangible before her.

Commoners were told to love the Emperor, who loved them in return. That the governor and his legion had their best interests at heart and could be counted upon to protect them. But in her experience, most people just wished to steer clear of the Empire and for it to steer clear of them. Even her parents didn't much care who ruled them from afar, as long as governor, archduke, and Emperor stayed firmly ensconced in their distant palaces, and well away from their little corner of the world.

As she neared the docks, she heard a hawker shouting. A small crowd had gathered round a raised platform and she moved in to see what was being sold. She spied the auctioneer first and recognized with a start the feline features and lightly furred visage of a rakasha—a cat changeling. This one was a nondescript beige in coloring, reminiscent of a mountain lion. His fang-like teeth made him menacing in the extreme.

A human fellow of middle age stood dejectedly on a wooden box beside the rakasha, a chain looped around his neck. An ugly black mark marred the fellow's right cheek, and Raina recognized the double chain-link symbol of the Slaver's Guild ritually applied there. She recoiled in distaste. He lifted his gaze briefly, beseechingly, to her. His desperation coursed through her, but there was naught she could do to help him.

Her family did not deal in slaves as a rule. Rather, her mother preferred indentured servants and gave them a fair opportunity to work off their debt. Lady Charlotte said people with hope for their futures worked much more willingly and well than slaves with nothing left to lose or to gain.

The bidding for the slave started anemically, and Raina moved away quickly from the auction. This river was larger than any she'd seen before. She overheard someone say that it was the confluence point of the Minon Wae and the Covin Wae, each a large river in its own right. She'd never seen the mighty Kamchatka River that flowed past Tyrel northeast toward the Wust. It was supposedly the largest yet discovered on this continent. Still, this river was plenty intimidating to her.

She read a crude sign pointing the way to a ferry crossing, and another pointing toward the harbormaster's office. Arv had told her to look for an honest-looking captain with kind eyes. Doubt in her ability to judge character assailed her as she hesitantly approached the boardwalk.

A gruff-looking dwarf was just shoving off, shouting irascible orders at his crew and looking completely disreputable. Good thing she'd missed his vessel, the *Tough Knut*. She searched for a likelier-looking ship. She'd nearly reached the end of the dock when a commotion erupted at the far end of the boardwalk.

She spied a pair of soldiers charging around the corner, weapons drawn. They raced to the edge of the dock and skidded to a halt, looking about frantically.

"Pssst. Over here."

Raina started. It sounded like that whisper had been directed at her. She searched around quickly.

"Don't look," the whispered voice bit out, disgusted. "Make your way over here casually, behind the wagon."

Her common sense ordered her in no uncertain terms to turn tail and run full tilt the other way. But there was something familiar about that voice. . . .

She peered around the end of the wagon and spied a golden-haired elf crouching in the shadows. "Cicero!" she exclaimed.

"Keep your voice down, for stars' sake," he muttered. He yanked her down beside him into the shadow of a stack of barrels.

"Are those soldiers after you?" she asked under her breath.

A grunt was her only answer. She'd take that as a yes. Cicero peeked past the barrels and then subsided next to her. "The barge just down there to our right is getting ready to cast off. We'll make a run for it at the last second. Timing will be everything. When I say go, take off running for all you're worth and don't look back or slow down for anything. Understood?"

"Not at all. What's going on?"

"No time to explain," he replied. "Just do what I say if you wish to remain free."

Alarmed, she nodded, securing her pack more tightly against her back, eyeing the barge Cicero indicated. He sidled along the wall of the warehouse, using stacks of crates for cover, and she followed along as best she could. They paused next to a straw pile, crouching huddled up to it.

Cicero stood and eased away from the wall. He mouthed silently, *Ready . . . Set*—

A jingling noise from an oxen harness very close by slammed them both back against the damp stone wall at their backs. She mimicked Cicero, who stood stock-still. Out of the corner of her eye, she spied soldiers milling in the road no more than twenty paces distant. Three more soldiers had joined the first two. They all looked to be reporting to one of the late arrivals. *C'mon, c'mon. Finish talking already and go away!* The first mooring line of their barge had just been cast off.

And still the soldiers chatted. They looked to be trying to figure out what to do next. The second line was cast off and thrown to the barge's deck. One more line to go. Time was running out.

The barge's crew cast off the last line with maddening slowness while she waited in an agony of impatience. The sailors picked up their long poles and walked to the front of the boat. Her muscles tensed. If she and Cicero were going to catch the barge, they had to go now.

With massive arms, the sailors jabbed the poles into the river bottom and commenced walking slowly toward the back of the boat. Cicero took a deep breath, and she did the same.

By inches, the heavy barge crept away from the dock. A balky ox on board bellowed as the vessel began to rock gently beneath his feet, and the captain shouted for one of his men to blindfold the animal. No help for it that the ruckus had drawn the full attention of the soldiers.

"Go!" Cicero ordered.

She went. As fast as her legs would carry her.

"Halt! You there! In the name of the Empire, halt!"

She and Cicero streaked across the road, cloaks flying. Footsteps pounded on the hard-packed dirt behind them. She gritted her teeth and ran for her life, concentrating fiercely on catching the barge before her. A gap appeared between the barge and the dock, some six feet of ominous, hungry-looking black water. Now seven feet. She barreled down the slope and clattered onto the wood dock. Eight feet. Nine.

It was too far for her to jump!

Cicero soared out into space in front of her. She had no choice but to do the same. One of the soldiers was tearing down the slope only a few yards behind her. It was the barge or a swim for her life. She took the last few steps at a dead run, flinging herself out into space, arms flailing.

Her toes just caught the edge of the barge's flat platform. Her momentum carried her forward, but her feet slipped and she lost purchase on the slippery deck. She began to fall, her shins sliding painfully down the ends of the planks into the water. She wasn't going to make it. Cold water closed around her legs. But then strong arms caught her under the armpits, rolling away from the edge of the barge and yanking her along. She was bodily dragged aboard in a heap, her sodden skirts dripping on the deck. She untangled herself enough to push up against a warm, strong chest. Cicero.

"Thanks be," she panted

Exasperated, he snapped, "Next time you choose to run away from home, do not wear a fancy dress with such a heavy skirt. Had you fallen into the water, it would have weighed you down and drowned you. Adventurers, even women, must needs wear practical clothing!"

The first thing that registered was the complete absence of peasant accent in his voice. He sounded as educated as her parents or herself. Only secondarily did she register that he hadn't shared with her exactly how dangerous his plan to jump for the barge had actually been.

As irritated as Cicero was about her dress, he wasn't half so irritated as the soldiers shouting on the dock behind them for the barge to come back to shore. Raina glanced back and shuddered at the nearness of her escape. Apparently, the soldier who'd nearly caught up with her had thought better of duplicating her jump. Which was just as well, since he and all of his comrades wore heavy chain-mail shirts. A fall into the river for one of them would've meant certain drowning.

"Gimme a good reason why I oughtn't do as them soldiers is shoutin' at me to and return to shore," a voice growled over her head.

Raina looked up. The barge captain. "Because they want to drag my friend off and imprison him or worse, when all he has done is help me out of a difficult situation."

The sailor shrugged. "They's Anton's men. Disobeying 'em is same as disobeying 'im. An' I ain't inclined to cross the guv'nuh'. 'E's a mean one, 'e is."

Raina winced. "Can't you tell them the current is too strong to turn around? Or that your cargo is bound for the governor and you dare not keep him waiting?" She gave the captain her best approximation of a kicked-puppy look—the one that always worked on Justin.

The captain's expression softened a tiny bit. "I shouldn't."

She poured all the charm she possessed into her voice. "But in your heart, you know it's the right thing to do. Please. Just this once."

Cicero piped up from where he sprawled beneath her, "Cut her a break, man. She has done nothing wrong. The soldiers were chasing me."

Raina scrambled off of him, mumbling an embarrassed apology.

He climbed to his feet, flashing her a rare, wry smile from behind those wise eyes of his. "We are willing to pay handsomely for passage downriver. I've enough gold to make it worth your while to . . . look the other way . . . regarding our manner of boarding."

The captain's eyes took on a cunning gleam that worried Raina. "Give it to me now."

Cicero laughed merrily. "Not a chance. I'll show it to you now. But you'll not get a copper until we set foot upon shore." Raina noted that Cicero's hand rested comfortably on the hilt of his sword.

The captain must have noted the same, for he scowled but nodded in agreement.

The pole men had pushed them out into the main portion of the river and the barge rocked gently as the current caught it. The soldiers onshore yelled insults and invective at the captain, their threats of what they were going to do to him upon his return growing ever more dire.

He glanced over at Cicero. "Ye'd best pay me well. I ain't gonna be able to put ashore in Castlegate Falls fer a while."

Cicero shrugged. "They're human. Short memories. In a few months, they won't remember a thing."

The captain, a human, too, grinned. "Aye, true enough, pointy ears. Fugitives like you two are as common as copper. Them soldiers'll find themselves a bigger fish to fry afore long."

Raina's heart dropped to her feet. She'd fled the Haelan legion. Disobeyed their orders to stop. She was officially a fugitive. The finality of the step she'd just taken struck her. Until now, she'd always had the option of identifying herself as Raina of Tyrel, a minor colonial noble, and she would have immediately had status and safety, not to mention a quick journey back home. But she'd just left all that behind. Her safety net was gone.

They drifted on what Cicero declared to be a stiff current. The barge traveled in an hour as far as they could have walked in half a day. The countryside as they drew closer to the capital was heavily settled, although it looked no more prosperous than the rural hinterlands.

Overnight, she and Cicero took turns napping because neither of them entirely trusted the captain not to slit their throats in their sleep and steal Cicero's purse. Raina did not ask where he had come by the pouch of coins in his absence from Mag and Arv's hut, and he did not offer an explanation. Now that they had money, she was relieved of the necessity to trade healing for passage. Which was just as well. Healers with her volume of magic were apparently quite rare and drew a fair bit of attention.

The barge rounded a bend late the next morning, and a city so vast she could not see the far margin of it came into view. *Dupree.*

Gold changed palms as the barge docked, and the captain grinned, appearing satisfied. Whether it would be enough that the fellow made no mention of them to the authorities remained to be seen.

She leaped across the short gap from deck to dock, nothing compared to the mighty jump she'd made to board the vessel. And yet she managed to catch her hem on a board and stumble headlong into a richly dressed and accoutered young noble who happened to be striding past.

He caught her as she staggered into him and righted her courteously enough. "Easy there!"

"I'm so s-s-sorry," she stammered. "I caught my skirt, and, well, you know the rest."

Her rescuer scanned her assessingly before answering her lightly, "No doubt, it was fate that threw you at my feet. I am Kendrick of Hyland."

She recognized the name. Hyland was said to be one of the largest and most powerful landholds near Dupree. As she recalled, the landsgrave's given name was Leland, though. This must be his son. His handsome, charming, womanizing son, if she had to guess. He looked as spoiled and entitled as his rank suggested he might be.

"And you are?" the young man prompted her.

She and Cicero had discussed this very thing. He had no confidence in her to remember to answer to a false name, and she had to agree. Thankfully, Raina was not that uncommon a name. They'd agreed she would use it but forego her title, henceforth. She dropped automatically into a curtsy. "I am Raina. It is my pleasure to meet you, kind sir."

Cicero glared at her over the young man's shoulder, and she realized belatedly that perhaps she should not have been so courtly in her response to Kendrick. She was supposed to be a commoner on her way to Dupree to look for work as a lady's maid. But it just felt . . . right . . . to address the young man thus. She always had a talent for instinctively knowing the best way to speak to others, whether to strike a formal tone or respect, or gently joke, or, as in this case, to flirt a bit.

Sure enough, Kendrick's eyebrows lifted in pleased surprise. He took a closer and more interested look at her. *Curses.* "Where are you bound in such a hurry, Raina? Have you time to tarry for a while?"

If she did not know better, she would guess he thought she was some doxy for hire by the hour—no matter that she was not wearing the Entertainer's Guild colors. The idea offended her more than a little. Bent on correcting his misapprehension, she replied a shade tartly, "As you saw, my traveling companion and I have just come ashore."

Kendrick eyed Cicero speculatively. "What sort of companion?"

It was a forward question. Not the sort a young gentleman asked of a young lady. But it was the sort of thing a noble could demand of a commoner, she supposed. "Family friend and protector," she replied, hoping that was evasive enough while appearing to give a reasonable explanation.

Cicero rolled his eyes at her over Kendrick's shoulder. She glared back. It was better than the fellow thinking they were lovers!

". . . on my way to make an urgent purchase," Kendrick

was saying. "If you would accompany me on my errand, it would be my great pleasure to dine with you afterward."

Raina's stomach growled on command, and Kendrick laughed. "It seems your belly accepts my offer." He ordered in a tone clearly accustomed to being obeyed, "Come then. I must hurry."

Had a pair of surly-looking soldiers not come into sight just then prowling the docks, she would have told this arrogant young man what he could do with his order. Instead, though, she fell in meekly beside him. Cicero followed just behind her, scowling and looking exactly the part of a long-suffering bodyguard. The three of them passed by the soldiers without incident, and Raina let out the breath she'd been holding.

Kendrick made his way to a jeweler's shop. Although it was somewhat less prosperous looking than she'd have guessed a person of Kendrick's station would choose to frequent. She was quite surprised, however, when he stripped off the many rings and brooches and necklaces gaudily adorning his person and presented them to the jeweler for sale. Kendrick obviously came from wealth. What could a young man of his station need gold for so urgently that his family would not simply give it to him? A gambling habit, perchance? Or maybe the purchase of female companionship?

"What will you give me for the lot?" Kendrick demanded of the jeweler.

He and the shopkeeper haggled a price, which, frankly, she thought was highway robbery on the part of the jeweler. But as a commoner she would not know such a thing and held her tongue.

Kendrick's next stop was a weapon smith's establishment. He went through the same routine, laying down two long swords, a beautifully inlaid bow, a short sword, and a pair of jeweled daggers on the counter for sale. This time it was Cicero who pulled a face at the final price.

However, Kendrick snatched up the coins hurriedly and headed for what appeared to be the worst neighborhood in Dupree. His destination was a large, run-down warehouse built of rotting wood.

Cautiously, she and Cicero followed Kendrick inside . . . to a slave auction of the worst possible kind. The slaves were filthy and half-starved looking, chained together in tight gangs of men, women, and children of various races. The slavers yelled harshly and treated their product little better than sheep, prodding at them with long canes, and striking them if they disobeyed. It sickened Raina to see it. The slavers here were white tiger rakasha and looked none too reputable. Even Cicero wrinkled his nose in distaste.

"Those are Kithmar slavers," he muttered to her. "Thieves, cutthroats, and mercenaries for hire when they're not slaving. They're one of the few changeling clans to join the Empire. I heard that they were royalty among their kind at one time, but I find it hard to credit."

"What is the story on those men over there?" she asked, gesturing toward a pair of well-dressed humans with prominent snake tattoos on their forearms. One of the men appeared to have a bodyguard, a burly troll born—part man, part troll. The other was accompanied by a beautiful young woman.

Kendrick muttered scornfully, "Those are Anton's lackeys. The one with the troll born lackey is Bogatyr, the Dupree Entertainer's Guild Master. He's probably here on the hunt for combatants for the Diamond."

She'd heard plenty about Diamond arenas, but her parents had never allowed her to attend a spectacle at one. They deemed the armed combat and gambling far too violent for a young girl's sensibilities.

Kendrick continued, "The other man is Kenzarr. The Dupree Slaver's Guild Master. That's his daughter with him. Mistress Richelle Devereaux. She's also with the Slaver's Guild."

Raina started to ask Kendrick what could possibly bring him to a place like this, but she had her answer as soon as she turned. He'd moved over to a row of slaves and was speaking with two young janns, a male and a female with the swirled markings of the elements on their skin. Brown stone coloring dominated in the big, muscular youth with a touch of red fire coloring, whereas the female was heavily blue water marked, with only a hint of stone coloring her visible flesh. As the girl moved, a striking iridescence shone in her water markings.

Kendrick moved toward the nearest Kithmar, a female, and Raina sidled closer to hear the conversation.

". . . willing to buy those two jann now and forego the auction block. What price for them?"

She could not hear the Kithmar's growled answer, but dismay was clear on Kendrick's features as he turned away from the slaver. Kendrick rejoined her and Cicero without comment. They waited through sales of a dozen slaves before Kendrick's male jann acquaintance was shoved up roughly onto the auction block.

The bidding was more spirited than it had been on any previous slaves. Apparently, his youth, health, and the known talent of janns for magic made him valuable. Not to mention his obvious physical strength. His brawny body was wreathed in muscles that made him look as strong as an ox.

Kendrick entered the bidding and refused to be topped. Clearly, he was determined to have this particular slave. Raina suspected that the fellow bidding up the price was in cahoots with the Kithmar, and she tried to tell Kendrick that, but he would not listen to a word she said, so intent was he on winning the auction. Finally, when the price had risen to triple what any other slave had gone for so far, the auctioneer declared the sale.

Kendrick sighed in relief. But as he counted out his coins to the slaver who came to give him the jann's leash, despair crossed his face. The elemental fellow's leash was passed to Kendrick, who immediately handed it over to the jann.

"I don't have enough left to buy Marikeen if she goes for a fraction as much as you."

The jann replied bitterly, "She'll go for double or more than I did. I heard the slavers mumbling last night of marking her for Anton's harem and making him hand over top price for her."

Kendrick frowned. "Maybe we can work that to our advantage." He rushed off to speak with one of the Kithmar, leaving Raina and Cicero standing with the collared and slave-marked jann.

"Uhh, hello," she said awkwardly. "I'm Raina. And this is Cicero."

"Eben," the jann replied shortly, his attention on Kendrick.

What did one say to a slave? Particularly one who was so brusque and seemingly unimpressed by his predicament? *So. How did you come to be enslaved?* Or, *I'm sorry your life is ruined. I hope you have a happy slavery.* Stymied, she chose silence.

Kendrick returned and announced under his breath, "I gave them the rest of my gold in return for their promise to wait a week before selling your sister to Anton. I told them I'd pay double what he offers for slave girls of her ilk."

"And they agreed?" Eben asked quickly.

"Aye. One week. That should be enough time to go home, explain what happened to my father, get the gold we need, and find the slavers."

Eben nodded. "Thanks be for my rescue, at any rate."

Kendrick replied, "Don't worry overmuch about Marikeen. The slavers won't mistreat her or mark her. She's too valuable unmarred and healthy."

Raina glanced over at the jann girl worriedly. Apparently, Marikeen had come to the same conclusion as Kendrick, for she looked supremely unconcerned. She was not chained with the other slaves and had been given a stool to sit upon. Her ankles were chained, but with fleece-covered shackles that would not rub her skin raw.

Kendrick tried to speak to her, no doubt to let her know he was working on securing her release, but three male Kithmar formed a wall and refused to let him approach her. She smiled jauntily at him and her brother, however.

Raina had to give Kendrick credit for his efforts to secure his friends' releases. She'd misjudged him, an unusual mistake for her. Or perhaps it was this new view from the bottom of society looking up that had wrongly colored her initial impression of the impetuous young noble.

As soon as they left the warehouse, Kendrick used his belt knife to slice the heavy leather collar off Eben's neck. Raina breathed a sigh of relief along with Eben.

Kendrick commented sourly, "Yon ritual slave mark may not prove so easy to remove, my friend. Let us try, though, shall we?"

Kendrick led the party, now increased by Eben's presence, deeper into the vast capital city to a huge square dominated by a single gigantic guild hall. It was painted a rich royal blue and accented with a gold stars-and-comets motif. It took up the whole of a city block, and she could only stare at its palatial dimensions. She had never seen the like before.

Raina was careful to completely power down her magic so that not even a hint of glow remained about her hands. The last thing she needed was for this bunch to snatch her off the street and demand that she serve them.

Funny how fast she'd begun thinking like a peasant. Her reluctance to reveal her magic begged the question of how many peasants with a latent talent for magic hid in the countryside, never developing their skill rather than serve the Empire. For a mage, the only source of training and advancement was usually within the Imperial Mage's guild—or for those with healing magic, the Heart.

She supposed, though, that life under the thumb of a guild was preferable to scraping and starving for most people. And after all, what other choice was there? The Empire was pervasive, all-knowing and all-powerful. She had not realized just how much so until she'd left isolated little Tyrel, tucked away on the edge of nowhere and barely touched by the Kothites and their empire.

She listened with interest as Kendrick inquired about having Eben's slave mark removed from his right cheek. Apparently, his chain links would require a second ritual to be taken off. Seventy gold was the price quoted to perform the ritual and provide the components from the guild's stash. Ritual components were various items magical in nature whose power was drained by a trained mage to achieve a particularly difficult magical effect.

"And the cost if I provide the components?" Kendrick asked, sounding taken aback.

Twenty gold was quoted for the casting alone. While Kendrick explained he would have to return home to gather the components and gold, Raina tried to contain her shock. She'd secretly been training to do ritual magic for years, and she'd had no idea the skill was worth so much. Mayhap working for a guild would not be so bad if they would share a reasonable portion of her earnings with her. She dared not ask the

Mage's Guild man any questions, though, lest she draw too much attention of the wrong kind to herself. There must be an indirect means of finding out the guild pay structures.

"We make haste for my father's home," Kendrick announced to her as they emerged from the guild building "You and your man are welcome to spend the night there while you get your bearings in the city," he offered.

Raina glanced over at Cicero for his opinion, and he nodded slightly. It was never a bad thing to travel dangerous streets in large parties with multiple swords at hand. Not to mention Kendrick's noble status would serve to protect them from rude soldiers or roving slavers looking to grab victims illegally.

She declared, "To your home then, my lord."

Will stared, slack jawed, as the *Tough Knut* rounded a lazy bend in the river and, without warning, the great capital city of Dupree sprawled before him. It covered the entire valley, from hilltop to hilltop, arcing around the wide blue harbor toward which the river flowed. Buildings seemed built on top of buildings, crowding one another nearly as tightly as people packed the streets. He'd never seen a tenth so many people in one place before, not even on the largest market days in Fort Southwatch.

"What business on Urth could so many people have all in the same place?" he demanded.

"Bumpkin," Rosana declared.

He scowled sharply at her. She might be right, but she did not have to point it out so bluntly. He pitched in to help throw the heavy mooring lines ashore and the captain clapped his shoulder in gruff thanks. Will and Roan Ironknot had struck up a friendship of sorts over the course of the voyage downriver. Will found the Kelnor's no-nonsense view of the world to be not far from his own forest-raised way of thinking.

"Safe travels to ye, boy. Don' forget, now. If'n ye got troubles, ye've but to ask me kind for aid. Tell 'em an Ironknot said you's good people."

Will replied, "If you ever reach the end of the Southwatch

Road, ask after Ty the cobbler and tell him Will said to show you his finest blade work." Stars willing, Will's father would be there to fulfill the request.

"Done." They grabbed each other's forearms in the dwarven tradition while engaging in a mutual back thumping that Will was certain would leave bruises on him. He leaped ashore and turned to offer Rosana his hand.

"I can jump myself," she declared.

"I'm sure you can," he replied patiently, "but my mother would skin me for not offering to assist you."

The belligerently independent gypsy actually reached out and took his outstretched palm. Her hand was small and soft in his and the warmth of her touch startled him. Her gaze snapped up to his, and her eyes were wide and surprised.

"Thanks be," she murmured as she stepped daintily ashore.

He mumbled something incoherent and was saved from having to say more by Roan tossing their packs across to them. He grunted under the impact. Cursed dwarf didn't know his own strength. Shouldering both packs, Will turned to follow Rosana down the long dock to the pier.

But at the end of the dock, a nasty surprise met them. An intensely officious-looking soldier blocked their way, announcing, "We have received word of a fugitive pair, a man and a girl who fled soldiers upriver two days past and departed by barge. Are you that pair?"

Will mostly forgot what a tiny thing Rosana was, due to the size of her personality. But she barely reached this Imperial soldier's shoulder as she drew up straight and replied formally, "I am on official Heart business, sir, and you block my way."

"Are you the pair who fled my men?"

Uh-oh. His men? This is some sort of senior trooper then? Will dived in to smooth the storm gathering on the soldier's brow. "I assure you, sir. We would never flee the rightful authority of the Imperial Army. We travel under the auspices of a Heart writ, which my companion will be more than glad to produce for your perusal." He threw a warning glance at Rosana that exhorted her to mind her tongue and her manners.

Scowling, she rummaged in her pouch and pulled out the letter from the Heart sister. The soldier took it and read it quickly.

"You're not them. I'm looking for a human girl and an elf. This says here you bear important tidings. What is your news?" he demanded.

"Did I not already tell you it was Heart business?" she snapped.

Will grimaced. While she might technically be within her rights to tell a soldier to keep his big nose out of a Heart matter, the practical reality was that Anton's legion trumped all other Imperial agencies in the colonies in actual power.

"Heart business is Imperial business. And Imperial business is *my* business, young healer." The menace in the soldier's voice belatedly seemed to register on Rosana.

"And who might you be, sir?" she asked a trifle more cautiously.

"I am Captain Krugar. If there is any news that affects the safety and security of Dupree, it will end up on my desk. What is it you plan to report with such urgency that the Heart will pass on to me, anyway? Have there been more orc attacks?"

"No common orcs!" Rosana exclaimed. "Boki!"

Krugar's gaze went saber sharp. "Do you know how to tell the difference between common orcs and Boki, child? This news is urgent and must needs be accurate. Be certain of what you saw and how you speak, or you will find yourself with the wrong kind of attention from some very important people, including myself and Governor Constantine."

Rosana wilted before the soldier's abrupt aggression, and Will could not help himself, his father's warnings against speaking be cursed. He dived in front of her to deflect the angry officer's interrogation.

"She speaks the truth, my lord. I saw the Boki, myself. I recognized their red scar markings from stories I have heard of the Boki insurrection that happened when I was a babe."

"Come with me, you two."

Krugar took each of them by an arm and bodily dragged them off the dock. His hand was huge and hard and strong, and the scowl etched in his brow made it clear he would stand for no shenanigans from either of them. Rosana wore an outwardly unconcerned expression, but Will saw the worry lurking at the back of her dark eyes.

His father's admonition to say nothing of the Boki attack but to Aurelius in the Dupree Mage's Guild rang hollowly in his ears. Now what was he to do? For all he knew, this fierce soldier was taking them to the governor himself to report their news. Rosana's Heart colors would not protect either of them if Anton Constantine was involved.

Dread settled like a boulder in Will's chest.

Raina gave up trying not to stare like a green kid from the country as Kendrick led them swiftly through the city of Dupree toward his father's town house. The city had *paved* streets. Gray stone houses crowded practically on top of one another, sharing *walls,* they were so close together. She'd never seen so many people! Their bustling energy swirled around her like a living thing. Who could have imagined a city would be this enormous and alive?

A tall wooden gate in an even taller stone wall opened at

Kendrick's shout and they stepped into a cobblestoned courtyard. The relative quiet in here was palpable after the jostling pedestrians without.

A servant mumbled a warning to Kendrick that his father was none too pleased by his absence and had given orders to have him report to his study immediately upon his return home. Kendrick gestured for them to come along with him. If his father was like her mother, she could understand his impulse to recruit strangers to deflect his father's ire. Raina followed Kendrick hesitantly, though. She had no desire to get caught in the cross fire of an enraged noble and his wayward son.

Cicero stopped just inside the door, murmuring for her ears only, "I shall tarry here in case we must make a speedy exit."

She nodded her understanding and followed Kendrick and Eben cautiously across the large, comfortable office to a huge stone fireplace. A few weeks past, she would have been completely at ease in the landsgrave's presence. But now, she was leery of his power to send her home or worse. Landsgrave Leland Hyland waved her down into a seat. A gesture of command not to be disobeyed. She sank into the stuffed and upholstered armchair with a sigh of delight. She had not experienced such comfort since she left home.

Her host looked to be of an age with her father. He was handsome, his hair just starting to turn gray at the temples. His gaze at his son was irritated, but Leland nodded pleasantly enough to her.

The landsgrave notably left his son and Eben standing before the fireplace like errant children. "How in stars' name did you two get mixed up with Kithmar slavers?" he demanded of the two young men without preamble. Arms crossed, he scowled back and forth between the pair, every inch an angry noble.

Uncomfortable, she took to studying the expensive rug, thick and hand knotted with an intricate pattern reminiscent of exotic lands. Hyland's office reminded her of her mother's solar. This space was larger and more masculine, with painted leather maps mounted on the walls and bits of armor and weaponry lying about. But it had the same air of purpose about it.

Eben explained shamefacedly how he'd accepted an order for expensive magical components from a client. The initial purchase cost from the supplier was more gold than he had, so he'd borrowed the money to make the buy. He'd taken delivery of the components, and he and his sister were transporting the goods to Dupree for delivery when their caravan was raided and the components stolen by masked attackers. The moneylender demanded payment and, when Eben couldn't deliver, he and his sister were seized and sold into slavery to cover the debt.

"Who was this moneylender?" Hyland asked tersely.

"Margen."

"And the buyer?"

"Anonymous. He wished to do the deal outside the Mage's Guild. I never saw his face and he never gave me a name."

"Mmm-hmm. As I thought," Hyland muttered.

"What?" Eben asked in alarm.

"You were set up."

"By whom?" Eben exclaimed.

Hyland ignored the question and turned to Kendrick. "And you—you were a fool to attempt to fix this without consulting me first. You've stepped in it to your neck. Stars only know if we'll be able to recover Marikeen after your amateurish dealings with the Kithmar."

As Raina had feared, Kendrick's clumsy attempt to

purchase Marikeen had greatly raised her value in the minds of the slavers who held her.

"We've got a week to buy her before the Kithmar hand her over to Anton," Kendrick replied defensively.

"And you believe those ruffians will honor their word?" Leland snorted in disgust. "They've been in bed with Anton for years. She's probably already been handed over to him."

"We have to rescue her!" Kendrick cried.

From what little Raina had heard of the governor, he was not the type to give up his personal toys easily.

"*You* will do nothing!" Leland snapped. "*I* will do what I can to save her." He paced his office restlessly. "The council meets in a few hours. Perhaps I can have a word with the governor. Buy her from him before he feeds her one of his cursed love potions. But I dare not show too much interest in Marikeen or she will never see the light of day again. Better, perhaps, to ask the Heart to intervene. Yes, I'll speak to High Matriarch Emberheart. Call in a favor . . ."

Kendrick and Eben exchanged worried glances.

"You two will have to leave the city. As long as you are here, Anton cannot relinquish Marikeen and save face. I cannot believe either of you were so foolish—" He broke off the nascent tirade in frustration. He seemed to realize the damage was already done and shouting about it would do no good. From what Raina had seen, Kendrick and Eben both felt deep remorse over the mess. Hyland must recognize that.

Leland ordered the youths, "Go count out enough gold to pay triple what the Kithmar quoted you for Marikeen. *If* I am able to buy her from Anton, she will not come cheap. When that is done, pack your gear."

The pair left the office, subdued.

The landsgrave stared pensively into the fireplace for

several seconds and then turned abruptly. "And who are you, child?"

Her recent adventures made Raina feel as if the appellation of "child" was obsolete, but her mother had long preached the value of being underestimated when dealing with a stranger. Raina replied meekly, "My friend and I bumped into your son by accident and traveled across the city with him for safety."

She looked over her shoulder for support and saw that Cicero was being politely, but definitely, detained by a capable-looking man-at-arms. What had she been *thinking* to bring him into the presence of a colonial noble? She *knew* he had troubles with the law. Was he about to get hauled off to jail or sold into slavery, too? Kicking herself for her stupidity, she fought the panic rising in her breast.

She stood and said carefully to Hyland, "Thank you for the hospitality of your home, and please relay our thanks to your son and his friend for their kind escort."

The man studied her in silence for long enough that she became acutely uncomfortable. But as she'd been trained to do, she waited as calmly as the undisturbed surface of a lake, her expression glass smooth and utterly still.

"Sit."

Curses. He was not going to allow them to leave so easily. She perched on the edge of her seat.

Hyland frowned at her. "You look familiar. Have I seen you before?"

"I do not think so. I'm not from these parts." Curse her mother for being so well known! Charlotte was called the greatest beauty in the west when she was younger, and Raina had oft been told she bore a strong resemblance to her mother.

"Where are you from?"

She shrugged. "The countryside."

Hyland pursed his lips. "Your diction is exceptional for a peasant."

She did not rise to the bait and said nothing in response.

Amusement glinting in his piercingly intelligent gaze, he finally leaned forward and pitched his voice low. "Who are you, really? You're no more a peasant girl than I am."

If she told this man she was a runaway from Tyrel, he would most certainly feel obliged to send her home. She opened her mouth. Closed it again. She had no idea how to answer him.

The landsgrave laid his hand on the small table between their two chairs. "Payment for escorting my son safely home."

He lifted his hand away and three gold pieces lay there. She stared, surprised. In the past few days, she'd learned just how much money that truly was. A year's worth of taxes for a peasant family. Often more than they could earn on an entire crop. The price of a good heifer, or a flock of chickens. A big flock. It also represented safe and comfortable travel for her and Cicero for weeks to come.

As tempted as she was to snatch the coins, she did not. "It was your son who escorted us, not the other way round."

"Please. Take the money as my personal thanks for services rendered."

She pushed the coins back across the table and said lightly, "Might I suggest that in future you not use that particular turn of phrase in the presence of a lady, lest she slip a dagger between your ribs for the insult?"

Hyland burst into laughter. When he eventually composed himself enough to speak, he chortled, "That is exactly how my lady wife would have said it. It is worth the gold to have been reminded of her . . . and to have been put down so soundly."

Despite his laughter, a shadow of grief lurked in his eyes.

He'd lost his wife, then. And clearly, he'd loved her well. Curiosity tickled at Raina. It was rare for people of education and wealth to fail resurrections; she would have asked why his wife had done so were it not for that lingering pain in his gaze.

"You are a mage," he announced.

She stared, stunned. "What on Urth makes you say that?"

"My wife was a mage. She had a way of moving her hands . . . you do the same."

Raina looked down at her hands, dismayed. She did have a habit of talking with them, but she gave away her magic with them, too?

Hyland continued, "You wear no guild colors. Why is that?"

Out of the corner of her eye, she caught Cicero stiffening. His hand crept to his sword hilt.

"Stand down!" Hyland snapped at her companion without bothering to glance over at him.

Cicero replied, "She is naïve. She knows not her worth to those who would take advantage of her."

The two men exchanged understanding looks that Raina could not fathom. Hyland dipped his head briefly. "She is lucky to have a man of your character at her side."

"Aye," Cicero answered briefly, "she is."

Hyland's attention turned back to her. "What about you besides your magic is so special that this free warrior chooses to lend his sword to your protection?"

Free warrior? An interesting turn of phrase. Was that Dupree-speak for a bandit? "I assure you, there is nothing special about me, my lord."

A snort from Cicero turned her head sharply in his direction. What was wrong with him? It seemed as if his allegiance had shifted firmly to the landsgrave in the space of a few seconds.

Hyland said more sternly, "It is time for us to speak frankly, young lady. Who are you?"

"With all due respect, I owe you no allegiance."

Warning glinted in his eyes. "Your impertinence is amusing up to a point, but do not test the limits of my good humor. Answer the question."

She looked him dead in the eye. "Sir, this is no game to me, I assure you. I have every reason to believe my life hangs in the balance."

"Did I wish it, you would already be dead."

"You are not the one who threatens my life."

"Ahh. I see." He studied her for a long moment. "You hide from someone. We will speak more of that in a moment. First, your name. Your full name. I will have it now."

Her stomach dropped precipitously. The colonies were not large, and the number of landed nobles few. Surely he knew Lady Charlotte or knew of her. He might even have heard of the disappearance of her daughter by now.

She closed her eyes for a pained moment. Had she walked right into her mother's trap? *Stupid, stupid, stupid.* She should've been more careful. Had she betrayed everyone who'd risked their lives to protect her? Mag and Arv? Cicero and Moto?

"Your name," Leland prompted gently.

She could not fail to hear the steel beneath his words. He would have her name, or he would get it out of her by force. A man of his power and wealth undoubtedly had ready access to potions that could force her to tell him anything he wanted her to.

She sighed. "My name is Raina. Raina of Tyrel. Second daughter to Lord Darren and Lady Charlotte of Tyrel."

He nodded. "I thought I recognized Charlotte in you. You have the look of her."

"So I have been told," Raina replied wryly.

"Do not be aggrieved. She is still considered to be one of the great beauties of these lands."

Perfect. Charlotte still won. Thanks to inheriting her face, Raina wouldn't be able to go anywhere without being recognized. Impotent fury at the misfortune of her birth burned through her yet again.

"How did you come to be in Dupree in the company of a kindari warrior?"

She sighed. "My journey began in Tyrel. My mother announced to me unexpectedly that she had arranged a . . . relationship . . . for me. I did not agree to it but was informed that I had no choice in the matter. As I was not willing to accede to my mother's wishes, I left."

"You ran away."

She nodded reluctantly.

"So it is your mother you run from?"

Close enough. Her mother and her mother's partners in crime. She nodded again.

"And your kindari protector?"

"He joined me largely by chance and has been kind enough to see me safely to Dupree." Eager to move past the tricky spot regarding Cicero's credentials, she continued, "We disembarked at the Dupree harbor, where I literally bumped into Kendrick on the dock. It was purely accidental that we crossed paths. We traveled across the city as a group while my companion and I gained our bearings. Since Cicero and I saw that war party of orcs running north, we have not wished to travel alone—"

"What war party of orcs?" Hyland burst out.

To her surprise, Cicero dived in to answer, "Boki. Two dozen. Led by a thane, moving north fast by night toward the Forest of Thorns. They passed up multiple targets of opportunity without attacking. My impression was that they were returning home as quickly as they could."

"What were they doing off their lands in the first place?" Hyland demanded. "They never leave the Forest of Thorns."

"These ones did." Cicero shrugged. "They weren't fleeing. They moved with far too much confidence for that. My guess is they accomplished whatever they left the forest to do."

Hyland was grimly silent at that news, mulling it over at length. Finally, he said, "So you met up with Kendrick and Eben at the docks. How did you end up seated at my hearth?"

"Your son was kind enough to offer Cicero and me shelter for tonight in your home."

The question the landsgrave asked next surprised and alarmed her. "Where do you come by your magical skills?"

How in stars' name had logic brought him to that pivotal question? Was he that frighteningly intelligent, or was it pure luck that he'd gone directly to the crux of who she was and from whence her problems sprang? Best to take the question at face value. "It is tradition in my family that any who show magical talent are trained somewhat in its use. Most of the females of my blood can use magic."

"How much can you do?"

"By that do you mean how many spells, or how much magical energy can I harness?"

"Spells are easy enough to learn. How much energy can you summon to you?"

She answered honestly, "A fair bit."

"Enough to perform, say, high-ritual magic?"

"I was able to do that before I passed my tenth summer."

He lurched forward in his seat, staring. "Truly?"

"Do you wish a demonstration?"

She'd asked it as a rhetorical question; hence she was startled when he replied, "Yes, I do."

It was her turn to blink. "I do not have in my possession a scroll or ritual components with which to cast high magic."

"Just summon the energy. Hold it in your hands and then dissipate it."

"It does not work quite like that," she replied dryly. "Once summoned, such magic is . . . restless. It attempts to return to wherever it came from. I may damage your office."

Hyland leaned back and linked his fingers across his stomach to observe. Clearly, he had no care for the destruction of his home.

"You show great confidence in me, my lord, to allow me to summon so much power in your presence. You cannot know that I will not launch it at you."

"I am generally a good judge of character, and you are no murderer. Since this test may well determine your future, I have confidence you will do your best not to harm me."

Determine her future? What did he mean by that?

"Whenever you are ready," he prompted, "show me what you can do."

It was a simple exercise, really. She focused her mind with the help of the talisman hanging from its chain around her neck, reached deep inside herself, and opened the mental barrier between her and the magic that pervaded every living person on Haelos. Magic flooded to her and through her in an exhilarating rush.

She channeled the torrent of power into the space between her palms, a hand span apart before her. In seconds the crackling, flashing ball of light was almost too bright to look at directly. He wanted her best, did he? She concentrated harder, drawing forth as much power as she could summon. The talisman grew warm, and then hot, against her skin.

And the magic kept on coming. She'd never left the gate full open like this and never for so long. Even she had no idea how much the well from which it sprang held. Her hands were forced farther and farther apart as the ball grew larger and larger. And still it came.

When her hands were spread well beyond the width of her shoulders, Leland finally called over the snaps and pops in her ears, "Enough!"

Without incanting the magic into any specific shape or flavor, she turned toward the fireplace and hurled the giant ball of energy into the flames. A great explosion flashed upward as the logs were blasted to splinters. She threw her arms up to protect her face.

From behind her, she heard laughter. "A fair bit of magic indeed, child. I have never seen the like." Leland laughed until he had to wipe tears from his cheeks. Eventually, still chuckling, he asked, "What are we going to do with you?"

A man-at-arms burst into the room in alarm, his sword drawn. Hyland gestured absently for the fellow to clean up the mess she'd made, and the soldier got to work sweeping up loose embers from the hearth and shoveling them back into the fireplace. The fellow laid a new fire on top of the resulting bed of coals and then left the room silently.

Hyland had fallen silent, his mind obviously working at full speed on an answer to his question of what to do with her.

Stunned by what she'd just done, Raina sat in shocked silence of her own. She'd known she was powerful, but she'd had no idea all of that was available to her. And the magic had still been coming when Leland called off the demonstration. No wonder the Mages of Alchizzadon were so hot and bothered to get their hands on her.

Leland shifted in his chair, raising his chin off his fist and looking away from the blasted remnants of the fire, which were just starting to relight. He gazed at her speculatively.

"You do understand," he commented, "that a mage of your power cannot be allowed to roam the countryside at large and unsupervised?"

She frowned. "Why not? I've been roaming around at large and unsupervised for some time, and your fire is my only casualty so far. I have control of my magic."

He sighed. "You will not be able to keep such power secret for long. When word gets out of your ability, more than your mother will be chasing after you. Every guild will want you. Brigands will try to kidnap you and force you into their service. For that matter, the governor himself will likely wish to press you into service, or even slavery, to him if he can lay his hands on you."

She frowned, finding the idea hard to credit. And yet Marikeen's predicament and cold, hard logic said Leland was correct.

"You are a valuable commodity, child."

"I have no wish to be a commodity. I would get rid of my magic if I knew how." Particularly since then the Mages of Alchizzadon would have no use for her.

Leland shrugged. "Wishing will not make it so."

He was right, and she was being childish to wish for the moon thus.

"You need a patron, Raina. Sooner rather than later." He sighed. "And therein lies the conundrum that has had me thinking these past few minutes." He gazed at her in compassion that was almost fatherly. A sharp pang of homesickness stabbed her.

"What do you know of the Heart?" he asked abruptly.

She shrugged. "What everyone knows, I suppose. They are the guild of healers. They control the Heartstones and, through them, resurrections. They live humbly but wield the power of life and death for each and every person within reach of a stone."

"Why is that important?"

His question had the sound of an academic exercise from one of her tutors, and she answered it in that vein. "Even our most resplendent Emperor cannot claim such reach."

Leland grinned widely. "I shall assume you did not mean that last observation treasonously, child. Although you are absolutely correct, you would be wise not to air it outside the walls of this room."

His eyes twinkled, but she thought she noted a hint of surprise in their depths. Not used to women schooled in political analysis, was he? She was beginning to understand just how strange the daughters of Tyrel really were.

"What do you know of the Heart's structure?" he asked.

Raina frowned. "There are three branches—the Heart proper, whose members maintain chapter houses and, in places that have them, manage and use Heartstones. Then there's the Royal Order of the Sun—the knightly order charged with protecting the Heartstones and healers. Lastly, there's the Order of the White Heart. They're wandering healers who travel the known world and try to convince people who've never seen a Heartstone that resurrections are a good thing."

He pursed his lips. "What else do you know of the White Heart?"

She shrugged. "Not much. We didn't get many of them in Tyrel."

"Members of the White Heart take an additional vow beyond the regular Heart oath. This vow sets them completely apart from the rest of the Heart. They promise, quite simply, to defend life."

She frowned. That was it? To defend life? What was so significant about that? Knights and even common foot soldiers swore to defend lives all the time.

Leland said, "Think on it. Not just certain people's lives. All people's lives. All living creatures' lives. No matter what race or side of the law. A White Heart member will render aid to a goblin as quickly as to a human, to a murderer as quickly as his victim. And it doesn't necessarily stop at humanoids. The more extreme White Heart members will become vegetarians and heal wild animals, monsters, *all* life."

She'd had no idea . . . the magnitude of such a vow staggered her.

Hyland continued, "Implicit in their vow to defend life is a secondary promise never to take life. In fact, most White Heart members take that vow one step further and interpret it to mean they shall cause no harm of any kind to any living being."

She blurted, "How on Urth does any White Heart member live more than a few weeks outside the walls of a city such as this if they will not defend themselves against any living creature?"

Leland laughed. "As I expected, you have immediately put your finger on the heart of the matter."

Raina leaned forward. "Do you mean that if a bear in the woods attacked a White Heart member, he or she would let the bear kill them rather than defend themselves? Or would they save themselves since they are a living being, too?"

His eyes twinkled. "Hmm, yes. That does get a little tricky. Can a White Heart member cast a sleep spell at the bear to save himself? Does that constitute attacking a living being? Does it place the sleeping bear in jeopardy from its own foes? Does the White Heart member incur a responsibility to guard the bear until it wakes up? These are all philosophical dilemmas White Heart members must address. This I know, however. Never take a White Heart member hunting with oneself."

Raina could not help but smile at his wry humor.

Leland continued, "You asked before how White Heart members travel over hill and dale in the safety they usually enjoy. The answer is twofold. First, to attack a White Heart member is to incur the wrath of the Royal Order of the Sun. And they are among the most skilled and feared warriors in the Empire." He added quickly, "And yes, that no doubt bothers the Emperor."

She blinked in surprise at how close Leland had just come to treason as he went on. "The second reason the White Heart is so safe is because nearly every sentient being on Urth knows their colors and generally wishes them no harm."

Raina echoed in dawning understanding, "Because they'll heal anyone who lives."

"Correct. A brigand or an ogre or a goblin is as happy to see a White Heart healer as any Imperial soldier or common peasant would be. They all receive healing without prejudice at a White Heart member's hands."

She turned that over thoughtfully. "An interesting group, this White Heart. But I should think the limits placed upon its members by such a lifestyle would be stifling. A healer would more or less live life as a walking healing station. Not to mention, I should think, upholding their vows cannot always be easy."

Leland nodded solemnly. "Despite the extreme protection offered by their colors, White Heart members are not known for dying of old age. They have a tendency to go places where no sane man would venture. And on the battlefield . . ."— he paused, obviously seeing memories in his mind's eye— ". . . they often end up between the lines, healing both sides as the carnage unfolds around them. It is not exactly the safest place to be, but it is where their vows send them."

Raina tried to picture doing that and failed. She shook off the grisly image. "So, my lord. Why do you feel a need to educate me so thoroughly on this specialized order within the Heart?"

He smiled broadly at her. "The circle of logic is complete. We arrive back at the beginning—at the matter of your safety."

"My safety?"

"Exactly. We have already established that I cannot in good conscience turn you loose to run about the countryside at risk from whoever manages to snatch you first." He continued, "How to protect a mage of your talent, then? The Mage's Guild would develop your talent to its full extent, but it would require you to stay here in Dupree for years of training. The guild would then exploit you shamelessly, selling your skills, keeping all of your earnings to make them rich. It is a viable option, but distasteful to me personally." He added reluctantly, "But perhaps that idea is to your liking. They would see to it you live a life of comfort and ease within a luxurious guild hall."

Picturing herself holed up in some dusty building casting rituals for the Empire until she burned out made her shudder. Although there was a chance that from within the Mage's Guild she could find a way to restore the Great Mage. But surely the Mages of Alchizzadon had already explored all of the Mage's Guild's knowledge thoroughly.

A grim smile flickered around the edges of Hyland's mouth as he seemed to read her distaste for the Mage's Guild option. "Then there's the Heart," he said. "As a regular healer, you would be expected to set up residence in a Heart chapter somewhere. Your movement would be restricted, and it would be no difficult matter for your mother to track you down and take you home by force.

The Heart would move to protect you, of course, but not quickly enough, I think. It is a big organization and its wheels turn slowly. Your mother could argue that you can be married and raise babes and still serve the Heart wherever your husband forces you to live."

Raina winced at that argument. Avoiding babes was the whole point.

"As I thought," Leland commented. "The White Heart, however, is a different story. The Royal Order of the Sun is directly responsible for the safety of White Heart healers and takes that responsibility very seriously. The Royal Order typically sends escorts with each White Heart member on their travels, in fact. At the first distress call from a White Heart member, they react instantly and aggressively. Furthermore, they retaliate swiftly to punish any who harm or hinder a White Heart member."

As a deterrent to future harm befalling other White Heart members, no doubt. She nodded her understanding and Hyland continued.

"In point of fact, most anyone who sees a White Heart member in trouble will rise up to defend him. Were you to join the White Heart, you could be assured that no one would dare touch you and risk the wrath of the Royal Order of the Sun."

Not even the Mages of Alchizzadon? The thought galvanized her. "How long is one required to serve the White Heart when one joins them?"

"White Heart members serve for life."

"What about a home? Family? Do they marry and have children like regular Heart members?"

"My lady wife was a White Heart member. But I will not

lie to you. Having a family while wearing the colors poses a difficult challenge. Loved ones are a weakness by which others might gain power over you. After all, could you stand by and watch someone kill your loved ones and do nothing to protect them?"

Raina stared at him. Yet he wished her to walk that path anyway? It felt as though she were bleeding out slowly from a mortal wound.

He continued on grimly, "For most, serving the White Heart is their one and only calling in life. My wife used to say that when she donned the colors, she ceased to exist as an individual. In effect, she became the tabard and what it represents."

Raina tried to speak normally, but her voice came out choked and halting. "And you . . . wish me . . . to do this?"

"How much do you want to avoid the fate others have planned for you?"

Enough to sign away her freedom for the rest of her life? To give herself over entirely to the White Heart, never to return home? Never to *have* a home? To be a wandering healer forever, living much as she had these past few days but wholly unable to defend herself? Ever?

Leland pushed to his feet and moved across the room to a large chest in the corner, which he opened. He lifted from it a folded cloth and shook it out, and she saw a white tabard, edged in blue and bearing a four-pointed blue star upon the breast. A white heart surrounded by white sun rays overlaid the blue star. "This is a White Heart tabard. My wife's. It also is a talisman for channeling magic."

"Surely you do not have the authority to induct me into a special Heart order," she protested.

"I do not. But I happen to know the High Matriarch of Dupree well. She will put you directly into the White

Heart if I ask her to, particularly given your extraordinary talents."

Desperation choked Raina. There had to be some other way . . . she couldn't give away her life like this!

Leland handed the tabard to her. "Put it on and you shall be safe."

She looked up at him, stricken. "But at what price, my lord?"

"Only you can answer that."

"If you had a daughter my age, would you ask this of her? That she sacrifice the rest of her life to this cause?"

He sat down heavily in his chair as if she'd struck him a grievous blow. "Ahh, child. You know not what you ask of me."

She gazed at him in anguish. He gazed back at her, his wise eyes sad unto the very depths of his spirit.

She managed barely a broken whisper. "But I'm only sixteen."

After that one stunning conversation with Talissar, Gabrielle did not see the kindari consort again for some time. It was almost as if he avoided her. But she supposed that made sense. He did say that he and his co-conspirators moved slowly so as not to get caught.

However, all of that changed when, yet again, she found herself drawn toward the wild garden. There was something about it that called to her. A compulsion to lose herself in its dark, mysterious shadows and thickets.

"Lady Gabrielle," Talissar's deep voice intoned from behind her one afternoon, late. "I feared I might find thee here."

She waved her guard off a little ways and turned to the kindari elf, curious as to why he chose to show himself here and now.

His voice low, charged, Talissar asked, "Hast thee ever been alone with Lord Tyviden Starfire?"

The question was a startling non sequitur. Rumors hinted that Starfire had been banished from court many years ago. "I beg your pardon?"

"I do not accuse thee of any impropriety," Talissar hastened to add. "It is just that this was a favorite rendezvous point of Starfire's."

Thunderstruck, Gabrielle glanced fearfully around the

total isolation of this wild corner of the Garden of Nations. Talissar had alluded to something similar the last time they met here, about a High Lord compelling women to come out here to meet him. *The dancing.* Her irresistible impulse to come out here alone and make herself dizzy—

"I see worry in thine eyes, Your Highness. Hast been alone with him, then?"

"Surely, if he influenced my mind, the effects would have worn off long before now."

The elf shrugged. "Kothites are timeless beings. Why would their powers not be the same?"

She admitted reluctantly, "I encountered him a long time ago. And we were not entirely alone. But he did . . . seem rather fascinating to me one night—"

"Of course," Talissar breathed in sudden comprehension. "I have long wondered what provoked thy knight to strike a Kothite noble. He saw Starfire attempting to influence thy mind."

Gabrielle's eyes widened in distress. "Are you saying that I come to this place because Starfire wished it so?" And had Starfire also enjoined her to dance in the forest? Did he laugh into his cups over a queen humiliating herself thus, even now? And then the rest of his words registered. *What knight?*

Talissar replied slowly, "I cannot be sure he is responsible. But take this." He removed an ancient-looking and exquisitely decorated gold amulet from around his neck and held it out to her. The medallion was embossed with eight sharp points, four large and four small, arranged in a compass rose. In the center, a large, green gem was mounted. She passed the pad of her thumb across it and a faint warmth emanated from the smooth stone.

"This is an Octavium Pendant. Symbol of the Eight,"

Talissar explained quietly. "Seek this symbol if thee ever hast need of me . . . or," he added significantly, ". . . of a friend."

She looked up at him sharply. He spoke of his conspirators, then. She nodded her understanding.

"Wear it awhile," Talissar suggested. "Its magic protects the mind from intrusions. See if thy compulsion to come to this place remains. If it does, then thee willst know it to be of only thine own desire."

"And if not?"

"Then thee hast just cause to worry that Starfire hast somehow influenced thy mind."

The pendant dangled, heavy, around her neck. She could swear faint warmth from it penetrated her clothing. *Starfire.* Without warning, the name rolled across her mind along with a flood of memories. A night at court long ago . . . a fist thrown . . . *Sir Darius.*

She reeled so violently that Talissar caught her arm in alarm to steady her.

"Is aught amiss, Your Highness?"

She reached into the bottom of her silk purse and rummaged until she came up with the strange ring she had carried around all these years, a bent and broken signet bearing the heraldry of Haraland upon it. Regalo hadn't recognized the ring, either. She had only known for all these years that it held a strange attraction for her. She could never bring herself to cast off the odd bauble.

The signet ring was his. Darius's ring. Given by him to me the night he was banished from court, his name stripped and replaced with the name, Krugar.

"How could I not remember?" she whispered, shaken to the core of her being.

"The Empire takes away memories. Takes history. Takes identities. It is how they steal hope from their subjects."

They stole my faithful knight, too, for the sole crime of loyally protecting me.

Something of her thought must have crossed her face, for Talissar smiled sadly in sympathy. Then he changed subjects abruptly, asking, "Perchance, rumors are true that inquisitors hast been seen in Haraland with psionic hounds?"

The magical beasts, bred to sniff out people with psionic abilities, had indeed passed through Haraland with their handlers. "Aye. Half a moon cycle past," she answered. "They stayed with us only a few days. They rested and resupplied, and then went on their way to the east."

"It is well that thy husband's thoughts and those of his subjects draw little interest from such guests."

"Indeed," she murmured. Talissar's meaning was clear. Regalo's mind must remain uncluttered with certain pieces of information so that inquisitors and mind sweeps by the Emperor yielded nothing to raise suspicion.

The elf spoke quietly and quickly. "Hast thee knowledge of a young woman, raised to noble rank, a female falcon avarian by the name of Syreena Wingblade?"

"I have heard of her," Gabrielle murmured. The avarians were a race of bird changelings not much in favor with the Empire. "Did she not start life as a common indentured servant and rise through the society rather spectacularly to attain a title or something like that?"

"Exactly. She is held up by the Emperor as a shining example of how a peasant can become an important and titled personage."

Now that he mentioned it, she did remember Maximillian lauding the avarian to the court some months back and calling for minstrels to write songs about her to be sung in pubs and palaces across the land.

"She must needs go to Dupree," Talissar announced.

"For what purpose?" Gabrielle asked curiously. "Is there trouble in the colonies?"

"I do not know," Talissar answered. "Sometimes, it is best not to ask. Better that most of us know only one small piece of the larger puzzle."

Ahh. This was the work of the Eight, then. She asked cautiously, "Is a posting coming available to Haelos, then?"

"Again, Your Highness, I do not know. That would be a question for thy husband, I imagine."

She nodded her understanding. She was to influence Regalo to argue in the Council of Kings in favor of posting the young avarian noble to Dupree. It sounded harmless enough. Certainly not the sort of thing that anyone could label treasonous. And it would not raise any suspicions, not even from her husband. "I will ask him," she answered simply.

Talissar gave her a short, formal bow and said loudly enough for her guard to hear, "It was a most pleasant surprise to encounter thee, Your Highness. Please give my warmest regards to thy lord husband."

"Of course. And please send Haraland's regards to Queen Lyssandra in Quantaine."

They traded formal bows and passed on their separate ways, him quickly and she more slowly and thoughtfully. *So. It had begun.* She knew not what "it" might be, but the Eight were active, and that meant some plot was afoot. In Haelos, no less. *Interesting. Very interesting indeed.*

Raina stared miserably at the White Heart tabard as Leland said persuasively. "Keep it. You don't have to put it on now. Think about it for a while. It is a big decision and one not to be made rashly or in haste."

Reluctantly, she held the cloth in her lap. But she was bloody well not putting the thing on! "You cannot know the

Heart would even have me as a member, let alone a White Heart member. I thought members of the Royal Order of the Sun and the White Heart had to serve in the regular Heart first and earn their way into the other orders."

Leland grinned at her. "You're an arch-mage. Do you have any idea how rare those are?"

Apparently not, for they were commonplace in her family. Yes, she was considered to be particularly talented among her kin, but not so much more so than the others that she was "rare."

Leland went on, "I guarantee the High Matriarch will grasp instantly how extraordinary you are and why you need the extra protection. Besides. She owes me a favor or two."

Raina frowned. *What sorts of favors?* She sensed hints of political forces at work that he was not admitting to. She could understand his wish for her not to fall into the hands of brigands or slavers. But why not the Mage's Guild or even the governor himself? Surely Leland would garner great favor in the eyes of the governor if he delivered a mage of her talent into Anton's hands.

Only one logical conclusion followed from the fact that he had not handed her over to Anton. Leland was no great fan of the governor and did not wish for the man to have her power at his disposal.

What was this? A hint of rebellion? Was Leland maneuvering her into a position to help with his own political agenda? If so, why then was he shoving her into the White Heart? Was the Heart itself preparing to oppose the Emperor in some way? The thought was staggering. Was the Eternal Empire showing signs of weakness from within?

"You're thinking so hard I can all but hear it, child. What goes on in that pretty little head of yours?"

She glanced up at Leland, startled, then pointedly across the room at his guard. "Nothing that bears repeating aloud, I assure you."

Leland looked first alarmed and then thunderstruck. "Who are you?" he half-whispered.

She was tempted to leave him hanging, but she sensed he truly did have her best interests at heart. "I am your friend, Sir Leland. You need have no fear of me."

He let out a snort of rueful laughter. "I think if I knew what was good for me I would be terrified of you."

Of her? Why? Because she saw too much? She said quietly, "I am my mother's daughter."

He nodded slowly. "Aye, you are at that. And yet you would forge your own path, free of her influence." He recited under his breath quietly enough that she didn't think he meant for her to hear it, "The son shall accept the father's fate, but the daughter shall refuse the mother's fate."

What did he mean by that? She frowned, but then he continued in a normal voice, "Allow me to tell you a little more of the White Heart."

"Are you so set on forcing that life upon me, then?"

He shrugged. "I merely offer you food for thought."

She made a silent gesture for him to continue.

"Members of the White Heart sometimes find themselves in a unique position to act as mediators between opposing parties."

Expecting another lecture, she was startled when he said no more. But then, her own analytical mind took over. *Of course.* They would be trusted by both sides in disputes because the White Heart would try to preserve the lives of everyone, no matter who the aggrieved parties were. The White Heart's goal in any dispute would be a peaceful resolution. To achieve that, they would have to push for a fair settlement for both sides.

Leland commented, "Mind you, only a few within the White Heart have the subtlety to take on this additional role. But you, my dear girl, were born to it."

It was her turn to snort. He had no idea how true that was. She leaned forward, pitching her voice low for his ears alone. "Tell me this, then. Does the White Heart dare to stand between the Empire and its foes?"

He jerked and went rigid in his seat, then relaxed only by slow and forced degrees. He sounded genuinely horrified when he finally choked out, "The Voice himself would not presume to openly defy the Emperor."

Openly? Did that mean the Heart would do so covertly, however? Aloud, she echoed, "The Voice?" The title sounded familiar, but she could not place it. Her studies had not focused overly much on the current Empire.

Regaining his breath a bit, Leland answered, "The Voice is leader of the entire Heart. The Light is the title of he who leads the Royal Order of the Sun, and The Pure leads your order."

"It is not my order, sir!"

"Not yet," Leland replied lightly.

A servant interrupted just then to remind the landsgrave of his upcoming council meeting. Leland nodded impatiently and turned back to her. "I dare not leave you alone, even in my own home."

"Surely I am not in that much danger," she blurted.

He grinned briefly. "Not at all. I simply consider you that big a flight risk."

Chagrin flooded her. She had indeed been planning to bolt at the first opportunity. Although, she had to admit, Leland's line of reasoning had her intrigued. Where was he going with all this hyperbole?

She reasoned aloud, "The Heart at large does not openly defy the Emperor. But the White Heart . . . it holds the deep affection of all the common people in every land, does it not? Out of gratitude for its long and peaceful service to them, it is in a unique position to draw together many traditional enemies to a single cause, is it not?"

Leland sucked his breath in sharply between his teeth. "Enough, girl. Say no more. Do not even think it. The Emperor's hounds are everywhere."

So. He begged for her silence not because he disagreed with her, but because he feared the Empire would catch wind of her ideas. She was on the right track to sniff rebellion in the offing. Leaning forward, she studied him intently. "This is the real reason you would force me into this tabard, is it not?"

His answer was hoarse. Heartfelt. "For love of the Lady, do not make me answer that, child."

Will was not reassured when Captain Krugar dragged him and Rosana to a sprawling, ornate pile of stone that looked exactly as he imagined the Emperor's palace to be. Krugar strode under the giant raised portcullis, and Will glanced up at its huge iron-clad teeth in dismay. It looked as if they walked into the jaws of a mighty beast. Mayhap that was not so far from the truth.

Krugar did not stop, nor turn either of them loose, even when a few troopers saluted him here and there. He strode into the great stone edifice situated in the middle of the broad bailey, through a shockingly extravagent anteroom of some kind, and into a huge hall.

"Sit. Stay." Krugar shoved the two of them down onto a

bench along one of the walls. He flagged down a soldier and ordered tersely, "Watch those two. Do not let them go anywhere."

Rosana threw Will a chagrined look sidelong. She'd been thinking about making a break for it, too, had she? Smart girl.

She leaned close and whispered, "Say nothing. We both fall under the *Kaer*'s protection. The governor would not dare do anything to us without permission from the High Matriarch."

"Why would she protect us?"

"I am Heart, of course. And you guard me."

She might be safe, but he was not the least bit confident that some stranger would gainsay the governor for him. His apprehension climbed as important-looking personages began filing to the hall and taking seats at an enormous table in the middle of the room.

He recognized various guild colors, and based upon the gray hair and aged visages of the men and women at the table, he surmised he was looking at the masters and mistresses of the Imperial guilds for the colonies.

People in other colors arrived, too. Rosana murmured identifications of a few of them—the Landsgrave of Delphi, Landsgrave Hyland. Landsgrave Talyn, a nulvari, dark elf. His holding, Talyn, was named after him as he was its first and only holder. His race's life spans were such that Talyn could expect to rule his holding for centuries to come.

A fourth man outfitted as a landsgrave sat down at the table. "Who is that?" Will whispered to Rosana.

"Gregor Beltane," she replied promptly. "Landsgrave of Lochnar." A gypsy landsgrave? Will had heard that a few gypsies remained loyal to the Empire, but he'd never seen one in person.

Over the next few minutes, Rosana identified a Heart

adept who temporarily ran the Dupree Heart, adding a murmured comment about the Dupree Patriarch dying recently under unexplained circumstances. Apparently, the Heart had its suspicions as to who was behind it given how she threw a dirty look at the governor's empty seat, which was more throne than chair.

Alarmed, Will pondered the ugly ramifications of the governor assassinating a high-ranking Heart member until she pointed out a handsome solinari just coming in. The shining golden skin of the sun elf was hard to miss.

"The yellow elf with pointy ears is the Mage's Guildmaster Aurelius," she murmured.

Will caught his breath sharply at that. Aurelius was the *guildmaster*? Will's father had sent him to speak to the highest-ranking Mage's Guild member in all of Dupree? He studied the elf closely and was stunned to realize that nearly all the blazons on the guildmaster's chest were identical to the ones he'd seen on his father's chest on that fateful night in Hickory Hollow.

Every chair at the table was filled, but for the grand one at the head of the table, and the people seated in them fidgeted. Until a tall door at the far end of the hall swung open, that was. Then everyone at the table stood and the commoners around the edges of the room knelt. Will followed suit clumsily and slid off the bench to the floor.

A herald loudly announced the arrival of Governor Anton Constantine.

Will peeked up from his kneeling position and was startled to see a richly dressed man wearing green trimmed with gold, balding and approaching middle age, step into the room. His chest was loaded with a gaudy array of blazons, most of which Will did not recognize.

But one of them caught his eye. His father had worn an

identical one that night in Hickory Hollow when Ty had donned all his old armor and weapons. It was round, with a turquoise-blue background with an irregular brown shape in the middle. It looked like a map of an island to him.

The man strode down the long hall toward the council table, checking when another man stepped forward without warning and blocked his path.

Will could not hear what the fellow spoke of with the governor, but it looked like a heated exchange. The man was well dressed, mayhap a craftsman or merchant.

"Get out of my way!" Anton snapped.

The man ignored him, continuing to press his point obstinately. His discourse was cut off by the *schwing* of a blade clearing its sheath. Anton whipped out a golden short sword and struck, fast as a snake, running the man through the heart.

The unlucky fellow and his unfinished speech dropped to the floor as shocked silence fell over the room. Anton yanked his blade free, the gold covered with blood. The Heart adept started to lurch out of his seat, but Anton swung the tip of the bloody sword in the fellow's direction.

"Sit." Anton bit out the order as if the Heart man were no more than a dog to be commanded.

The adept sat.

Anton casually wiped his blade on the dead man's trousers. A large pool of blood was spreading rapidly underneath the man's torso, forcing Anton to step back from the bright red pool. The governor gestured a pair of soldiers over to dispose of the body. "When he resurrects—if he resurrects—fine him five gold."

"For what offense, my lord?" one of the soldiers asked.

"For bleeding on my floor," Anton replied dismissively.

Will stared, appalled to the core of his being, as the

governor strolled the remainder of the distance to the head of the table. Not one person at the table moved or spoke. Anton had just *killed* a man in front of them all, and they'd *let* him.

As Anton settled upon his throne-like seat, a nulvari woman slid out from behind it and emotionlessly ordered servants to mop up the pool of blood.

"What crime did that man commit?" Will whispered frantically to Rosana.

She shrugged. "He got in the governor's way."

"By the Lady," he breathed. "And that was enough to warrant killing a man and fining him so much?"

"Welcome to Governor Anton Constantine," she muttered back.

The man's death cast a pall over the proceedings as the business meeting commenced. Eventually, however, the subject of a rich vein of recently discovered minerals in the Ice Wall, apparently a great mountain range somewhere far away from Dupree, came up. The parties at the table commenced haggling vigorously over it.

The Forester's Guild claimed the surface lumber, and the Miner's Guild claimed the minable ore. But then the branch of the Forester's Guild that regulated hunters and trappers weighed in and wanted a portion of the forest set aside for them to ply their trade. The Mage's Guild accused the miners of wanting to keep any magical crystals they found for themselves. The Merchant's Guild protested at having to pay for road construction to the region. In response, the landsgraves declared that the merchants should bear the expense unless the landsgraves were cut in for a share of the revenue.

It was at that point Will began to develop a headache. Rosana seemed fascinated by the exchange, but his gaze roamed the hall. He spied an incongruous face across the hall from where he sat—a striking blond girl of nearly an age with him, maybe a few years younger. She looked on the verge of bolting at any moment. He knew the feeling. She glanced over at him, and he nodded at her in commiseration.

"You know her?" Rosana whispered.

"No. But she looks nearly as uncomfortable as me."

"Relax. I will not let any harm come to you."

He smiled a little at that. Rosana seemed fiercely protective of those she cared about and he supposed the trait made her a fine Heart healer. His attention was yanked back to the council table as the governor's voice cut sharply across the bickering.

"Enough. Since none of you can agree on anything, I declare that these mines will fall directly under my purview. All of you will surrender to me the usual percentages of your proceeds from the region, plus taxes of course. You shall share the costs of road building equally, and those, too, shall be subject to the usual tolls payable to me. Are there any questions?" The governor sounded well pleased with the proceeding. As he should be, Will supposed. He'd just taken a huge chunk of income for himself.

Although the others at the table attempted to hide their dismay, it was palpable in the room. That, and resignation. As if the governor seized vast territories and resources for himself on a regular basis.

"Let us move on to other business," Anton announced in a bored tone. "Captain Krugar, you said you have news?"

The soldier who'd dragged Will and Rosana off the pier stepped up to the long table at the governor's right hand. "Yes, my lord. The Heart has sent in a report of a Boki sighting on the Southwatch Road. This independently corroborates my own men's report of an orc attack."

The Heart's adept spoke up immediately. "I have received no such report!"

"I met yon healer at the docks, and she spoke directly to me," Krugar retorted, pointing at Rosana.

All eyes in the room turned in their direction. She shrank close against Will's side, and an urge to put a protective arm around her surprised him.

"Step forward, girl," Anton ordered.

Rosana threw Will a frightened glance but did as ordered.

"Give us your report, then," the governor demanded.

"Uhh, yes, sir. As you wish, sir." She dropped a little curtsy and about fell over in her nervousness. A few desultory chuckles wafted up while the governor rolled his eyes.

"I, umm, traveled with Brother Angelo and Kirchen and Moricello. Kirchen and Moricello, they guarded us. We have no Royal Order in our little chapter house, so we hired guards. But they were good boys. Honest. They wouldn't steal from the Heart—"

"The orcs?" Anton snapped.

Will saw Rosana's cheeks turn pink.

"Sorry, Your Highness, uhh, Your Governess, uhh, sir. So. We traveled the countryside seeking donations of supplies for the *Kaer*—umm, the Heart. Food is scarce after the hard winter we had, what with the drought and taxes—" She broke off in horror and visibly had to collect herself before continuing, "Our stores, they ran low."

"Get to the point," Anton growled. "The orcs. Where were they?"

"Oh. Yes. Of c-c-ourse," she stammered. "We traveled the Southwatch Road, way out at the far end of it near a bump in the path called Hickory Hollow. . . ."

Will bristled a bit at having his home denigrated thus, although he reluctantly allowed that the hollow was, in truth, little more than the intersection of two footpaths and a few muddy streets lined with miserable huts.

"We threw a wagon wheel and lost most of the afternoon repairing it. We chose not to camp, but rather to head for Hickory Hollow, because the Wylde Wood is a dangerous place at night. We feared wolves or bears, of course, but not orcs. We had no idea Boki would be in the area. I mean really, who could have imagined that—"

"Enough already!" Anton yelled. "What of the cursed orcs?"

Will jumped along with everyone else at the outburst, but not nearly as hard as Rosana jumped. An urge to go to her and protect her from the governor's wrath washed over Will. Visions of a golden blade drenched in gypsy blood danced menacingly in his mind's eye. He watched on helplessly as her face grew even redder.

"The attack came after dark. Maybe, uhh, two hours after. All of a sudden, orcs rushed out of woods at us. They were screaming—"

Anton interrupted sharply, "How many?"

Rosana frowned. "I do not know. I, uhh, maybe panicked a little. They were very big and green. And smelly. They stunk like pig manure—" As laughter broke out, the governor looked on the verge of ordering her put to death. She added hastily, "Four. Maybe five orcs."

"Continue."

She was clearly rattled by the governor's constant interruptions. If the fellow would just let her tell the story, she would no doubt give over all she knew. Will scowled in Anton's general direction as she plowed onward.

"Well, they rushed us. And shouted really loud. Like a war cry." Without warning she let out an ululating howl that made everyone jump first and laugh second.

Anton looked ready to explode, but Rosana stumbled on heedlessly, "Kirchen and Moricello, they fought, or tried to fight, at least." She warmed to her story a bit more and used her arms to gesture as she added, "The orcs were very big. Strong. Fast. They carried giant axes. Never have I seen axes so huge—"

Yet again, Anton snapped. "Yes, yes. Get to the part where you decided this raiding party was Boki!"

"Umm. Right. Well, they were ferocious fighters. And they wove things in hair—you know. Teeth and bits of bone, and . . . and . . . ," she added in distaste, ". . . and cut-off ears. Human and elf and . . . and . . . other ears I didn't recognize."

Anton's palm cracked down on the table. Will jumped, but not nearly as hard as Rosana did. The governor roared, "This is what you bring to me as proof of an invasion, Krugar? Teeth and ears?" He turned his wrath on Rosana. "And you? Have you ever seen an orc before, girl? Are you sure it wasn't just a few goblins shouting? Or is this mayhap a filthy gypsy ploy to extract compensation out of me for something that didn't even happen?"

Rosana stammered, "B-b-but I didn't make up the attack. A brother and two guards are dead."

"And yet you walked away completely unharmed?" Anton growled. "What flimsy scam is this?"

Will's jaw clenched. Rosana looked near tears.

Beltane growled from his seat, the sound resolving into an angry outburst, "Just because the girl is gypsy does not make her a liar or a thief. Are you willing to risk another green-skin insurrection? Green fires still burn across the colony in remembrance of the last one."

Will stared at the landsgrave, shocked. *Since when did such a highborn take up the defense of anyone to such a man as Constantine?*

"She has no proof!" Anton raised his voice, drowning out all other protests. "How do I know the Heart hasn't sent a charlatan to trick me into sending troops and supplies to a chapter that's failing to support itself properly? I am no hot-headed landsgrave who overreacts to every outrageous rumor to reach my ears. I am governor, and I require proof before I act."

Someone from down the table, the Heart adept, half-rose out of his seat. "Here, now. There is no cause for accusations against the Heart. A young healer has come in good faith to report an attack upon a Heart caravan. The Heart is entirely within its rights to request support from the Imperial Army to investigate this attack—"

Anton cut the adept off. "Where is her evidence? You expect me simply to take this gypsy at her word and send out an army in response?"

"She is Heart—"

"She is not *the* Heart!" Anton roared. "You people may be able to throw your weight around in Koth, but this is *not* Koth, boy! I am in charge, here."

The adept fell back into his seat looking stunned. Will glanced around the long table. Everyone looked shocked, in fact.

The Landsgrave of Lochnar leaned forward. "What she describes sounds enough like an orc raiding party to me that I think we should have a look into it."

"Since when are you such a big orc hunter, Beltane?" Anton snarled, his voice oily with threat.

"If the Boki have left their forests, we need to know right away and, furthermore, see to our defenses. Immediately. Lest we have another insurrection.

"Commit troops to an investigation right now, Lord Governor, or I shall send my own men," Lochnar demanded.

"You do not give orders around here, Beltane."

The landsgrave pushed his chair back. Stood up. Said

through a clenched jaw, "Then I shall depart and go where I *do* give the orders. And I will see to the defense of my own people." The implication was clear that Anton would not do the same and take care of his subjects.

Following Beltane's furious departure, uncomfortable silence fell around the table.

A look of something Will might name chagrin crossed Anton's face, followed by a momentary flash of rage in the direction of Lochnar's empty chair, come and gone so quickly Will almost thought he imagined it.

Anton leaned forward aggressively and growled at Rosana, "If you're lying to me, girl, Heart tabard or no, I'll strip your colors and sell you into slavery before this day is done."

He would do it, too. Of that Will had no doubt. Panicked, he jumped to his feet and cried out, "She's telling the truth! They were orcs, I tell you. I fought one myself. And they were Boki. I saw the red scars on their foreheads!"

Glaring fiercely enough at him to make Will's knees knock together in terror, Anton gestured sharply for a soldier to bring him to the council table. Shaking, Will stumbled along beside the guard. The fellow shoved him forward to stand beside Rosana.

She threw him a sidelong look of both wonder and gratitude that he would take up for her like this. He was shocked as well. But something protective, possessive even, moved in him at the notion of her being frightened and badgered. He straightened to his full height and smiled down at her reassuringly. The room fell away as she smiled back shyly at him in dawning awareness. Oh, yes. He would go to the Imperial Seat and back for her if necessary. And he would certainly face Anton Constantine for her.

"Who are you?" the governor demanded.

"Umm, I'm Will, uh-h—" he stuttered, unsure if he should

give his full name or not. His father had long insisted that Will never, ever tell his real, complete name.

"Whatever. Tell me of these orcs, and make it good, or I'll make a slave out of you, too."

Will cleared his throat and started over. "I wanted to stand watch for Hickory Hollow with Adrick. The hollow's at the southwest edge of the Ring in the Wylde Wood."

Anton gave the barest nod of recognition, and Will forged on, "I went home to get permission to do it, and when I returned to the knot above the hollow, Adrick was dead. An orc had just gutted him with a spear. The orc attacked me next."

"You defeated a Boki warrior?" Anton scoffed.

"Not exactly. He broke my spear, but I tripped him with the shaft. He fell and hit his head. Knocked himself out. I went over to see if he was dead or not, and I saw an irregular reddish scar in the middle of his forehead as clear as day. I heard more orcs coming and ran for the hollow to warn everyone."

"Then what happened?" Anton asked dismissively.

"Near two dozen of them, plus a bunch of other greenskins, dragged everyone outside and burned the village. The Boki thane killed Lars in single combat."

"You recognized a Boki thane?"

His father might be dead, but Will was not about to give up Ty to the governor. "Not me. One of the villagers said something about the Boki leader being a thane."

"Yet you not only lived but also escaped this supposed thane of the Boki." Anton sounded as skeptical of Will's story as he had been of Rosana's.

"I ran," Will replied firmly. Why he didn't mention his parents he wasn't quite sure, but it seemed right not to do so. "From behind a hedgerow, I saw them firing huts and gutting Lars and . . ."—he gulped and continued, ". . . and eating body parts. That's when I fled for the woods and did not look back."

The room had fallen completely silent as everyone listened intently to his tale.

He continued, "I ran for a long time. Eventually, I came upon the Southwatch Path. I must have circled around to the south of the hollow. At any rate, I saw an overturned wagon on the road. I approached it and found Ros—Novice Rosana—alive but unconscious. As she previously stated, her three companions were dead." He added defensively, "I checked them myself."

"But you have no idea whether goblins or orcs attacked them?" Anton challenged.

"The two guards were hacked nigh in half. I've never seen a goblin strong enough to do that. And we get plenty of goblins in the Wylde Wood. Plus, the Boki were sending patrols out into the woods by the time I fled. I had to hide from a few of them."

"Poppycock," Anton pronounced.

"I speak truth." Frustration overflowed his gut and into his voice as Will added, "Novice Rosana speaks truth!"

He started as his voice rolled forth, deep and powerful. That was how his father had spoken the night of the Boki attack in the woods. A voice of command. A voice designed to carry across the chaos and noise of a battlefield. A voice so powerful it could be heard in the spirit itself.

"Where . . ."—Anton half-rose to his feet, his own voice gathering power—". . . in the name of Koth did you learn how to do the Dragon's Roar, boy?"

Will gaped. He had no idea what to say, for he had no idea what this Dragon's Roar might be. "The . . . what?"

Anton leaned forward aggressively, staring. "You look familiar, boy."

Equal parts shocked and terrified, Will stammered, "This is the first time I've ever left the Wylde Wood, sir, uh-h, Your Lordship, uh-h, my lord governor. I don't see how—"

Anton's stare swung to Aurelius. "Is he one of yours?"

Aurelius held up his hands as if to disavow any knowledge of Will.

Anton pressed harder, "Your guild knew nothing of this boy who throws out a powerful Celestial Order of the Dragon ability so casually?"

"No, Governor, I had no idea a youth of such talent was in the city." The solinari rose to his feet, scowling. The elf appeared displeased at this surprise even more than the governor. Aurelius added direly, "I shall take him immediately to be tested."

All eyes fixed on the Mage's Guildmaster pacing toward Will. For his part, Will gulped in dawning dismay.

From down the table, the man Rosana had identified as the Landsgrave of Hyland announced abruptly, "In the meantime, I volunteer to send a force to investigate the Boki. If orcs have broken the peace, all of Dupree could be in grave danger."

The lizardman girl, Sha'Li, stood utterly motionless in the darkest shadows the alley had to offer while her partner in crime picked the lock behind her. She wasn't half-bad at popping locks, herself, but Kerryl Moonrunner had insisted on doing it himself. Far be from her to tell a nature guardian of his stature what to do, however. And she did have the advantage of blending into the shadows better than he did. Her black scales made her all but invisible in these low-light conditions.

Pinky-white human. He would laugh if he knew she thought of him thus, but she would never dream of voicing it aloud. It was not the way of the lizardmen to mock their superiors. At least it was not how she and her clutchmates of Clutch Ol'lu had been raised.

A shockingly accurate cricket chirrup noise behind her was the signal that Kerryl had opened the warehouse door. She eased backward, watching all the while for the town guard or an untimely passerby. But the mouth of the alley remained deserted. She slipped into the inky interior of the warehouse and Kerryl closed the door quickly behind her.

There would be a guard roaming in here somewhere, but he was the least of their troubles. She had no doubt that Aurelius Lightstar and the Mage's Guild would guard their truly valuable treasures with only the most dastardly of traps. It was for those Kerryl had brought her along tonight.

She was grateful for the chance to prove herself. If she did well enough, she might finally earn her Tribe of the Moon mark. All full Tribe members wore the stylized moon-and-stars symbol prominently on their right cheek. Of course, if she failed tonight, if she set off the guild's traps, she would die. Many aspired to the mark, but few succeeded. The seven tenets of the Tribe of the Moon were not easy to uphold.

Her reptilian eyes were well suited to the dark and she had no trouble seeing Kerryl wave his hand to indicate she should follow him. As they moved out, she gazed around the cavernous space. It was large enough to hold a small house, she estimated. Strange how so large a place could feel so claustrophobic. It was the crates and barrels and boxes stacked so high and close, she supposed. Give her an open sky and a nice, smelly swamp any day over this. Aurelius could have his hoard. Except for a few bits of it that did not belong to him, which was the whole point of breaking in.

Kerryl had told her earlier that somewhere in here would be a special area, magically protected and trapped within an inch of its life. It would be there that Aurelius stored the prize

Kerryl sought. Moonrunner could take care of the magical protections, but he needed her to disarm the traps. First, though, they had to find the special stash.

Twice they had to duck behind crates and freeze while the guard bumbled past. Clumsy, loud human. She noted scornfully that he followed the same track through the piles of goods and took exactly the same amount of time to make each circuit of the warehouse. No self-respecting rogue would ever be so predictable.

She'd followed Kerryl in careful silence to the far wall of the storeroom before she spied the faintest of magical glows emanating from behind a tapestry hanging on the wall. The tapestry depicted a heroic battle of Imperial forces defeating the Dominion—the dangerous animal changeling horde that occasionally poured from its island stronghold to bedevil Koth and its colonies.

She touched Kerryl's sleeve and pointed to the glow. He nodded, murmured some sort of incant under his breath, and the magical glow behind the tapestry winked out. He gestured her forward to search for a hidden door while he took up a watch position.

As she moved past him, she noted a pair of mice skittering out from behind a barrel to sniff at his feet. Kerryl chittered under his breath at the rodents. She wondered why she shuddered whenever he spoke to animals and if he was telling them to keep an eye out for the second guard, who had yet to show himself. She wondered briefly what animals had to say to humans who could talk with them.

She peeked behind the tapestry and spied a door. No hinges, so it opened inward, away from her. She pulled out her thin-bladed dagger and ran it gently around the door. Two wires, both chest high, one on each side of the door, acted as sensors against its opening. She quickly ran a crossing wire between the two, then carved out a small notch and slipped a pressure pad against the hinge-side wire. Using her knife blade, she held pressure on the other wire as she tested the knob. Unlocked. A sure sign of a trapped door.

She eased the portal open just enough to slip a small mirror inside. *Ahh. Clever mechanism mounted on the other side of the door.* She would have to—

A cricket chirruped behind her. *Dregs.* That was Kerryl. She flattened herself next to the door and prayed that she wasn't disturbing the hang of the heavy, dusty tapestry lying against her. An urge to sneeze climbed her nose, torturing her until she near died from the tickle. Another chirrup. The guard on his rounds had passed. She mashed her hand over her face and gave vent as silently as she could to the mighty sneeze she'd been holding in.

She went back to work on the intricate trap, concentrating fiercely. Her entrance into the Tribe rested upon defeating this mechanism, and she would do anything, *anything,* to become a member of that elite force.

Eventually, when she poked the mirror through the gap, she spied nothing to indicate that any active traps remained on the door. All that was left to do was open it and pray some attack wasn't launched at her from across the hidden room or that a poison gas didn't explode in her face. The predictable guard had just passed again, which gave them seven minutes or so until they needed to worry about his return.

"Pick me up you will when I drop?" she breathed.

"Aye."

She eased the door open. No warning glyphs screamed, and no gas traps discharged. She took a cautious step into the small treasure chamber. Golden and jeweled platters, chests, vases, and chalices were jumbled about just like she would have imagined in a dragon's lair.

"So much gold there is!" she exclaimed quietly.

"Bah. It is a distraction. Aurelius hopes to deflect ignorant thieves away from the real treasure." Kerryl began setting aside the gaudy baubles quickly. "Help me. We need to get into the chests below these useless piles of gold."

"What seek we?"

"A pair of bracers. Leather. Decorated with animal shapes and signs. A mantle with the same sort of decorations around the hem. And a staff intricately carved with animal figures all around."

Those sounded like items created by or for the Great Circle. She nodded and commenced digging through the first chest. It was only gold coin. Hundreds of pieces. More than she and all her clutchmates could hope to see in ten lifetimes. The temptation to pocket handfuls of it was great, but tonight was about impressing Moonrunner, not enriching herself.

"Ah hah!" Kerryl exclaimed under his breath. "There you are." He lifted a curved leather piece from a chest. It was brown and looked old, but the leather was well oiled. Crude, almost runic, images of animals cavorted along its surface.

"What is it?" she asked.

"One of the Bands of Beasts."

"What does it do?"

"This one gives the wearer power to command beasts that would otherwise not obey."

She gaped. What beasts did not obey Kerryl already? It was said the Hunter in Green was the most senior nature guardian in these lands and Kerryl Moonrunner his most powerful apprentice.

"If Aurelius had the other items, he would store them with this. He must not have them. Too bad," Kerryl commented regretfully. "And now we must find the focus item for a ritual, Sha'Li."

"The . . . what?"

Kerryl spoke impatiently as he wrestled open a big chest. "A chalice. Made of wood. Decorated with inlaid ivory. It should have some sort of runes or symbolic drawings upon it."

She might have asked what the chalice was for or what a focus item did, but the guards would be back soon. Instead, she focused on the search. They grew sloppier in shoving aside priceless objects to get to the chests below. She opened chests full of silver and jewels and more gold, glowing crystals, and some filled with strange mechanical objects she didn't recognize. Finally, she threw open a lid and stared down at an ornate chalice covered in intricate designs and whorls of ivory. Silvery runes were worked into the complex patterns covering the surface of the drinking vessel.

"Found it!" she called.

Kerryl moved over to her quickly. "Good girl." He picked up the chalice and examined it closely. "Yes, indeed. This is it."

He moved over to the open chest of glowing crystals and scooped up as many as his pouch could hold.

"What are those?" she asked.

"Mana crystals."

Ahh. She'd heard of those. They powered magic spells and rituals. They were passing rare.

"Have you taken something for yourself?" Kerryl asked abruptly, startling her.

"No, sir. My mission this night is to aid you."

"Yes, yes, that's noble and all. But you should take something. . . . I know just the thing. . . ."

She glanced around, overwhelmed by the riches. She would have no idea on her own of what to take. Something small that would fit in her pouch, she supposed. Maybe gold or gems. Would they be marked, though? Could they be traced back to the guild's treasure horde? She lifted a green wreath made of gold-edged leaves that, for all the world, looked alive, fresh, and crisp. The wreath looked about of a size to wear upon one's head.

Kerryl lurched. "Is that—" He squinted and looked more closely and then laughed a little. "No, it isn't the Crown of Gandamere. That is just a trophy from some recent tournament. Gave me a start, there, for a moment, you did."

He rummaged in the chest the bracer had come from and lifted out a dull metal cube not much larger than his hand. "Cold iron," he announced.

She frowned. Cold iron was renowned for its ability to harm and ward off fae. Did the box hold an item of fae making, then? Kerryl set the thing on the floor and lifted the small woodsman's hatchet from his belt. She jumped as, abruptly, he swung the hatchet and hacked the little cube nearly in two. He reached into the pieces of it that had fallen apart and pulled out an entirely innocuous-looking disk of wood.

It was about the length of her thumb in diameter and round. The rings of a tree's growth were visible in its lightly polished red-brown surface. The whole of it was covered with strange sigils that looked very old. That was all she saw before Kerryl swiftly ran the pad of his thumb across the edge of the hatchet blade and blood welled. He held his thumb over the disk and let his blood drip onto it until the surface was red and slippery. He held it out to her.

"Take it. Give it to the elders of your tribe. I have woken it as much as I can, but they will need to attempt to finish the process. Maybe they succeed, maybe not."

"What must they do?" she asked, startled.

"They will know."

She took the blood-slippery disk he thrust at her and slipped it in her pocket. A mouse commenced chittering frantically in the corner, and Kerryl cursed. Quickly he kicked the remains of the iron cube into the corner behind a treasure chest.

"Time to go," he bit out.

Sha'Li darted out of the treasure room on his heels. They darted past the tapestry and into the shadows behind a stack of crates. The guard had a companion this time around, and the pair pulled back the tapestry and commenced arguing excitedly. One seemed to think there'd been a break-in, and the other that a worker had merely been lazy and not properly set the traps. She and Kerryl crept farther away from the pair.

She heard the *schwing* of a sword being drawn. A second sword was drawn more slowly. Kerryl slipped behind bolts of cloth piled high, and Sha'Li rolled behind a wine cask as the arguing guards headed this way.

The pair passed, and she and Kerryl raced silently for the door they had come in through. Locked. They were trapped in the building. She reached into her pouch for her picks, but a shout went up behind them. Apparently, the disturbed treasure horde had been found. Running boots pounded toward them as she reached frantically for the door, cursing. Lock picking was not a speed sport.

"No time for that," Kerryl grunted. "Get back."

She leaped back from the door just in time to avoid a great blast of magic he hurled at the panel. Wood exploded in every direction with a mighty crashing, splintering sound. Kerryl leaped into the gap while she stared, slack jawed.

"Run or die!" he snapped.

While the council dithered well into the evening and long past time for his supper, Anton Constantine's mind raced. As countrified a bumpkin as the boy before him clearly was, the youth's story had the ring of truth about it. And that cursed gypsy girl, for all her tongue-tied panic was no different. Worse, everyone seated at the council table had surely heard the same ring of truth.

Krugar had neatly sidestepped him by bringing the gypsy and the boy directly to the council instead of to his private chambers. Had he gotten ahold of the pair before anyone else heard the tale of a Boki raid, he could have quietly killed the lad and disposed of the girl. Problem solved. *But no.* Now he had to deal with whatever the Boki were up to. Publicly, no less.

Scowling at Krugar, he said rather more pleasantly than he felt, "Thank you so *very* much for bringing this matter to the council's attention, Captain Krugar."

The whoreson rendered a short, ironic bow too insolent to be mistaken for respect, but not so rude as to call for punitive action. Krugar knew full well he'd maneuvered his superior into having to confront the cursed Boki.

What were those orcs up to, anyway?

Leland Hyland, the old bulldog, wasn't about to let this bone go. The landsgrave leaned forward aggressively and said, "I suggest the Haelan legion, led by one of Krugar's eight lions, supplemented by troops from the landholds, investigate."

"You speak of raising an army," the Landsgrave of Delphi replied in alarm.

"Do you not recall the last Boki incursion?" Hyland retorted sharply. "They nearly destroyed us all."

Anton scowled. But those cursed Boki hadn't managed to destroy the Landsgraves of Hyland, Delphi, Lochnar, and Talyn like he'd paid them to. Nor had the Boki killed Aurelius as they'd promised to.

Instead, Hyland, Aurelius, and De'Vir had managed to turn the tide of battle at the last minute and unexpectedly drove the Boki back into the Forest of Thorns. Who'd have guessed those three were capable of rallying their troops with such heroism? They'd fouled up all his best-laid plans, curse them. *He* was supposed to be the rescuer of Dupree. *After* the Boki laid waste to his enemies and took blame for the wholesale looting with which he'd planned to enrich his personal coffers.

But no. The wondrous threesome had to go and save the day all by themselves. Fury raged in his breast even now to remember the glory they'd stolen from him. And now they were sitting there, all smug, demanding that he send out one of his senior military officers in Dupree to confront the Boki. Krugar, of course, was the most senior officer in the Haelan legion, and the next tier of officers below him were the Lions.

Down the council table, the Landsgraves of Delphi and Talyn weighed in, agreeing to contribute to an expeditionary military force. Anton's own sergeant at arms was excitedly tallying up how many men he could gather and outfit for war immediately, which did nothing to calm the council members.

Even Aurelius chimed in, offering up all of the Celestial Order of the Dragon knights he could round up on short notice to provide combat-magic support for the expeditionary force. Anton sneered into his sleeve. Of course, the whoreson offered up his dragons. He'd have been ordered to do it anyway. Trying to come off all noble and patriotic was Aurelius? Since when did any sun elf care for a blessed thing beyond his own fancy hide?

Anton felt the tide turning inexorably against his plans. These fools were determined to rush out and confront the Boki before the orcs laid waste to Dupree again. He could order them not to fight the Boki, but how would that look? Word would get back to Maximillian that the governor refused to defend the colony. Even Ammertus would not be able to protect Anton if he did something so obviously opposed to the Empire's best interests.

Did the Emperor ever feel constrained by the idiocy of his courtiers like this?

How to turn the thing to his favor?

His speculative glance shifted to Hyland, by far his most bothersome landsgrave. Leland had thwarted him at every turn over the years, always arguing for the good of the people, shaming Anton into humanitarian acts and generous decisions that Hyland *knew* galled him. If the Boki could manage to kill Hyland this time around, the collateral losses of a full-scale Boki invasion would be well worth the cost.

Not to mention a war would distract everyone from his new venture in the Ice Wall. Maximillian and the Imperial guilds in Koth would never notice the failure of that region to produce income for them. Every bit of it could go straight to his own coffers.

For that matter, he could levy all sorts of special taxes to finance the defense of Dupree and seize any resources he wished for "the war effort." Oh yes. A war would be tremendously profitable.

A second green insurrection it was, then, led by the Boki. And this time around, he would see to it they followed his instructions to the letter and that the outcome was to his exact specifications. He would send a message by secret means this very night to Ki'Raiden. And this time he would withhold payment until *after* they killed everyone on the list he gave them.

Despite her worry for Will, Rosana yawned as the council wrangled over every last detail of who would do what and how much and when and report to whom in preparing an expeditionary force to march out and drive the Boki out of Dupree. She'd always imagined going to war would be much more glorious—swords waving and grand speeches and distraught damsels kissing the brave warriors on their way.

At long, long last, however, the meeting broke up. Rosana stood and stretched her stiff joints. The governor's benches were none too comfortable..

The Heart adept approached her immediately. "I'm off to the Heart." He added under his breath, "If you know what's good for you, that is where you will go without delay, as well."

Rosana nodded fractionally in acknowledgment of his warning.

"Walk with me, Novice."

Will nearly had to run to keep up with the guildmaster's long strides out the main gate of Anton's residence.

They passed through the gate and Will stopped in his tracks, stunned. *What on Urth?* The entire population of

Dupree seemed to have emptied into the streets, and the city was lit up with torches and lamps and lanterns.

Was tonight some sort of festival he was not aware of? The crowd buzzed angrily, though, and he caught snatches of rumor—guild storehouse looted. Soldiers searching the city, beating and arresting any caught with booty. Mobs fighting back against excessive force. Emergency curfew going into effect. This was no festival. It was a riot!

Aurelius swore under his breath and plowed into the melee.

Alarmed, Will plastered himself to the solinari's heels. If there was violence afoot, the safest place in the colony would be at the back of its most powerful combat mage. But Will had a terrible time keeping up with the sun elf, who was moving swiftly and keeping his hood pulled well over his face. In minutes Will had no idea where they were. If he became separated from the elf now, he would be hopelessly lost in the sprawling city.

He was soundly jostled, elbowed, and cursed at before a wide avenue opened up before him, one entire side of it flanked by a long, ornate building, stone below and half timbers above. The trim was intricately painted in royal blue and gold. At night, the magical glow around the structure was plain to the naked eye.

Guildmaster Aurelius hurried up the broad steps, waved his hand briefly, and the great magical shell around the building lowered at his command.

The power of the casual hand gesture stole Will's breath away. Dread anticipation over what the solinari would do to "test" him made his steps slow and his heart pound as he followed the man up the long steps.

This was it. The point of no return.

What of his father's quest? If he went into yon building and learned more of it, he would have no choice but to press on.

He could turn away right now. Leave. Go find Rosana or a nice girl like her, settle down, and live a quiet, normal life, which, after the past few days, sounded pretty blessed good. Of course, that would also mean he would spend the rest of his safe, boring life wondering what would have happened had he found the courage to dare greatly.

The Heart adept hurried away from Anton's great hall with Rosana as if the place made him vaguely ill. She knew the feeling. Her knees still felt on the verge of collapse. Had Will not stood up so bravely for her, she did not want to think what would have happened to her.

"Come along then, Novice," the adept ordered with thin patience. "We must not stay where we are not welcome, and the governor has made it clear he bears no love for us." He exclaimed as they reached the mighty portcullis, which was coming down ponderously, already halfway lowered, "What is this?"

Her heart lurched. Were the two of them to be detained, then? Terror exploded in her bosom. But then she saw past the portcullis and noticed people racing past in every direction. To her untrained eye, it looked as if the world were ending.

"Oh, good grief," the adept muttered. "Not another riot. Come. We will have need of every healer this night. There will be cracked pates and broken limbs aplenty afore this mischief is ended. Cursed governor barely controls his troops in the best of times. But turned loose to restore order, they'll behave little better than savages themselves."

Wide-eyed, she crowded close to his side as the adept dived into the seething mass of people crowding the streets.

"A healer, a healer . . ."

"I'm wounded, Heart. Magic, please . . ."

"We've wounded over this way. . . ."

It was a mess. Everywhere Rosana looked people with bloody faces and limps and cradling injuries hobbled past. She didn't have the first idea who to begin healing. A fellow with a bloodied lip and what looked like a broken jaw staggered into her, knocking her hard into the adept. The wounded man made a garbled noise like a choking turkey.

She drew forth power to repair the man's face. It came easily, for the Heart's energy was orderly, powerful, in the city with its Heartstone and high concentration of Heart members.

But before she could cast it, the adept snapped, "Save your mana. There'll be much worse than him who need your healing this night!"

"Worse? Where?"

"They'll bring the bad ones to the Heart. Such violence Anton breeds. It'll come to no good, I tell you. The man's a menace."

Rosana's jaw dropped open. She did believe she'd just heard a Heart member mutter treason. Of course, in the fellow's distress at the number of wounded around him the comment could certainly be forgiven. But her heart warmed to this fellow more than a little at the sentiment.

A tangle of limbs, weapons, and shouting spilled out of an alley and into the street before them, nearly overrunning them both. Rosana recoiled, but not quickly enough. A ball of glowing energy twisted her way through the air, striking her on the shoulder. As it began to sink into her being, however, she recognized it as curse magic and expelled it from her being. Not only did her kind have a gift for creating such magic; they also had a gift for shrugging it off.

A soldier in the Haelan legion's black and gold peeled away from the brawl. "To me, Heart!" he yelled. "This way!"

The adept grabbed her elbow and shoved her toward the soldier, who took off running. Someone took a swing at them from a doorway with something thick and clumsy—a club of some kind—and the soldier's sword flashed up to deflect the blow.

"Hurry," the soldier urged them.

They burst out into a large square, and on the far side of it she spied the large whitewashed structure that must be the Heart building. Its shell of magical protection glowed brightly, illuminating the entire square in a soft white light.

"Thanks be to thee, soldier," the adept panted. "Who are you? What is your name?"

"I am Kel. A friend of the Heart. You should be safe enough here if you stick to the lighted places."

"The Heart will remember you. If you ever have need of us, you have but to ask."

The soldier nodded briefly and turned to face the square. Only small pockets of fighting were noisy around the edges of the big space.

"Thank you, Kel!" Rosana called as the soldier plunged into the crowd and disappeared from sight.

The crowd was heavy, and the number of wounded exponentially higher here than in the streets behind them. The adept dived into the crowd, dragging Rosana along by the elbow lest she become separated from him.

"The Heart is here!" the shout went up, and was accompanied by voices cheering.

He commented in irritation, "It is most likely my own healers cheering at having me back so they can dump this mess in my lap."

Grinning, she barged along beside him.

Not far from the Heart's front door, however, they ran across a group of gravely wounded people. They'd been laid out in a row before the Heart's doorstep almost like corpses on a battlefield.

"Oh, for the spirit of Nature," the adept griped under his breath. "When will Anton learn to rein in his troops?" He raised his voice in brisk command, "Who's in charge, here?"

A harassed-looking woman of middle years looked up gratefully from where she bent over a still, pale form. "Thank the stars, you're back. We could use your mana, Brother."

He shed his cloak, shoving it at Rosana to hold. "Do you know the life spell?" he asked.

"I have been taught it but have never really cast it."

"Looks like you get to learn on the job. Pick a body and dive in, Novice."

With that, the adept shouted, "Where is Brother Lizmorn? We have need of his potions!"

A lizardman wearing the Heart colors materialized, a handful of glass vials in hand. Rosana stared at this Lizmorn fellow, shocked. Although she supposed it was no more shocking for one of his race to be in the Heart than for one of her race. Neither was well loved by Koth.

"Take these," the lizardman said, shoving a few vials into her hands.

"What are they?" she asked, not seeing any written labels on the vials.

The adept spoke from beside her. "Lizmorn's kind do not learn to read easily. Our native brother has devised a color-coding system for identifying healing potions. See those white stripes on yours? You've got simple healing potions, good for a minor injury or staving off death for a bit." He gave her a little shove toward the many waiting victims. "Go."

He turned his back and commenced restoring life to the body nearest to him.

The old panic clutched at her, freezing her mind and body

into immobility. What if she messed up? What if she wasted her mana and someone died because of it? Doubts piled on top of one another until she could hardly breathe beneath them all.

"You! Healer girl! Get over here!"

She looked up swiftly at the sharp order.

A richly dressed rakasha, who looked like a white tiger changeling, was waving at her imperiously. His whipcord tone of voice cut through her panic enough that she was able to move her feet.

"These two have been dead for more than three minutes. I need them both lifed. Now."

She looked down and saw the body of another sumptuously dressed white tiger rakasha. The race of cat changelings was exceedingly uncommon in Dupree. The dead one's hand still clutched a thin golden chain that ran to a matching collar around the other victim's neck—a dead girl, a female jann with strikingly iridescent blue skin for the most part. The girl was nearly of an age with her and so beautiful Rosana's teeth ached to look at her still face.

"Who are they?" she asked as she knelt between the two.

"My master and a gift for the governor."

Her gaze narrowed. She'd heard about the governor's tastes. That he poisoned women to make them wildly in love with him and then did unspeakable things with them.

She frantically reviewed the incant for a life spell in her head. She could do this. Taking a deep breath, she began the process of clearing her mind and reaching into the ethos around her for spiritual energy.

"Hurry, girl! My master will have to resurrect soon."

Irritated, she murmured the focusing incant, using its cadence and rhythm to shape the magic in her hand. She finished the incant and slapped her hand down upon the slave girl's chest, vigorously projecting the energy into her.

The slave girl lurched upright as she drew in a gasping breath. Wild-eyed, she glanced around as if waking from a nightmare. "Be easy," Rosana murmured. "You live. I got to you in time."

"Get on with it, girl! Heal my master!" the antsy rakasha cried behind her.

Taking her sweet time, Rosana started to draw another batch of magic but then stopped. "You know, this would work better if my target weren't clutching a metal object like that." She pried the end of the leash out of the dead man's hand and passed it to the slave girl, who took it in shock, her eyes a mile wide. Rosana lifted her chin infinitesimally in encouragement.

"Go on, do it!" The rakasha was all but jumping up and down in panic.

Truthfully, Rosana did not believe she had the capacity to draw enough magic to herself for a second life spell. But she was not about to tell the agitated man with the big sword on his hip that.

Careful not to accidentally tap into her own spirit and making sure the cat-man's undivided attention stayed fully on her, Rosana did her theatric best reciting the incant, shaping all of the charge she was able to gather, and throwing it down into the rich man's chest.

Nothing happened. He was now beyond the aid of her magic. Only a resurrection would bring him back now. It was coldhearted of her, but she could not find it in her conscience to care overmuch that a slaver had died.

As a Heart member, she was obliged to do her best to save lives, but she was still a gypsy, too. Her kind had been pursued and bedeviled by slavers forever. And gypsies were not known for their forgiving ways. She pushed aside the frisson of regret that she had let down her Heart colors as she pushed to her feet and murmured an apology to the cat changeling who'd summoned her.

The rakasha guard was distraught that his master had not come back. He demanded to know where the Heartstone was and whirled to head for the Heart building, his long, tufted tail swirling behind him.

The drain of attempting a second life spell pulled at her. She had no more magic for this night and felt instinctive warning creeping into her consciousness that further casting would destroy a piece of her spirit. The physical exhaustion of being at the end of her magic pulled at her as well.

But she could still render basic first aid. She reached into her pouch for a rolled bandage and knelt beside a youth with a badly gashed arm. It looked like a sword had hacked it. As she wrapped the wound, a golden collar clattered to the cobblestones at the edge of the Heart building. The leash was still attached to it, but there was no sign of its wearer. Smiling a little to herself, Rosana tied off the bandage.

W ill passed through tall double doors painted royal blue with four-pointed gold stars the size of his outspread arms upon them, a long comet's tail arcing away from each star. He stopped just inside the Mage's Guild.

A large, threatening man stood just inside in full chain-mail armor. The cloth tabard covering his mail shirt was the guild's royal blue with an embroidered gold dragon rampant upon it. He moved quickly to interpose himself between Will and Aurelius.

"I am Drake Bruin. Celestial Order of the Dragon. State your business, boy."

Will's jaw dropped. The Celestial Order of the Dragon was the sect of warriors designated to protect and serve the Imperial Mage's Guild. Recognition of the colors and heraldry washed over him. Ty's blue and gold armor. Ki'Raiden demanding that the "dragon" show himself. *My father must have belonged to the Celestial Order of the Dragon.*

Aurelius had already hurried across the main room and his robes were just disappearing up the steps. Will was on his own.

The guard looked him up and down suspiciously and repeated more sharply, "State your business, boy."

Will's jaw tightened against being called a boy. "I have a message for Guildmaster Aurelius, if you please."

"What is the message?"

Will answered carefully, "I am charged with delivering my message to him alone and no one else."

The guard took a long, suspicious look at Will's face, his frown deepening the longer he studied Will. Much as Anton Constantine's had. But eventually the knight replied gruffly, "Then you'd best see the guildmaster."

Will took another step into the room and became aware of a sympathetic vibration in the air that resonated deep within his spirit. His kind of magic lived in this place.

He looked at the wall where the guardian was fiddling with an elaborate lock, maybe a palm's span across. Its brass surface was carved with swirls and curls. The fellow returned a similarly decorated key to a hook beside it. That must be a magical lock. And it raised and lowered the marvelous shell of protective magic around the building!

Will's hand rose toward the wondrous contraption, but the drake snapped, "Don't touch the wizard's lock!"

Will jerked his hand back.

"You may put your pack there on the floor. This way."

Will dropped his pack by the door and followed the drake up two flights of stairs. He glimpsed books, mages conversing quietly among themselves, and even one hunched over a table, painstakingly copying a scroll. Ahh, how he'd love to become one of them. He'd been fascinated by tales of magic ever since he could remember. No wonder. It ran more deeply in his blood than he'd ever known. But none of the theory of magic, nor the history of it, nor the deeper study of it had been made available to him. The gall of his father's refusal to teach him soured his gut as he climbed two more flights of stairs.

He nearly bumped into Drake Bruin's back as the knight stopped abruptly in front of a closed door. The portal had a bright aura about it, distinctively yellow. His escort knocked upon the portal through the glow.

"Enter!" a resonant voice called from the other side of the door. The yellow glow blinked out.

The drake ushered Will inside. "This lad says he has a message, Guildmaster Aurelius. For your ears only."

The sun elf looked up from his work, his amber gaze measuring Will narrowly. "You may go, Bruin."

The drake frowned at the dismissal but left the room, closing the door with a disapproving thud.

Aurelius, who upon closer inspection was no youngster, leaned back in his chair and studied Will intently. "Have I met you before? You have a familiar look about you."

"No, sir, we have never met."

"And yet you know a rare and difficult skill, taught only to a knight of the Celestial Order of the Dragon. Where did you learn the Dragon's Roar, boy?"

"I don't know, sir. I just . . . did it."

"Who are you? Where are you from?" Aurelius demanded.

"As I told the council, I come from Hickory Hollow." He

passed over the thorny question of his identity and plowed forward with delivering his father's message. "The hollow has been attacked by orcs, and everyone in the village has been killed except me. But there is more to the story, and it is this I was charged with relaying to you, sir."

"Indeed? Then by all means, tell your tale."

"Ki'Raiden, Sixth Thane of the Boki, led the attack. And he demanded that the yellow dragon show himself. He declared the villagers little more than sheep and of no interest to him."

The elf's eyebrows shot straight up. In Will's experience with his mother, such an obvious display of surprise was rare. The guildmaster interrupted, demanding, "Do you know to whom this Boki referred?"

"I believe I do, sir."

Aurelius stared at him a long time, myriad emotions flitting across his golden features. Finally, he asked, "How did you manage to survive and escape?"

"We—my parents and I—ran when the Boki came. My father had an emergency stash of weapons and armor in the woods. He and my mother stood and fought the Boki that I might flee. At my father's command, I came as fast as I could to deliver the message to you. Only you." He hung his head. "I didn't know what to do when the governor's captain dragged me and Rosana before the council. I dared not lie." He added, blurting defensively, "And I could not stand by and let them throw her into slavery. She spoke the truth!"

"Exactly how many orcs attacked your village?"

"Upward of two dozen, plus some ogres and goblins who were with them."

The guildmaster asked carefully, "And who might your father be?"

"Ty the cobbler."

"Of Hickory Hollow," Aurelius finished dryly.

"Aye."

"Dost know why he sent you to me?"

"He said I must continue the quest in his stead. That you would know more about it and could tell me how to proceed."

The guildmaster flung himself backward in his chair, staring in open shock. Eventually, he muttered, "Did he now? He judged you ready, then?"

Not bloody likely. Ty had never judged his only son ready to do much of anything. It had always been chores and more chores, always pushing, always demanding. But Will had never measured up to his father's ridiculous expectations. Of course, now he understood why his father's standards had been so unattainable. The man had been no cobbler at all. He'd been some sort of battle-mage knight for this man and his guild. *And the Empire.* The thought was bitter in his heart.

Will answered honestly, "I doubt he found me ready. It was simply that he had no choice in the matter. Ki'Raiden was coming for us, and he knew he was going to die."

"Did you see your father's body?" Aurelius asked grimly.

"No. My mother struck me with a fear gas poison to make me run before they engaged the thane."

Aurelius grinned, momentarily giving his features a surprisingly boyish cast. "That doth sound like Serica. Efficient woman."

"You know my mother?" Will blurted.

Aurelius didn't bother to answer. Instead, he leaned back. "So your father sent you to me, did he? Did he tell you to ask me for training?"

"No, sir."

That occasioned another smile from Aurelius, this one rather more wry, however. "Arrogant whoreson thought he taught you more than I could, did he?"

Will had never heard his humble father called arrogant before. It gave him pause. That last night, though, when his father had been snapping orders and toying with Boki warriors, Will supposed he'd seen a flash of a man who could be labeled arrogant. Or maybe just supremely confident.

"If you don't mind my asking, Guildmaster, who was my father to you?"

"He was my right-hand man. More than a friend. Like a son to me." A pause as a distant look entered the elf's golden eyes. "Did he tell you that I adopted him?"

Will's jaw sagged. No speech came to him. This man was his adopted *grandfather*? His mind could not process the meaning of it.

Thankfully, Aurelius filled in the silence by explaining, "Solinari culture places great emphasis on family lineages. It is vital to bring honor to your family name and to pass that name on to your children. My career and . . . events in my past . . . have made it nigh impossible for me to have a family of mine own, however."

Will frowned, not understanding.

"Females of my race able to bear offspring are exceedingly rare, for one thing," Aurelius responded to his unspoken question. "For another, some years ago I drew out and absorbed the magics of the Hand of Winter to save my commanding general from being consumed by it. Some of Winter Lord's curse still resides within me. Ice magic and my gift for fire magics do not mix well."

Who on Urth was the Hand of Winter? Hearth tales were told in Dupree of the Lord of the Harvest, who was a friendly fae lord with a pumpkin for a head. He visited the region each autumn to ensure a bountiful harvest. Was a winter lord similar, somehow?

Aurelius continued, "I have been close to the De'Vir

family for centuries. When young Tiberius came along, so extraordinarily talented, I suppose it was natural that I should form a particular affection for him. I took over his training personally, and I confess I pushed him mercilessly."

Will snorted. That must be where his father learned how to be such a hard taskmaster.

Aurelius's voice became almost hushed. "For my people, the highest expression of our race is to achieve everything of which one is capable. Only then can one's name be etched upon the Naming Stones at the top of Mount Sohlaya."

Will recalled his mother speaking of this mountain once. It was in the Sunset Isles and was the heart of the solinari culture. A circle of standing stones crowned the mountain, one for each great solinari clan. And great heroes within the clans, upon their final death, got their names carved on the stones. As a child, he'd thought it sounded like an awful lot of work just to get one's name on a rock. But standing before a solinari now, seeing the longing in his golden gaze when he spoke of being remembered forever, Will understood a little better.

Aurelius continued, "Over the years, your father and I became a fighting team, he the warrior-mage and me the straight combat-magic caster. Tiberius was implacable. Invincible. A force of nature upon the field of battle. If a fight was unwinnable, he was the one person who could see a way through to victory, no matter how improbable the odds. He was instrumental in turning the tide of the Boki insurrection."

Will would like to hear more of how his father personally defeated the Boki during the invasion sixteen years ago, but Aurelius was not done speaking.

"Anton was furious that we defeated the Boki."

That made Will stare. Why would the governor be angry that invaders were repelled? Aurelius gave Will no pause to ask, however.

"Of course, we completed your father's naming ceremony in Koth. We attempted a polymorph upon Tiberius here to make him into a solinari, but unfortunately, Anton's hired mercenaries found us before the ritual could be completed."

Such a transformation from one race to another was possible? Will had never dreamed of such a thing. Will interrupted, shocked, "My father was to become an elf?"

"Aye. Your mother, of course, we did manage to transform—"

Wait. What? His mother had begun life as a human and only later become a silvani? Why had his parents never bothered to tell him? Likely for the same reason they'd never bothered to mention that his father was one of the greatest warrior-mages in the colonies.

Aurelius was still speaking. ". . . Anton's thugs also found us before I could name Tiberius's infant son. As the eldest member of our family in the colonies, the task of naming all offspring of the line falls to me, you see."

That infant son had been *him*. It felt strange to Will to think of himself as a babe in the presence of this man.

"So, in point of fact, young Will, you have no name."

"My father said once that he wanted me to be called Villerius." Will had protested against it, however. He'd thought it sounded far too stuffy for a cobbler's boy from Hickory Hollow.

"A fine solinari name."

Which explained why it had sounded so stuffy!

"Until the solinari naming ceremony can be completed, however, you are neither Villerius nor De'Vir."

It was no great loss in Will's mind, but Aurelius's voice was laced with significance. The solinari seemed to expect a response from him, so Will shrugged a little.

Aurelius challenged, "If someone associated with the

Empire were to ask you your father's full name, how would you answer?"

"I would say his name is Tiberius. Tiberius De'Vir."

The effect of those words upon Aurelius was startling. The man's gaze went utterly black and he lunged out from behind his desk so quickly that Will barely saw him coming. One second the solinari was seated in his chair, and the next he had his hand upon Will's throat, squeezing so tightly he could barely breathe.

"Never . . ."—the strong fingers tightened upon his neck— ". . . *ever* utter that name if you wish to live. That name is Death upon the lips of any who speak it. If you wish to live, you are the son of Ty the cobbler, and no more. Do you understand me?"

Galvanized, Sha'Li darted out after Kerryl as the first guard took a wild swipe at her with his sword. She raced pell-mell down the alley after Moonrunner. His dark green cloak billowed out behind him like bat wings.

They reached the mouth of the alley and he bit out, "We need to split up." He gave her a shove to the right as he bolted left.

No time to argue or even think. The guards were almost on them. She took off running in the direction Kerryl shoved her while a hue and cry rose behind her and spread, picked up by townspeople and soldiers shouting of thieves at the Mage's Guild storehouse. She ran until the stitch in her side was so severe she could not walk, let alone run. Besides, to be seen running when a hunt was on for a thief was more dangerous than not. She slowed and dived into a darkened doorway to catch her breath. Now what?

The faint, distant shouts changed in tenor. She eased closer to the street to listen. A roar had overtaken all the other sounds. Something to do with a guild storehouse being breached. Of it not being guarded.

Well, of course not. The guards had chased her and Kerryl from the structure. Glee entered the tone of that roaring mob. As of many, many people joyfully anticipating robbing their oh-so-beloved empire.

But then a new sound intruded upon the celebration. Boots running in unison. Like a mass of soldiers quick-timing their way to the warehouse. More sounds ruptured the night: Battle cries. The screams of wounded. The cries of a mob fleeing. Of soldiers pursuing. In short, Dupree was in chaos.

Just the sort of chaos she could hide within and slip away from here. So far, the street before her was relatively quiet. Only a few townspeople had raced by earlier.

At least she had nothing of value on her person from the warehouse. Just that stupid little piece of wood. No one would miss it or know it for Aurelius's, right? Still, to be safe, she'd better dump the stupid thing where no one would find it or associate it with her. A woodpile across town. Or a trash heap.

She should just walk out of here as if she'd done nothing. That was it. Play it cool and pray the warehouse guards had not seen that a black-skinned lizardman girl was one of the thieves who started this whole riot.

She stepped out of the doorway.

And all but ran into a patrol of soldiers.

"There's a lizardman! Get her!"

Swearing, she took off running again. If they caught her, she'd never get her Tribe mark. Not to mention, she would be *so* dead.

Raina hurried along beside the Landsgrave of Hyland through chaos unlike anything she'd ever seen before. Apparently, there had been some sort of break-in at a guild warehouse, dozens or hundreds of locals had partaken in a looting spree, and now Anton's men were chasing them down in a vain attempt to recover the stolen goods.

She desperately wished for Cicero's sword and steady countenance at her side. But he had prudently elected not to accompany her to the governor's council table.

"Oh, for stars' sake," Hyland muttered in irritation. "Cannot Anton even manage to keep order in his own city? He has an entire army at his disposal."

"It appears to me," she offered hesitantly, "that Anton's army is contributing to the overall disorder rather than containing it."

Hyland threw her an aggrieved look. "Aye. Just so. The legion has no discipline at all. It is a disgrace." He added as a running mob of youths wielding clubs raced past, jostling her into him, "Move to my left side and stay by me as if we've got a paste of stickiness joining our cloaks."

She nodded and did as told. "Why the left side?" she asked as the street quieted once more.

"Most swordsmen fight right-handed. A backpack healer should stay left, out of their way and behind their shield, but close enough to pump healing and magical shields into the warrior as they need it."

"Could you show me how to do that, sometime?" She was always eager to learn more about the many ways of using magic.

He snorted. "You may get to practice it before we reach my house across town. We have to pass through the Great Square, and if I know Anton's sergeants, there will be a full-blown brawl in progress there."

In fact, the brawl was just winding down when they reached the main square. She recognized Captain Krugar bellowing orders and personally shackling soldiers who failed to stop fighting immediately. Problem was, townspeople kept taking potshots at the soldiers and restarting the hostilities.

Hyland took one look at the scene and drew his sword. The blade glowed as he strode forward, shouting out orders of his own. Raina was intrigued that the townspeople seemed prepared to obey his command to disengage when they completely ignored the governor's men.

Between Hyland and Krugar, the two mobs were separated quickly. And that was when the carnage became fully apparent. Dozens of people lay on the ground bloodied and broken. Some appeared to have been trampled, others run through with bladed weapons, yet others simply beaten to a pulp.

Hyland glanced over his shoulder at her. "You know all the standard healing spells?"

"Yes, my lord."

"Then have at it."

How on Urth was she supposed to deal with a dozen or more dead and what looked like a hundred badly injured spirits?

Hyland must have caught her look of dismay, for he instructed, "Life the dead and give the dying the minimum healing necessary to keep them alive. If you've stabilized everyone and have any magic left, go back through and fix the most seriously injured."

She took a deep breath and called magic to her. Although the density of humanity was high in this place, only a portion of them were natives of this continent, tied to it in the same way she was. But there were enough of them. She drew their spiritual power to herself like a cloak.

There was no time for delicacy in delivering healing. She moved from body to body, combat casting life spells as fast as she could incant them. Thankfully, there were only eleven actual dead upon the ground. She got to all but one of them in time to prevent a resurrection, and that fellow had likely been beyond a life spell before she arrived in the square. As Hyland had instructed, she turned her attention to the dying next, casting just enough magic into them to keep them alive.

She was starting to feel fatigued and hungry as the toll upon her mind and physical body rose, but there were injured people everywhere she looked. She dug deep and continued to draw magic to her. Pull, incant, cast. Over and over, she cast basic healing magic. The faces blurred together as she grew more and more exhausted. Finally, when she was too tired to move around, a nearby voice gave an order for the wounded to be brought to her.

As she drew near the end of her resources, someone put a strong, gentle arm around her shoulders to support her while she gasped the incants and forced the magic out of herself and into her targets.

And then it was over. No more injured people remained in front of her. With huge effort, she raised the back of her hand to mop the sweat off her brow. She gazed around and realized two things: first, Hyland was the one with an arm around her, holding her upright almost entirely of his accord, and second, a strange, almost reverent, silence had fallen across the Great Square. Everyone she could see was staring back at her. Like she was some kind of freak.

"Why are they looking at me?" she murmured to Hyland.

"You really have no idea how unusual you are, do you?" he responded.

She didn't know how to answer that, nor did she have the energy left to figure it out.

"It has been a long time since an arch-mage took the field." He shrugged and added, "Not to mention they are not used to a healer of your power turning her resources upon commoners when Anton's men are about."

She frowned. Why wouldn't a healer heal commoners?

"You must be hungry," Hyland continued. "My wife was always ravenous after a long healing session, and she couldn't do a fraction of what you just did. Come, child. Let us get you under a roof. You're done for the night, anyway." He added under his breath, "After healing half the town, you should be done, at any rate."

She turned to accompany him from the square and that was when she spied a man lurking in the shadows at the edge of the square. A man who made her blood run cold. A tall man wearing a dark cloak. Was that blue, mayhap? *They've found me.*

His eyes practically bugging out of his head, Will struggled frantically against Aurelius's claw-like grip on his jugular but to no avail.

The guildmaster flung Will away from him and commenced pacing the office in high agitation, muttering to himself in a tirade Will only half-understood.

Shaken, Will straightened his shirt and rubbed at his throat. What was that all about? Had the solinari not just finished telling Will all about the proud tradition of his father's name and the honor it was for Ty to have been given it? He surreptitiously eyed the glowing door and a possible escape from the crazy guildmaster.

Aurelius explained carefully as if it were of utmost importance that Will understand, "If you were, in fact, the son of that . . . person . . . I would be required to arrest you and hand you over to the governor forthwith for execution. Not only was that person sentenced to death, but all of his family and issue were also. It is all well and good to speak of the past, but that man is dead, and were he to have had children, they would surely have been put to death by now as well."

Will stared in utter shock. There was a death sentence active against *him*?

"If, stars forbid, the son were to survive and inherit any of the father's talent for certain rare skills like, oh, magic, learning how to use it would be strictly illegal. I would have to exercise my full authority as Guildmaster of the Imperial Mage's Guild of Dupree to put an immediate end to such training and turn the child over to the authorities. Do you comprehend me, boy?"

Will nodded fearfully. He clasped his hands behind his back, terrified that by some stray glimmer they might give away his ability with magic. Aurelius must have noted the movement, for he nodded knowingly. "So, tell me, Will the cobbler's son. Can you cast magic?"

"I've . . . uh-h . . . never been formally schooled," he stammered.

"That is not what I asked. Can you cast magic?"

"A little. After a fashion."

"No, no, no!" Aurelius bellowed. "Have you not listened to anything I've said?" He moved toward Will threateningly. "Where is your talisman? Hand it over."

"Talisman?" Will repeated, confused.

"Yes. Your talisman. The magical object you use to focus your mind and call magic to you. Give it to me."

"I have no idea what you're talking about," Will retorted. He had no weapon at hand, but an instinctive compulsion to protect himself surged to the fore. His hands whipped up as the guildmaster stalked toward him, a ferocious scowl on his face, his skin gleaming metallically in the lamplight. The solinari drew within about two body lengths of him—his effective range with a repelling spell—and Will mentally pushed him back. The elf halted mid-step, leaning forward but coming no closer.

"Ahh. There it is. The stone in your bracelet. That is your talisman."

Will stared at his own wrist. His bracelet? His father had given it to him when he was a boy. Before he learned how to summon magic. The stone had been a gift from Adrick, and Ty had braided it into a leather wrist band for him. Recollection of his father asking if he'd had the bracelet on that last night when the hollow was under attack flashed into Will's mind. *That* was why his father had asked. He'd checked to make sure his son had one of these talisman things so he could cast magic.

Aurelius stepped back and gave a curt nod. "You look like the type to whom force magic might come naturally. The Dragon's Roar is sound magic, but De'Vir was a skilled kinetic mage. Apparently, you share his talent for it."

Kinetic magic? What was that? Were there different types of magics, then? Everyone knew of spirit magic, of course, but that was special. "Uh-h, begging your pardon, but I was never taught force magic."

The solinari went silent, staring at Will speculatively. Eventually, he commented cryptically, "Better. Cautious, he was. Smart. Sit, boy. I will return in a moment." The elf swept out of the room.

What on Urth? Now the guildmaster was back to being friendly to him? His brain felt whiplashed. Did he dare make his escape now? Or would the knight from before be standing outside the door to keep him here . . . assuming Will could even figure out how to pass through the glowing magic protections upon the door in the first place? Will tugged his sleeve down over his wrist band, hiding his talisman from sight. He glanced around, spying the only visitor's chair in the office, a four-legged wooden stool with a vertical back of narrow slats. He sighed. Like it or not, he was effectively caged. He perched on the uncomfortable stool like a naughty schoolboy.

Truth be told, he was a little surprised he'd hit the guild-master with that spell. In his limited experience messing around with magic in the woods back home, it was an inexact science at best. He'd initially assumed that casting magic would be like throwing a rock. It would travel straight and true at his target. But he'd found it to be more akin to tossing a pitcher of water toward a target. Magical energy curved and twisted and bent with a mind of its own once loosed. It took great force of will to drive the magic forward to a target with any accuracy at all.

He'd heard the great battle mages could deliver magical damage at a range upward of a hundred feet. Mages like his father, he thought bitterly. He had a hard time crediting such rumors, though. He'd been practicing in secret for years and his effective range was no more than twenty feet.

The guildmaster did indeed return in a minute or two. He promptly sat down at his desk and removed a blank sheet of parchment, a fresh quill, and an inkwell out of a drawer. Will watched in silence as the elf trimmed a quill and unstoppered the ink pot.

Aurelius poised his hand over the page. "Have you any name besides Will?"

"You know full well that my family name is De'V—"

Aurelius cut him off sharply. "We've already covered this. You. Have. No. Name. Am I clear?"

"But—" He broke off. His true identity must disappear forever if he wished to live, apparently. He said hesitantly, "Perhaps you could spell out my name for me, Guildmaster?"

Aurelius smiled broadly. "Will is an easy enough name to spell. Common. Cobblerson is too cumbersome for a last name, though. How about something shorter? To the point.

Cobb." He scribbled on the sheet of parchment before him. "Yes. Will Cobb. That is how your name is written."

Will had no wish to run afoul of the Empire. But apparently, the fact of his birth had already put him on the wrong side of the law. The solinari bent his attention to drafting several long paragraphs. Will tried to read the script upside down, but the print was too small and ornate to decipher.

Aurelius sprinkled sand on the document and, when the ink was dry, blew the sand back into its stone box. He finished the document by melting bright blue wax at the bottom and pressing the ring on his right-hand middle finger into the cobalt puddle.

"This is my report upon your magical testing to Anton."

Will leaped out of the chair. "My father did you a favor! He sent me to you for help! And you wish to reveal my magic that he tried so hard to hide to his greatest enemy?"

"Far more is afoot here than a simple raid by orcs. Ty the cobbler did the right thing to send you to me. And now I do the right thing in return." Aurelius shrugged. "Unfortunately for you, the only way to ensure the complete silence of the son of Tiberius De'Vir would be to kill him. Tiberius was well known. Anton despised him. And after your stunt in the council with the Dragon's Roar, you are known as well. It is exceedingly fortunate for you that you are this other person, Will Cobb and that your talent for magic is limited."

Limited? Exactly how many untrained youths walked in here doing this Dragon's Roar thing?

"The Mage's Guild will, of course nurture what little talent you have. But you are far too old to ever train up fully."

Impotent rage at his father rose up in Will's chest before he caught the twinkle in Aurelius's eyes. *Oh.* The anger drained away, leaving him sad. His father's name was all he had left of him. It felt utterly wrong to cast that off like a ragged shirt. It was who he was. This was how the Empire repaid its loyal servitors? Do it a favor and it casually stripped you and your family of everything it was for its own convenience?

In the midst of his confusion, something took shape within Will, a nascent sense that he did not deserve what was happening to him. If he did not go along with changing his name and casting off his father's legacy, he would die swiftly and brutally at the hands of the Empire, sicced on him by his father's adopted father. After watching his friends and neighbors be slaughtered like sheep, he was not about to stand here quietly and allow the same to be done unto him.

"How can this be the right thing to do?" Will demanded. "His name is all I have left—"

"You never had his name. It was never yours. And it is not yours now," Aureilius responded with terrible urgency. "These are the *facts,* boy."

The guildmaster's expression remained intense. In desperation, Will cried, "But what about the Sleeping King? My father told me to finish the quest. To find and wake him before freedom dies. Before memory of hope is lost—"

That got a reaction out of the solinari.

Aurelius snarled and advanced upon Will with naked fury glittering in his blazing golden eyes. Will's hands rose up of their own volition in front of him. What had his father gotten him mixed up in? Had Ty known this would be the outcome of this interview? Had he sent his son here to die?

"Do not speak of that again!" the solinari snarled in palpable threat.

In his burgeoning horror and terror, a surge of magic rose up in Will greater than anything he'd ever experienced before. He did not stop to think. He merely let instinct take over.

He gathered the energy into a great, burning ball and hurled it at the elf menacing him.

Kaboom!

The explosion nearly knocked Will off his feet. It did knock Aurelius off his. It blew the guildmaster backward a half-dozen feet, in fact, slamming him into the bookcase with enough force to send disintegrated books and incinerated bits of parchment flying every which way. Flaming paper rained down like burning snow.

Will turned in panic for the door. It was not glowing. He didn't stop to ask why but merely bolted through it. Footsteps pounded on the stairs, coming up fast, along with the telltale jingle of chain mail. *The drake, Bruin.* Will raced down the hall to the stairs nonetheless. It was the only way he knew out of the building.

Will jumped down the steps two and three at a time. He rounded a bend, took a great leap, and jolted as Bruin careened into sight in front of him. Will lowered his shoulder and let his downward momentum slam him into the guard. Both of them went tumbling, but Bruin was on the bottom and wearing heavy armor, and he got the worst of it by far. Will regained his feet and tore onward while Bruin struggled to untangle his armor and hoist himself to his feet.

Will burst into the common room and raced straight for the intricate lock he'd spied upon his arrival. The key still hung on its hook beside it. *Thanks be to the Lady.* He snatched up his pack, ripped the key off the wall, and jammed it at the big lock. It slid into its slot easily and turned smoothly.

The front door ceased glowing. Bruin burst out of the stairwell and Will dived for the door. He made it outside onto the stoop before Bruin caught up with him. The guard grabbed and Will ducked, as slippery as any pickpocket dodging capture. But the guard did clip his shoulder, spinning him off balance and sending him tumbling head over heels.

Will was too off balance already, too startled by the unexpected impact, to control the fall like Ty had taught him. He landed in a heap at the foot of the guild steps, banging his knees painfully and scraping his palms on the rough cobblestones. He staggered to his feet and stumbled a few steps before regaining his wits and balance.

A quick movement caught his eye—a dark shape barreling at him from the alley beside the Mage's Guild. He braced himself instinctively, throwing up his forearm to absorb the blow. Something—someone—slammed into him, nearly knocking him off his feet again. He grabbed on to the other person to steady himself and was shocked by the inhuman face only inches from his. Covered with fine black scales, the creature looked more like a swamp monster than any sort of humanoid. But then a frantic gaze met his, eyes so black Will could not tell iris from pupil, and the terror glinting in them was entirely humanoid. A lizardman girl.

He felt the creature's hands move between them, groping for Will's pocket. A quick, almost imperceptible nod and the creature tore out of his grasp with incredible strength and raced away. Will turned in the opposite direction and ran. He didn't look back. He just ran.

He didn't stop until he was so out of breath and the cramp in his side so sharp that he had no choice but to stop. He crouched behind a rainwater barrel in a narrow alley, completely lost, his sense of direction blown. He listened carefully but heard no pursuit. For now.

He probably had that lizardman girl to thank for drawing off any who might have pursued him. Wherever she was, he wished her a successful escape. He was fairly certain the reptilian creature had put something into his pocket as opposed to picking anything out of it during their brief collision. He stuck his hand in his pocket. Sure enough, he felt a foreign object there. He pulled it out to have a look at it.

It was a thin, round disk, a thumb's length across, bulging slightly in the middle. It appeared to be made of some sort of red-brown wood. Were it not for that swollen center, it would look like a cross section of a tree branch. As it was, it looked more like an oversized seed of some kind. The whole of it was covered with fine, carved sigils that were incredibly intricate and ancient looking. And . . . that was odd . . . the disk was faintly warm. A tingle passed through his hand as he rubbed his thumb over the highly polished disk.

Just then something heavy crashed squarely into the middle of his back, throwing him forward.

"Gotcha, boy."

Will took a large, staggering step to catch himself. Something caught his side with a glancing blow, spinning him to the ground. He landed awkwardly, his right hand still clutching the wooden disk, trapped awkwardly under his chest. Searing pain shot through his upper body. It pierced him with agony so intense he could not draw a breath.

Had he been stabbed?

Will gasped at the pain ripping through his lungs. His heart felt as though it had burst and was pouring his life's blood out upon the ground. He rolled to his side and grasped frantically at his chest, feeling for a wound. His shirtfront was intact. He craned his head around awkwardly to see if there was blood upon his back. What little he could see was muddy, but not bloodied.

"Get up, you lousy piece of filth. Attack my guildmaster, will you?"

Dregs. Bruin. Will opened his mouth to speak, but the

agony in his chest was so intense he couldn't force air out to make a sound.

Bruin bent down, reaching for him. Using the tactics his father had pounded into him over years of practice, Will rolled fast, not away from but toward his attacker, slamming into the man's legs. The guild man toppled over him, his armored shins smashing Will's ribs and making him grunt in pain. But he kept rolling until he was clear of Bruin's tangled form.

Will leaped to his feet and took off running once more. At first he attributed the daggers of pain in his chest to the excessive running for his life. But as he stopped and slowly caught his breath, the pain intensified rather than dissipating. He opened his shirt to check for some injury Bruin might have inflicted without Will's being aware of it. The man worked for wizards and sorcerers, after all.

The agony centered on a single spot just to the left of Will's breastbone, about the height of his heart. He looked down. *Odd.* The wooden disk the lizardman girl had slipped in his pocket was stuck to his chest. He gave it a tug. It didn't come off.

He tried to wedge a fingernail under the edge of the flattish medallion, but it was plastered fast to his skin. And every time he tried to peel it off, the pain intensified. The thing felt as if it was slowly burning a hole through his flesh and muscle to the bone. What manner of strange object was this? What had that lizardman girl done to him?

Aurelius studied Bruin, who stood before his desk, brushing mud off of himself in disgust. His vaunted elven control slipped a notch and he asked the knight anxiously, "But he got away, though?"

"Yes, Guildmaster. As you ordered. You do realize I'm going to be harassed for years to come about letting a mere boy give me the slip like that?"

"I thank you for your sacrifice, Drake Bruin—and for your superior acting skills. Did the boy believe the ruse?"

"Oh yes. He was convinced I meant to kill him then and there."

"Perfect. And my message? You found the gentleman in question and were able to deliver it?"

"Aye. Selea said he would do as you asked. He said it was good fortune, indeed, that he happened to be in the area to aid you." Bruin added somewhat reluctantly, "And he said you would owe him a large favor for this night's work."

Aurelius nodded, wincing. He leaned back in his chair behind the charred and splintered ruins of his desk. A wry smile twitched at the corners of his mouth. "This desk is kindling. The boy packs a punch, doesn't he?"

"Like his father," Bruin commented quietly.

"Aye. Tiberius was the most talented battle mage I ever had the privilege of fighting beside."

"Agreed." Bruin was silent for a moment, then said reflectively, "Will the son live up to the father, do you think?"

"If we are to survive, he must exceed the Dragon's skill, Bruin. He must."

"Was the news he brought you so dire, then?"

Aurelius looked candidly at his drake, unable to conceal his deep unease. "I have a bad feeling about it. Very bad."

Anton hated skulking around Dupree in the middle of the night like some common criminal. He was the governor, for stars' sake. But there was one man on this forsaken continent who wielded more power than he, and it was to this man, who had summoned him, he went. Anton pulled his dark cloak and nondescript clothing closer to him, darting from shadow to shadow so as not to be seen.

At least the curfew had finally taken effect. He wanted with every ounce of his being to head for Aurelius's storehouse and finally glimpse the extent of the treasure within. Lust for the taxes he could levy on the undeclared property coursed through his blood, thick and hot.

And the small treasure room in the back . . . if that room had been breached . . . to see Aurelius's greatest magical treasures. Ahh, he would give his firstborn child to have his pick of that horde. He could all but taste the schemes of that insufferable solinari that he could upend. Emptying the special treasure room's contents into his own coffers could be disastrous to Aurelius. Set the whoreson back decades. The power he could gain . . .

But instead, here he was creeping along like a sewer rat. Summoned . . . summoned! . . . to speak with Kane. The cursed assassin had interfered with Anton at every turn ever since they'd both arrived in Dupree on the same ship.

He'd sent letters through channels weeks ago to the Imperial Assassin's Guild requesting a new round of assassinations. More specifically, he'd demanded writs for right of vengeance. He'd expected to meet with Selea Rouge, rumored to be a local master assassin, so the nulvari could deliver his writs to him.

But instead, Kane himself had answered. He was said to be master of the entire Dupree Assassin's Guild. What did it mean? Surely the assassins weren't trying to signal some sort of break with the Empire. But lo, the possibilities if they were . . .

Kane had been specific. Anton was to come alone. No guards. No girls. Although why he'd bring women to this sort of meeting Anton had no idea. Exactly what kind of governor did Kane think he was, anyway? It did hint at his reputation back in Koth, though.

Anton nodded in satisfaction. He intentionally cultivated rumors that he was an incompetent libertine accomplishing nothing of worth in Dupree, which had turned out to be not a particularly productive or profitable colony. It kept other Kothite nobles from rushing over here to replenish their coffers.

More important, his poor reputation lowered the Emperor's expectations of income and productivity from him. All the more for his own coffers—unless some rabble broke into a rich guild storehouse and took booty that he coveted for himself, curse them all. He would crush the perpetrators slowly and publicly for that. A stern lesson to the people of Dupree not to tangle with their empire's gold—

"You are late."

Anton jumped violently as a disembodied voice came out of a lane between two buildings. "Who goes?" he demanded.

"Do you answer the call or not?"

He did not appreciate being treated like some lackey. "I am here aren't I?" he snarled.

"Then come with me."

He rolled his eyes at the heavy mystery surrounding this rendezvous and followed the cloaked figure deeper into the alley. An unmarked door opened before his guide, who stepped back to let Anton enter alone.

He looked around a plain, low-beamed room. A fireplace provided the only flickering light, and two tall-backed, stuffed armchairs sat at angles to each other before the fire. Other than that, the room was completely bare. He moved around the chairs and was not surprised to see a man seated in one of them already, an average-looking fellow of middle age.

Anton didn't bother to memorize the features. He'd heard that Kane never allowed his true face to be seen by any who did not die immediately upon seeing it. No doubt tonight's facade was the result of a potion of disguise, anyway. Tricky recipe to master. Rare. Expensive. But this was Kane.

Anton took the second chair. He didn't bother to ask if they had privacy. This was the Assassin's Guild. Of course their business would be conducted in complete secrecy.

"Governor."

"Guildmaster." He noted with satisfaction that the assassin did not correct the rank. *So.* He finally had confirmation that Kane was the guildmaster. Slippery whoresons, these killers. Even that simple a piece of information was a closely guarded secret. "You wished to speak with me?"

"I require evidence before I can sign a writ approving right of vengeance."

A man of few words, this Kane. Anton said equally briefly, "I have it."

"Do you wish to pursue single deaths or something more permanent?"

Anton raised his brow to express his annoyance at being made to state the obvious. "I wish to eliminate all of the people on my list permanently."

"Permanent death is a different matter. We do not make a routine practice of signing over permission to non–guild members to pursue such a goal. To do so encroaches greatly upon our purview."

Even in matters such as this he could not escape guild wrangling? Anton marshaled his irritation enough to answer reasonably politely, "I will not object to your people carrying out the assassinations as long as my targets are removed permanently."

"What you seek is difficult to achieve."

"But not impossible. With persistence and repeated deaths, entirely achievable."

"An expensive endeavor."

He didn't bother to respond. He was the governor of Dupree. His resources were more or less unlimited.

A gloved hand reached across the space between them expectantly. The black leather was so thin and perfectly fitted that it looked like skin painted on Kane's hand. "Your list."

Anton rummaged in his belt pouch and came up with the list of names. He passed it over.

Kane perused it in leisurely fashion. "Do you invoke the right of vengeance, Governor?"

"I do." It was good to be governor. He had the power to declare his own right of vengeance against anyone who dared to cross him.

The hand was held out expectantly once more. Silently

Anton laid a sheaf of parchments in the hand. The required proof that his targets had all earned vengeance from him. It was mostly a formality for him to produce it. As governor, he could fabricate any evidence he needed and there was no one to gainsay his word.

However, the protocols must be followed. When Kane signed a writ, he was vouching for the validity of both the contract and the evidence for the contract. Should the writ later be proven invalid, Kane would die for it and not the customer contracting for the assassination. It kept the guild from running around killing anyone whom it chose. Or at least that was the reasoning. Whether it truly worked that way or not was anyone's guess.

Kane perused the documents at length. Eventually, he murmured, "Your evidence is adequate."

Not necessarily real, but adequate. After all, this was not an Imperial court of law. Kane required only enough documentation to cover his hide should someone challenge his signature on the writs.

The guildmaster added unexpectedly, "I have an asset ideally placed to execute several of these contracts."

Anton itched to know who the asset might be and which of his enemies was exposed, but that was not how the guild worked. Show too much curiosity and you were likely to become a target yourself.

"There is one target I wish for you to deal with personally, Guildmaster."

"Which one would that be?"

"The first name on the list."

"Ahh." A world of understanding was packed into that single syllable. Then, "That will be a difficult contract, indeed."

Anton didn't have a care for the difficulty of it. He was sick and tired of his enemies thwarting him, and it was time they were removed once and for all. If the cursed Boki couldn't do the job, he would see to it himself.

Kane said quietly, "I will execute that contract personally, as you request. However, there is something special I will need for the job. And I believe you are ideally suited to provide it to me, Governor. You are an accomplished alchemist, are you not?"

Anton nodded in the affirmative. He would move heaven and earth to give Kane whatever he needed to get that particular job done. But when the assassin named his requirement, it gave even him pause. Whether the assassin planned to use the item in doing the killing or merely take it in payment for the killing Anton did not know. He knew better than to ask.

He answered quickly, "I will get it for you."

Kane named an additional price for the other killings that would beggar most men. But he was not most men. He was Governor Anton Constantine, and he'd been looting Dupree for many years. Anton nodded and raised his right hand in solemn promise. "We have a deal."

"Done."

Will had to get moving. But he felt terrible. His head swam and he alternated between shivering and sweating. He'd emptied his stomach long ago, but his body still heaved as if he had not. He felt on the verge of collapsing but dared not stop moving. Soldiers ranged throughout the city still, looking for looters and rabble-rousers. Twice he heard troops capturing and beating their victims close by.

He had to find the Heart building. Rosana would expect him there. And maybe he could get some healing for whatever ailed him.

He dragged himself along with the vague idea of also

finding the black lizardman girl and getting her to take this stupid wood thing off him. His thoughts limped in desperate circles along with his feet. But he found no answers in the town's muddy bowels.

Despair swallowed him. He had no supper, no roof over his head, and no coin to buy either. His message was delivered, his grand quest finished before it began. The man who was supposed to help him had instead taken away his name and threatened to kill him. His parents were dead, his home destroyed. What was he supposed to do now?

A tavern. Maybe he could tuck himself into a corner and go unnoticed for the night. Maybe work for a meal. A shout went up ahead of him, and three soldiers broke into a run, rushing toward him.

He backed up a few steps, ducked into a side street, and ran for his life. If he was lost before, now he was turned around and confused to boot in the maze of narrow, dark streets. He didn't run far; he was simply too exhausted to go on. He crouched in a fetid alley, dizzy with sickness and fear.

He ducked behind a pile of empty, decrepit barrels. Something—someone—had just slipped into the alley from the far end. Someone up to no good, if the way the person was sliding from shadow to shadow was any indication. The cloaked and hooded stranger stopped in a recessed doorway not far ahead of him and froze there, nearly invisible, as if waiting to meet someone.

Will debated what to do. He dared not reveal himself to the dangerous-looking stranger. Then another figure came up from behind Will, gliding past his hiding place silently, and he was left with no choice but to stay put. The second person was shorter and stockier than the first. But he, too, wore a dark cloak and deep cowl.

The first figure waited until the second was abreast of him before stepping out of the doorway. Shorty lurched.

Whispered snatches of a whispered conversation floated to Will.

". . . entire southern quadrant and west wall locked down . . ."

". . . riot down by the Red Boar Inn . . ."

". . . army's on a rampage . . ."

Then Shorty whispered brusquely, "I have a job for you—"

"Who and how many?" Will thought he heard a sigh in the tall stranger's whispery voice.

"Three for you. There are others, but I can take them easily enough."

The tall one muttered, "The writs?"

Shorty rustled under his cloak and produced a narrow leather tube. "Here. Signed by Kane himself."

Will bit back a gasp. The name was legend. These men weren't common murderers. Worse. Much worse. They were Imperial assassins if they were passing around writs of execution. He was *dead* if these men discovered him eavesdropping on Assassin's Guild business.

The scroll tube disappeared under the tall one's cloak as he murmured so frigidly Will felt the cold ripple across his skin, "Consider it done."

The short man nodded tersely and departed, slipping away into the night. After Shorty had disappeared, the tall figure strode directly toward Will's pile of barrels. Stopped before it.

A harsh voice slid from the darkness of the hood. "You may come out, now."

Will hesitated for an instant, but the shadowy figure glided unerringly to his hiding place and loomed above him, waiting. Menace wafted off the figure like vapor curling off ice.

Dead. I am dead. He'd survived a Boki attack and a homicidal guildmaster, but there would be no escape from this faceless assassin.

Surreptitiously, Will unbuttoned the loop holding his dagger down. And there was always his uncertain magic. Pitiful protection against the danger emanating from the tall form before him. Reluctantly, he stood.

"How much did you hear?" a half-whispered rasp demanded.

"Nothing," Will replied nervously.

"You lie." A pause. "But I don't suppose it matters. Anton's soldiers will kill you long before they stop to question you on who or what you've seen."

Maybe it was fatigue that made him reckless. Or maybe he was just too sick to have a care for his well-being. Will blurted, "Why don't you just kill me here and now? Then I can't carry any tales."

The tall form visibly recoiled. "I have no writ of execution for you. You are perfectly safe with me until I get one . . . or until you threaten me and my . . . associates."

A delicate way of putting it. Will replied carefully, "Truly, sir. I only heard a few snippets, and they made little sense."

An almost soundless chuckle. "Now that was honestly said."

Silence descended upon the alley. Faint sounds drifted to them on the night air of shouting in the distance. A ruckus of some kind, but far away.

"You must get off the street," the stranger announced.

"Actually, I was thinking the same thing. If you know a place where I can go, I'll gladly avail myself of it."

"You look sick. The Heart is the destination for you, methinks."

Hope flickered in his breast. Was it possible that this

menacing stranger would take him exactly where he wanted to go? Careful not to sound too eager, he replied, "Actually, I do not feel well."

"Come, youngling."

Youngling? That was an elven term. Was this person an elf then? Or was he just using the word to throw Will off?

The cloaked figure continued, "We must go. Now." His voice dropped into a bare whisper. "Evil comes this way."

A chill snaked its way down Will's spine. The dire warning had a prophetic ring about it. "What sort of evil?" he breathed.

"Pray you never learn of it firsthand. But I fear that will not be your fate—for I believe it comes for you."

Evil? Coming for him? Will had no more time to wonder what his impromptu companion meant, for the man froze abruptly.

The hooded figure breathed, "Get down."

Will dropped into a crouch, easing back into his original hidey-hole while the stranger swept past him and into a doorway across from Will's position. The man's black cloak blended seamlessly into the shadows. Will was startled at how totally the tall stranger disappeared. One moment he was there, and the next he wasn't. Had Will not seen him hide in that alcove, he'd never have known the man was there. It was uncanny. And, frankly, unnerving.

A pair of soldiers turned into the alley from the nearest end, walking and talking noisily. ". . . see the look on 'is face when that crone whacked 'is knees wit' 'er broom?"

The second soldier guffawed as the pair strode past Will and the cloaked stranger's position. "Bet the old witch won' do that again. 'E laid her flat, 'e did."

The two soldiers swaggered on down the alley, laughing. They passed no more than an arm's length from the cloaked man and never saw him. Will let out a relieved breath as the soldiers rounded the corner and disappeared from sight.

The stranger materialized out of the shadows like some sort of specter. "Let us make haste to the Heart."

He probably shouldn't follow the cloaked man like a lamb to the slaughter, but his mind was so fuzzy he could think of nothing else to do. Besides, he got the distinct impression it would be the last foolish thing he ever did to cross this man.

They made their cautious way across Dupree over the next half hour, easing from shadow to shadow, pausing often to listen for approaching soldiers. The city was crawling with them, and the only townspeople risking crossing the army's path this eve were being as furtive as Will and his secretive guide. The way the stranger avoided detection bordered on unnatural.

After giving him a strict order not to move from his current hiding spot, the stranger left him in a dark shadow and slipped around a corner. Several minutes passed and Will's curiosity got the better of him. He crouched low to peek around the corner of a building. Great flying dragons, it was a guild square! With soldiers lounging at even intervals all around the open space.

He spied out the guild hall's trim and then fervently wished he hadn't. He was plastered against the outer wall of the Slaver's Guild. Had he just handed himself over to an Imperial Slaver?

Syreena Wingblade reveled in the stiff breeze ruffling the white feathers that covered her scalp where humans would have hair. An urge to spread her arms and fly nearly overcame her. Not that avarians could actually fly. She could soar for a short period of time and even land lightly out of it, but the peregrine falcon portion of her spirit still longed for true flight.

"You have everything you need for your journey, Lady Wingblade?"

She turned to the handsome kindari who had been so courteous to her since she arrived in the Imperial Seat. On behalf of the Queen of Quantaine, Talissar had lent her rooms within the queen's quarters, and he'd even provided a carriage and escort for her down to the docks and the Black Ship *Courageous*. Not that she, as an Imperial noble, needed protection. Who would dare to harm her and incur the wrath of the Empire, particularly at the foot of the Seat of Eternity itself?

A sailor cried a debarkation warning, and Talissar murmured, "Safe journey to you, then, my lady."

Strange journey, more like it. As far as she could tell, she was being posted to Dupree to be some sort of official observer. Of whom she knew not, although she could guess. The governor, Anton Constantine, had a dodgy reputation in Koth. He had an even dodgier reputation in their mutual home kingdom of Culdroone. In fact, her family had been destroyed by the very cabal Anton's family was rumored to control, the Coil. It had been her family's debt to the Coil that landed her in indentured servitude.

Although she supposed she should hold no grudges given how her life had worked out. Her indenture contract had been purchased by a minor noble so she could be a companion to his daughter. Saving him and his daughter from a bandit attack had earned her freedom and enough recognition to be appointed steward to a young ogre chieftain. She'd helped him ascend his nation's throne and ultimately earned her noble title. And here she was, on her way to monitor a Coil scion. Odd how her life had come round full circle.

She half-suspected that someone or some group had pulled strings to get her sent here.

For whom she was supposed to observe she knew not. Her guess was the Council of Wind, a secret avarian group. Regardless of who'd maneuvered her over here, undoubtedly her purpose was supposed to be to observe Anton Constantine. Despite being effectively banished to Haelos far away from court, he was nonetheless a powerful player in Kothite politics—and not just for his Coil ties. His wealth was rumored to be immense, as were the untapped resources of this young colony on a giant, largely unexplored continent.

The efficiency with which the ship's crew cast off and got under way impressed her. They did not hoist sails, as close to the mountains as they were; the winds swirled far too unpredictably in this valley for safe sailing. Rather, they relied on water elementals to propel the ship forward for now. She expected that, if the wind didn't do the job once they reached the open sea, air elementals would be called to fill the sails and propel the Black Ship across the mighty Abyssmal Sea with all due haste. The Merr who controlled the undersea realms had never submitted to Koth and were rumored to have chased the Empire out of their watery domain in no uncertain terms. It was not wise to tarry overlong upon Merr waters.

Talissar had mentioned that the journey to Haelos should take three months, plus or minus, depending on the weather and winds. She hoped to spend that time learning more about the Black Ships and their awesome capabilities. She knew they contained the finest technology the Empire had acquired, but from whence it came was a closely guarded secret she secretly hoped to unravel.

The *Courageous*'s captain, Lord Captain Kodo, had invited the ship's guests to a welcoming dinner that evening.

Perhaps he would tell her more of his vessel then. In the meantime, she had brought a book with her to pass the time. A history of Dupree. Or at least as much of a history as the Emperor wished for his subjects to know of it. Such was the power of the Kothite Empire. Nothing had preceded it, and nothing would ever follow it. The Kothites were truly eternal.

Sometimes she wondered idly what life might have been like if there was a "before Koth." Would there have been freedom of thought? Independence? Choice? Or would those concepts have been as foreign then as they were now?

Mayhap recently colonized Dupree would shed some light on the mystery. Haelos had only been discovered and brought under the Emperor's fist less than two centuries ago. With a natural-born historian's eagerness, she turned her gaze to the north.

A powerful hand slapped over Will's mouth, stifling his yelp of startlement, yanking him back against a tall, lean body that felt made of living iron. "I told you to stay put."

Panicked, Will took a deep breath to slam the cloaked man with all the magic he had.

"Power down, boy," the stranger bit out. "You will draw attention we can ill afford. Have patience. We are nearly to safety. But first we must pass these slavers."

The very lack of concern in the man's voice was all that kept Will from blasting him. What did this man know about magic that Will didn't? Obviously, he had some defense against it that made him oblivious to it.

Will's terror surged again, however, at the man's next words. "Hold out your wrists so I can put these manacles on you."

"No!"

"Keep your voice down!" the stranger snapped.

"I will not let you handcuff me and lead me to the Slaver's Guild like a witless sheep!"

"I'm taking you to the Heart, which is in the next square over, and past those guards is the quickest route to get there. The manacles are a ruse to get past them." He added dryly, "Somehow, I think I'll pass better for a slaver and you a potential slave rather than the other way round."

Will stared into the black void of the hood doubtfully. He didn't trust this assassin for a second.

Apparently, Will's reservations must have shown in his eyes, for the stranger murmured, "If I meant to kill you, I would not be so unsubtle as to leap upon you here and now and slit your throat."

"Unsubtle?"

The tall man didn't answer, but a distinct aura of exasperation rolled off his silhouetted form. And for some reason, Will took comfort from it. It wasn't the emotion of a murderer or an avaricious slaver. He threw caution to the winds and asked, "How would you kill me if you were being subtle?"

"A bold question, boy."

In for a copper, in for a gold. "Too bold for you to answer honestly?"

The stranger made a sound almost like choked laughter, but his answer, when it came, was delivered in a silky tone a man might use to seduce a beautiful woman. "If I wished to kill you subtly, I would appear to help you. Gain your trust. Turn you over to other apparently trustworthy people, who might or might not realize they were doing my work. I would maneuver them wittingly or unwittingly into leading you into a trap. The sort of trap that, when it killed you, all who heard of it would know it to be an unfortunate accident. No questions, no suspicions, no associations or trail of blame that could possibly lead back to me."

The assassin spoke of murder as reverently as if it were the highest of art forms, and he a master practitioner. His words and demeanor sent chills down Will's spine.

The stranger said lightly, "The city is crawling with soldiers this night. If I were to kill you now, your body would be discovered quickly and a hunt for your killer initiated. It would make for an . . . inconvenient . . . getaway. If, indeed, I had decided to kill you, your death would be inevitable. I would have no need to be in a hurry about it."

Will believed without question that this man could do as he said. Something the assassin had said did pique Will's curiosity, however. Why would a manhunt be initiated for anyone who killed him? He was a no-account youth from the hinterlands. To the authorities, his life was less than meaningless. Certainly not cause for a manhunt. Unless something had happened regarding him and his news of the Boki attack that he was not aware of—

"Is there news this evening?" Will asked cautiously.

His companion went stock-still. "What do you mean?"

"I was merely curious," he replied hastily. "A great many soldiers seem to be out and about."

The cloak lifted slightly as if the stranger shrugged. "All the more reason to get you off the street." He held out the manacles once more. "I swear upon my word of honor, I will not lock these. Look." The stranger attached the metal bracelet around his own black-gloved wrist and seemed to snap it shut. "Twist your wrist, so, and it pops open."

Clever. "Are those trick manacles?" Will asked.

"No, they're real. It's all in half-latching them. If someone ever cuffs you, turn your wrist sideways as the bracelet is locked, and the latch may only partially catch. Hold out just one wrist. I'll show you."

Will became so absorbed in learning the twist and flex

trick that he momentarily forgot where they were and the stakes at risk.

"Got the hang of it?" the stranger murmured.

"Aye. Let's do it," Will replied jauntily.

"Not so brave, lad. This night calls for caution." He added wryly, "Subtlety." He glanced out into the square and then back at Will. "Remember this. Bravery is not always the best course of action. Patience, prudence, and cunning are also virtues."

Will nodded, perplexed at the teacher-like tone the man had taken with him. "Right then. On with the manacles."

Will fancied he caught a flash of white inside the hood as if the stranger smiled. But then the cold metal bracelets clasped around Will's wrists and the moment was at hand to stroll forth among all those soldiers. *Slave-like. Act slave-like.* As the stranger attached a short rope to the manacles by which to lead him, Will couldn't suppress a shudder.

They stepped out of the alley.

Immediately the nearest set of guards came to attention and one of them stepped into their path. "Who goes there?"

"An Imperial Slaver on official business!" Will's companion snarled. "Who dares stand in my way?" The cloaked stranger straightened to his full height, seeming to gain several inches in height and breadth all of a sudden. He cut an imposing, if not downright intimidating, figure towering over the tallest soldier by a good hand span.

The soldier backed away hastily. Will's companion gave a sharp yank at the rope. Will stumbled forward and went down to his knees.

"Get up, you lazy cur!" his captor snapped.

The soldiers laughed as Will climbed to his feet awkwardly without the use of his hands. He'd torn one knee of his pants, and cold mud slid down his shin as the rope yanked once more. This time he was ready for it, though, and managed to keep his feet. The stranger's long strides carried him past the Slaver's Guild so quickly Will had to jog every few steps to keep up.

A voice called from behind them, "Oi there! I thought you said you was on Slaver's Guild business."

The stranger stopped so fast Will ran into him from behind. It earned him a sharp elbow to the ribs and another snapped admonition, this time to watch where he went. Will doubled over in pain. Carrying the act a little far, wasn't the guy?

The stranger turned deliberately. Stared down the soldiers before enunciating clearly, "This slave is sick. I'm taking him to the Heart to get him cured so I can sell him. Have you got a problem with that?"

On cue, since he was already bent over, Will made a heaving sound. It was not entirely an act. Out of the corner of his eye, he saw the soldiers leap back.

"Uhh, right. We'll be letting you get on with it, then. Don' wan' no contagion spreading through the city."

Without deigning to reply, Will's companion whirled and strode onward, dragging Will along behind him like a lamb on a leash. They passed down several side streets and emerged into another square, this one dominated by the giant, white-washed Heart building with its jaunty red and yellow trim. A red heart was painted dead center on the front door, five straight red points and five curved yellow sun rays arrayed around it.

The cloaked man took off his glove to pound on the door, and Will stared in disbelief at the coal black skin of his temporary captor. Was he a nulvari? One of the fabled dark elves of Under Urth? The glove slipped back on, and the black-on-black flesh disappeared.

A healer opened the portal, peering out into the night. "We are not dispensing potions to purify blood from the effects of liquor tonight owing to excessive demand. Come back on the morrow if you've a severe headache and we'll give you a powder to ease the ache in your skull." The door started to close.

"Hold," the cloaked man said with unmistakable authority. "I come on other business. Tell the High Matriarch a friend calls."

"How did you know she is here? She has only arrived within the hour!"

"Just give her my message!" the nulvari snapped.

"And what is that friend's name?"

"Give her this." The stranger held out his fist and Will glimpsed a brief, metallic flash but did not see what object was contained within the grip. A ring mayhap? Or a token of some kind?

It was no more than a minute until the healer was back at the door. "One moment, please. I must drop the shield."

"Be quick about it. This is no night to have your wizard's lockdown," the stranger admonished.

"Enter," the healer directed from out of sight.

Will followed the stranger inside the Heart chapter house. It looked much like the Castlegate Falls Heart common room at a glance, albeit less threadbare. A common room dominated the ground floor, and several people wearing the Heart's white tabards ranged around it tending to people in various stages of injury and healing.

These sorts of magics were foreign to Will, and he watched in fascination as a mage worked, a glow trickling from both his hands where they lay on a man's clearly broken forearm. The patient moaned and writhed a bit but didn't seem to be in unbearable pain as the bones were being knit back together

The cloaked stranger murmured, "You may release the manacles."

Will did so with alacrity. He was roundly sick of being hauled around like a piece of meat. That was enough of slavery for him, thanks be.

Another flash of white indicated the stranger had smiled deep within his cloak. "Disliked shackles, did you? Never forget what they feel like."

"Yes, Master," Will said with a bite of sarcasm.

His companion's head whipped in Will's direction. *What?* What had he said to merit such a reaction? After all, the fellow was preaching at him like a schoolmaster.

The healer who'd let them in returned. "Follow me. High Matriarch Lenora is waiting for you."

Stars! Who was this cloaked man he'd taken up with to merit an instant audience with the highest-ranking healer in the entire colony, and late at night at that? Not to mention the nulvari had faced down the soldiers in Slaver's Square as if he were the governor himself.

Will followed the men upstairs, a few guttering candles in sconces lighting their way. Their Heart guide knocked on an age-blackened door.

"Enter!" The female voice was warm. Pleasant. But strong. And it turned out to belong to a human woman with blue, twinkling eyes and dark hair mussed as if she tugged at it often.

Will's companion stepped forward, his black cloak billowing like the wings of night itself. He pushed his hood back to reveal a shock of brilliant red hair in stark contrast to his midnight black complexion. *Nulvari.* Will stared at the elf. His kind were exceedingly rare in these parts. At least aboveground.

The High Matriarch cried out in obvious pleasure, "Selea. Welcome! And who have we here?" She had spotted Will.

For his part, Will gaped in shock. *Selea? Could it be?* Was this the man his father had named as one of his companions on his quest to find the Sleeping King? An assassin? What in stars' name had his father been doing keeping company with one such as this? Not to mention this cold stranger hardly struck Will as the type to go haring off across hill and dale in search of some mythic sleeping king. The more he learned of his father, the more questions piled up about him.

If only Ty were alive to explain all of this. To tell Will everything. He missed his parents almost more than he could bear at times. He would even be glad for his father's stern visage and frequent criticisms if Ty were but alive to deliver them.

Selea spoke, interrupting Will's despondent thoughts. "I bring you a lad in need of healing and a safe place to spend the night."

He really wished they'd all quit referring to him as a lad, or boy, or youngling.

"Is he in trouble with the law?" Lenora asked shrewdly.

"Not that I know of." The elf fixed his sinister gaze on Will. "Are the authorities looking for you?"

"Nobody even knows my name," Will answered carefully. He wasn't exactly sure where a lynch mob featuring the Celestial Order of the Dragon and the Mage's Guildmaster ranked on the scale of official or unofficial, but he didn't particularly feel like asking.

The matriarch shot him a penetrating look. "I hear evasion in your voice. But given the company you arrived in, I will take your word at face value for now." Her voice and expression abruptly waxed serious. "Know, however, that I will not allow you to abuse the sanctity of this house and its special status within the Empire. We do not harbor criminals."

Will frowned. He knew little of the Heart. "What special status?"

The healer smiled warmly once more. "That question requires a very long answer. Suffice it to say that the House of the Healing Heart enjoys a certain . . . standing . . . in the Empire."

"How did that come to be?" Will asked, ever curious.

"An equally long answer. Another time perhaps." She turned back to the dark elf. "What danger follows this young man that you bring him to me?"

Selea shrugged. "I cannot say for certain. An old acquaintance asked me to look after him."

Who in Dupree knew of him to ask this strange man to take care of him? Aurelius? But he and his knight had tried to kill Will—

Of a sudden Selea's comments about how to kill him subtly took on new and alarming significance. The elf had already gained his trust and brought him to trustworthy people! "Why you? And why this boy?" Lenora demanded bluntly.

"Rumors and portents," the nulvari answered vaguely.

"What's this?" the matriarch blurted, startled. "What portents?"

"Mostly mumbo jumbo. But so many seers are reporting similar visions and prophecies that there may be some small value in listening to them."

The matriarch's blue eyes twinkled. "Yon boy looks like a simple street urchin to me. A sick, hungry, tired, and filthy one. Hardly the stuff of portents and prophecies, old man."

Old man? Will glanced sidelong at the nulvari. He certainly didn't move like an aged person.

"Who gives these prophecies of yours?"

Selea shrugged. "I am not at liberty to say."

Lenora looked over at Will with renewed interest. "Well then. I guess you're spending the night here, young man."

"Thank you." He gave the pair the short, formal bow that his mother had taught him.

The nulvari startled Will by returning the bow courteously, as elven etiquette dictated.

Lenora waved off the formality. "So tell me. Who is out to harm you?"

Perhaps it was the exchange of bows that put him in mind of it, but an evasive response born of inspiration that was purely his mother's smooth social skills struck Will. He answered lightly, "My mother, I should think. When she realizes I have not returned home this night, she'll grab up the nearest frying pan and come looking for me with murder on her mind."

Lenora chuckled while a dagger of white-hot grief shot through Will's gut. If only she were alive to do such a thing, he'd gladly let her catch him.

The matriarch turned back to the nulvari. "What does the oracle speak of?"

"These lands lie at a crossroads. Great events come together to create a crisis. A long quest nears completion, and it shall lead to death."

Will jolted. Surely the prophets did not speak of his quest! He was done with all of that. He just wanted to get this stupid piece of wood unstuck from his chest and go home. No heroics for him, no sir.

Lenora asked sharply, "Has the governor gotten wind of this?"

Selea answered dryly, "I doubt the governor pays heed to

any prophecy. He believes he has complete control of all that occurs on Haelos."

The High Matriarch shook her head. "Arrogance has been the downfall of the great before, and it shall be again." She led the way back to the common room. On the way down the dark stairs, Selea hung back a little, blocking Will from joining the matriarch ahead of them.

Will took the opportunity to whisper quickly to the nulvari, "You knew my father."

"Did I?" Selea asked blandly. "I know a great many people."

Urgently, sensing he had little time to banter with this elf, Will asked, "Where would you look if you sought a sleeping king?"

Selea stumbled and jerked himself upright with a quiet curse. "I'd look in his bed, boy."

"Where would you tell the son of Tiberius De'Vir to look?"

"Any De'Vir would know to search in the heart of the Forest of Thorns for both king and crown. But the De'Vir's are dead." He moved away from Will rapidly, pulling up his hood as he hurried down the stairs, effectively concealing his face and race once more.

When they arrived in the common room, Will thanked Selea for his safe escort and got back a single terse nod and the distinct impression that the fellow would rather not have Will bow to him again in the elven fashion in this public venue. Likewise, the assassin gave him no more chance to mention his father or ask questions.

As quickly as he'd appeared to Will before, Selea slipped out into the night and disappeared. *Probably was off to find himself one of the poor sods named on his writs and kill him. Could the Heart interfere in an Assassin's Guild matter?* Will was tempted to find out and tell Lenora of the writs he'd seen delivered earlier, except some small kernel of a wish to survive held him back.

Selea hurried through the night feeling as if a ghost breathed down his neck. Depths below, Tiberius's boy was just like him. Impatient, aggressive, confident to a fault. Quick-witted, though. And eager. Perhaps Aurelius's assessment of the lad was not so far wrong. The solinari thought there was a chance the lad could pick up the quest where his father had left off. Maybe even complete it. Still, the boy was barely off his mother's apron strings.

Or was it merely that he had grown old? He passed a hand across his face. His reflexes were not what they once were. He had given thought to retiring more than once, lately.

Leland's town house loomed and Selea knocked quietly upon the door. The guard recognized him on sight and let him in quickly.

"Is he awake?" Selea asked without preamble.

"Yes, sir. In his study."

He didn't need the man-at-arms to show him the way and told him so quietly. Selea passed through the comfortable home and wondered briefly what it would be like to live in one place for years on end. To put down roots. To surround himself with familiar and comfortable things—

—*Bah*. It was softness to think thus. He was not done for just yet.

He opened the study door to let himself in and his old friend glanced up from his desk. Leland leaned back in his chair, smiling broadly. It had taken Selea years, but he'd trained this human not to engage him in the fist-pumping and back-thumping hugs that his race seemed to favor. He supposed their excessively short life spans made them prone to those dramatic displays of emotion.

"Selea. What brings you to my home at this unholy hour?"

"I saw De'Vir's boy."

That made Leland jump out of his seat. "He's here? In Dupree?"

"I just delivered him to the Heart. Something is wrong with him."

"Wrong? How?"

Selea shrugged. "I'm no healer. But the boy's sick. Looked like some sort of slow poison to me."

"What kind?"

He shrugged. "I did not recognize its smell."

Leland rolled his eyes. "If you do not know the poison, I doubt the Heart will do better. I would trust you over any healer in this land to recognize a poison and its source."

It was true enough. The great assassins did not rely only on their blades to kill. The art of killing lay in using the best means to accomplish the end. Sometimes a contract must seem an accident, while others it must loudly proclaim itself to be an assassination. He shrugged at Leland. "Mayhap it is an actual sickness."

"If so, the Heart will take care of it."

"Not this, I think. It was complex. Powerful." He hesitated and then added, "Old."

"Old disease?"

He spread his gloved hands wide. "I merely report my impressions."

"What would you have me do?"

"The lad is going to need special treatment. Expensive healing. He did not strike me as having the resources to finance his own cure."

"Ahh, yes. The age-old dilemma of healing for the rich while the poor die in droves."

"It is no dilemma!" Selea snapped. "It is merely the way of the world."

"It is the way of the Empire," Leland corrected.

Selea chose not to reply. The nulvari nation was closely aligned with the Empire, and he had spent his life in service to that same Empire. His honor-bound featly oath was given to an Imperial guild, and above all, nulvari valued their honor. Regardless of his personal opinion of the Empire, he was still its creature, no matter how reluctantly he might serve. Although that did not guarantee he always worked toward the Empire's ends by the same means as it might wish of him.

"I may have something—someone—who can heal De'Vir's boy," Leland announced, interrupting Selea's grim train of thought.

"Who?"

"An arch-mage has wandered into my home. A young healer. If anyone has the power to cure the lad, it will be her. She sleeps now to restore her powers, but I will take her to the Heart in the morn."

Selea nodded briskly, his errand accomplished.

"Is there any other news?" Leland asked.

It was kind of Hyland not to ask for specifics but rather to let him dictate what information he was at liberty to share. He answered carefully, "Ki'Raiden led the attack on Hickory Hollow where one Ty the cobbler resided."

Leland sucked in a sharp breath at that. "That must be the Boki war party we've received reports of. Why do orcs move against our old friend after all this time?"

"The Boki hold their grudges as well as anyone."

"It must be more than that," Leland declared.

"Like what?" It was Selea's turn to probe delicately for news.

Leland replied, "Mayhap their soothsayers are seeing the same portents that ours are. Something big is on the move. Powerful. Ancient forces step into the game."

Selea nodded slowly. That was in line with what he was hearing. A deep game was in play now. Deep enough for him to activate his sleepers? To call in decades' worth of favors? "What is De'Vir's boy up to?" he blurted uncharacteristically.

"The way Aurelius describes it, the lad plans to take up where we left off."

So. The boy truly had known what he asked when he'd whispered of a sleeping king. "Does he stand a chance of succeeding?"

Leland shrugged. "You tell me. You've met the boy. I have not."

Selea weighed the thing, making quick mental lists of the pluses and minuses of the boy's character. Finally, slowly, he said, "He might. With the right help, he just might."

Leland answered simply, "Then let us see to it he gets the help he needs."

Selea nodded in a decision more momentous than Leland knew. *It is time.* The long years of waiting were over. It was both a relief and a fearful thing to know the moment of final action was upon him at last.

He took his leave quickly, slipping out into the night that was his true home to move the next piece in the game he now knew for certain to be afoot. How had the Boki found Tiberius after all these years? The possible answers were few and the likely answer obvious.

A deep game indeed . . .

High Matriarch Lenora called out, "Novice Rosana! Your young man has finally arrived."

"Will!" a female voice squealed.

He barely had time to brace himself before Rosana flung herself at him as if she had not seen him in years. She was as slender and lithe as a doe in his arms, and a strange warmth passed through him at her open display of affection and concern. Mayhap it was his fever worsening.

"You look terrible," she announced with her usual bluntness.

He grinned down at her. "And you are more beautiful than ever."

She cast her gaze down at the floor as a pretty blush climbed her cheeks. Will stared at her downcast eyelashes. Never had he seen any so long and luxurious. She blinked. Time slowed and the moment stretched out in slow motion. Her eyes fluttered open as gently as a butterfly's wings in the first light of morn. The room and its noise faded away, leaving the two of them alone in an otherworldly place where faint whispers of a natural magic older than time twined around them, invisibly drawing them to each other.

"Have I finally found a way to silence you?" he teased gently.

She looked up at him, her black eyes snapping with laughter, her mouth opening on a retort, but Lenora interrupted briskly, "Feed the boy and then show him to a bed. He looks like he could use some rest."

Will flashed a grateful grin at the matriarch, then followed Rosana to the kitchen. She wore a dress tonight and not the sturdy traveling clothes of before. Her waist was tiny, her shoulders narrow. The only girl even close to his age back in the hollow was Helga Larsdotter. She was fully a hand taller and broader than Will and she'd been as strong as a lumberjack . . . not exactly a paragon of petite femininity.

As Rosana gestured for him to sit at the long trestle table

while she ladled up a bowl of what smelled like mutton stew, he was stunned by the effect just gazing at her had upon his breathing. Or maybe it was just his illness worsening. Her mouth—a thoroughly lush affair—curved into a little smile, causing a dimple to wink merrily in her cheek. She was the most ravishing creature he'd ever laid eyes on.

"Any news of my family and your friends?" he asked.

"No." She set the bowl of stew before him and he glanced up in time to catch tears spilling over onto her cheeks before she dashed them away. His own heart fell like a stone. The meal, so enticing a moment before, looked completely unappetizing of a sudden.

"No one?" he whispered. Not her colleagues? Not his parents? None of the other villagers from the hollow? *No one?*

"No one. I checked the death logs myself." She sat down on the bench beside him. "Eat. You look like you need strength."

For her, and only for her, he forced a spoonful of the hot stew down. Another. And another. How much he ended up eating he could not remember later. Enough to ease the gnawing ache in his gut at any rate.

"Better?" she asked eventually.

The meal had made the worst of his physical symptoms pass. But it had done nothing for the hurt in his heart. Not wishing to disappoint Rosana, however, he answered stoutly, "Better. I vow, my stomach near gnawed a hole through my spine before I got here."

"What took you so long? I was sick with worry, what with the rioting and violence earlier."

She was worried about him? The warmth of the bracing meal spread well beyond his belly of a sudden.

"Something passing strange happened to me tonight. . . ." He felt foolish telling her a piece of wood was stuck to his chest and he was afraid to pull it off. Heat climbed his neck and spread across his face.

"You are hurt?" she asked in quick concern.

Better to just show her. He untied the neck closure of his shirt and exposed the disk of wood.

She leaned forward, interested. Stars above, she smelled of vanilla. "What is that?"

He shrugged, feigning a casualness he did not feel. "I don't know. I was hoping you could tell me."

She scooted close to him. Her small hands were warm and soft against his chest, and abruptly his heart beat far too hard against his ribs. He yelped as she tried to wedge a fingernail under the edge of the disk to pry at it. Embarrassed, he mumbled, "I already tried that. It is stuck fast."

"How did it get there?"

"I picked it up"—his face felt hot at the half-lie but he forged on—"and then I fell with it in my grasp. It just . . . stuck . . . to me."

"Have you tried an alchemical solvent to release the glue that holds it in place?"

He hadn't thought of something like that. Unfortunately, alchemical potions were hard to obtain. And even if a solvent was available, he had no coin to purchase such a thing. His face burned even hotter.

"We have solvents in the storeroom, upstairs. If you're finished eating, we shall try one, yes?"

He followed her up a narrow servants' stair, glad that his forest-trained eyesight adjusted quickly to darkness. Only a single candle on each landing lit the way, and lithe shadows of his escort danced upon the walls. She led him to the third floor and then down a dark hallway to a low, iron-banded portal.

"Hold the door open while I light a candle," she murmured.

He stepped forward, close enough that her scent wrapped around him again, warm and delectable. The heat and nearness of her drugged him until he could hardly think as they slipped inside the storeroom.

She muttered over her shoulder, "Help me search the alchemy globes. We're looking for a poison labeled 'alchemical solvent.' Try this shelf of contact poisons."

The shelf at eye level held long, narrow boxes, each holding a row of round glass globes the size of plums cradled in a bed of straw. Some of the globes were cloudy, some clear; a few held brightly colored gases within. There must be thirty of them. He cast his gaze lower to other shelves holding various bottles and jars of pourable and drinkable poisons. He'd never dreamed the Heart had such riches!

As he examined labels where Rosana indicated, he was grateful for once to his mother for forcing him to learn to read despite his loud and frequent protestations that it was a worthless skill he would never use. His parents had taught him in secret and exhorted him never to let anyone know he could read. They said it would give him an advantage in life when people assumed he was not literate because he was a peasant. It wasn't that reading and ciphering were illegal. They were merely too time-consuming for peasants to learn in the midst of their daily race to survive, and hence associated only with the wealthy and those who had attained rank within the Empire.

The labels contained both the name of the contents and the expiration date of each. He noticed that none of the solvents were more than a handful of months old. Alchemy must expire in about the same time frame as potions and scrolls, then. Their magics usually held for no more than a year or so. Unless, of course, they were stored in special—and rare—containers that could protect magic from draining away.

"Here it is!" Rosana exclaimed, carefully lifting a narrow bottle.

Will held the candle for her while she relocked the storeroom behind them. Then she blew out the light to conserve it. Something he'd expect of a frugal housewife but not an Imperial guild member.

"Is the Heart not as wealthy as the other guilds, then?" he asked.

He made out the silhouette of Rosana's shoulders shrugging ahead of him. "We do well enough. But if you had a choice between spending your gold on candles or on potions and scrolls to save lives, which would you pick?"

"I see your point."

"Being a healer is not about wealth or power. Well," she amended, "we are powerful but not in the way you might think."

"In what way?"

"The *Kaer* heals common people. Births their babies. Mends broken limbs and cures diseases and infections that otherwise kill common people. And we do resurrections, of course. Who is the average peasant going to love more—an Empire that takes his bread and coin in taxes, or a House of Healing Heart that saves his life and asks only what he can afford to pay in return?"

Will chewed on her words as they neared the staircase. Her comments, although they made perfect sense, danced dangerously close to treason. But then, the gypsies had been hounded and harassed by the Empire since anyone could remember. She had reason to dislike the Empire. Still, he'd had no idea the Heart held such a powerful position until she pointed it out. He asked thoughtfully, "Does the Heart have need of force casters, perchance?"

"Why do you ask?" Rosana replied, startled.

He shrugged and hoped he looked casual.

"The Heart looks mainly for casters of spirit magic. Force is mostly a battle magic. Not sort of thing we use much around here. But maybe the Royal Order of the Sun could use it."

"Who are they?"

She rounded on him in surprise. "You've never heard of the Royal Order of the Sun?"

"I grew up in the woods. We didn't get many visitors."

She shrugged. "The Royal Order is made up of guardians and knights who protect Heartstones and healers."

Ahh. The Heart's version of the Celestial Order of the Dragon. He asked curiously, "Who'd want to hurt healers?"

"Not many people. The Royal Order spends most of its time protecting stones."

"Heartstones are used for resurrection, right?" he asked. He felt smart for being able to toss out that tidbit.

"When a spirit absorbs a stone's magic, it gains enough strength to re-form body and inhabit it."

"An entirely new body?" he asked, shocked.

She nodded. "No matter how badly injured before death, a whole and healthy new body form, assuming spirit strong enough to journey back through stone—with guidance of healer trained how to use it, of course. Not all spirits come back, though."

"Why not?"

"We not know for sure."

"How does a Heartstone work?"

She shrugged. "Stone make light visible in spirit realm. If spirit see it, spirit can go to it. Draw energy from it to resurrect."

He frowned. "What is it?"

"Magical stone. Some say sentient."

"If it's sentient, why would it allow spirits to drain energy from it for resurrections?"

Rosana laughed. "Now you know great mystery of Heartstones. Emperor give large kingdom to anyone who answer question, I expect. He love to cast off Heart and force common people to depend on him alone for healing and resurrection."

Now, *that* was outright treason. "Have a care what you say," Will muttered sharply under his breath. "Such words will get you killed or worse!"

Rosana glanced up at him from under her thick eyelashes. "You not tell on me, would you?"

His breath caught in his throat and he shook his head, struck dumb by her mild flirtation. He eyed the lime green goop clinging to the rim of the solvent bottle she unstoppered and managed to choke out, "Do you know how to use that stuff?"

She grinned. "Easy as pie. You pour over thing you unstick. It reverse effect of all paste or glue. And no, I not know how it work, Curious Will."

His mother called him that sometimes. However, at the moment he was distinctly uncurious to find out what that green mess would feel like against his skin. If the horrible pain when the wood disk had attached to him was any indication, this was going to burn like dragon's breath. Not only did he dread the pain, but moreover, he had no desire to whimper like a babe in front of Rosana.

"Come sit near fire where I see better," she ordered briskly. "And open shirt more."

He did as she directed with trepidation, steeling himself against what was to come. He was gratified, however, to see her gaze drink in his muscular chest. Cutting and hauling timber for the Hickory Hollow lumberjacks kept most of the young men there in excellent condition. And then there had been the endless chores Ty had made Will do over and over.

Carefully, she poured some of the green substance over the disk, catching the excess in a cloth she held below it. Other than being faintly cold against his skin, the solvent felt like nothing more than syrup dripping down his chest.

"See if it pry loose now," she directed.

He reached up and tried to pull it off.

Nothing.

He tried again, scraping his fingernails painfully at his skin in a vain attempt to gain purchase on the blasted disk. Again, nothing. It felt rooted to his body as if it had grown into him.

Rosana leaned back, staring down at the disk, confounded. "Never I see such thing. I think another healer must look at it."

In short order every other healer in the house examined his chest and expressed interest in his problem. However, none of them had any solution to offer, and none of the others had dimples and smelled of vanilla.

Finally, the adept who had taken over running the house until a new patriarch could be appointed commented, "I think we'd better show this to the High Matriarch."

Forthwith, Will and his gathered audience trooped upstairs to the same office he'd gone into when he first arrived in the building.

Lenora looked up in surprise as the lot of them tromped into her impromptu office. "What's this?"

"We have a conundrum, High Matriarch," the adept explained. "This boy has a strange affliction which none of us have been able to cure or even identify. We were hoping you might take a look."

"By all means. If you were sick when arrived, you should have told me, young man. Riots notwithstanding, we are here to heal all who walk through our doors," she said kindly.

By way of answer, Will pulled back his shirt, inured now to the idea of showing the wood disk to strangers. High Matriarch Lenora studied the disk as the other healers relayed everything that had been tried on it so far. And then she did an odd thing. She laid her palm directly on the disk, her fingertips cool on Will's flesh around it, closed her eyes, and murmured a half-intelligible incant, something to do with detecting spirits.

Her eyes flew open, and she jerked her hand away from Will with a start. "Well then. I think I may have found the problem."

Will looked at the healer expectantly.

"Yon disk of wood is sentient."

CHAPTER

17

Raina expected to fall unconscious from exhaustion when she finally collapsed in one of Hyland's guest beds, but she struggled to sleep, and when she did her dreams were restless.

She knew this place. The dryad grove where she and Cicero arrived in Dupree. But it was different, more . . . alive. A subliminal groaning filled the air as if the rowan trees were speaking with one another. In fact, when she looked more closely, they were. Small animals chattered back and forth, their language frustratingly just beyond her understanding.

And there were other creatures. Otherworldly ones, some monstrous and some beautiful. In her dream, she strolled around the margins of the grove under the great trees ringing the circle.

She passed a stand of heavy brush and was startled to hear a female voice emerge from the undergrowth. It said in perfectly understandable human speech, "What do you seek in this place, dreaming human?"

Was the unseen woman talking to her?

"Yes, I speak to you. What other dreaming human do you see in this place?"

"I do not understand."

"You seem to understand me perfectly well. What do you seek?"

"Who are you?" Raina demanded.

A trill of laughter. "I am Rowan."

"Where are you?"

"Why, right before you, of course, silly child."

Raina blinked and, in a single closing and opening of her lids, was able to make out a face among the clustered leaves before her. It was almost as if the face were made of leaves, so perfectly did it blend in with the lush greenery around it.

"I see you!" Raina cried out in delight. Although why she was so delighted in her dream, she could not quite say.

The one named Rowan smiled beguilingly. "Tell me what you seek."

She frowned. "I do not know what you mean."

"Of course you do," Rowan replied brightly. "We all know in our heart of hearts what we truly seek."

"It's a secret," Raina whispered, finally understanding.

"But this is a dream," Rowan whispered back. "Anything you say here will not leave this place or this dream. I can keep a secret. I keep many secrets."

"Like what?"

The green-faced lady laughed. "If I told you they would not be secrets anymore!" Her emerald green gaze was beseeching. "Please tell me yours."

Her voice was so pleasant, so enticing, that Raina had no desire to resist. "I seek great magic," she confided.

"You have great magic. I sense it within you."

"No, no. Bigger than what I have now."

Rowan's face fell. "Oh. I had hoped for something more special from the one who managed to wake me," she murmured, disappointed.

"I woke you? How?"

"You woke my wand, of course." The leaf-faced woman leaned a little closer. "You may keep that for a while, by the way. It's mine, but you will need it, someday."

"For what purpose?"

"I cannot tell. It's a secret," the lady answered with a conspiratorial twinkle in her green eyes.

"The magic isn't for me," Raina explained, returning to their earlier conversation. "I need it to save someone else. My sister and . . . and my future daughters. And maybe my aunt if she's still alive. But I fear she is not."

"That's better, then," the leafy lady said encouragingly. "What kind of magic do you seek?"

"I'm not sure. I think it needs to be very old and very, very powerful." Raina added hopefully, "Do you know anyone with that kind of magic?"

"I did once."

"Who?" Raina asked eagerly.

"The Great Circle."

"What is that?"

"Not a what. A who. They were the great tree lords of the forest."

"What happened to them?"

The green-faced lady's face grew unbearably sad. "They turned on one of their own. They did not understand that his anger and violence were a natural part of the cycle of life, and he hurt someone. They destroyed Bloodroot, but in so doing, they destroyed the balance and destroyed themselves. The Mythar was gone and was not there to fix the balance. The Great Circle is broken. No longer complete."

"Oh, dear," dreaming Raina sighed. Then she brightened, saying, "I have heard of this Mythar. Is he still alive? Who is he exactly?"

A gentle laugh. "He is . . . was . . . the lord of all the nature guardians."

"Where can I find him?"

"He is lost. We cannot find him no matter where we look."

"Where did you lose him?" Raina asked curiously.

"He used to visit the Great Circle sometimes. We saw him there, mostly. Perhaps that is where we lost him."

"Where did the Great Circle live?"

"They liked the Forest of Thorns, the Wylde Wood, and the White Wood."

"Is the Mythar dead?"

"We do not believe so. He has gone beyond us, though. Perhaps he is with his mother."

"You mean beyond the Veil, in the Void, where the permanently dead go?"

"No, no!" Rowan snapped a little irritably. "With his mother, the Green Lady."

Raina was starting to feel a little exasperated. "And who is she?"

"She is a what, not a who," Rowan replied with infuriating good cheer. "She is the life in everything around us. The breath in our lungs, the renewal in rain, the birth of new life in seeds, the death in winter's frost."

"So the Mythar is dead, and has returned to nature instead of to the Void."

Rowan shook her head emphatically in the negative. "We would sense him if he were with the Urth. We have lost him. We misplaced him." She frowned prettily and added, "He had the magics of which you speak, too. Very old and very powerful. If you could find him for us, we would be very grateful. And we would ask him to share his magic with you."

"Would he listen to you?" Raina asked curiously.

The green one looked offended. "I am a princess of the

Green Court. What male does not listen to me? Even the Mythar is not entirely immune to my charms."

For some reason, the spirits around the green-leaf-faced lady found that idea hilarious in the extreme. Laughter of every shape and sound rippled through the grove joyously, and even Rowan could not scowl for long and joined the laughter.

Raina drifted on that tide of happiness, wishing with all her heart never to wake and leave this magical place.

But she did wake up. Abruptly and disoriented. Little remained of her strange dream except an absolute certainty that she needed to find this Mythar, and that the place to start looking for him was in the Forest of Thorns.

Will stared in shock at High Matriarch Lenora. "It's alive? A sliver of wood is alive? That's absurd."

"Mayhap," Lenora replied, "but I sensed two spirits within you when I cast a spell of detecting spirits upon you. Unless you are already possessed by another and would like to tell us of it now, yon disk has a spirit."

Will shook his head in disbelief. "As far as I know, I am not possessed. So how do we get it off me?"

"Well now. That could be a problem. When it attached to you, was there any discomfort?"

Will nodded warily.

"A lot of discomfort?"

Reluctantly, he nodded again.

She frowned. "As I feared. That thing may have already grown into you in some way."

Will stared, dismayed. That did not sound good at all. "Now what?"

"Now you sleep. It is late, and my guess is that it will require ritual magic to remove that from you. I do not have the components or the scroll to cast such a magic here. Mayhap, the Mage's Guild has them."

"If I do not obtain this ritual?" Will asked cautiously. No way was he going back to the Mage's Guild to ask for help.

"You may be stuck with it on your chest until you die and resurrect. Even then, it may not come loose, however. If it has attached to your spirit in some way, it could very well resurrect with you. It would help if we knew from whence it came."

Great stars. How on Urth was he supposed to research where a random lizardman girl he had never seen before and would likely never see again had obtained this stupid hunk of wood? He had no desire to go traipsing around the Empire with this thing stuck to him!

The depth of how adrift he'd suddenly become washed over Will. He had no home, no family, no means of employment, no prospects. How was he supposed to pay to fix this problem, let alone supply himself and travel into the Forest of Thorns in search of a legend? He needed gold. Resources. Information. Hopelessness broke over him. Would he end up pressed into the Haelan legion or enslaved, or worse?

A commotion downstairs interrupted discussion among the healers of his interesting problem. An excited voice floated up the stairs announcing that Lord Justinius had stopped in to check out the Heart's security.

Will looked over at Rosana questioningly. *Who is Lord Justinius?*

Her face lit up by way of answer. She grabbed his hand and bodily pulled him out of the office toward the stairs. "I never see him before," she blurted, blushing. "Hurry. Come!"

"Who is he?" Will demanded as she dragged him down the stairs at a dangerously fast clip. "Is he a ritual caster?"

"He commands Royal Order of Sun. He work for Voice."

"Voice? Who is that?"

"Voice lead entire Heart," she explained impatiently. "And Lord Justinius—he battle caster, not ritual caster."

They burst into the main room, or at least into the edge of it, for the place was suddenly crowded to bursting. A cadre of big, dangerous-looking men in the Royal Order of the Sun's white tabards, decorated with red shields behind their heart and sun emblems, filled much of the common room. It appeared that every healer in the Heart had also crowded in, and commoners off the street jammed the remaining corners. Lord Justinius was the biggest of them all, a massively powerful warrior with dark hair going gray at the temples. His sword, shield, and armor glowed brightly with magic, as did his hands.

"Welcome, my lord Justinius!" the High Matriarch cried out in greeting. "To what do we owe this great honor?"

"We received tidings of trouble in the city. We came in from the field to check upon your safety and security."

"All is well, here. We run somewhat low on supplies, but that is not unusual after a night like this."

"And the Heartstone?"

One of Justinius's knights piped up, "I have checked the locks. It is secure, my lord."

"Thank you, Sir Christian." Justinius turned back to the high matriarch. "I have heard rumors of a new healer in town. A girl of spectacular ability. Who is she?"

"Only new girl we've gotten the past few days is Novice Rosana. Where is she?"

Someone shoved her forward, but she was holding Will's hand so tightly that he was dragged forward as well.

"How many life spells can you cast in a single day, Novice?" Lord Justinius asked her kindly enough.

"One, sir."

His dark eyes flickered in disappointment, but he still

smiled and nodded in approval. "Keep practicing, then. Your skills will grow quickly under High Matriarch Lenora's tutelage." To the high matriarch he murmured, "This is not her. Talk was a spirit arch-mage had come to Dupree."

"An arch-mage? There hasn't been one in my lifetime," Lenora replied. "But I'll certainly keep an eye out for one, my lord."

"Excellent. I'm off, then. Back to what we were doing before news of the riots reached us. My men will, of course, share what scrolls and potions they can spare to see you through the next few days. Give her all the Delphi marked potions and scrolls you have. That batch is nearing its expiration date. Best to use it up here, where we know it will do some good before the magics drain away."

The knights stepped forward one by one to empty their pouches. When they were done, the crowd of knights swept out of the Heart, and abruptly the building felt empty. Hollow. The day's excitement and the strange malady Will had suffered on and off caught up with him of a sudden, and he was glad to curl up in a bunk in one of the alcoves lining the Heart's common room.

He had barely laid his head on the thin, musty pillow, his eyes barely closed, when strange images began to dance in his head, more vivid than any normal dream, not quite hallucination, and not quite imagination.

The images were dark and violent. Some thinking part of him registered surprise that the battle his dreaming mind conjured was not that of Hickory Hollow. Rather, he saw a huge field, bordered on opposing sides by two great armies, one composed almost entirely of elves, the other made up of various greenskins. And trolls. Lots of trolls. The center of the greenskin line was dominated, though, by a regiment of orcs bristling with weapons. Orcs with red symbols that looked like outspread tree roots tattooed on their fore-heads.

The two armies did not battle each other. Rather, all eyes were directed to the center of the field where two lone fig-ures dueled. One an elf, the other a troll, the crowns upon their brows declaring them to be kings among their kind. The elf's crown, predictably, was made of what looked like living green leaves edged in gold.

As Will looked on, the elf lunged forward and, with a mighty thrust of his sword, impaled the troll upon it. In so doing, however, he opened himself up to a vicious slash from the troll's axe from shoulder to opposite hip.

Both men toppled over to their deaths simultaneously. The armies roared with one voice, whether in glee or dismay he could not tell. A cadre of elves rushed forward from one side, and the orc regiment charged forth from the other side. Will winced, waiting for the clash of battle, but instead, the two forces made for their respective fallen champions.

The orcs hefted the body of the gigantic troll onto his nearly body-length shield and commenced carrying him from the field in a rough procession. A chant rose up from their throats, taken up quickly by the rest of the greenskin army. "Roo. Dath. Roo. Dath."

Will didn't know the meaning of the syllables, but the greenskins roared it over and over, adding in the clanging of clubs, axes, spears, and swords against shields and the stomps of armored feet until the cacophony was painful to the ear.

As they pulled back from the battlefield, the more quiet grief of the elves became audible. A lament rose from the elven army, made loud by the thousands of throats issuing it.

The entire elven army knelt in its grief. And then a shim-mering appeared in the air before the fallen king and his grieving guards. The shimmering took on a greenish cast, and from within it a figure stepped forth of a young and terribly beautiful lady. She looked human, but not entirely. Her figure was wreathed in a glow of green light, and her clothing was adorned with living leaves and flowers.

She spoke in a normal voice that somehow could be heard across the entire field. "I am sorry for your loss this day. But know this. I can and will save your king."

Oh, great. Now he was dreaming about kings, too. At least this one had the good grace to be dead and not sleeping eternally.

The phalanx of elves surrounding the body of their leader looked up hopefully.

The lady continued, "Give me his body, and I give you my word. He shall not perish permanently. I shall use all my power to keep him safe."

The elves glanced around at one another, unsure, muttering among themselves.

One of them called out, "But, my lady, Gawaine's spirit has flown. Our healers saw it leave him!"

The lady's voice rang out, terrible in its power, "Do not underestimate my abilities, mortals."

The elves bowed their heads in apology for doubting her. As no one seemed to have any more objections to voice, the lady glided to the body of their fallen king. As if he weighed nothing, she scooped up the elven king in her arms. She turned away from the army and made for the green shimmering that still hung in the air.

From his dreaming vantage point Will could swear he saw the lady's skin glitter faintly, almost as if covered by tiny metallic bits. He also saw her smile in dark triumph, her back turned to hide the expression from the grieving elves, as she swept through the portal and disappeared.

Heat spread outward from his chest, an uncomfortable itch beneath the wood disk. It grew into a piercing blade of burning agony that finally roused him from his strangely vivid dream.

Rebellion surged within him as he awoke. *Father, I cannot take up your quest. Aurelius will not stand for it. He issued a death warrant for me, for stars' sake! Selea suggests I take up the search in the heart of the Forest of Thorns, but it is certain death to go there. You are dead and cannot make me change my mind. Begone with your cursed hallucinations!*

Something rumbled deep inside Will's mind. Almost a chuckle. A wordless promise by some otherworldly spirit to have his way with Will, like it or no. And the first order of business was to go north. To the Boki lands. Where his father and the others had left off searching for the Sleeping King sixteen years ago.

R aina found the procession the next morning across Dupree with Hyland, his son, Kendrick, Kendrick's jann companion Eben, Cicero, and a half-dozen guards deeply reminiscent of when Lady Charlotte used to take the children into Tyrel City to shop with their assorted nannies and watchdogs. She found it odd how familiar moving with an entourage was and yet how foreign to her now. The fall from grace was so very easy in this empire.

The Heart building was not far from Hyland's house, and the walk did not take long. Long enough, though, to see broken storefronts, looted warehouses, and the sullen faces of the townsfolk.

Raina was not entirely certain why Hyland insisted on her visiting the Heart building this morn. She hoped it did not include an aggressive sales pitch by some high-ranking Heart personage to join the White Heart. It had been awkward enough to turn down Hyland. He'd insisted on her taking his wife's White Heart tabard anyway, and she had stuffed it into the farthest, deepest corner of her pack.

The Heart common room was crowded when they arrived. A brightly shining solinari with golden skin was there, along with a squad of big, armored men wearing the Golden Dragons of the Celestial Order of the Dragon on their royal blue tabards. Any number of healers loitered about, and two fellows wearing the red shield on their tabards behind their Heart emblems—Royal Order of the Sun—watched everyone carefully.

They piled inside adding to the crush. Only then did Hyland reveal his purpose in coming here.

"Raina, there's a youth here with an unusual malady. I would like you to try to heal it."

"What illness could I possibly heal that Heart healers could not?" she asked, surprised.

Hyland shrugged. "I am no healer."

The High Matriarch looked younger than Raina would have expected of someone of such rank. Lenora's eyes lit with interest, and mayhap even recognition, when Hyland explained that Raina was an exceptionally talented young healer.

"Come this way, my dear," Lenora said gently.

Raina followed the High Matriarch across the room to the hearth, where a perfectly healthy-looking youth sat beside a lovely dark-haired healer. She recognized the pair. They were the ones who'd caused the fuss at the council meeting by reporting an orc raid.

Raina eyed the young gypsy with interest. That could be her life—living in a Heart house, sitting with patients, fetching potions, and patching wounds. The girl, who turned out to be called Novice Rosana, seemed reluctant to leave the handsome young man's side.

"This is Will Cobb." Lenora explained. "He's lately come out of the country with a strange affliction. Show her."

The youth, a tall, lanky boy on his way to being a large, powerful man, threw her a long-suffering look. He reminded her of Justin, and a pang of missing her childhood sweetheart stabbed her sharply.

Will opened the top of his shirt, and she leaned forward with interest to examine what turned out to be a thin disk of wood partially grown into his chest. A lip of his skin formed a ridge around the edge of the disk. It reminded her of a piece of jewelry with a thin rim of precious metal ringing a gem to hold it in place.

"Does it hurt?" she asked doubtfully.

"When people pry at it, it does."

She grinned at his aggrieved tone. He sounded just like Justin. She looked up at the matriarch. "What am I supposed to do to this thing that you cannot?"

Lenora shrugged. "Mayhap cast more magic into it than I or any of my healers can. Landsgrave Hyland says you've a fair bit of power."

Novice Rosana muttered, "Who'll life him when you people kill him?"

Personally, Raina agreed with the novice. She was no expert at these sorts of things. It looked like a job for a ritual-casting healer. But she did not air her untrained opinion. "Do you mind if I touch it? she asked Will. "I promise not to pry at it."

"Have at it. Everyone else here has poked at it."

She reached out to touch the disk of wood. It was satin smooth beneath her fingertips, with only the faint ridges of the carvings upon it marring the surface. It was also warm.

As if it were alive. *How odd.* "Do you feel it tingling?" she asked Will.

"Sometimes."

She rubbed the pad of her right thumb across the seductively smooth surface and jolted as something poked her painfully in the hip. She looked over her shoulder sharply. But no one was there. Where had that jab come from, then? Her pouch rested on her hip right over the spot where she'd been stabbed.

Had she accidentally forgotten to sheathe her herb knife? She reached her left hand into her pouch to check. The instant her fingers touched the bumpy stick of wood stowed there—the Wand of Rowan—it was as if lightning shot up her left arm, across her shoulders, and down her right arm into Will's disk of wood.

"Ouch!" he yelped at the same moment she yanked her hand away from the wand singeing her fingers.

"What did you do?" the High Matriarch demanded.

"I . . . nothing . . . I just touched it," she answered. She wasn't eager to explain where she'd gotten ahold of a powerful magic item like the wand hidden in her pouch. Particularly since she supposed she had technically stolen it from Kadir that night in the barn.

"Can you remove the disk?" Lenora asked.

"If I had a ritual scroll and the components I might be able to cast something to take it off, but I have no idea what ritual to even try."

"Just cast some healing into it," the matriarch suggested.

"How much?"

"As much as you can."

Hyland dived in quickly. "Why don't you just start trickling healing into the disk, Raina? The matriarch can tell you when to stop."

She glanced sidelong at him, her eyes twinkling. Careful to keep her left hand out of her pouch, she commenced guiding a thin stream of healing magic into the disk of wood. There were two methods of delivering healing—gathering a big wad of magic and throwing it into a target all at once in a fast, painful explosion of healing or trickling in the magic less painfully but much more slowly. The first method was used mostly in combat when warriors needed immediate and radical healing to stay alive and continue fighting. Apparently, it was excruciating, and only the life-and-death demands of the battlefield could induce most people to endure the agony of fast healing,

Which wasn't to say that slow healing was that much less painful.

Will, however, seemed unaffected by her magic. "Are you feeling this?" she asked him in surprise.

"No. Whatever you're doing is going completely into the wood."

She frowned and upped the amount of flow. "Are you all right?" she murmured.

"As a duck in water," he answered jauntily.

"Open the gates a little," Hyland muttered to her.

She nodded and increased the flow of magic significantly. Will's only comment was, "The disk is getting warm."

"Let me know if it gets uncomfortable," Raina replied, pouring magic into the disk at nearly the power level she would perform a ritual-magic casting.

"Is it loosening up at all?" Novice Rosana asked anxiously.

Will reached up to give the disk a tug and shook his head in the negative.

"Enough, child," the matriarch told Raina. "As I thought. That thing's going to require a ritual to remove. But thanks be for trying. By the by, child, if you're planning to run around casting that kind of healing magic, I'm going to have to insist you join the Heart. The Empire can't have healers of that kind of power roaming free and not properly inducted into one of its guilds."

Raina threw Hyland a distressed look. He answered smoothly for her, "I've spoken to her already regarding that, High Matriarch. She understands the Empire's position on unregistered mages and is taking a few days to consider her options. Personally, I think the White Heart would be ideal for her."

"Indeed?" Lenora replied sharply. She looked back and forth between Hyland and Raina intently. The High Matriarch nodded and said slowly, "Yes, Landsgrave, I concur. The White Heart makes sense. I would happily approve such an appointment. Do you wish induction into the Heart and directly into that order, child?"

Raina answered in alarm, "I have made no decision, High Matriarch."

"We would love to have you in the Heart in any capacity you choose," Lenora said sincerely. "I promise we would do well by you—"

Blessedly, Hyland interrupted the unfolding sales pitch with, "Sadly, my son has business elsewhere this morn and must leave presently. If you will excuse me, I wish to make my farewells to him."

"Of course," the matriarch responded. "So, young Kendrick. How are you doing for healing potions? It seems I'm forever having to resupply you."

"But I use them on other people, mostly," Kendrick protested.

"So you say," the matriarch replied tartly. But Raina saw the glint of affectionate humor in the woman's eyes. Rosana was sent to fetch a handful of healing potions. While they waited for her return, Lenora asked Kendrick, "Where are you off to now, rapscallion?"

"To Talyn. My friend, Eben, and I have business there."

Raina glanced over at the jann sympathetically. She had not heard whether or not Landsgrave Hyland had been able to learn something of Eben's missing sister, Marikeen.

"Talyn, is it?" Lenora commented. "Last I heard, Patriarch Hiru Nightblade is up that way. Give him my greetings if you see him, would you?"

Kendrick grinned and nodded. Infectious charm the young man had. But Raina's affection was back in Tyrel with another charming young man who likely did not even know she'd had a crush on him.

Will asked, "Talyn is near the Forest of Thorns, is it not?"

At mention of the Forest of Thorns, Raina perked up. It was there she wished to go with all due haste. If her strange dream was true, it was where she would find the Great Circle that might have some idea where to find the Mythar. If this lord of the nature guardians had enough olde magick to restore the Great Mage and could be talked into sharing it, mayhap she could finally go home again.

"Aye," Eben answered Will's question. "Talyn includes the southern margin of that forest."

"Might I go with Kendrick?" Raina asked hopefully. "I should like to see more of Dupree."

Cicero threw her a questioning look but made no comment.

Hyland smiled broadly. "I would rest easier knowing my son travels with a healer of your talent. And it might be wise to remove your skills from the roving eye of—"

Hyland did not finish the thought, but she had no doubt he referred to the governor. Out of the corner of her eye, Raina caught Rosana whispering in Will's ear. He nodded and whispered something back in return. Her heart ached to see how close the two of them were. It reminded her of Justin and herself.

Hyland asked for parchment and quill to pen a letter to the Patriarch, and the matriarch led him away. Raina turned to Cicero and murmured, "Would you be willing to visit the Forest of Thorns with me?"

He made a face of distaste. "Willing, but not eager. Why there?"

"I had a dream. I think I might be able to find what I need there."

"And what exactly might that be?"

Raina had never been the type to rely overmuch on her dreams, and she felt silly answering Cicero's question. But she owed him the truth if he was going to put his sword and his life to the task of protecting her. She answered reluctantly, "The Great Circle."

Cicero visibly started—a dramatic reaction out of an elf, even a demonstrative kindari. "What need have you of that?" he demanded under his breath.

"To help me find the Mythar and solve the problem that forced me to leave Tyrel." Suspicion knotted in her gut at the suddenly closed expression on Cicero's face. She asked, "Do you know something of the Great Circle?" It would make sense, after all. The kindari were forest elves. If any would know of the great tree spirits, it would be them.

He shrugged. "It has not made an appearance in a long time."

She wondered what constituted a long time in kindari lore. "What more can you tell me of it?" she asked eagerly.

But Cicero was forestalled from answering by the solinari stepping up to Raina. The elf half-bowed formally. "If I might have a moment of your time, youngling?"

"Of course . . ."—she took in the five stars on his shoulder—
". . . , Guildmaster. How may I be of service to you?"

"Perhaps you might turn your magic to a small favor for me?"

"Of course. What can I do for you?"

He planted the tall, beautifully carved staff he had been leaning on before her. It was made of some rich, dark wood covered in intricately carved vines. The weapon was topped by a rose so perfectly carved as to be indistinguishable from a real rose in full bloom. Only the wooden grain in the petals gave away its true composition. She'd seen some stunning carvings in her day but nothing came even close to the exquisite workmanship in this staff.

"I brought this here for the High Matriarch to attempt to reawaken. It should take care of Will's problem with that wood disk. However, Lenora's other duties have required her to expend her magical energies elsewhere already, today. Are you perchance, ritual magic capable, youngling?"

Raina nodded respectfully. "Yes, Guildmaster. I am."

"And are you familiar with awakening artifacts?"

"Yes, Guildmaster." In fact, it was a relatively simple procedure and did not even require a full ritual to complete. She'd mastered the technique years before. "What can you tell me of the magics within this staff, Guildmaster?"

"They are spiritual in nature."

She nodded confidently and took the wooden staff into her hands. It was as smooth and sleek as mink, and warmth coursed through it. Yes indeed, the magic within it did have the feel of spiritual energy.

"Do you know how much it will require?" she asked as she poured a fair bit of energy into the staff.

He shrugged. "I do not."

Surprised that the artifact had not already awakened given the magic she'd just cast into it, she took a deep breath and gathered magic to herself once more. After the past few days, it was growing easier to draw large amounts quickly. Where her fists grasped the staff, a white glow began to dance across the surface, highlighting the sinuous carvings until they looked alive.

The more energy she cast into the staff, the hungrier it felt. It vibrated in her grasp and grew almost too hot to hold as it absorbed everything she could throw at it. The carved rose atop the staff began to glow a soft green color, and the gem nestled within its petals shone as brightly as a beacon.

She stared at the staff, mesmerized by its terrible beauty. All at once, it jerked in her hands as if attempting to escape her, wildly more powerful than she could control. She staggered back, her magic faltering.

Rosana, who was directly behind her caught her to steady her, catching her shoulder blades with a forearm and the staff with her free hand.

But as soon as the gypsy's fingers closed around the staff, a tremendous flash of green energy exploded, enveloping Rosana in a nimbus of emerald light. Blindingly bright, the energy passed through the gypsy so strongly that Raina fancied that her friend became transparent for an instant, lit from within by that brilliant green glow.

Rosana gasped but could not seem to find her breath. Raina did not dare touch her friend while that strange and powerful magic was coursing through the gypsy. Finally, the glow subsided—what seemed to be minutes later—disappearing at a spot just under her shoulder.

"Oww!" the gypsy exclaimed, rubbing at the spot just above her heart.

The High Matriarch snapped at Aurelius, "And what, pray tell, was *that*? What have you done to my healer?"

The elf stared, first at the gypsy, then at the staff, and then at Raina. "In all honesty, High Matriarch, I do not know. I meant the magic for Will."

"Guess!" Lenora snapped.

"The staff was created to remove taints or curses. Perhaps to restore a person to their natural state."

All eyes turned on Rosana. She blinked back at them, looking afraid. "I do not know of any taint upon me. I feel no different than before. Just a little blinded by that bright flash."

Lenora performed first aid upon the girl quickly and, thankfully, pronounced her unharmed by the magical blast. Raina was relieved. She did not believe she had any more big surges of magic left in her this day.

Hyland pushed forward through the gathered crowd, looking worried. "Is aught amiss?" he demanded.

The High Matriarch replied, "Nay, Landsgrave. I believe no harm was done. But," she added tartly, "I'll thank you to get that thing out of my guild, Aurelius."

The solinari bowed formally, collected his men—and the now quiet staff—and departed from the building. The last glimpse Raina caught of the sun elf's face was of a man completely flummoxed.

Raina turned back from watching them go to see the High Matriarch whispering to Hyland. They both looked grave. What had put that look in their eyes?

In the general chaos of the final preparations for their party's departure for Talyn, she got no chance to ask Landsgrave Hyland about it. She did, however, notice Hyland drawing his son aside to have a brief conversation that put a grave look on Kendrick's face as well.

The moment came to leave, and Raina thanked Hyland sincerely for his assistance. For his part, he wished her *safe* travels. She did not miss his emphasis on the word "safe," and gave him her promise to do her best.

Kendrick and Eben led the way, and she and Cicero brought up the rear. They were not a dozen steps beyond Healer's Square, though, when Eben turned to Kendrick and demanded, "What news did your father have of Marikeen?"

Raina eavesdropped with interest as Kendrick answered, "Anton swears he has not seen or heard of your sister. The Kithmar claim that she escaped last night during the riots."

"Where is she, then?" Eben demanded in frustration. "Why did she not come to your house? I'd lay odds the Kithmar lie and still hold her. We must find her and rescue her!"

"Agreed," Kendrick replied. "Last the High Matriarch heard, a party of slavers was headed north. Talyn lies in that general direction. Let us go there and see to getting that mark off your face, and mayhap we'll pick up the trail of the Kithmar clan while we're at it."

"You have the components?" Eben murmured low enough that Raina barely caught the question.

"Aye," Kendrick muttered back.

Raina was glad the jann would be getting the ugly black chain-link symbol removed from his face. It was a jarring reminder of the Empire's power that a free man could, through nothing more than a bit of bad luck, end up enslaved forever. Eagerness to finish her task and return home rolled over her. She looked forward to being as far away from the Empire's politics and danger as she could get.

Hyland looked over the troops Anton had added to those the landsgraves had been ordered to assemble for a march north into the Forest of Thorns. The governor's soldiers were a motley bunch, but no worse than the rest of the army, he supposed.

Anton had never been one to put overmuch by way of resources into training or equipping his troops. The whoreson probably feared a coup from within the ranks of his men. And for good reason. They were treated dismally and paid worse. Which likely accounted for the rampant corruption and tendency of Anton's legion to be both greasy of palm and light-fingered.

Supply wagons lumbered around the corner into the crowded courtyard, pulled by teams of oxen. Even the beasts who served Anton seemed more stubborn than normal. Hyland waited patiently while the drivers hauled at the beasts until they formed a rough column.

He looked up on the ramparts to where Anton's first advisor stood, overseeing the whole operation. Ceridwyn Nightshade's strikingly red hair stood out sharply against her black, nulvari skin. As she'd instructed him to do earlier, Hyland signaled her that the troops were ready to go. She nodded, but then surprised him by indicating that the force should hold its position.

Now what? Hyland started when Anton himself came out into the courtyard where the troops had been mustered. And the man was wearing a chain-mail shirt, no less. *What is this?*

"I have decided to accompany my army north," the governor announced. "And you, Landsgrave, shall accompany me."

Only by dint of many years' worth of military self-discipline did Hyland's jaw not fall open.

Fully aware of the shock he'd just delivered, and no doubt relishing every cursed moment of it, Anton continued, "I shall lead this expedition and see to it the thing is done properly. You shall command the troops and lead them into battle, but I will be the field general and direct your movements."

Which was to say, Anton would take credit for any successes they had and blame *him* for any and all failings. Hyland barely managed not to roll his eyes in disgust at this arrangement as Anton strutted to the front of the column of soldiers.

He muttered under his breath, "So. The Viper returns to the nest."

"I beg your pardon, sir?"

Leland glanced at the startled young soldier beside him. "Nothing." It was a nickname Anton had earned during the first Boki insurrection. The usual translation of the Boki's nickname for Anton was Strikes like Viper. Leland's own names for the man were substantially worse.

He and Tiberius, Aurelius, and Selea had been on the verge of unraveling the big mystery the Boki guarded in the Forest of Thorns when Anton, in his avarice and lust for power, had to go and draw down the entire Boki army on all of their heads.

So close, they'd been. Inside the hidden cave, within literal arm's length of the key to the legend of the Sleeping King. It was supposed to be a stealth mission. Until, of course, Anton decided to beat them to the prize with all the stealth of a charging bull. Then the guardians of the secret—if that was what the creatures that had attacked them had actually been—had driven them from the chamber. Were it not for Selea's extraordinary skill with swords and Tiberius's speed with a magical incant, they would all have died. The four of them had barely escaped with their lives. Too bad Anton had escaped with his as well.

Leland shook his head, chasing away the bitter memories. The Boki had no doubt moved their treasure to someplace even more remote and closely guarded.

And somewhere out there were his son and a handful of

inexperienced youths who had no idea the hornet's nest they were about to kick. Kendrick had been eager enough to pursue the quest when Hyland had asked it of him this morn. The boy had grown up on whispered stories of the mythic king and no doubt found the whole notion of being a hero thrilling. As for Hyland, stone-cold terror described his reaction to his son attempting to breach the Sleeping King's resting place.

What choice did he have but to send him, though? What choice did any of them have? Anton could not be allowed to find the key to the Sleeping King. The whoreson would not hesitate to hand it over to Maximillian. And then all hope for deliverance from Koth would be lost.

It was close enough to lost already. Barely any being alive had any memory of freedom from the fist of Koth. Words like "dignity," "happiness," and "opportunity" had all but ceased to have meaning. Who would save them when no one remembered anything but life in Maximillian's iron grip? Who would even know to fight against it?

Hyland hated sending his son into the fire, and he had no doubt Tiberius had hated doing it as well. But who else was there? He and his boon companions were past their primes. Old men. Lacking the vigor and heart for grand adventures. Like the Urth around them, their lives were fading, drained away drop by drop by the Empire. Time wore a man's spirit down, it did. And the cursed Kothites knew it. They won by simply outlasting their foes.

Only the long-lived races—the elves, what few dwarves had managed to avoid the Empire, and rare races like the janns and paxans—stood a chance of retaining any memory of freedom or could even imagine a world without the Kothite Empire.

The despair of the past long years settled heavily upon his

shoulders. But as he had always done, he squared them and took a deep breath. His own star might be fading, but by the Lady, he'd help the youngsters if he could.

One thing he knew from his many years as a landsgrave. Rulers came and went. But the land and the common people—the ones tied to the land for their survival—remained. They always found a way to carry on, even unto the end.

The motto on his personal coat of arms conveyed that very sentiment, in fact. *We find the path.* He'd endured famine and pestilence, marauders and monsters, even the death of his wife and stillborn daughter. But to have to endure Anton Constantine making a run at the last hope for freedom from Koth . . . again . . . the fates were more cruel than even he'd reckoned on. The governor *must not* find the Sleeping King.

He turned for the great portcullis, wincing at the stiffness in his back. He still gave his knights all they could handle on the practice fields, but his vigor was slipping away from him. He only hoped he would live long enough to see his own troops through this latest expedition of Anton's. He smelled a plot afoot. There was more to this foray into the Forest of Thorns than Anton had revealed. He feared it might even be more than seeking the Sleeping King. *What are you up to?* he asked his nemesis silently.

Leland calculated his odds of living out this expedition. Not high. But then, he never had expected to die of old age. Heroes—and troublemakers—never did.

H ey! Wait up!"
Will turned, waiting for Rosana to draw close. She pushed back her hood and grinned up at him, her dark eyes sparkling.

"We're out of sight of Heart, so now I can walk beside you," she explained.

"Why couldn't you walk with me before?"

"It's not proper for me to show interest in a young man."

His heart swelled at being called a man, even if a young one. "Why not?" he asked, curious.

"As a novice, it's expected that I will devote all my attention to learn the healing arts."

"You seem plenty skilled to me," he replied loyally.

"Not like her," Rosana replied, her gaze sliding to the pretty blonde in front of them.

He shrugged. "You're good enough for me."

Rosana gifted him with a brilliant smile.

"What was that business back at the Heart with that staff exploding?"

"No idea."

"It didn't hurt you, did it?"

She frowned and lowered her voice. "Something strange happened."

"Do you need healing?" he asked quickly.

Still frowning, she pulled back her tabard and the neck of her red blouse to reveal her left collarbone. Just below it, a small tattoo rested. It was a bouquet of four roses, one red, one white, one black, and one green. They were beautifully detailed, not the usual crude drawings he associated with most tattoos. Her skin beneath the ink was creamy and smooth.

"Look. That's strange, yes?"

"What's supposed to be strange about it? It's a beautiful tattoo."

"Yes, but I'm only supposed to have three roses."

He grinned down at her. "The tattoo artist must have been sweet on you, then, because you got a fourth rose for free."

"The green rose was not there before today."

His smile faded. "What are you saying? That a fourth rose just . . . appeared?"

She nodded, her eyes wide with worry.

"Does it hurt?"

"No. And it looks exactly like the other three roses. How can that be?"

"Where did the other three come from?"

She shrugged. "I've had them for as long as I can remember."

"And now there are four." It *was* odd that all four roses looked as if the exact same artist had rendered them. "It's a mystery," he announced.

"I don't like mysteries."

"Me, neither." He looked up and lurched, startled to see how far behind the party they had fallen. "We'd better hurry. Kendrick and the others are almost at the city gates. We need to pass through with him if we want to be assured of the guards giving us no trouble."

They lengthened their steps to catch the small party in front of them.

"Did the High Matriarch believe your excuse of needing to deliver a message?" he murmured.

Rosana murmured back, "You haven't heard? We gypsies are born liars." She laughed gaily and he joined her. The morning was warm and sunny, a fine day to go for a walk with a pretty girl.

He said lightly, "I hear this is a long journey, so I hope you're a good storyteller. I get bored with only myself to talk to."

She laughed again. "Oh, I have plenty of tales to tell. Shall I tell you of the Boki insurrection and how the heroes of Dupree defeated them?"

He nodded, interested. Although entertaining, her story didn't tell him anything he didn't already know. An army of greenskins, led by the Boki, had roared out of the wilds from all directions toward Dupree, killing, looting, and burning everything in their path. "Why did the greenskins attack the colony like that? Had too many colonists arrived? Or did the colonist do something to make them angry?"

Rosana's voice lowered to a bare murmur. "Rumor has it that someone made a deal with them. That a traitor paid them to attack the colony."

Will stared at her, dumbstruck. The death and destruction of the insurrection had been horrendous. People still spoke about how terrible it had been approaching twenty years after the event. Who on Urth would pay to make such a thing happen?

The attack had nearly wiped out the entire colony before the Haelan legion miraculously turned the tide and beat the invaders back. Apparently, the battle-magic casters of the Imperial forces had saved the day. Had his father been one of those casters? Surely he had. And yet Ty had never breathed a word of it.

Rosana took up the tale again. "Afterward, the Heart decided that it had better learn more about the native tribes and try to build some sort of alliance, or at least peace, with them. They sent a White Heart emissary, Brother Balthazar, to go to the Boki. He was to teach them about Heartstones, learn their ways, and make friends with them."

Will burst out, "Why in stars' name would anyone want to make friends with a pack of rabid beasts like the Boki?"

"They're not rabid bea—" She finished lamely, "Oh. That."

"Yeah. That." The murder of his family and the total destruction of his village. Furious that anyone could defend the Boki in any way, he sped up. She kept up, but he ignored her. They almost caught up with Kendrick and the others before Will demanded angrily, "Why would the Heart make peace with honorless curs like the Boki?"

"They may be violent, but the Boki have honor," she replied in surprise. "Buckets of it."

"No, they don't." Images of the carnage he'd witnessed flashed through his mind's eye.

"Then it was not Boki who attacked your village," Rosana stated firmly.

Something deep inside Will rumbled that she spoke true about Boki honor. Enough so that he did not argue back immediately. How could he be so sure of something like that?

He didn't like the deeper implication of her words. If these Boki were so blasted honorable, why did they attack Hickory Hollow? Was it revenge against the Dragon Knight who'd defeated them? That didn't sound particularly honorable. Had the Empire *and* the Boki wanted Ty dead? Who—what—was his father?

Kendrick and the others were glad enough for the extra company when they asked to join the traveling party, and numbering six now, they passed out of the city without incident. The roads were excellently maintained so close to the capital, and they made good progress despite their late start. The sun arced overhead and then behind them, casting longer and longer shadows as night grew nigh.

The kindari Cicero, who seemed to consider himself the young arch-mage's personal protector, finally announced to the party, "If you desire a fire, we'd best stop and light it now. By full dark, we'll need to put it out."

"Boki?" Will asked.

The kindari shrugged and replied evenly, "Other things for now. We should not encounter orc sign until we draw near the Forest of Thorns."

Kendrick spotted a likely clearing just off the road and the party veered toward it. Will efficiently gathered deadwood and built a fire while the others made camp. Rosana scoured the woods nearby and returned with a cloth full of fresh greens. The tender spring shoots made a delicious addition to their bread and cheese.

They sat beside their small fire for a time, staring into its cheerful flames. Rosana hummed a couple of songs in the old rhythms of her people, one a rollicking tune she refused to sing the words to on grounds that it was too bawdy for her to admit to knowing. The second song was a lament, so sad it hurt to hear.

"What was that about?" he asked after surreptitiously swiping at his eyes.

"My people's lost home."

"Lost?"

"The story goes that we gypsies had homeland long time ago. The song hopes that someday we'll find it again."

"How do you lose a homeland? Did you gamble it away?" Will asked.

Rosana snapped, "Gypsies are not gamblers and pickpockets. We have a code of honor, you know. And, shocking news, most gypsies live by it!" She sounded offended.

He mumbled, "Sorry. I'm a little on edge tonight."

A rather awkward silence fell around the fire. Eventually, Eben and Kendrick commenced murmuring quietly to each other, speculating about where the Kithmar would take Marikeen if they captured her again. Raina asked Cicero about something that he told her he didn't want to talk about here and now. The blond healer looked a little miffed. Rosana scooted over beside Will on the fallen log he'd turned into a bench and, beneath the folds of their cloaks, shyly twined her fingers with his. He froze, thrilled and nervous, unsure of what to do and frantic not to do something to make her move away from him.

Gradually, holding her hand became more natural, and he

relaxed . . . a little. He listened absently to the forest's night sounds, the rhythm of it as familiar as his own voice. Rosana grew drowsy and leaned her head upon his shoulder. Her eyes drifted closed and she dozed, soft and warm against his side. It was the first time since he'd fled Hickory Hollow that he had felt at peace even for a moment. He relished the sensation.

Full dark stole near, and Cicero put out the fire. Rosana woke and, with a sleepy smile for him, crawled into her bedroll. Her eyes closed immediately as she went back to sleep. He envied her the ability to rest so well. His troubled dreams of the night before made him leery of sleeping tonight. Reluctantly, he settled into his own bedroll. Eben took the first watch.

Will jerked awake abruptly some time later. What had roused him? He lay still, listening intently to the forest sounds. He detected a discord in the night's melody. It was faint. Nothing a town-bred person would ever notice. But he was born of the woods, and tonight his senses seemed sharper than usual.

He rolled out of his bedding, bunched his cloak, and pulled his bedroll over it to make it look as if he still slept there.

Eben was nowhere to be seen. He must have moved off into the woods a bit or maybe was walking about to stay awake. Will eased his dagger from its sheath and picked up his staff. He still carried the thing on his back as a reminder of home. A pang of grief struck him at the memory of Ty giving him the weapons. Grimly, he slipped into the shadows. Stealth wasn't in his nature—he'd rather confront his enemies head-on. But the Lady help them all if this was a Boki raiding party.

He felt strangely at home in the darkness, slipping in and out among the trees as he sought what lurked out here. He circled wide around where he thought he'd heard a noise or, more accurately, a damning lack of noise where the crickets and spring peeper frogs had gone too silent.

The fact that he spotted the vague shape at all was testament to his weirdly improved senses. The would-be attacker was well hidden, crouched within the spreading branches of a lingon bush, berryless at this time of year. The figure was perfectly still, a study in shades of black. It wasn't that Will saw the ambusher as much as felt him. He felt out of place in the fabric of the woods, much as a fragment of straw woven into a piece of wool was part of the weave, yet not meant to be there.

The shadow moved toward the circle of sleeping figures, and Will followed, the texture of the leaves beneath his feet flowing up his legs and into his awareness. He adjusted each step instinctively, bypassing twigs that would've snapped, dry oak leaves that had dropped since the last rain and were still crunchy. He even found himself breathing in time with the spring peepers' rhythmic croaks as they started up their chorus once more. He was of the woods and the woods were of him. When had *that* happened?

He was curious to see what the black figure planned to do. Was this a scout of some kind for the Boki? Or a thief? He ought to raise an alarm and rouse the party. But some compulsion within him stopped him from doing so just yet.

The intruder crept forward in admirable silence. Will waited patiently as the figure crouched for long minutes studying the cluster of long lumps on the ground. Eventually, the person eased forward . . . directly toward Will's bedroll. *Interesting. No, not interesting! Cursed worrisome.* What did this person want with him?

The figure held out both fists, and claws abruptly gleamed dully in the faint starlight.

He eased forward to within a half-dozen body lengths of the attacker. Will couldn't believe the fellow didn't sense him yet. The figure rose slightly, as if easing cramped circulation in his legs, or perhaps preparatory to moving abruptly.

The attacker lifted the deadly claws high over Will's bed-roll.

Will coiled to spring upon his would-be killer, but at the last second the attacker's arm paused. The claws lowered slowly to the person's side. Will dared wait no longer. He leaped forward, snaking his arm around the intruder's neck, the cold steel of his knife biting into flesh.

As quick as lightning the attacker grabbed Will's forearm and bent over sharply, attempting to throw Will over his shoulder. Ty was known to do the same when he wrestled, and the move was only partially successful. Will grappled with the fellow, who thrashed wildly in his grasp. A claw streaked back toward him. Will dodged the strike, using the attacker's own body to block the vicious attack.

The man was wiry but strong. *Really* strong. Inexorably, Will felt his grasp slipping. The attacker was going to wiggle free, then turn and finely dice him with those deadly claws. *Not good.* Who would protect Rosana when he died?

18

Selea slipped down the darkened servants' passage quickly. The tunnel, constructed of common brick, was low and rough, barely clearing his head for all that he was tall for an elf. Anton did not waste the fine materials in his Blood Palace on servants. Neither did the governor waste resources on security in this part of his residence. Which was handy for Selea's purposes this night.

He slipped out of the crude brick tunnel and into a larger hallway, this one constructed of rough-hewn stone. The door he sought was made of thick oak planks and sturdy iron hinges, but neither slowed him down much. He quickly picked the lock and slipped into the dark chamber.

A woman's voice came out of the darkness, not from the bed, but rather from the high-backed armchair by the fire. "Is that you, Uncle?"

"It is. And how do you fare, Lady Nightshade? It has been a while since we've spoken." Selea sank into the chair facing hers before the hearth.

Ceridwyn Nightshade, Anton Constantine's first advisor and as red-haired as he, answered dryly, "I am well. At least as well as can be in this viper's nest."

Selea smiled slightly at the reference to Anton's nickname,

The Viper. It was well-earned, and not just for the snake mark on his forehead or on his crest. "Have you any news for me?"

"Why are you in such a hurry, Uncle? Shall we not trade a few pleasantries, perhaps share a hot drink before we get down to business?"

"You would chide me?" he teased gently, allowing the merest hint of reference to his age beyond hers to creep into his voice. She might outrank him significantly, for he was a mere master of his trade while she was second-in-command of an enormous, if largely untamed, land. However, he was still her elder by decades, and they were kin.

She, of course, caught the the true source of his remark instantly. "What has happened?" she asked quickly.

"I merely recall the first rule of the Hidden Province," he answered obliquely.

"As do I." She recited,

> "Honor is spirit, together as one.
> Honor is fabric, invisibly spun.
> Honor is victory, silently won.
> Honor is all, the rest forever shun."

The were both silent for a moment, contemplating the guiding rule by which all their kind lived and died.

The she added wryly, "And I recall the second rule as well: never forget rule number one."

He smiled at the joke every nulvari child knew. Ahh, how he missed home, sometimes. But he had chosen to come live among the humans and their endless, frantic struggles for wealth and power and fame.

Ceridwyn fiddled with her signet ring bearing the distinctive blazon of House Night, and finally turned the conversation to his purpose in being here, commenting, "The Emperor receives the same reports you do, Uncle. I withhold nothing from you."

"You report directly to Maximillian, now?" Selea asked in surprise.

"A lowly first advisor in a distant colony? Hardly. My reports go through channels."

He nodded in understanding. It was the way of his race to prefer being the people *behind* the people behind the throne. Invisibility was prized in the Hidden Province. Real beauty rested in the art of manipulating kings without ever touching them directly.

"You have news, then?" he asked.

"I believe I have discovered what Captain Krugar has spent the past fifteen years traveling the colony in search of."

"Indeed?" It was an enduring mystery where Krugar came from and what his true purpose in being here was. It was unlike the Emperor to send one of such obvious skill and competence so far from court to languish in the worst legion in the entire Imperial Army.

"He let slip to me that he has long sought an escaped prisoner."

"For fifteen years?" Selea responded, surprised.

"Apparently."

"The identity of said prisoner?"

"I do not know. But I believe him to be a former Imperial military officer. Which may explain Krugar being sent after him." She added as an afterthought, "Oh, and I am told this prisoner is jann. And powerful."

Imperial Army. Jann. Powerful. An impossible possibility exploded across Selea's mind. *Surely not.* The man he thought of was *dead.* "When did this prisoner arrive in the colonies?" he asked urgently.

"The last prisoners were transported to Dupree sixty-five

years ago. This fellow must have been here at least that long."

The timing was right. General Tarses had been a jann and, stars knew, powerful. Selea had personally witnessed the general absorbing the essence of an ice elemental lord during the Pan Orda campaign. Granted, Aurelius had to dive in and lend magical help to keep Tarses from being subsumed within the elemental. But it still had been an impressive feat on Tarses's part to absorb even a portion of an elemental lord's powers.

If Tarses *did* still live and he *had* escaped, that would certainly merit Maximillian sending someone of Krugar's talents to recapture him.

His mind awhirl with the implications of this news, he mumbled distractedly, "Any other news to share?"

"Anton is alarmed by reports of a Boki raiding party in the south. He was not expecting the raid and does not know its cause, which angers and worries him. He has sent Captain Krugar to the Forest of Thorns to investigate why the Boki attacked an outlying village like that."

The reference to the Forest of Thorns jerked Selea's attention fully back to the conversation at hand. "Does Krugar have any hidden agenda other than the escaped prisoner?"

"Not that I am aware of. Have you information regarding some other task he might have been given?" she asked shrewdly.

"Nay."

"But you will let me know if you discover one?"

"Aye, of course," he answered.

"In the meantime, Anton appeases the landsgraves by letting them mount an expeditionary force to the Forest of Thorns."

A full expeditionary force? Not good. Not good at all. De'Vir's boy was about to head that way in search of what Tiberius, Aurelius, and he failed to find sixteen years ago.

Aloud, he asked, "Anton *lets* his landsgraves go? My impression is that they have no great enthusiasm for such a venture. They do not wish to provoke another native insurrection like that last one. The landsgraves seem to feel this expeditionary force of theirs is necessary for the safety of the colony."

And better that the landsgraves do this thing than Anton, who had a gift for infuriating and provoking people.

Ceridwyn nodded her agreement. But then she said, "I am certain that Anton has no stomach for war with the Boki. My guess is that he has secret allies among them. But the populace will howl if Anton does not make the point to the Boki that they will only be tolerated so long as they stay within their forest."

"Has he lost control of his Boki allies, then, or have his cronies within the Boki been overruled by their peers?" Selea mused.

"I do not know, Uncle."

They both stared at the fire for some time, considering the implications of a secret deal between Anton and portions of the Boki leadership.

Eventually, Ceridwyn shrugged. "Anton intentionally weakens the landsgraves, of course, by ordering them and their subjects on what is bound to be a bloody mission, and furthermore, forcing them to pay for the expedition out of their own coffers. As usual, Hyland sees through the ruse. But his hands are tied. The Boki must be confronted."

A silence fell between them, and he relished it. Most humans labored under a distressing compulsion to fill pauses with meaningless babble.

Eventually, Ceridwyn murmured, "Have you had any communication from our friends of the Shadow?"

"Nay. Cauchemar and his servitors have been quiet of late. Truth be told, I have heard little the Hidden Province."

He thought fondly of the nulvari homeland deep in Under Urth. He should go back for a visit when he retired. Aloud, he said, "The only directive I have received is that we are to continue to monitor the situation closely. A number of powerful forces seem to be converging on Haelos toward some unknown purpose."

"I have heard the same from other sources, albeit unreliable—soothsayers and seers mostly. Even Anton seems uneasy. Earlier this evening he called for the old military reports from the Boki insurrection to be brought to him. He spent the evening poring over the maps his commanders drew."

Maps, eh? What did the canny whoreson seek on the old maps? Mayhap the location of that grove from so long ago? The one Tiberius had conveniently failed to draw on the maps of the previously uncharted Forest of Thorns?

"Nothing the governor does or says go unobserved?" Selea asked.

"I have been watching him for twenty years. I do know how to do my job," she replied mildly.

No more needed to be said, so he rose to his feet and let himself out of the chamber silently.

Desperate, Will pressed his knife harder against the attacker's throat. And belatedly became aware that the person's skin felt oddly resistant under the blade. Cool and slightly . . . metallic. That wasn't skin. It was scales.

Recognition exploded across his brain. *The lizardman*

female. This was the same wiry frame beneath his hands as yesterday. The same smooth, unnaturally cool scales. The same desperate strength.

A foot hooked behind his right ankle and he started to go down. But from somewhere unconscious within him the proper technique to counter the sweep came to mind and he executed it—not perfectly, but well enough to keep his feet. Startled at his success, he yanked the girl upright.

"What're you doing here?" he growled in her ear.

"My treasure. Taking back," she grunted as she strained against him.

He released her abruptly and she stumbled forward, crashing to her knees. The noise and disturbance brought the others awake and they leaped up in various degrees of readiness for combat. Rosana was the last to wake, and she looked badly disoriented as she roused slowly.

"I ran into this girl yesterday in Dupree," Will announced. "Literally. She's the one who gave me the wood disk."

Rosana's gaze shifted to the lizardman girl in interest. "Where'd you get it?" she demanded.

The lizardman girl remained silent, oozing surliness. Kendrick lit a small oil lamp with some sort of flint and steel device he pulled out of his pack. A circle of golden light illuminated the clearing.

"Where's Cicero?" Raina asked abruptly.

Eben replied, "He took the watch after me."

"The kindari in the woods, you mean?" the lizardman girl asked. "Knocked him out I might have."

Raina lurched. "Where?" she demanded.

The lizardman girl pointed over her shoulder. Raina wasted no time plunging into the darkness, and Will was relieved to see Kendrick follow her, sword drawn. The healer didn't strike Will as particularly capable of protecting herself. He turned back to the lizardman girl. "Why did you give the disk to me?"

"Give it to you I did not. Your pocket I used to hide it from those cursed soldiers." She stared at him defiantly for a moment, then added, "Give it back!"

"I wish I could."

The lizardman girl jolted. "Sell it you did not?"

"Nope. Still have it."

"Then hand it over." Her voice grew more truculent by the second.

"I can't. It's stuck to me."

The lizardman girl frowned. At least he thought so. With that fine mesh of scales covering her entire face, it was difficult to make out the nuances of her facial expression. "What mean you, 'stuck'?"

Will sighed. He reached for the top of his shirt and peeled the garment back to reveal the wooden disk stuck fast to his chest. The lizardman girl took a step closer to him. He groused, "If you know how to remove this thing from me, by all means, please do it."

Her right hand snaked out lightning fast and snatched at the disk.

"Ouch!" he exclaimed, jerking back. It felt like she'd tried to rip off a patch of his skin with her hard, sharp fingernails.

His eyes widened as her nails extended into dangerous-looking claws and lifted toward him once more. He reached up instinctively to bat her hand away. No way was he letting her slice into him with those things!

"Weak human," she complained. "Alchemy we use, then." She reached into her pouch and pulled out a small glass vial filled with lime green liquid.

"If that is a solvent, we already tried it, and the stuff didn't work," Will announced. The lizardman girl frowned momentarily, and then her face lit up. She pulled out another vial. The glass was brown, so Will could not see the color of its contents. "What's that?" he asked warily.

"Acid," the lizardman girl replied confidently.

"No!" Rosana cried out.

Will threw a protective hand over the disk. The smooth, warm wood felt good under his palm. Inexplicably, he was comforted by the feel of it nestled below his collarbone. "Nothing you can do will remove it," he declared.

"Gone and done it, you have now!" the lizardman girl flared up.

"I didn't do anything!" he retorted. "I fell on it, and the blasted thing stuck to my chest. It's not my fault. I just want it off me." Although as he said the words the slightest uncertainty rippled through him. *I do want it off, right?*

"What do we do, now?" the lizardman girl demanded.

Rosana's eyes widened of a sudden. "Run!" she screamed.

Raina screamed as a half-dozen armed men rushed out of the woods toward her. They were dressed rough like bandits, but their blades were high quality. Gleamed with recent sharpening. Were well tended. Instinctively she drew magic to herself, but she had no idea whatsoever how to use it in combat. Nonetheless, the massive, crackling ball of energy between her hands gave the charging men pause.

In that breath of reprieve before they killed her Kendrick jumped in front of her, sword drawn. The attackers resumed their charge. Weapons clanged and men shouted. Eben materialized beside Kendrick, forming a wall in front of her all by himself with his muscular bulk.

Although her companions were clearly much more skilled

than their foes, there were a *lot* of bandits. Her father used to say often that quantity would overwhelm quality every single time on the field of battle.

Her initial impulse was to hide, but the sight of the first actual fighting she'd ever seen was so morbidly fascinating she didn't immediately seek cover. She stared, unable to tear her horrified gaze away from the grisly scene. One bandit dropped. Then another.

Out of nowhere, Cicero charged forward, taking a position on Kendrick's right side. His sword flicked in and out like the tongue of a hungry beast, seeking flesh and blood and finding it again and again.

More bandits charged into the tiny clearing, Her companions laid into the attackers and mowed them down like tender spring grass. Kendrick had clearly trained with master swordsmen. His technique was elegant, efficient, and deadly, even to her untrained eye. Cicero's style, while less refined, was honed by actual, life-and-death experience, and the right end of the line of attackers was thinning rapidly. Eben also held his own through raw strength and power alongside Kendrick, although he began to show small nicks and cuts before the other two.

Another wave of attackers, this group mostly made up of rakasha swinging their claws, charged. With their shorter blades, the cat changelings closed aggressively, pressing in hard upon her companions. Raina spied her protectors' arms growing battle weary and bloodstains beginning to blossom on their clothing.

Eben, on the left flank, was closest, so she made her way to him and laid her hand on his back. "We have no time to do this gently!" she shouted over the noise of combat. She slammed a bolt of healing energy into him.

The jann grunted in pain, but his nicks and wounds

disappeared. He nodded a quick thanks as he dived with renewed vigor into the fight.

She made her way behind Kendrick and Cicero to heal them as well. It took a few minutes and several rounds of combat healing into her friends' backs, but the ranks of bandits gradually dwindled. The sounds of clashing metal and men's cries grew less deafening. Maybe they were going to make it after all.

And then, without warning, no fewer than a half-dozen heavily armed shapes ran out of the trees from behind them, right into their midst.

Her relief evaporated in a rush of ice-cold terror. Those were *not* bandits. They were soldiers. Wearing the black and gold of the Haelan legion. *Anton's men.*

Powerful arms wrapped Raina in a crushing hold and slapped a hard hand over her mouth. She struggled like mad, but the attacker overpowered her with ease.

With her mouth covered, she couldn't utter any incants. Without incants, she could cast no magic. And without magic, she could not help her friends. Panicked, she looked around and saw that all three of her friends were down on the ground and similarly restrained. At the end of the day, their foe's numbers had just been too great for them. Various bandits and rakasha sat on her friends' chests or stood on their necks. They were the roughest, meanest-looking ruffians she'd ever laid eyes on. The soldiers didn't look any more reputable. She and the others were going to die.

W̲ill scrambled for his dagger, knowing even as he fumbled to draw it that the small weapon was completely useless in combat against longer weapons. But it was all he had on him. His staff lay beside his bedroll, useless.

Rosana cried out an incant and a bright flash of magical

light flew wild, slamming into a tree with a shower of sparks. A black figure raced past him, momentarily halting the headlong rush of the bandits toward them. The lizardman girl was fleeing the scene by practically barreling through the middle of the bandit line. *Coward.* One of the attackers peeled off to follow her running figure, but the remaining brigands resumed their advance.

Will assumed a fighting crouch. Not that it would do him a cursed bit of good. At least he got to stand and die like a man. Three bandits squared off against him and Rosana.

"Get behind me," he muttered to her. She edged closer to him, trembling so badly he could see her shaking.

Grins spread across the assailants' ugly faces. One of them muttered something under his breath and the other two laughed. Will didn't need to hear it. Oh yes. He was going to be good fun indeed for these whoresons—a mouse in the jaws of tigers.

The smallest of the bandits, still a powerful man with a broad chest and massive arms, stepped forward. He gave an experimental thrust with a spear, and Will leaped away from its hungry tip. The bandit thrust again, this time a powerful strike that would've gutted Will had he not dodged nimbly out of its path. The watching attackers laughed, and the one with the spear scowled.

Spear Guy howled a battle cry and charged. Will retreated fast, but not fast enough. The bandit's arms came up and forward with obvious intent to imprison Will in a crushing grasp. A flying object whooshed past Will's ear and a tinkle of breaking glass came from the vicinity of the man's chest.

Will's opponent staggered forward, slamming into him. They crashed to the ground and Will, on the bottom, grunted as the air was smashed out of him. Whatever that alchemical gas had been, it had been strong to drop this ox of a fellow.

Will shoved at the bandit and was stunned when the fellow's arms loosened without resistance. He gave another frantic heave. The brigand rolled away, a telltale hole eaten through his clothing. Acid. The lizardman girl must have thrown some at this poor sod. The bandit looked dead, or at least bleeding out. Either way, he would not be rejoining the fight without some serious healing.

Will leaped to his feet in time for one of the two remaining bandits to peel off and run for Rosana. Will shouted in a feeble attempt to draw the attack to himself as he struggled to free his legs from beneath the downed bandit.

He watched helplessly as the brigand charged Rosana, a sword raised over his shoulder. The weapon swung in a deadly arc. At the last moment the fellow turned the blade, striking her in the left ear with the flat of the blade. It sent her flying. She landed, crumpled, in a motionless heap. Rage and terror exploded in a fury of white light behind Will's eyelids and he finally managed to pull free of the deadweight upon him.

Something glinted overhead, rushing down toward him. Will rolled away from the mace that buried itself in the spongy earth beside his head a bare instant after he dived out of its path. He finished the roll and gained his feet, panting.

He sidled left, away from the stalking bandit coming in from his right. The fellow looked plenty mad now. The one who'd hit Rosana closed in from the left.

Will took a step backward, feeling around with his foot. *There.* Rosana's pack. He jumped backward over it, dropping his dagger as he landed in a crouch beyond the leather rucksack. He grabbed the hilt of her short sword and whipped it out, swinging wildly. The blade slowed his attackers enough that he was able to take a few more steps backward and scoop up his staff with his left hand. *Better.* At least he would die now for lack of skill and not for lack of weapons.

He had no training beyond what his father had taught him with staves, but what the attackers didn't know wouldn't hurt him. Their advance stopped abruptly as they assessed him anew.

He swung Adrick's staff lightly before him, testing its balance. He stood lightly on the balls of his feet as his father had drilled him endlessly, poised to react to the slightest movement from either assailant. He wished the terrain were more open than this. All the brambles and brush were not conducive to a long weapon like his staff.

Just as the assailant on his right lunged, another alchemy globe whizzed past, burying itself in the fellow's belly. Sha'Li must be close to risk the expensive alchemy in this cover-laden terrain where her targets could dodge so easily. Of course, with Will keeping the bandits' attention firmly on him Sha'Li's odds of hitting her targets went up greatly.

The wounded bandit roared in pain and fury as he charged, lifting up his mace as he came. Will planted a foot behind himself for balance, raised the staff overhead, and braced, taking the mace swing squarely in the middle of its shaft. The sturdy wood held, and the spiked ball slid off its metal-clad tip with a hail of sparks and a metallic screech.

Yanking the staff down, Will lunged forward and past his attacker, swinging a flurry of blows low and fast with his weapon on his way by. He rapped the bandit hard on the knee-cap and the fellow howled, hopping in pain. That was the greatest weakness of the staff. It was made for disabling a foe, not killing one.

A shout from behind caused Will to whirl, staff instinctively outstretched. He staggered as a rushing bandit slammed into him, bowling him over. Narrowly avoiding landing in the campfire, Will rolled away frantically from the flames and back to his feet.

A glob of black flew past almost too fast to see and splatted against the attacker's face. The man went down, screaming and clawing at his face. Will traced the path of the attack back to its source. The lizardman girl. It looked like spittle. He nodded a quick thanks to her for the help. Her timely alchemy and that spit had likely saved his life.

Rosana. What of Rosana?

Raina forced her eyes to stay open against a cowardly urge to squeeze them shut and pretend they were not all about to be skewered or worse. But then a strange thing happened. It was as if the trees themselves came alive and a half-dozen slight beings stepped right out of the trunks. Laughter tinkled in the air like tiny bells. *Dryads.*

The hand covering her mouth fell away from it as shouts of what sounded like disgust and dismay erupted from the throats of the raiders.

The faerie females with skin in hues of green and gold and dressed scantily in bits of clothing made from leaves and twined vines stepped right up to the bandits and soldiers, practically draping themselves on the furious fighters. Raina was shocked to see how quickly the tension drained from the men's shoulders. How fast gleams of ensorcelled lust lit their eyes. Those dryads might not be physically strong, but mentally they were lethal.

"Come with us if you wish to live," one of the dryads trilled in Raina's companions' general direction.

Raina and the others followed the fae creature with alacrity a little ways through the forest. Suddenly a glade opened before them, glowing in the moonlight. It was circular and beautiful and ringed by rowan trees—

"I know this place!" Raina exclaimed. She turned to Cicero, who stood warily behind her, eyes downcast at the ground. "This is the grove where the wand brought us!"

"Great," he grumbled.

For their parts, Kendrick and Eben looked around in wonder. One of the dryads strolled up to Kendrick and stroked his cheek with her palm. He smiled like a pup in love, and Cicero groaned under his breath.

Eben did his best not to look directly at the enchanted females, but when one of them breathed something unintelligible in his ear his gaze jerked to her and he was lost as well, grinning wider than any fool.

Their attackers had not followed them into this place. They must know of its charmed nature.

"Thank you for saving us," Raina said in relief.

One of them waved an indolent hand. "Oh, it is not you we save. But you are welcome, nonetheless."

"Will and Rosana!" Raina cried out suddenly. "We must help them!"

Will jumped to his feet and raced to Rosana's side. He rolled her over gently onto her back. A lump the diameter of his palm had already raised itself on the side of her skull, but she was breathing normally and didn't seem to be bleeding anywhere.

He heard someone approaching from behind and spun to face this new threat. He looked up. A breathtakingly beautiful female figure dressed in nothing but green leaves stepped forward. The firelight revealed her skin to be gently green in hue as well.

His jaw dropped. The staff wobbled, abruptly heavy and clumsy in his hand. "Who are you?"

He did not know whether to stare at the *green* female or

look away from her scanty attire. To worry more about the threat this strange creature posed or about Rosana lying unconscious on the ground. To attempt to render aid to her or leave her be. In the end, confusion froze him in place.

A ruckus erupted as Cicero, Eben, and Kendrick, in that order, burst into the little clearing followed by two more of the green humanoids. "Are you safe?" Cicero rasped.

Will gestured down at Rosana. "She's out cold, but she'll live."

Raina rushed over to the gypsy girl and knelt beside her, examining her quickly. "The swelling is outward. This is good. Although she should not remain unconscious for any longer than can be helped." She laid her hands on Rosana's head and commenced trickling a stream of white magical energy into her injury. Will was so grateful he felt vaguely nauseous.

Eben looked down at a prone bandit at his feet and announced, "What should we do with them?"

Kendrick frowned. "I do not think those were simple bandits. They fought like trained soldiers."

"Anton's men?" Eben asked tersely.

Kendrick nodded grimly. "It would be just like him to disguise his men like this so he can get away with attacking lawful subjects."

Raina murmured distractedly, "A few of the men who attacked us actually wore Anton's colors. But they were definitely working in league with these bandits."

Those were *soldiers*? Horror exploded in Will's gut. He would be put to death or enslaved forever for attacking the governor's men! They all would. He told Raina urgently, "There's one over there . . . I don't think I killed him . . . can you heal him?"

She moved quickly to the bandit Will indicated and cast

the required healing magic. The fellow lurched and sat up, looking around in disorientation, and Will was so relieved he could cry. The soldier/bandit blinked exactly twice before a dark shape slid out of the shadows and struck him on the back of the head with the butt of a dagger. The bandit fell over.

Will's jaw dropped. "You didn't kill him, did you?" he demanded.

"Of course not," the lizardman girl replied scornfully. "He'll wake up in a little while."

Raina moved around the clearing silently. She rendered enough aid here and there to keep any of their attackers from dying, and each time one of them regained consciousness the lizardman girl clocked the fellow on the noggin just hard enough to knock them out. Will thought she took altogether too much pleasure in doing so.

One of the dryads cooed, "Come with us, young ones. We have food and drink and will not let those bad men bother you."

Without stopping to ask the others what they thought of that idea, Kendrick grinned and plunged into the trees after the females. Eben went after his friend all too willingly. With a shrug, the lizardman girl followed.

"I do not like it," Cicero announced.

"We'll be careful," Raina murmured. "And we girls are immune to their charms. If you boys start acting strange, we'll rescue you."

Rosana giggled and Raina joined in.

"That's not funny," Cicero ground out.

Will's sharp ears picked up the sound of movement beyond the clearing. And after the ruckus of the past few minutes, no animal in its right mind would be moving around out there like that. "Funny or not," he muttered, "I think more soldiers come. We'd best go with the dryads unless you fancy being overrun and killed."

The kindari let out a long-suffering sigh and turned to follow the others.

Gabrielle looked down the high table at the Imperial inquisitors seated below her. High Lord Inquisitor Laernan had insisted on sitting below with his men rather than at the high table with her and Regalo. She admired the gesture—it was the sort of thing her own lord husband would do—but she could not help fearing the quiet, polite man. He was, without question, the most infamous torturer in the Empire.

Rumor at court was that he and Endellian were close. The princess generally kept company with a small cadre of the offspring of the archdukes, and, of course, her own brothers and sisters, of whom Laernan was one. It was a strange position that particular group found itself in, heirs to titles held by immortals—eternal limbo. At least Laernan seemed to have found himself a useful niche at court.

Gabrielle's gaze shifted to the Emperor's Master of Hounds. Another frightening individual. He apparently had figured out how to breed specific lines of mastiff-like hounds who could track and hunt down extremely specific targets. Certain hounds tracked down fae creatures. Others tracked psionically capable beings or elementals. Apparently, the pack he'd brought to Haraland hunted Children of Fate.

Which was a serious problem. A Child was known to live in the local area. She must get word to the man as soon as possible. And in the meantime, she must delay the master from running his hounds. Gabrielle motioned the castle steward near and murmured to him, "Open a cask of our best wine and keep it flowing to our guests."

"Yes, Your Highness."

Regalo glanced over at her, his right eyebrow lifted in question.

She answered his unspoken question innocently, "We would not want the Emperor to think that we show his servitors anything other than our most lavish hospitality, would we?"

Regalo made a sound of agreement.

Mentally, she winced. He must not suspect anything. Not if she wished him to live . . . which she desperately did. He must never find out that she had received an anonymous note just before the meal with a crude compass etched in its wax seal that suggested that the latest search for Children of Fate be thwarted as much as possible.

She could certainly understand the logic of keeping the gifted seers out of the Emperor's clutches. Forcing him to operate blind was a clever tactic. But why now? He'd been using Children of Fate seers for as long as anyone at court could remember. Her curiosity bordered on painful in its intensity, even though she knew it likely that her questions would never be answered.

Her mission was merely to serve in silence and secrecy. To knock a chip or two out of the foundation upon which the Eternal Empire rested. She must satisfy herself with that. To do more would risk drawing too much attention to herself, if not outright discovery. And that would be disastrous. All the work of her co-conspirators would be for naught if Maximillian caught wind of their slow, careful work.

Who knew how many years' worth of effort would be wasted? Her guess was that the Eight's work stretched back for centuries, if not longer. The thought was mind-boggling. But how else could anyone stand against the Emperor? It would take the combined efforts of generations of resisters to defeat him.

Regalo commented casually, "Did I tell you that the Master of Hounds has trained a new type of hound and two of them are with him? Laernan came in person to see them hunt."

She had ducked in the stable earlier to peek at the great fawn-colored beasts whose heads came easily to her waist. She'd assumed they were psionic hounds bred and trained to sniff out psionic abilities within people. It was said the hounds could smell a psionicist a league away and could track one up to five days after a scent trail was laid.

"Special hounds?" she asked lightly. "What do they hunt?"

He tore off a chunk of bread and spread berry butter on it as he answered, "Prophets and seers, apparently. Children of Fate, in particular."

Her fingers went white around the chalice she clutched. "How do you suppose he trained them to do something like that?"

Regalo swallowed the bread before answering, "No idea. Impressive, though. Apparently, a Child has been tracked into Haraland. High Hunter Lovak and High Inquisitor Laernan are taking the beasts out tomorrow to finish the hunt. Thought I might ask to go with them and see the hounds in action."

"What hour do you leave? Should I have Cook serve breakfast here or prepare rations for in the field?"

"After breakfast will be soon enough to start out, I'm sure. No need for these things to be uncivilized affairs. After all, they hunt humans, not wild animals."

She made a noncommittal sound as her mind raced. She must get word *now* to the Child of Fate in Haraland to hide. Or, better, flee. Whom could she trust with such an errand? Deeter. One of Krugar's men. He'd retired from the army a while back. Worked as a gardener, now, on the castle grounds. "An early breakfast on the morrow. And a picnic I should think for during your hunt. Shall I have Cook pack a supper as well?"

"I think not," Regalo replied casually. "How long can it take to hunt down one fugitive seer once the Emperor's hounds pick up the trail?"

She restrained an urge to run as she excused herself and left the room.

Will looked around in wonder as the dryads ushered the party into their magical grove. It was fully as beautiful as the hearth tales said faerie places were. A strange sense of familiarity came over him as he looked around this place and its exotic occupants. He'd never seen a dryad or a dryad grove before, yet he recognized this place.

"This is a mistake, I tell you," Cicero muttered. "Handing ourselves over to these sorceresses is madness."

"Relax and enjoy the moment, man," Kendrick replied, busking Cicero on the shoulder. "They're beautiful and like us. Enjoy their charms a little. It would be an insult not to."

Rosana rolled her eyes. "Just because a pretty lady offers you poison candy doesn't mean you ought to eat it."

"Exactly," Cicero agreed fervently.

The good-natured bickering continued as the dryads laid and lit a fire, produced a metal spit, and commenced roasting a delicious-smelling cut of meat. Will recognized the scent of venison. His mouth watered in anticipation.

He studied the faerie creatures surreptitiously. They appeared young and as inhumanly beautiful as the hearth tales described. They dressed in brief green skirts made of what looked like leaves. Their upper bodies were adorned only with lush garlands of ivy and flowers. Tantalizing glimpses of the curves of their breasts riveted his attention.

Cicero made a sound of disgust. "Do not make eye contact with them, human. They will ensorcel you in seconds."

Will looked over his shoulder at the elf, who still gazed steadfastly at his toes. "Really? I thought their effect on men was only the stuff of bedtime stories."

"We *are* the stuff of bedtime stories, you gorgeous young thing," one of them cooed.

"For pity's sake," Rosana grumbled. "Do they charm women as well, Cicero?"

"Nay. Just males. It is satyrs that women must worry about."

Will noticed Sha'Li grinning like a well-fed cat. Suspicion blossomed in his gut. "Are these dryads dangerous?" he asked bluntly.

As soon as the question came out of his mouth the answer bubbled up from somewhere deep in his mind. The dryads would not attack unless attacked. They could be exceedingly dangerous in a fight because of their ability to enslave males to their will. But in and of themselves, they posed little risk. Knowledge rose unbidden in his mind that the tree a being was bound to helped shaped their spirit, and rowan trees imbued a spirit with peace, idealism, and a drive to defend against the storm and evil magics. However, dryads were not above toying with males and amused themselves by charming men into being their love slaves.

How he knew all that he had no idea. But he was certain of the knowledge. Mayhap the other spirit inside him was whispering to him somehow.

Or mayhap he was losing his mind. No one in the Heart had uttered the word "possession" when High Matriarch Lenora announced that a second spirit was trapped within Will, but the possibility of it had hung heavy in the air. And Rosana *had* been adamant about coming with him on this journey.

Was she here to keep an eye on him? To take action against him if he should prove to be possessed? Would she kill him if it came to it?

Cicero snorted. "Depends on who you talk to whether or not they think dryads are dangerous. The women of my clan think they're deadly."

This made the dryads laugh with a trilling, dove-like noise.

"Come share our fire, my lovely young warrior," one of them said to Will. She sidled close to him, trailing an impossibly soft hand across his cheek. As she pressed her body against the length of his, he started when her knee lifted gently, her inner thigh caressing the front of his leg.

Rosana cleared her throat. "With all due respect, ladies, he is not exactly yours to crawl over."

One of the green nymphs shot a glare in the gypsy girl's direction. "He is yours, then? Bound to you by sacred vows?"

"Well, no—"

More laughter. "Then he's certainly free to play with us again, you silly human."

Rosana flared up, "Leave him alone."

"Temper, temper," one of them taunted lightly.

What did she mean, "play with us again"? he opened his mouth to ask, but looked up sharply at the sound of some sort of commotion just beyond the ring of rowan trees. That sounded like soldiers. He motioned urgently for silence and the male members of their party edged toward the shadows, weapons drawn.

He caught snatches of the whispered argument between Anton's men.

". . . know that place. It's Hawksong Grove. Haunted it be."

". . . 'taint haunted. Fae infested, it be."

". . . Dryads in there? . . . Ain't getting paid enough to tangle with them green witches. . . ."

". . . can't go in there."

". . . *won't* go in there!"

". . . they's gotta come out sometime . . . assuming them witches don't kill 'em all. I say we wait. . . ."

Kendrick motioned Will and the others away from the margin of the clearing and back to the fire. The younger Hyland announced, "We're safe so long as we stay in here. But Anton's entire army could surround the grove and we would never get out." He didn't sound too broken up over that prospect. Will rolled his eyes.

Eben commented in his baritone hum, "We eat and rest, and leave under cover of darkness, then?"

"The sooner the better," Cicero responded. He glared at Kendrick and added, "And no looking at them. We'll never get you out of here if they manage to charm you more deeply. Understood?"

Kendrick sighed. "But they're so pretty. And so friendly. We must stay and protect them!"

Cicero groaned and Will echoed the sentiment.

"No dalliances," Eben declared. "Marikeen is missing, and I've got to get this blasted mark off my face." A pause. Then he added more uncertainly, "But they are lovely, are they not? And frail. They could use some decent warriors to protect them from Anton and his men . . ." His voice trailed off as one of the dryads all but climbed his big body and commenced whispering in her ear.

"Agreed," Kendrick declared. "We will stay and protect the dryads from Anton's men."

Cicero traded significant looks with Will, who nodded back grimly. The two of them were agreed. When it came time to leave, they would knock Kendrick out if they had to.

The four of them headed back to the fire. As the party seated itself on logs rolled into a circle around the blaze, Will risked glancing at the dryads. Their skin undulated in hue even as he watched from a pale mint color to the rich emerald of summer leaves. He couldn't really tell them apart, so regular and similar were their facial features.

One of them slid closer to Cicero on his log, and Will noted with amusement that a fine sheen of perspiration had broken out upon the elf's brow as he struggled to keep his eyes off the creature now practically sitting in his lap. For Will's part, two dryads wasted no time cuddling up to him and making cozy.

"Mmm, you're warm."

"Oooh, strong muscles. Hard and bold."

A soft hand raked through his hair.

As Kendrick and Eben flirted back freely with the creatures, clearly lost in whatever spell the dryads had placed upon them, Will frowned. While these sprites were certainly easy on the eye, he found himself unimpressed with their aggressive flirting. He reached up to gently disentangle one of them from around his neck. "Sorry, ladies. Not interested."

The one who did most of the talking reared back. "You do not like females?"

Sha'Li snorted with laughter, and Rosana and Raina grinned broadly.

"I like girls just fine, thank you very much."

"Then why are you not interested in me? Am I ugly? Do I repel you in some way?" The dryad seemed genuinely distressed that he wasn't falling all over himself to become her plaything. Will glanced up at her, then realized his mistake. Her emerald green eyes pierced into his, capturing his gaze and holding it as power poured forth from her.

Will frowned. Looked away from her and over at Cicero. "You okay, buddy?" he asked the elf.

Cicero had his eyes tightly squeezed shut now, and sweat

poured down his face. "Must . . . not . . . look . . . ," the kindari gritted out from between clenched teeth.

Will looked back at the dryads draped all over him. What was the big deal? This time he looked directly at the females. Both of them frowned in concentration, obviously doing their best to do whatever it was they did to most men.

He shrugged. Grinned apologetically. "Sorry, ladies. You are very attractive, and I appreciate your interest. But I've had a long day and I could use some sleep. If you don't mind, it looks like my friends have had about all they can take, too."

All three dryads froze, staring in shock. He stared back at them, perplexed by how confounded they seemed.

"Who are you?" one of them whispered.

"I am Will. Uhh, Will Cobb."

"You are well named. Will, indeed," another murmured.

The one who appeared to be the leader of the pack stared at him long and hard. Finally, she said soberly, "I know not who or what you are, young human. But I will tell you this— and it comes from a servant of the Green Lady herself, so I speak truth. Someone dangerous comes this way. And he comes for you, strange human."

That was the second time someone had told him that. Will snorted. "So what's new?"

The dryad stared at him intently, not as if trying to control his mind but as if willing him to take her seriously.

"All right. Fine," he replied to her unspoken demand, "I believe you. I will have a care for my safety."

She nodded, relieved.

"Do you know who comes for me, then?" he asked her.

"Nay. I only know the message I was given. Safe travels unto you strange human." As one, the dryads rose gracefully, stepped up to the nearest tree trunks, and disappeared into them. Just melted right into the solid wood.

Will stared. "Did they just—"

"Tree walk," Eben replied, relief that the creatures had left palpable in his voice. "They move from tree to tree that way. They're forest spirits."

Will jolted. The world as he knew it shifted upon its axis. He'd heard stories of tree walkers but had always guffawed at the tales, knowing them to be pure fiction. But if dryads truly did exist . . . what other legends and fairy tales of his childhood might also be true?

Like stories of long-ago kings sleeping in wait for a time when they would be needed once more. Until now, his father's quest had been a hypothetical thing. He had been going through the motions out of respect for his parents' memories. But of a sudden it hit him: What if their quest was *real*? What if a king did exist with the power to throw off the yoke of Koth?

And of more immediate concern, what other magical or fantastic creatures were out here lurking in the forest? He glanced at the ancient rowans around him, suddenly feeling like a stranger in a strange land. What else didn't he know about these woods . . . or about the wider world?

Raina was too keyed up after the bandit attack to sleep for the remainder of the night. Which was why, deep in the night, she heard Kendrick creep away from his bed and one of the dryads emerging from her tree quietly coo in greeting. Raina rolled her eyes and stuffed her fingers in her ears.

She woke a little before the gray of dawn, and while Cicero scouted out the locations of Anton's men the others quietly broke camp. Whatever hold over Kendrick and Eben the dryads had before, it appeared to have been released. Likewise, if their pursuers had posted any guards in the night, they were all sleeping like babes, now. Whether from lack of discipline among them or the machinations of their dryad hostesses, she could not tell. Either way, she was deeply relieved that they would not have to fight their way out of the grove.

The party slipped quietly from the grove and Cicero led them around the sleeping bandits or soldiers or whatever their attackers had been. The dryads did not make another appearance, for which the male members of their group seemed relieved.

That annoying lizardman girl insisted on tagging along. Something about not leaving until Will handed over that wooden disk of his to her. Raina wished he could just do it and get rid of the surly female. But no such luck.

Their odd little party set out, everyone watching everyone else with veiled suspicion to one degree or another. Not exactly an auspicious start for this journey of theirs. Rosana was furious with Sha'Li for attacking Will. Will was angry at the lizardman girl on Rosana's behalf. Eben was angry at Kendrick for dallying with the dryads, Kendrick angry at Eben for being angry, and Sha'Li was angry at everyone, it seemed.

They trudged along, mostly silent through the morning, for which Raina was grateful. It was better than the bickering her brothers—her half brothers, she corrected herself bitterly—would have engaged in under the same circumstances.

They stopped for lunch, and the conversation turned to what threat the dryads might have been trying to warn Will of the previous night. The consensus was that a superpowerful dryad who could command Will's mind was en route to restore the dryads' reputations. For some reason, she and the other girls in the party found the whole notion much funnier than the fellows did.

The party was less tense through the afternoon, but quiet

as fatigue set in. Not long after they'd started looking for a likely spot to stop for the night, Cicero abruptly called a halt, studied what looked like some random scratches on a tree, and, without explanation, plunged into the trees. He returned a few minutes later, grinning widely.

"What?" she demanded.

"Follow me. We will sleep safe from Anton's soldiers this night," he declared.

Perplexed, she and the others followed him off the path and into heavy woods. The trees were huge here. Old-growth forest. Somehow, this stretch of timber had escaped the ravages of the Forester's Guild.

They picked their way through dangerous tree roots and thick brambles for several minutes. Without warning, a half-dozen elves dropped out of the trees around them. Raina noticed intricate russet-colored swirls decorating their faces. *Kindari.* Cicero must have seen their sign along the margins of the road.

Cicero murmured under his breath. "The ursari. Bear clan." Louder he said, "Greetings, cousins. I am Cicero of the arachnari."

One of the elves stepped forward. He was tall and held an axe in his right hand, but the blade was behind his body in a nonthreatening fashion. "Ho, long legs. Do northern stars take away your sorrows?"

Cicero replied, "Would that they could. We travel in search of a lost friend. And this night, we seek safe shelter."

"Then come with us and be welcome," the big elf replied.

In short order the kindari had invited the party to their village, tucked into the hillsides and roots of the largest trees in the forest.

They were ushered into a large roundhouse, some sort of gathering place for the village. The construction was beautiful, with arched wooden ribs that looked carved directly from tree roots climbing to a point in the center of the high ceiling. The wood-paneled walls were carved with gorgeous representations of nature—vines and flowers and fanciful creatures. It was a room worthy of any king, tucked here among the trees.

Food and drink were brought, and dinner was a merry affair with laughter and song aplenty. The kindari embraced life with zest, not shying away from displays of emotion like their cousins of other elven persuasions. They laughed loud, freely shed a tear at a sad song, and seemed more at ease in their skins than any other elves she'd met.

After everyone had dined and the assemblage was served mugs of bracing hard cider, the kindari elders and travelers settled down around a bonfire to trade news.

Raina sat quietly, listening to the events of the day. The big news was that an expeditionary force from Dupree marched north to the Forest of Thorns and was wreaking havoc along the way, requisitioning whatever food and supplies it wanted. She wondered how these forest dwellers managed to get such current information way out here. Word had it the governor was leading the force personally. The idea concerned the ursari greatly.

Rumor also had it the governor was looking to provoke a war with the Boki. The kindari elders, led by a fellow with a thick head of snow-white hair, predicted that in his ambition and greed Anton would use the invasion as a free pass to steal all the gold and other resources he could lay his hands on. Or worse, he might attempt to make a great conquest of the Forest of Thorns, an endeavor the ursari scorned as folly.

If Anton truly provoked the greenskin tribes, it was generally agreed that the Empire would be forced to send a large

Imperial legion to Haelos to quell the hornet's nest Anton would stir up.

Cicero chimed in, "The way I hear it, the governor is unbalanced in the head. Kothite nobles always seem to be a little off, if you know what I mean."

This from the man whose friend and colleague had ranted about her bringing down a kingdom, compliments of a vision from his dragon lord?

Knowing nods bobbed all around. Several ursari spoke in quick succession while she was momentarily distracted by the reminder of the elf Moto's disturbing prophecy.

". . . The people of the Black Flame go a little mad with power when they come to Haelos. . . ."

". . . If the Viper knows what's good for him he will stay clear of the sky people of the Ariannas. . . ."

". . . But if he fells the nomads then all the Valelands would be his for the taking. . . ."

". . . The Wyldes will be lucky if he stays occupied high of Dupree. . . ."

". . . the Lady knows the Boki will draw much blood. Fighting in the thorns is madness."

A momentary silence fell. Kendrick leaned forward, grinning with surprising violence. "Personally, I'd like to see the governor try the full might of the Boki. If anything, their strength has grown since the last time he quelled them. They'd crush Anton."

Eben argued, "I dunno. I've run my caravans through the Forest of Thorns, and those orcs are always brawling and squirmishing among themselves."

The white-haired elder replied sagely, "Ahh, yes. Wolves fighting over a single bone are fierce individually. But such a pack will rend the bear that comes to their supper limb from limb. The Lords of the Boar have an entire forest under their control and all of its power."

Rosana piped up, "Like our violent little colony is not the same way if properly provoked?"

The ursari elder shrugged. "We make our homes in a dangerous land. Those who live here must keep their reflexes and swords sharp to survive."

Cicero commiserated, "Better perilous freedom than safe and certain servitude. Is that not what our kind always says?"

The elder nodded slowly. Raina's head was in a whirl. These people were speaking treason. Casually! Surely there was an informant somewhere in their midst. Merely thinking these sorts of thoughts was a crime punishable by death. Her parents had no love for the Empire, but never . . . ever . . . would one of them utter aloud anything like these folk were chatting about over mugs of hard cider.

Furthermore, the vitriol dripping in the kindari's voices at any reference to Koth was breathtaking. The Empire was all-powerful. All-knowing. One did not gainsay it. Ever. And yet, these wild people dared to speak their minds.

A staggering exercise of freedom.

Freedom. A notion for which she had a new and utterly profound respect after her own narrow escape from unwilling servitude to the Mages of Alchizzadon. She *had* to find a way to rouse the Great Mage. And sooner rather than later.

Aurelius peered surreptitiously out the window of his office high in the Mage's Guild. He spotted the individual he awaited entering the far side of Eldritch Circle. How could anyone miss the man? Not only was he a head taller than any other person in the open space, but he still moved as gracefully as a dancer, still exuded an odd sense of utter calm in the midst of a great storm, still wrapped himself in an aura of deadly menace.

But from this vantage point Aurelius watched most of the people in the plaza completely failing to notice one of the most feared assassins on either shore of the Abyssmal Sea. Shaking his head, he headed downstairs to greet his guest.

When a knock sounded upon the guild's outer door, Aurelius brushed aside the apprentice on door duty and opened it himself. He grinned at the faint shoulder twitch that was his guest's only indication of surprise.

"Come in, you old reprobate." Aurelius laughed. "Are you wearing that getup to frighten small children, or do you seriously think it hides your identity?"

Selea shrugged out of his voluminous hooded cloak and passed it to Aurelius. He stripped off the black gloves that completed the ensemble. "It seems to do the trick. So,

Aurelius. I am surprised to find you here. You do not accompany our illustrious governor?"

"What's this? Is your spy network failing you?"

The nulvari grinned, his smile all the whiter for his midnight dark face. "Go ahead and think that, my friend. We'll see who's still standing in two hundred years."

Aurelius had no illusions as to why Selea had come to visit. The nulvari had come to collect on the favor owed him and would finally demand answers. Answers Aurelius had avoided giving the assassin for sixteen years. Selea followed him into his office complete with its new desk, making no sound whatsoever with his passing.

Aurelius ushered Selea to the pair of new armchairs he'd brought in after De'Vir's boy blew the place to bits, propped his feet on the raised hearth before the fire, leaned back, and feigned a casualness he was far from feeling. "What can I do for you, my old friend?"

"I seek answers to questions you already know I am here to ask."

Like most nulvari, Selea could be incredibly obtuse when he chose. He was a master at speaking around a subject, at conveying vast amounts of information without ever once mentioning a thing directly. And vice versa, he could talk for hours and never actually reveal a thing. Interesting that he indulged in no pleasantries today, no subtle wordplay, no hints or innuendos. The reappearance of the names De'Vir and Ki'Raiden in the same week must have worried Selea as much as it worried Aurelius.

Seeking to delay the real issue, Aurelius asked, "What news of the boy?"

In much more typical Selea fashion, the nulvari answered a question with a question. "What do you know of the lad?"

He temporized, "I'm assuming this conversation is

between two friends and not the representatives of our respective guilds?"

"Of course."

Even Aurelius, who'd known Selea for some two hundred years, had no idea what Assassin's Guild rank the man held. But his assertion that this was not a guild matter seemed to relax the nulvari. Ever the cautious one, he was. Didn't entirely trust his closest acquaintances, even after centuries.

Selea finally ended their verbal dance by saying bluntly, "I sought out the boy as you asked. Delivered him to the Heart. And at my request, Lenora duly let him slip out with that gypsy girl he came to Dupree with. As we expected, they headed toward the Forest of Thorns. My informant reports that your boy caught up with Hyland's son before they even passed through the city gates."

"Excellent," Aurelius murmured. "On what pretext did Lenora let the boy go?"

"I suspect all she had to do was leave the door unlocked and look the other way." Selea added reflectively, "That boy gravitates to trouble like his father did."

Aurelius rose and went to the liquor cabinet. "Your usual?"

"Indeed."

He poured honeyed mead into a pair of tall glass mugs and carried them back to the fire. The two men sipped in silence, contemplating the flickering flames for several minutes. It was a pleasure to be in the leisurely company of another elf. Humans were always in such a blasted hurry. They talked fast and moved fast, racing through life like madmen. Of course, with so little time to live he supposed they had cause.

"Why this particular chain of events?" Aurelius murmured. "Why now?"

Selea frowned to show he'd heard the question, but the silence stretched out while he considered his answer. Finally, the nulvari murmured back, "Perhaps it is merely coincidence."

"Cursed improbable coincidence that the Boki leave their forest for the first time since the incursion, De'Vir's boy shows up out of nowhere, and Anton goes tearing off to the Forest of Thorns on some flimsy pretext. You'll forgive me if I'm not that big a believer in random chance."

"What's your take on it, then?"

Aurelius shrugged. "Something's afoot. Something having to do with that twice-cursed Boki grove and the legend surrounding it."

"Like what?"

"I haven't the slightest idea." He huffed in frustration. "I even resorted to consulting a seer about it."

Selea's brows shot up, as well they should. Aurelius had long been a proponent of logic in all things, and soothsayers were anything but.

"What did you learn?"

Aurelius sighed. "I wish I could say it was all stuff and nonsense, but I cannot. She said the blade heats in the fire and awaits only the beating of its edge. I take that to mean the players are nearly in position and some great event is nearly upon us."

"What event?" Selea asked.

"No clue."

"Did she say more?"

Aurelius rolled his eyes and quoted, " 'In the glow of the sun will hope endure, whilst they battle dread for an ancient cure. She who waits will, too, play her part, half a light will grow to fill the heart.' "

"What does that mean?" Selea asked.

"I haven't the slightest. I can tell you the seer had no

memory of telling me those words when I repeated them back to her, though."

Selea jerked upright. "She didn't remember her own vision after she spoke it?"

Alarmed, Aurelius answered, "No." A pause. "Why do you ask?"

Another long silence ensued as Selea's formidable mind worked on something. Aurelius was patient, however. Finally, the nulvari replied slowly, "I caught a whiff of an incident at the Imperial Court some time back."

At court? What in the world did that have to do with their current problem?

"A bare whisper," Selea continued. "Years ago. From the innermost circles of power. That a prophecy killed a seer. Have you ever heard of such a thing? And now you speak of a seer forgetting her vision immediately after giving it?"

"Is something wrong with the Veil that is causing seers to fail?" Aurelius asked in surprise.

"Nay. Exactly the opposite. I think the seers are getting something exactly right. Something powerful enough to erase itself from their minds or even kill them."

"All my seer indicated was that the event is near. But what event?"

The two men stared at each other. What event indeed? And why were all the players from another event, long past, suddenly converging again? Aurelius listed them in his head. Himself. Selea. Hyland. Tiberius De'Vir—or at least his son. Anton. Even the Boki and their blasted grove. Aurelius asked Selea, "Do you know where the Boki raiders are, now?"

"A few rumors have come in of Boki scouting parties. They seem to be seeking something or someone specific. They are not engaging in their usual killing and looting. And there was that one large raiding party seen moving fast to the north. Fast enough not to bother sacking any crofts. One would assume they made for home."

"Did they find what they were after, then?"

Selea shrugged. "They wiped out Tiberius's village. One must assume they killed our old friend."

Sorrow stretched out, silent and painful between them for a time. He had quietly checked the Heart death logs and no one matching Ty's description had resurrected recently. Aurelius had already grieved the loss of his adopted son once, long ago, but this time seemed so much more final. Only his previous centuries of life and loss gave him the strength to endure it. It was the price of living among humans. They lived and died so very quickly.

He finally broke the silence. "What is really going on behind the stage of this play? Who pulls at the puppet strings?"

Selea countered, "Who would benefit by bringing all of us back together? What does that being have to gain by it?"

A log burned through just then, its halves collapsing with a burst of sparks. The blaze flared up briefly, then settled back to a sluggish flicker. *An interesting word choice, that. What being* indeed? Selea thought greater powers were involving themselves in the affairs of humans? Such a thing had not happened in a very long time.

"I think," Aurelius said carefully, "that someone wants us to finish what we began."

"And what, exactly, was it that we began?" Selea shot back.

Aurelius winced. He'd known this conversation would come to this. That the price for the assassin's help with De'Vir's boy would be the secret he and Tiberius had guarded so closely for all these years. "I don't suppose you'll accept that it is Mage's Guild business and leave it at that?"

"I accepted that once. I will not do so again. The last time you nearly led me to dishonor."

Aurelius sighed. If Selea deemed this a matter of honor, he would not budge. He had come for answers and would not leave without them. Nonetheless, Aurelius tried one last time to divert the nulvari. "The Boki are slaughtering innocents. It is up to us to find a way to stop them. Is that not enough?"

Selea's voice was deceptively gentle. Chiding, even. "Surely you know that slaughter is no argument to sway me, of all people."

Aurelius closed his eyes and pinched the bridge of his nose. It did not alleviate the dull ache starting behind his eyes. "I take my word and my oaths no less seriously than you, Selea. What you ask of me is tantamount to betraying my oath to the Mage's Guild."

"Which part of it?"

Aurelius snapped, "Does it matter?"

Selea replied promptly, "Nay, it does not."

They traded commiserating looks. Living by a strict code of honor could be a many-horned pain in the arse sometimes.

Finally, Aurelius broke the stalemate. "I will tell you as much as I can. You will have to fill in certain blank spots for yourself, however. After that, I leave it to you to decide whether or not to help me finish this thing."

Selea nodded, the only movement disturbing that uncanny stillness of his.

"When I first arrived in the colonies and realized the magical nature of the land itself, I immediately suspected that there might be more to this continent than the Empire realized. Much more. I sent several of my most trusted people forth to learn what they could of this land and its past. I had no way of telling how much history the Kothites had successfully expunged."

Selea made a wry face. "If my limited research is any indication, the Empire has vastly underestimated Haelos."

Aurelius nodded. "On that, we are agreed. I sent my Dragon north into the Forest of Thorns, which rumor said was an especially dangerous—and magical—place."

"Tiberius?" Selea interjected.

"Aye. He brought back word to me of a land guarded by fantastic creatures—gruesome magical constructs, talking trees, and the fiercest greenskins ever encountered. I sent a request to my superiors for resources to research the contents and magical properties of this place. Governor Volen got wind of the discovery. He made a stink that the guilds were becoming too powerful, too independent."

Selea chimed in, "And as he was the duly appointed representative of the Emperor, this could not be tolerated."

Aurelius nodded. "He ordered us to leave the Forest of Thorns alone and, furthermore, set his first advisor, Anton, to keep an eye on us. But of course, what poor Volen didn't count on was Anton starting a war with the Boki."

"One that conveniently killed Volen," Selea commented wryly. "You've proof that Anton engineered the Boki incursion?"

Aurelius pulled a face. "Anton's too smart for that. But why else would the Boki come roaring out of their trees, kill the governor and most of the landsgraves who were giving Anton trouble, and then pull back into the Forest of Thorns? The Boki had no argument with the colonists. Their paths had never even crossed for the most part. There's no question in my mind but Anton hired them to do his dirty work."

Selea nodded slowly. "I have long thought his violent campaign to avenge the death of Volen seemed . . . contrived."

"Not only did it make him look good to the Emperor and emphasize his innocence in knocking off old Volen, but it also gave him a perfect excuse to poke around the Forest of Thorns for whatever secret treasure Tiberius had stumbled across."

"Was there a treasure?" Selea asked quietly.

"Still is one. And to anticipate your next question, no, I do not know what the Boki guard so fiercely. But they are willing to die to the last man, woman, and child to protect it."

"You're sure Anton did not find it?"

"Positive. He was chased out of that grove before we were. He never even made it into the cave. I'm convinced the Boki moved whatever it was they hid soon after that debacle, anyway. Even if Anton returned to the spot later, the treasure was long gone before he came back."

"Any idea what the treasure is?" Selea asked casually.

A little too casually. Aurelius looked his old friend directly in the eye and answered honestly, "I do not know."

"Any guesses?"

Aurelius laughed. "I've got plenty of those. I've had many years to come up with a long list of possibilities." And because he was not eager to elaborate upon that list, he asked in a diversionary feint, "I never did understand why you were sent to accompany me on that original expedition."

Selea leaned forward. "Since we are sharing confidences today, I suppose it does no harm to tell you. I was sent along to investigate a request for an assassination writ on you. The evidence presented to the guildmaster was . . . questionable . . . and I was sent to see if the charges had merit. Should you show anything other than utmost loyalty to the Empire, a writ would have been issued for your death."

Aurelius stared, stunned. "Who tried to buy the writ?"

"Who else?" Selea answered elliptically.

Of course. Anton. The whoreson. Aurelius looked at the assassin quizzically. "Then why am I not dead?"

Selea's gaze went blacker than his skin. "The First Rule. I cannot say more."

Aurelius was shocked. He had in no way demonstrated utmost loyalty to the Empire in that grove. By all rights, he should have been dead in short order. Behind his back, Selea was called the killer who never failed. Aurelius silently blessed whatever quirk of nulvari honor that had interfered with Selea making a report that would have resulted in a writ of execution on him all those years ago.

The only person to suffer out of that's day's work was . . . *of course.* An explosion of understanding detonated in his head. *Tiberius.* Despite his own glowing reports on how Tiberius had conducted himself in the Forest of Thorns, the knight had inexplicably been stripped of his title, charged with a host of crimes, and sentenced to death.

"Did you divert attention away from me and onto Tiberius instead?" he blurted.

"Not I," Selea answered blandly.

Who then? An image of another nulvari came to him, one close enough to Anton to whisper in his ear. Ceridwyn Nightshade. Selea's cousin and both of them from House Bat. Did she and the assassin seated beside him conspire together from time to time? Blood was particularly thick among the nulvari, even more so than most elves.

All these years later, he did not know whether to thank the nulvari or curse them. *Ah, Tiberius.* Ever the loyal soldier. They'd all used him ill, and he was no exception to that. The knight had silently accepted disgrace and become a fugitive to protect his adopted father and his guild. Pain and pride sluiced through him in equal measures. Tiberius was surely worthy of his family's name.

"What more can you tell me of that odd fellow who helped us escape the forest?" Selea was asking.

"That nature guardian? What did he call himself?"

"Greenbeard," Selea supplied.

Aurelius would never forget the shock of seeing the forester. Ostensibly human, the fellow had actually had moss growing in his beard and veins colored green beneath his skin. He had seemed part plant and part human, and he had not been much more civilized than a forest creature. But he had called off the guardians of the grove and guided their little party clear of the remnants of battle. Or, by that time, the remnants of slaughter. The Boki had utterly destroyed Anton's army and not been merciful in the doing of it. They did not appreciate their lands being invaded and had let it be known in no uncertain terms.

"I know nothing more than you, Selea. He appeared out of the trees, led us out of the forest, and then disappeared back into the woods. Strange fellow, to say the least."

"Tell me more of this political stink over your researching the grove," Selea murmured.

Aurelius gave himself a mental shake. "The Forester's Guild claimed the grove, as all forests fell under their control. Never mind that not one of their loggers would set foot in the Forest of Thorns for fear of dying a swift and terrible death at the hands of the orcs there. Then the Miner's Guild got into the fray. They claimed to be in charge of harvesting all magical components. If there were any magical properties to the place, they wanted to go in first and gather whatever was to be had."

"I'm surprised the Heart didn't find a way to throw its hat into the fight," Selea commented dryly.

Equally dryly, Aurelius replied, "Oh, they did. They claimed they ought to go in first and be allowed to convert the residents of the Forest of Thorns to the Heartstones. Once the natives were properly civilized, then the rest of us could go in and engage in peaceful trade with the forest's inhabitants."

Selea rolled his eyes. Aurelius thought he heard his companion mutter under his breath in nulvari, "Self-righteous do-gooders."

Aurelius echoed the sentiment. His guild was forever competing with the Heart over who would control the magics, scrolls, potions, and magical components so necessary to both of their crafts. He picked up the thread of his story again. "At any rate, representatives of various guilds went en masse on Anton's expedition to see this magic grove. They treated it like some sort of glorified picnic outing."

"And conveniently forgot about the magical constructs and talking trees?" Selea asked wryly.

"Not to mention the army of orcs," Aurelius added while he pondered how to gloss over the next part. He'd been ordered in secret by his Mage's Guild superiors to lead the expedition astray, not to reveal to the group where the actual magical site was located. But such an order was strictly the private business of the guild, even after all these years. Revealing that communiqué skirted the very edge of outright disobedience to the Empire.

He spoke carefully. "As we drew closer to the grove, resistance by its defenders grew steadily more determined and dangerous. It was decided that it would not be in the general interest to make a direct approach to the area. After the battle of the plant-men and the were-bears—" He broke off. "Were you present for that?"

Selea nodded, his expression grim enough that he could indeed have been there. It had been a massacre. Nearly half the expeditionary force had been killed in that one brief, bloody battle.

Aurelius continued, "After that, a panicked retreat was

called. Parties got separated from the main force. Skirmishes further scattered our troops throughout the woods. It was chaos."

"I remember it well."

Time for another delicate evasion. "Tiberius and I fought as a team that day. Eventually, we found ourselves alone. He recognized a landmark and informed me that we must be all but upon the site we sought."

"How convenient," Selea murmured.

Not surprisingly, the nulvari didn't buy the half-truth for a minute. But, thankfully, neither did he press the issue. It went without saying that Tiberius and he had intentionally left the main force of Anton's soldiers to seek out the grove in the midst of the mess.

Aurelius continued grimly, "We made our way into the grove, the two of us. Just as we reached the clearing, a skirmish broke out on the other side of it. It did not go well for the colonial troops. A cadre of orcs—I found out later it was Boki Blood Lords led by Ki'Raiden—rolled through the squad like they were raw recruits. Hyland was the lone survivor of that fight. When he realized he was the only man alive, he fled and ended up with Tiberius and me. We three hid. The Boki elite guard was drawn to another fight on the other side of the grove, and we were not found."

Selea grinned. "So. It was not superior skill over the Boki Blood Lords that gained you entrance to the grove, but rather dumb luck."

Aurelius grinned. "Aye."

"How did you get past the tree guardians and plant-men?"

"I do not know. Maybe because we were so few and so weak by then, they did not see us as a threat. Speaking of which, how did *you* gain entrance to the grove?"

Selea smiled. "I, too, . . . evaded . . . the Boki. As for the plant guardians, I captured a dryad and threatened to kill her if they did not let me pass. Lady Elysia was none too amused to have my blade at her throat, I might add."

"How did you resist her charms?" Aurelius burst out in disbelief.

Selea pursed his lips. "Trade secret. Sorry."

Another time, Aurelius might have argued strenuously that this knowledge was of utmost importance to the Mage's Guild. They'd been trying for decades to come up with some defense against the devastatingly effective gaze attacks of the dryads. But today he let it go.

"How did you kidnap a dryad, then?"

Selea shrugged. "It was not my first time to work in the Forest of Thorns."

Aurelius stared, stunned. *To work?* Selea had been there before to assassinate someone? But who? The only known dwellers of the place were Boki—

"You assassinated a Boki?" Aurelius blurted.

Selea frowned sharply as if to say that Aurelius knew better than to ask such a thing directly. And indeed he did. His solinari mind raced. *Who among the Boki would rate an Imperial assassination other than a thane, and a high-ranking one at that? Who on Urth would contract and pay good gold to see a thane killed? Who could use internal strife among the Boki to his or her advantage—*

Anton.

If he asked any more questions, Selea might very well get up and leave, and Aurelius desperately needed Selea to agree to help him. Instead, he commented lightly, "You have known for a long time, then, the true nature of our governor."

Selea said not a word, but very slowly, very subtly, nodded his head in the affirmative.

Unbelievable. Anton had assassinated one of the thanes,

either to sow discord among the Boki or to make way for a thane he supported. Was it possible that the governor had been in collusion with the Boki for all these years? How was any other conclusion possible? But, of course, there was not a shred of proof. Writs of assassination were strictly secret and stayed secret even after their execution. The guild would never cough up the writ, even to prove Anton's complicity with the Boki.

Aurelius's mind whirled over the scale and audacity of Anton's corruption. *And Selea had known about it all this time.* No wonder the nulvari had bent his ironclad rules of honor to protect Aurelius and to hang Aurelius's knight out to dry instead. Selea must have sensed Aurelius's deep disapproval of Anton right from the beginning and decided a Mage's Guildmaster who disliked Anton and would thwart him at every turn was more important than sacrificing a bit of his honor . . . and a knight. Aurelius, frankly, was humbled. He knew just how seriously the nulvari took their honor.

"You are silent a long time, my old friend," Selea said gently.

Aurelius took a moment to trace back the thread of the conversation. They'd been talking about how they each gained entrance to the closely guarded Boki grove. He shrugged, "And then you joined us in the clearing. You know the rest."

Selea wasn't about to let Aurelius get away with that. "Actually, I would like to hear your version of 'the rest.' I saw several things I did not understand that day. I have wondered much about them."

Rather than tell all, Aurelius took instead the tack of asking, "What didn't you understand?"

"We found the underground chamber and went in. What were those creatures that attacked us?"

Aurelius closed his eyes and saw the beasts as clearly as if it had been yesterday. Some resembled mythic creatures, but most were simply grotesque. He answered honestly, "I do not know what they were. The stuff of our worst nightmares."

Selea frowned. "When we cut them down, they transformed into those ghost-like things."

Aurelius winced. Here went another guild secret. But he could probably justify it to his superiors as the sort of information a top-flight assassin could conceivably need someday. "I believe those were phantasms. They took the shape of our worst nightmares and when they neared death, they reverted to their natural forms."

"Dream creatures?"

Aurelius nodded reluctantly. Thankfully, Selea pressed no more on that subject. Instead, he asked, "They were calm at first, but then raged all of a sudden. What set them off?"

"We must have touched some trigger or set off some sort of trap."

"What was that door on the far side of the room? I thought I saw writing upon it."

Aurelius exhaled carefully. "Neither I nor Tiberius ever made it across the room to take a close look at it."

"What did those creatures guard, then?"

"I do not know." Another half-truth. The door—or more accurately the place it led to—was undoubtedly the thing they guarded. He changed the subject smoothly. "As you well know, the phantasms chased us out of there before we could do much besides fight, and then run, for our lives."

Aurelius schooled his face to its most passive, relaxed, open expression. He dared not make eye contact with the oh-so-perceptive assassin, and stared into the fire instead. *Please, by the Lady, let him not ask any more questions.* The door might have been across the room, but the writing upon it had been large and clear. Only he and Tiberius out of the four men in the room had the skill to read the magical writing, and read it they had.

The door was definitely extra-planar in nature and involved transporting people to someplace . . . else. He and Tiberius had talked and talked about it on the return journey to Dupree. Their best guess was that the place behind the door was not the treasure itself. Rather, whatever—or whoever—was in that place beyond the door was the great and closely guarded secret of the grove.

And now, all these years later, every portent the fates could throw in his path pointed back at the grove.

"What do you propose to do, Aurelius? Broach the guardians and attempt to gain entrance to the grove once more?"

He leaned forward, looking intently at his companion. "We know what we're up against, now. Why not try it?"

"I am thinking of retiring, not embarking on heroic quests."

Aurelius made a face at him. "Your skills have not diminished an iota. On that I would bet my life. You are not called the Emperor's Blade for nothing."

Selea rolled his eyes. "I assure you, the greater part of my reputation is speculation and rumor."

"Which makes your work that much easier."

"I repeat. I am retiring."

Aurelius leaned back, commenting sardonically, "Of course you are. Assassins are always left to their old ages in peace. Once you declare yourself out of the game, no old vendettas will come looking for you. You can let down your guard and relax. Why, I wager you won't even bother to carry a dagger, will you?"

Selea came as close to a glare as he ever did to any real expression.

Aurelius grinned unrepentantly. "As I was saying. You and I could do it. We could get into that grove again and discover its secret. Furthermore, I think we're supposed to. The hand of some greater power is clearly at work here."

"And perhaps we are a couple of vain old fools, wishing to be in the thick of events once more, manufacturing portents and signs that tell us what we wish to hear."

Aurelius huffed. "I'll grant you that we may both be vain, but when did you become old or a fool? The last time I checked, I was neither."

Selea shook his head. "We were lucky last time to escape with our lives. Very lucky. Do you not remember the Boki guards ringing the grove? Or those trees snapping their branches back and forth like giant whips? How are we to defeat them? And once past them, how are we to vanquish the nightmares and phantasms?"

"I believe they will make way for us. I think they want us to find whatever's in that chamber."

Selea exclaimed, "And now you are mad in addition to old and foolish!"

"Mayhap I am. But do you not wish to know the secret? To give it one last try?"

Selea shook his head. "No. I wish to live out a long and quiet retirement."

In desperation, Aurelius threw his final argument at Selea's feet. "I may not know what is in that grove, but I know this. It is extremely valuable and powerful, else it would not be defended thus. Do you really want it to fall into the hands of Anton Constantine?"

"You are so sure he'll make a run at it?"

"I wouldn't bet a shaved copper that it won't be the first place he goes once he reaches the Forest of Thorns."

Selea sighed heavily. "I wouldn't take that bet, either. My sources speculate that he has an agenda beyond defeating the Boki in this foray to the Forest of Thorns." He was silent a long time. Aurelius waited him out. Finally, with deep reluctance, Selea said, "If Anton moves on the grove, I will stand with you."

Aurelius nodded. There was no need for handshakes between them to seal the deal. A nulvari's word was given. While Selea stared morosely into the fire, Aurelius went to the door and called for food.

They talked of inconsequential things over supper. But when they had finished eating and pushed their plates away, Selea commented without preamble, "Why did you send the boy in that direction? Do you suppose Tiberius told him where the grove is? If so, why not let him have a go at the chamber? After all, he's expendable."

"Maybe. Maybe not."

Selea looked startled, which meant he was mightily surprised indeed.

Aurelius continued reluctantly. He hated to open up yet another touchy subject with Selea so soon after gaining a major concession from him on the last one. "The seer I hired said a few additional things in her forgotten trance. She said the son would fulfill the father's fate and the daughter would refuse the mother's fate. What if the son is Tiberius's boy?"

Selea let out a long-suffering sigh. "What kind of nonsense is that? This is why I never deal with fortune-tellers or soothsayers. They babble enough to make you think your gold was well spent."

Aurelius grinned reluctantly. "You're probably right. But still. To have Tiberius's boy emerge out of the blue, having crossed paths with the Boki . . . It was Ki'Raiden himself who led the raiding party if the boy's report is to be believed. You have to admit it does look more than a little like young Will is the son who would fulfill the father's fate."

"And the girl?" Selea asked.

"I have no idea whom the fortune-teller spoke of."

"De'Vir's boy has a good head start upon us." Selea sighed heavily. "I hate having to travel fast."

During a lull in the conversation, many of the young kindari made their way outside to smoke their long, thin pipes. Cicero, Kendrick, and Eben joined the exodus, and on their way out pried Will away from Rosana's side to join them.

Raina made her way to where the white-haired elder sat in a chair of bent wood, intricately woven. "I would ask you a question, good sir."

He gestured to a low cassock at his left elbow and waited silently as she perched upon it and composed her thoughts. "What can you tell me of the Green Lady?"

The elder answered readily enough, "We are thankful to the Green Lady for all of her gifts." He shrugged. "She is the living heart of our lands, the trees, the stones, the creatures all. She whispers in the winds. She paints in the blooms. How does a lady of pages come to know of the Lady Green?"

She spoke carefully. "I have heard this name in conjunction with other names. References to beings who would protect the land from . . . outside influences."

"What beings?" he asked directly. Bluntly.

She sighed. *So much for delicacy.* "The Mythar, for one."

"Ahh."

She waited, but the elder added nothing more. Finally, she asked, "What can you tell me of him?"

"The words of my people are for my people alone."

"Why not? Does not the land belong to all of us and all of us to it? Why would a guardian of the land not be the guardian of us all?"

The elder stared hard at her. She became aware that abrupt

and total silence had fallen among all the kindari within earshot. He planted his chin on his fist and stared into space, deep in thought. An elf nearby cleared his throat and, when the elder glanced up at him, gave a tiny jerk of his head to indicate that he should get rid of Raina so they could talk.

She intruded upon the silent exchange with quiet determination, "This matter concerns me directly. I would prefer to remain for the entire discussion, if you please."

Looking intently at the necklace she always wore around her neck, the kindari elder asked, "What have pages taught you of this Mythar, little flower?"

If she wanted answers, she was clearly going to have to come clean with this elf. She answered reluctantly, "I wish to find him and wake him up. I need to borrow some of his magic to solve an old and vexing problem within my family."

Exclamations of shock and dismay erupted around the fire.

The elder's mouth twitched with suppressed humor. "We wonder if the flower can survive the storm that is to come."

Someone said from the darkness beyond the fire, "She is not of the Green. This is not her path—"

Raina cut the voice off with a smooth diplomacy her mother would have been proud of. "But many paths can lead a person home. The problem within my family is dire and I will walk this path to the Mythar with or without your help."

Silence fell, interrupted only by the quiet crackling of the fire.

"What ails your family, little flower, that needs the Mythar to cure?"

Raina winced mentally. "I have need of olde magick to wake someone who can release my family from an ancient promise. Until then, the women of my family are trapped into unwilling servitude to this promise. You can ask Cicero if I speak truly."

The white-haired one replied mildly, "No need. I recognize clear skies when I see them and know full well that thunder follows lightning."

"Will you help me?"

"If this be your path, little flower, we cannot walk it for you. But we can give you signs to guide your way." The elder looked around at the gathered elves, who seemed to have increased greatly in number all of a sudden. "Speak now, Children of the Bear if you challenge my telling of the old words."

The silence that followed was turbulent, disgruntled even, but no one broke it.

The elder gave a short nod. "It is settled." He shifted to face her more fully. "From the time when the Green was new again pass the words of legends old."

Raina nodded. The magnificent library she'd been educated within survived mostly because it had been carefully protected from the ravages of the Empire. Come to think of it, the Mages of Alchizzadon might have had something to do with that.

The white-haired one spoke, his voice paper thin with age. "The mark of the Great Spider Zinn was given to the warriors of the Green who called home a place named Gandamere. This place, where all elves lived in the Great Circle, did the Mythar rule until he fell in battle to the Darkclaw of Ru'dath.

"A Green Lady, wreathed in the power of the woods, came to the Zinnzari, bearing hope that their king might yet be saved. She demanded that the king's guard bring his body to her. But her promise turned as grey as the storm clouds when the king was left in an enchanted slumber. Ever bound to their king, the Zinnzari promised to serve the lady so that the Mythar might one day return. In the service of Hemlocke, the Great Green Dragon, they remain to this day."

Raina listened, enthralled. "Do your legends say anything about where he can be found?"

White Hair frowned. "The place remains in shadow but light shows through the clouds in dreams."

"What do they say?" she prompted.

"Dreams are not like pages, little flower. There are no maps where you dare to walk."

"Please."

He sighed. "Under the blood of thorns, the Lords of the Boar hide their shame and glory. You seek a green place of peace and power."

"Where is this place?" she asked eagerly.

"See what is not on the pages of your learning, little flower, and you will know the truth of it."

"And these Boki warriors? What is their connection to the Mythar?"

The elder shrugged. "Words of old say the fates of the people of the green are entwined like the roots of a great forest. But there is much mist."

She nodded, already lost in thought. In her experience with fairy tales and legends, they usually were built around a core of truth and then exaggerated or distorted so greatly that they ultimately bore little resemblance to the original truth. So what were the key facts of this legend that would not have changed?

A great king, known as the Mythar, had fallen in battle and not quite died. He existed now in some state between life and death, which she supposed constituted sleeping.

This business of Boki warriors guarding the Mythar worried her. Apprehension crawled across her skin at the thought of who, or what, they were. "Do you know how I can find these Boki?" she asked reluctantly.

The elder snorted. "In the shadow of blood leaves the Boki hunt their prey."

"Will they help me find and wake the Mythar?"

Thunderous silence was her only answer. She sighed and stood up. "Well, I will cross that bridge when I come to it. I thank you for your help." She bowed formally to White Hair.

Will's head buzzed and his stomach threatened rebellion as he crawled into one of the hammocks these forest elves favored. Their tobacco was strong, albeit more smooth than any leaf he'd ever tried. Not that a few stolen puffs of others' pipes back in the hollow made him an expert. His mother would've tanned his hide had she ever caught him smoking.

Head throbbing with pain, he closed his eyes in hopes of stopping the hut from spinning and was just drifting off to sleep when a small noise jerked him back to consciousness. The leather flap over his door lifted aside.

"Rosana?" he murmured.

A trill of laughter was emphatically not Rosana. He sat up fast, overbalancing the flimsy hammock, which spun around and dumped him unceremoniously on the floor. The giggle became a full-blown laugh. He scowled up at what turned out to be a stunningly beautiful young woman wreathed in shadows. Her clothing appeared made entirely of leaves and foliage, and he thought he spied bits of leaves and twigs in her hair. *Not another dryad!*

She bowed deeply to him. "Greetings, gifted one."

"What can I do for you?" he asked as courteously as his dizziness, nausea, and bruised ego would allow for.

"Ask rather what I can do for you," she half-sang.

"Why do you call me gifted?" he asked.

"You have an old spirit. This is a gift, is it not?" she asked playfully.

He got the impression she was speaking in riddles, but he couldn't even find a riddle to solve in her odd words.

"Is this the only gift you speak of?" he asked suspiciously.

She clapped her hands together joyfully as if he was terribly clever. "Of course not! You travel with another spirit who has recently received the greatest gift of all. Her true nature has, at long last, been revealed. That is a gift to you as well, is it not?"

"What female do you refer to? Speak plainly, please."

"Why, the healer, of course."

He rolled his eyes. "Which one? The dark-haired one or the golden-haired one?"

"The dark one."

Rosana? Alarm quickened his gut and he took an aggressive step forward. "What about her nature?"

"Her connection to the land, her true origin. You know. Her *nature* . . ."

The fae creature trailed off as if she dared not say more.

"What of her origin?" he asked.

"A wonder has been created. Like a bloom in spring, it will blossom into a marvelous flower."

Where was Rosana from? Who were her people? What made this unearthly creature so nervous about Rosana that she would not or could not speak of it?

The dryad was speaking again. ". . . tree spirits are said to be older than time. Between them, they governed all living plants and formed the Great Circle. Each of the great spirits represented some specific aspect of nature—birth, growth, death, rebirth."

She stopped as if waiting for him to acknowledge that he followed her so far. He nodded, confused at her abrupt shift of topic, and she continued, "Between them, they maintained balance in all of nature. One of them represented the destructive aspect of nature. The others, not understanding, turned on him and ousted him from their midst. Their minions destroyed him, scattering his fragments across the lands." She spoke urgently as if trying to convey something important without speaking of it directly.

Will frowned. "What does this have to do with me?"

The strange girl stared hard at Will, her eyes drilling into him with sharp intelligence. "You tell me. Why you? I want to know."

A chill chattered through Will as something dangerous entered her gaze. Abruptly an air of threat hung about her. He had no idea what, exactly, she was asking. Hence he had no idea how to answer her.

Just then a disturbance erupted outside, breaking the tension of the moment. Someone was shouting, and an abrupt flurry of activity erupted. The young woman spun toward the door.

"Why do you speak of this Great Circle to me?" he demanded of her.

She spoke quickly, in a whisper. "The Forest of Thorns, human boy. Stay alive long enough and journey deep enough in the forest, and you may find it. Let the tree spirit guide you." And on that note, she slipped disconcertingly into the tree trunk beside her and disappeared.

The ruckus was so loud across the way at the council house that he could hear the gist of it from here. A young kindari took great gasping breaths in the middle of a fast-gathering crowd as he relayed urgent tidings.

. . . Imperials . . . killing all travelers . . . had word a kindari village was harboring a party of outlaws . . . questioning everyone and taking prisoners . . . headed this way within the hour—

Sharp orders were barked out for the village to rouse itself and flee. Something grasped his arm of a sudden, and he whirled, his dagger in hand.

It was Sha'Li. She whispered two short sentences, but it was enough. "Boki I smell. We go now."

Soldiers *and* Boki were hunting them? He groaned under his breath. She jerked her head to indicate that he should follow her. She waited impatiently for him to duck inside the cave to fetch his pack. He glided into the shadows with her, doing his best to match her soundless passage. She really was quite stealthy.

Will made out a thick cluster of bushes ahead. Something was wrong with them, though—a dark clump in the middle of them that was not of the bushes. "Who goes?" he breathed.

"Me," a familiar, frightened voice whispered back.

Rosana.

He joined her beneath the bush, and she immediately huddled close. His heart warmed. Too bad his stomach was not following suit. It felt terrible. His head ached and he felt slightly feverish, too. He made a solemn mental vow never to smoke kindari leaf again.

Sha'Li took off once more, presumably to fetch the other members of their party. While they waited, Will wrapped his arm around Rosana's shoulders and pulled her closer, whether to comfort her or himself he couldn't tell. Kindari were streaming out of the village, disappearing into the forest as quickly as he spotted them.

A twig snapped off to their right. He whirled, battle ready, brandishing his dagger and spear.

"This way," a new shadow ordered curtly.

Cicero. And the rest of their party was with him, including Sha'Li. The kindari moved off swiftly through the trees, running along some path only he could see. The footing was smooth, their way uncluttered by deadfall. How long they raced silently through the woods Will could not say. But he was out of breath by the time the elf finally stopped. The others were panting, too.

"Are we safe?" Will murmured.

Cicero shrugged. "As safe as can be, considering that both the Boki and the Empire seem to want badly to kill us."

Raina murmured, "Do we dare continue into Talyn? It is our known destination. Won't the governor and his men go there first looking for us? Perhaps we should skip any settlements and head directly for the Forest of Thorns."

Will threw her a startled look. He'd expected that she and her elf would depart from the party on other travels at some point. What was *her* business in the dangerous forest?

Kendrick and Eben protested immediately, and Kendrick's voice won out. "We must go to Talyn to look for Eben's sister. The Patriarch is there and can remove Eben's slave mark, too. Besides, Anton will figure the last place we'd go is where we said we would. You heard the scout's report. The governor is calling us a band of outlaws."

Kendrick made sense.

Rosana added, "Maybe the Patriarch can help Will, too."

Will turned to her, suspicion exploding in his breast beneath the wood disk. Help him with what? Removing the disk? Or declaring him mentally unstable? "What orders did the High Matriarch give you?" he demanded.

She blinked, looking startled. "I beg your pardon?"

"What were your exact instructions regarding me?"

"No instructions. We were to sneak out of Heart together. No one was to know that we left."

"And you do not think we escaped a little too easily? Why would the Heart let you come with me? To watch me? Why do they care where I go or what I do?"

"I do not know." She added when he scowled, "Honest. I know nothing beyond what I've told you."

One side of his brain shouted at him to trust her and not attack her like this. But the other half of his brain smelled subterfuge in her words. If she was not lying, then whoever had let them slip out of the Dupree Heart so easily and with full packs of supplies had an agenda of their own. What did the Heart want with him? Suspicion roared through him. The Heart was the Empire's pet dog.

A quick vote among the party members yielded a consensus for Talyn. Will abstained while his thoughts whirled angrily.

Cicero announced quietly, "To Talyn it is, then."

Will was impressed by the kindari's secret network of trails through the countryside. Mostly the region was parceled into farms and small steadings. Every now and then a patch of woods like the one the kindari village had been in broke up the fields and pastures. They circled wide around a few villages that reminded Will painfully of Hickory Hollow from a distance.

It rained on and off throughout the day, making their travel damp and cold. Near sunset, though, the clouds cleared somewhat and the temperature dropped sharply. Based on the sun's position, he was able to tell that Cicero led them in a generally northerly direction. But beyond that, Will was lost.

Not that he could summon the energy to care. His fever had worsened and his stomach hovered on the verge of revolt. Raina even gave him a big dose of healing magic, but it made him feel no better at all.

They headed for a wooded patch that would give them cover for the night. The scrawny trees were dank, stinking of rot, the ground spongy underfoot and the branches slick with slime. The trees were not properly thinned and trimmed to provide knot-free boards for fine furniture, and a general feeling of neglect hung about this place. It was entirely unlike the neatly tended forest about Hickory Hollow. Given their all-night march, the group had agreed to stop before full dark today to hunt for a decent meal and get a good night's rest.

Between them all, they had a respectable camp laid, a fire burning, and a stew heating over the blaze in no time. Cicero and Kendrick disappeared into the trees to set warning trip wires around their camp, collect firewood, and generally scout out the area. Eben took care of the last details of making camp.

Will, as accustomed as he was to hard outdoor work, was worn out. He felt ill and weak, and the stew did not smell the least bit appetizing. He felt better, though, when he spied even the indomitable Sha'Li drooping in fatigue. He was merely overtired. At least their exhaustion prevented them all from snapping at one another. Everyone would perk up when they got some hot food in them.

Not long after the entire party had returned to camp, Will's preternaturally sharp ears picked up a sound nearby. Or maybe he sensed a foreign presence first. But either way, he snatched up his staff and was on his feet in time to see a dryad step lightly out of trees and into the clearing. Will rolled his eyes. *Not this again.*

The males of the party groaned while Sha'Li grinned, Rosana looked ready to hurt someone, and Raina sat back to observe the show. They were all too tired to fend off the machinations of another dryad tonight.

He said patiently, "My lady, if you wish to stay in camp, I need you to give me your word that you will leave my male friends alone and make no attempt to charm or enslave them."

The familiar laughter trilled, but the creature nodded her promise to behave.

Will looked up sharply as more rustling became audible in the shadows beyond the fire. "Who goes there?" he demanded sharply. "Show yourself!"

Three ursari stepped out of the trees wearing expressions of chagrin. "The human has sharp hearing," one of them commented wryly.

Cicero spoke low to the trio and reported, "They insist the dryad has not charmed them. Rather she asked for their protection that she might reach you safely, Will."

"Me?"

The dryad interrupted, "The wind has whispered to me of a strange young man who shrugs off our magic like it is nothing. I came to investigate."

Will turned to the warriors skeptically. "She *asked* you to protect them?"

"Aye. In the name of the Lady."

Cicero sucked in a sharp breath. Will turned to him questioningly, and Cicero explained, "Invoking the Lady among my kind is serious business. We do not take it lightly, and neither do her kind." He nodded in the direction of the dryad without making eye contact with her.

Silence fell in the clearing.

"Have you eaten?" Will asked the faerie. He doubted the dryad would take him up on a bowl of common stew, but his mother had been a stickler for courtesy. You always offered to share your meal with a guest.

"Thanks be unto you, Will Cobb. But I do not hunger." She added, "At least not for what you seem willing to offer."

He hadn't introduced himself, yet she knew his name. He sighed. The dryads were definitely gossiping about him among themselves. He studied her more closely. Her skin was noticeably more golden in tone than any dryad's he'd seen so far. It shimmered as if gold dust were sprinkled across it. She seemed more . . . mature . . . than the others. Self-possessed. If there was some sort of hierarchy among dryads, he'd lay odds this one was a noble of some kind.

Her gaze, which had roamed around the clearing, swung back to him. He looked away hastily, considering whether or not he dared look this one in the eyes. *What the heck.* He already had her promise to leave the other males alone.

"Watch my back," he murmured at Eben.

The jann's eyebrow arched faintly, but he nodded slightly.

Will looked back at the golden dryad. Her gaze was amber, warm and joyous. She exhibited none of the intense concentration the other dryads had used on him, merely a certain wry humor. Her very lack of an attempt to ensorcel him was more appealing by far than the best efforts of any of the others.

Something surged up within Will so quickly he had no time to stop or hide it. He knew this dryad. She was a noble of the Green Court and chief among the dryads of this part of the wood. "Elysia?" he asked incredulously.

The dryad jolted. Alarm flitted across her face, chased by curiosity. And then anger took her over. She surged around—or maybe through—the fire in a trice, her hand unexpectedly strong and fierce on his throat. "How do you know my name, boy?" she snarled.

The party would have jumped to its collective feet, but the ursari warriors abruptly loomed over them all threateningly, weapons drawn, making it clear that any interference on their part would get them hurt or worse.

Elysia's inhuman fury was fully roused, and he needed no special powers to sense death in her molten gaze. Will blinked at her, startled. "I haven't the slightest idea. Your name just . . . came to me."

"How, human? Who are you?"

"I am Will Cobb. Of Hickory Hollow in the Wylde Wood. In the west," he added lamely.

"Did one of my kind tell you? Did one of them break the Silence?"

"The Silence? What is that?"

"Answer my question!"

"None of your kind spoke your name to me. In truth, until a few days ago I did not believe your kind existed."

"Then how? How do you know my name?" She gave him a little shake by the neck, glaring deep into his eyes, searching for answers.

Anger boiled up unbidden in Will's gut. How dare she treat him thus? He'd done nothing to merit an attack from her. "Let me go!" he ordered in a voice that shook the spirit itself. Like the Dragon's Roar but different, deeper, older, more powerful.

The dryad's hand leaped away from his neck like he'd physically flung it off. She staggered back, staring first at her hand and then at him. She whispered, "Is it truly you?"

"I don't know what you're talking about," he mumbled back in his normal voice.

"Lord Bloodroot. Is it you?"

Alarm speared through him. Would the dryad try to harm him if she knew a piece of a tree spirit was trapped within him? What would his own companions do if they knew? Her hand shot out and she tore back the top of his shirt. Reverently, she touched the disk of wood on his chest lightly.

"Oh my lord, it is you," she whispered too quietly for the others to hear.

He answered the dryad urgently, "I'm not this other fellow. I'm Will Cobb, I tell you!"

Elysia bowed low. "It is my great honor to stand before thee once more, my lord. We thought thee gone forever. Others have tried and tried to free you, but your spirit was bound. We knew not how nor where nor by whom."

Although his impulse was to roll his eyes, Will choked out, "It's only a piece of a tree spirit."

"You do not hold a piece of him, human; you hold *him*. His core. Yon is the piece of heartwood that holds his spirit."

"What is all this about spirits?" Rosana demanded.

The dryad ignored the gypsy and demanded of Will, "How are you not *dead,* human?"

Rosana interrupted even more forcefully. "Dead? What?"

The dryad stared at him wonderingly. "No human should be able to withstand the power of that one's spirit. It should have rent your puny spirit to pieces. And yet, you live."

Did she speak truth, or was this some trick of her kind? Suspicion warred with certainty deep in his gut that she spoke the truth.

"Long have we waited for the prison that bound Lord Bloodroot to be broken. Long have we waited for the forest lord to find a host. Now that you are awake, we deliver a message and a task."

Will snapped, "A task? I do not do your bidding, dryad!"

The dryad responded, "This is not my bidding, human. It is *his* bidding for you. I am but the messenger."

The tree spirit inside him was giving him orders via dryads now? Will frowned, not liking this development in the least. "Deliver your message then."

"To you shall the secret be revealed, long forgotten by all but she who once kept it. Retrieve that which is lost; find it, but do not claim it. It is not yours, yet you must give it freely."

Will blinked. Replayed the words in his mind. Then he grumbled, "Did I ever mention how much I hate riddles?"

The dryad's lips twitched in humor. "Nonetheless, you must solve this one, human." She gazed at him expectantly, as if waiting for him to question her. *Very well then.*

"Whose secret is it?" Will demanded.

"It belongs to the last one bonded to this living continent."

"Could you be a little more specific?"

She shrugged, dislodging the garlands covering her chest in a most distracting manner. "I speak of the Mythar, of course."

Will couldn't help but notice how Raina lurched upright at the mention of that. He asked, "And this Mythar is who, exactly?"

Elysia sighed. "Ignorant boy. The Mythar is lord of all the nature guardians."

"You said he was bonded to the land. Past tense. Is he dead?"

"No, but he is lost to us nonetheless."

Will rolled his eyes. Couldn't any legendary heroes from the past just die like normal people? Did they all have to enter some strange sleeping state?

Raina interjected, "Is this lost Mythar of yours by any chance an elf who was also once a great king of an elven nation?"

Elysia seemed annoyed at the intrusion in her conversation with Will, but snapped, "He was an elf!"

Raina pressed, "So, the Mythar and the Sleeping King might be one and the same person?"

The dryad shrugged. "We call him only Mythar. We have no care for mortal kingdoms and titles."

Will stared at the blond healer across the fire. If Raina was right and the Mythar and Sleeping King were one and the same, it was a good sign that these magical creatures were trying to help him find the fellow, right? Maybe his quest was not entirely doomed, after all.

Elysia was speaking again. "I was told only to seek he who bears our lost lord home, for he and his boon companions would have the power to uncover the secret which must be revealed if we are all to survive."

"Who, exactly, told you to seek me?"

"The Green Lady."

"Is she a dryad as well?"

That made the dryad laugh until tears ran down her cheeks, but no clearer answer than that was forthcoming from the faerie. He supposed, given the degree of her humor, that this Green Lady person must not be a dryad.

Will glanced at the rest of the party. His "boon companions" looked as flummoxed by this unexpected message as he felt. "Do any of you know who this Green Lady is?"

Raina answered, "I am given to understand that she represents the entirety of nature and living things, mayhap the Urth itself."

Elysia seemed to delight in adding cryptically, "The Green Lady has not forgotten her son."

Will scowled. Stars above, he hated it when people talked in circles! "Will you please give me a clearer answer than that?"

Elysia laughed, a rich, contralto ripple that made him shiver with delight. "I like you, human. Perhaps when you have grown up a little more we might . . . come to know each other better."

If he was not mistaken, she'd just propositioned him. And given that Rosana made a sound in the back of her throat not unlike that of a dog growling over a bone, he was fairly certain he made no mistake. Well, wasn't this turning out to be an interesting evening?

His head whirled with it all. That and the whole rot about him being some sort of chosen one who was supposed to find some lost thing but not claim it, then keep it but give it away. Never mind that he hadn't a clue what he was supposed to do with this *thing* between finding it and getting rid of it.

He asked the dryad, "Assuming I can solve this riddle of yours, what am I supposed to do about it?"

"All in due time."

"I also really hate it when people answer my questions like that, all mysterious and evasive."

"I but speak the truth, impatient human."

"Where am I supposed to look for this secret?"

"All will become clear."

"When? How?"

"Patience, Will Cobb."

He bit out, "I'm running exceedingly short on that at the moment, lady dryad. Won't you give me a direct answer to anything?"

She placed a gentle hand upon his chest, laying it directly over the wooden disk of Bloodroot. "You have all you need to do this task. Let your heart"—she pressed down lightly on the disk—"be your guide. A chain of events has been set in motion by forces greater than you or me. And for whatever reason, you have been thrown into its path. I can only tell you this. Do your best to succeed, Will Cobb. The fates are not kind to those who fail them."

He demanded, "What fates are these who make me their tool? I have no desire to be anyone's pawn."

She replied sadly, "Nonetheless, that is exactly what you are, young human."

He scowled at her, thoroughly annoyed. He just wanted to get the stupid disk off his chest and go home. Except the cursed disk refused to let go and he had no home left to go to. Other than those two small, rather inconvenient details, everything was just perfect.

"You are not alone in your quest. You have friends and allies of whom you are not yet aware, grandson of Hickory. We have been watching out for you for a long time."

"Some lot of good all these invisible friends have done me so far," he grumbled.

"Who do you think tripped that Boki scout next to the grandfather hickory and saved your life back in your hollow?"

Will stared at her, stunned. "That was you?"

"Aye. Just so."

"Whose bidding did you do to protect me?" he demanded.

Ignoring his question, Elysia spoke quietly. Soberly, even. "I shall leave you now. Safe travels and my apologies for any . . . inconvenience . . . my kind might have caused you"—a glance over at his companions—"or your friends. I shall see to it you are not disturbed by my kind again."

As a murmur of fervent thanks went up from the male party members at that news, the dryad evaporated back into the trees. The kindari warriors who had accompanied her nodded silently, turned, and disappeared into the night.

Sha'Li sighed. "Miss it I will, watching Rainbow Boy, Mister I'm-a-noble, and Captain Pointy Ears squirm like worms down their shorts they have."

Rosana replied grinning, "Be nice!" She turned to Will. "What in stars' name did she speak of? What secret are you supposed to find?"

Will shrugged. "I have no idea. You know as much about it as I do."

Sha'Li commented snidely, "In green methinks the boys will be dreaming for weeks to come."

Kendrick scowled. "Jealous because you're black and scaly?"

"Closer come, and say that."

"Hah!"

Sha'Li's scales lifted. The effect was similar to that of a bird ruffling its feathers. "Think you a scrawny human like you can take me?"

Raina stepped between them hastily as the two bristled at

each other. "Who's hungry? The stew smells ready. Here, let me serve it up." She thrust bowls of hot stew into Kendrick's and Sha'Li's hands, effectively ending their spat. They subsided, sulking into their bowls.

"What name did that yellow dryad call you?" Rosana asked Will. "I did not quite catch it."

He had no intention of confessing to them that he might be possessed by some crotchety old tree spirit. He did detect—and secretly enjoy—the hint of jealousy in Rosana's voice, though.

He answered casually, "It was nothing worth repeating. But the good news is they won't be bothering us anymore. The golden one is some sort of noble among her kind. If she can't bewitch me, I think they all will give up trying."

"But she said she would come back sometime to see if you are interested in her then, yes?" A definite note of resentment had crept into Rosana's voice now.

Will laughed. He couldn't resist teasing, "There are worse fates."

The party ate in silence for a few minutes, the rest of them wolfing down the stew. Will picked at it halfheartedly.

A rustling sounded from off to his left.

Eben threw a disgusted look at the forest in general. The jann hummed around a mouthful of stew, surly. "I thought you said the dryads were going to leave us alone. Sounds like your girlfriend is already back. With more of her friends this time."

Will sighed. He was really getting tired of this. Why did he have to be a cursed dryad magnet? He peered into the darkness. And smelled them before he saw them. Rotting meat. And then his disk started to burn so fiercely it stole his breath completely away.

Orcs.

The brush all around them erupted. A half-dozen howling orcs charged them, clubs raised and blood in their eyes.

Will spewed out the mouthful of stew he'd just taken and threw his bowl at the nearest orc as he scrambled for his staff. *Dregs!* Where had these beasts come from?

An orc swung a war club at Will, who parried the blow with his longer staff and riposted with a quick jab to the creature's exposed shoulder. The orc staggered back, clutching his arm as Will looked around frantically. The seven in his party had been attacked by at least as many orcs, all bearing the irregular red forehead markings of the Boki, and two of his number were healers and not combatants. This was bad. Very, very bad.

My lady, that wounded fellow who was found in the woods this morning is asking for you."

Gabrielle looked up in surprise at the servant boy. "Me? I am no healer."

The boy shrugged apologetically. He obviously had no more information than he'd just given her. With a sigh, she rose, made her way across the bailey to the infirmary, and ducked into the small cottage built off by itself to isolate diseases from the castle population. A Heart adept looked up as she entered.

"Thank you for coming, Your Highness. This man is refusing treatment until he speaks with you."

"In private," the gravely wounded man gasped.

Gabrielle's ever-present bodyguard made a sound of denial behind her as she studied the man. He looked like any other peasant, roughly dressed and work hardened. With great effort, he moved his right hand from under the blanket and laid it on top of the wool, wrist up. She spied the crude tattoo inside his wrist as she was obviously meant to, and her stomach clutched.

"I will speak with this gentleman alone," she declared. "Please leave us."

Her guard protested, but she raised a hand, cutting him off.

It was not often she pulled rank, but tonight she did so. "I insist," she said with quiet authority.

The healer and one extremely unhappy knight backed out of the cottage. When the door had latched, she turned quickly and knelt at the side of the man with the eight-pointed compass tattoo. "Have you a message for me?" she murmured low.

"News. Must get it to the Eight. Have you a way to pass it to them?" The man did indeed sound as if he were on his last legs.

"Yes, of course." If Talissar was not one of the Eight's inner circle, he would surely know one of their number.

"Insurrection brews on Haelos. Factions there test Anton's strength. Move against him indirectly. They will drain the colony's resources and, furthermore, draw Imperial attention. Force Koth to send reinforcements."

"Is that all?" she asked.

He nodded, and then his eyes rolled up into his skull alarmingly.

"Adept!" she called out urgently. "Come quick!"

The healer, hands glowing, and her guard, sword drawn, rushed inside the cabin.

"He's died," she reported. "I shall leave so you may do your best to revive him."

The adept nodded, already gathering magic for a life spell. She swept out of the infirmary quickly. She had no wish to be present when the fellow fully regained consciousness. Her desire to question him, to learn more of the mysterious Eight, was nigh overwhelming.

She fingered the Octavium Pendant Talissar had given her. She'd worn it continuously since her memory of Darius returned. She would not risk forgetting her loyal knight and his supreme sacrifice again. In addition, her impulses to dance embarrassingly in the Emperor's gardens had not returned since she donned the talisman. Of course, neither had Starfire returned to court since he was ordered by Maximillian to walk the Ice Bridge all those years ago.

Clearly, the Eight's plans centered around the colony of Dupree. And given the urgency of the fellow's message, she could only assume that the Eight's plans might be nearing fruition in Dupree. Was the collapse of the first buttress holding up the Empire closer than she had realized?

She strolled back to the castle thoughtfully. She started at the noise of a trumpet announcing the arrival of guests to the castle. Any time Imperial nobles came to the outer kingdoms, local nobles flocked to get face time with members of the court, to make contacts and maybe gain favor.

She called to the steward whom she spied hurrying toward the bailey, "Who is it?"

"Brialla of Aurenhorn and her brother, Idrys."

Gabrielle's heart near skipped a beat. Brialla was the kindari daughter of Talissar and the Queen of Quantaine. Idrys Bowyn was Brialla's twin, a silvani. Surely no mere coincidence accounted for Talissar's offspring arriving here at the same time as both Laernan and a messenger bearing news for the Eight. Did the twins work for their father's cause as well, then? Neither twin was often at court. It was possible they avoided the scrutiny of the Emperor—

Gabrielle ordered the steward, "I will meet them personally. Show them to my solar. Have refreshments sent up immediately." He veered toward the kitchens while she glanced up quickly at the sun. Lunch was perhaps an hour gone by. How much longer her husband and the psionic hunters would be afield was anybody's guess. If the twins had business from the Eight to conduct in Haraland, it would have to happen fast.

The entourage piled into the bailey noisily, and she waited impatiently for the twins to separate themselves from the others. Soon enough a handsome pair of youths stepped forward and bowed formally to her. She returned the bow and then said warmly, "Welcome to Haraland. My lord husband is afield, but I will be honored to entertain you until his return."

Under her breath, Brialla murmured, "That suits us well, as our business is with you, Your Highness."

"Ahh," Gabrielle breathed. Louder, she ordered servants to show the entire party into the great hall and bring food and drink for all the travelers. In short order she led the twins to her private office and closed the door. A light snack was already laid out and waiting. She served the twins herself.

"How may I help you?" she asked bare moments after she handed her guests their plates and goblets.

Brialla fingered a pendant nearly identical to Gabrielle's and murmured, "A ship will make port soon in Haraland, and we have passengers and cargo that must needs be aboard when it sails again."

A coastal nation, Haraland was renowned for its deepwater port and fleet of oceangoing vessels. "What ship do you have in mind?"

"The Black Ship *Courageous*. It makes shore one last time before crossing to Haelos."

She started. The Black Ships were another matter entirely. Imperial harbormasters and longshoremen loaded and unloaded the mighty juggernaut-class vessels personally and saw to their comings and goings separate from all other ships passing through.

"Have you these passengers and supplies with you?" she asked.

"Aye. Several avarians you can recognize by the white swans on their heraldry. And various items in their baggage . . . mostly magical in nature. Nothing that would draw the attention of an Imperial inspector, of course."

"I will have a word with Regalo. He can have a conversation with the Imperial harbormaster. He will see to it the passengers and their baggage make the ship."

"My thanks, Your Highness. Whilst my sister and I are here, is there aught we can do for you?" Idrys asked quietly.

"In fact, there is. A Child of Fate, a stargazer of no small talent, has emerged in Haraland. High Lord Inquisitor Laernan and the Emperor's Master of Hounds arrived yester eve and already hunt her."

Idrys lurched upright in his chair. "Do you know the whereabouts of this Child? We must get her out of Haraland immediately!"

"My thought exactly. I can tell you where she last was and who I sent to take her away. Any aid you could render, any diversion to the hounds, would be immensely helpful."

"Consider it done," the twins murmured in unison. They rose in graceful and perfect unison as well.

"Might we trouble you for inconspicuous clothing?" Idrys asked.

As Gabrielle nodded, Brialla added, "And is there, perchance, a . . . discreet . . . way to leave the castle?"

"Of course. Follow me."

Will took a quick, assessing look around the firelight clearing. Unless he did something creative and unexpected, this fight was going to go against them very fast. Even in the few seconds it took him to look about, his companions were all but overrun.

Rosana was holding her own at the moment. The combination of her colors, her brightly glowing hands, and the most colorful stream of invective he'd ever heard issue from a female mouth seemed to have frozen the orcs before her in place.

The brush was thick around them, though, making use of magic nigh unto impossible except at very close range. The heavy foliage provided abundant cover to duck and hide from bolts of magic or thrown alchemy globes. Cicero seemed to be thinking the same thing, for he drew his short bow quickly. Arrows would fly true through underbrush. The heavy brush was also going to make movement difficult. Swinging his staff was going to be a problem. If only he knew the first thing about fighting with a sword! But his father had never deigned to teach Will bladed combat.

Sha'Li hadn't run. Backed up against a tree, long claws extended from her fingers, she swung them in continuous and vicious arcs before her. As he glanced her way he saw her spit. A stream of black fluid streamed from her mouth and smacked the orc nearest her on the face. The beast screamed and collapsed to his knees, his hands tearing at his skin as if acid ate at it.

Will's gaze shifted to Kendrick, whose sword flashed so fast Will could hardly make out his weapon. Still, a wall of orcs was advancing on the young warrior and would overrun his position in a few seconds. Raina was gathering a massive ball of magical energy behind Cicero, but what she planned to do with it Will could not guess. As far as he knew, she had no skill with combat spells.

Eben fought with his back to a tree, and Kendrick was making his way toward his friend. They were both excellent fighters and would give the orcs trouble unless and until a magic caster took them out.

Kendrick yelled over his shoulder, "Aim for the joints of their armor or their heads, Will! Your staff will be of no use against their hide armor!"

Will gripped his staff tightly in his hands and charged. The temptation to shout a battle cry was great, but he bit it back. Better to surprise his enemies than warn them of his coming.

Staff flailing, he plowed into the nearest Boki and managed to bowl the beast into another one. Both orcs staggered, snarling, and got tangled up with each other. Will's staff slammed into the first orc's throat, a harmless-looking little move, but the creature went down, gasping. Apparently, orcs had breathing parts in roughly the same spot as humans.

The second orc stumbled back, shoving the weight of his companion off of himself. Will jumped forward, up and under the orc's blade, and jammed the end of his staff into the side of the orc's head. He whirled and threw up the staff, barely managing to parry the swing of a two-handed axe from another orc, presumably aimed at cleaving Will's head in half. Luckily, he caught the blade on the metal-covered portion of his staff and it was not cleaved in half by the orcish axe.

The axe slipped off his staff and sliced the laces off his shirt but otherwise did not harm him. Will fell to the ground, rolled, and, as he somersaulted past the orc, swung hard at the beast's ankles, connecting with the bones there with several fast blows. The orc went down, roaring in pain. Will's staff fouled in the underbrush and he frantically yanked it free.

He rolled to his feet, planted his staff, and vaulted into yet another Boki, feetfirst. His boots connected solidly with the creature's chest. The beast staggered back, shouting what sounded like invective in his thick accent. Holding his staff in the middle, Will swung his staff furiously, battering at the orc with both ends of the weapon. Will could not kill the beast, but mayhap he could drive it back into Kendrick's and Eben's swords. Before Will could accomplish that, however, the orc toppled over with one of Sha'Li's alchemy globes broken against his back.

The lizardman girl stood only a few feet beyond the fallen creature. She nodded briefly and whirled away, seeking more targets.

Will spun around as he heard Rosana shout some incant that involved burning blood and curses. That orc dodged the spell from Rosana easily enough in the heavy brush but pitched forward seconds later with a trio of arrows sticking out of his back. He took several staggering steps and plowed into Will, knocking him over and landing heavily on top of him. His staff trapped between them, Will shoved in desperation at the orc.

The Boki grinned at Will, showing sharp, yellow teeth, blackened along their edges. He opened his mouth wide as if to bite Will's nose off. Rosana shouted something about weakness above them, but he could not count on her to hit the broad side of a barn, let alone an orc in battle.

Will had to escape, now. Otherwise, he was in serious trouble. No sooner had he thought it than he thought he felt a slackening in the orc's hug of death. Rosana must have managed to hit with her weakness spell. A look of confusion entered the orc's eyes, and Will heaved for all he was worth. He put enough distance between them that he was able to jerk his knee up sharply.

The orc wore some sort of hard codpiece to protect his privates, but the awkward angle at which Will struck it seemed to drive the cup sideways, its hard rim pinching something soft and imminently pinchable. The orc squealed, jerking up and away from Will. Which was enough to free Will's left hand. He smashed his fist into the Boki's ear once, twice.

The orc bellowed and rolled away. Will kicked his feet up into the air, arched into a backbend, then whipped his feet down, snapping his torso upright. He slashed down and back with his staff and sparks flew as its iron tip scored across the orc's blade. But the blow held the beast in place for the instant Will needed to wrench his dagger out of his belt and plunge it into the orc's neck. A spurt of hot blood sprayed him.

Will looked up. One of the Boki had Rosana pinned against a tree and held a knife to her throat. Will's impulse was to lurch toward her, but he would never reach her in time. He prayed her magic was sufficient to the task of defending herself. She commenced incanting something about disarming a weapon. He hoped it worked.

Will locked gazes with another orc who looked like the leader if the quantity of battle scars on the beast was any indication. Hopeful that his companions could take care of the rest of the orcs, Will closed on the leader.

The big orc snarled, and an answering smile curved Will's lips. The consciousness of the other being within him surged forward, and Will let it run free within his veins. He relaxed his mental guard and gave himself over to it. He hardly recognized his own voice when it emerged from his throat, deep and rough. Shaggy. "You think you can take me? Why don't you try, then?"

"Du'shaak!" The challenge in the orc's voice wasn't nearly so certain this time.

Will's eyes widened when the alien wildness within him made him laugh . . . and throw the staff onto the ground almost halfway between him and the orc. He threw his body forward in a jumping, pivoting step, then flung himself backward onto his hands in an acrobat's handspring. It was a trick he'd performed for his buddies back in Hickory Hollow a thousand times.

His right hand landed on the staff as his feet flew over his head. He landed on his feet, rebounding high into the air, executing a 180 turn midair. The handspring had the effect he'd hoped for. The Boki stared, openmouthed, at the mad youth now charging him.

Calling upon all the training his father had ever drilled into him, Will attacked the orc with every ounce of his strength and speed. He incorporated Kendrick's advice to aim for joints and the Boki's head. Will got in a couple of solid blows, enough to slow the beast a tiny bit. But the orc was stronger and bigger than Will and forced him back until his feet tangled in brambles and brush. He tripped. And started to go down.

Without warning, the tip of a blade poked forward through the orc's chest. The creature toppled over, and Kendrick stood behind him, withdrawing his sword smoothly as the orc fell.

"Thanks be," Will panted. Using his staff, he pulled himself upright and turned to face the next threat.

It was over.

A circle of bloody bodies lay around the spot where Kendrick and Eben had made their stand. Cicero and Sha'Li panted side by side, a giant tree at their back, a pair of dead orcs before them. Will stepped forward to check the orc down at Rosana's feet, but she whipped out her own dagger and brandished it.

"Don't kill it, Rosana," Will said wearily. "You should not kill anyone, not wearing those colors." Not to mention it was not honorable.

A reptilian voice hissed from the far side of the fire, "Kill him, gypsy!" Eben nodded in agreement with the lizardman girl, and Will turned to Kendrick for support. As he was a noble, however minor, his opinion was the only one that ultimately mattered beyond the Heart member's.

Kendrick shrugged. "They attacked us. I say we kill them." Sha'Li interrupted, "Never do they randomly strike a target. Around this camp they could have gone just as easily. Why attack us do they?"

Had the Boki attacked here for the same reason they'd attacked Hickory Hollow? Was there something, or someone, here that they wanted? What could this motley bunch possibly have that any Boki would want? Surely these orcs had no way of knowing Will carried his father's blood in his veins.

This pack of orcs had been carrying barely more than the hides on their backs and a few supplies. Which meant this was likely a scouting party, come south out of the Forest of Thorns. Why would the orcs have scouting parties outside of their traditional territory unless they hunted something or someone specific?

Rosana shrugged. "I know not why they attack us, but that one intentionally spare me. It was my Heart colors. . . . Will, we cannot kill this one."

She turned her dark, pleading gaze upon him. How could he say no to her big, sad eyes, her compassion? Her innate kindness? And yet these were the monsters who'd decimated Hickory Hollow. They deserved to die, did they not?

He turned to Kendrick. "What would we do with a Boki prisoner?"

Sha'Li snapped, "Kill him you must. Vicious foes are these Boki. Do not let the gypsy girl's fluttering eyelashes out of common sense talk you!"

Will drew breath to answer when, without warning, the disk on his chest went searingly hot against his skin. *A warning, perhaps? Against what? Or to do what?*

"They are enemies of the Empire," Kendrick declared as if that answered everything.

"Bah!" Will burst out. *Imperial law be cursed.* He had no will to kill a defenseless creature. He stepped away from the unconscious Boki.

But before Will had taken three steps back, the lizardman girl leaped forward and, with her claw, slit the orc's throat. Nausea and rage rolled through Will so thick and hot he could barely remain on his feet.

Rosana glared at the lizardman girl in fury. "I cannot believe you did that!"

Sha'Li stared back implacably. "What had to be done, I did. This world is kill or be killed." Rosana continued to glare in righteous fury, and Sha'Li added defensively, "Resurrect he will. Strong spirits have orcs, and close enough to Forest of Thorns we are for his spirit to reach shamans."

Will wasn't used to living near enough healers or Heart-stones for death to be such a casual thing. In his experience, death was permanent and something to be feared, not a casual inconvenience.

He surged forward to confront Sha'Li. "Pull another stunt like that, and the next time my blade is at your throat I'll show you the same mercy you just showed that orc."

Kendrick jumped forward to pull Will back from the hissing lizardman girl. "Hey, now. No need for threats. She did what she thought was right. I can't say as I entirely disagree with her. The Boki did attack us first. We've the right to defend ourselves with lethal force."

Will was too conditioned not to cross nobles to argue with the young man. But that orc had been defenseless, and killing a downed foe was different from killing in the heat of a fair fight against an armed enemy. Shock that he was taking a Boki's side in any dispute rolled through Will . . . along with a vague sense of . . . approval.

Sha'Li turned away from him and Rosana with a shrug. Eben grunted in what sounded like support of the lizardman girl, and the two of them traded grimaces that might pass for smiles.

Raina spoke up. "Eben, how can you side with her? She just murdered that orc in cold blood! Killing greenskins makes them hate humanoids and kill us in retaliation. Violence only begets more violence."

"You're not White Heart until you put on the colors," Kendrick defended his friend.

"That orc was going to murder *us* in cold blood. Good riddance, I say," Eben added. The basso humming undertone of his race was more pronounced than usual in his voice.

"Angry you be at him, why?" Sha'Li interjected. "I did the deed." She slid over toward Eben's side as he nodded his agreement with her.

Will looked back and forth between the two. A jann and a lizardman allies? Now *there* was an unlikely pair.

A foreign rumble of humor bubbled up within him at the notion and Will jolted. How much was the entity within the disk manifesting himself? Was that why Will's senses had been so extraordinarily sharp recently? What else would the thing do to him? Would the entity drive him mad? Take over his mind . . . or worse?

The thought chilled him to the marrow of his bones.

Sha'Li spoke into the heavy silence in a low, urgent murmur. "Go we must. Now. The noise of battle Anton's men will have heard. Investigate they will."

Only now, after the heat of battle faded, did Will feel remorse for harming the orcs he had in the fight. He would never grow used to killing any living thing. As it should be, he supposed.

There was a brief argument while Cicero and Sha'Li disputed who could best erase their trail, and it was decided that both of them would cover the party's tracks. The group set out with Will in the lead, the countertrackers bringing up the rear.

For the first few minutes their only goal was to get away from the site of the skirmish. But then Rosana murmured from behind Will, "How do you know where to go at night?"

Will did not. But he closed his eyes for a moment, probing within his mind for Bloodroot, who lay quiescent at the moment. Then a single, overwhelmingly joyous thought suffused Will. *Home.*

Dead certain of his course all of a sudden, Will angled slightly to his left and strode confidently into the blackness. Toward a home he'd never seen before, which was not his, but in which he knew every stream and stone and tree and could picture each as clearly as if he stood beside them. He could all but smell the familiar sweet-sharp scent of pine sap and oak tannin.

His steps lengthened until Rosana called out for him to slow down, and even Sha'Li complained that she and Cicero could not erase their trail that quickly.

Impatient with his frail human body, Will's urge to race for home was nigh unto uncontrollable. But when he promised that other, foreign part of him that he would get him home as soon as humanly possible if he would but let Will set the pace and manage his own body, the tree spirit relented. Will slowed to a more reasonable pace and that other awareness retreated, only reasserting his presence to make minor course corrections now and again. Exhausted without Bloodroot to goad him, Will stumbled along on sheer willpower.

Soon now. Soon he would be home, and all would become clear. The human boy would understand why he'd been dragged halfway across the northern colony and endowed with skills few mortals ever mastered. The human would also understand what was required of him in return. No matter that it would likely cost the boy his life. Given what was at stake, the boy was entirely expendable.

Will grumbled as a twig or mayhap a root poked him in the back, and he shifted in his bedroll. It had been a long, cold hike, and he was delighted to be hunkered down, warm at last, in his bedroll. Something poked him again. It felt like a finger jabbing in his ribs. Okay, he hadn't been moving. If that was another dryad—

Something slithered past his nose, fast, and he lurched upright, grabbing for his staff. *Where is it?* The weapon was not at his side where it had been when he lay down. He groped frantically for it as another something long and sinuous, the thickness of his wrist, whipped past his head. The flying thing impacted something large behind him, wrapping around it with a solid thwack.

"Oww," someone complained.

"Who goes?" Will bit out sharply. Curse it, he still hadn't found his staff! His dagger came to hand and he scooped it up as he leaped to his feet to face the intruder.

"Call off your blasted weeds," the voice complained again.

"Sha'Li? Is that you?"

"Yes!" the lizardman girl hissed. "Off me get them!"

Will stepped forward in the gloom, peering at what confined her. Vines. Thick and green, they looked like the giant serpent his father had shown him once in the Southwatch market. The vines constricted around her much like the snake had around the hapless rabbit its handler had tossed it.

"What happened to you?" he asked the lizardman girl.

The others were rousing, sitting up sleepily in their bedrolls behind him. Kendrick charged back into camp from where he'd been sitting watch a little ways out in the wood.

Sha'Li snarled something unintelligible, sibilant and angry.

Although he didn't understand the words, that other awareness within Will reacted with sharp caution. Will circled around her to have a better look at the twining vines. As he moved behind her his foot kicked something hard. He glanced down, startled to see his staff. He bent down and scooped it up. How had that gotten way out here behind Sha'Li?

In front of him, she gave a violent heave, using her strength to attempt to rip free of the entangling vines. Another vine streaked out of the darkness from his left and whipped tight around her waist. *What on Urth—*

Rosana burst out, "You tried to kill him!"

Will's gaze snapped to the gypsy in surprise and then back to Sha'Li. To Rosana, he demanded, "Why do you say that?"

"Why else forest attack her? Trees and plants, they protect you."

Will stared at the gypsy. Her statement was preposterous. And, yet, it made perfect sense. He looked back and forth between Rosana and Sha'Li. Cautiously, he asked the lizardman girl, "How did my staff come to be behind you?"

"There I threw it, moron."

He stared, shocked. "You did try to kill me, then?"

"Mine is that disk, and tired am I of waiting for it. Want it back, I do."

"I told you. It has grown into me. It cannot be removed."

"If you live, maybe not. But remedied that can be."

Will drew back sharply from the venom in her voice. "You would kill me over a stupid piece of wood?"

"Anything but stupid is that disk. This, both of us know."

"That's not the point. Is it really worth murder?"

She hissed, and he took a prudent step closer to a tree he could duck behind if she chose to spit at him.

Sha'Li snarled, "Not for you was that meant! For the shamans of my people was it taken. Who are you, Will Cobb? Why hunt for you do Boki, and doing their best to kill you are Imperial soldiers? Why fear you do the dryads, and why giving you messages about the Mythar are they?"

"I have no idea."

"You lie, human."

He stared at Sha'Li, who stared back accusingly. She was right, and he respected her for her blunt honesty. But he dared not tell any of them the truth. It would make all of their lives as forfeit as his. No, ignorance was their best protection. Reluctantly, he conceded, "You may be right. But for your good, I must not say more."

Kendrick, to Will's surprise, interjected, "Why mustn't you? Why shouldn't the lizard know what she fights for?"

Sha'Li snapped at him, "For myself I fight, human!"

Kendrick snorted. "Now who lies?"

Sha'Li's only answer was to fling herself against the vines.

The living ropes visibly tightened themselves even more snugly around her. Mildly, Will commented, "You'd better stop fighting those vines or they'll crush the life out of you."

"Call them off!"

He looked at Sha'Li in surprise. "How?"

"Talk to them."

"Talk—to plants?"

"To everything else you talk in these cursed woods."

Eben and Cicero snorted behind Will in what sounded

suspiciously like laughter. He glared at the lizardman girl. "That's not funny."

"Yes, it is," Rosana responded in undisguised amusement from behind him.

"Just because I'm immune to dryads doesn't make me some sort of freak."

"Yes, it does," Cicero disagreed. "And then there's the way you suddenly know which direction to travel. And the way the tree limbs move aside for you to pass by—"

"They do not!"

All his companions answered simultaneously, "Yes, they do."

He stared at them in dismay. He cast his mind back to their pell-mell flight from the scene of the earlier fight, and then the long march through the night to this hidden glade. He didn't remember ever having to dodge a low-hanging limb. And now that he thought about it, how had he known this tiny clearing was tucked behind that seemingly solid wall of brambles? How had he known just the right spot to lift the tangled vines and slip into this protected place?

He'd just . . . known.

Rosana was speaking quietly. ". . . if I didn't know better, I would say that disk of wood has possessed you."

He frowned. "But I'm me. I'm not him. He doesn't possess me."

"Him who?" Sha'Li demanded.

Will scowled at her. "I told you, it's better if you don't kn—"

"Bloodroot," Cicero answered from behind Will. "That was the name the golden dryad called you. Lord Bloodroot."

Will whirled to glare at the elf. "You know nothing of it."

"I know Lord Bloodroot belonged to the Great Circle, and that his companions turned on him. I know his tree got cut up into little pieces and scattered all over the continent. And I know the Boki have been running around trying to collect the pieces of him and restore him for as long as my ancestors have lived in these forests."

Will reeled. The Boki searched for the pieces of Bloodroot? Was that why they were chasing him? Did it have nothing to do with his father's quest to find the Sleeping King, then?

Rosana asked Cicero, "What is the Great Circle?"

"A council of elder nature beings in this land. Tree spirits. They guard—or at least they did in the old legends—the land and all living things upon it."

"One of those is stuck to Will's chest?"

"Well, the spirit of one at any rate."

Sha'Li struggled fruitlessly, and the vines tightened mercilessly until she was forcibly stilled, gasping for breath.

Will bit out in what he now knew to be a small version of the Dragon's Roar, "Let her breathe, for stars' sake."

The vines slithered, easing their hold somewhat, and a cold feeling spread outward from Will's gut. The vines had just obeyed his command. What was he turning into? His companions stared at him with varying degrees of wonder and fear. He could hardly blame them.

"What else do you know of Bloodroot?" Will asked Cicero soberly.

"Is it safe to build a fire?" the elf asked.

Will cast his awareness outward. The forest for a league all around was at ease, free of intruders. "Aye. It is safe." But why did the elf want a fire? To hold back the forest should it decide to attack the rest of them?

Cicero nodded briskly and went about the business of laying and lighting a small fire. The others drew near it, holding out their hands eagerly to the heat. For his part, Will felt none of the night's chill.

"Hey! Cut me loose. Attack you I will not again."

Will eyed Sha'Li warily. "I would suggest you keep your word, or else the trees will tear you limb from limb."

Rings of white showed around the dark slit irises of her eyes as she stared at him, frightened. She nodded her understanding.

"Release her!" Will ordered in the roar.

The vines unwound themselves in a wriggling mass, falling to the ground to lie there motionless, as innocent as any other forest vine. He stared at them in dismay as Sha'Li bolted out of the circle they made. What was happening to him?

This lizardman girl spoke hastily. "Look, Will. Nothing have I against you, personally. Just business this is. That disk I need back. Before kill us all your enemies do."

"Why do you need it so badly?" he asked curiously.

"To prove a task I have completed."

"To whom? And for what purpose?"

Sha'Li balked at saying any more. She shook her head, but Will caught the fear and determination in her eyes. Whatever she had planned for the disk, she was dead set on having it. She fired back, "What seek you in these woods, Will?"

It was his turn to balk.

"Tell her," Rosana urged him.

"Yes. Tell her," Raina chimed in.

He whirled on the two of them. "Maybe you two should tell me, since you seem to know so much. Why are both of you out here running around the woods with me, risking your lives for no apparent reason?"

The healers stared at him with matching guilty looks on their faces.

"At least Sha'Li's been honest with me from the start. She's here for the disk and she's never made any secret of it. But what of you two? What do you want from me?"

Rosana confessed first. "Truly, Will, Matriarch Lenora told me only to look after you. Nothing more."

"But why?" Will demanded.

She looked him in the eye and said seriously, "I swear by the burning of my gypsy blood, I would tell you if I knew."

As Sha'Li settled by the fire well away from him, Will turned his gaze on Raina. "What of you? Why are you here?"

She answered reluctantly, "I seek a source of olde magick, and I have reason to believe this Mythar fellow might have the magic I need."

She sought the Sleeping King as well? Will stared, shocked. She looked back at him defiantly.

He spoke slowly. "It seems we work toward the same end. Mayhap our reasons are different, but it would appear our goals are one."

He nodded at her, and she nodded back. They were agreed, then. They would work together to find her Mythar who was also his sleeping king.

Cicero had made it clear he was here purely to protect Raina. Kendrick and Eben were with the party only until they reached Talyn, but in the meantime they sought sign of Kithmar slavers having passed this way, stars forbid, with Eben's sister. And the pair had been generous with their swords in defending the party.

Will looked around the circle, making eye contact with each of them in turn. An odd bunch, they were. All outcasts in their own way. Mostly without family or homes. Brought together by chance and circumstance—*or maybe not chance at all.* The idea exploded across his mind with the force of a revelation. Was it possible that this inexperienced, fractious bunch was not random?

They hardly struck him as a band of heroes. More like the

scrapings at the bottom of life's barrel. For better or worse, though, they were the only ones in a position to find the Sleeping King if it was possible at all. Will was certain the fates could have chosen better. But who was he to argue? He was just a nameless boy from the outer lands.

And he did have to admit, despite their squabbles, when blades had been swinging, these people had risked their lives for one another. And they seemed prepared to go forward into the Forest of Thorns, each for his or her own reasons. If they might have to die for him, he supposed they had a right to know why he was here. Or at least a piece of it.

He sighed and chose his next words carefully. "My father entrusted me with a quest and asked me to finish it when he could not. It's based on a ridiculous tale and common sense says it's not even real. But, it was his dying wish and I swore to do this thing. I'm likely out here on a fool's errand that could get us all killed."

Rosana asked, "What this quest?"

He shook his head. "I cannot tell you. My father swore me to silence."

Cicero leaned back, stretching his feet out toward the fire. "But he did not swear me to silence. Care if I make a guess at what you are about?"

Will shrugged.

"It has something to do with Bloodroot and the Great Circle, or else that disk would not have chosen you to stick to. Sha'Li, you said you had it in your possession for several hours, and it never stuck to you. Correct?"

The lizardman girl nodded, looking distinctly surly.

"Perhaps Bloodroot wants your help in reconstituting his body. . . ."

As the elf trailed off, Rosana piped up, "I think no. You

say Boki try that for very long time already and it no work." She looked intently at Will. "What quest interest Bloodroot enough to latch on to Will?"

Kendrick stared at the gypsy and then at Will in dawning shock. He blurted, "Surely not."

Will blinked at him. "Surely not what?"

"You do not seek the Sleeping King, do you?"

Where on Urth had Kendrick heard of that? *Oh, wait.* The son had heard it from the father the same way Will had from his own father. "Landsgrave Hyland told you of him, I gather?" Will asked in resignation.

"Actually, no. I eavesdropped on my father when I was a boy. I heard him talking about it once with a solinari."

"Aurelius," Will declared. *Of course.* The son of a landed noble was too valuable to risk on a quest for the Sleeping King. But Will, the son of the disgraced and outlawed Dragon, was not.

Eben chimed asking, "Who is this sleeping king?"

Kendrick answered eagerly, causing Will's ingrained sense of secrecy to wince. "He was an elf. The king of a great elven nation called Gandamere that spanned most or all of this continent. He fell in battle against a troll and nearly died. A mysterious lady came along and saved him, barely. He fell into an endless sleep somewhere between life and death, and there he has remained ever since."

Will stared. What Kendrick described *exactly* matched Will's dream a few nights back. How was it possible he'd dreamed of events he'd never heard of until now? The answer was sour in his mind. *Bloodroot.* The tree spirit had given Will that dream. The whoreson must have waited until Will's mental defenses were down in sleep and slipped the dream into his mind.

Will asked, "Does legend say how this guardian will wake?"

"Or when he is supposed to wake?" Rosana chimed in.

Kendrick shrugged. "The legend is vague about those things. It goes that the Mythar will awake when the land would perish without him. As for the how of it, I have never heard anything."

Will asked soberly, the other one within him radiating certainty that this other tale was the key to everything, "Who is the keeper of the knowledge of how to wake him?"

Kendrick answered heavily, "The Boki." The other members of the party, save Raina, squawked in dismay.

Kendrick continued, "My father and Aurelius spoke of how close they'd come to finding the Sleeping King in a grove deep within the Forest of Thorns. The grove was guarded by powerful Boki warriors. If you want to find this sleeping king, you will have to ask them. Assuming they let you live long enough to even speak to them and do not kill you the second they hear your question."

Which was to say, they were all doomed.

W ill stopped to camp when the others forced him to but only because they flatly refused to take another step without food and rest. The needs of the physical body were of no meaning to him, vaguely registered pangs subsumed in his driving need to get home. Too restless to sit still, he went into the woods to gather firewood while the others set up camp.

In the rare moments when Will was aware of his body, he felt terrible. His health was deteriorating rapidly. He'd lost weight until his clothes hung on his frame. His cheeks felt gaunt, and he could hardly eat without becoming violently ill. If he did not know better, he would say he was dying of some wasting disease.

Rosana insisted on healing him every time they stopped

to rest, and the Heart-calibrated vibrations of her magic did make him feel somewhat better for a time. Except something subtle had changed in her magic since they left Dupree. He couldn't put his finger on how it felt different. But it did. Regardless, he deteriorated quickly between healings. Quickly enough that she even broke down and asked Raina to heal him.

The blond girl's magic felt different upon his skin. Whatever source she drew her power from, it was not the same as Rosana's. Which was odd, given that they both used simple healing magics upon him. Rosana's magic seemed to work best when directed at the wooden disk, whereas Raina's was most effective upon Will directly. Between the two girls, they managed to keep him patched together. But just barely.

Raina hit upon using magic to clear poison upon him, and that seemed to help a bit longer than simple healing. Even then the girls' magic had a fraction of the effect upon him that it should have had. Only the sheer volume of magic the two of them were able to pour into him seemed to be keeping him alive.

Rosana suggested that perhaps the party should slow down and rest more. But he knew the suggestion was for his benefit and not hers.

He was having no part of that, however. Will led the party's frantic rush toward the Forest of Thorns. He told himself a tale about merely being eager to end this quest and return to a normal life, and that it was not Bloodroot spurring him on. But it did not take an ancient forest lord to point out that Will was lying to himself.

It was a relief to pretend he still had a family, a home, a normal life, to return to, and it was toward that fantasy he raced. It was easier than listening to the tiny voice in the back of his mind whisper at him to accept that his parents were dead and his friends and family slaughtered, as if death and destruction were nothing out of the ordinary, all part of the cycle of life.

Of course, death was all around. He, himself, killed animals for food and for furs to warm him. He'd helped the loggers in the hollow cut down living trees to build homes and furniture, and they all harvested plants to eat. Without those other deaths, he could not live himself.

He understood that nature encompassed both birth and death and that without both the cycle would fall out of balance. Starvation, overpopulation, and disease would run rampant if death ceased, and then every living thing would finally die. But, he argued with himself, there was also a proper time for everything to die. It was not right when death claimed a living being prematurely.

Bloodroot all but snorted in response, as if to say, *Who's to say what's premature and what's not?*

Will challenged, "Is it right, then, that somebody killed you and chopped you into little pieces? Was it your time?"

The surge of rage that rose in his gut nearly knocked Will off his feet. He staggered against a tree and had to catch himself against it.

Will commented dryly in his mind, *Right. That's what I thought.*

Bloodroot's presence retreated into sulky silence, and suddenly the rigors of the journey caught up with Will full force. His limbs felt like logs and his eyelids were abruptly so heavy he could barely hold them up. He staggered back to camp, dumped his armload of wood, and collapsed onto the bedroll Rosana had been thoughtful enough to lay out for him, unconscious before his head hit the ground.

Will and his companions kept the same grueling pace for the next several days, traveling until they collapsed from exhaustion each night. Were it not for the others forcing him to stop now and again, he feared that Bloodroot would have driven him literally to death. Were it not for Rosana and Raina's constant healing, he was certain he would have died. Every time they stopped, one or both of them came over and laid hands on him.

The others slipped the three of them extra rations, which was probably why the healers didn't keel over as they drained themselves again and again. The party traveled mostly in silence, too exhausted to chat and too nervous about being attacked to make noise that might draw attackers.

There was no guidepost announcing that they had crossed into the Forest of Thorns, no clear dividing line between settled lands and untamed wilds. Over the course of a day, the last few clearings retreated behind them and the trees blended together into thick, continuous forest. The trees shifted from fast-growing birch to swaths of pine and then to stands of old-growth oak, huge and gnarled and ancient, their limbs tangled overhead.

When they crossed a small stream flowing out from between two giant boulders late the next morning, the landmark sent a surge of exultation through Will that nearly made him leap for joy. "We're here," he announced. "The Forest of Thorns."

The healers pulled their cloaks closer about themselves while the others clutched their swords a little more tightly. Sha'Li cast a suspicious glare at the massive trees crowding close to the path. Whoever was responsible in this part of Dupree for keeping the trees cleared back from the road ten paces on each side wasn't doing his job. At all.

Rosana looked around curiously. "Where are the thorns?"

Cicero answered, "Thorn is the title of the shamans within the Boki."

Eben looked over his shoulder sharply at that. "The Boki have shamans?"

Sha'Li replied, "Think you they live like savages?"

The jann shrugged. "It is not something I think much on. They act like savages, so why would they not live like savages?"

Bloodroot snarled inside Will's head. *Fond of the Boki, was he?* Will couldn't see why. Eben was right. They *were* savages.

Cicero muttered, "We'd best look sharp and move quiet. They'll kill us first and ask questions later."

The party slowed its breakneck pace, emphasizing stealth over speed now. That night, they ate cold rations and slept in shifts, with two people standing guard at all times. To Will, the night sounds were sweet music to his ears. It was as if each cricket, each trilling whip-poor-will, were an old friend welcoming him back.

With his new awareness, Will heard the slow groans of the grandfather oaks speaking to one another, almost, but not quite, within his comprehension. He felt the vibrant rhythms of the woods . . . and gradually became aware of something else. Something disturbing.

Bloodroot hadn't been in these woods for a very long time, and perhaps that was why Will noticed a difference in the tapestry of life around him. While the others slept, he lay awake thinking, trying to figure it out. Something felt wrong, but he couldn't quite put his finger on it.

Frustrated, he threw off his cloak to sit directly on the cold ground. Its damp chill seeped through him until his fingernails turned blue. But it wasn't enough. He tore off his clothes—shirt, trousers, boots—until he was completely naked. He lay upon the ground, spread-eagled upon his belly, and let his awareness become one with living Urth.

It was threatened, his Urth. A slow attack encroached upon the land, eating at it from within the way a termite attacked a tree. Panic filled him. Death was natural and healthy. But this . . . this was wrong. Alien. Not of nature. Not of Urth. This death bore no hint of renewal. The forest was in danger.

What had the others done in Bloodroot's absence to let the forest come to this pass?

What others? Will seriously wished his mind would quit conjuring up such nonsense.

Renewed urgency to find his tree-body and be restored to his former power surged through him. The Great Circle was horribly out of balance. It was high time and more for Bloodroot to resume his place within it. The boy needed to hurry up and make it happen. And maybe while he was at it the human should wake the Mythar as well. The land could use its greatest guardian right now.

Thankfully, the other one within him allowed Will to sleep when his shift on guard duty ended. It was clear that Bloodroot's presence within Will was too much for his fragile human body. He was killing the boy by slow degrees. The arch-healer was a boon. Not only did she help the boy, but she also was giving him enough strength to hold back his full powers from destroying the boy outright. Without her impressive power and its unusual source, he would be trapped in his heartwood once more, awaiting a spirit of sufficient strength and resolve to withstand him for a time.

If only he were whole—he could give the boy such strength and vitality as he'd never known. How was he ever to accomplish what must be done with only this frail, naïve human to work with?

When Will woke the next morning, the new day was chill and wet, with a slow drizzle dripping down through the trees, making all of them miserable. A fine mist, not exactly fog, hung in the air, reducing visibility to no more than a dozen lengths of a man in any direction and muffling sound like a thick fleece blanket.

They huddled around the tiny pit they'd dug to contain a small cook fire and conceal its light from hostile eyes. How Cicero had gotten it started with the available tinder as soaked as it was Will had no idea. They set up a watch rotation that excluded Will so he could get some extra sleep, and he laid down close to the tiny blaze. The heat of the fire drove back the bitter chill he'd been unable to shake since he'd realized he was stark naked and so stiff with cold he could barely move last night. Bloodroot was going to be the death of him yet.

R aina eyed Will worriedly as they resumed their trek. He did not look good. His skin had taken on a sickly, gray tone, and if she looked closely she saw dark veins crept beneath his skin like tree roots through the ground. She'd never seen the like.

More practically, Will shivered periodically as if he had a fever, and he barely ate anymore. Half the time he spoke, he did not sound like himself. She would lay odds the spirit within that disk had possessed him, or at least was in the process of taking him over.

She was giving him literally every bit of healing energy she could summon. Well, him and that disk. As soon as she'd started healing it directly, Will's decline had seemed to slow a bit. If she was not mistaken, the constant casting of all the magic she possessed was gradually increasing her overall capacity. It was still not enough to get ahead of Will's wasting sickness, however.

For some reason, Rosana's magic seemed to affect him

differently than hers. It was as if each of their magics had taken on a different, and necessary, flavor to heal Will.

Cicero, Kendrick, and Eben veered away from the party from time to time, making side trips to hunt while they hiked. Now and then, Will dragged himself off into the woods as well. But he never returned with any game. He'd left on one such excursion when she took advantage of his absence to move up beside Rosana.

She matched her stride to the pretty gypsy's. "I'm worried about Will," she murmured. "If there's aught I can do for him, you have but to ask." As she expected, the dark-haired healer cast her an equally worried look in response.

Raina commented, "Anyone can see he likes you. A lot." She added, "You're lucky. The one I like is very far from here. I miss him terribly."

"Tell me of him," Rosana murmured. "It will help to pass the time."

Raina regaled the gypsy girl with some of her and Justin's wilder exploits as children. Several times, Rosana had to slap a hand over her mouth to keep from laughing aloud.

Raina noted Sha'Li sidling closer to hear the stories, but the lizardman girl remained surly and uncommunicative. Lizardmen were widely regarded as savages within the Empire, unfit even to be slaves. Although as strong as oxen, they were said to be too stubborn, too stupid, and too time-consuming to break to the yoke to be worth anything in the slave markets.

They lived in freshwater marshes, rivers, and lakes, their settlements underwater, which meant they mostly avoided contact with land dwellers. From what Raina knew, lizard-men were green or gray in coloration. Sha Li's shiny black scales must be some sort of anomaly. If she was odd even among her own kind, that might explain her prickly demeanor. Although the way Raina heard it, most lizardmen were unpleasant sorts.

It wasn't until midafternoon and a chance comment Raina made about the Great Scholl Swamp north of Tyrel that Sha'Li finally joined the conversation. "Scholl, you say?"

Raina blinked at the first words from the lizardman girl since lunch. "Aye."

"Any of my kind are there?"

"Lizardmen? I assume so."

"No. *My* kind."

Raina glanced uncomprehendingly at the hopeful look on Sha'Li's face. She asked carefully, "You mean of your color?"

"Yes!" the girl snapped impatiently.

"I do not know," Raina answered regretfully. Were black lizardmen rare among their kind, then? Outcasts, mayhap? Was that why this girl was alone, far from the waterways that would usually hold her kind?

"Of strange monsters and terrible creatures in your swamp do people speak? Touched by death and tainted by strange magics?" Sha'Li asked.

Surprised, Raina replied, "Yes, as a matter of fact, people do speak of such things."

Triumph gleamed in the lizardman girl's black, vertical-slitted gaze. "I knew it."

Raina frowned. "What does that mean? Are your kind . . . tainted in some way?"

Sha'Li hissed and long, vicious claws abruptly protruded from the backs of her hands. Cicero leaped in front of Raina, his sword clanging clear of its sheath. The sound rang loudly through the trees, bringing the entire party to a sharp and horrified halt. Raina jumped back as Kendrick's sword joined Cicero's in front of her, forming a steel barrier between her and the lizardman girl.

"Stand down, you two," Raina bit out. "The fault is mine. I said something to offend Sha'Li without knowing I did so." She bowed her head formally to the lizardman girl. "My apologies."

Sha'Li blinked and her claws began to retract slowly. "To me you apologize?"

"Why wouldn't I?"

"Lizardman I am. Human you are."

Raina frowned, not understanding. "But I offended you."

Sha'Li shook her head. "Your kind apologizes not to my kind."

Raina retorted indignantly, "You are a living, thinking being with as much right to polite treatment as anyone!"

Sha'Li stared. A ring of shocked white glistened in her eye sockets.

Raina was inexplicably irritated. "Look around you. They have pointed ears, and brightly colored skin, and funny accents, yet they get respect. Why not you? So you have scales"—she glanced down cautiously—"and really big claws. Do you not have a heart? Does not blood flow through your veins? Do you not have thoughts and feelings? You're not any different from the rest of us."

"But stupid your kind call my kind—"

"—and stubborn and lazy," Raina added sharply. "I suppose that's why you're such a skilled countertracker and can throw alchemy with unerring accuracy. Why you work so hard making and breaking camp and carry twice the weight of any of the rest of us. And it's why we all trust you and travel with you."

The lizardman girl stared at Raina for a long moment. "Ignorant human. Ways of the world you know not." Sha'Li scowled but not with the vehemence of before.

The lizardman girl touched her right cheek unconsciously,

and Raina wondered again at the gesture. What was its significance?

Sha'Li surreptitiously studied the human healer. Did the girl mean what she'd said earlier? That lizardmen had the same sensibilities and should earn the same respect as humans? Of course, *she* knew that to be true, but did any other humans agree with Raina?

Cicero mentioned to Sha'Li after dinner that he'd spotted a little stream a few hundred feet from their camp if she'd like to go dunk herself. The thought of being underwater, of rehydrating her horrifically dry, itchy skin, of recovering to full strength in the healing embrace of water, was too much to resist. With a nod of grudging thanks to the kindari, she slipped out of camp and headed for the stream.

Normally, her kind spent a third or more of every day underwater, which helped them maintain optimal health. She didn't even want to think about how long it had been since she'd gone for a swim or even a simple soak.

She stripped out of her garments and slipped into the tiny rivulet. It was barely deep enough to cover her and freezing cold, but she would take it. The water tasted fresh and sulphurous on her tongue. Spring fed, then. Using the gills on her neck for the first time in days, she breathed in great, cooling lungfuls of water and practically gurgled aloud with joy.

The stream was not large enough to do much more than wave her hands back and forth in it and kick her feet a little. It was not a proper swim, but even the tiniest swish of water across her skin made her shiver in delight.

Cicero had muttered to her on her way out that he would come get her in time for the last watch. She had *hours* to rest and rejuvenate herself between now and then.

The time passed all too quickly. Something sharp poked

her shoulder, and she woke from the most refreshing rest she'd had in weeks. Cicero's wavy form was visible above the surface of the water in the faint light of a new moon. He sheathed his sword as she sat up and shooed him away so she could dress in privacy. He rolled his eyes and departed for his bedroll. She would stand watch the rest of the night until dawn.

She made her way back into camp with a smile on her face . . . not that the pinkskins would know it. They were terrible at seeing the facial expressions of her kind. Someone had rigged a small tent of green leaves over the fire. It diffused both smoke and glow from the fire to make it hard to spot.

The others formed a tight circle around the fire, greedily absorbing its meager warmth. She moved off into the forest and had barely found a comfortable tree to lean upon when she became aware of something moving in the wood.

Whatever it was moved fast, part of the night itself. She used her outstanding night vision to search for the creature as she raced silently toward the campfire. She burst out of the trees and was in time to see two bolts of magical energy strike Rosana and Raina.

The noise of it—mayhap the muttered incants or else the crackle of magic striking flesh—roused Cicero, who was probably just dropping off to sleep anyway. He gave a shout and leaped to his feet. A shadowed figure cleared the trees on the far side of the clearing and struck Cicero on the back of the head with the butt of a long sword. The kindari dropped like a rock.

"Get up!" Sha'Li shouted to the others. "Under attack we are!"

She ran forward, seeking the shadow, but the attacker had already darted back into the trees and disappeared from sight.

Eben and Kendrick roused, and Eben gained his feet first. A flash magic in the shadows followed by a disturbance in the air aimed at the jann's back announced the position of a caster in the shadows. The spell struck Eben but dissipated harmlessly in a shimmer against some sort of magical shield surrounding the jann. The magic briefly shone like sunlight shining off a lake and then disappeared. *Ahh. An elemental shield.*

Eben whirled and took a swing with his mace at something behind him in the shadows. Metal slithered off metal armor and Sha'Li whipped out a throwing knife, cocking her arm back. If only she could see the attacker!

She glimpsed Eben, Kendrick, and Will charging through the trees as flashes and clear trails of magic marked their passage. The caster must be incredibly powerful to be spraying this much magic about. A faint, metallic odor began to tinge the air from all of it.

Eben ran close to her hiding place, his skin the stony gray color and texture of granite. It was a protective shell his kind were able to form around themselves for short periods of time. He paused, crouching behind a tree, and his right hand began to glow slightly as he called elemental magic to himself. But a bright burst of magic exploded around Eben and, just like that, the protection dissipated.

This caster was too good. If Eben could not protect himself from the withering volleys of magic, he would never be able to close to weapon range fast enough to take out the attacker. If only the caster were showing signs of running short on magical energy. But the rapid-fire magical attacks were not slowing one bit in frequency.

Another streak of disturbed air marked the flight of a magic spell. It struck Eben with a flash of bright light. She watched in dismay as the jann gave a surprised grunt. His mace fell from his fingers. Eben stood for a moment staring down in shock at a smoking hole in his tabard. His knees buckled.

Kendrick charged, shouting. She spotted the outline of the attacker just as Kendrick jumped at the fellow and unintentionally blocked her line of fire. Cursing, she darted forward to help the young noble.

He fared no better than his jann friend. The attacker must have recognized the quality of swordsman before him, because a particularly bright glow abruptly shone beyond Kendrick. A gently curving line of disturbed air, a quick flash of the spell hitting its target, and Kendrick froze in an awkward half lunge. Sha'Li cursed under her breath.

She spied Will creeping around a tree trunk looking for the attacker, who remained frustratingly hidden in the shadows. A glow flashed at Will, who barely managed to dive behind another tree in time. She slid along the edges of the clearing as well, seeking cover, but the forest floor was frustratingly clear. Perfect for casters, but not for a rogue like her.

Will dodged a flurry of magic attacks, leaping and diving and rolling for a good minute as the caster blasted spell after spell at him. Will sent a few back, but he had nowhere near the range or accuracy of his assailant. Then, without warning, a streak of magic flashed past Will's guard and slashed across his chest. He grunted and went down on one knee. Showing no mercy, the attacker raced forward, closing the distance, and threw another spell at point-blank range at Will's back, laying Will out flat.

The only effective way to stop a competent combat mage, besides putting up a wall of some kind, was to strike him with some sort of long-range attack, or to close right on top of him and strike him down fast, before he could turn and blast his attacker into dust.

Sha'Li flung a globe of acid with all her strength toward the source of the magic bolts and immediately reached for another precious globe. Her target half-turned, however, and with a broad grin in her direction slugged down a liquid alchemical potion of his own. A shimmering shield of protection against alchemy surrounded him as quickly as her acid burned the previous one away.

"Nice throw!" the attacker called appreciatively.

"Kill him!" Kendrick shouted. Obviously, whatever magic confined his body in that strange, motionless pose did not extend to his vocal cords.

Sha'Li lurched, halting the release of her next alchemy globe by the barest of margins. That voice was familiar. She stared, shocked. "Kerryl? Kerryl Moonrunner? Is that you?"

"So much for going unrecognized," the nature guardian replied wryly.

"You know this unclaimed whelp?" Kendrick demanded disbelievingly. "Was this all an elaborate trap you've been leading us into? Is he your partner in crime?"

"Not this night!" she snapped at him. "What business have you with us, Moonrunner?"

"Just doing my job. Protecting the forest from the dangers that lurk within it."

"My friends these are," she declared. "No danger do they pose to the forest. For them I vouch."

"So noble you've become, young Sha'Li. You wear your Tribe mark well."

"If ever I get it," she grumbled.

"But you have it already," he replied, tilting his head at her as if perplexed. She stalked forward into the circle of firelight.

"Tease me not," she warned him. Had the mark appeared in the past few days when she could not see her reflection to know it? "Kendrick, see you a mark on my face? A moon-and-star symbol?"

"No."

She glared at Moonrunner. "If a joke that was, funny it was not."

"I'm serious. The mark is already upon your spirit. All that remains is for you to feel as if you have earned it. It will appear spontaneously upon your cheek. I do not jest: I sense it. You are Tribe of the Moon, now."

Her jaw sagged.

"Release me!" Kendrick demanded.

Moonrunner glanced over at the angry youth. "Come away with me, Sha'Li. Wander the wood with me. Help me save these idiots from threats they cannot even begin to imagine. Be my apprentice."

Her jaw dropped even farther. Kerryl Moonrunner himself was offering to train her? The scales on the back of her neck stood up of their own volition at that. The honor of it, the things he could teach her—

Moonrunner pulled out a dagger. "Give me a moment to kill these intruders and we will be on our way, you and me."

"Stop!" Sha'Li cried. "Kill them you cannot. My friends these are!" She didn't know who was more shocked at that, her or Moonrunner. Or mayhap Kendrick. He managed to look thunderstruck within his confinement spell.

"These are strangers!" Kerryl snapped. "Outsiders who do not belong here. They are not your friends."

"Yes, they are." She pointed down at Raina, prone on the ground. "Yelled at me just this afternoon that one did about how more respect from humans my race deserves."

"She lied," Moonrunner replied flatly.

Dismay ripped through Sha'Li. He could not kill her friends. That was not the way of the Tribe of the Moon. Its first tenet was to protect the innocent. Tenet number two was to defend the weak. Her companions looked extremely weak at the moment from where she stood—every one of them was incapacitated or worse.

"Surely you understand, Guardian Moonrunner. In Tribe of the Moon I desperately wish to be. And if right you are, I *am* Tribe. Let you kill them I cannot."

The nature guardian frowned at her. He looked so completely calm and reasonable that, of a sudden, she saw madness in his gaze. He showed no anger. No doubt. No remorse whatsoever over his decision to kill the others. That was not normal, was it? Particularly when someone you knew to be decent and honorable was arguing passionately against you making the kill.

"Healers are those two," she explained desperately. "Girls younger than me. And that one, the elf: purely as protector to the blond girl he acts. The jann over there his sister tries to find and rescue. Taken by slavers she was. And that one"— she jerked a thumb at Kendrick—"his friend helps. The boy you struck down: the disk of wood you gave me he wears, now. Bad people these are *not*."

Moonrunner's gaze remained unaffected. Implacable. His only response was to mutter, "I did see the Kithmar and their minions, yesterday. Those rakasha were running hard like they had somewhere important to be."

"Please, Guardian, I beg you. Kill not these people. As a favor to me! Without me, no Band of Beasts would you have gotten. Owe me you do."

Moonruner's unblinking stare finally flickered. He pointed at Will. "That one I already know from when he was a boy. Forces greater than I have long had plans for him that I shall not interfere with. But the others die."

She pressed the tiny opening as hard as she could, "The

Tribe has ever been your friend, Kerryl Moonrunner. If murder these innocents you do, see to it I will that the Tribe of the Moon knows of your crime. Turn on you we will. After you we will come."

The nature guardian guffawed. "It is the Tribe's work I do, Sha'Li. They will thank me one day when they understand what I do. But I do owe you. As a favor to you, I give you their lives. All but one of them. Choose which one I shall take."

She stared at him, appalled. He was unquestionably insane. "Choose I cannot—"

"Take me," Kendrick demanded. "Kill me. Spare the others."

Sha'Li's head whipped around to stare at him. He was a spoiled rich boy. Son of a noble. Why would he volunteer himself to die?

"Why you?" Moonrunner challenged.

"It is my right to do so. I am a noble and these others are commoners. It is my *duty* to protect them. To sacrifice myself if called upon to do so in their behalf. Kill me, you crazy freak."

Moonrunner hesitated, and Kendrick launched into what could only be described as a creative tirade of insults questioning everything from Moonrunner's parentage to his body odor.

But instead of infuriating the nature guardian into attacking, Kendrick's invective made Moonrunner burst into merry laughter. "I like you, boy. I like your spirit. Enough to take you, I think. And you are skilled with a sword. Yes, you will do nicely." He glanced over at Sha'Li. "We have a deal, then? I take him and you may have the rest. And my debt to you is repaid in full."

She looked over at Kendrick doubtfully. He glared at her,

battering at her with his words. "Take the deal, Sha'Li. I insist. It is the right thing to do. You and I both know it. I mean it. Do it."

"All right!" she burst out. "Fine. Your deal I accept, Moonrunner."

"I have one last request," Kendrick announced.

The nature guardian paused in the act of reaching for him, whether simply surprised or acquiescing she could not tell.

Either way, Kendrick spoke quickly, with terrible urgency, directly to her. "Tell the others not to come after me. Understood? I am young and strong and will resurrect. Who knows? I may catch up with all of you, later. Tell Eben of the Kithmar slavers moving in the forest, but tell them to finish Will's quest, first. Above all, they must finish the quest. You understand me, Sha'Li? Do *not* follow me."

"Oh, I do not plan to kill you, boy," Kerryl purred. "Oh no. I have better plans than that for you. Plans you will thank me for."

She frowned, not understanding at all as Moonrunner swept forward and slapped an open hand on Kendrick's chest. He incanted a spell too quietly for her to hear, and the human youth slumped, unconscious, within the magical restraints upon him.

Sha'Li said quickly, "Magic I do not have to heal the others. Let them die you cannot. Not our deal that was."

Moonrunner reached into his waist pouch and tossed something small and glittering at her. She caught it with one hand as he growled, "Use that wisely and they will live." With that, he grabbed the young noble's sword, heaved Kendrick over his shoulder, and jogged off into the night.

Frantically Sha'Li examined what he'd thrown her. A glass vial holding a potion of some kind. *Please Lunimar, let it be a healing potion.* She noticed the vial was color coded and silently thanked Brother Lizmorn for color-coding this one. *Now how did it go?* She swore under her breath, trying frantically to remember. Blue for life potions, black for spirit forms. Yellow to cure diseases. She could not remember what green stood for. This one bore a strip of white . . . straight healing. She ran over to Raina, rolled the girl over, and poured the clear liquid down the human's throat, praying that it worked.

The healer coughed. Opened her eyes, disoriented. "What happened?"

"Attacked we were," Sha'Li bit out. "Heal the others."

Raina jumped to her feet and moved fast around the fire, healing everyone. Eben was the only one who'd been killed outright, but the healer lifed him as easily as she woke Rosana from Moonrunner's sleep spell and roused Cicero from the unconsciousness caused by the blow to his head. Will was declared dying but not dead, and Raina dumped a bunch of healing into him last of all. He leaped to his feet like the others, wild-eyed and looking for an enemy to attack.

Chaos ensued as everyone demanded to know what had happened, bombarding her simultaneously with so many questions she could not answer any of them. But eventually she got a word in edgewise.

When she got to the part about Kendrick telling them not to go after him, though, the party fell totally silent. She finished delivering his message as close to exactly how he'd said it as she could.

After a long, heavy silence, Eben finally burst out, "That sounds just like him!"

Raina replied, "What will we do?"

Sha'Li was inclined to go after Kendrick. As annoying as he'd been and as often as she'd argued with him, she had to respect the way he'd insisted on being the one Moonrunner took. He didn't have to do that, but he hadn't hesitated. His heart was nobler than she'd given any human credit for.

Will and Raina reluctantly admitted to wanting to continue their quest for the sleeping-elf guy. Rosana was for giving chase to Moonrunner and rescuing Kendrick. But then, she was Heart. It made sense she would feel that way. Sha'Li was glad for the support. Cicero threw up his hands and said he'd do whatever the party decided. He was only along to keep Raina safe.

They all turned to Eben. It fell to him to break the tie. She did not envy him the choice. His best friend or his best friend's last request.

CHAPTER

24

Raina woke with a heavy heart in the first gray light of dawn. The others seemed equally depressed as they choked down strips of dried meat and erased the signs of their camp preparatory to moving out. She noted that Eben was quietest of all. In the end, he'd honored Kendrick's request not to chase after him immediately. But to have lost both his sister and his best friend who was like a brother to him . . . it was a heavy burden to bear. She worried that he still might do something impulsive and draw down their little party by yet another skilled sword it could not afford to lose.

When she was not fretting about her traveling companions, she fretted about how she was to convince the Boki to let them wake the Mythar. She must find a way to appeal to the Boki's honor, which they seemed to hold so dear. If only she knew more of their mythology regarding the one they guarded. Mayhap she could find a way to use their own Boki legends to prove it was time to wake the sleeping one.

The group had promised one another stoutly that, if Kendrick was not back in Dupree waiting for them when they returned, they would come back here and rescue him. She sincerely hoped that was not necessary. She'd liked the landsgrave's son. Although a bit impetuous, Kendrick had seemed to have a brave and good heart. Much like his father.

Cicero and Sha'Li took turns erasing the party's tracks and serving as rear guard as they moved out in the gloom. Most of the time, Will took point, leading the way. Or rather, Bloodroot's spirit led the way, unerringly finding the least difficult path through the increasingly rugged terrain.

How much longer Will could go on like this was anybody's guess. Raina's training suggested that he should already be dead. She could only assume that some combination of her magic and Rosana's, Bloodroot's stubbornness, and Will's determination was what kept him going.

The deeper they journeyed into the Forest of Thorns, the more frequently the front or rear guard signaled for the group to halt and hide. Late in the afternoon, they crouched by a trickle of water sluggishly seeping up out of the ground to drink and refill their water skins. Eben and Cicero slipped away into the woods while the rest of them rested to scout for a spot to bed down.

Without warning, Eben burst into the little clearing, panting. "We've got a problem." Cupping his hands around his mouth, he let out a caw that sounded like one of the local grackles.

Raina started at the harsh noise. "What was that for?"

Sha'Li muttered, "Calling in Cicero."

Sure enough, the kindari burst into the clearing at a dead run in a moment, sword drawn. "What's amiss?" he demanded.

Eben replied with a single word that struck terror into Will's heart. "Anton."

"How far?" Cicero asked the jann tersely.

The jann hummed urgently, "Maybe two hundred yards behind us, I spotted a scout. He'll be working ahead of the main force by a bit. I estimate a half mile to Anton's main force."

Raina looked at her kindari guardian and said in dismay, "I'm going to have to run again, aren't I?"

The elf nodded grimly. She groaned under her breath as she shouldered her pack and tucked her skirt up around her knees. If Anton caught her, at best he would send her home to her mother and the Mages of Alchizzadon. At worst, the governor would make her his slave. She'd heard Eben and Kendrick muttering about how Anton fed women love potions and then engaged in lascivious orgies with his love slaves. She shuddered at the thought and panic beat at her ribs.

The good news was that an army was not likely to move fast in terrain this rough. Cicero set off at a steady jog that had Raina chomping with impatience to go faster. But the wisdom of the kindari's pace was evident when they were still jogging along an hour later. The elf finally called a halt when full dark made the forest floor totally impossible to see. She was grateful to stop tripping and stumbling every few strides.

The group huddled together over the napkin Rosana unfolded. It held the last of the calorie-dense cheese bread they brought with them. She tore off big hunks of it and passed them around. Raina approved of Rosana's decision to feed everyone well. This was no night to be stingy with sustenance. They'd been going a day, a night, and another day with only a few hours of rest.

Cicero spoke quietly. "I'd suggest we sleep for a few hours, and then move on. We'll need all the head start we can get on Anton if we're to stay ahead of him."

Eben nodded grimly. "From what I make of the man, he'll move fast and drive his troops mercilessly. Patience is, mmm, not his greatest virtue."

Wry humor hung in the air from the obvious and unspoken retort to that comment: *Anton Constantine* has *virtues?*

Rosana burst out, "What does that snake want out here?"

The kindari shrugged. "Don't know and don't care. I just don't want to get caught by the viper."

Raina fervently agreed with that sentiment. For all she knew, her mother and the mages had already reported her missing to the Imperial Army. And for all intents and purposes in Dupree, Anton Constantine was the Empire.

She passed the last of her healing into Will and then hunkered down in her bedroll in the cold and dark, the night sounds even more ominous than usual. Every twig snapping or leaf rustling made her heart jump with trepidation. She napped, but it seemed like she'd just closed her eyes when Rosana gently shook her awake.

Every time she woke up, she felt miserable. The amount of healing she was doing on Will and Bloodroot was straining her mind's and body's abilities to recover. She did her best not to complain, but each day she felt weaker as her magic grew stronger. She consoled herself with the fact that Will undoubtedly felt much worse than she did.

She eyed the youth surreptitiously as she packed her bedroll and tightened her boots. Will staggered through each day seeming not to care much where Bloodroot led them all. She only wished their journey would end soon. Before they all collapsed of exhaustion and the constant, gnawing fear.

Cicero issued strange instructions prior to their moving out tonight. *Build a fire. Leave signs of a camp. Stoke the embers well.*

"What are you about?" Sha'Li growled, sounding surlier than usual.

The kindari answered, "If Anton's soldiers find our camp, they will think it only recently abandoned and believe us much closer than we are."

Raina approved of the cunning. What would she have done

without her faithful protector? She certainly never would have made it this far. Not once had he complained of the hardships helping her had brought him, nor had he once mentioned compensation of any kind for his service. All she could pay him with was her friendship, and that she gave the kindari without reserve.

The group got into the spirit of deception immediately, laying out hasty beds of boughs and pine needles to indicate that they'd slept in this place. Then, moving carefully, and with their countertrackers meticulously erasing their trail, they slipped out of the clearing. When Cicero judged them well clear of the camp, they moved out more quickly.

Night travel was slow and hard going. But better that than death at Anton's hands or in an Imperial slave galley, however.

Raina pondered whether or not Anton was hunting them, specifically. Their little party could not possibly be that important to him. Surely Anton had not gotten wind of what they sought.

In her more grim moments, she wondered if it was possible that Anton was out here for the same reason they were? To find the Sleeping King? Although, as he was the Emperor's man, Anton's goal would no doubt be to destroy this supposed king and any threat he might pose to Maximillian.

Or mayhap Anton was merely looking for a fight. Stars knew, the Boki would give him one.

Night became morn and morn became day, and still they trekked onward. It was moving toward sunset and everyone was staggering with exhaustion when Eben threw up a fist ahead of them, signaling frantically for all of them to get down. Raina, almost too numb to comprehend the signal, stumbled, stared stupidly for a moment, and belatedly dived behind the nearest clump of brambles. *Now what?*

Silence settled around her and her companions. Too much silence. Whoever came this way would sense their presence in the absence of chirps and clicks and random noises of the woods. Worried, she caught Will's apprehensive gaze and pointed at her ear.

He frowned for a moment and then nodded in sudden comprehension. She watched as he laid his hands upon the ground and closed his eyes in concentration.

She didn't fully understand who Bloodroot was, but unquestionably the spirit was deeply connected to nature. Will's face went even grayer and more haggard as the spirit within him encouraged the creatures of the wood to resume their normal chorus. In a few moments the usual buzzings and chirpings resumed.

Raina sagged in relief. As soon as she got within reach of Will, though, she was going to have to pour a bunch of healing into him and his disk. He looked terrible after the effort of allowing the tree spirit to function through him like that.

They were never going to get out of this mess alive.

Will panted, each breath painful. Regaining control of his mind after relinquishing it to Bloodroot like that was almost more effort than he could manage. But Raina had been right. If the forest went silent around them they were all dead.

It was no more than a minute after the crickets and frogs started singing once more when abrupt silence cut through the forest. This time it was not of their doing. His senses shot onto high alert. He smelled them first. He would never forget that effluvia of rotting meat.

Orcs.

The Boki patrol came into sight, four of them, moving in casual but nonetheless vigilant formation. They moved like creatures on their home turf, not expecting trouble. But then, all of a sudden, the one in front's heavy-jowled head swung up sharply, an upthrusting tusk glinting. He lifted his lumpy green face to the wisp of breeze and took a long, loud sniff. He grunted something that sounded suspiciously like "hoomans."

Dregs. Will gripped his sword more tightly and thought fiercely, *I don't care if these are your people or not, Bloodroot. If they kill me, they kill you. Stay out of my way if this comes to a fight.* An inarticulate snort in his head was all he got back.

The other Boki stopped and sniffed as well. After a spate of urgent grunts two of them wheeled around and headed back to the north from whence they came. The other two sprinted south, straight at Will and the others, hidden in the underbrush. He tensed, readying himself to meet the charge. He would take the leader. Will was ready to spring out and face his foe. A dozen more strides and the orc would be within weapon range. A half dozen. Three strides. Two.

And then the orc barreled past, not even slowing down as he passed Will's hiding place. Both of the Boki pounded on by, charging south and disappearing from sight within a few tense seconds.

What on Urth was that all about?

Will and the others crouched in their hiding places, holding their positions for several minutes, awaiting the possible return of either group of Boki. But gradually the sounds of the forest resumed around them—and without any help from Bloodroot. The party crept out of hiding and huddled together, and the others looked fully as perplexed as Will felt.

Eben spoke first. "The two who went north were going back to warn their tribe. The others went south, following the scent of humans."

Cicero nodded. "Anton's army. The orcs must've picked up the scent of the larger party of humans behind us. It probably masked our scent, or at least mingled with it such that they didn't realize we were right here."

Raina laughed under her breath. "Who'd have ever guessed I'd be thrilled to have a squad of the Haelan legion on my tail?"

Cicero replied grimly, "Oh, it is no mere squad. It is a full battalion if I don't miss my guess."

Will turned on the kindari in dismay. "How do you figure that?"

"Animals flee before large parties of humans much like they would before a wildfire. Based on the number and type of displaced creatures I've seen moving through the woods, I can estimate the size of the force and its direction of movement."

It was the sort of logic Adrick would have used. Will thought back also to his father's endless lectures about historic battles of old. If Anton was out here to confront the Boki, a line of battle would emerge where the two forces met and clashed. Their little party needed to move out of the way and not end up caught between the two armies as they charged headlong toward each other.

And in the meantime, they still had to find the remains of the Great Circle . . . wherever they might be hiding. But they'd also had practically no sleep in two days, and they were all exhausted.

Will spoke quietly. "I think we need to find a good hiding place and get some real sleep. There are about to be two armies running around out here, and it's going to take all of our skill and strength to avoid them both."

The others agreed, and if he was not mistaken, looks of relief passed around. Cicero told them to stay put while he looked for a likely spot. He returned in a little while and led them into an area of chokingly thick, nearly impassable underbrush. The going was painfully slow, for they dared not leave even a single thread behind to mark their passage through the thick brambles. But, by the time full night had fallen, they had made a cold camp, ranging their bedrolls in a tight defensive circle under cover of a stand of thorny holly bushes with thick evergreen leaves that made a dense cover over and around them.

It was dangerous to stop like this, but they had no choice. Not one of them had the strength to go on. Raina had poured a massive amount of magic into Will around sunset, which made him feel marginally better, but she'd been stumbling along in utter exhaustion ever since. Maybe if Kendrick had been here and given them some stirring speech of courage and perseverance it might have convinced them to find a way to press on. Will had never expected to miss the young noble, but Kendrick had grown on him over time. Their attacker had no doubt killed Kendrick by now and Hyland's son had already resurrected in Dupree. His father would be exasperated, but Kendrick was probably sitting in a pub right now hoisting an ale and flirting with a barmaid while the rest of them ran for their lives out here.

But without Kendrick's boundless energy to inspire them, the party members could not muster the energy to do aught but close their eyes and pass out.

Leland's breath hitched as a scout burst into the command tent, panting. Clearly, the soldier had news of their quarry. With all his being, Leland wished to avoid the battle to come. Krugar, in the middle of his daily report, fell silent. Anton ordered imperiously, "Speak, scout."

"They've been spotted again. Due north of our position and on the run."

On the run? Boki didn't run. Ever. They stood and fought their enemies. And usually won, of course. Who, then, did Anton have his scouts tracking? Horror exploded in Leland's chest. Surely not the very party he and Aurelius had sent forth into these woods. *My son.*

"What of the Boki?" Leland asked the scout.

"Sign, but no sightings, my lord."

"Who, then, did you see?" Leland asked as blandly as he possibly could. Meanwhile panic clogged his throat.

The Kithmar scout's nose twitched, and his yellow-eyed gaze darted to Anton and back.

It was all the answer Leland needed. Helpless fury washed over him. Even Anton knew Leland would fall on his own sword before he would kill his own son and Kendrick's companions. But forcing Leland to actually choose between family and duty—Anton always had been a master at finding and twisting the knife in a man's gut.

Anton answered casually, "While we're hunting green-skins, we might as well take out some bandits and outlaws while we're at it. Put a bounty on a renegade and these cats suddenly turn into fine trackers."

The Kithmar scout growled in eager anticipation. Leland couldn't tell if the creature was lusting harder for blood or gold. But the avid greed in the rakasha's feline eyes worried Leland. A lot.

Once, he'd been the adventurer on the run, simultaneously fleeing Anton's forces and racing toward glory. Once, he and his comrades had been young and eager, sure that they were fated to save the world from the Kothite scourge. If only he were Kendrick's age again—

Wishing would not make it so. Leland had had his shot at glory. It was time to move aside for the next generation of heroes. But knowing it did not make his heart yearn any less for the thrill of the chase, the taste of glory on his tongue, the clash of battle in his ears.

Truth be told, his son and the others faced an even more difficult challenge than Leland had before. For one thing, the force chasing him thirty years ago had worn Imperial Army colors and been constrained to a certain degree of civilized behavior. But this bunch that Anton had hired . . . Leland barely stopped his lip from curling in disgust. The good governor had dug to the very bottom of the midden pile of humanity to come up with these Kithmar rogues, brigands, and outright assassins he'd brought with him into the Forest of Thorns.

Worse, at the governor's order, nobody wore uniforms or colors of any kind, not even Anton himself, thereby negating what few rules existed for honorable behavior in combat. How Anton had gotten wind of Tiberius's boy, Leland's own son, and a young arch-mage on a quest Leland had no idea. Eben was excitable, but could handle himself in a fight. And the girl's kindari watchdog seemed to have a level head on his shoulders. The inexperienced gypsy girl could be a liability, but at least she wore Heart colors. That could prove useful. *They'd be all right . . .* but the assurance rang hollow in his own ears. *Five against an army of five hundred? Particularly* this *five hundred?* And that was assuming Anton didn't have more mercenaries that he didn't know about lying in wait in the woods.

Of course, it went without saying that Anton's real goal was to find and seize for himself the fabled Boki treasure of the Forest of Thorns.

Perhaps worst of all, Anton had declined to bring along a

single Heart healer on this unofficial expedition of his. Not only did he likely wish to avoid the Heart reporting back to the Empire through its own channels on this escapade of his, but Leland also suspected Anton hoped the majority of his force would die out here beyond the help of resurrection. Two birds brought down with one stone. Anton would have his treasure and his glory, and he would rid the colony of many of its most troubling bandits.

Leland glanced across the tent at Selea, lounging indolently in the corner. The nulvari showed no reaction to the latest report of a small party of outlaws moving deeper into the forest. But surely the irony was not lost on him, either. Aurelius, on the far side of the table, was outwardly composed, but Leland thought he detected a hint of tightness about the solinari's jaw.

Another one of Anton's petty revenges—insisting that the three of them travel with him . . . to witness the end of all their hopes and dreams for freedom in their lifetimes. Oh yes. Anton had been more than happy to include Aurelius and Selea in the expedition when they'd unexpectedly shown up in camp two nights ago, to rub their noses in their failure thirty years ago and in his triumph now where they had failed. *Whoreson.*

Anton was gleeful at the news of the latest sighting. "A night march tonight and we shall finally catch some little fishies in our net." The governor's sly gaze landed on Leland. "What on Urth could fugitive outlaws be after out here?"

Leland shrugged as casually as he could muster. Anton knew as well as any of them what the adventurers attempted. Anton was merely under the mistaken impression that the treasure they sought was monetary. In that, at least, Leland held a trump card over the governor.

Anton continued, "We can't have rogue bandits running

around like this provoking petty wars with greenskins. We must crush these renegades. And we must teach all the heathens of this barbaric land a lesson about who rules this place." Anton's voice rose. The governor did love to get himself all worked up. "I say when and where my subjects may go. No one breathes in these colonies without my permission!"

Krugar cleared his throat. "Your mercen—men—have been on forced march for the past three days. They will be dropping in their boots by the morrow."

Anton waved a careless hand. "Cull the weak, Captain."

Krugar tried again. "If we move in force to capture this party of outlaws tonight, we will likely engage Boki. I have no exact count of how many orcs are out there—the scouts I sent out to get a head count are overdue on their return."

That threw a damper into the gathered leaders of the various groups of thugs that formed Anton's cadre. Boki were formidable warriors. The usual practice was to count one Boki as the equivalent of five seasoned Imperial soldiers. Who knew what the odds would be against this cobbled-together force, however? Given the bandits' lack of experience working as a single, disciplined military unit, Leland guessed the Boki counted more realistically at eight to ten of Anton's men to one of the orcs. And they were defending their homes, most dangerous foes indeed.

Renewed worry for Kendrick and his companions stabbed Leland. If a substantial orc force had moved to intercept the little party of adventurers, their situation was grim indeed. Boki before them, Anton's mercenaries behind them.

The parallels to last time were eerie.

Thankfully, Anton was not so worked up yet that he could not hear reason. The governor scowled at Krugar. "Very well. We will wait for your scouts to return with a Boki head count. And then we move to grab the renegades."

Leland sent an urgent plea out to the party, so young and inexperienced for the task laid upon them. *Run, children. Fly like the wind.*

Will slept heavily, and the others seemed to do the same. Dawn found him feeling worse than ever, but it mattered not. When Rosana would have examined his health, he batted away her hand, forced himself upright, and plodded on once more.

They journeyed deeper into the Forest of Thorns, and a wilder and more primordial place he had never seen. Even if he tilted his head back and stared until he became dizzy, he couldn't make out the sky through the towering maze of distant limbs. If all the members of their little band joined hands, they still would not circle the mightiest of the trees growing in this place. When he laid hands on them, their black bark was as hard as steel, their spirits older than time. If they lived at all, their greenery was so far overhead as to be invisible beyond the limbs above.

The tree roots posed a formidable obstacle. Many of them stood waist high, smooth and sloping and too wide to gain purchase upon. The travelers resorted to boosting and hauling one another over the largest of them, but it made for slow and tiring going.

The eyes of the forest never left them. Will felt its gaze constantly and jerked at the slightest sound, grabbing for his staff so often he finally resorted to carrying it in front of him at all times. He noticed that Cicero did the same with his bow and even Rosana clutched a dagger in her fist as they scrambled, climbed, and crawled through the tangle of mighty roots.

An ambush here would be ridiculously easy to spring upon them. They were forced to rely on the silence of the place and

Will's own, odd, intuitive feel for the nearness of orcs to know when danger was nigh.

Every few hours, an internal warning fired in his head and he signaled the others to dive for the nearest hiding spot, waiting in tense silence for they knew not what to attack them. Before long all of their nerves were frayed.

In the afternoon the forest primeval gave way to slightly smaller girthed trees. And, with the increased light from above, carpets of ferns and velvet moss took hold. The resurgence of green and growing things marked a return of life to this place, and Will breathed a deep mental sigh of relief.

He muttered to his other self, "Tell me you're not one of those monsters in your original form."

He sensed a grunt inside his skull as if those had been mere saplings behind them.

Rosana startled Will by asking, "You talk to self again?"

He sighed. "No. I'm speaking to Bloodroot."

"And he speak back to you?"

He caught her worry, but answered evenly, "Not exactly. I get impressions. Feelings. But not actual conversation."

She looked vaguely relieved. "My teachers always tell me, 'Never speak to voices in your head.'"

It was Will's turn to wax sarcastic. "And did they teach you anything else?"

"Yes. Never ever accept power from voices in your head."

Will didn't know whether to worry or laugh. He was not possessed . . . he hoped. The powers Bloodroot had given Will were helping them. Without his new ability to find forest tracks, or speak to the animals, or his immunity to the charms of dryads, they would never have made it this far, nor would they be on their way to the Great Circle itself.

He said lightly, "Obviously, your teachers never had a tree spirit stuck to their chests."

Rosana shook her head, her dark gaze worried. "It come to no good, Will. You mark my words. Someone get hurt before this finish."

He responded lightly, "With you here to look after us? Never."

She snorted. "Raina, she make me look like amateur healer. If we live through this, she will be cause of it."

Will glanced over at Raina, who was impatiently blowing a wayward strand of hair out of her face and looking more like an awkward adolescent than an arch-mage at the moment. He asked under his breath, "How powerful is she?"

Rosana shook her head. "Never have I seen like her. And I see plenty big healers and high-magic casters in my day. She, how you call, a freak."

"Well, at least she's our freak, eh?"

Rosana shrugged, not looking especially thrilled with that concept. He reached out and rubbed the back of his knuckle down the line of her cheek. "You'll always be my favorite healer."

"You big flirt, Will Cobb."

He grinned at her, doing exactly what she accused him of. "And you love it. So no complaints from you, my gypsy rose."

The blush that leaped to her cheeks and the sparkle that lit her eye were a sight to see. He drank them in eagerly, storing them away in his memory against a time when he and Rosana might be apart. Although it was becoming increasingly hard to imagine a single day without her cheerful countenance and steady warmth at his side.

The tree-giants grew more scarce, and a rather more normally proportioned forest sprang up around them. But with it came increased danger. Nearly every hour one of their scouts signaled for them to take cover.

Over a cold snack of raw, edible roots and dried strips of

smoked rabbit meat, Eben and Cicero discussed in whispers battle tactics appropriate to their party's experience and abilities. Will worried periodically that the colorful jann might be some sort of spy. He kept taking all those side excursions by himself ostensibly to hunt. But for all they knew, the elemental creature could be laying a trail for Anton and company to follow straight to the party.

The whites of Sha'Li's eyes showed continuously, a sure sign that she was deeply uneasy. Even Rosana and Raina, normally whispering up a storm with each other, fell silent as the afternoon waned.

Just after sunset, as they began to search for water and a place to hunker down and hide for the night—for it could no longer rightly be called making camp—an unearthly noise echoed through the air all around them. Part roar and part screech, it was deafening and froze all of them in their tracks.

Cicero roused himself first, pointing up toward the sky and signaling frantically for them to take cover. Crouching under the arching boughs of a white pine tree, Will did not see what passed overhead. But the slow, rhythmic whoosh of enormous wings made him exceedingly glad that he did not.

When the creature had passed, the party huddled together. Raina was first to whisper, "What was that?"

No one replied. Cicero finally said reluctantly, "If I didn't know better, I'd say that was some sort of draconic creature."

Will's eyes about bugged out of his head. "You're saying that dragons really exist?"

The kindari shrugged. "I've never seen one myself, but I've heard stories."

Will retorted, "And there's one in these woods?"

Another shrug from Cicero. "Not my home woods. I could not say."

Sha'Li piped up, "Green I thought I glimpsed as that creature flew over."

The elf frowned. "Lore has it that the green dragon is asleep. If that is true, then the green's minions should not be out and about, either."

Sha'Li snapped, "Supposed to be asleep is this king of yours, too. And yet, a wakeup call we are here to give him. Maybe for your dragon someone did the same!"

Cicero scowled. "The green is not mine. She is the province of the zinnzari."

Will noted that Raina's head snapped toward the kindari at that remark, but she said nothing. What was a zinnzari, anyway? Some other magical creature he'd never heard of?

Unnerved by that unearthly scream, the party was too jittery to stop. They continued on grimly in the dusk.

Leland was lying on his cot, trying unsuccessfully to catch a nap before whatever this night brought, when one of his men burst into his tent. He jerked upright. "Has a scout returned with a head count on the Boki?" he asked tersely.

"Aye, m'lord."

Leland grabbed his sword belt and, as he strode out of his tent toward Anton's, buckled it on. He had a bad feeling about this.

The scout had only just reached Anton's headquarters and clutched his side, muddy and panting, trying to catch his breath enough to give his report. Leland glanced around quickly. Aurelius and Selea were already there. They must have stayed after the earlier meeting for dinner with Constantine. They were braver than he to dine with the devil.

Anton snapped at the scout, "Give me your report now. If it's satisfactory, I'll see you healed if you keel over!"

The young soldier panted, "War party. Boki. I counted fifteen. Found their camp. Here." The scout stabbed at the map spread out on a folding table. "They were packing up to move. Heavily armed. Lightly armored."

Leland had never known the Boki to wear a lot of armor. The orcs had their own tough hides to protect them. He frowned. *Only fifteen?* That didn't seem right.

As Anton's face lit with glee, Leland grimaced. The governor would not appreciate him throwing a bucket of cold water on this good news. Nonetheless, the lives of his men were at stake.

He sighed and cast himself upon his proverbial sword. "My lord governor, this report worries me."

Anton's gaze swung to him, a thunderous frown gathering on his brow. "Why say you so?"

"Only fifteen? Surely, they know full well that we are a force five hundred strong out here. Why would they send so few? Even they cannot be so arrogant as to believe that is a sufficient number of their kind to defeat us."

Anton's cheek twitched in irritation, but Leland continued doggedly.

"They bait a trap. They dangle a small force before us to entice us to attack. Were our scouts to press deeper into the forest beyond this party, they would find the main body of the Boki force. I've no doubt that force is sufficient to crush us all."

"You whine like a frightened old woman, Leland!" Anton snapped. Constantine cast a furious gaze around the tent at the others present. "Gather your men and prepare for battle. We march on the Boki now."

Desperate, Leland started to protest, but Anton cut him off with a sharp slash of his hand. "Follow my order, Hyland, or we shall pause long enough to hang you from the highest tree I can find."

Leland was careful not to look over at Aurelius or Selea. This was exactly what Anton had done the last time. He'd come out here seeking treasure, unaware that the only treasure was a sleeping king, not gold and jewels. But as soon as the Boki had shown up, Anton couldn't resist the temptation of winning glory in battle.

Of course, back then few had realized the true might of the Boki. But this time Anton had no excuse. He'd met the orcs in battle. How many of Anton's men would not survive this night? A hundred? Two hundred?

The potential loss of so many sickened Leland. Even if they were the lowest of the low, they were still people. They had families and loved ones. And many of them would die this night because Anton refused to listen to reason. No man had the right to let his arrogance cost so many so much.

Anger hardened in Leland's gut. If he survived this fiasco, he would take action against Anton. Leland knew not how or when, but he would see the man taken down if it was the last thing he did. And likely it *would* be the last thing he did. For to attack the governor was to attack the Empire itself.

So be it.

W ill blinked awake, disoriented. Why was he lying on the ground? Raina was crouching over him. His arm tingled painfully like tiny needles were stabbing it. She must be healing him. *Not that it would do any good.* She muttered low, "Anton's men are almost upon us. Can you move?"

"Do I have any choice?"

"Sha'Li could probably carry you and keep up."

"I'll stand on my own two feet."

"Let me give you a little more healing before you get up. You're as weak as a kitten." Raina's hands and arms glowed nearly to her shoulders as she pulled in a particularly large charge of energy. He braced himself for its pain, but she was getting quite good at pouring it into him with a minimum of discomfort. Either that or he was too numb with exhaustion to feel anything. As the magic jumped into him sharply he gathered into enough energy to sit up. Raina reached for his arm to help him to his feet, but Rosana intervened smoothly.

"I'll take care of that," the gypsy murmured. She startled him by throwing a little healing into him as well. Anton's force must be really close for Rosana to have done that. She stepped back and Eben and Sha'Li unceremoniously hoisted him to his feet.

"Run now if you would live, human," Sha'Li muttered into his ear. "Otherwise, that disk I'll cut out and your remains leave for the Imperial jackals."

With Cicero leading the way, they took off into the night, running for their lives. They didn't bother countertracking. He noted also that Cicero did not set a steady, sustainable pace. This was an all-out sprint. Anton must have been no more than a stone's throw from their position.

Old man, if you can help me, now is the time to do it.

Of course, Bloodroot was actually the source of Will's progressive weakness and illness. A human body simply wasn't strong enough to withstand the spirit of a tree lord. What had Bloodroot been thinking to choose Will for a host? Not that the whoreson cared if he lived or died, Will supposed, as long as he got home.

They ran for fifteen minutes or so, stopping only a few

seconds at a time to listen for pursuit. Sha'Li snapped for them all to have respiratory failure less loudly so she and Cicero could hear. Will did his best to comply, but his head felt as if it would split in twain and white spots danced before his eyes.

Cicero was the first to murmur, "I hear troop movements. Sounds like they're deploying for a battle."

Sha'Li nodded. "Aye. Forming a line Anton's men are. About to engage the Boki he is." She added under her breath, "Idiot."

Eben said grimly, "They should remain occupied with each other for some time. We need to put as much distance between them and us as we can manage."

Will dutifully followed the others as they took off racing through the trees. Even Rosana had no trouble outpacing him. How he kept up with the party he had no idea. Probably a combination of panic and sheer, stubborn determination to survive.

Will's muscles screamed for rest. His mind screamed for escape from this nightmare. He wanted no more part of this quest. He wanted to go home. To crawl into his bed in the loft of his parents' cottage. To wake up in the morning to the smell of bacon frying and hear his parents' cheerful voices. But the night and the trees and the terror stretched on and on, a black, never-ending abyss that had swallowed them all.

During one of their infrequent rest stops, Raina muttered in his general direction, "Did I hear you say the Sleeping King was guarded by the Boki? And the Boki have been trying to collect the pieces of that thing on your chest for a long time, right? Do you suppose Bloodroot knows something about the Sleeping King?"

She had the energy to think, let alone reason? He mumbled, "If he does, he hasn't shared it with me."

"Can you ask him?" she pressed.

"No." He added, "I'd hate to think I've been carrying around the location of the king all this time inside my head." *Did you hear that, you old fossil? If you know, you'd better show me.*

"Who else could know something, then?" Raina asked reasonably.

He huffed. "I don't know. I don't know anything. Except that my father and his friends nearly found the king a long time ago, and he was in this forest, guarded by Boki."

Cicero called for them to move out, and Raina and Will's conversation ended. But at the next rest break, Raina picked up where she'd left off. *Persistent girl.*

"If they wished to see him woken and could do it themselves, they already would have. Which means one of two things then. Either they do not wish him woken, or someone else needs to wake him."

"But which?" Will muttered.

She shrugged. "Only way to know is to ask them, I suppose."

He snorted. "As if they would answer a bunch of pinkskin adventurers like us."

"Speak for yourself!" Sha'Li hissed.

Finally, a little before dawn, Cicero called a halt by raising a closed fist. The group stopped gratefully, the healers flopping immediately to the ground. Will would have done the same, except Cicero gestured him, Eben, and Sha'Li close.

Cicero asked the jann, "Are we far enough from the Imperials to take a few hours' rest?"

Eben considered briefly. "Aye, but we've another problem. If I haven't gotten myself all turned around in the course of our flight, we've run right down the throat of the Boki force."

Will stared in horror at the jann. "You're kidding."

Cicero replied grimly, " 'Twas that or be taken by the Imperials. They were spreading out in a line behind us and flanking us on each side. I deemed a swift and honorable death in combat against Boki preferable to what Anton Constantine would do to us."

Eben shrugged. "I cannot argue with that."

Will demanded, "So what now? We hand ourselves over to the Boki and give up?"

"Keep your voice down," Cicero bit out low. "Now we hide. We stay absolutely still and silent and hope the battle passes us by."

"That's not much of a plan—" Will started hotly.

Eben cut him off. "Nay, but it is all we have. Rosana and Raina are done in. They can't run another step. Frankly, it is miraculous they didn't both collapse hours ago."

Cicero pointed at what Will thought to be the north. "The Boki are that way. Let me check that way"—the elf pointed east—"for a hiding place."

The others nodded, then as one looked at him. Will frowned. Since when had they appointed Cicero leader of this ill-fated expedition? Will took a deep breath and said as calmly as he could, "Let's do it."

Cicero moved off through the trees. For his part, Will slid to the ground beside the nearest tree, leaning back against its trunk in utter exhaustion. Maybe it wasn't such a bad idea to just give up now and turn themselves over to the Boki. At least they might be able to talk their captors into giving them a hot meal before they were slaughtered or sold into slavery. He closed his eyes, idly envisioning the Boki's shock if he strolled into their camp and roared in tree-speak for a bowl of stew.

Actually . . .

No.

Nonetheless, the idea did have a certain merit. . . .

Leland waited a few paces behind Anton, well to the back of the formation. It was exceedingly strange being so far from the front line as this. Leland always led his men in person. Not so with Anton, and certainly not with this motley force of cutthroats and assassins.

They'd only caught a fleeting glimpse of a few Boki warriors through the trees, but then they'd disappeared.

"Where are they?" Anton growled.

A good question. A half-dozen scouts had been sent out in various directions, but none had sent a signal back that the enemy was in sight.

Without warning, a signal came from dead ahead. The enemy was moving left to right parallel to Anton's forces at a high rate of speed. In quick succession the next two scouts in line reported the same thing, as the Boki force apparently raced east.

"Hah!" Anton crowed. "They have learned the identity of their attacker and flee before me like spineless cowards!"

Leland frowned. The Boki were neither spineless nor cowards. In fact, tradition had it that no Boki warrior fled from any fight. Ever. They would die rather than retreat. He would bet his entire holdings and everything in them that the Boki did not flee them now. Which begged the question, what exactly were the Boki doing?

And then it hit him.

Boki scouting parties had been out here well before Anton's force arrived. Which meant they were already looking for something. Or someone. Like a small party of adventurers bent on disturbing the tomb of their sleeping king, mayhap?

The Boki would never flee from Imperial soldiers, but they

would most certainly take off in hot pursuit of their prey. Which meant . . .

. . . The Boki must have spotted Kendrick and his companions.

Panic all but drove Leland to his feet shouting for his men to go after the Boki and engage them—anything to divert them or at least slow them down. At the last moment, he restrained the impulse.

Instead, he leaned toward Anton and murmured, "If the Boki do, indeed, flee us, then they give us their unprotected backs. Do we attack, my lord?"

Anton glanced sharply at him, clearly surprised at the aggressive suggestion from his reluctant landsgrave. "Aye. Sound the call. We give chase. Engage the Boki and kill them all!"

Leland rose from his position, sword raised high, and shouted the order to his men. He prayed no one died needlessly in this maneuver, but what choice did he have? His son and the others, Ty's boy and the arch-mage girl, must live. They must escape the Boki and be given a chance to complete their mission. The fate of the colonies and all who lived there might very well rest upon their shoulders.

As Leland expected, finding and engaging the rear guard of the Boki was more difficult than it sounded. The forested terrain made a traditional battle impossible. This would be an extended skirmish for the most part. Command and control was going to be a nightmare as Anton's troops scattered through the woods.

Worse, the orcs were on their home turf and they were strong and fast. Plus, they didn't seem interested in fighting Anton's men in a major, force-on-force battle. Nonetheless, the soldiers managed to force a few Boki to turn and fight.

Much more in the manner Leland was accustomed to from

them, the Boki stragglers fought furiously and to the death. Suspicion settled in his gut that they were acting as sacrificial lambs to delay Anton. Even when the Boki were swarmed by a dozen men at a time, it still took long and costly minutes to kill each one. Leland could only pray that somehow Kendrick and his companions had managed to avoid the rushing Boki force behind them.

Will's better judgment was still managing to overrule his wilder impulses by a whisker when Cicero called a halt in the thicket the kindari had found for them. It was Will's turn to take first watch and he settled in the shadow of a giant hickory tree, careful to make sure he was not comfortable enough to drift off to sleep. He could swear Adrick's staff, made of hickory heartwood, warmed a little in his hand.

The woods were tense around him. The night creatures did not go about their usual business, and alarm calls were more prevalent than mating calls among the frogs and night birds. Bloodroot's extraordinary ability to read the sounds of the forest might be absent, but Will had learned enough from the tree spirit to know the enemy was close. Very close.

What was he doing out here? He was going to die. And for what? A legend? What could anyone do against the might of Koth? Even if this sleeping king did exist, what could one man do against so great an enemy?

He had no business running around out here with armies and orcs. He wasn't skilled enough or experienced enough to survive, let alone prevail against such foes. What had Ty been thinking to send him on this quest? It was too much to place upon the shoulders of a youth his age. Either his father had thought too highly of him or else Ty thought so little of his only son that he'd been willing to sacrifice him to a mad dream. Will reflected bitterly that it was most likely the latter.

Snap.

Will jolted to full alert, watching intently in the direction the sound had come from. He commenced counting in his head. When he'd reached thirty, he heard a faint rustle of leaves. And another.

He eased backward, moving arhythmically. Step. Pause. Step-drag-step. Long pause. Gliding around the far side of the giant tree trunk at his back, he placed the hickory between himself and whoever was out there.

The irony of being alone in the woods at night in the lee of an ancient hickory while Boki roamed the forest was not lost on him. The more things changed, the more they stayed the same. He eased toward his companions, clicking and chirring under his breath to mimic the insects around him. *Odd.* He'd never learned how to do that. Maybe Bloodroot was still there after all, waiting and watching.

The others lay in a tight cluster under a spreading patch of broad-leafed muscat vines. Will tapped everyone's feet and they all roused quickly, alarmed.

"Anton's army comes," he breathed. How he knew it was Imperials and not Boki he had no idea, but didn't question it.

Sha'Li complained, "Why cannot we hide here, and for it to pass we wait? Then south we can head and far away from all this go?"

He echoed her sentiment entirely, but answered grimly, "If Anton catches us, he'll kill us all. Slowly and permanently."

The lizardman girl grumbled, "A better chance we'd stand by far of living if the Boki caught us. Into their camp we should walk and hand ourselves over. At least a decent night's sleep we'd get before into slavery they sell us."

Will stared hard at her. "Actually, that's just what I was considering doing."

"Are you insane?" Rosana cried under her breath.

Eben waved her to silence. "We have to move. Whoever's out there draws near."

The party eased into the night. They crept along for several minutes in silence, pausing every few minutes so Cicero could slip away behind them and check for pursuers.

Rosana picked up their previous conversation exactly where she'd left off, declaring in a whisper, "Are you mad to consider giving yourself to the Boki?"

"No. I think they'll recognize the spirit of Bloodroot and want to talk to us about where I got the disk."

Sha'Li hissed, "Tell them you must not!"

He snapped back, "I think we have no choice but to ask the Boki for help. And unless I tell them about Bloodroot, they will kill us all!"

"What help do you seek from the orcs? Help saving us from Anton?" Raina asked, "Or help with our quest?"

"Both," Will answered grimly.

She stared at him long and hard. "Sir Leland will help us. And there are others who would as well."

Will frowned. "But Hyland and the others do not know where to find the Sleeping King. I think the Boki do."

"Are you sure?" Raina asked doubtfully.

Will met her gaze solemnly. "Not at all. But I think going to the Boki is the only way for us to get out of this alive."

She took a deep breath and exhaled heavily. "I think you are right."

Rosana looked back and forth between the two of them desperately. "You can't be serious! We can't just march into a Boki camp. It is suicide!"

"No more suicidal than staying out here and waiting for Anton's men to find and slaughter us."

Rosana's hand slipped into Will's and grasped his fingers

painfully tight, making her opinion of the whole idea crystal clear.

Eben spoke up. "I hate to say it, but I have to agree with Will. Never thought I'd consider surrendering to the likes of orcs, but better that than Anton's assassins getting their blades on our throats."

Cicero shrugged. "I've escaped orcs before. I can do it again."

Sha'Li hissed, "For sheep is slavery. Not for my kind!"

Eben grunted, "Everybody knows your kind make terrible slaves. You're too surly and dense to train properly to any but the meanest task."

Sha'Li's scales lifted. "Stupid you call me?"

"No more arguments," Cicero whispered. "Boki are fanning out from the north to our east and west flanks, and Anton's men are matching the maneuver from the south. We're surrounded and trapped. We must choose an army to hand ourselves over to, and soon."

Will replied, "I believe we are agreed. The orcs it is."

Cicero stood. "All right then. To the Boki. Follow me."

Stealthily, they eased northward. Will was concerned about his inability to speak or understand the heavy accent of the orcs. He hoped one of the Boki would speak clearly enough for them to communicate.

Twice they heard the sounds of skirmishing and veered away from the shouts and clanging. Cicero started a quartering pattern, zigzagging left and right as they maintained their generally northerly course in an attempt to locate the Boki encampment. They could use a little dose of Bloodroot's familiarity with this place long about now, but the tree spirit remained frustratingly silent within Will.

After maybe an hour of fruitless searching, Cicero lifted

his head suddenly. Took a long sniff, turned, and headed un-erringly to the north and east. Will's pulse spiked. *Last chance to back out of this madness.*

A faint, familiar odor tickled his nostrils unpleasantly. His impulse was to duck and hide. To creep away. To save himself and the others. But he fought the impulse. Resolutely forced one foot in front of the other. Ever since that night so long ago in Hickory Hollow, his path had been leading him to this—a direct confrontation with the monsters who'd killed his parents and slaughtered everyone in his village. It was as it should be. A fitting end to his long journey.

But he was still scared stiff.

Please let them run not into a club-happy Boki perimeter guard who swung first and asked questions later. Please let this scheme not have been a colossal mistake.

Whether some greater being heard Will's plea or whether it was nothing more than dumb luck, they managed to reach the edge of a medium-sized clearing filled with crude Boki shelters with their heads still attached to their bodies.

Cicero glanced over at him questioningly and Will nodded back. He turned to face Rosana. He did not know what to say to her. So instead, he pulled her close and kissed her hard and quick, full on the mouth. And praise the stars, she kissed him back.

He let go of her and stepped out into the moonlight.

Great galloping stars in heaven. The encampment sprawl-ing before him must house hundreds of Boki warriors. An-ton thought to defeat this army? Will shuddered to picture the size of the force Anton must have brought with him.

Within seconds, a half-dozen orc guards had spotted Will. A shout went up, and within a few more seconds the entire camp was on full battle alert.

He murmured over his shoulder, "I think it is safe to say

we've got their attention." He felt the others move up behind him in a tight cluster. Will lifted his hands away from his sides, raising them slowly to clasp them behind his head lest the orcs think he might cast magic. He walked boldly toward the Boki. Might as well not earn the beasts' contempt before they killed him.

Shock poured through him as Raina moved up beside him, head held high. She strode beside him like she was the Emperor's daughter herself. *Brave girl. That, or incredibly foolish.*

"Let's end this," she muttered. "Let's find this king and wake him up. I've had enough of these games."

Will snorted. "Me, too."

She replied, "Head high, Will. You were chosen by a great tree lord for this quest."

He pictured his father that last night, a great warrior in command of the battle, and did his best to channel Ty. He squared his shoulders and walked boldly beside Raina toward he knew not what.

"Soo-ren-duhh, hoo-mans!"

He refrained from rolling his eyes. As if it weren't already obvious that surrendering was precisely what they were doing. He muttered down at his chest, "Okay, old man. Tell them who you are."

Nothing.

Two of the Boki charged, clubs drawn, and Will fought with every ounce of his being not to run screaming from them. Visions of that night in Hickory Hollow, his first sight of these monsters bursting out of the brush, washed over him. The horror of it was fresh again. The terror. The fear for his family. The blood—

"We're all going to die," Rosana wailed from behind them.

Leland tried twice to talk Anton out of taking the fight to the main Boki force, which had indeed been spotted to the north of their position. He failed, of course. A person would think Anton had learned from past mistakes. After all, no one had ever accused the man of being thick.

But Anton wanted no part of Leland's advice. Frustrated, he returned to the front lines—a thinly stretched formation that couldn't possibly withstand a direct assault by the Boki— and continued hunting the Boki rear guard.

Anton was being lured into a trap as surely as the sun would rise in the morn. And the governor seemed not to care one bit. Leland supposed it was possible this was an elaborate scheme to murder him, Aurelius, and Selea. They all held enough rank and titles that they would be very difficult to put to death openly. It was also entirely possible that Anton sought to start a war. For what purpose, though, Leland could not fathom. Either way, this madness would surely end in blood.

The pair of orcs were almost on Will, their weapons raised high over their heads, their eyes aglow with bloodlust. He feared Rosana was right. They were all going to die. *Blood-root! Talk to them!*

Still nothing.

Do I have to be at the point of dying before you bestir yourself to save us both?

"Dead meat we are," Sha'Li muttered.

To Raina's credit, she did not flinch even once as the orcs charged them.

At the last moment before the Boki warriors slammed into them Eben shouted, "We're here to see the Sleeping King!"

A huge greenish-brown orc pointed out Rosana's tabard and grunted something that sounded like, "Bal. Tha. Zar."

A disgusted groan went up among the other Boki. What was *that* all about?

They were hustled none too gently in a tight cluster, surrounded by a cadre of hostile guards to a fire burning in the center of the sprawling camp. It threw off a dancing, even cheerful light, in marked contrast to the grim visages of the Boki pouring into the space. The fire circle was crammed with Boki, male and female, all big, muscular, armed, and dangerous looking. Will felt puny among them. He might have attained most of his adult height already, but he had yet to fill out as a man and still retained the gangly cornstalk leanness of youth.

An aged Boki with dozens of bones twined into his matted hair stepped forward, and right behind him the last person Will would have expected to see in this place: a large, jovial-looking human wearing a soiled White Heart tabard.

"Who are you?" Will blurted. He was backhanded across the face for his troubles, a casual swipe that laid him out on the ground.

He picked himself up slowly and dusted himself off as one of the Boki guards pulled Rosana forward and grunted, "Balthazar."

The White Heart man exclaimed to Rosana, "Good heavens, child, what madness brings you here?"

"I would ask the same of you!" she retorted.

"I am Emissary Balthazar of the White Heart. I live among the Boki to teach them of the Heart. I know their ways and how they think. I can help you communicate with them."

Apparently, the fellow had done his job, for the sight of Rosana's tabard had stayed the orcs' clubs. One of the orc warriors, a big fellow with scars all over his arms, grunted something in not quite intelligible common.

"He wishes to know why are you here," Balthazar translated.

"We seek asylum from Anton Constantine," she replied to the White Heart brother.

A hiss went up at the governor's name that nearly drowned out Balthazar's groan.

Rosana glanced over her shoulder at Will and he nodded encouragingly to her. "And," she continued in a lower voice to Balthazar, "we seek the Sleeping King. He might also be called the Mythar. We want to wake him up. Perhaps the Boki can tell us where to find him?"

Balthazar frowned. "Are you sure this is what you wish to ask them? They will kill you for it."

"It is, in truth, why we are here," she replied. "Will, he can explain more."

Will stepped forward to do just that, but the Boki who'd slapped him shoved him back into line with the others.

Balthazar commenced speaking rapidly in syllables flavored heavily with a Boki accent. It seemed to be taking him entirely too long to repeat what Rosana had said, but eventually a roar of rage went up among the orcs and the nearest ones brandished clubs in the party's direction.

Balthazar leaped in front of their little cluster, his arms

spread wide. He shouted for their hosts to halt and the orcs paused in the act of surging forward. The White Heart man muttered over his shoulder without looking away from the furious mob, "If there is more to your story that might stop the Boki from killing you all, now is the time to tell it. And quickly."

Will stepped forward again, and again was shoved back.

Cicero tried next. Perhaps his kindari heritage and kinship with the forest would earn him a measure of respect among the orcs. "Surely, the Boki know of the threat to the land. Surely, they feel the attacks upon the forest, feel the damage. We wish to help stop all of that."

A few of the shamanically decorated Boki nodded as Balthazar translated. The murderous mood of the mob eased a fraction.

"And?" Balthazar prompted.

"And," Cicero added, "they need to hear what my human friend has to say."

All eyes turned to Will. *Any advice? Anything, Bloodroot?* The tree spirit within Will was stubbornly silent. He huffed. *Fine.* He would do this himself.

Will reached for his laces and opened his shirt wide.

A gasp went up.

Balthazar turned all the way around to stare at Will's chest. "What is that?"

Will lifted his chin at the Boki. "They know. Tell them it is not merely a piece of Bloodroot. It is heartwood. I hold his spirit within me."

Balthazar turned to an aged Boki whose dress was adorned liberally with teeth and bits of bone, as if he were a shamanic thorn. "Is this possible, Thar'Ok?"

The old Boki shuffled forward slowly and laid a huge, calloused hand over the disk. He stared into Will's eyes for long seconds. And then slowly, very slowly, nodded his head once. Twice. The thorn grunted a single syllable. "Troo."

The orcs went wild. Whether they shouted in joy or outrage or utter disbelief Will could not tell. His companions huddled closer to him as Balthazar shouted to be heard, "He said you speak truth!"

"They will help us then?" Will asked.

A long discussion followed among the Boki leaders, if size and number of scars indicated seniority among these creatures.

Balthazar stepped aside with Will and the others while the debate raged on. The White Heart member spoke in a low voice to them. "Since you are here, I have a message I need relayed to the Heart in Dupree. I do not know if any or all of you will leave this place alive, so I am going to break Heart protocol and tell you all in hopes of the message reaching its intended destination."

Will and the others nodded at Balthazar.

The White Heart man murmured low and fast, "I have good reason to believe that there is a traitor in the colony. Someone who double deals with the Boki and stirs them to violence."

Will started. "Are they not already plenty violent enough on their own?"

Balthazar shook his head. "That's the thing. The Boki warlord and other most senior leadership of the tribe have no interest in provoking Anton or in invading the colony. And yet, someone incites certain . . . more angry . . . factions within the Boki to do both. I believe payments are being made by the traitor to ensure that another insurrection happens."

"Who is the traitor?" Raina asked in a hush.

"It has to be someone at the highest level of colonial government, with enough resources to buy himself or herself a war, and with a vested interest in benefitting from another greenskin invasion."

Even Will could not miss the emissary's implication. Anton was behind paying off the Boki to invade Dupree.

"Are you sure of this?" Rosana asked.

Balthazar shrugged. "I do not have direct evidence. But I have lived with these people for fifteen years and more. I know them extremely well. And it is clear to me that I speak the truth. I have overheard arguments about it. I have seen fights among the Boki themselves over whether or not to proceed with another insurrection, and during those fights, accusations have been made by Boki with no reason to make such accusations were they not true."

Raina frowned. "The Heart cannot make a direct accusation against the governor without witnesses or tangible proof."

Balthazar threw them all a frustrated look. "It is why I have not spoken up before now. But I believe an invasion is imminent, and the colonists must prepare themselves lest there be another slaughter like before. I cannot in good conscience remain silent."

"You should come to Dupree. Make a report yourself," Raina urged him.

"The Boki will not let me leave. They know I have seen too much. Whoever is dealing with the traitor blocks my departure in the Boki council, and the others do not want their dirty laundry aired to the outside world."

Rosana nodded solemnly. "We shall see to it that your message is delivered as soon as we get back to Dupree."

Will winced. Just what they needed. To get embroiled in yet more political wrangling, particularly against the governor himself.

Someone yelled for Balthazar and the White Heart member left them to go speak to the Boki elders. Eben used his height to look over their captors and report on what he saw. "I think they want to kill Will and take the disk. Balthazar seems to be arguing that killing Will won't detach the spirit within him from the boy's spirit."

"Tell them Balthazar is right!" Rosana cried.

Raina added urgently, "Tell them I am a ritual caster and Balthazar speaks truth. Will's and Bloodroot's spirits are joined as one. Only a major ritual might separate them."

Might? Will stared at the arch-mage. *Might?* He could be stuck with this tree spirit forever? Although the way Will felt now, forever might not be more than a few days away. The crowd of orcs parted and several heavily scarred, older Boki approached the party, still arguing.

Thar'Ok threw up his hands in obvious disgust. He stomped over to Will and grunted, "Hoo-man. No wuh-thee. Give Bloodroot ovuh."

"Not worthy?" he repeated. Balthazar nodded behind Thar'Ok.

"I did not choose Bloodroot. He chose me," Will stated slowly and clearly.

"No wuh-thee. Know too much. Kill hoo-man."

Something broke within Will. A dam of rage he'd been holding back ever since that night in Hickory Hollow. Ever since Adrick collapsed, dead, with a Boki spear through his belly. Ever since he watched Lars gutted like a sheep. Ever since he realized his parents had sacrificed their lives for him. The rage surged up in him like a tidal wave, swelling until he could barely contain it.

The mob pressed in on them from all sides, brandishing mostly wicked-looking clubs, but a few axes and pikes glinted among them. Sha'Li hissed behind him, and a rock flew out of the crowd, striking the lizardman girl in the side of the head. She cried out in pain.

Will's rage spilled over. His entire being went white-hot with it and red rimmed the edges of his vision. He shoved forward between Eben and Cicero, batting them aside like flies. He raised his right hand high beside his ear and let go of his rage, hurling a massive ball of magic into the pile of logs burning at Scar Arm's feet.

The bonfire exploded. Literally. Blazing logs went flying every which way. Glowing embers made a stunning fireworks display overhead before they began raining down upon everyone around them. Hoarse screams erupted from the Boki as they scattered in all directions, dodging the burning missiles. Where there had been a bonfire moments before now there was only a shallow, ash-lined depression in the ground.

Darkness fell upon the clearing as the debris finished raining down. A few logs still burned here and there upon the ground, but no other light illuminated the shocked faces of the Boki. Still, it was enough to see them all staring at him, stunned.

"I'm the one who was chosen to wake the cursed king!" he snarled from between gritted teeth. "Chosen by my father, and chosen by Bloodroot himself."

The vignette was still for a moment more, and then Scar Arms called out several commands in orcish. The Boki leaped into action. Some went to fetch torches, others quickly laid a new bonfire and got to work lighting it, but the majority stamped out the small fires burning across the clearing and checked the roofs of the huts for smoldering embers.

Eventually, the bonfire was restored, the camp made safe, and the Boki reassembled around Will and the others. But this time the guard from before stood well back and showed no inclination to lay a hand on him. Will stood at the front of the group, and all eyes were upon him now.

Thar'Ok was the first to speak. "Who be thee, hoo-man?"

"I am Will Cobb. I hail from the Wylde Wood, and I have been brought here by my companions and by Lord Bloodroot to wake the Sleeping King."

His announcement was met with deep silence. It occurred to him that they had not laughed at his words. In fact, they seemed to take his announcement entirely seriously. Almost as if this sleeping-king legend was real, after all.

"Why Boki buh-leef thee?" Thar'Ok challenged.

Why indeed? Will didn't believe it himself. He was just a boy who'd had a crazy father and been in the wrong place at the wrong time. The whole string of events that had brought Will to this place at this moment could add up to either co-lossal bad luck or the hand of fate. The Boki could take their pick. He didn't much care which it was.

He shrugged. "I am here, am I not? Believe me, it was no easy feat to stay alive and get here. Were I not bound by my quest, I would never be mad enough to walk into your camp and hand myself over to you. "

"Hoo-man stoo-pid come hee-uhh."

He had to smile sardonically at that. "I agree."

"Where hoo-man get?" Scar Arms demanded, his club raised in one hand, his other stubby green finger pointing at Will's chest. Will registered vaguely that the dark red wood of the weapon was strikingly similar in color to the disk upon his chest.

"I fell on it, and it just . . . stuck to my chest."

"Why Bloodroot choo' thee?" Thar'Ok asked, incredulous.

Will shrugged. "I haven't the slightest idea."

He thought maybe Thar'Ok looked awed for a moment, but he wasn't sure, for the orc turned away quickly and began conversing in grunted undertones with Scar Arms. Before long, a number of other Boki had joined what turned into a pitched argument. The orcs with stuff in their hair seemed arrayed against a half-dozen big, scarred warriors made from the same mold as Scar Arms. More wood was brought for the fire and the discussion almost came to blows more than once before their dispute was finally resolved.

Balthazar reported, "The warriors disagree with shamans in this matter. The warriors think Will should die, but the shamans think he should be given a chance to complete his quest."

Raina, who had never once budged from his side, drew in a sharp breath. She murmured, "So. The Boki do know where the Sleeping King lies."

She spoke urgently to the White Heart man. "Ask them why Bloodroot would attach himself to my friend and lead his steps to this place if he did not wish for them to help us?"

Balthazar looked regretful as he relayed the response. "The warriors have decided. Will Cobb is not the One."

Desperation wrapped around Will's throat. He was so close. Somebody in this mob obviously knew something about the Sleeping King and was just being stubborn about telling him of it. If only he could prove he was who he said he was—

"Let me fight for it," he blurted. "Honor combat. Let me prove that I'm the One."

Balthazar's gaze lit with interest. "I do not condone combat, but they will kill you all, otherwise. Perhaps this way only you die, boy." Balthazar translated quickly, sounding as if he negotiated for the lives of the others. Another argument ensued, this one blessedly much shorter and less heated than the first.

"Are you sure, Will?" Raina asked doubtfully. "Everything is at stake, here. *Everything.*"

"Can you think of any better solution?" he retorted.

A sigh. "No."

"Then I fight. Maybe I die; maybe Bloodroot decides to get off his leafy arse and help me win."

Balthazar turned to Will triumphantly just then. "Done. The Boki accept your offer of honor combat. In return, your friends live."

A shout went up among the Boki. Three syllables, repeated over and over. For her part, Raina grabbed him fast and slammed a bolt of healing magic into him that hurt like fire for several seconds. He appreciated the sentiment, but he doubted anything would help him, now. At least her casting caused the Boki to stand a little farther back from her as well.

Eben murmured beneath the din, "I think they're saying something about 'to the pit.'"

"What's that?" Will asked back.

"I have no idea. But the title seems fairly self-explanatory, does it not?" the jann replied wryly.

Will had been afraid of that. Many hands reached out for him, dragging him forward roughly.

He barely had time to call back over his shoulder to Raina, "Don't let Rosana watch!" before he was hauled out of sight of his friends and swallowed in a seething mass of green-brown bodies. They led him to the edge of the village and a clearing that reached into the woods beyond the huts.

"Yon be pit, hoo-man!" Thar'Ok shouted in his ear on a fetid breath that all but knocked Will over.

He looked where the orc pointed and saw a giant hole in the ground. It was mayhap thirty feet across and ten feet or so deep. A single rough, wrist-thick rope hung down the side of the earthen pit.

"Choo' weapon, hoo-man!"

Will reached for the staff still shockingly slung across his back, and he drew it forth, brandishing it across his body. It might be primarily a defensive weapon, but it acted as a shield of sorts in a pinch. And it was the one weapon with which he was truly comfortable. He would need every bit of his skill to make a decent showing before he died in this fight. It was a foregone conclusion that he would lose, of course.

He swung the staff experimentally and remembered wryly his mother saying that he had all the tools to become as great a warrior as his father. Little had Will known then of what she spoke. Who would have guessed that threshing and sweeping and mowing could teach a boy the rudiments of combat? Too bad Ty had never deigned to finish his training.

"This staff will do. And I have a name, by the way. It is Will Cobb."

Balthazar stepped close to him. "The rules of the fight are that there are no rules. This is a fight to the death."

Will nodded his understanding. He'd expected no less. Still, it was intimidating to hear the words.

The healer added fervently, "And for stars' sake, make it good."

He could do this. He'd fought Boki before and won. Of course, he'd mostly relied on stealth, surprise, and a hefty dose of luck to beat them. It had been the swords of others who finished off his opponents, though. Did he have it in himself to kill if it came to it? To look another being in the eye and take his life in cold blood?

Too late to back out, now.

While a bevy of orcs planted dozens of torches around the top of the pit, Will stepped into the loop in the end of the rope. A single Boki casually lowered him as if he weighed no more than a babe. A ring of avid orcs leaned over the edge, jostling for position to see the fight. It was a miracle none of them fell into the pit with him.

He spotted Eben and Cicero in the crowd but saw no sign

of the girls. That was good. He stood an excellent chance of dying this night, and he did not want Rosana to carry that memory with her forever.

"Where do I go to resurrect, White Heart?" he asked.

"Go to the Light. Your spirit will know what to do."

He eyed the Boki warrior who'd been chosen to face him. He looked young—if a bumpy-faced, leather-skinned, undershot-jawed orc could look young. He had a collection of scars to be sure but nowhere near as many as the thanes who'd argued over him.

A young warrior, then. Proven probably, but not their best. Will supposed he should be grateful that they were trying to give him a fighting chance. Either that or this fight was so far beneath their honor that they'd passed the combat down to someone too junior to refuse the fight.

Will sighed. He could only do his best and hope it was enough. It wasn't like he could count on Bloodroot to help him, after all. It took him about two heartbeats to realize his best would be little more than a pitiful joke against this warrior. Across the packed-dirt circle, the Boki they'd sent down the rope to face him had pulled out a pair of axes and wielded one in each hand, swinging them as easily as if they were extensions of his arms. Will gulped.

"Arm self, hoo-man!" someone yelled down from overhead.

Will gave his staff a nervous swing. It banged clumsily against his boot. *A little help, Bloodroot? This is your quest, too.*

But only thunderous silence echoed inside Will's head.

I swear, if you abandon me now, I'll never help you again.

But as the young Boki stepped forward into the middle of the pit, it appeared that was exactly what Bloodroot intended. Will was on his own.

He glanced up at the circle of Boki overhead, a massive wall of leathery green writhing in the glare of the torches. Someone started a rhythmic grunting and the others quickly picked it up until the din was deafening.

Will's opponent touched his forehead with the crossed axe heads. "Ki'Rig Agar," the orc announced.

Will saluted back, touching his forehead briefly with the tip of his staff. "Will Cobb." He was tempted to give them his father's name, but he wished to get out of this thing alive and kept the identity of his sire to himself. Nonetheless, he silently dedicated this combat to the memory of his parents. He swept the staff across his body, gripping it in both fists, and assumed a ready position. The Boki did the same.

They commenced circling each other slowly. The grunting overhead rose to a howl so loud it hurt Will's ears. Cursing under his breath, he braced for the Boki's charge. At least he got that part right. The warrior roared and came running, his axes swinging like a windmill gone wild.

Will threw up his staff and caught a mighty blow on the shaft. He bent beneath the attack and slid to the side, deflecting the worst of the force, turning the parry into a riposte with the tip of the staff in a single movement his father had taught him a lifetime ago with a scythe. It wasn't as smooth as when Ty did it, but it served well enough. He jabbed the Boki in the ribs, and he fell back to regroup.

The Boki leaped in on the attack again and the tips of Will's staff flickered like candles in the wind, barely managing to counter the orc's rapid swings. His staff work was not fancy, but was sufficient to keep him alive for a few more breaths.

He jumped forward this time, but the orc was fast. And strong. The middle of Will's staff and the Boki's axe handle locked over their heads, and the orc easily pressed Will's back into an arch that forced him to retreat stumbling. The Boki pounced and Will barely got away, catching himself on the ground with his left hand to keep from falling outright.

He might be quicker than his opponent, but the orc was definitely stronger. And worse, the Boki seemed to know how to use it to his advantage. Ty would have told Will to look to his footwork and stay well clear of the larger, more powerful opponent. Thing was, in this tiny pit he had nowhere to go. Will dusted off his hand and settled into light balance once more. *Come on, Bloodroot. A little help here!*

The Boki gathered himself for a major attack, jaw thrust out, gaze determined. Despite his superior speed and agility, Will wasn't at all sure he could beat this focused Boki.

He tried to summon the fury he'd held close in his heart ever since that night in Hickory Hollow, but for some reason it was not coming to him. He leaped away from two more concerted attacks, and the Boki above began to jeer. *Whatever.* He was not here to put on a good show. He was here to survive. To prove his worthiness to finish his quest. His father's quest, that was.

Where was his righteous anger? His grief and fury at the loss of his parents? The burning need for revenge that had sustained him throughout the journey so far? Had even his rage failed him when he needed it most? What had the fates—and his father—been thinking when they chose him for this quest? He could not do it. He was not strong enough, or brave enough, or constant enough to see it through, apparently.

Frustrated, he fended off his opponent as best he could. But in the end, he didn't stand a chance. Gradually, his defenses buckled beneath the punishing force of the Boki's twin-bladed assault.

The Boki's axe heads continued to pick up in speed and come ever closer to slicing him in two. A terrible suspicion took root in Will's gut and gnawed at what little confidence he had that the orc was toying with him.

Fury rushed through him. Of a sudden he found another level of skill within him. One where he was faster, better balanced, more aware. His staff battered at the orc relentlessly, whacking the orc in a dozen places. Will knew from firsthand experience at his father's hand that no one blow would defeat the orc, but the sum of the bumps and bruises added up over time.

He did not mortally wound the Boki; but he did seem at last to give his opponent pause. The jeers from above faded gradually. After a nifty move where Will planted one end of the staff against the wall of the pit as the orc charged, letting his foe drive his own gut hard onto the opposite end of the staff, the jeers fell silent, altogether. Will's opponent staggered back, grunting in pain and gasping for air.

A new shout went up—distant, not from the ring of immediate onlookers. In that exact moment, he saw desperation enter the gaze of the orc across from him. Saw the moment of decision. Saw the feint that disguised the leap. Both axes chopped down at his neck, one from either side. Will dropped low, trying to catch both blades on his staff. At the last instant the Boki saw the ploy and reversed direction with his left hand, arcing around to swing low and up beneath Will's guard.

It was a suicidal move, for it gave Will the entire left side of the orc's chest, open and undefended. Lightning-fast, Will yanked his dagger free of his belt. He plunged the blade forward and down with as much strength as his tired arm could muster. Too late, he saw the other axe coming up under his elbow to gut him. He leaped back. But not soon enough.

He felt nothing. One second his knife was driving hungrily into tough Boki flesh, and the next everything went black.

Raina looked up sharply as a Boki thorn burst past the pair of guards watching them. It looked like the shamanic fellow who'd spoken with Will earlier, but she couldn't be sure. The orcs looked much the same to her.

Agitated, the thorn waved at them in what looked like a gesture to come with him. What on Urth was going on?

Rosana was the first to her feet. Raina was alarmed when the orc took off running, and with a glance of alarm at each other she and Sha'Li took off after the Boki and Rosana. Had Will been injured or killed? Was the thorn summoning the Heart healer to fix him? Guttural roars echoed through the night and her alarm grew. What had the Boki so riled up?

As they ran toward a circle of torches and a seething mass of bodies ahead the shouting grew louder and she fancied she heard the clanging of weapon blows. Was the duel still going, then? Confused, she hurried onward.

"What's happened?" Rosana panted desperately at Raina as she drew even with the gypsy.

Raina shrugged sympathetically. If it had been Justin who might be wounded or dead right now she'd be out of her mind.

That was definitely the sound of swords screeching on

metal among the orcish screaming. Had some sort of brawl erupted? Was Will all right? What of Cicero and Eben?

Their orc guide stopped abruptly. Raina craned to see around his bulk. They were at the edge of the encampment and black night yawned away from them into the forest. As her eyes adjusted to the deeper dark of the woods she saw, with shock, that Boki were running every which way. It appeared for all the world like the camp was under attack.

She spotted a cluster of orcs hoisting a pair of bodies out of some sort of hole in the ground. Both bodies flopped bloody and motionless onto the dirt in unnatural poses that did not belong to the living. Horrible certainty erupted in her gut that Will and his opponent were both dead.

Screams and groans and clanging metal registered vaguely, but Raina had no attention to spare for those as she raced across the clearing toward Will. Rosana's hands began to glow. Raina followed suit, summoning her white-hued healing magics as she ran.

A Boki warrior who looked like some sort of sub-thane grunted a series of what sounded like commands to the cluster of orcs around the two bodies. Most of the Boki followed him away into the woods. One of the remaining Boki, a thorn, leaned down and planted a hand on the dead Boki warrior's chest, muttering something in orcish as his hand glowed bright white.

The dead orc lurched, took a great, heaving gasp, and sat up, looking around wildly as Raina, Rosana, and Sha'Li skidded to a stop. The other body was indeed Will, and he did indeed look quite dead.

Rosana dropped to her knees beside him with a wail of distress. She reached out to heal him, but the thorn grabbed her wrist and shook his head threateningly.

Balthazar trotted up just then and took in Rosana and the shaman glaring daggers at each other. He spoke quickly. "It is the custom not to heal the dead after honor combat. The fight is to the resurrection."

"Then why did they life Will's opponent?" Rosana snapped, her voice vibrating with fury.

Balthazar asked something in unintelligible grunts and listened to the grunted reply. "Anton's forces attack, and they need every able-bodied warrior on the lines. They had no time to wait for Ki'Rig Agar to resurrect."

The young Boki, apparently Will's opponent, interrupted with an angry outburst.

Balthazar murmured, "Yon warrior is asking much the same. If he lives, his opponent should also live. He's threatening to kill himself if they don't let you heal Will."

Raina stared at the young Boki in shock. Yet again she was stunned by the depth of the honor in these creatures.

Balthazar translated the warrior's angry tirade, " 'Where is the honor in living when this human dies? If I live, so shall he! We fought to a draw. Both live or both die.' "

The orc raised his axe and held it away from his neck, the blade pointing ominously at his own flesh. He glared around at the orcs still crowding near.

Raina looked back and forth between the gathered Boki as a short, terse argument ensued. Finally, the orc holding Rosana's wrist loosed it with a gesture to Will's corpse.

Raina laid her hand over Rosana's. "I know you care for him. But let me do this. In case it takes . . . extra."

The gypsy hesitated for an instant, then nodded reluctantly.

Raina laid her hand on Will's chest, called power to her, and murmured the incant to shape life magic. A single thought formed in her head as she released the blast of magic.

Please let this work.

Will jerked upright, swearing, before he realized he was conscious and before it dawned on him he must have been unconscious. He registered Rosana sitting on her heels nearby as Raina lifted her hands away from him. But then the gypsy flung herself upon him, sobbing, and nearly knocked him over again.

He hugged her tightly and rasped, "What happened?" A flash of memory came back to him as the words left her mouth. A deadly axe blade coming up under his guard . . . he looked down at his left side. His shirt was torn and blood and gore adorned its ragged edges. But his flesh was whole.

"Ki'Rig Agar—" he started. He glanced up in alarm and spotted the young Boki standing not five feet away from him with an axe blade next to his neck. "Are you all right?" he blurted to his foe.

Balthazar translated his question and the young Boki warrior's response. " 'Aye. Fine now. Thee?' "

Will nodded. "Alive. Well fought."

As the Boki said something Balthazar rolled his eyes. The White Heart healer translated in disgust, " 'It was a good fight. But not finished. It was a draw. Honor was neither won nor lost. Your spirit is strong and will feed Bloodroot well.' "

Will blinked. He'd salvaged a draw out of that mess? Not bad for a kid from Hickory Hollow with no real dueling experience. "I will remember your name, Boki."

"I know yoo' name, Willcobb."

"Two names. Will. Cobb." He climbed painfully to his feet. He hated this wobbly, weak feeling. Perhaps Raina could give him a little more magical healing. Okay, a lot more magical healing.

The Boki warrior yanked at his jerkin and a ripping sound ensued. He held his palm out to Will, and a carved wood emblem lay there.

"My warr-iuh mark. If no good enuf' beat choo, me no wea-uhh. You keep fo' now. One day, I take back."

Will snorted. "You can try."

The two warriors traded broad grins.

The young Boki thane warrior thumped Will on the shoulder with a meaty fist, as Balthazar translated, "'Another day, Will Cobb. We will finish our fight, yes? See who's the better warrior?'"

Will grinned and gripped the orc's forearm while the Boki crushed his in return. "As long as it's not to the death next time."

"Oh, for the love of the Lady," Balthazar muttered under his breath before translating the orc's grunted reply. "He says it's not a fight if it's not to death."

Will should've expected no less of a Boki. "Another day, then."

To his surprise, the Boki only took time to nod once and then turned and sprinted away from them. "Where's he going?" Will asked Rosana.

She turned her tear-streaked face to him and threw herself against his chest again. Startled and pleased, he wrapped his arms around her.

"Are you really all right?" she murmured.

"I am now. Right as rain. Perhaps one of you could spare me a little more of your healing energy, though?"

Rosana reached out for him, but Eben came charging up just then, shouting fit to raise the dead, and she jerked her hands away.

"We've got to go! Run! Hide!"

Cicero whipped around to face the jann, sword materializing in his hand in an instant. "What's going on?"

"Anton. He and his men are attacking in force. They've got the camp nearly surrounded."

"I must go," Balthazar announced. "Duty calls." He took off running toward the loudest fighting.

Cicero swore under his breath and Will heartily echoed the sentiment. "Which way, Eben?" the kindari asked quickly.

"It's chaos out there, and none of the Boki will stop to give me directions."

Will was dizzy and weak, yet he must do something. But what? He steadied himself against the nearest tree trunk while he tried desperately to get his bearings. He didn't even bother asking Bloodroot for help. The whoreson had completely abandoned him.

He noticed the tree trunk beneath his hand was warm to the touch and vibrating slightly. *What the—* He lifted his palm away just before a green female creature stepped out of the tree directly in front of him. He jumped about a foot straight up in the air.

"This way," she ordered in a low, worried tone. She moved off quickly toward the blackest part of the forest. Will and the others looked at one another. Eben and Cicero shrugged while the girls scowled. What better option did they have? At least the dryads seemed to have a vested interest in protecting Will as long as he held Bloodroot's spirit.

The party took off running to keep up with the swift-moving dryad. She led them through a hideous thicket and waited impatiently for them while they crashed clumsily through the brambles and tangled vines. Finally, the party disentangled itself and could proceed onward.

The sounds of battle were distant here. Muted. As Will's

recent bout of death caught up with him and he paused, exhausted, to catch his breath the dryad drew close to speak to him.

"Listen, Will Cobb, to what I say. Normally, I would be more . . . circumspect . . . about this, but time is short and this is important."

Since when was any dryad direct about anything? Startled, he straightened from his bent-over, panting posture. "I'm listening."

The other members of the party drew near as well, and as a testament to just how urgent the dryad's message was, she spared not even a glance for Cicero or Eben. "Your quest is urgent, Will Cobb. The Green Court needs you to succeed, but we are bound by the Accord not to interfere in the affairs of humans nor to restrict your freedom of choice. Thus, I cannot offer you direct help. Even my speaking to you may be a violation . . ."—distress entered her voice—". . . but so be it. If I am destroyed, it will be for a worthy cause."

Will stared. *Destroyed?* "What is the Green Court?"

"It is a fae gathering of nature-aligned beings."

"Fae!" Sha'Li squawked. "Listen not to her, Will. A trick this is!"

The dryad threw a glare at the black lizardman girl but, interestingly, did not attack her as Will would have expected. Instead, the tree faerie said urgently, "He whom you seek must be awakened, and soon. You must convince the guardians of these lands to lead you to the Laird of Dalmigan. He can take you to the one you seek."

"Who is the Laird of Dalmigan?" Will asked.

"You shall know him by his black lion. He helped the Elder protect the Sleeping King. Beware the image of Unkareg which would keep you from him."

"What is Dalmigan?" Raina asked.

"And Unkareg?" Will added.

The dryad pointed at the ground at her feet. "This place is Dalmigan, now called Talyn, now home to the Forest of the Thorns."

Will thought he followed that. Dalmigan was an ancient name for where they now stood. "So, we are close to where we can find the Sleeping King?"

"Aye."

"Where is it? Show us!" Will demanded.

She shook her head in the negative. "My kind are bound by the Accord. Were I to do what you ask of me, the Accord might be violated. Not only would I be destroyed by the keepers of the Accord, but so would you."

"Then what use are you to us?" Will exclaimed in frustration.

The dryad lowered her voice to a conspiratorial whisper. "The Thorns are not bound by the Accord. They have seen the same portents we have. They, too, seek the one who can complete the quest."

She reached out with a finger to touch the wooden disk through Will's tattered shirt. "By this sign shall they know you." She laid her hand more fully on the disk, frowning. "The power of Lord Bloodroot is killing you. He expends nearly all of his remaining power to bolster your weak human spirit. Do not waste his sacrifice by failing, boy."

Bloodroot was keeping him alive? The whoreson was doing a cursed poor job of it as far as Will could tell.

"Hurry, human. The Kothites' lackey draws near. He must not find the king first or all will be lost."

"What do you mean by 'all'?" Will asked suspiciously.

"Everything. Everyone. This continent, and mayhap all of Urth, will perish."

His jaw dropped. All of that rested upon his shoulders? "I cannot do it—" he started.

The dryad cut him off with an angry slash of her hand. She looked around the party fiercely. "All of you were brought here for a reason. All of you have lost your homes, your names, your families. I know not why or how, but you have been chosen. It all comes down to you."

Will gulped. What on Urth had they stumbled into the middle of? How much bigger was this thing than even he had any idea of? "We cannot do it. We're not experienced or powerful enough," he protested.

The dryad shrugged. "Nonetheless, you must find a way. It is what heroes do."

He snorted. "I am no hero. I am more dead than alive and can barely keep my feet."

"Mayhap I can help with that." She laid her hand on his chest, and a brief compulsion to lean in to her touch, to lose himself in the emerald depths of her intent gaze, washed over him. Was this what the others felt when they were around dryads? No wonder they sweated so badly.

The dryad frowned, breaking the momentary spell. "Your sickness is beyond me, human."

"How's that?" Rosana asked quickly.

The dryad scowled at her and answered shortly, "Lord Bloodroot poisons the boy."

"He *what*?" Rosana squawked. "That's it. That disk is coming off your chest now—"

The dryad literally stepped in front of Will and seemed to grow in size. "You will not touch him nor Lord Bloodroot. My lord does not mean to kill the boy. It is just that the human is not of sufficient constitution to bear the power of a treant. I assure you, Lord Bloodroot does everything in his power *not* to kill his host. But their union is . . . difficult."

As Rosana's hand moved away from her dagger the dryad turned back to Will. "I will do what I can to strengthen you. It will not be much, though." She laid her hands on him and a green glow emanated from her. It tingled, but not unpleasantly, and he did feel a tiny bit less horrible.

"Thank you," Will murmured.

The dryad threw Rosana a sidelong glare, then leaned forward quickly and shocked Will by kissing him on the cheek.

As she did so another strange tingling passed across his entire body for an instant, different from her healing. It was as if a wave of something like magic, but not magic, clung to him. Rosana jumped forward, practically snarling, and the dryad thrust out a hand. A burst of green nature magic exploded from her fingers like a miniature bolt of lightning, striking the gypsy squarely in the middle of the chest.

"No!" he cried, lurching toward Rosana. But the magic merely absorbed into her body and seemed to have no effect on her.

The dryad stared at the gypsy, a stunned look on her face, and then back at Will. "Passing strange company you keep, human. Chosen, indeed . . . ," she muttered under her breath.

And then the dryad leaned forward once more and whispered into his ear, "If you would wake a king, give his crown to him—"

She popped out of existence on the beginnings of a wail and disappeared before their eyes.

Eben commented dryly, "I guess she said too much."

Who or what had the power to snatch away a magical creature like a dryad in an instant? Was that same power watching him?

Into the ensuing silence Cicero said, "So, I gather we have

to go find a Boki thorn and ask him to take us to wherever we can find this Dalmigan guy?"

A general groan went up. Eben groused, "We just got away from the battle. Are you suggesting we wade back into it?"

Rosana spoke up reluctantly. "I can go back and find someone."

Cicero snapped, "You assume that Anton's mercenaries will honor your Heart colors. That may be an extremely optimistic assumption!"

She stared at the kindari in dismay as Will piped up, "I think we should go together. The dryad seemed to think we were all critical to the success of whatever she wants us to do."

The group reluctantly turned to retrace its path toward the battle behind them. They'd barely taken a dozen steps, though, when completely without warning a big Boki stepped out of the shadows directly in front of them. Will about leaped out of his skin. For big, clumsy-looking creatures those orcs could sure move quietly.

"Come," the orc grunted.

The creature said the single syllable like he knew exactly where Will and the others needed to go and like it was his job to get them there. Had the dryads said something to this guy, too? At least the orc was edging impatiently away from the sounds of battle.

"Do we follow him?" Rosana muttered.

"In for a copper, in for a gold," Will replied. By silent consensus the party turned and followed the orc deeper into the forest. As soon as the orc saw them following he broke into a ground-eating run.

Will groaned. If he ever got out of these woods he was never running another step as long as he lived. He grew light-headed in a few strides and faint within a few more. Were it not for the healing the dryad had given him, he would have keeled over. He blinked hard, focused on Rosana's white tabard, and ran with every ounce of strength left in his body. It did not amount to much.

"Fast-uhh," the orc urged.

But Will was done. Even the girls passed him by and had to slow down to wait for him to catch up. As he staggered the last steps in him the orc suddenly dived off the rough path they'd been following. Literally dived. Headfirst.

Too exhausted to question it, Will followed suit. He landed on a leaf-covered slope, which broke his fall but also sent him tumbling head over heels down a short incline, probably no more than a few feet high but too much for him to navigate in his weakened state. He fetched up hard against something tough and smelly—the orc. Will grunted as Eben slammed into him on the left. The orc sat up, grabbing at handfuls of mud and smearing them on his face.

Cicero bit out, "He's camouflaging himself. Quick, everyone smear mud and crushed leaves on any exposed flesh. Rosana, ditch the white tabard."

Rosana shot Will a stubborn glance and he muttered, "Just cover up the white with leaves for now." He helped her partially bury herself.

From beside him Eben murmured, "Here they come."

Leland ran through the woods as ordered, disbelief uppermost in his mind. This frontal attack upon a major Boki settlement was beyond folly. He could not fault Anton's argument that it was time to bring this thing to a close. But this was not the way to finish it.

Anton bellowed at the leaders of his ragtag crew, offering a gold each for Boki hides and refusing flatly to allow a retreat from this battle. It was a fight to the death. The various slavers, bandits, and barbarians arrayed around the clearing flinched. Even Leland felt the mental power Anton was unwittingly—or maybe intentionally, knowing him—blasting them with. Stars, Leland hated dealing with Imperials.

Anton shouted derisively from somewhere behind them for the contingent of rakasha slavers to move farther forward and quit lagging like cowardly women.

Leland swore he heard a faint, ominous growl issue from the back of the tiger changeling's throats. *So.* Dissension in the ranks was setting in. Perhaps, if there were enough defections from the battle, Anton would be forced to withdraw.

A scout burst out of the trees before him and Leland pulled up short.

The fellow panted, "Boki camp. Just over the next ridge. Three hundred or more greenskins. They were holding some sort of council when I left. Lots of shouting and axe waving."

Anton's black eyes glittered with greed and Leland looked away in disgust as the governor announced, "They rally their forces to attack us. But we shall attack them first. Sound the charge in two minutes."

Leland blurted, "Three hundred Boki? And us with less than five hundred half-trained irregulars and mercenaries? We'll be slaughtered."

Anton wheeled on him in fury. "You would gainsay me? You, old man? I suppose you know better than I what to do? If you're so smart, then you shall lead the charge, Leland. Out front. Like a proper battle commander."

Leland stared, stunned. It was pure suicide. And it was also an order from his liege lord. Very slowly, Leland straightened to his full height. His spine went ramrod stiff. He clicked his heels together and gave a short military bow to Anton. "As you command." He could not bring himself to call the whoreson *my lord*. But Anton did not seem to notice.

Leland pivoted and headed for the tiny clearing where his men were currently catching their breath. *Stars, my men.* He was responsible for them. And by opening his big mouth he'd just cost them their lives. They were all going to die, and there was no healing to be had out here. None. He'd doomed them all.

His men sat up, alarmed when he joined them. He said heavily, "I have been ordered to lead an assault on the Boki encampment just over yon hill. Three hundred or more Boki have been sighted."

"That is madness—" one of his sergeants started.

Leland looked over at him grimly and the man broke off. Leland said quietly, "Aye. Madness it is. But Anton has ordered it. I want all of you to stay behind with the main body of troops. Follow the sergeant when I have gone down. He will see you safely through the battle. Stick together and you may live to see your families again."

"We follow you through fire and forest, Landsgrave!"

"Hyland boughs do not break!"

"Hyland hearts together!"

The men pulled out their blazon sashes and slung them over their shoulders, proudly displaying the badges and marks of their service to Hyland.

He smiled in genuine gratitude at his men's loyalty. "I thank you for the sentiment, gentlemen. But this day, I die. I refuse to take your lives as well. You have my orders." Resolutely, he reached into his belt pouch and pulled out his tabard, unfurling the white stag of Hyland upon a field of green. If he died this day, he would do it in his colors, by the Lady.

He turned and strode away before they could argue further. Before they could spy the tears burning in his eyes. He did not shed a tear for himself. He'd awaited this day almost eagerly for twenty years and more. Nay, he wept for the better life he had failed to bring them, the freedom he'd promised himself he would give to his people before he died. But it was not to be. If he could buy Kendrick and Raina and the others even a few minutes more to escape the carnage and complete their quest, then he was glad to die.

Raina smelled an unholy stench to her right. Cicero, beside her, cursed on a breath of exhaled dismay.

Her eyes well adjusted to the dark, she made out a mass of green, muscular, gnarled flesh lurking in the forest. Had she not spent the past few hours staring at more just like them, she likely would not have picked them out, so well did they blend into the shadows and underbrush. She grimaced at the foul smell of them. The nearest ones looked to be liberally smeared with grease of some kind, maybe bear fat from the rancid odor.

And then Anton's forces burst out of the forest on their left and stopped at the top of the rise, waiting.

Horror exploded in her breast. She and the rest of the party were about to have front-row seats for the main battle.

Leland studied the battleground Anton had chosen, a clearing covered by a dense canopy of green far overhead, but relatively open below. It was on the small side. Leland estimated only about a hundred combatants from each side would fit into this space. Not that it mattered how many of Anton's men were brought to bear upon this fight. Against a hundred Boki, Anton would have need of a thousand Imperial soldiers to stand a chance. Surely the whoreson knew that. The governor was scared half to death of Boki. Why this fight? And why here? Why now?

Perhaps Anton planned to send his men against the Boki

in waves. Except, of course, Boki had the stamina to fight all day and half the night without flagging. Leland frowned. Unless Anton planned to flank the Boki and send in forces from the sides . . . although the east flank was bordered by what looked like an impassable hedge of brambles running down a small incline. Leland checked the west margin of the clearing. It was no better for passability.

He scowled as understanding broke over him. This was a diversion. Anton planned to occupy the Boki force here with slaughtering Leland and his hired army while Anton and a few of his personal guard circled wide of the fight and went after the Boki treasure. Leland smiled bitterly. He would not be alive to see it, but at least he had the satisfaction of knowing Anton was doomed to disappointment.

A scout came sprinting out of the north and Leland winced at how young the lad was. Barely more than a boy.

"Boki coming. A lot of them."

"How long?" Leland asked tersely.

"One, maybe two minutes behind me."

That was not long. But perhaps for the best. It was not a good thing to dwell too long upon one's imminent death. Leland turned and strode down the line of worried soldiers behind him, standing along the south edge of the clearing. He paused before his contingent of Hyland men, who looked strange to him swathed in nondescript cloaks instead of the green and gold Hyland colors. They had flatly refused to leave his side.

"Remember," he murmured to his sergeant, "stay well back. You are *not* to follow me to the front of the line. That's an order. This battle is but a diversion for Anton's real objective. It is not worth dying for. Understood?"

The soldier nodded, a surly look on his face.

Leland moved on. The man would get over it in a few years

when he was alive to see his children grown and grandchildren frolicking at his feet.

Leland did not have much time to find what he sought, and he passed quickly down the line. *There*. A squad of barbarian warriors arrayed in full battle paint and the leather loinskins they preferred to fight in. This group was thirty strong, with a half-dozen archers more behind the main force.

This crew had been bickering and scrapping among themselves the entire march out here, but when a common enemy presented himself before them they would band together and fight as fiercely for one another as brothers.

"Sons of Rage, hear me!" he shouted. "Your blood calls out for battle. You were born to it like wolves to the wood. A mighty pack you are, and even the mighty bear falls to the power of your pack!"

With each shouted word, the barbarians yelled louder, brandishing their weapons and stamping their feet until they'd whipped themselves up into a fine frenzy. *Perfect*. These barbarians were possessed of their kind's ability to battle rage. He would need their rages today.

"We battle the bringers of the Green Fire this day! Snuff their lives like so many torches and *our* fires will burn this night, not theirs!"

Another hoarse shout.

"These monsters seek our doom, that they may feed their trees with our blood! If blood must flow like water, then make it Boki blood!"

Another enthusiastic roar.

He glanced across the clearing and thought he spotted the gleam of sharpened metal through the trees. It was time.

"Then to blood and chaos and glory we go! Charge!" Leland shouted with all his might. Raising his sword, he turned and ran pell-mell toward the Boki army before him.

The Boki met his charge, roaring out of the trees in force. Gads, there were so many of them. But his stride never faltered; his pace never slowed. Thankfully, the barbarians behind him were so bent on blood that they never hesitated. Which was exactly why he'd chosen them to lead the charge.

He drew close enough to see the open maws, the yellow tusks, of his foes, to smell the meat the Boki had eaten for breakfast. He grasped his sword in both hands.

"Freedom!" he bellowed.

He engaged the enemy. And counted the blows until Death found him.

He'd been plowing into Boki flesh for about a minute when he caught a glimpse of green out of the corner of his eye. And gold. He almost didn't catch a wild axe swing on his sword in time as he half-turned to stare in shock. As it was, a shallow slice appeared high on his left arm. He felt no pain from it, though, and classified it as not serious enough to impair his fighting.

In the next momentary pause in the Boki's attack he took another look. A wedge of Hyland colors was making its way to him. His men. They'd ignored his order and were coming to join him in full Hyland regalia.

"Noooo!" he shouted. He waved them back violently with his free arm, but they kept on coming. A giant Boki leaped into his path and he was forced to bend all of his attention to the warrior before him. No untrained youth was this orc. The Boki's eyes were ferocious, rimmed in red fury. Leland was forced to give ground under the enormous power of the orc's blows. His wrists ached and his fingers were fast going numb under the punishing flurry.

He felt the surge of support at his back more than saw it. And then Hyland swords joined the fray, flicking in and out beside him, picking off the orcs pushing his flanks.

"Go back!" he screamed at his men.

"We stand with you!" the sergeant shouted back.

"You die with me!" he retorted to no avail.

Dismay lodged in the pit of his stomach, but there was no time to do more than register it vaguely, for the Boki he fought was slowly but surely breaking down Leland's defenses. A nick opened up on his lower calf and he vaguely felt blood running into his boot, making stepping on that foot a squishy affair. His mind shifted into an oddly detached state, observing the proceedings from afar.

So. This was the face of his death. He'd always assumed it would be an Imperial soldier who killed him in the end, although maybe he wasn't so far wrong. His duel with the Boki had turned enough for Leland to glance off to his left to where Anton hid in the trees, far enough back from the fighting to be safe himself, watching. Grinning with glee to see his old enemy dying like this, no doubt.

Two of his men pressed close and teamed up with him to drive the Boki warrior back. For the moment. The orc would collect two more Boki to even the fight and would return soon.

"Get back!" Leland bellowed. "They will match as many warriors as we present to them with the same number of theirs! Let me do this alone!"

But his men either did not hear or chose not to. More of his men swarmed around him until a total of ten joined him. He tried to spot which two had already fallen or been beaten back, but the fighting was too chaotic for him to tell.

The Boki had correctly identified him and his men as the tip of the spear of this attack and were concentrating all their forces upon the knot of soldiers in green and gold. Leland couldn't believe his men had dared to defy Anton and donned their colors for the fight. But it was comforting to be surrounded by his own colors in this, his final battle.

It was too late now to send his men back to safety. Their fate was sealed. They would meet at the Heart, then.

Raina shoved her fist into her mouth to keep from screaming in horror as she spied the leader of the charge onto the battlefield. *No. No, no, no! Not Leland.* He'd been kind to her. Helped her when he did not have to. Had looked out for her best interests. He was decent and honorable and noble!

What was he doing out there, charging into the face of a huge Boki army? He would *die*.

Eben groaned on her left, "Oh no. Not my lord. What is he thinking?"

The Boki kept pouring out of the trees and the two forces clashed in a tremendous crash of noise and shouting and clanging metal. In a few seconds the groans and screams of the injured and dying joined the din.

The battle was gruesome. Raina saw men gutted and beheaded, saw limbs flying up into the air spraying perfect arcs of scarlet blood. She saw dying men trampled into the mud. And in the midst of it all she could not take her eyes off Sir Leland, fighting like a man possessed in front of the entire Imperial force.

Eben was muttering and groaning continuously, literally quivering in need to join his liege lord and defend Sir Leland. Cicero shifted place to lie beside Eben, placing a firm hand upon the jann's shoulder.

"Steady, man. You could not help him anyway."

"But he's like a father to me. I already lost Marikeen and Kendrick. I cannot lose him, too. He is all the family I have left."

Eben's grief washed over Raina like ice water.

Cicero murmured sorrowfully, "Hyland's already dead. The Boki have brought at least a hundred warriors to this grove, and Anton's engaging about the same number of his own men. You know as well as I do that they'll be cut down to the last man out there by the Boki."

Raina did moan aloud then. She could not sit here and watch Sir Leland and his men slaughtered like sheep. A strong arm came around her shoulders and she leaned into Cicero, burying her face against his chest.

Sha'Li hissed angrily from her right, "What is Anton about? Why doesn't he send all his men? He lets these ones die like fish in a barrel!"

Eben snarled, "He's a coward. And a whoreson. He has always hated my lord. He sent Sir Leland out there alone and undermanned intentionally! I'll kill him—"

"Easy, Eben," Cicero murmured, getting a firmer grip on Eben's upper arm. "We have our own quest to think of. None of us can afford to throw ourselves upon our swords. We must stay together and, regretfully, stay out of this battle."

Eben swore violently. Raina echoed the sentiment in her head. It was not fair. It was cruel and unjust and vicious of Anton to take his revenge upon Leland in this manner.

"Ahh, stars!" Eben cried under his breath in agony. "The Boki elite take the field!"

Raina looked up from Cicero's shoulder.

Leland and his men squared off against a force of nearly a dozen Boki warriors, all of whom looked nearly twice the size of the humans arrayed before them. Unquestionably, that was at least a sub-thane leading the force of elite Boki warriors. The two forces charged each other.

The fight was violent and bloody. And fast. The Boki warriors sliced through Leland's men as if they were babes, cutting them down with brutal efficiency. Leland was the last left standing, and the largest Boki of them all charged him with a roar.

The fight slowed to a near stop in time as Raina took in the unfolding nightmare. The Boki feinted high with his right-hand axe. Leland raised his sword, bracing the blade with his free hand to take the blow. The axe slammed into the blade and sparks flew. But as the weapons connected, the Boki swung his left-hand axe. It started low, nearly at the ground, and swung up in a slow-motion arc. It bit into Leland's groin and traveled up the length of his entire body, eviscerating him from stem to stern in a single horrendous blow.

"*Nooooo!*" Raina screamed.

Leland froze. The Boki's axes fell to his sides. Leland staggered back a step. Looked down at his own dismembered body. Looked up at his foe. Nodded once. Smiled. And collapsed. Dead.

"Nonononononononono . . ."

Raina wasn't sure if she moaned the syllable over and over or if it was Eben. Or maybe both of them.

"A healer. Where is a healer?" Cicero bit out frantically. "Why doesn't one come to him?"

Sha'Li answered bitterly, "We've been scouting the Imperials for three days. Have any of you spotted a single Heart tabard among them?"

The others' only answers were grim, damning silence.

The lizardman girl snarled, "Anton brought no healers on this expedition! What better way to ensure that his mercenaries fight for their lives?"

Raina stiffened in fury. Sha'Li spoke the truth. And it was outrageous. Irresponsible. Criminally negligent. Make that plain criminal.

Then Raina cried out, "Rosana! You wear Heart colors. You can go out there onto the field of battle and heal him! Hurry! His spirit only has a few minutes!"

The gypsy shook her head, the look in her eyes agonized. "I cannot. The Boki do not let anyone heal their kills. Not even the Heart. They would cut me down the moment I set foot upon the field. Even if I took a spirit form to get to Leland, the Boki surround his body. As soon as I took solid form to heal him, they would cut me down."

Raina's flash of hope dissipated in her mental wail of despair. He was lost then. Leland was well and truly gone. Grief ripped into her until she felt as eviscerated as his mangled corpse.

She looked on in dismay as the Boki thane commenced chanting something. He pulled something long and thin out of somewhere on his person. It looked like a small stake carved of the same red wood as his club. The thane finished his chant and slammed the stake down into Leland's body, through his heart, and into the ground below. Raina turned her head away in horror as the thane lifted his head and roared in exultation.

"What about you?" Eben asked suddenly from beside her.

Raina lifted her gaze to him. His face was a multihued blur behind her unshed tears. "I wear no colors. I would stand even less chance than Rosana of making it to his body alive, let alone being allowed to heal him."

"But what of the White Heart tabard in your pouch?"

Raina stared. Hope and dismay erupted in her gut in nearly equal parts. *No. Not that.*

Eben continued urgently, "The Boki know Balthazar and let him live among them. They will honor those colors. You could get to Hyland. You could save him."

Stars, but at what cost? The rest of her life? Except it was

Leland. Mentor. Friend. Father-protector to them all. Guardian of their quest. The quest—Hyland had sacrificed himself out there to buy them time to complete the quest. As soon as the thought struck her she knew it to be so. She *owed* Hyland. They all did.

She closed her eyes. Reached deep within herself for the strength to do this thing. It was the right thing to do. The only thing to do. She looked up at the battlefield and could not see Leland's body through the mud and blood and clashing warriors. But she felt his spirit slipping away even as she hesitated.

"Hurry," Eben urged.

She looked up at Cicero. For just an instant she let all the despair in her spirit show in her eyes. A flash of sorrow reflected in his. Then he nodded his encouragement.

And she opened her pouch.

The pristine white fabric spilled out into her hands and she fumbled with the cloth, trying to unfold it and find the front. In her haste to get the thing on before she could chicken out she could not get it over her head. Many hands helped her, and in a moment the four-pointed blue star with its white heart and sun rays was centered boldly upon her chest. She smoothed her hand down the unfamiliar insignia. Her mind refused to accept what her eyes saw.

"What do I do?" she asked Rosana blankly.

Rosana cried, "Just run out in the middle of the fight and start healing. They all will leave your colors alone. Heal everyone who needs it, no matter their race nor which side they fight on. Since the Boki allow Balthazar to live with them, I think they know the rules and will let you heal their kills."

She looked up at the raging battle doubtfully. "I'm supposed to walk out into the middle of that?"

"Aye. You are White Heart now. No one touch you."

Rosana muttered a fast incant and cast a glow spell on Raina. Against the pristine white of her tabard, it lit the night like a torch. "Go!" Rosana gave her a little push.

Sha'Li and Cicero pulled back the brambles to make an opening for Raina. She stumbled forward. Stood upright. And started forward, terrified.

The nearest combatants hitched in their swings as they caught sight of her. Both the rakasha and the Boki who were fighting disengaged from their combat and stepped back to let her pass between them. She walked forward, dimly noting the sounds of their resumed combat behind her. *Heal everyone.*

Leland. Must get to Leland.

She fixed in her mind's eye the last place she'd seen him and broke into a run, aiming straight for him. The ground was rough, and she tripped several times over what she hoped were tree roots but suspected were not. Once a hand even reached out to steady her when she would have fallen in a patch of blood-soaked mud. She did not stop to thank the warrior, for Leland lay somewhere before her, dead, a stake through his heart.

Shockingly, the battle seemed to part in front of her like butter melting away from a hot knife. She judged she'd nearly reached the spot where he went down and pulled up to have a look around for him. A fierce knot of fighting centered upon the spot where Leland and his men had been mowed down. How was she ever to get through that? She flinched as a sword swung perilously close to her head.

"Gads, White Heart! Apologies. I saw ye not!" someone yelled from her left.

She gathered all her remaining nerve and stepped forward. "Make way for the White Heart!" she shouted.

The effect of her words was stunning. Boki and human

alike fell back, lowering their weapons to let her through. It was surreal, passing through the battle almost as if she were a brightly glowing ghost, surrounded by gore and violence but touched by none of it.

She continued forward, stumbling over something soft and slippery. She dared not look down to see what it was. She was hanging on to her sanity by a thread as it was. She spotted a pile of green and yellow obscured by the churned filth of the battlefield. She leaped forward, searching frantically for the familiar visage and graying hair of her mentor. *There.* She fell to her knees beside him and used the hem of her pristine tabard to wipe the mud and blood off the slack face. It was Leland.

His face was pale. Peaceful.

She laid her hands upon his two shoulders, barely all of him that was intact, and quickly recited the incant to call forth life-restoring magics. The energy rushed painfully through her and into Sir Leland.

Nothing happened.

Nothing happened.

She did it again, drawing more magic forth from within herself, blasting him with a burst of life magic a full-sized dragon could not ignore.

And still Leland lay there, lifeless. Dead. Gone.

She rocked back on her heels in disbelief. He couldn't be gone. He'd genuinely cared for his people. For her. Given her wise advice. Protected her from those who would harm her or take advantage of her. *Please resurrect,* she begged his spirit. But something within her doubted that he wished to return to this world of pain and suffering, not when his beloved wife waited for him so patiently beyond the Veil.

The fog that had momentarily shrouded Raina's mind began to shred. Screams and blood and bodies began to register upon her stunned senses. With awareness came tearing grief so sharp it caused her physical pain. A keening wail rose up in her and found voice, rising to mingle helplessly with the moans of the dying. Her innards felt as though they might fall right out of her and she clutched her middle in agony. *No. Nononononononono . . .*

But the bloody truth sprawled before her eyes, undeniable. Sir Leland was dead. She had reached him in plenty of time for the magic to work, and she had given him more than enough of it. Maybe that stake had made his spirit irretrievable. Now she had to trust him to the miracle of resurrection and Leland's own will to live.

She noticed spatters of blood upon her clothes, obscene against the whiteness of her tabard. She scrubbed at them, succeeding only in smearing the blood into crimson streaks across her front.

Putting on the White Heart colors had been a waste. She'd given up her freedom, her future, her dreams—everything she'd fought so hard for—and it had all been for naught. She'd failed to save the one person in the world who'd ever shown her a parent's selfless love, completely free of any ulterior motive or hidden agenda.

She'd failed. Utterly and completely.

As she knelt in the mud, her hands lying useless in her lap, her shoulders gradually slumped lower and lower as if a great load and then a greater load still were being piled upon them. And at long last, she finally cried. For her lost childhood, her lost home, her lost family. For everything and everyone she'd run away from in her desperate quest and for the unbearable price of it all.

CHAPTER

27

Will jumped as Eben groaned beside him. "No. Oh no. Not my lord. Aaah, my lord—" The jann started to rise up from his hiding place, but Cicero and Sha'Li leaped on the grieving jann and forcibly held him down.

"Eben," Cicero muttered urgently, "there's naught you can do now."

Will frowned over at Rosana. He thought he spied tears glistening on her cheeks. "What's happening?" he whispered to her.

"Raina, she reached him in plenty of time. Which means the landsgrave's spirit refused to come back when she tried to restore his life."

"What does that mean?" Will pressed.

She gazed at him sorrowfully. "Hyland is dead. His spirit must resurrect if he is to return. If and until that happens, Landsgrave Hyland is gone."

"Oh." It felt like someone had just hit Will in the gut with a heavy rock. He looked out at the ghostly white form of Raina rocking back and forth on the ground over Hyland's crumpled form. "We should go to her."

Sha'Li snorted. "Look you at the same battle I do? A killing field it is. No mercy, no quarter. And not so well the pinkskins fare. Slaughtering everything crossing their path are those Boki."

Will gazed out upon the battle, stricken. She was right, of course. But it felt wrong just sitting here, letting all this death unfold before him. Thing was, there wasn't really anything their little party could do to stem the flow of a battle encompassing hundreds of combatants. And more important, they were so close to finding the Sleeping King, and that must take precedence—

Will's brain hitched. He flashed back to the anguish and determination on his father's face as Ty had led them away from the massacre of Hickory Hollow. This must have been exactly how Will's father had felt, the thoughts he had been thinking, that awful night.

It was a hard thing, knowing that a goal you held dear was more important than the lives of dozens of your friends and neighbors—or of hundreds of soldiers, who'd done nothing wrong but follow orders. It sat ill within Will. But what choice did he have? Since the moment his father had revealed the existence of the Sleeping King, Will's path had been set. He could not stop until he found the king or died permanently in the attempt.

He jolted when a whispered word floated out of the darkness behind him. "Willcobb."

Stunned, he half-turned on his belly to look over his shoulder. Thar'Ok and a half-dozen Boki warriors loomed in the shadows behind him.

"What—" Will stared.

The orc shaman waved him urgently to silence, then gestured for all the members of the party to come to him. With varying degrees of trepidation and suspicion, Will and the others complied. Thar'Ok drew them several dozen yards away from the main body of the battle.

"Willcobb. Now be time."

Will stared at Thar'Ok. "I beg your pardon?"

"Go now. Wake king."

"But I don't know where to go—"

Thar'Ok cut him off. "We show. Come now."

"But Raina—our healer—"

"She Balthazar," the orc intoned in disgust. "We bring. You go."

Will looked to the others questioningly. His inclination was to trust the Boki. Stars knew, Thar'Ok didn't have to come out here and expose himself to danger from Anton's men like this. The others in the party hesitated, but eventually they all nodded. Sha'Li was last to join in.

Will answered for all of them, "All right. We go. Lead on."

The orcs turned and melted into the night with Will and his companions close on their heels.

Something touched Raina's foot. She jumped and looked behind her to see a badly mangled arm attached to a bloody shoulder that led to an even bloodier face with desperate human eyes looking out of it.

"Please, White Heart. Save Hyland's men."

Oh, stars. The rest of them. With alacrity Raina reached down and threw healing into the man to stanch the worst of his bleeding and stabilize him enough not to die.

"You knew him?" she asked hoarsely as the man gasped in pain beneath her hands.

"I am . . . was . . ."—a groaned curse—". . . his sergeant at arms. He told me to stay back and the others to stay with me, but I couldn't let him die alone. I led the men to 'im. And now they's all dead."

"Where? Show me?" Raina asked urgently. Of a sudden it was incredibly important to find Leland's men and save as many of them as she could. The sergeant crawled over to a corpse a few feet away. "There be Donal," he pointed out.

She hit the young man with the same healing that had failed on Sir Leland, but this time her target blinked his eyes open almost instantly. She choked back a sob. Six more times she used life magic, and all six times it worked. Why, oh why, couldn't it have worked on Sir Leland? On the remaining men, she threw enough healing into them to fix the worst of their injuries and see them safely off the field.

The last one sat up with a jerk, raising his sword to swing at the hamstrings of a nearby Boki.

"Stand down!" the sergeant barked to the fellow. "Lower your weapon!"

Raina frowned up at the soldier, startled.

The sergeant shrugged. "Sir Leland saw to it we knew the rule."

"What rule?"

He frowned that she did not seem to know the tenets of her own order, but nonetheless explained. "Tradition holds that if the White Heart heals a man and he departs peacefully from the battle, his opponents will let him withdraw unharmed. But if my men reengage in the fight, we be fair game to die again. Not to mention we risk the displeasure of the White Heart, who do not take kindly to spending their precious magic saving a man's life only to have him throw it away again."

Ahh. A good rule. She could see the sense of it.

"May I just say how good it is to see my mistress's tabard abroad again. You wear it well, young lady."

She shook her head, unable to speak past the sudden lump in her throat.

Hyland's men all rested their weapons on top of their

heads. She assumed that was some sort of signal to the Boki that they intended to withdraw from the fight without engaging any further. The men started to move toward the south end of the battlefield, and Raina stood up with the idea of leaving with them.

The sergeant spoke to her gently. "Your work is not done, White Heart. Many more wounded and dying lay upon the field. Until your healing is spent, you must stay."

Raina looked around in dismay at the carnage. *Of course. Heal everyone you see, regardless of race or affiliation. . . .*

He continued, and she could almost hear Leland's voice saying, *Heal without prejudice, green and pink, flesh and fur, alike. The Boki are living creatures and as deserving of your skill as me and my men.*

As the sergeant limped away with his men she took a deep breath, turned, and reached for the dead orc lying at her feet, minus the entire right side of his head. She laid her hands upon him and blasted him with a life spell. The Boki did much as Leland's men had done. He blinked awake, face now intact, looked confused, spied her tabard, and comprehension lit his black eyes.

He nodded and grunted something in orcish that sounded like an expression of gratitude. He climbed to his feet and held a hand down to her. Startled, she took it. The orc hoisted her to her feet and then some, nearly sending her flying with his strength. Another grunt that sounded apologetic and then the fellow put his sword on his head and jogged off the field. Stunned, she watched him go. And then she turned to the next corpse, another Boki.

She worked her way in an expanding circle around the field, doing her best to conserve her energy and give each man just enough magic to save his life. How many humanoids and orcs she healed she had no idea. She decided then and there never to keep count of such things. How long she stayed upon the field she also had no idea.

But when her magics were completely drained she staggered, exhausted, toward the brush from whence she'd come. She'd only taken a step or two beyond the clearing, though, when a big, meaty—and very green—hand clasped her upper arm. The same orc who'd tried to lead them past this place before.

"Come. Willcobb."

Startled, she stared up at him. He was going to take her to Will and the others? She nodded her understanding and followed as he veered toward the north end of the battlefield. A great cry went up from behind her. "Kidnapping . . . White Heart in trouble . . . green whoresons abuse the colors! . . ."

She only caught snippets of it, but it was enough to tell that Anton's men took umbrage with a Boki escorting her off the field like this. She would have turned to reassure them, but the Boki was dragging her forward so quickly she could barely keep her feet.

Nonetheless, someone caught up with her, because all of a sudden something swung past her from behind and slammed into the orc beside her. He staggered, but the blow did not draw blood. The orc released her arm and whirled to face his attacker. Raina did the same.

It appeared to be some sort of barbarian. He looked human, but his face was covered in complicated whorls of red-brown paint. "It's all right," she tried. "I go with him voluntarily."

But the barbarian either did not hear her or did not understand her. His attention rested solely upon the orc before him. The two combatants rushed each other and Raina stumbled back momentarily from the fury of their fight. She stepped forward and tried again. "It's all right—" It did no good.

The two fighters disengaged only when, frustrated, she physically stepped between them. It was a foolhardy maneuver, but she was lucky. Both men had enough control of their weapons to check their blows mid-swing and not decapitate her.

She shouted, "Stop!"

The Boki frowned at her for a moment and then sighed. "Bal-tha-zar?" he asked reluctantly.

Huh? "Uhh, yes. Sure," she tried. "No killing."

He nodded in disappointment. "No kill. Bal-tha-zar."

She turned to the barbarian. "No killing," she repeated forcefully. She pointed at her tabard and then at his weapon and then shook her head in the negative. The barbarian frowned and pointed at the Boki, then drew a finger across his neck.

"No!" she exclaimed. "For lack of any better demonstration, she reached out and tucked her arm into the Boki's elbow as if he were a dance partner about to escort her onto the floor. The barbarian's eyes bulged. She waved him away with her free hand and then turned and commenced dragging the Boki off the field with her.

She glanced back over her shoulder once, and the barbarian still stood there, staring at her in shock. Yup, she could hear the rumors now. The White Heart healer was dating a Boki.

The Boki glanced down at her in definite humor. "Bal-tha-zar. Cray. Zee."

What else could she do? She nodded in the affirmative and kept on walking.

When they cleared the battlefield her orc escort shook off her hand and took off running. Wherever he was going, he wanted to get there in a big hurry. Exhaustion, both physical and emotional, dragged at her.

The Boki stopped twice to wait impatiently for her to catch up with him, but there was no help for it. Draining her magical energy like that had drained her physically, too. And she had not a drop of magic left to cast into herself and mayhap give herself more strength to run faster.

The third time she caught up with him, she gasped before he took off running again, "How much further?"

"Soon."

She sincerely hoped "soon" in Boki terms meant a matter of minutes. Because that was just about all she had left.

And that was when the fighting broke out on their right.

The Boki jolted and put on a burst of speed that demonstrated just how much he'd been slowing down for her. Cursing under her breath, she followed, ducking out of sight behind a cluster of oak saplings. The Boki stopped and she did the same, panting.

He gestured at the direction the sound of fighting was coming from and then pointed at her tabard. "You go . . . Bal. Tha. Zar?"

She laughed without humor and held up her hands, which were definitely not glowing in the deep gloom of night. "No magic. All gone."

"Ahh. Go qui-uhht."

Stars willing, "quiet" also meant "slow."

For a big creature the Boki moved with shocking stealth. She did her best to mimic his silent passage through the wood but wondered at the value of doing so, attired as she was in white that stood out like a beacon in the night. They had to circle wide twice more around skirmishing. Luck favored them, though, and they moved away from the fighting until it was only a distant murmur behind them.

Who was out here, sneaking around in small, thief-like groups, and why? Did Anton know the lair of the Sleeping

King was close by? Had he sent his men out looking for it? Leland had said Anton believed the Boki to be guarding a great treasure trove. Was that what his men searched for?

If so, that meant the main battle behind her had been nothing more than a ruse! Leland had died for nothing more than a distraction—

Fury erupted in her heart. The governor had murdered Sir Leland as surely as if he'd wielded the sword that killed Hyland himself. It was wrong. How were the people supposed to live under a ruler who valued life so little? She was White Heart now, her prime tenet of existence to defend life. And Anton Constantine was anathema to everything she stood for.

Her thoughts flashed back to Moto and Mag and Arv and the kindari villagers who lived on the fringes of society rather than accept the yoke of Koth. *Freedom indeed. A most worthy goal.* She did not know what she could do to support their fight, but she would find a way. Someday. Somehow.

They topped a ridge and her Boki guide stopped abruptly, enough so that she ran into his back. "Sorry," she mumbled.

"Shhh." The Boki clicked his tongue in a rapid pattern several times and then fell silent. He repeated the insectoid sounds once more. In a moment the clicking sound came back, but in a slightly different pattern.

Her escort moved forward confidently. Raina frowned. A sophisticated signaling system for supposedly stupid beasts. She was rapidly coming to the conclusion that these Boki had been vastly underestimated by the Empire. All her life, she'd heard nothing to contradict the idea that greenskins in general were intellectually inferior to the humanoid races. But clearly, it was not so.

They stepped into a small clearing and she spotted Thar'Ok. Or at least she thought it was Thar'Ok, the most senior of the Boki shamans.

He spoke roughly, "We wait for worst fight go by. Rest. Be some time."

She swore under her breath and stared at the party of orcs standing silently around her. She started, though, when Thar'Ok abruptly started mumbling into thin air. The other orcs moved aside a little and the shaman knelt. *What on Urth?* For all the world, it looked like he was starting a field resurrection.

Sure enough, in a few minutes the body of an orc had formed at Thar'Ok's feet and become solid. In a few more minutes the resurrected orc took a gasping breath and lurched upright.

Huh. She'd never thought to ask how greenskin races healed their dead. Could they speak with spirits as well—

She jumped to her feet and asked Thar'Ok urgently, "Can you speak to the dead?"

The thorn blinked at her in surprise. "Big magic. But yes."

"I need to speak to a dead pinkskin spirit. He died well. But he refused to resurrect for me. I'm completely out of magical energy. I used it all healing your warriors and mine. I *must* speak with this spirit. Convince him to come back."

"Whoo be he?"

"Landsgrave Leland Hyland."

"Him big figh-tuh."

"With big honor," Raina added. "Like you. Please. If you wish me and my friend to wake the Sleeping King, you will do this for me. We're not going anywhere for a while. You said so yourself."

Thar'Ok frowned and reached out to poke her tabard gently. "Bal. Tha. Zar."

She nodded and waited, holding her breath.

"I do. For Bal. Tha. Zar."

She sagged in relief.

"Three ask. Only." He held up three thick fingers to illustrate his meaning. She nodded impatiently, understanding. A spell to speak with a spirit only allowed the caster to ask three questions, no more. No conversation. Just the questions. And, of course, the spirit was not required to answer honestly. Although she doubted that would be an issue with Leland. He was honest to his core.

While Thar'Ok muttered to himself and commenced gathering magic, she thought frantically, preparing the questions she would have the thorn ask Leland. How to convince him to come back to this world when she knew for certain he did not wish to do so?

The orc cast the magic, and Raina looked around expectantly. Where was Leland's spirit? As a spirit caster, she ought to be able to sense its presence.

"Is he here?" she asked urgently. "Did his spirit come to you?"

"Ahh. There he be," Thar'Ok sighed.

Raina looked around again. She didn't see him. Was Leland hiding himself from her? It would be like him. Could spirits do that?

"Ask," the thorn grunted.

Raina spoke carefully. "Landsgrave Leland, were you ordered not to resurrect?"

Thankfully, the thorn didn't seem to have to relay the question to the spirit, for in a moment he shook his head in the negative. Thar'Ok muttered, "He say no. Ask two."

She took a deep breath. And now for the key question. "Does Sir Leland know where a man named Kerryl Moonrunner took his son, Kendrick, after Moonrunner kidnapped him?"

Thar'Ok frowned. "Spirit very . . . move much. Talk to self. Mad. Scared, maybe."

Excellent. "And my question? Does he answer it?"

A pause. "He not know. Ask three."

She thought fast. If Leland didn't know before he died that Kendrick had been kidnapped, then that meant he had received no ransom demand. Either Moonrunner had killed Kendrick, in which case the youth had likely already resurrected, or the fellow still held Kendrick alive. But why? For what purpose?

She asked her third question. "Does Leland understand that he must resurrect if he is to help us find his son and save Kendrick from whatever Moonrunner has planned for him?"

Thar'Ok looked off into space for a long time. Long enough that Raina began to get very nervous. If only she could see Leland! "Is he still there?" she whispered. "Does he answer?"

At long last, the thorn murmured, "Aye. He unner-stan."

She fell to her knees, emotionally emptied. She'd done her best. Now she could only hope and pray his spirit chose to make the long journey back to the land of the living.

"We go now," Thar'Ok rumbled above her.

Would this nightmare never end? She gathered herself to rise and a rough green hand appeared before her face. Grateful, she took the thorn's hand and let him help her up. Kindness from an orc. How much more upside down would her world turn before this was all said and done?

The cadre of orcs fanned out in front of and behind her, and they moved out cautiously into the dark.

It wasn't long before her escort led her into another small clearing much like the last one. Except this clearing held familiar faces. Rosana rushed forward to wrap her in a sobbing embrace. Raina was too drained to respond in kind, but she did hug the gypsy back weakly. She looked up over Rosana's shoulder and spied Eben, his eyes bleak.

"I'm so sorry," she murmured, brokenhearted. "I did my best. But it wasn't enough—"

Cicero cut her off. "We all saw what you did out there on the field. No apologies required."

Sha'Li added pragmatically, "Weak was his spirit. Eager to die." She added somewhat less sarcastically than usual, "In peace could he die knowing that his madness we carry on."

"It is not madness—" Will started hotly.

"I spoke to his spirit—" Raina started at the same time.

"Hush, both you," Thar'Ok said forcefully. "Anton near."

Raina started in alarm, and Will whispered, "How near?"

She breathed to him, "On our way here, we heard several groups of his men creeping around in the dark."

Thar'Ok grunted, "We go. Hurry."

They moved off to the north into terrain that commenced rising and falling in ever steeper slopes. A big orc warrior moved up beside her to guide her. Will startled her by falling in beside her escort and striking up a whispered conversation. "So, Ki'Rig Agar. You have helped me yet again. Am I to be in your debt forever, Boki?"

The orc grunted, "Wake king. We even. But still finish fight someday."

Will grinned. "Deal."

The pair of elves crouched side by side, dark cloaks obscuring their forms until they were part of the night, shadow without form or substance. Aurelius looked over at his old friend and wondered if Selea was experiencing the same déjà vu that he was.

"And now we are two," he murmured.

Selea nodded slowly. "I will miss Leland if he chooses not to resurrect. He had the best heart of us all."

"Aye," Aurelius answered reflectively, "he did at that. Humans are possessed of a unique generosity of spirit."

"Perhaps it comes from having to live and die so quickly."

"Mmm," Aurelius replied. "It would be a great tragedy if he does not live to see his dream to fruition."

He felt, rather than saw, Selea's shrug under his black cloak. "He knew his dream was in motion. DeVir's boy has taken up the gauntlet. And Leland found the girl and put her into the perfect position to influence events in the years to come."

"He always did have a knack for that sort of thing."

The two elves fell silent for a time. Aurelius could not fathom what Selea contemplated, but his mind was full of the possibilities of the girl—the first arch-mage to emerge in generations, trained in politics and diplomacy, and operating within the special immunity of the White Heart colors. Yes indeed, Leland did have a gift for stirring the pot.

And in the meantime, Tiberius hadn't done a bad job, either, of setting massive events into motion with his son. It was hard to imagine that the boy might soon succeed where they had all failed. Perhaps the hand of fate was guiding the younger De'Vir, after all.

A handful of youths, hailing from all corners of the realm, perfectly prepared to fulfill great destinies, brought together in a single place and time to pursue a common goal. What were the odds? How could the greater beings not be pulling at least a little at the strings of this night's events?

It did give an old elf pause to wonder where he fit into the grand scheme of it all. He murmured to his companion, "What is Anton thinking? Running his mercenaries around out here like this is madness. The Boki will hunt down Anton's men and crush them like so many helpless rabbits."

"As long as one of his men succeeds, the others are

expendable. Anton only needs a single person to bring him the location of that which he seeks."

"It's cursed frustrating knowing we're so close to it—again—yet we have no idea where it is."

"Patience, Aurelius. We will find it."

"How?"

"Anton's got the wrong of it. He should not be following his men. He should be following those who know where the treasure lies. Those who will rush to guard it from his men."

"The Boki?"

"Aye."

Aurelius chuckled under his breath. "Of course. Let the orcs lead us to the hiding place."

"In spite of your noisy conversation, old friend, I hear several groups of orcs moving generally in a northward direction. Unfortunately, Anton's forces appear to be moving that way as well. Let us do the same."

"Once more, then, we shall all gather to confront the fates: Anton, the Boki, and us, the ever intrepid fools."

"History does like to repeat itself."

"Let us hope for a better outcome this time."

Selea retorted grimly, "I place little faith in hope!"

"Perhaps. But what else do we have? A handful of children, totally untried, in whose hands rests the fate of us all?"

Selea shook his head gloomily. "We are doomed."

Thar'Ok led the way deep into the heart of the forest. Will noticed Ki'Rig Agar surreptitiously holding up a hand by his ear yet again in what Will thought might be some sign to ward off evil. The whites of the Boki's eyes gleamed in the dark and he was acting positively jumpy. All the Boki were acting that way.

Will chastised himself. What had he expected? That the Sleeping King would be laid out in a pleasant grove they could stroll into and merely give his shoulder a shake? Of course the place would be protected in some way. Defended by something or someone dangerous. But it was not reassuring knowing that the king's guards scared the green off of ferocious Boki warriors.

They joined a larger group of Boki warriors in the bottom of a tiny vale bounded on each side by a rocky slope. Giant trees ringed the little bowl, and even in the scant starlight they looked strange and twisted. Thorns as long as Will's forearms pointed downward at close intervals along the trunks. Their bark was cracked and thick, a dark, bloodred color. The branches high overhead were gnarled and massive, and nestled among the leaves were more o f those vicious-looking thorns. A lone squirrel was visible a dozen arm lengths up one tree, notable for how it was impaled upon a thorn, dead. *Bloodthorn trees.*

The orcs already in the grove bristled with weapons and looked as nervous as his escort. Will was relieved to spot Balthazar among them. If Will and his friends were slaughtered out of hand for being here, at least they might stand a chance of getting life spells.

Ki'Rig Agar, still beside him, pointed across the vale. "Ovuh they-uhh."

Will squinted, trying to make out exactly what it was the Boki was pointing at. He saw only boulders scattered like trash all over the steep slope at the base of the biggest tree of all.

"Ahh," Cicero sighed. "Clever."

Thar'Ok grunted something low and Ki'Rig Agar spoke up more loudly. "Willcobb go. Fine' king. Now."

To punctuate the orc's declaration, the sounds of a skirmish erupted behind them. Every head snapped around toward the sound, and a half-dozen Boki warriors raced to the southern lip of the bowl to take up defensive positions.

Ki'Rig Agar gestured at the cadre of warriors with him. "We stan' hee-uhh. Die foh yew. Go. We figh' again one day. Do not fay-uhh, Willcobb."

Do not fail indeed. He got the distinct impression that failure would mean death for them all.

Cicero led the way briskly toward the randomly strewn boulders littering the hillside on the other side of the bowl-shaped vale. Or maybe not so random. As they drew practically within touching distance of the stones, Will spotted a narrow vertical opening behind an overlapping formation of boulders. It was tall enough to admit him, but barely wide enough to squeeze through.

Sha'Li moved aggressively toward the opening. "Finish this thing now, shall we? Yes?"

Will grabbed her to hold her back. If she went, Rosana

would expect to go, and there was no way he was letting her die tonight. "No. Not you, Sha'Li. I would not risk all of our lives."

The lizardman girl hissed and yanked her arm free with shocking ease. He was so weakened he could barely stand. How on Urth did he expect to face whatever threats awaited them within that dark opening?

"Keep all treasure for yourself, you would?" Sha'Li demanded. "I think not."

He huffed. "The only treasure we seek this night is the Sleeping King. No matter what we find inside, he must be our only goal."

The lizardman girl replied grudgingly, "Fine. No looting. Go now, we shall. Yes? Before comes Anton."

"Don't talk to me about hurrying. You're not dying of slow poisoning," Will grumbled back.

Sha'Li's simmering anger evaporated into a toothy grin. Why she found that funny he could not fathom. Cold humor to match her cold skin, he supposed.

They paused at the bottom of the slope and Cicero asked the orcs in general, "Does the passage stay this narrow all the way to its final destination?"

Ki'Rig Agar shrugged and looked around at the other warriors, who also shrugged. Thar'Ok was brought forward to help.

Will was first to speak. "Do you know how the king is protected?"

Thar'Ok spoke carefully, enunciating each syllable clearly. "Yonder is the Bloodthorn tree of Gir'Ok. Our greatest warriors are interred beneath such trees so their blood may nourish and strengthen the Bloodthorn. We give trees power. They give us powerful weapons." He pointed at a reddish wooden club being wielded by one of the biggest warriors close by.

Will hissed at that and eyed the mighty Bloodthorn tree towering overhead. "Is this his tree?"

The Boki laughed at that. Balthazar was the one to answer, "This is a tiny sapling in comparison to Bloodroot's tree, apparently. No, this is Gir'Ok's tree. He is the greatest Boki thorn of them all, a contemporary of ancient kings, and many of his descendants are interred here with him."

"Ancient kings?" Raina piped up. "The ancient king we seek?"

The thanes around them hesitated, and then nodded their heads reluctantly in the affirmative.

Thar'Ok was speaking slowly again. ". . . end of this passage is the burial chamber of great thanes and thorns of the Boki."

Will blurted, "Surely it is not that simple. We merely go into this burial chamber and find the king?"

Balthazar asked the question and the Boki broke out in rumbles of orc laughter. Will would take that as a no, it was not that simple. He demanded, "What else can they tell us of what we will face?"

"Nothing," Balthazar answered soberly. "The whole point of the thing is for you to prove yourselves worthy. If you fail, you were not meant to wake the king."

Will was certain he knew the answer, but he asked Balthazar anyway, "And what happens to us if we fail?"

"You die."

As I thought. "I go in alone," Will announced.

His companions actually laughed at him.

"I am serious."

"So are we!" Rosana snapped.

Cicero commented, "We have come this far together. I say we finish this thing together."

A chorus of agreements greeted that statement.

Eben spoke soberly as Will fumed. "Sir Leland spoke to every soothsayer he could find in the past few months. They all spoke similar prophecies. A person with no name, with no home, would do something important. Something to do with an ancient king." He looked around the party significantly, then continued, "Who here, for one reason or another, has no name and no home?"

"Me," Raina replied promptly.

"Me," Rosana added.

"Me," Sha'Li answered a little reluctantly.

"Me," Cicero added quietly.

Eben turned to stare at Will. "And me. We all meet the requirements of the soothsayers. I say we go in together."

Cicero murmured, "At least one of us must live to reach the king. Are we agreed that no matter who it is, we will not give up until one of us finds him?"

Will gulped. Cicero was suggesting that they each be willing to die. He said low, "If anyone needs to resurrect, go to Rosana or Balthazar. The Heartstones in Tallyn are probably being watched."

The others nodded grimly as the kindari set out a quick marching order. "Me first. Eben next. Then Will, Raina, Rosana, and Sha'Li." Cicero looked around at all of them. "Ready?"

Will nodded along with the others.

"Let's go, then."

The dark maw of the Boki tomb loomed ahead, swallowing Will's companions one by one. He caught the admiring, even wistful, gaze of Ki'Rig Agar upon him. This was madness. Pure madness. They were all going to die. The certainty was bitter in his mouth.

None of the hearth tales he'd heard ever spoke of the story's hero thinking his adventures were suicidal folly and that his companions had lost their minds to continue on with him. Had his father ever felt like this? Or had he been so lost in the imagined glory of finding the king and freeing the colonies that he'd never seen the grim reality of failing and dying? Maybe at the end . . . with his wife about to die and his son fleeing for his life . . . no, probably not even then, knowing Ty.

And so it was, with the taste of death on his tongue and a curse in his heart for his father, that Will entered the narrow tunnel.

He heard the others shuffling ahead of him, feeling their way in the dark. He reached out to touch the wall of the cave, a distance of only a few inches, and recoiled at the cold, seeping slime thick upon the wall. Stars, how he hated being underground like this, half-smothered by the weight of Urth pressing down upon him.

His gut clenched in a sharp cramp. Whether it was the life-draining effect of Bloodroot within him or merely fearful anticipation of what lay ahead he could not tell.

"It glows ahead and appears to widen somewhat," Cicero whispered.

Will relayed the information to the others behind him. The passageway did indeed widen enough to accommodate the width of his shoulders, and he was relieved to turn and walk normally instead of shuffling along sideways. But roots still hung in his face, caressing him uncomfortably as he passed. He used his staff to push them aside. He thought he saw a tree root shift, serpent-like overhead, but he was forced to look away by the clods of dirt that rained down on him of a sudden.

Dregs. It was as if the hill itself were alive and attempting to repel them from its depths. Cicero cursed ahead of him and Sha'Li echoed the sentiment from behind. They sounded as jumpy as he. If only the Boki had told them more of what would face them in here.

He noticed the faintest glow at the edges of his vision. He squinted in the inky dark. It seemed as if the glow came from ahead of him, somewhere down the tunnel. Eben stopped in front of him abruptly and Will nearly plowed into the jann, so focused was he on the glow.

Eben half-turned and whispered in Will's ear, "Cicero says there's a wide spot. We're to follow him close and pass through fast."

Will dutifully passed the message along to those behind him. When they'd clustered up tight, all hanging onto one another's tabards, Cicero rushed forward, charging the wide spot in the tunnel. Will burst out into the larger space, his sword in his right hand.

Nothing moved immediately, but he did notice that the walls seemed to be covered in some sort of bumpy, faintly glowing substance. The light it gave off was dim, but adequate to see by as his eyes adjusted to it. Mushrooms. Growing so thickly that the stone walls of the tunnel completely disappeared beneath the glowing fungus. They encroached upon the margins of the floor where dampness seeped off the wall, standing thigh high.

Perhaps they could pick one and use it as a makeshift torch. Will reached for the nearest small one, about knee high.

From behind him Sha'Li hissed a warning sound and said, "Touch not the fungus."

Too late. He'd grasped the stem and given it a good tug. The mushroom came loose easily in his hands, but as he lifted it a poof of foul-smelling dust puffed out of it and into his face. A green light flickered briefly across his skin, repelling the dust and then blinking out of existence as he dropped the mushroom and staggered back.

"What was that?"

Cicero, whom he'd brushed past to pick the mushroom and who was standing directly behind him whipped out his sword. "Get back!" the kindari cried out. "That dryad means to kill us!"

Will frowned. *What the—*

Other mushrooms commenced coughing out dirty gray powder into the air. He ducked and passed beyond the directed sprays as shouts erupted behind him. He turned around brandishing his staff to face chaos. The entire party was shouting about various monsters . . . Raina was hollering about spider monkeys attacking her; Rosana was in a panic of some sort of magical hound attacking her. But all he saw were mushrooms, and they weren't attacking anyone.

Frowning, he stepped toward his companions with the intent to suggest that they had lost their minds. But something heavy banged into his back and he whirled, startled. A hanging root as thick as his arm had struck him solidly. Something whipped around his waist and he snatched at it. Another root, snaking around him and squeezing . . . hard. Something grabbed his ankle.

"The roots are attacking!" he yelled as he hacked himself free with his dagger.

But his companions were busy swinging wildly at thin air and seemed oblivious to the threat. He charged back toward the group, slicing at the attacking roots as he went. His own companions were perhaps the biggest threat as they yelled and ducked and swung their various weapons wildly.

Cicero, cursing up a storm about green women, was shooting arrows at mushrooms as fast as he could draw and loose them. Each mushroom he hit collapsed in on itself with a loud, drawn-out screech of escaping air.

A root wrapped around Rosana, pinning her arms to her

sides, and Will commenced sawing at it above her head. His dagger finally sliced through the root, and the end of it fell away from Rosana to the floor, where it writhed like a dying snake. Will recoiled from its thrashing length, yanking Rosana back from it as well.

She stared at him, unseeing, and took a swipe at him with her dagger. He leaped back, narrowly avoiding being gutted.

"It's me. Will!" he cried out.

Her eyes did not indicate the slightest recognition of him as she ranted about not letting the magical hounds catch her. She was too far lost in her hallucination to know him. The next time she swung at him, he grabbed her wrist and gave it a hard enough twist to force her to drop her dagger. He scooped up the weapon and tucked it in his belt as he bodily dragged her to the end of the passage.

"Stay here," he ordered. "The hounds will not find you if you hide here and are absolutely still. Do you understand?"

She nodded and crouched down in a feral pose.

Will dived back into the chaos. Timing his attack carefully, he leaped close behind Cicero and snatched the elf's quiver from his back. Cicero turned and took a vicious swing at him with his bow. It connected hard across Will's back and nearly knocked him off his feet. But thankfully, his metal-ringed jerkin prevented the blow from doing any real harm. It stung like a stripe of fire, though.

"This way, Cicero," Will urged. "We can form a defensive line over there by Rosana and kill the dryads together."

Cicero nodded and darted to Rosana's side. "Give me my arrows back."

Huh. Not a chance. He dived back into the fray and grabbed for Raina next. She was perhaps the most dangerous of them all, for she was completely unskilled with a sword and swung the one she was clumsily wielding in both hands completely unpredictably. She was ranting something now about mages in blue cloaks not getting her.

The roots had noticed her and several small ones had wrapped around her left ankle and were twining into her hair. He waited until she'd about knocked herself off her feet with a huge roundhouse sword swing, and then jumped forward to pluck the weapon from her hands. He had to hack her free from the roots while she struggled, but he managed not to cut her to ribbons.

"Come quick," he ordered. "The mages will not find you over here."

He did not know how long his thin logic would hold up against the bizarre visions gripping his companions, but he desperately hoped it would be long enough to get them out of here and away from any new puffs of hallucinogenic dust from the mushrooms.

He eyed Eben and Sha'Li doubtfully. Eben was every bit as skilled a fighter as he, and Sha'Li was not only strong and good with blades, but had that whole poison spit thing going. How was he to disarm either one of them? As he watched, though, Eben backed into a hanging thicket of roots that reacted sharply, whipping around his limbs, immobilizing his arms, and all but pulling his feet out from under him. The jann screamed and thrashed, but the harder he fought, the tighter the roots squeezed.

"Stop fighting!" Will shouted.

Right. The jann completely ignored him. The roots tightened so hard, though, that by the time Will reached him Eben was completely immobilized and gasping horribly for each breath. Using his dagger, Will slipped the narrow blade between Eben's shirt and the biggest root constricting the jann's chest. Will had to saw at it, but the razor-sharp blade eventually bit through the fibrous root and it fell away from the jann.

It took a few minutes, but by using the sword he'd liberated from Raina he cut the jann free. In the meantime, Will had to duck behind Eben twice to avoid attacks from Sha'Li. Her claws actually raked aside several of the roots holding Eben, although Will highly doubted that was her intent.

Eventually, Eben staggered clear of the mass of writhing root parts. He was starting to frown in confusion and stared around the dim passage as if he had no idea where he was. Grimly, Will turned his attention to the raging lizardman girl. One thing was for certain. He would never wish to face Sha'Li in combat. She was lightning fast and graceful as a deer as she fought her invisible demons, her claws flicking in and out among the roots so fast he could barely keep his gaze upon them.

The roots thrashing around her were not able to gain any purchase on her because of those claws. What she saw in her mind Will did not know. But it clearly terrified Sha'Li, and she just as clearly believed herself to be fighting for her life. There was no way he was going to be able to subdue her.

But thankfully, as he watched, her claws began to move less desperately, and she frowned around her.

"Where went the—" She broke off, confused.

"Hallucinations," Will replied shortly.

Sha'Li muttered something under her breath in hissing syllables that sounded suspiciously like curses. He turned to check on the others, and they were all looking around in confusion and embarrassment.

"Well, that was fun," Cicero remarked sarcastically. "My arrows?"

"Are you yourself?" Will asked cautiously.

The kindari merely pulled a disgusted face and stuck out his hand. Yup, Cicero was back to being his usual uncommunicative self.

"Are we all well?" Will asked.

Rosana looked like breathing was painful, and Raina was holding her left foot so the toe just touched the ground. Eben looked a little worse for wear, but all in all, they were all alive and ambulatory. It could have been worse. He held Rosana's dagger out to her and she took it wordlessly.

"Shall we continue?" he murmured.

With deep breaths all around and some resettling of armor and weapons, the group nodded. It went without saying that they would not touch any more of the glowing mushrooms, which continued to grow thickly upon the walls. As for the hanging roots, they avoided touching the things as much as possible. When it was absolutely necessary, Will gently draped roots back and away from their path with the tip of his staff, moving slowly and as nonthreateningly as possible in the process. Only one root attacked him, and it was his fault. He'd gotten careless and flipped the small root aside too fast. It whipped back and struck him across the face, leaving a thin, bloody line across his right cheek.

All the roots nearby stirred, as if interested in the smell of blood. But Rosana wiped off his cheek quickly and, pulling a little tin from her pouch, smeared a salve on it to stop the bleeding. The rustling roots subsided.

They eased forward cautiously for what seemed like an hour but was probably no more than a few minutes, this time with Will in the lead. He stopped and reported over his shoulder, "There's a chamber ahead. Big. Lots of roots. I can't see all the way across it. More mushrooms on the walls, so there's light to see by."

Very carefully, he stepped out into the space. It felt enormous after the tight confines of the tunnel. His companions joined him, staring as one into the massive cave, its ceiling lost in the darkness overhead.

Although the space was clearly large, it was choked with roots hanging down, some as thick as pillars and appearing to support the rough roof of the chamber like great, wooden columns. Other roots were smaller, mayhap the diameter of his arm. They dangled snake-like, writhing very faintly, hanging thickly enough that he could not see more than thirty or forty feet ahead.

He took several cautious steps forward. And that was when he saw the bodies tucked in among the roots. Dozens of them in various stages of decay. Orcs. Warriors in full battle dress and shamans decked out with bones and claws and teeth in their dead, dry hair and around their skeletal necks. The corpses seemed oddly deformed, even for orcs.

He looked closer and spied tree roots growing around and through the skeletons. Some roots appeared to embrace the skeletons, while others pierced right through rib cages and eye sockets. Some of the most decayed skeletons appeared nearly engulfed in sarcophagi of thick roots, while the newer bodies with flesh still clinging to them were only lightly gripped in twists of vining roots.

"Are they safe to touch?" Raina murmured as the dead stared silently at them.

"Let us not find out what traps the Boki have laid among their dead," Eben declared.

Will examined the roots more closely. In the faintly green light they looked chocolate brown, but he suspected in stronger light they would be the same dark, bloodred color as the tree above. The roots were peppered with thorns, too, albeit smaller than those protecting the tree aboveground.

Raina murmured, "There's got to be more to this place than that passage and some bodies. Why else all the fuss about keeping this cave secret?"

The group crept forward into the chamber, gently pushing

aside hanging roots and slipping around the larger ones anchored to the floor. He didn't know who bumped what first, but there was a faint rattle of armor as if someone had jostled the corpse of a Boki warrior. It was followed immediately by an odd noise, like a puff of air sharply expelled.

"Oww!" Sha'Li yelped.

He turned fast, staff in hand, and was startled to see a trio of small barbs sticking out of Sha'Li's upper arm. The barbs looked like wooden needles, maybe the length of his finger.

"That cursed root shot thorns at me!" Sha'Li exclaimed. She yanked the barbs free of her tough skin and threw them down in disgust. Cicero knelt and picked up one of the thorns gingerly to examine it. He lifted it to his nose and frowned.

Eben commented wryly, "At least we know now what happens when you disturb the dead."

Raina was looking around the jungle of roots thoughtfully. If he'd learned nothing else about her, it was to be worried when she waxed thoughtful.

"What?" he asked her cautiously.

"Which one of these bodies do you suppose is Gir'Ok?"

"Look for the oldest one of the bunch, the most covered in roots, and that'll be him, I imagine. Why does it matter?" Will asked.

"Balthazar said Gir'Ok was a contemporary of our ancient king's, right?"

"Aye."

"If I were going to hide a clue about how to find the Sleeping King in here, I would put it with the body of one who knew that king. That way I could find it again."

"You make my head ache with the things you think about!" Will retorted.

Cicero piped up, "But she does have a point. Are we to

wander around in here until these cursed roots crush us or shoot us dead with poison thorns?"

"Why think you those be poison?" Sha'Li asked quickly.

"Smell this." Cicero thrust the thorn he held under her nose and the lizardman girl pulled back sharply.

"Poisoned, it is," Sha'Li declared.

"Good thing your scaled hide is so tough and those barbs didn't penetrate your flesh," Cicero commented.

Rosana pointed off to their left. "That one over there looks old."

Eben added, "But the one just beyond it has an older type of sword with it. See that curve in the blade? Ancient smiths made swords thus. Your orc has a straight-edged blade."

"Fine!" Rosana snapped. "You find the oldest, deadest, most root infested orc corpse in the place. I'm going to sit down and smell the daisies."

Will grinned reluctantly at her waspish humor. They all were feeling the strain. "Let's spread out a bit and have a look around. I should think this Gir'Ok fellow's body was elaborately clothed for his burial."

Raina laughed without humor. "They're all old and elaborately clothed to me. Why don't you experts in weaponry search while I try to find any other clues that might be here?"

The group spread out, moving gingerly into the giant chamber. They slipped sideways among the tightly packed roots, and Will silently prayed that it would not come to a fight in here. His staff would be less than useless in these tight confines.

In a few places, Will came across roots that had been tied back to form openings in the curtain of growth. He slipped through them, inspecting body after body. The place smelled of worms and decay. And death—musty and repellent. The chamber was maze-like, and it was easy to get turned around. He fancied a person might get lost in here and die of thirst before they ever found their way out.

He did note that none of the dead thanes bore Bloodthorn clubs. Mayhap those were too valuable to bury with the dead and were instead passed down to living thanes.

"Over here!" Cicero called out eventually. "I may have found something."

Will slowly worked his way across the chamber to the sound of Cicero's voice. The corpses in this section of the tomb were all no more than skeletons barely recognizable within tangles of heavy roots. Definitely old.

He was last to join the others, who stood before a large corpse. The rotting remains of a tooled leather breastplate were covered in row after row of ancient blazons. One of them, in the center of the corpse's chest, was made of crystal that sparkled and winked as if lit from within.

"That's a paxan blazon," Cicero murmured, pointing at the brightly shining crystal. "Where would some orc come into possession of that and furthermore wear it with pride?"

Cicero was right. This was no common Boki warrior.

Upon the skeletal brow of this orc was a circlet bearing a large, cabochon gem with an eight-pointed star around it. No other orc body in this place wore anything of the like.

Will reached out gingerly to touch the gem and the disk on his chest burned fiercely in response. He staggered back from the circlet, gasping in agony.

"Do you ail?" Rosana asked in quick concern.

"You mean more than the usual dying bit?" he responded dryly. "I think Bloodroot recognizes this corpse."

Eben said, "Does that mean we've found Gir'Ok?"

Cicero asked reflectively, "What is his message for us about the Sleeping King, then?"

The group circled slowly around the ancient orc's resting

place. The roots were especially thick around this skeleton, growing toward it as if feeding hungrily upon its essence. In addition to the circlet on his brow, a pile of tribute at his feet included plates, goblets, jewelry, and rotted chests full of ancient coins.

Raina murmured, "Amazing that none of this treasure has been touched over the centuries."

"Kill anyone who touched it those cursed roots would," Sha'Li grumbled, sounding thoroughly disgruntled.

Will grinned at her chagrin.

Raina murmured, thinking aloud, "A clue to the Sleeping King would not be obvious. It would be hidden. Obscured in some way." She stepped right up next to Gir'Ok's remains to study them closely.

Frankly, Will found the way the tree roots grew through the body's skull and chest cavity ghoulish.

"His hand!" Raina exclaimed suddenly.

Will jumped at her outburst. "What about it?" he asked. What little was visible of the bones was bleached white and fragile looking.

"Every other orc's hands in here are pointed down. Gir'Ok's right hand is pointing up."

Rosana shrugged. "He was probably the first orc interred down here. Maybe it was a sign of honor to him that he's the only one pointing up toward his tree."

"Yes, but look at his fingers," Raina argued.

Will examined the bones wrapped around the hilt of what looked like a ceremonial dagger. "What of his fingers?"

"The other orcs' bones grip their swords loosely. That's because there was once flesh on their hands. As the flesh decayed away, the bones became loose around the handles. But Gir'Ok's hand bones grip his staff tightly. These bones were placed around that weapon well after the flesh was gone from his hands."

Sha'Li made a sound of distaste, and Will echoed the sentiment. But he took a closer look at the small, crumbling bones wrapped around the staff and had to reluctantly allow that Raina was correct.

Eben stared upward into the tangle of roots overhead, and Will followed suit. He saw nothing but darkness and dirt and more tree roots than he could count. The jann murmured, "Whatever is up there has no doubt been obscured over time by the growth of more roots."

Will replied, "Then how are we to know what is up there, if anything?"

All of them stared up into the morass fruitlessly until Sha'Li declared, "Only one way to know." And without further ado she grabbed on to a wrist-thick root and shimmied up it.

"Beware the thorns!" Rosana cried.

"Think thee so?" Sha'Li replied sarcastically. "Thick skin, I have."

In moments the black lizardman girl had blended into the shadows above and disappeared. Her muffled voice drifted down eventually, "High ceiling."

"Do you see anything?" Raina called up.

"Dirt. And more cursed roots."

Will grinned. But then a moment later Sha'Li's voice drifted down to them, and her words erased his smile. "A strange cluster of roots I see. Curled in upon themselves like a mother's arms, as if something valuable they cradle." And then, "Higher I must climb to reach it." The strain of physical effort was audible in Sha'Li's voice.

All of a sudden a flurry of air puffs exploded overhead.

A spate of hissed syllables followed, and it did not sound as if Sha'Li were singing the praises of the Bloodthorn roots. Chips of wood began to rain down, and the roots around them swung around in obvious agitation. Will jumped back with the others out of range of the thrashing roots.

Eben cursed as a root grabbed his leg, and the jann hacked at it with his sword. About the time he freed himself, Sha'Li jumped down from above, landing in a crouch right next to Will. He jumped about a foot straight up in the air on a cry of surprise.

She grinned at him, her teeth gleaming white in her black face. "A surprise I have."

She held out her hand and in it lay a wreath of green leaves slightly wider than Will's hand. The leaves were pristine, fresh and bright green, even in the scant light of the mushrooms. He looked closer and realized a thin line of gold edged each leaf perfectly. Thin, flattened wires of gold twined in and among the leaves in a delicate, intricate pattern.

"What is it?" he asked, blankly.

"His crown," Raina breathed. "The crown of a king devoted to the land."

Now that she mentioned it, the circlet of twined leaves did look somewhat like a headpiece. "Is it magic?" he asked disbelievingly. If this crown was real, did it mean a king who'd owned it truly did exist as well?

All this time, all this suffering, all his doubts . . . had the quest been real all along? Did the Sleeping King really wait for them to wake him? Was there hope for a different, better future? The idea unfurled within him like a banner, waving strong and brave in a freshening breeze. New strength coursed through him as he stared down at every perfect leaf of the Sleeping King's crown.

Rosana reached out to touch the crown reverently. "It must

be magic. How else would living leaves survive down here in this darkness?"

Eben added, "Not to mention, each leaf is unharmed and tipped in gold. No normal leaf would survive being painted in molten metal. Those should have shriveled and died from the heat. That must be worth a fortune."

"Sell it we do not, merchant!" Sha'Li snapped.

Funny that she, of all of them, would be first to dismiss the option of profiting from this extraordinary find.

Will did a double take as he noticed something odd in the dim shroom light. A gray outline was visible upon the lizard-man girl's right cheek. It looked like a crescent moon criss-crossed by an eight-pointed star symbol. Where had that come from? In another time and place he might have stopped to ask. But as it was, he merely murmured, "Now what?"

They all looked at one another blankly. After a moment Raina began walking around Gir'Ok's corpse once more. "It has to be here," she muttered. "Another clue."

Stubborn girl. Wasn't the Sleeping King's crown enough?

Cicero observed, "We could wander around this place for weeks and never find everything it conceals. We are missing something."

Raina picked up the hem of her white skirt and reached out to rub Gir'Ok's armor. Sha'Li leaped forward quick as a cat between Raina and the nearest hanging roots and cursed as a half-dozen thorns shot her in the back.

"Oh! Sorry," Raina murmured. "Good stars above, Sha'Li! What happened to you?"

Will looked over sharply at the lizardman girl and belatedly noticed that she looked like his mother's pincushion. Dozens of finger-length thorns stuck out of her hide.

Raina reached forward to pull one out, but Cicero grabbed her wrist quickly. "The thorns are poisoned. I am wearing gloves. Let me get them." Raina yanked her hand back, and Cicero commenced carefully pulling the thorns out of Sha'Li and laying them aside.

When the task was done and Sha'Li's colorful cursing had subsided, Raina said, "Can we cut away the roots from Gir'Ok's chest? I think I see something interesting."

Eben did the honors while Cicero with his sword and Sha'Li with her claws beat off the roots that would have attacked the jann. In a few minutes Gir'Ok's chest cavity came into sight. Or, rather, a leather breastplate, inlaid with another round gem to match the one in Gir'Ok's circlet, covered the crumbling ribs of the remains. A raised series of ridges embossed into the leather formed the shape of a stylized eye with the gem at its center. It stared back at the party balefully.

"Creepy how it watches you," Rosana muttered.

"Maybe it's not watching us," Raina murmured. "Maybe it's looking at something. After all, his hand was pointing up at the crown."

As one, the group turned to follow the unseeing gaze of that giant eye across the chamber.

Rosana whispered, "I think I see something moving over there—something big."

Will replied in a hush, "I saw it, too."

Sha'Li's claws extended with a faint slithering sound, and Will, Cicero, and Eben followed suit, brandishing their swords. They crept forward in a tight cluster toward that hint of movement. A bulky shadow moved across the faint glow of the mushrooms and they all froze.

Sha'Li hand signaled for the rest of them to hold still while she investigated. Cicero signaled something back to her and the lizardman girl nodded. She peeled off to the right while Cicero slipped off to the left.

Rosana eased up next to Will's side, and he felt her trembling against him. A desire to put his arm around her, to draw her close for comfort, struck him. But until they knew what that . . . thing . . . was he needed to keep his hands free to fight. He glanced down at her reassuringly and noted that Rosana's hands were glowing in the folds of her skirt.

Cicero and Sha'Li returned far too quickly for Will's peace of mind. Cicero reported, "There's a magic circle of some kind. Inside it is a gigantic mottled gray wolf with two heads."

"A two-headed wolf?" Will echoed skeptically. Such things did not exist! They were the stuff of hearth tales designed to scare children into staying inside at night.

Sha'Li nodded. "Dangerous, it looks. But unable to leave the circle, I think."

Raina whispered, "Can we go around it?"

Will stared at her. "Why would we want to do that? Better to avoid two-headed wolves, completely, I'm thinking."

"Gir'Ok's eye looks in that direction. Whatever we seek must lie beyond the circle and the wolf . . . wolves . . . wolf."

Stars, he hated it when Raina was logical like that.

Cicero whispered, "The circle does not go all the way to the wall on the left. I think there is a narrow path around it. We would have to hack through some roots. Beyond the circle there is a dark patch in the cave wall where no mushrooms grow. It is perfectly circular in shape."

"A door, mayhap?" Eben asked.

"Maybe." Cicero shrugged. "It is worth investigating."

Rosana whispered, "And you're sure this wolf-creature cannot leave the circle?"

Sha'Li answered, "A path is worn in the floor around the perimeter of the circle as if the beast prowls it."

They eased forward and to the left with Cicero in the lead. Having to move so slowly through the jungle of roots was maddening to Will until he heard the deep, rasping breath of something *huge* in front of them. Abruptly his feet wanted to drag even more slowly than before.

"There," Cicero breathed.

Will looked where the elf pointed and his mouth fell open. It was indeed a two-headed wolf. It stood half-again as high as a man and easily twice as long as one. Its coat was shaggy and gray in the dim light, its paws the size of Will's head. And its fangs . . . both mouthfuls of them . . . were nearly the length of his sword and gleamed dangerously. Only a shockingly thin band of light in the dirt of the chamber's floor separated them from the monstrous creature.

Worse, the beast was awake. Its yellow eyes glowed in the darkness and its heads swung side to side, independent of each other. Both noses took long, loud sniffs. Abruptly the beast growled, the vicious rumble striking terror into Will's heart.

Snarling, the beast rushed the side of the circle nearest them. Surely a mere line in the dirt could not contain such a monster! Will braced to die as the beast slammed into an invisible barrier, snapping and snarling in impotent fury. Spittle frothed at its mouths as the wolf lunged again, clawing at the air before it in rage.

Will eyed the narrow strip of dirt bounded on one side by the magical circle in the dirt and a wall of mushrooms on the other. *Great. Don't cross the circle or else be torn to shreds. Don't touch the mushrooms or be rendered mentally incompetent and likely to wander into the aforementioned circle. Don't overly disturb any roots or else be squeezed to death . . . or, if really unlucky, shot with poison thorns.* "This is going to be fun," he breathed.

"Hey. You've got a staff!" Raina retorted. "I glow in the dark in this white tabard and have no magic."

She is out of magic? Dismay coursed through him as Cicero picked his way precariously through the narrow alley of safety. If the agile elf barely made it through there how were the rest of them supposed to make it? Will had been counting on Raina's nigh unto endless reserves of healing magic to fix whatever injuries they incurred in this hall of horrors.

"Landsgrave Hyland? The battlefield? Remember?" Rosana murmured to him. "She wiped herself out. It will be at least sunset on the morrow before her energy stores renew themselves."

He rolled his eyes as Eben commenced the treacherous walk past the narrow spot. He stumbled and nearly fell into the circle and staggered back into one of the fungi. Only

Cicero lunging forward and yanking him down to the ground prevented Eben from charging the wolf in the circle and being torn to shreds. The party waited in tense silence while Cicero wrestled the jann for several long minutes until the hallucinogen wore off.

Rosana went next. She was small and agile and only had one tense moment when the wolf lunged at her skirt which had apparently crossed the margin of the invisible magical barrier. She barely managed to yank it back in time to keep the beast from snagging it and dragging her to her death.

Raina went next, and her White Heart tabard snagged on a root, which promptly wound itself tightly in the fabric. Raina was forced to pull out her boot knife and saw painfully slowly through the tendril of root. But finally, she was free and continued on.

It was his turn. Why did his body have to go all weak and uncooperative on him just now? *Bloodroot,* he warned, *I need my strength.* Stars, he hated sharing his body with another spirit!

He followed the course the others had taken but nearly lost his balance as the wolf lunged at him, snapping and clawing mere inches from his face. The fetid odor of its breath nearly knocked him over as the wolf opened its gigantic maw, displaying dozens of deadly fangs that could no doubt rip a man in half with ease.

Finally, the circle began to curve away from the wall, and he had a few more inches in which to navigate his way forward. And then he was beside the others. While Sha'Li brought up the rear, making the traverse look easy, Will looked around. Eben had moved over to the circular dark patch on the wall and was studying it intently.

"Over here!" the jann called.

"Keep your voice down!" Will snapped.

"Why? The wolf's wide awake."

True. In fact, they had to raise their voices to be heard over the steady stream of whines, growls, and snarls emanating from its dual heads.

"It's a door," Eben announced. "And this carved bit here, in the middle, is a lock. It has slots for two keys. I do not know what these other markings are."

Will stared at the intricate spider's web of lines crisscrossing the surface of the door. It looked like wood, but so smooth and black and polished that he might mistake it for stone at a glance.

"The workmanship is amazing," Eben said in awe. "It must be priceless."

"If we find the king and wake him, I promise you can carry out this door and sell it, merchant," Will said.

Eben grinned over at him. "I would have to wrestle Sha'Li for it first, and she would kick my arse."

"Forget that not, Rainbow Boy!" Sha'Li snapped.

Rosana and Raina grinned. The moment of levity was interrupted, though, when Sha'Li announced, "Yonder are the keys."

Will looked where she pointed and groaned. The wolf was standing on its hind legs and pawing some fifteen feet in the air, which was why Will caught the faint glint of metal at its neck under its furry chin. Will looked closer and spied a circlet of metal around each of the beast's necks. Collars.

"Let me guess," he asked. "Keys hang from each collar."

"Aye," Sha'Li answered grimly. "Fast I am, and the keys I can steal. But the beast I cannot defeat."

Cicero commented, "You need a distraction. But what on Urth could keep that thing occupied for long?"

"Can we even enter that circle?" Rosana asked.

Raina fielded that one quickly. "Almost all magical and

ritual circles can be crossed unless they are specifically designed to prohibit a being from entering or leaving. Like Fido, over there. Circles do not act at all like magical walls, which prevent all beings from crossing them."

Cicero shrugged. "Even if we could get into the circle, that beast would rip us to shreds."

"Maybe not," Eben piped up.

Will stared at him, startled. "What do you have in mind?"

"I can turn to stone temporarily. The beast will not be able to do me harm while I concentrate. If I were to get it to bite me and be forced to hang on, could you get the keys, Sha'Li?"

The lizardman girl stared at him with new respect. "Steal them I could."

Eben nodded and stepped up to the edge of the circle. He made fists of both hands, pressed the knuckles together in front of his chest, and closed his eyes. He appeared to take a deep breath, and then the color of his skin did indeed begin to change in the sickly light. The multicolored whorls and swirls from before faded, leaving a dull, gray sheen over all of his exposed skin.

"I am ready," Sha'Li announced.

Eben stepped forward. His foot passed easily through the circle, and the beast wasted no time grabbing Eben's leg and yanking him up high into the air. The jann brought his fist down hard on the beast's second nose, and immediately the second head grabbed him by the arm. The two heads shook savagely, doing their best to tear Eben in half. But to no avail.

Sha'Li moved fast, leaping onto the beast's belly and climbing its fur like a flea. The beast shook itself as if registering her presence, but then Eben swung his free fist again and clobbered the beast in the side of a head. The wolf's answering snarl was muffled as it chewed fiercely on Eben. But Eben's concentration held.

"The first one I have," Sha'Li grunted. Will had to admit, she was very good at her roguing craft. Of course, if she hadn't been quite so light-fingered and hadn't stolen Bloodroot's disk in the first place Will wouldn't be hovering on the verge of death now.

Will held his breath as Sha'Li clung to one of the wolf's necks precariously. The beast was still whipping its heads from side to side in an effort to dismember Eben. The lizardman girl leaped and Will gasped as she flew from one neck to the other.

The wolf let go of Eben's leg to snap at its other neck where Sha'Li now clung.

"Watch out!" Raina shouted.

Sha'Li swung below the neck fast, barely missing being the wolf's lunch. The beast yelped as it bit itself and lifted the head still holding Eben's arm high while the other mouth snapped ineffectually at the neck where Sha'Li now hung. The lizardman girl actually used the jann as a shield, ducking behind his flailing body as the wolf tried to grab it with its snapping jaws.

Cicero managed to get in a good blow with his bow across the top of the wolf's free nose that made it yelp and then snarl. Distracted from Sha'Li, it grabbed Eben in its second mouth around the middle of his body. Will couldn't imagine the crushing power of those massive jaws. But so far, the stoneskin was holding

Will held his breath as the lizardman girl hooked her feet in the beast's metal collar and hung by one hand from a fistful of fur, using her free hand to fiddle under the beast's chin.

"Got it!" Sha'Li crowed in triumph. She swung down, using the momentum of the wolf's thrashing head to throw her toward the edge of the circle. As the free beast lunged at her with its mighty paws, Sha'Li rolled fast, crossing the thin light barrier at the last possible second before the beast's claws snagged her. The wolf's body smashed into the barrier and the beast screamed in pain and fury.

Will looked up at Eben. "Okay. You can come out now."

"Umm, small problem," Eben grunted. "If I drop my stoneskin, the wolf will crush my arm."

Rosana frowned. "So keep your stoneskin up until the wolf tires of trying to eat you. When it lets you go, you can walk out of there."

Raina spoke up. "It doesn't work that way. Keeping up a magical effect like that takes intense concentration. Eben can only do it for a few minutes at a time if I had to guess. And that wolf doesn't look even close to bored with the idea of killing him. Eben's stoneskin will fail before that beast turns him loose."

"She's right," Eben grunted.

From behind them Sha'Li announced, "Fit the keys do. This lock I can open."

"Not yet!" Will exclaimed. Stars knew what threats lay beyond that circle of strange wood "First we have to free Eben from this cursed beast."

"Can we distract it?" Rosana asked practically.

Cicero bent down, picked up a clod of dirt, and hocked it at the beast's nose. It ignored the missile completely. "I do not think so," Cicero answered grimly.

The wolf lay down, covering Eben's legs with its giant paws, and commenced chewing on the jann with his free mouth as if he were a bone. A tough, annoying bone.

"This is not good," Eben said in tones of rising alarm.

"Sha'Li, can you go back in there and distract the wolf?" Raina asked doubtfully.

"I doubt it. I got past its guard the first time because both mouths were full with Eben. But the wolf's free head is tracking me now."

Will looked and noticed that indeed the wolf's free head was keeping a sharp eye on the lizardman girl, its jaws open and waiting for her to make a mistake.

"Can you reach the edge of the circle, Eben?" Raina asked. The jann's legs lay not far from the glowing line of safety.

"Maybe I can get a foot across, but that's about it," the jann grunted. He sounded like he was about at the end of his ability to hold the stoneskin.

Will suggested, "What if we lasso Eben's foot, and, the instant his stoneskin comes down, we yank him out of there? Maybe the wolf will be surprised enough by his change that it won't bite down on him right away."

Nobody had a better idea.

"I can't hold up my stoneskin much longer," Eben panted. He struggled for the next few seconds to angle himself until one of his feet rested outside the circle. It was the best the jann could manage. Using a length of thin, tough root that Will chopped off fast with the dagger Ty had given him so long ago, he lashed the root quickly around Eben's boot.

"Everyone, grab Eben's leg or the root," Will instructed.

"It's fading," Eben gasped.

"On the count of three, let it go. That's when we all pull," Cicero bit out. "One. Two. Three!"

Will jerked as hard as he could on the root-rope as the beast lurched and both heads whipped toward Eben, jaws snapping together like great bear traps. Eben let out a horrible scream. The group crashed backward as Eben slammed into them, narrowly avoiding hitting the mushroom wall. They all rolled away from the glowing fungi fast as Eben let out another horrific scream. Hot blood shot everywhere.

Raina and Rosana leaped forward, working feverishly and speaking in half sentences.

"Know regeneration?"

"No."

"Stop the bleeding."

"Got it." A pause while Rosana poured magic into whatever great injury they worked over. Will had no wish to see it. Then the gypsy muttered, "Bandages. My pouch."

Raina rummaged around at Rosana's hip and emerged with a roll of white cloth. All the while, Eben moaned in agony. The sound was terrible to hear. Will watched the two healers work in grim silence for several minutes.

Then Raina announced, "I think we have another problem."

"Beyond his arm being ripped off?" Rosana echoed in dismay.

Will lurched. He moved to stare around Rosana and, sure enough, there was only a heavily wrapped stump where Eben's right arm should be. He shuddered, nauseated at the gruesome sight.

"Smell his breath," Raina said.

Rosana sniffed and then sucked in a sharp breath of her own. "What is that?"

"Plague. Magical and powerful," Raina said low.

"What does that mean?" Cicero asked tersely.

"The wolf's bite was diseased. Eben will die by degrees over the next few hours or days."

"But you can cure disease, can't you?" he demanded of Raina.

"When I have magic, I can." She stared down at Eben, who was writhing in mindless agony beneath Sha'Li's restraining hands. "But I don't know if I could cure that. It's empowered magic. Very nasty stuff. It would likely take a ritual to fix.

And yes, I know how to cast the ritual, but I don't carry around the scrolls or components for such things."

Will grimaced. Cicero's words from before they entered this place a lifetime ago echoed through his head again. *One of us must live to reach the king.* The true meaning of that phrase struck Will now like a physical blow. Was this really worth it? Eben was horribly maimed and dying. Who would be next?

He looked up at the door in hatred. Why did it have to be him to do this thing? Why all of them?

He opened his mouth to tell the others they should turn around and go back. Find a cure for Eben. Leave this madness and be safe. He would go on alone. But just then Sha'Li cracked open the circular door. As she did so the lighted circle behind them, the one containing and restraining the two-headed dire wolf, blinked out of existence. With a vicious snarl the beast charged straight toward them.

Anton wanted nothing more than to roar in fury and frustration, but to do so would call down more of those twice-cursed orcs upon him and his men. It had to be here, somewhere close by, whatever it was the Boki guarded so fiercely and his enemies coveted so greatly. The concentration of orcs was growing steadily greater and the fight the greenskins were putting up growing steadily more desperate. Oh yes. He was very close indeed to their treasure.

But there was one monumental problem with that. If he wanted to be the first to lay his hands on it, he was going to have to move to the front lines and actually lead his men. In the point position. Where it was dangerous. He might be lethal throwing his gas poisons, but he could only deliver one at a time. If several orcs attacked him simultaneously from close range, he was dead.

Something rustled just ahead and he froze, his heart pounding like a smith's hammer. The only thing he hated more than being afraid was being deathly afraid. Something grabbed his right elbow from behind and he jumped straight up in the air. He realized only belatedly that it was just Krugar. Snickers erupted and then abruptly cut off behind him. *Whoresons.* He glared daggers at Krugar's men, daring the next one to make a peep and live.

"My lord, I smell Boki," Krugar announced. His nose wrinkled in distaste. "And they stink of fear."

An anonymous voice muttered, "Ain't no Boki stinkin' like 'at. 'Twere our guv—"

Anton whipped around. "Who speaks?" he hissed.

Guilty—and fearful—silence hung thick in the air of a sudden. He glared at Krugar. "Pick one of your men at random and kill him."

Krugar nodded impassively, his expression stony. He turned and gave his men a long, assessing look. His gaze settled on one of the soldiers near the back of the line. Krugar stepped forward, sword raised.

"I didn't say it!" the soldier exclaimed. "It was 'im!" The soldier pointed at one of his comrades.

Without breaking stride Krugar continued forward, merely changing his target. His sword swung in a fast, deadly arc. It sliced neatly through the culprit's neck at a shallow downward angle. Anton watched in detached fascination as the head, still upright, slid off the neck and then tumbled to the ground, rolling to land at his feet. Blood spouted everywhere, drenching his boots in hot, sticky fluid. Shock registered in the single eye staring up at him.

Krugar remarked dryly, "Apologies, my lord. It was a clumsy blow to send the head and blood in your direction."

Krugar snapped an order over his shoulder, "Remove the corpse from the governor's sight!"

Distaste for the messiness of all of this rolled over Anton. He preferred to pull unseen strings and manipulate his subjects from afar. Dirt and blood and sweat were so . . . messy. It was all well and good to quash unrest, but this was too direct for his taste. Maximillian was thinking too small with his whole "stop any rebellion before it starts" mentality. Better to let a little upheaval unfold, and all the more profit to be had in crushing it.

Why merely stamp out a nascent rebellion when a person could give it a little rein and let the instigators draw out other rebellion-minded people into the open? Better to let a few more fish swim into the net before yanking it out of the water.

Besides, if there were reports of unrest brewing in the colonies he could claim a need for more resources to fight it. More gold to line his pockets. And if he heroically stopped a rebellion on behalf of the Empire he might even win enough status and goodwill from Maximillian to earn a higher noble title. He nodded in satisfaction. It was a much better plan than merely finding and killing local instigators, now.

And in the meantime, he was going to find the secret Boki treasure and not report a single copper of it to the Emperor. Too bad Aurelius and his faithful lapdog, Tiberius De'Vir, weren't here to lead him straight to the treasure like they had the last time.

A twig snapped nearby and he whirled, fist cocked back, poised to throw the gas globe in his hand. Krugar and his troops whirled as well, weapons at the ready. They waited for long seconds for a horde of Boki to burst out upon them, but nothing moved.

Anton lowered his trembling hand, realizing in alarm that

he'd been clutching the gas globe so tightly he could've accidentally broken it and released the instant death gas poison within it upon himself.

Gads, but he hated all of this being one with nature. He hated creeping around in the dark. He hated being drenched in cold sweat. He hated whoresons who thought to beat him to his treasure and take it for themselves. And most of all, he hated orcs. When he found their cursed treasure and took it for himself he was going to send an army into these woods to annihilate every last one of the greenskins.

And then, let rebellion come.

But first, the treasure.

G o, go, go!" Will yelled at the others as he and Cicero dived for Eben to throw him through the doorway. They leaped through the portal and the three girls were already throwing their combined weight against it, hauling it ponderously shut.

The great metal latches clanged into place just as something huge and furious slammed into the other side of the wooden panels. The door shuddered but held against the weight of the great wolf. "Praise the Lady," Will panted. "That was close."

"Uhh, Will?" Rosana muttered. "We may have a small problem on this side of the door."

He straightened from Eben's prostrate form and looked around quickly. A thin mist hung in the air, and wherever this place was, it was daylight bright. How that could happen underground he knew not. And then he spied what alarmed Rosana. A gigantic, green hulk was advancing toward them menacingly through the fog.

The hulk stood thrice as high as a man, moved upright on two legs, and had a massively thick, powerful torso. The creature appeared to have four arms, all of which brandished weapons. The beast was hideously ugly. He had green, bumpy skin, but a deeper, clearer shade of true green than the orcs, who tended to muddy and yellow tones. He had tusks as well, bigger and more of them than an orc. His facial features were heavier and less humanoid than the Boki's. He wore a loin-cloth, a belt, a necklace, and a crude headband of some sort.

"What is it?" Raina breathed in dismayed awe.

"Troll," Cicero bit out. "Big one."

And without Eben, they were down a critical warrior to take on such a creature. Will swore under his breath. Would this nightmare never end? He looked around fast. No apparent obstacles. Even footing on level ground. No cover that he could see.

Sha'Li said low, "If behind him I can go, more effective I shall be."

Cicero nodded. "We'll distract him for you. C'mon, Will. Let's go beat us up a troll. He won't be fast, but he'll be strong. Really strong."

"Right. No problem. That thing's huge." *Maybe we could annoy him to death.*

The kindari shrugged. "It's us or him. As for me, I'd rather live."

Cicero was right. No sense moaning about the inevitable. They were going to have to defeat this beast or die trying. Will reached for the sword he'd picked out of Raina's hands earlier but, eyeing the beast's tough hide, thought better of it. A blade would not give Will any great advantage against this mountain of gristle.

Not that a staff would fare any better. But at least he might be able to channel a little magical damage if he got lucky. If only he fully understood how he'd used the staff that night in Hickory Hollow to channel magical damage and could call it forth on command! Aurelius had talked a lot of theory at him about intent and concentration, but he'd had precious little real experience with channeling magic.

He took up the old threshing stance Ty had drilled into him over the years that gave him the best balance on his feet.

The beast roared something incoherent that sounded like a trollish insult and charged. Cicero slid over to take on the two left-side arms while Will slid to the right.

Raina crouched protectively over Eben, although Will doubted she could do anything to protect the jann other than use her body as a shield. Rosana planted herself in front of Raina, a short sword in her left hand and magic glowing in her right.

"Save your power for healing!" Will called to her as he moved closer to the pair of troll arms.

At least the creature had only one head. Mayhap the three of them could take turns attacking when his attention was distracted elsewhere.

For her part, Sha'Li eased off to one side unobtrusively. There were no physical objects for her to use for cover, though, and the bright white mist did nothing to conceal her black form. It would fall to Will and Cicero to keep the troll's attention entirely on them while she positioned herself for a back attack.

To that end, Will shouted a stream of insults as he charged forward to engage the beast. He ducked the troll's first weapon, a club ponderously swung at him, and raised his staff to meet the second weapon, a hybrid axe with a long, narrow blade that lay close to the shaft for nearly half its length. No tree cutter, this axe. It was purely a weapon for killing.

The murderous blade shaved a thin curl of wood off Will's staff below the metal-clad part as it sliced down the length of his weapon. The power behind the blow nearly swept Will off his feet. Had he not deflected it down his staff's length like that, he'd have been thrown a dozen feet or more.

Cicero grunted from nearby. This creature had to be four or five times as strong as a man. No way would they be able to defeat him by brute force. Panic began to vibrate in Will's gut. And with it came magic. It crackled through his fingers and down the shaft of his staff in golden bolts of energy.

The next swing of the troll's mighty club passed by, and Will lunged in close behind it, jabbing the tip of his staff at the troll's hip. Will connected with the solid wall of flesh, and the force damage crackled off the staff and into the beast. The troll lurched in surprise and gave a roar of fury.

Sha'Li jumped onto the beast's back and stood on the troll's belt while she raked the back of his head with her right claw. The troll spun around to face his new threat. He nearly threw off Sha'Li, but she clung tenaciously to the monster's back.

Will darted in to pummel the beast's ankle, knee, and ribs, anywhere bones might rest close below the surface of his hide.

Cicero leaped in as well and took a swipe at the beast's hamstrings with his sword, and the troll's leg partially collapsed. He staggered and took a backward swipe with his lower arm that forced Cicero to jump back with all the speed and agility the elf had.

Will walloped the knee before him with his staff, willing magical energy into the blow as well. Only a weak bolt of golden energy flowed down the staff, but it was enough to make the troll howl. Will was appalled as he darted backward to see the wound left by Cicero's sword already healing over.

Rosana called out frantically, "He spontaneously heals himself! We must figure out what flavor of magic will kill him!"

As if they had multiple flavors of magic to choose from.

They had Will's force magic and Rosana's curse magic. Period. He caught sight of Sha'Li drawing her claw back and taking a big swing at the beast's neck. Her blade appeared to bounce off the beast's hide, but it caught the troll's necklace of teeth, claws, ears, fingers, and various other body parts from Will knew not what.

The necklace clattered to the ground, and as it did so Will noticed something odd. It was as if the troll's facial features became slightly less distinct.

"Did you see that?" Raina cried out.

"Yeah," Will grunted as that cursed club swung at him yet again. He dodged, but the troll adjusted his strike at the last minute and Will took a glancing blow on his left shoulder. It spun him all the way around and he staggered, trying desperately not to fall.

Raina cried out, "I think his spirit is tied to his items! Remove his clothing and weapons and you may weaken him!"

Rosana interjected quickly, "Can we leave the loincloth on him?"

Will's humor faded as the beast half-turned toward Will to follow up on his advantage, and Cicero lunged in to stab at the beast's momentarily unguarded side. The blade lopped a few pouches off the troll's belt, but did no other damage.

And yet the color of the troll's skin faded somewhat and the wartish bumps upon him diminished in prominence. Raina's theory seemed true.

Will and Cicero darted in and out frantically trying to remove other clothing and personal items, but the troll seemed to have caught on to their tactic.

"What's happening?" Sha'Li hissed from her perch on the troll's back.

Raina replied urgently, "He's fading whenever he loses his stuff. Can you cut his clothing off from where you are?"

"Easier said . . ." Sha'Li ducked the wicked axe blade the troll winged over his back at her. It skimmed down her scaled back harmlessly. ". . . than done."

Frustration coursed through Will. If only he could shape his magic into something truly powerful. But Ty had never deigned to teach Will how to do any real battle magic spells, or perhaps never dared. In his anger at his own failings, he became aware of more golden energy dancing down his staff. *Huh.* Was it somehow tied to his emotions? He had no more time to consider it as the troll's battle-axe whooshed toward him.

Will threw up his staff to meet the blow wishing with all his being that he could disarm the troll of his cursed axe. His staff connected solidly with the axe, and then all but flew out of his hands. His fingers went numb from the force of the blow, but the axe went flying and the troll scrambled after it.

Cicero and Sha'Li leaped on the troll's distraction to go after his possessions. Sha'Li knocked the headband off the troll's head while Cicero sliced at the troll's belt with his sword. As the accoutrements fell to the ground the troll almost melted before them. He was still a troll, and he still towered many feet over Will's head, but his features became indistinct. It was as if Will looked at a generic representation of a troll and not an actual troll.

Regardless, the creature still had that giant club and was still swinging it wildly back and forth. Will had to fall flat on his face to avoid the low swing that came at him next. He was so weak and exhausted that jumping back to his feet was more than he could manage. If only the wasting sickness of Bloodroot hadn't sapped all his strength!

He looked up in time to see a black, shiny claw come around the troll's neck from behind and slice across his throat hard and deep. Will expected a gush of blood, but instead a gray, almost gaseous substance spurted from what should be a mortal wound. The troll staggered toward Will and looked to be in grave danger of falling on him. Raina leaped on Will, grabbed his shoulders, and rolled away frantically, dragging him with her as the beast toppled over at their feet.

"Thanks," Will panted.

"No problem," she panted back.

Cicero plunged his sword into the beast's chest and called urgently to Sha'Li, "Get that club out of his hand!"

The lizardman girl had no sooner knocked the club loose than the troll began to . . . dissipate. His body turned to smoky wisps and blew away like fog. Will stared in disbelief. He'd felt the blows of that club, the strength in those massively muscled arms . . . and yet they were disappearing like mist burned off by the morning sun.

"What the—" Rosana started.

Eben surprised Will by croaking weakly, "Phantasm."

Raina stared at the jann. "That was a dream creature? Does that mean we are in the dream realm?"

Eben's gaze shifted to the door and Will's gaze followed.

Cicero murmured, "I know that silk. It comes from Vaestros. He is the dream-weaver spider. Scion of Zinn, the Great Spider."

Raina moved to the panel and traced the intricate web of lines etched into the wood panels with her fingers. "Then this must be a dream catcher," she whispered.

Will had heard of those. His mother used to hang one in the window if she left it open at night. She'd told him it kept phantasms from creeping in and stealing his dreams. He looked back quickly at where the troll had fallen. Phantasms were *real*? Hearth tales described them as denizens of the dream realm and capable of taking on the appearance of anything or anyone.

Will turned back to Eben to ask him what else he knew of this place, but the jann's eyes had lost focus and were glazed over with pain once more. Will noted that the jann's normally colorful skin was going grayer by the minute. They had to find healing for him, and soon.

"What is this?" Sha'Li asked. She'd moved far away enough from where the troll had fallen that she was starting to be swallowed by the mist. From what Will could make out of her, she appeared to be staring hard at something.

Cicero moved toward her and Will joined him. He stopped short, though, when he spied the wall before them. It was solid but violently uneven. It looked made of crystals colored yellow and white and orange and red and even shot through with a translucent hint of blue in a few places. All the colors of fire. As soon as he thought of that it dawned on him that the crystals looked exactly like flames, made substantial and frozen forever in a dancing pose.

"It looks like crystallized fire," he murmured.

"And forms an arc around us," Raina announced.

Sha'Li commented, "I'll bet there is no opening in it and we are trapped." She took off to the right, following the wall into the mist.

"Feel like going the other way with me?" Cicero muttered to him.

"Why not?"

They followed the curving wall of crystallized fire back to the stone and dirt wall containing the circular door. They followed it to where the girls crouched beside Eben, checking his bandages.

"How is he?" Will asked.

Raina answered grimly, "He worsens rapidly."

"We have to get out of here and find him help soon," Rosana added in dismay.

Will squeezed her shoulder comfortingly, and Rosana rose to her feet and turned in to his touch for a quick hug as Sha'Li materialized out of the mist.

"No opening," the lizardman girl announced in disgust. "Too slippery and tall it is to climb. Smash through it we must."

Rosana frowned. "It's not a good idea to destroy a magic thing. Bad things happen when magic gets set free."

"A better idea you have?" Sha'Li snapped.

Rosana huffed in frustration. "No."

Will shared her sentiment. He didn't like the idea any better than the gypsy, but what choice did they have? They couldn't just sit here and wait for Eben to die. Time was of the essence and they needed to press forward.

"We cannot leave him here, alone," Raina announced, gesturing down at Eben, who appeared to be barely conscious. "I will take him back to the surface."

Once she'd put on the White Heart tabard she'd seemed to embrace its tenets with gusto. Still, he hated to split the party.

Rosana piped up, "You go forward, Raina. I will take Eben back. I have a little healing for him."

"I have no healing at all!" Raina protested.

"You have knowledge. You go on."

Raina's spine stiffened stubbornly, and Will sensed an argument forthcoming. They had no time for this!

Thankfully, Cicero laid a hand on Raina's arm, which seemed to shock her into silence. "Rosana is right," the elf murmured soberly. "Let her go. She, too, is bound to heal the injured and cure the sick. And she can defend herself . . . after a fashion."

The fight went out of Raina's spine and Will sighed in relief. He nodded his gratitude at Cicero, but the elf merely gave

Will a worried look back. They were sending the last of their healing out of the cave. It was a desperate measure. But they had no choice. The clock was ticking.

Rosana declared firmly to Raina, "This is your quest. Not mine. I'll go back with him."

"What of the wolf?" Will demanded. No way was he letting her go back into that chamber of the dead if the wolf was still loose.

"Haven't you noticed that it is no longer attacking the door?" Raina asked.

"Mayhap it's lying in wait for someone to come out. All the more reason for Rosana and Eben not to go out there!" he retorted.

"Let us take a peek and see if we can ascertain where it is and what it's up to," Raina suggested.

Will sighed and gave in for lack of any better idea. "Fine. Sha'Li, if you could unlock the door, I'll have a look."

Cicero, Sha'Li, and Raina put their shoulders to the door in preparation to shove it shut if the beast should attack. Will pulled on the heavy portal and it slid open a few inches. No attack. He opened it a bit more. Still nothing. Finally, he opened the door far enough to peer very cautiously around the panel.

He straightened in surprise and pushed the door open a little farther to look again. "The circle is back up and the wolf is within it." He moved out of the doorway far enough to hock a clod of dirt at the beast's nearer head. The dire wolf lunged at the circle, snapping and snarling, but did not pass through it. "It's caged once more," Will announced.

"There you have it," Rosana replied in relief. "Eben and I will make our way back to the Boki and Balthazar. They will heal Eben."

Will doubted the White Heart man would have any mana left by now, either, but kept that pessimistic prediction to himself. Eben needed the hope. "All right," Will conceded reluctantly. "Be careful. Do not disturb the roots nor touch the mushrooms—"

"I came in the same way you did," Rosana chided gently. She laid her palm briefly on his cheek and whispered, "Come out of this cave alive, Will Cobb. I would take it much amiss if you did not return."

He smiled quickly and nodded his promise to do so; then she was spinning away and thrusting her shoulder beneath Eben's armpit. "Let us go, Rainbow Boy," she said jauntily.

So brave she was. Plucky. His heart swelled with affection for her. She was the kind of girl his mother would approve of. His mother, who'd sacrificed her life that he might complete this quest. The great, circular door closed behind Eben and Rosana. *And now they were four.*

Will said heavily, "If we are going to do this, we might as well do it quickly. Any ideas for passing over, under, or through yon wall?"

"Use your staff," Raina suggested. "If you can channel some magic down it, breaking the magic of the wall may not destroy you."

He grimaced and gripped the weapon hard. His strength was waning and with it his ability to call magic. A thin stream of gold wandered down the staff. He took a deep breath and thrust it at the wall.

The crystals reverberated from his blow, but did not shatter or even appear scratched. Oddly, though, the vibration continued on for longer than it should have, chiming loudly, almost like it summoned something.

"Not good," Sha'Li said under her breath, taking a step backward.

"Not good at all," Cicero echoed, backing away from the wall.

Will looked up, and out of the mist above the wall a creature was materializing. It looked like a drawing Will had seen once of a great sea monster, except atop this one's massive body were multiple massively long necks, each capped with a vicious reptilian-looking head and rows of glittering, deadly teeth. It was *huge*.

"What. On. Urth. Is. That?" Raina asked in awe.

Sha'Li answered shortly, "Hydra."

Will added, "And this one is not wearing clothes and items that might weaken it to remove."

Just then one of the four waving heads opened its mouth and blasted a gout of fire over their heads.

"A fire hydra make that," Sha'Li corrected herself.

"As if that makes it any better?" Will exclaimed.

"No choice we have, Will Cobb," Sha'Li declared. "Proceed we must until succeeding or dying, yes?"

Without bothering to wait for an answer the lizardman girl charged forward bravely, claws before her, for the belly of the beast. It wasn't a bad idea in theory. The hydra's underside appeared to be the only part of the creature not covered in red shiny scales the size of a soldier's shield. And perhaps Sha'Li thought her own scaled hide would protect her from the monster's fiery breath. Will had to admire her directness and complete disregard for personal safety.

But as she neared the hydra one of the heads swooped down and exhaled a gout of flame that completely engulfed the lizardman girl, blocking her from view. Only the roar of the fire, ten times as loud as any smith's furnace, filled the air. It went on for many long seconds, freezing Will's feet to the ground in horror.

When the creature lifted its head, its fiery attack finished,

Sha'Li was no more. Where she had stood there was only a small pile of gray ash flecked with black. The casual thoroughness with which the beast had eradicated her stunned Will speechless. They would never be able to defeat this beast. They were finished.

Raina slapped a hand over her mouth and didn't quite succeed at containing her sob of grief and horror.

Will looked shaken to his core, and even stoic Cicero looked dismayed. What on Urth were they to do next? Her selfish quest to break the curse upon the women of her family was not worth all of this death, even were she not wearing the White Heart colors.

"Obviously, we cannot fight it," Will declared with patently false confidence. "We have nothing left to fight it with. We must think of a way to pass by it."

But how? She was completely out of ideas. Out of courage, out of belief in the rightness of what they did. The cost was too high. It was time to end this madness. She opened her mouth to say so but was forestalled by the hydra making a strange, rusty sound. One of the heads had opened its mouth, but instead of fire, oddly formed syllables of . . . speech? . . . emerged.

She strained to understand the beast, making out something along the lines of, "It is in the air we breathe, the earth we stand on, the water we drink, and the fire that warms us. It is always and forever, never waning, never fading. It is what you feel in your heart, what you know in the deepest part of our spirit, and what you believe in your wildest dreams. Only its purest form can tame me."

Will breathed, "Have I lost my mind, or is that thing trying to talk?"

"You have not lost your mind," she muttered. "I think it's a verse of some kind."

The head repeated the taunt, "Only its purest form can tame me."

"Or a riddle?" she added doubtfully.

There was something familiar about the words. Their rhythm. The singsong flow . . . She could not place it.

Will lurched beside her all of a sudden, as if a blast of memory had just slammed into him. He said in wonder, "My mother said something like that to me just before—" He broke off, then continued painfully, "Just before she and my father died protecting me."

"What else did she say?" Raina asked urgently. "Think, Will. It is important."

The hydra head repeated the cryptic description and Will blurted, "Magic. It's as pure as lady's breath. Legend says the Green Lady's final breath upon the land became a flower."

Raina didn't have the slightest idea what he was talking about. She looked around frantically for flowers, however. Within view, a few small, nondescript flowered weeds grew.

Beside her, Will muttered to himself, "Lady's breath. Lady's breath . . ." He cast his gaze around the scattered weeds. He dashed over to a small, unassuming clump of plants bearing simple white flowers and pulled off a handful of stems.

"You're going to fight that monster with flowers?" Cicero asked skeptically.

Will waved the flowers at the beast, and Raina privately thought he looked passing silly. Not to mention nothing happened.

The beast repeated the verse. And it sounded noticeably impatient. They were missing something.

"Are not offerings to fire creatures usually burned?" she suggested.

Will blurted, "Of course. This plant is used for incense, sometimes. Quick. Flint and steel, Cicero."

The elf pulled out his fire stones and in a minute had a small twist of dead grass burning on the ground before him. Will touched the lady's breath to the small flame. A thin line of smoke curled up from the leaves, its distinctive sweet aroma filling Raina's nose. A feeling of wellness washed over her. All three of them waved their hands to waft the sweet smoke toward the beast.

The hydra dissipated almost the same way the troll had, but this time fading into a cloud of burning flames. But no heat radiated from the misty fire, which was large enough to engulf a cottage. Nonetheless, the three of them fell back against the dream catcher door, cringing away from the spouting blaze.

As the fire billowed above them like a length of silk in a strong wind, the tinkling of crystal shattering echoed all around. The great flame had pushed back the mist enough for her to see the wall of crystallized fire crashing down all around them.

As the gust of smoke and fire dissipated, something red and glowing became visible on the ground where the hydra had lately stood. It was slightly larger than her fist and looked like a lump of molten glass fresh from a blast furnace.

It ebbed and flowed like a living thing, but never lost its spherical form. It was shot through with the same colors of fire of the wall and hydra. It pulsed, almost like a beating heart.

As the white, featureless mist began to close back in around them, Raina took a single, curious step closer to the glowing . . . thing . . . before a piece of the mist broke off from the rest and engulfed the glowing gem. The mist rushed away on a gust of wind that she saw but did not feel. And where it had been, the fiery gem was gone. Eerie, childlike laughter, as of a little girl giggling, echoed around them, coming from every direction at once.

"What on Urth was that?" Will demanded.

They all looked at one another and shrugged. "Sha'Li would be furious that the mist grabbed her treasure, though," Cicero observed dryly.

Will grinned reluctantly, and Raina followed suit.

As if any of them except the bold lizardman girl would have been willing to touch that strange, pulsating crystal, let alone attempt to carry it out of here. A moment of silence came over all of them as they silently mourned Sha'Li's death. Raina fervently hoped the lizardman girl would resurrect successfully. Her surly demeanor had rather grown on Raina. She would miss Sha'Li if she failed to return from beyond the Veil.

Raina already missed the irascible lizardman girl's presence. Who'd have guessed Sha'Li would have grown into her actual friend somewhere along the way? In the meantime, they must not let Kendrick's, Eben's, or Sha'Li's sacrifices be in vain. They *must* complete this quest.

If only they knew how much more stood between them and the Sleeping King. Raina was exhausted and Will looked ready to drop any second. Cicero didn't look much better. Her magic frustratingly was refusing to regenerate at all. She knew such things took time and rest. But she really had need of at least some of it, now. Not that needing it helped bring back one bit of it.

Will and Cicero were nicked and bloody, the tips of their swords all but dragging in the dust with their fatigue. How were any of them going to find the strength to confront any more challenges? Of course, the answer to her question was obvious. They simply had to find a way. *Everything* depended on it.

She sighed and asked, "Are we ready to move on?"

She watched in admiration as Cicero squared his shoulders resolutely and turned to face forward. *Thank the stars for the elf.* He might not be the most powerful fighter ever, but the kindari's spirit was indomitable. If he had the strength to keep going, then so did she.

Will trod forward warily and she followed suit. Given how each guardian of this place seemed progressively bigger and stronger, she deeply dreaded what came next. They'd gotten this far on little more than luck. And given Sha'Li's fate, their luck had apparently deserted them now, too.

Raina did not want to know what awaited them ahead in the mist. One thing she was sure of: death was in the air.

W hat are they doing?" Aurelius whispered to Selea.
The carnage in the clearing below was hard to fathom. Anton and his men had attacked in force, but the Boki had responded with a heroic stand worthy of epic poetry to commemorate it.

More Boki were streaming into the bowl-shaped vale, and Anton's mercenaries were being cut down like wheat before scythes. They literally lay in piles on the ground, and no attempt had been made to revive or heal them. Coldhearted whoreson, Anton.

Selea rose from his crouch, peering over a pile of rockfall.

The nulvari whispered back, "Anton gathers his men for a new attack. They must have spotted the entrance to the tunnel."

Aurelius would not have spotted the entrance had Selea's sharper eyes not picked it out earlier. Anton's scouts must have found it in the midst of the fighting and managed to report back to him. Aurelius stared down at his nemesis, surrounded tightly by a phalanx of the Kithmar's most brutal warriors.

The tragedy was that, even if someone did kill Anton, the Emperor would merely replace Constantine with a governor who might even be worse. The only answer was to eliminate the entire Empire. But it was a task so huge, so daunting, Aurelius could hardly imagine where to begin. If this gambit failed . . . if the Sleeping King was destroyed . . . all hope would be lost. There must be *something* he and Selea could do to help De'Vir's boy and his companions.

At his feet, Anton's forces pushed inexorably forward, forcing the Boki lines to give way. If Anton reached that tunnel . . . "Do you still refuse to involve yourself in this fight?" he demanded of the nulvari assassin beside him. Without question, Selea could turn the tide of this battle.

Selea threw him a deadly look. "Do you truly wish to see what happens when you force a nulvari to choose between two conflicting oaths?"

"Some things are bigger than your cursed honor, nulvari. And those children inside that cave succeeding in their quest is one of them."

Selea stiffened and fury radiated off him, but he made no other response. Which was probably why Aurelius lived to draw his next breath, much to his surprise.

A noise carried to their position that he did not need Selea to interpret. Shouting. Reinforcements were arriving from beyond the ridge to their left, roaring battle cries. But for which side did they fight? Agonized impatience flooded him as he waited to see the allegiance of the warriors who would top the ridge.

"If you will not do what must be done, I will." Aurelius ground out. "Move aside, Selea."

The nulvari threw Aurelius a look that he had absolutely no idea how to read. Maybe that was icy rage. Or mayhap disdain. Or mayhap resignation. Or mayhap all three. Selea spoke urgently. "Your thinking is too direct, old friend. This is Anton we deal with. Misdirection is required, and so far, the Boki have failed to do so."

"What do you suggest?" Aurelius snapped. At least the nulvari was engaging in strategic thinking about how to defeat Anton. It was better than nothing. But it still was not action to help De'Vir's boy.

Instead of answering him, Selea stretched out on top of the pile of rocks they currently hid behind and rolled silently down the far side. As Aurelius watched, shocked, he spotted Selea crawling off into the trampled brush. What was that wily assassin up to?

Whether or not Selea would actually enter the fight when the moment came was anybody's guess. But at least he'd made his old friend do more than just observe from the sidelines.

Stay alive, younglings. Everything rests upon your shoulders now.

Raina peered ahead into the mist, but saw merely featureless white upon white upon white. They began walking forward. *At least we made it away from the door, finally.* But gradually, as they walked, the mist began to turn gray, and then a faint green. She began to notice texture underfoot. As if the hard ground gave way to softer soil. And then to a suggestion of grass.

"Are those trees?" Cicero murmured, peering off to the side hard.

They stopped walking and she thought she might just be able to make out the vertical columns of tree trunks.

"Reminds me of the Wylde Wood in a bad fog," Will murmured. "I do believe you are right, Cicero."

A few more minutes of walking brought them into a wooded valley. The path was narrow and bounded on each side by trees and lush ferns. It was unlike any forest she had ever seen, beautiful and verdant. Tyrel was an arid land prone to stunted trees with leathery, dust-grayed foliage.

"Have you ever seen a place like this?" she asked Cicero.

He nodded, "Aye. Long ago. In an unsettled land far west and south of here, untouched by the Kothites. But never have I felt such . . . life energy . . . flowing through a forest."

Now that he mentioned it, this place did throb with life. It was invigorating. Refreshing. It almost seemed wrong to experience this place after the terror and death their companions had so lately faced.

Cicero froze ahead of her, listening.

Now what? She froze as well, straining to hear what his sharp elven hearing already discerned. *There.* A rhythmic breathing sound, as of something huge bearing down on them hard.

Will lifted his staff defensively and Cicero's sword rose to the ready as a tall, rapidly moving shape rounded a curve in the path ahead and charged them. As her companions braced for combat she cried out, "Wait! The black lion's head!"

Will planted his staff on the ground, and Cicero lowered his sword as a massive black lion, bigger than a bull, bore down on them. A man rode on its back, one hand twined in the creature's bushy black mane. The other hand held a giant spear, longer than the mighty beast he rode.

Poised on the balls of her feet in preparation to dodge the massive, speeding apparition, Raina awaited its approach.

"Whoa, Aegenis," the rider ordered his lion firmly. The beast planted his hind paws and scrabbled with his front claws to slow himself. Clods of dirt and turf flew up as the lion slid to a stop no more than two of the knight's spear lengths from them.

"Who goes?" the knight demanded. "Dost the Elder send thee with tidings? And the Chosen One? How dost he fare?"

"The Elder?" Will asked cautiously.

"Aye. He who bears the symbol of the seeing eye."

"Gir'Ok?" Will responded.

A snort of derision. "Gir'Ok served the Elder, but is no more. He has not lived in more years than have count. Identify yourselves or die, strangers!"

Raina dived in. Perhaps she would fare better with him than Will or Cicero. She asked formally, "Do we have the honor of speaking with the Laird of Dalmigan?" She did not recognize any of the many blazons crowding his chest, but their sheer number indicated that they'd likely found the laird himself.

Sure enough, the knight bowed over his lion's neck with a flourish and replied courteously, "Fair demoiselle, I am he. Prithee, mightest thou honor me with thy name that I might praise thy beauty?"

"I am Raina. Uhh, Initiate Raina of the White Heart." She stumbled a little over the title. Its source was still too painful to speak of calmly. "And there are my companion, Will Cobb, and Cicero, my friend and protector."

"Come thee not with the blessing of the Elder, then?"

"No, my lord. Many people have helped us and led our footsteps to you, but sadly, not the Elder."

"Whence knowest thee my name, then?"

"A dryad named you, sir. She told us to seek you out, in fact."

"A faerie, is it? Are times so desperate, then, that the fae courts involve themselves in the affairs of men?"

"I fear it may be so, Lord Dalmigan."

The knight dismounted and knotted his reins around the animal's neck. "Rest, Aegenis," he murmured.

The Laird of Dalmigan was heavily armored in plate mail from neck to ankles. He carried a massive gold shield with a black lion's head embossed upon it, and the sword at his hip hung nearly to the ground. He appeared to be a human of early middle age, but vigorous.

His keen gaze took in Cicero quickly and then settled on Will. As she watched, the knight's eyes widened in surprise. He blurted, "You bear a portion of Lord Bloodroot's spirit?" Dalmigan looked impressed. "Thou hast not wandered upon this place by chance, then, hast thee?"

Will answered, "No, sir. It is not chance that brought us here. It has been an arduous struggle to find this place."

"Long have I guarded these lands, and thou beist the first to come upon it. Only those with nothing can pass into this place."

"With nothing?" Will quieried.

"Correct. No magic, no skills, no strength. Only spirits washed clean of all urthly abilities may pass into this place."

Raina laughed painfully. "I am sorry to say that describes us to a tee. I am completely without magical energy. My friend Will hovers on the verge of death and is all but without the ability to do more than walk. And my boon companion, Cicero, looks so exhausted he can hardly hoist his bow, let alone swing his sword."

"Just so," the laird nodded. "Hadst thee attacked me, or possessed the ability to attack me, I would have slain thee where thee stood."

"How long have you been here, good sir?" Raina asked curiously.

"Time has no meaning for me in this dreaming land. Others tell me thousands of years have passed away in the living lands."

Thousands of years he'd been here? He looked mighty well preserved for someone so ancient.

"Why comest thee, young sir?" the knight demanded of Will.

"We have been sent to find and wake the Sleeping King."

Dalmigan's eyes didn't so much as flicker in surprise. "Why seekest thou His Majesty, then?"

Will jumped on that. "You do not deny his existence?"

"I guard his existence, boy. Wherfore wouldst I deny it?"

Excitement leaped in her belly to match the exultation on Will's face. "Where is he?" Will demanded. "Let us finish this thing."

Stubbornness flashed in the knight's eyes. Raina stepped in quickly to ask more diplomatically, "What must we do to prove our good intentions to your satisfaction, Laird Dalmigan?"

"Tell me why thou wouldst wake the king."

A frisson of excitement passed through her, as if the finger of fate drew lightly down her spine. Close. They were so very close, now. "Is this king of yours also called the Mythar by some?"

"The Lord High King of Gandamere is also ruler and protector of the natural realm within his lands. I do believe the title the forest creatures gave him is Mythar."

She'd never heard of a kingdom of Gandamere, but now was not the moment to split historical hairs. She was not in a hurry to tell this noble knight that her reason for being here was to take some of the king's magic to solve her own problem. Her instinct told her Laird Dalmigan would not be impressed. She glanced sidelong at Will. "Perhaps you would like to explain your reasons for waking the Sleeping King?"

Will answered slowly, "I will try. I first heard of the Sleeping King from my father. We were under attack by Boki and—"

Dalmigan interrupted, exclaiming, "The Boki still live?"

"Aye," Will answered. "They guard the chamber which leads to this place."

Raina added, "And they ferociously guard the secret of the king's existence."

Dalmigan nodded in satisfaction as Will continued, "My village was under attack by the Boki, and my mother and father made a last stand to let me escape. Just before the Boki closed upon them, they told me of their quest to wake the Sleeping King and bade me to finish it in their stead."

"And why didst thy parents seek to wake His Majesty?" Dalmigan prompted.

"For everyone. For Urth. The Empire of Koth has crushed the spirit of its subjects and systematically destroys the land. The Emperor has ruled for so long that few remain who remember a world without Maximillian. A world with hope. Where the word 'freedom' had meaning. We need the Sleeping King to lead us out from under the Kothite fist before all hope is lost."

Dalmigan studied the three of them long and hard. At length, he finally said, "This is a worthy reason. However—"

They never got to hear Lord Dalmigan's "however," for a new sound intruded upon the silence. It was as if a great ship approached across unseen water nearby, its sails snapping and flapping in a stiff wind.

The knight cursed under his breath and barked at his lion,

"Under the trees, Aegenis! Hurry!" The lion's head whipped up and the animal bolted for the cover of the trees.

Cicero's sword whipped up and he bit out, "Who comes, knight?"

"If yon glimpse of green lies not, Hemlocke sends her minion to investigate. If you have drawn *her* attention, then the three of you obviously must finish your quest."

"Who is Hemlocke?" Raina panted as they ran for the cover of the spreading tree boughs beside the path.

"The Green," Dalmigan replied low and hard. "She durst not come herself. It would draw too much attention to this place. But apparently, she would risk sending one of hers to destroy thee. We must ascertain how dangerous a creature she has sent. 'Twill tell us how great a threat she doth deem thee."

Within moments a huge, winged creature came into sight. Covered in scales with leathery wings, it looked reptilian. *Draconic.* Great stars above, was that a dragon? Raina stared in disbelief. She'd read of many wondrous creatures in her studies, but of them all, the one she'd never *dreamed* of seeing was a dragon.

"Drakken," Dalmigan breathed. "A great one. Well then. A most serious threat Hemlocke perceives in thee."

Will and Cicero looked as astounded as she. Drakken were mythic creatures, said to be made of Dragons much like a golem, and only slightly less powerful than their legendary creators. Or so the hearth tales went. To her knowledge, no living being had seen an actual dragon in ages. Literally, *ages.* And a single age was measured in thousands of years.

"I will face this beast in combat, young adventurers, whilst thou flee with all haste. I shan't defeat the beast, but mayhap I shall grant thee time enough to reach thy destination." He whistled low for his lion, which crashed out of the underbrush momentarily. "To my death I ride, then. These thousands of years as guardian of the grove come down to this moment. For the promise of hope, I ride!"

"Wait!" Will blurted as the knight made to mount his steed. "Where is the king? Where do we go from here?"

"All paths lead to the king, boy. Make the leap of faith!"

The drakken, no doubt attracted by their sound and movement, swooped down in a deadly dive toward them, its great, toothed maw open hungrily. Dalmigan spurred his lion, and the pair charged forward to meet the drakken in mortal combat.

"C'mon!" Will shouted at Raina as she stared, aghast.

"We can't leave him!" she cried. "He's sacrificing himself for us!"

Cicero gave Raina a light shove. "Go. I will stay and help him as best I can. We will fight the drakken together."

Not Cicero. Not her stalwart Cicero on whom Raina could always depend. It was too much. This final blow would break her. "I cannot lose you!" she cried.

"I have resurrected before and will do so again. Go!" he shouted over his shoulder as he ran forward to meet the beast at the knight's side.

Will grabbed Raina's arm. "Do not let their sacrifices be in vain. Let's go!"

Heartbroken, Raina did the only thing she could as the huge creature's leathery wings blotted out the light above. She turned and crashed after Will into the forest. The sounds of battle and terrible, inhuman screams erupted behind them.

Creatures began to materialize out of the trees around them, clawing at them as they tore past. Grasping fingers reached for her ankles to trip her, for her eyes to blind her. She ducked and tripped, staggered, and righted herself, but always she ran on. In spite of his weakened state, Will's longer legs allowed him to keep ahead of her as they fled through the rapidly darkening forest.

They ran flat out for several minutes before Will's steps flagged. She pulled up beside him and gasped, "Where are we going?"

"He said all paths lead to the king. We'll find a path and follow it."

And as if his words conjured one, a narrow path opened up before them, running at an angle to their current direction. Will veered onto it and Raina dived after him. Mist began to form around them, but not the bright, white fog of before. This cloud was dark and cloying, smelling foul and sliding unpleasantly across her skin.

The last, dim green light of the forest gave way to the colorless darkness of the gloaming around them. Worse, that awful flapping sound became audible again. She dived under what might be some sort of overhang beside Will, and they plastered themselves close to the cold, slimy surface at their backs. A gigantic shadow glided low overhead.

"Is that the same drakken from before?" she whispered.

"I don't think so. This one looks even bigger than the last one."

She hoped desperately that the appearance of this second drakken meant Cicero and Dalmigan had survived and somehow defeated the first one. "We must hurry," she breathed. "If these monsters are going to keep coming until we find the king, Cicero's and Dalmigan's lives depend on us."

The weight of so many's blood upon her hands sat almost too heavy on her spirit for her to go on. But that weight was precisely the reason she *must* go on.

The second monstrously huge drakken flew out of sight into the putrid cloud and Will nodded at her. They took off running again with renewed desperation. Invisible hands continued to reach for them, and she spied a massive cliff rising ahead. It was smooth and gray and looked formed of a great upheaving of granite from the earth.

They pulled up short before its base, staring up at the smooth, several-hundred-foot-high wall.

"Can we climb it?" she asked doubtfully.

"No handholds. It might as well be a mirror, it is so smooth. Not a chance we can scale it." Will looked left and right, and the wall stretched away from them in both directions. "We cannot go back. The drakken are behind us. But I do not see a way around this."

Screeches and clicks and all manner of inhuman noises rose up behind them, closing in fast from all directions. The creatures of the darkness were almost upon them and would tear them limb from limb.

She said, staring at the cliff, "Dalmigan said to make the leap of faith."

"What does that mean?" Will snapped.

"Are we supposed to . . . leap up the cliff?" she asked slowly.

"It is no crazier than anything else in this place—four-armed trolls and crystal fire, hydras and immortal knights," Will grumbled. "How do we do this?"

They both took an upward leap and landed unceremonious on their feet.

"Umm, problem, Will."

He turned around with her to face outward. Monstrous creatures were materializing rapidly out of the dark mist. And they looked dangerous and hungry. It wasn't just their bodies these creatures wanted to consume. It was their spirits they drooled for. Will swung his staff in a desperate arc around them both, and it passed harmlessly through the insubstantial bodies of the mist creatures.

But as she looked on, the forms were becoming more solid. Something sharp raked across her arm, and it *hurt*.

Will winced beside her, his staff flailing wildly. "There are too many of them," he panted.

He sounded as exhausted as she felt. They had nothing to use to defend themselves. They were going to die if they didn't get out of here *soon*.

"We have to *believe* it will work and . . . jump!"

"On the count of three?" Will gasped.

She cried out, "One. Two. *Three!*"

They jumped a little ways in the air and landed right back on their feet once more.

"Nothing happened!" Will cried. "Now, what?"

She was out of ideas. Despair washed over her, threatening to crush her. They could not endure so much, sacrifice so much, come so close to their ultimate goal, only to fail now.

There *had* to be a way. But what? Dalmigen said to take a leap of faith. What if the leap wasn't the thing? Maybe faith was the key.

She spoke quickly as the hideous creatures around them became fully corporeal and solid, snarling and snapping as Will flailed at them with his staff. "Not only do we have to believe this will work, we have to have faith. Hope. Reach deep inside yourself and know in your bones that everything will turn out all right. After all, we've made it this far. Right?"

"Right," he grunted as he fought off the claws and snapping jaws closed in on them from all sides.

"We've got this," she encouraged him. "Let's just try the leap one more time."

CHAPTER

31

Anton screamed in fury as the trees came alive, branches whipping, and vine creatures began to writhe around them. Now the forest itself helped guard the Boki treasure? Its worth must be beyond compare! Furthermore, he must be almost upon it.

Another cursed wave of Boki charged over the ridge ahead. Would they never stop coming? But then he spied the composition of the charge. Female orcs. Old orcs if their heavily scarred hides and faded coloring was an indication of age. And half-grown orcs. Their women and children had been hiding beyond that ridge all this time? And they chose to engage now? His eyes narrowed as he stared at the charging Boki. They were not brilliant military tacticians. But they might send out a charge in a last-ditch effort to destroy him as his men approached that ridge.

Abruptly it was imperative that he see what lay beyond the hill. For surely that must be the spot where the treasure was hidden. This vale must have been the anteroom to the actual treasure chamber, obviously. But now that the Boki force was losing, they made a desperate charge with the last defenders. Oh yes. He must get over that ridge right away.

Krugar yelled for his men to fall back and take up a

defensive formation, but Anton shouted to belay that order and bellowed for his men to charge.

The orcs had moved together in front of him, shoulder to green shoulder in a veritable wall of living rage. But he could meet rage with rage, by the stars.

How dare they turn on him like this? Where was the Ki' with whom he had his arrangement? The Boki were supposed to put up token resistance out here. To retreat from this battle and then invade the outlying holdings of his most irritating landsgraves in a few weeks! Of course, he had neglected to mention his own plan to loot the Boki treasure horde in the process. But still. They'd had a cursed deal! No surprise the green whoreson was absent, the traitorous cur.

If he couldn't find the Ki', how was he supposed to get the supplies he needed to make what the assassin, Kane, required to finish off his greatest enemy? Nothing was going as it was supposed to out here. And that would *not* do. It was time to change the rules of the game.

He was within a single arrow's flight of perhaps the greatest acquisition of his life, and no orc army was stopping him, curse it. He swore viciously under his breath. He would kill every last one of them himself if he had to.

"My chest of globes!" he yelled. He was not a master alchemist for nothing. If they wished to taste of gaseous death, so be it. A soldier ran up to him with the wooden chest and its rows of carefully padded glass globes within. Enraged, he stormed forward, globes filled with expensive and rare death gas poison dancing in his fingers.

H ere goes nothing," Will muttered resolutely. He stopped swinging his staff and let down his defenses entirely. Hope. Faith. He could do this.

He closed his eyes and imagined himself flying up the cliff face like a giant hawk. And jumped as hard as he could.

A yank at the back of his tunic snapped his eyes open. The crowd of dark creatures had fallen away beneath his feet, howling in outrage. The cliff face was soaring past and he looked down in shock as he realized he no longer stood on the firm ground. *What on Urth? Or rather,* not *on Urth?* He looked up and saw the white-feathered belly of a massive bird. He craned his head to see more and spied the short, hooked beak of a falcon.

A quick glance to the side revealed Raina's clothing firmly clutched in the talons of a giant white falcon as well. A look of wonderment filled her face as she smiled over at Will. For all he knew, the birds were going to fly them well above the ground and drop them to their deaths. But at this point, there was not a thing he could do about it. He took his cue from Raina and looked around, determined to enjoy the flight before dying.

How many times in his life he'd enviously watched birds soar through the skies he could not count. Everything looked different from here. Smaller. Less important. But at the same time, the wider world seemed grander. Limitless.

How long the flight lasted he could not say. But he memorized every second of it to remember in his old age . . . if he managed to survive. The top of the cliff slid past his feet, and a thick carpet of green stretched ahead of them on this new plateau. If possible, it was even more lush and verdant than below the cliff.

His falcon folded its wings all of a sudden and dived for the trees like an arrow, but ten times faster. It was terrifying and exhilarating seeing the ground fly up at dizzying speed. Wind tore through his hair and made his eyes water, and he'd never even imagined moving so fast, let alone ever hoped to experience such a rush.

At the last possible second before slamming into the ground the falcon threw out its wings and back-flapped with a furious motion. The talons at his back released and Will fell. He had just long enough to brace for a horrible splat before his feet hit the ground. He landed in a deep-kneed crouch, and Raina did the same beside him.

Alive. They were still alive. Raina gasped beside him as if that happy circumstance surprised her, too.

He looked around at where the birds had chosen to deposit them. It was a grove. The most beautiful grove Will had ever seen, in fact. More so even than the dryads' grove. The grass was a perfect carpet of emerald, with patches of wildflowers nodding here and there, vibrant in their garments of pink and yellow and blue and white. Dappled shade dotted the edges of the glade, although from whence came sunlight to make shade Will had no idea.

But then a movement caught his eye. It was a man. Standing on the far side of the grove, contemplating a small, brown sparrow as it sat in a tree and serenaded him for all it was worth.

The man was tall. Broad. Built like a warrior. Fair skinned but dark haired. As he turned his head to stare at them, Will noticed the elven shape to his ears. Not that there was any doubt that the elegant features and noble bearing were anything other than elven.

"I thought he was supposed to be asleep," Will muttered.

"We don't know if that's him," Raina muttered back.

The elf turned fully to face them. Surprise definitely lit his dark eyes, but he said courteously, "Long has it been since I was graced with new visitors, even longer still since one who does not bear the mark of Zinn came here."

Raina bowed her head in the elven way, a show of respect for an elder. Will did the same beside her. After all, his mother hadn't raised him to be a total barbarian.

"I am called Raina."

The elf cocked one brow and returned their nods regally. The fellow certainly looked like a king. And then that perceptive gaze was aimed at Will. "And you, young sir? Who are you?"

"Uhh. Will. Will Cobb they call me."

"But that is not your true name?" the elf asked sagely. "There is power in a true name. One must be cautious in giving it away to strangers. You are wise to be circumspect."

"And you, sir?" Raina asked breathlessly, "Might we inquire as to who you are? We have come a very long way on an arduous journey seeking one such as you."

Rosana moaned as she sensed yet another spirit hovering nearby seeking resurrection. Sha'Li's body had finished forming moments ago, and the lizardman girl was just blinking back to consciousness.

Sha'Li jerked upright to a seated position and Rosana fell back off her heels and rolled onto her back clumsily as she threw herself clear of Sha'Li's wildly swinging claws.

"It's just me, Sha'Li," she complained. "Put those things away."

The claws slithered into the lizardman girl's fists and disappeared from sight. "What hap—" Her face clouded with memory. "Oh. The hydra."

"A hydra?" Rosana squawked. How was Will ever going to survive a hydra that could kill tough-skinned Sha'Li? Terror gripped her until she almost could not sense the new spirit. *Please, please, let it not be Will.*

Eben, who had already finished resurrecting, passed Sha'Li some clothes from his pack. Not that she needed them particularly with that covering of scales all over her body.

Nonetheless, Sha'Li snatched at the garments when Eben held them out to her over his turned shoulder.

"I sense another spirit," Rosana announced.

Eben groaned. "What do you suppose is happening to them in there?"

Sha'Li answered promptly, "Dying, I expect. Huge was the fire hydra and with ease did it kill me."

Rosana restrained the wail climbing her throat and turned to the new spirit, which felt male. *Oh no.* "Do you wish to be resurrected?" she asked the disembodied spirit aloud.

A strong affirmative feeling rolled off it.

She closed her eyes and began the focused concentration of a field resurrection. She could help a spirit find its way back to this realm, guide it in re-forming a body for itself, but she could not restore its skills. Only time and rest would do that.

Slowly, slowly, the spirit hovering close coalesced a body from the life energy she drew together and offered up to it. The process took nearly a quarter of an hour, but gradually a male body formed. Eben and Sha'li covered it with the lone blanket Eben happened to have in his pack when they fled Anton's forces so long ago. It felt a lifetime away from this place.

She worked over the body for a few more minutes and facial features began to form.

Cicero.

She sagged in relief that it was not Will, and then guilt assailed her for being glad the kindari had died instead. Like Sha'Li, Cicero woke up fighting. His fists flailed around him, but Rosana was prepared for it this time and knelt well back from him as he revived.

"And what happened to you?" she asked as soon as the elf was fully in possession of his faculties.

"Drakken," the elf bit out.

Great galloping curses. Will and Raina must surely be dead by now. It was only a matter of time before their spirits showed up here, too. And she was running dangerously low on magical energy to help them.

The elf gestured for them to come closer. As he and Raina trod the short grass, Will restrained an urge to kick off his boots and tickle his toes in it. The beauty of this place was more soothing than a hot bath or his mother's hugs.

A great sense of well-being washed over him and he stumbled in shock. After feeling so terrible for so long, he'd forgotten what healthy was like. Stars above, he'd felt *awful* before. But now . . . now it was as if a great weight had been lifted off of him. Lightness and vigor surged through his veins and into every corner of his being.

He followed Raina's lead and stopped a respectful distance from the elf, who was even taller and more powerful up close. He'd never seen an elf of such proportions. His mother had been slight, light boned. Even Cicero, a warrior among his kind, was shorter than Will and leaner. But this elf made Will feel puny.

Their host smiled a little, but the expression did not touch his dark, fathomless gaze. "I am but a dream. A memory of one who once was but is no more."

"Are you a phantasm, then?" Raina asked in disappointment.

"No. I am not an elemental of Nod."

She replied, "I do not understand. You stand there, and smile, and speak of your own will. How can you be only a memory?"

"This is the dream plane, child, and this is not my physical body. This is merely a dreaming manifestation of my true self."

"What of us? Are we merely dreams, too?"

Will frowned. He didn't think he was a dream. He would never have dreamed the monsters they'd faced in this place on his own.

"Nay, you are here both in body and spirit. You traveled to this realm through physical means, yes?"

"Yes, sir."

Will had no great interest in the metaphysical properties of this place. A cure for that which was killing him lay more heavily on his mind. He said a touch impatiently, "We have undertaken a very long, very difficult journey, and several of our friends have died that we might reach this place. Your name, sir. Might we have it?"

"I am called Gawaine. Gawaine Valshaer."

"Do you, by any chance, go by the title of the Sleeping King or the Mythar?"

"I had not thought of being called the Sleeping King, but I suppose it is possible such a name could have been given to my memory. As for the other, I was called Mythar in my day."

Will's heart leaped. They'd done it! They'd found the Sleeping King! Raina glanced over at him, her expression jubilant.

Triumph. Relief. Sadness. They all raced through him. Ahh, if only his father had lived to see this day. Mayhap Ty finally would've been proud of his son.

"And why have you come on your long and arduous journey to seek me then, my young visitors?"

The elf moved to a moss-covered bier about the height and length of a fainting couch and sat down upon it with easy grace. Raina surprised Will by crouching down to run her hand through the cool green blades. She smiled up at their host. "Would you mind if I sat here?"

Gawaine smiled, the warmth of it reaching deep into his calm gaze. "Not at all. Be at ease in this place. You are safe."

Will flopped down beside her and finally did give in to the urge to unlace his boots and kick them off. The greensward was even cooler and softer than he'd expected. He felt young and carefree all of a sudden.

"I ask again. Why have you come here?" Gawaine's tone was still pleasant, but Will sensed a bit more steel beneath the question this time as the elf studied them.

Will looked over at Raina. She was the one skilled with words and pretty speeches. She glanced at him and he nodded at her.

She spoke carefully. "We have come in search of a legend. A sleeping king who is said to wait in the long sleep of the eternal dreamer to be woken once more."

Gawaine's gaze went closed of a sudden. Not exactly hostile, but cautious. Will thought he heard the elf breathe under his breath, "It is time, then?" But Will wasn't sure.

Raina continued, "The Sleeping King is said to be an elf. One who lived long ago and who fell in battle. He was put into a magical sleep of some kind and laid to rest until Urth and its creatures should have need of him once more."

Gawaine frowned openly now. "And you have determined that now is the moment? In what way does Urth need this king?"

Raina searched for words. "A . . . blight . . . has come upon the land. It is slowly killing Urth and its people. Those who know of it fear it. They believe that, if it is not stopped soon, Urth will be too far gone to recover."

Concerned now, Gawaine asked, "What is the nature of this blight?"

Raina looked over to Will for help. He gave it a try. "The Kothite Empire stretches across the whole of Urth. They strip the land for its wealth and they unbalance the cycle of life and death."

Gawaine shrugged. "With time and care, that is easy enough to repair. Urth is a resilient place and tends to return to balance if left alone."

Raina dived in. "Urth's people have nearly forgotten what freedom means. What hope is. Many do not even know the words. How will balance be restored when they do not remember what it looks like?"

"Ahh. Now that is a problem," Gawaine murmured. "And how is this king of yours supposed to set that aright?"

Will answered, "By leading us to freedom from Koth, of course."

Gawaine made no reply to that. He merely stared off into space as if he had not a care in the world.

Frustrated, Will blurted, "He's also supposed to cure me of the poison that is killing me."

That got Gawaine's attention. "What is the source of your poison?"

Will opened his shirt and the elf king stared in open surprise. "I knew I sensed a familiar spirit. I just could not credit that a fragile human such as you could tolerate so powerful a being. Particularly a malevolent spirit of such magnitude."

Malevolent? That explained a great deal. He'd been right to despise Bloodroot, then. To blame him for not helping in key moments. For sickening him and not caring one whit about driving him to the point of exhaustion and even death.

Will poked at the cursed wooden disk burrowed into his skin. "This malevolent spirit is killing me. Can you remove it?"

"Young Will. If Lord Bloodroot wished you dead, you would already be dead. In point of fact, for you to have withstood his presence at all Bloodroot must have actively been working to keep you alive. Of course, you undoubtedly have a natural ability to channel magic and an affinity for the

Green as well, or even Bloodroot's efforts would not have saved you."

"Nonetheless, can you get rid of this thing?"

"That sliver of wood is no longer the issue. Even at a glance, I can see that Bloodroot's spirit is deeply entwined with yours. That is the crux of the matter. The more you drew upon Bloodroot's power and the more he manifested through you—which I assume you both did, else why would he have attached to you at all?—the more you were exposed to his curse. And the sicker you would have become."

"What curse?" Raina interjected.

"Bloodroot is—was—the embodiment of death and destruction within the Great Circle. Emotions such as hatred, fear, and rage were his tools. He was the dark force that balanced the lighter forces of nature. This is the curse I refer to. A heavy burden indeed for a young human to bear. But what he does here and now I do not know. Clearly, the Great Circle has been broken in my absence."

Gawaine sounded deeply distressed at that.

Raina must also have sensed the elf's disquiet, for she asked gently, "What was the Great Circle?"

"The Great Circle is the representation of the Green Throne. It is made up of the eldest of treants, the great beasts of Urth, and totem spirits. They maintain—maintained—the balance and looked to the well-being of nature on behalf of the Green Lady. Lord Bloodroot was one of them. But given that a piece of his heartwood resides on your chest, and his spirit within you, Will Cobb, I can only assume he has been destroyed. If that is so, then the Great Circle is no more." He added heavily, "The circle was my responsibility as Mythar to defend." Grief wreathed the elf's features. "Not only did I fail my people with my death, but apparently I failed the land as well."

"Would restoring the Great Circle restore balance to Urth?" Raina asked.

Gawaine shrugged. "I doubt it would be as simple as that, particularly given the scale of the destruction if Lord Bloodroot's current condition is any indication. For the task of repairing Urth to have fallen to children such as yourselves speaks of dire times indeed."

Will blurted, "My father passed the quest to me. He was about to be killed by Boki and it was his dying behest to me."

Gawaine merely nodded.

When Gawaine did not elaborate about the Boki, Will asked, "What can you tell me of this disk?"

"It is Bloodthorn wood. That is a piece of Bloodroot's tree, a piece of the heartwood from the exact center of the tree. Bloodthorn is renowned for its poisonous thorns, sap, leaves, and, of course, poisonous fruits if not prepared properly. Even the wood of the Bloodthorn bears traces of death and destruction within it that make for fierce weapons. Clearly, you have had excellent training to channel both its power and its darker emotions successfully. I would urge you to continue that training if you wish to retain the disk."

"Retain!" Will exclaimed. "It is my fondest wish to be rid of this thing and the spirit within it!"

"If that is your choice, Will Cobb, I will honor it," Gawaine replied gravely.

"Why on Urth would it *not* be my choice?"

"Unlike me, you are actually here in this place in totality, both physically and spiritually. This grove is designed to trap spirits, but with your bodies here, you can walk out of it if you choose. That is such a small piece of Lord Bloodroot's physical form that it could not carry his spirit out of this place were he disconnected from your body. If I remove that piece of him from you now, his spirit will be trapped here eternally with mine."

"What of me?" Will asked.

"Assuming that separating the two of you does not kill you, your body and spirit will return to Urth and you will go on as if nothing happened. The temporary health you are experiencing here will be fully restored to you back there. However, it is unlikely that Lord Bloodroot would ever be able to return to Urth."

Will failed to see the downside of that proposition.

Gawaine continued, "Make no mistake. This place may be beautiful, but it is my prison. And it will become Bloodroot's prison, as well."

"Why is that bad?" Will demanded. "If he is as malevolent as you say, isn't it a good thing to trap him here, forever?"

"Bloodroot represents part of the natural order of life. Dark though he may be, his is an important part of the cycle of life, death, and new life. If Bloodroot does not go back to the material plane with you, the Great Circle can never be reborn nor ever be complete."

"Which means what?" Raina asked warily.

"Which means my mother—the Green Lady, you call her, the essence of nature itself—will be weakened even more, and this Empire of yours will be able to gain a permanent foothold on Haelos. The Kothites will gain power over the living land itself."

"And if I keep this cursed disk upon my chest and Bloodroot's spirit within me?" Will asked reluctantly.

"There is a chance the Great Circle can be restored, and the damage caused by these Kothites to the land can be repaired. On a personal note for you, Bloodroot can teach you to be more than you will ever become on your own."

Will stared. He thought back to the extraordinary senses

Bloodroot had channeled through him. The extraordinary knowledge of woodcraft. The enhanced awareness of nature. His ability to speak with animals. The way the dryads deferred to him. All of that could be *his* and not just borrowed from the parasite within him?

Gawaine was speaking again. "Removing Bloodroot from you may kill you. If you die here—which means your body becomes separated from your spirit within this grove—your spirit will also be trapped here. Forever. It will bond to one of those trees over there, and you will never again see the young lady who inspires the deep feelings I sense within you."

Panic clawed at Will over the notion of never seeing Rosana again. He had to get back to her!

Gawaine continued, "Likewise, leaving Bloodroot attached to you will ultimately kill you when you return, unless you find a mortal cure for his poison."

Kill me? He was dying in truth, then?

"Frankly, I'm surprised you lived long enough to find me."

Will jerked his chin in Raina's direction. "Without her healing and the healing of another, I would already be dead."

Gawaine studied Raina intently for a moment, and then comprehension lit his face. "An arch-healer. Convenient that you two came together. Or mayhap not convenient at all. The fates do seem to have taken quite an interest in you two."

Raina answered quickly, "Not in us, Your Majesty. In you. Everything and everyone who has helped us has done so with the intent of seeing us wake you."

Gawaine was silent for a time while Will's mind whirled with the implications of the daunting future looming before him.

Eventually, Gawaine said gravely, "This must be your choice, Will Cobb. I will not tell you what to do. This time and these events are your destiny. What you choose, the world you make, is your responsibility."

"Do you know the cure for Bloodroot's poison?" Raina asked quickly.

Gawaine nodded. "I can tell you the ingredients and how to make the antidote. But I cannot manifest it outside this grove. My power is completely contained within this place. It is why I can make your friend healthy and whole, here. But he will return to his weakened state as soon as you leave my presence. You will have, at best, a short window of time upon your return to cure him."

Will was still stuck on the elf's previous words. It was his choice? Shock rolled through him. Since when did any peasant under the fist of the Empire have a choice in any but the most menial decisions?

This *king* would let him make so momentous a decision by himself? Surely Gawaine wanted him to take Bloodroot back. To repair the Great Circle. And yet the king did nothing to sway him, merely answering his questions and laying out the facts that Will might choose for himself.

It was a staggering exercise in freedom.

As an unfamiliar sense of power, of control of his destiny, coursed through him, Will suddenly understood his parents. *This* was what they fought for. This was what they had died for. And this was the quest they had set him upon. They wished for all people to have *this*. The rightness of what they did—what *he* did—sank into his bones and became a part of him in that moment. With it came certainty. His path in life was set, and now it remained only for him to walk it.

"Can you do it?" he asked Gawaine. "Can you free us all?"

Gawaine stared at him long and hard before finally answering slowly, "I cannot promise to succeed. But I can promise to try."

A few yards away, a tree suddenly began to move as if a strong wind rattled its limbs. Will jumped up in alarm, for not a breath of air stirred across his skin. Raina did the same beside him. But Gawaine remained seated as if nothing were amiss.

"Ahh," the elf murmured, "Bloodroot manifests. I thought he might once he realized doing so would not kill you, here."

Will stared as the knots and whorls in the tree bark shifted subtly, taking on the vaguest of humanoid aspects. It was not exactly a face, and yet the suggestion of eyes and nose and mouth appeared upon the wood.

The mouth cracked open slightly, revealing raw, green pith beneath the bark almost like the inside of a mouth. A deep, gruff sound grated painfully upon Will's ears, vibrating through his body until he had to restrain an urge to move away from the discomfort of it. "Willcobb."

"Bloodroot?" he blurted. "Is that you?"

Gawaine commented, "This is somewhat closer to his true form than he is capable of on Urth at the moment."

"Willcobb," the voice rasped. "I can help you save your friends. The one who was taken . . . Kendrick. I know him. I know where this captor lives. I can help you find your friend if you take me back—"

Gawaine surged to his feet. "Stop that, Bloodroot!" he ordered sharply. "This has to be his decision entirely. No coercion. No blackmail."

The tree's limbs drooped slightly, almost as if Bloodroot bowed to Gawaine. Bloodroot rasped slowly, "Mythar, without me, the boy will be hard-pressed to find his friend. Kendrick was taken by Moonrunner, keeper of the Wolf."

Gawaine's eyes lit with recognition, but he stood firm. "Nonetheless. The boy's choice must be his own. He must take full responsibility for whatever happens, going forward.

Fate has set a possible path before him. But his destiny is his own. Success or failure, life or death, with you or without you—it is his choice."

Bloodroot fell silent. The tree lord radiated displeasure at Gawaine's command, but clearly was not going to disobey the Mythar.

Into the silence, Will asked, "If I were to keep Bloodroot within me, what would happen?"

Gawaine answered, "Because time works differently here, I cannot tell you how much time you would have on Urth to find a cure for yourself before you are overcome. Maybe months. Maybe minutes."

Will replied, "What of my friends? Eben's sister is possibly in the clutches of slavers. If Eben dies, who will rescue her? Kendrick was taken by this apprentice guy. Kendrick's father, Landsgrave Hyland, has died and may or may not resurrect. With him gone, who but us will rescue his son? Will my other friends' sacrifices be in vain? Eben dies even now of a wasting disease; Sha'Li died facing the fire hydra to reach you. Cicero is no doubt dead at the claws or teeth of a drakken—"

"What color?" Gawaine interrupted sharply.

"Green," Will answered.

The king frowned heavily, but he spoke evenly enough. "If you go back, you may be able to help your friends. With Bloodroot's help, you might stand a better chance of succeeding."

The rest of that statement hung unspoken in the air. *Assuming you do not die first.*

Gawaine might be bent on giving Will a choice, but it was really no choice at all. His feet were already set upon this path, and he would not leave Rosana. Would not abandon his friends. Would not give up this sense of hope ever again. He could never meekly serve the Kothite Empire having once tasted the savory bite of freedom upon his tongue.

"I will keep Bloodroot," Will announced.

Gawaine looked relieved but sad at the same time. "I wish things were different. I would gladly stay here forever if it would give you your freedom. But these are the fates written in our stars. Greater hands than mine dealt you the hand you now must play. Know this, Will Cobb. Your path going forward is your responsibility alone and no one else's."

Will nodded soberly. "I would have it no other way."

"So be it."

Aurelius ducked back behind an outcropping of rock and hoped against hope that Anton and his men didn't see where that blast of force magic had come from that mowed down a dozen of the most powerful rakasha mercenaries where they stood. It had been a foolish and dangerous stunt, but he *had* to do something to even the fight.

Anton, curse him, had been tossing those glass balls of airborne death like candy at babes. Each tinkling strike of shattered glass had resulted in a Boki dropping dead instantly. Anton had thinned the Boki lines to a fraction of their original strength, and his mercenaries had all but overrun the ridge.

Selea, crouching beside Aurelius once more, stared at him in shock. He shrugged. He'd warned the nulvari he planned to do whatever it took to help De'Vir's boy and his friends.

Shortly after Selea had scared a century off Aurelius's life by appearing at his side like a ghost, the Boki had mounted a charge over the ridge and into the vale that had succeeded in drawing Anton to chase after them. Once the governor had engaged in hot pursuit, the Boki force had melted back over the ridge and out of sight. The sounds of battle were fading beyond the ridge as the combat drew farther and farther from this little valley. Someday he must remember to ask Selea how he'd convinced the Boki to make that deceptive—and effective—charge. For surely it was the clever nulvari's doing.

"Who goes there?" Krugar roared in their direction.

Aurelius cursed under his breath. He should have known the Imperial Army officer would know exactly where that blast of force magic had come from.

With a glare for Aurelius, Selea stood and stepped around the boulder. *What is this? Betrayal from my old friend? After so many years? Had I misjudged Selea so badly? Is all lost? Our secret quest unmasked?* All those questions and more tore through Aurelius's shocked mind in the blink of an eye.

Aureilus was stunned when the nulvari shouted back at Krugar, sounding badly out of breath as if he'd just raced up. "Look to the governor's flanks. It is a trap. Large Boki forces approach on both left and right! Look to your defenses!"

Selea's shouted warning threw chaos into the undisciplined ranks of soldiers. They ran pell-mell toward the center of the line and Anton, hemming in the governor with a crush of his own men that effectively prevented him from throwing his gas poisons at the enemy.

Abruptly understanding Selea's gambit, Aurelius stepped out, too. "Boki! They're coming! Dozens of them!"

Selea strode forward and skidded to a stop in front of Krugar. "You must take up a defensible position. Your rear is completely vulnerable and more Boki than I can count are out there! Mayhap beyond the ridge there is a place. But this bowl valley is a death trap."

Krugar nodded in frustrated agreement. A highly trained tactician, he needed no convincing to get out of this place. With Anton temporarily trapped and overrun by his own troops, Krugar seized the moment to order his own men and all the soldiers within hearing to relocate over the hill and form a defensive formation.

Selea's ploy worked brilliantly. Anton was swept along with his panicking troops and disappeared out of sight beyond the ridge. Selea's surprise appearance also seemed to have broken the battle rage that gripped Anton and made the governor aware of the vulnerability of his position. Nothing like a little trickery to turn the tide when brute force failed.

Aurelius turned to his old friend and murmured under his breath, "Since when does your code of honor allow a nulvari to lie?"

Selea's white eyebrows shot up practically to his snow-white hair. "I never lie."

"You told Anton more orcs are coming."

"I did not lie. There is a forest full of orcs coming. It's just a question of when they will get here. The Boki will die to the last man, woman, and child to protect this place." Aurelius grinned broadly as Selea continued, "It is certainly no lie that Anton's flanks are exposed. One might safely say this entire expedition has left his drawers flapping in the breeze, in fact."

"You sly dog—" Aurelius started.

"You two," Krugar ordered briskly, "make yourselves useful and look to the defense of the flanks."

"Of course, Captain," Selea murmured politely. "It would be our honor."

Raina started as Gawaine's rather intimidating attention turned to her. He said evenly, "I gather your purpose in being here is not merely to heal your friend."

How he knew that, she had no idea. She also had no idea how to begin asking the favor she wished of him. Given what he had already told Will of how his spirit was trapped within this grove, she doubted he could help her anyway. Instead, she asked, "What can you tell us of your reign?"

"To tell you all of it would take a long time even in the way time is measured here."

"Can you tell us a little of who you were, at least?" she replied.

"I was a king in my day. I ruled over a great and peaceful nation known as Gandamere."

That was the name the Laird of Dalmigan had used. Odd that she'd never run across it in all her studies of history. Had it been expunged from the history books, then? Interesting that the knowing of this man and his kingdom seemed to threaten them. It was strange to think of the Empire having vulnerabilities, but it must have some. It just worked very hard to hide them, apparently. Or was his kingdom so old the Kothites did not know of it?

Gawaine continued, "All races were welcome in my lands. But the troll king grew jealous of my country's prosperity and invaded Gandamere. I failed to take him seriously enough at the beginning, and the mistake was a costly one. It was a bloody war. Too long. Too many lives lost. He drove deep into my lands and the war did not go well."

Will interrupted, blurting, "Rudath. That was the name of the troll king, was it not?"

Gawaine looked at Will in surprise. "Yes, it was."

"And in honor combat, you killed him the same moment that he killed you. Orcs served in his army along with trolls. I dreamed of it not long ago."

"Did you, now?" Gawaine asked thoughtfully. "I wonder who gave you the vision. What else did you see?"

Will answered eagerly, "The orcs were called the Night Reavers. When Rudath died, they were freed from unwilling slavery to him. Their descendants came to revere you as their liberator."

Raina asked carefully, "Did they revere him enough to become the guardians of his resting place?"

Gawaine gifted her with a smile for her cleverness. "I am told the Night Reavers' descendants go by the name Boki."

She asked quickly, "Who tells you about the current goings-on in our place and time?"

He gestured toward the trees. And called out, "Show yourselves, my faithful guardians!"

She gasped as dozens of elves stepped out of trees, heavily armed warriors, battle mages with brightly glowing hands, archers, and more. How she had not seen them before she had no idea.

"These are the zinnzari."

"The Children of Zinn?" Raina blurted. The old, white-haired kindari elder, had mentioned them. They served the Great Beast Spider, named Zinn.

Gawaine nodded. "The same. My elite personal guard. They and their descendants bind themselves to me in life and join me in death. When they die permanently, their spirits come to this grove where they continue to guard me for eternity. As they arrive, they share what they know of the goings-on in the material realm. Their perspective is limited, but it is more than nothing."

Will moved away from them, perhaps to examine the elven guards more closely. Or perhaps he wished to converse with Bloodroot, who sulked silently in his tree. Gawaine commenced strolling along the margin of the trees, and she took the opportunity for private conversation with him to ask, "Have you ever heard of a human king, a great mage named Hadrian?"

"Yes, of course. He was before my time, but I know the tale of his reign."

"Hadrian is said to have fallen into an eternal sleep of some kind, although not the same as yours, I believe. I am told it would take an infusion of ancient magic to wake him. If you were free of this place, could you give him such an infusion?"

"Possibly. It would depend on what put him into that sleep. And I am far from free of this place. Why do you ask this of me?"

"My family, the women of my family, are tied to him by an order of mages who serve his memory. I wish to break that bondage and free my sister and future daughters from this fate."

Gawaine frowned. Stopped walking and held out his hand to her. "If I may?" he murmured.

She laid her hand in his palm. Massive energy pulsed through him. It was as if she touched the combined life force of all living things on Urth. She gasped as his fingers closed around her hand, their warmth and vibrant magic overwhelming her senses entirely. And something deep within her, equally vibrant and pulsing with life responded, welling up from some source she knew not.

Gawaine looked nearly as startled as she felt. He held her hand a moment more and then released it. She stumbled back, shaken to her core by the brief contact.

He spoke slowly, as if testing each word before he said it to see if he would be allowed to utter it. "Hadrian was a great mage, even for our time. Devoted to his people. When the great destruction of Haelos came, he appears to have taken measures to protect his subjects."

"What great destruction?"

"Suffice it to say that there was a great battle that nearly destroyed this continent utterly."

"How did Hadrian protect his subjects?" she prompted when Gawaine did not continue.

"You say the females of your line have been tied to him since the time of his death?"

She nodded. "That is what I have been told."

Gawaine nodded as well. "I believe that Hadrian bound his power to his bride, and his bride's life force to his people. Your life force. And that of your ancestors and your descendants."

She stared. "I do not understand."

"The greatest gift of female life energy is, at its essence, the giving of life. Birth. Renewal. I believe Hadrian tapped into that. I gather one of your ancestors was near him or with him at the time of the great attack?"

Raina answered dryly, "It was their wedding day. They were about to marry."

"Even so. Hadrian tied his bride to his people. Enhanced her female life force with his magic and bonded it to his subjects to save them from destruction."

Raina stared. No one had ever hinted at such a thing to her. And to her knowledge, not to her mother or sister or any of her ancestors who would have written such a thing down.

Gawaine continued reflectively, "Such a feat must have been a tremendous drain upon him. Is it possible that he lies now in a torpor from which his spirit is too magically weakened to recover rather than an actual sleep?"

"It is entirely possible," she replied in dawning understanding. "The mages who guard him claim to be attempting to strengthen the magic of the women of our line that we might someday bear his children. Perhaps they refer obliquely to using our magic to wake him that he might have children."

Gawaine said quietly, "Over time, knowledge is inevitably lost. Facts become history, history becomes legends, legends are bent and changed, and finally they are lost altogether as they fade into the mists of time."

Was it possible that the Mages of Alchizzadon did not know about this bond of Hadrian's doing? Had the facts of it faded into their current legend of breeding a bride for a dead king, rather than protecting a line of women bonded to a people to save them?

"What would happen if the bond broke?" she asked breathlessly.

"I do not know. What I sense of this bond in you leads me to believe, though, that your well-being, your power, is still directly tied to the well-being of Hadrian's people—or at least their descendants. If they are strong, you are strong. If you grow weak, they will weaken."

"What would weaken me?"

"Diluting the bond, I expect. If the women of your line were to marry men of little or no magical power, to have children outside of the bond, those things might weaken the magic of your line and, hence, weaken the bond. You, however, are quite strong magically. I sense no dilution at all in you."

Had the Mages of Alchizzadon wittingly—and eventually unwittingly—protected Hadrian's bond through their breeding program, after all? Had their efforts to strengthen the magic of the women of the House of Tyrel strengthened the bond itself? Were they *not* the villains she'd believed them to be?

She frowned, sorting it through. The mages did the right thing, even if they did not know the truth of why their actions were good. It was reasonable to assume that Gawaine had the right of it: that over time the facts had been lost and the current tradition evolved in their place.

But it was a hard thing to let go of her hatred for the

blue-cloaked mages. They had still planned to force her into a relationship she did not want and to force her to produce children to continue the family lineage. Those things she could not forgive.

She looked up at Gawaine in anguish as the rest of it struck her and Justin's dear visage flashed through her mind. "Then I must never marry of my own choosing. I cannot have children with the man I would love lest I weaken the bond with Hadrian's people and weaken us all."

He took a quick step forward as if he would comfort her. His hands lifted, but in the end he did not touch her. He only said gently, "Nothing is writ in stone in life. You may yet find a way to have everything you wish for. There is always hope."

She did not see how he could be right. If the well-being of an entire people rested upon her and her sister to protect, she could not risk weakening the bond. Ever.

Gawaine's voice pierced her silent grief. "In the meantime, you seem to have landed in the perfect position to strengthen your bond to the people and for them to strengthen you."

She looked up at him quickly. "How is that?"

He gestured at her White Heart tabard. "Healing others strengthens you, I should think."

Funny how the fates worked. She had desperately wanted to avoid the White Heart, and yet here she was. Doing the one thing that would best serve the bond she did not know she bore.

She looked up into Gawaine's dark, wise gaze. "What happens if I die permanently?"

"It would likely diminish the spirits of your people. Mayhap the bond would jump to another female of your line. Or it could just end."

"To what effect?" she asked reluctantly.

"Perhaps nothing. Perhaps utter destruction."

She winced at that. *Well then.* Apparently, she would not be seeking a way out of the White Heart anytime soon. Nor would she be seeking to interrupt the Mages of Alchizzadon's practice of only allowing the women of her line to breed with the most powerful mages who were also natives of Hadrian's lands. She highly doubted she would ever consent to have children with one of them, however. Mayhap she could find another way to preserve the bond and have a family on her own terms. She prayed that she would be allowed the time to figure it out.

She took a deep breath as a great weight lifted from her heart.

Raina glanced across the clearing at Will, where he spoke quietly with Bloodroot. "What must I do to cure Will?"

Gawaine studied her intently for another moment before shifting subjects with her. "You must find a sanguine fruit from Bloodroot's tree. Not any Bloodthorn, mind you, but *his* tree. The one he inhabited, or at least the remnant of it. Unfortunately, I do not know where you will find it."

She nodded her understanding and attended closely as he listed off several more ingredients. He finished with, "You will need to find a master potion maker to mix the antidote. And you will need to hurry."

"How much time do we have?"

"I do not know. It will depend on any number of factors . . . how much he has tapped Bloodroot's powers and interacted with him, how strong the boy's constitution is. How much healing you can cast into both of them . . . Weeks. Days. Maybe hours. His spirit appears very weak."

"And what of you?" she asked low.

"What of me?"

"How do we free you from this place? The peoples of Urth have grave need of you."

"I know little of this Kothite Empire you speak of. Not all within it may be my enemies."

She snorted. "They will most certainly think of you as their enemy." She added belatedly and apologetically, "Please forgive me for speaking so bluntly, Your Majesty."

He made an impatient face as if apologies from her were entirely unnecessary.

"Please call me Gawaine. My kingdom is a distant memory now." She nodded as he continued, "That choice still lies ahead of me. If my path should lead me there, I will declare them ally or enemy when the time comes."

As if there were any doubt how he would declare himself once he saw the devastation wrought by the Kothites upon their subjects and upon the land.

He smiled faintly as if reading her thoughts. "Even so," he murmured.

"That reminds me," she blurted. She fumbled in her pouch and came up with the perfect wreath of living, gold-edged leaves, uncrushed in spite of its sojourn in her crowded pouch and her recent violent exertions. "What of this?"

Gawaine's face lit with pleasure. "My crown." He added with a sigh, "My regalia is all that remains of Acadia, my mother."

He reached out for it, and the moment his fingers touched the fresh leaves resting in her hand something powerful, magical, streaked through her. Something *really* powerful. A spark of enormous magic, orders of magnitude beyond anything she had ever felt before.

She clutched one side of the wreath convulsively, and interestingly enough, Gawaine did the same to the other side. She stared up at him and he stared down at her. Shock registered in his dark eyes. She felt it too. A sense deep down in her bones that the two of them shared a link. She didn't know how or why, but it drew her to him with inexorable force.

"What was that?" she whispered.

"A connection made," he murmured. "One of great power. Fate, even."

. . . a sleeping king fated to thee as thou art fated to him . . . Moto's prophecy came to her abruptly. She'd assumed Cicero's friend spoke of the Great Mage, Hadrian. But had he spoken of *this* king instead? *What on Urth?* Of a sudden, butterflies filled her belly.

Gawaine did not take the crown; rather he pressed it back into her now-trembling hands.

"But it is yours—" she started to protest.

"Not here. Not yet."

"I don't understand—"

"It is not time."

"You do not know what goes on outside of this perfect grove. How can you be so sure it is not time?" she exclaimed.

He did not answer, but rather looked over to Will. "I believe they have finished conversing," he commented.

What did he mean? A connection made? What kind of connection?

Will glanced up and caught them watching him. He muttered one last, inaudible thing to Bloodroot and started across the grassy space to join them.

She asked low, "What is fated between us?"

Gawaine stared at her intently, as if peering straight into her soul. "As I told your friend, fate is what the stars place before us. Destiny is what we choose to do with that fate. Apparently, you and I are fated to meet again." He paused, then added low, "That pleases me."

To her vast frustration, Will's arrival cut off any further conversation in that vein.

"My apologies for keeping you waiting," Will intoned politely.

Gawaine murmured back courteously. "Raina inquired about freeing me from this place. It would be prudent, I think, for both of you to hear this."

As Gawaine began to speak, it felt as if something huge . . . moved . . . in the cosmos. As if some gigantic chain of events had been set in motion. And this moment, these words, were the first link in it. If fate did exist, she and Will had affected it in a measurable and significant way by coming here. But to what end? Where would the chain lead them?

She listened with every cell of her being as Gawaine explained, "I do not know where my physical body lies on Urth. But I do know the green dragon, Hemlocke, keeps it. Find her and you will find my body. It is my physical form you must wake if you would free my spirit from this prison."

Will nodded, listening as intently as she.

"This, too, I know," Gawaine continued. "Hemlocke has bound the zinnzari into her service in return for allowing them to guard my body. Find the zinnzari and they will know how to find Hemlocke."

"Who, exactly, are the zinnzari?" Raina asked.

"You named them the Children of Zinn, already. And to anticipate your next question, I do not know where to find Zinn. You said before that the Kothites have broken the Council of Beasts. Perhaps Zinn lives, perhaps not."

"The zinnzari are a clan of kindari, then?" she blurted.

"I believe they have become such with the passing of much time, yes."

"How do we find the zinnzari?" Will piped up.

Gawaine nodded at the crown she still held. "Use that to find the other pieces of my regalia. My shield and sword, my bow, and my signet ring may still exist. I expect there will be zinnzari near at least one of them."

Raina was daunted at the prospect of yet another dangerous quest. But it was not as if she or Will could walk away from this. It was her duty to help the people of this land, and he had sworn to wake the Sleeping King. Neither of them had yet fulfilled their vows.

Gawaine was speaking again. ". . . this warning I give you. Be extremely careful who you trust and who you ask for help. Even the Great Circle cannot be trusted. Much has changed in my absence."

"Is there anyone we can trust?" she asked.

"The Elder . . . if you can find him. But I do not know what form he currently takes. He is a body walker and takes on a new race and form in each incarnation."

"The same elder whose symbol is an open eye?" she queried.

"That is him," Gawaine confirmed.

"All right then," Will said stoutly. "Find the zinnzari to find Hemlocke. Find Hemlocke to find your body. And how will we wake you once we find your body?"

"You will need an antidote to eternal slumber." Gawaine listed out a set of components they would need to create the enhanced potion, and Raina memorized them carefully.

To Will, she said, "The first order of business is to cure you. *Then* we find the zinnzari."

"The *first* order of business," he corrected, "is to get out of here alive. I don't know about you, but I do not fancy fighting any more drakken or fire hydras or giant trolls on the way out."

Gawaine chuckled. "I might be able to help with that. I am not entirely powerless within this realm."

"Is there any way we can contact you again that does not

involve fighting our way back in here and facing all those monsters?" Raina asked.

"This is my dream, and you have entered into it and become part of it. Using the connection the fates forged between us, I believe I shall be able to enter your dreams from time to time, as well. If you do not object."

Truly? "I do not object," she breathed.

"I will contact you when I can, then. Safe travels and best of luck to both of you."

And with that, Raina was falling, or at least it felt like falling, as featureless white mist rushed past her. Without warning, solid ground materialized beneath her and she thudded onto cold, hard ground a few feet in front of the great circular wooden door with its spiderweb of dream-catcher etchings. Will grunted beside her as he sat up.

"How are you?" she asked as she took inventory of her health. The fall and landing did not appear to have caused her any harm.

"I feel terrible," Will groaned. "I did not realize how bad I felt until the effects of the poison were removed for a little while."

She nodded sympathetically and helped him to his feet. "We'd better get out of here before any more monsters show up and try to eat us or cook us."

They tugged on the door, and thankfully it opened slightly under their hands.

"Wait," Will whispered. "Let me check for that cursed dog."

She waited nervously as he peered around the corner.

"In its circle," he reported.

They eased through the portal, sticking close to the wall without touching the glowing mushrooms. They pulled it shut behind them and Raina heard the latches tumble into place. It sounded as if they scrambled themselves automatically.

"One second," Will whispered. "I want to try something."

She watched impatiently as he laid hold of the two nearest hanging roots and closed his eyes. A great moving mass of roots began to move toward them, and she cried out, "Stop whatever you're doing. They're going to kill us!"

The great two-headed wolf lunged at them of a sudden, snapping and snarling ferociously, and Raina jumped reflexively.

Will's eyes opened. "Look." He pointed at the door and she was stunned to see a wall of roots weaving across it as she watched. It was unsettling seeing the tendrils moving like sentient beings.

"What did you do?" she asked in wonder.

"I asked the tree to hide the door to Gawaine's resting place. Or maybe Bloodroot asked. Or both of us. But it worked!" Will declared triumphantly before staggering against her a little.

"You're too weak to be pulling stunts like that," she chided. "You heard what Gawaine said. Channeling Bloodroot's powers speeds up your poisoning."

"Yeah, but that was cool."

She rolled her eyes as he moved off in the dim green glow of the mushrooms.

The shock of being back in a danger-fraught cave full of dead orcs and deadly roots was terrible after the utter peace and beauty of Gawaine's grove. "Where do you suppose the others are?" she asked in a hushed tone.

"Outside with Balthazar, hale and healthy, I hope."

They crept around the margins of the ritual circle, trying, and failing, not to cringe as the two-headed wolf lunged and snarled furiously at them from a distance of only a few handspans. She searched the beast's necks and did not spot the keys hanging on its collars. With the door hidden and its keys gone, she prayed the secret of Gawaine's grove would be safe until they could wake his body. In the meantime, she was more than ready to get out of here. A forest full of Anton's troops and warring Boki sounded like a pleasant stroll through a park compared to this place.

She spied the particularly thick tangle of roots that marked Gir'Ok's resting place. Will angled left confidently, and she did not question his unerring navigation skill, although she worried about its cost to his health. She spotted a pair of hanging roots recently tied back to make a triangular opening. That was Cicero's work. *Thank the stars.* They were almost out of here. Will held the vines back lightly for her with his staff and waved her forward.

She ducked through the opening and pulled up hard as the tip of a sword nicked the underside of her chin. Her panicked gaze slid down the length of the weapon—

—The sword clattered to the ground and Cicero wrapped her in a quick, hard hug.

"Thank the Lady," she breathed as she hugged him back. "You survived!"

"Nay. I died, all right. Rosana just finished resurrecting me."

The gypsy girl stepped out from behind him. "If you'd gotten here two minutes ago, you'd have seen him as naked as the day he was born."

Will swept forward and wrapped the healer in a hug that Raina suspected nigh crushed Rosana. Although the crushing looked mutual. Raina turned away as Will drew back far enough to kiss the gypsy.

"Sha'Li!" Raina cried. "You resurrected successfully. Oh, thank goodness!"

The lizardman girl took a hasty step back. "Kill you I shall, if you try to kiss me."

Raina fetched up laughing. Surly as always, Sha'Li was. "And Eben?" she asked quickly. "How does he fare?"

"I am alive," the jann replied from the shadows beyond the lizardman girl.

"Better he is after death!" Sha'Li retorted.

Raina was confused. "How is death better?"

"His arm he has. And his plague he has not. Ready to go is he—"

Cicero interrupted, "Speaking of which, now that we are all here, I think we should be on our way out of here with all due haste. The Boki die outside even now defending us."

The party headed out with the kindari leading the way. They dodged the vines, mushrooms, and orcish corpses almost without thought as they moved through the dim chamber.

"What happened after you fled the draaken?" Rosana asked Will ahead of her.

"There is much to speak of. But later, when we are all—"

His voice faded suddenly as his knees buckled, and he toppled over without warning.

Raina lunged for him, but Rosana was quicker and dropped to her knees beside him, hands on his chest. "Dead!" the gypsy cried out. "And I do not have enough mana to renew him!"

"I do not think your magic would help him at this juncture," Raina replied grimly. "He has been poisoned by Bloodroot, and it is no ordinary poison. Gawaine said we would only have a short time to heal him. But I had hoped we could at least get out of here and have a few days or weeks to make the antidote."

"Gawaine?" Cicero asked.

"He's the Sleeping King—" Raina started.

"You found him?" Cicero, Eben, and Sha'Li exclaimed in unison.

"Later!" Rosana snapped. "We must do something. We cannot let Will just die."

Raina cursed her tabard for draining herself earlier so that now she could not help her friends. If only she had a life potion in her pouch. But all she had in it was—

She fumbled frantically in her pouch and came up with Gawaine's crown. "Put it on him. Maybe its power will restore him."

Rosana jammed the crown on Will's head, and Raina waited impatiently for something to happen.

"Nothing!" the gypsy bit out. "We have to do something!" She tore Will's shirt open and slammed her palm down on the wooden disk. "Help him, curse you!" she cried.

Rosana jumped, yanking her hand away from the disk as if it had burned her.

"What?" Raina asked quickly.

But the gypsy ignored her and hesitantly put her palm back on the disk. A look passed over her face as if she was listening intently to something.

"Is Bloodroot speaking to you?" Raina asked urgently. "What is he saying?"

"There may be a way . . . a spark within me . . . I do not understand. . . ."

Raina got the impression Rosana was not talking with them. "Who is it, Rosana? Are you communicating with Bloodroot?"

"What spark?" Rosana demanded. She listened for a moment. "Oh, my. I did not know. Surely, you are mistaken. . . ."

It was frustrating not being able to follow the conversation only Rosana heard in her mind.

The gypsy muttered, "Such is the Accord that I must agree

three times. . . . Well, ask then, and quick!" she snapped. "Yes, of course I will pay the price. Any price. Just do it."

Raina frowned. What price would Bloodroot demand of Rosana? Raina wasn't at all sure that was a good thing.

Rosana's voice rose in frustration. "Yes, yes. A piece of my spirit. I understand. Get on with it."

A piece of her— "Rosana!" Raina cried "Have a care what you agree to!"

Rosana was intoning low and fierce, "Lo, do I solemnly swear to accept thine aid, Lord Bloodroot. Lo, do I solemnly swear to give up whatever part of my spirit is necessary to save Will Cobb. Lo, do I make this agreement of my free will, without coercion, trickery, or deception. Lo, do I swear to abide by this agreement unto end of time."

Twice more Rosana repeated the vow in spite of Raina's protests and pleading not to do it, to think before she leaped, to question Bloodroot more thoroughly as to what the price would be before Rosana agreed to pay it.

Then the gypsy announced, "The deal is struck. Bloodroot will help."

"At what cost?" Raina demanded frantically. "What have you done?" Gawaine had described Bloodroot as a malevolent spirit. Rosana didn't need to be making deals with one such as that.

"I do what I must. I love Will."

The gypsy laid her palm over Bloodroot's disk once more and closed her eyes. Raina actually sensed the piece of Rosana's spirit being torn from her. The gypsy moaned in pain and shuddered, but did not lift her hand away from Will and the wooden disk.

Raina thought she spied a faint, green aura about Will and Rosana for a moment, hovering at the very edge of her vision. But then it disappeared.

Will's entire body shuddered much as Rosana's had, and he took a great, heaving breath as life returned to him. Rosana collapsed on his chest, whether of exhaustion or relief Raina could not tell. Will's arms went around the gypsy.

"What happened?" he croaked.

Eben answered, "We lost you there, for a minute. But Rosana made some sort of deal with Bloodroot and he saved you."

"Ahh, no," Will groaned.

"What just happened?" Raina demanded of the gypsy. "What did Bloodroot take from you?"

Rosana lifted her head and helped Will sit up before answering, "I'm not sure. It felt like a piece of me I did not even know was there got taken and passed through Bloodroot to Will."

Will nodded, frowning. "It feels as if the three of us—Rosana, Bloodroot, and I—are . . . linked . . . somehow."

Rosana nodded. "Yes, we share this thing, together."

Will and Rosana exchanged smiles. Secret, lovers' smiles. Raina looked away, the pain in her own heart too great to bear. She was never going to have that. Could never have the family she'd always wanted.

She set aside her grief to ask Will, "How do you feel?"

He took inventory and answered, "About like before. But not dead. And yet, something is different. It is as if Bloodroot rests more easily within me."

She did not like the sound of that. Had Bloodroot found a way to take firmer control of Will? She dreaded learning what the tree spirit had in store for him next. "Shall we be on our way before you keel over again, Will?"

They assumed a marching order with Will in the lead. Their working theory was that the Boki outside would not kill him on sight. But they might take one of the others' heads off before they realized the entire party was coming out of the tunnel.

As they approached the faint light of the exit Cicero muttered from ahead of Raina, "Only the Lady knows what we shall face outside this hellhole, but it cannot possibly be any worse than in here."

Cicero was wrong. Will pulled up short in the tunnel entrance. Dawn was just breaking through the tree-tops, and the carnage around the tunnel entrance was unbelievable. Bodies lay, literally, in piles in and around the scrambled boulders lining the vale, and fighting continued on top of the corpses. Humans and orcs and rakasha sprawled together, racism forgotten in death.

A pair of figures rose up from behind the nearest boulder, ghost-like in the gray half-light. Will whipped his weapon up, as did Cicero and Eben at this new threat. He looked down the length of his staff and was stunned to recognize the face at the other end.

"Guildmaster Aurelius?" he asked in disbelief.

"Did you succeed? Did you find him? Is he awake?" the solinari bit out under his breath.

"Partially. We spoke with his spirit and know what we must do next to wake his physical form and free his spirit."

The two elves' faces lit in triumph.

Will reported, "I have closed the way to the king. Even if the governor enters the cave and vanquishes its defenses, he will not find the king."

Aurelius and Selea looked relieved at that news.

"How goes the battle out here?" Cicero asked.

Selea answered, "The Boki will gain the upper hand now that they do not have to throw all their best warriors at defending this vale. But it will be slow and bloody work."

"Landsgrave Hyland? Did he resurrect?" Eben asked quickly.

The nulvari answered dryly, "Strangely enough, his men have not engaged in combat near the governor for some time. I could not tell you if he leads his men once more or not."

Cicero snorted from behind Will, who shared the sentiment.

Eben spoke urgently. "We must find him. We have news. Kendrick has been taken. Kidnapped and likely killed by a madman."

Aurelius asked sharply, "What madman?"

Will replied, "The apprentice to the Hunter in Green."

"How know you that?" Sha'Li demanded sharply.

"Bloodroot told me. He offered to help us find this apprentice guy and Kendrick if I kept his spirit within me."

"A spirit resides within you?" Aurelius blurted in alarm.

They had no more time to talk, though, for Selea bit out low and hard, "Get down."

Everyone obeyed with alacrity, and Will spied a small rakasha force creeping silently across the far side of the vale. They moved like rogues. Or assassins.

"Where do they go, sneaking about like that?" Aurelius whispered.

"Shall we find out?" Selea replied under his breath.

The two elves moved out, and without bidding, the rest of the party followed. The rakasha pack was small, only three strong, two males and a female. White tiger changelings, which marked them as Clan Kithmar. The trio paused at the top of the far ridge, scouting ahead, and then moved off through the trees.

"I know them," Selea breathed. "They're slavers. Scum of the worst sort. Female's called Mara. The big male is Gorath, and I don't know which brother the third one is."

Will moved up beside the two elves as they paused in the same spot the rakasha had recently vacated. Dead bodies littered the grove before them. He whispered to the nulvari, "Do you see where the cats went?"

"That way." The nulvari pointed off to the left through the trees.

"But the fighting sounds to be off in that direction," Will questioned, pointing to the right.

"Nonetheless, the Kithmar move away from the battle."

"Why would they avoid the fight?"

"I have no idea," Selea murmured. "Let us follow them and see what we can learn."

Whether Selea actually tracked the Kithmar or guessed at their path Will could not tell. But the dark elf moved unbelievably quickly through the woods, forcing the others to nearly run to keep up with his swift strides. That was, until the elf screeched to a halt and Will plowed into the nulvari's back. Selea threw Will an irritated glance, but made no other sound. The assassin sank slowly toward the ground, and Will mimicked the movement, as did the others.

When they were all crouching next to a heavy stand of brush, Selea breathed, "The Kithmar search for Anton."

Why? Raina mouthed.

"How can you tell?" Will asked at the same time.

The nulvari chose to answer neither question but merely continued, "The governor has broken away from his troops and moves stealthily, with only a few guards, through the forest."

"Does he seek the treasure horde he believes the Boki have out here?"

Selea frowned. "If so, why would he move away from the vale the Boki led him to?"

"Where it *is* hidden," Will added.

"Either way," the nulvari replied, "I am curious to know what our esteemed lord governor is up to, skulking about in the woods like this."

"As am I," Aurelius growled.

Personally, Will had no desire to tangle with the governor. In fact, his impulse was to run away from Anton as fast and far as he could go. But both Eben and Raina seemed interested in tagging along with the elves. Will supposed the party stood a better chance of surviving this day and the battle raging around them with the two powerful elves than without them. Rosana threw him a doubtful look but shrugged.

"Come," Selea ordered. "Everyone stay low and move as quietly as you can."

Will's mouth twitched toward a smile at the subtle derision Selea laced into that last remark. The party sounded like a herd of thundering oxen to him, too, these days. This must be how the forest heard the passage of humans through its green corridors.

Cicero whispered, "Where are the Kithmar, now?"

"They've split up as if perhaps they lost the scent of their prey," Selea answered.

Scent, huh? If that was how rakasha tracked prey, how did the nulvari do it?

Sha'Li was staring at the ground just ahead of them. "Is that a countertrack sign, just there?" she asked no one in particular.

Selea looked where she pointed and responded, "The Kithmar are not erasing their tracks."

Aurelius added, "But Anton likely would have someone erasing his tracks if he's up to something sneaky."

Sha'Li had already slithered forward on her belly to the other side of the stand of underbrush. Will gathered she was following the trail of the countertracker's marks. After one last glance around the dim forest, Selea stood and strode forward to join the lizardman girl. They conferred in whispers and then, as a pair, moved forward quickly. Will had no idea what sign they followed, but both of them moved confidently now.

What could the governor be up to in the Forest of Thorns, breaking away from his army secretly like this? Apparently, they were about to find out, for Selea held up a fist abruptly to signal a stop as Sha'Li froze without warning ahead of them. She looked like a hunting predator who had just spotted its future dinner. The charged stillness of explosive violence clung to her.

For his part, Selea turned to ice. Cold concentration poured off his back like fog rising from an icy lake. Slowly, slowly, Selea eased forward. Cicero followed suit, step by cautious step. Will mimicked the elves' achingly slow progress with care for utter silence. It seemed to take an hour, but in a minute or two he knelt behind a fallen log no more than a stone's throw from Anton Constantine himself.

The governor was having quiet speech with a Boki!

Will eased up to peer over the log and all but fell over when he got a good look at the orc. There was a long, vertical scar over the Boki's right eye. *Ki'Raiden*. What on Urth was that particular Boki thane doing meeting clandestinely with Anton like this?

And then Will spied the sword hanging from the thane's hip. The curved, milky white blade gleamed as if lit from within. *Dragon's Tooth*. Will's father's sword! Grief and fury ripped through Will and he coiled to spring at the whoreson who'd killed his father and stolen his sword.

Eben and Cicero literally had to lie on top of Will to keep

him from attacking. The silent struggle went on until Rosana managed to breathe in his ear, "We will all die if you give away our position. Do you want *me* to die?"

It was an underhanded tactic, using his feelings for her against him, but he subsided reluctantly. One day he would kill Ki'Raiden. He would get back his father's sword and he would avenge Ty's and Serica's deaths. Just not this day.

Finished fighting? Cicero mouthed at him.

He nodded, and the elf and Eben rolled off of him cautiously.

Fury still bubbling in his gut, he turned his head slightly to hear the murmured conversation better. It lay right at the edge of his hearing, but he managed to tune out the random forest sounds and was able to make out most of the discussion.

Anton was speaking. ". . . give me Tiberius's sword."

"No," the Boki grunted. "Dis foh' my fathuh.'" Anton opened his mouth to respond but Ki' Raiden cut him off. "No ahh'gue. Mine."

Anton huffed. "Have you at least got the sanguine fruits?"

"Uhh-huh. You gah' maps?" Ki'Raiden grunted in reply.

What was this? The governor was doing some sort of trade with the Boki? To what possible end? Aurelius and Selea looked thunderstruck.

Will and the others watched as the Boki pulled out a small skin, unwrapped it to reveal a handful of bloodred fruits about the size of plums. The orc handled them carefully, using the skin to prevent his flesh from ever touching the fruits. He rewrapped the fruits and handed the whole thing over to Anton.

In return, Anton pulled a rolled parchment out of his vest. It looked to be several sheets of vellum rolled tightly together and held by a ribbon.

"All heah?" Ki' Raiden demanded.

"Yes, yes. The defenses of Talyn are all there. Both outlying lands and the keep's protections. You know what to do, right?"

Ki'Raiden grinned, flashing tusks and teeth. "Uhh-huh."

Selea edged backward on his belly, and everyone in the party followed suit carefully until they were well away from Anton and Ki'Raiden. They waited tensely where they were as Anton and the Boki parted ways and disappeared toward their respective forces.

"Now what?" Will whispered.

Selea answered, "My old friend and I have to rejoin the governor's forces and see if we can prevent a wholesale slaughter out here. If we can turn this fight around, we might just be able to dissuade the Boki from retaliating for this ill-advised attack with an invasion of the settled lands like they did the last time Anton sashayed out here to engage them."

Will had not finished absorbing that shockingly blunt observation before the two elder elves had disappeared into the trees. And just like that, he and his companions were alone once more. Silence settled around them and the members of the party traded looks of exhaustion and relief. They'd done it.

Rosana repeated Will's question. "Now what?"

Eben was first to speak. "We cannot leave. Kendrick is out here somewhere. And if I know my liege, Landsgrave Hyland will resurrect and come here immediately to search for his son. If we could find him and his men, we could get some healing."

"And food," Sha'Li muttered.

"And swords to protect us," Cicero added.

Will looked around, getting his bearings. For a moment he recalled the first time he was lost in a wood, fleeing Boki. So much had changed since then. He had changed. "Hyland died back that way. If his body has dissipated from the battlefield, we will know he has already resurrected."

Everyone nodded at Will, and he was silently elected their de facto scout. He moved out slowly, relieved not to be running through these woods for his life for once.

Maybe it was the dragging fatigue, or maybe he placed too much trust in his Bloodroot-enhanced senses, or maybe Krugar's men were just too good. But all of a sudden the woods around them exploded with soldiers brandishing weapons.

Will jolted and his staff began to come up, but then the sheer number of swords pointing at them registered. That and the fact that everyone in the party was completely without skills at the moment.

At least their captors were human.

"'Oo in the bloody winds be ye, and whot in curses be ye about, a-wanderin' out 'ere?" a gap-toothed soldier wearing a sergeant's rank demanded.

"Um, we're lost," Will replied as casually as he could muster.

"Lost? *Lost?*" the sergeant sputtered. "'Oo ever 'eard of a bunch o' kids goin' lost in these 'ere woods?"

Will improvised as the faces hardened around them. This bunch was going to kill them first and ask questions later if he didn't come up with something good, and fast. "We're looking for Landsgrave Hyland. We have important news for him regarding his son."

"So ye strolled on out in the middle of Boki lands to tell 'im?"

It sounded ridiculous to Will, too. But he nodded firmly. A chorus of voices burst out around them.

"Preposterous!"

"Take 'em to the boss."

"Aye. He'll be interested in these ones."

"Arrest 'em!"

Many voices took up that phrase, shouting for their arrest.

The sergeant nodded and straightened his shoulders. "By order of the guvnuh of Dupree, I place 'ee under arrest. Surrenduh them weapons!"

Will had no choice. He handed over his staff. His attempt to keep his belt dagger failed, though, when a soldier gestured to it as well and held out an expectant hand. They were patted down and all their weapons seized. He felt naked without any weapon whatsoever.

There was a commotion over whether or not to arrest Raina, and the soldiers settled on ordering her detained but not actually arrested. While the rest of them summarily had their hands tied behind their backs, she was allowed to stand unfettered beside them. Not that she could do a thing to help them until her magic returned. And even then, now that she was White Heart it wasn't as if she could single-handedly engineer an escape.

Not that any of the six of them were in any condition to resist the governor's men. It was laughable, really. They were treated as dangerous criminals when they could barely stand upright and four of them had resurrected within the hour and were barely clinging to life.

The soldiers tromped noisily through the woods toward some unknown destination. The squad of Imperial men seemed confident that its numbers would protect it from attack by the Boki. Personally, Will thought they were fools for thinking thus, but far be it from him to say so.

In about a half hour, they were dragged into a makeshift camp. Guards had been posted around the clearing, and soldiers lounged at rest or nursing wounds all around.

The sergeant marched them over to a small folding table with a cluster of men around it. One of them looked up, irritated, as the sergeant cleared his throat. Will winced in recognition. Krugar.

"Well now, what have we here?" Krugar commented. He peered back and forth between Will, Raina, and Rosana. "You again. What are you three doing out here . . . and with friends?"

"They sez they's lookin' fer Hyland," the sergeant answered for Will.

"Is that true?" Krugar asked shrewdly, staring down Will.

"Uhh, yes, sir. Hyland's son has been kidnapped and we believe his captor brought him in this direction. We were hoping to find Hyland and help him mount a search."

"You expect me to buy such a thin excuse?" the soldier asked, not unkindly.

"Well, yes," Will answered. With more force he added, "It is the truth."

"I highly doubt anyone who is not Boki will be alive in these woods by the morrow. The hornet's nest is well kicked."

Privately, Will had to agree.

"There is more to this story than you are telling me, boy. You shall return to Dupree as my prisoners and we will sort it out, there. The governor will want to hear the entire tale of how young Kendrick was kidnapped."

Despair coursed through Will. For all he knew, Anton had arranged the kidnapping and would kill them for having survived it. Will tried to come up with an argument that would sway Krugar, but drew a blank. And in the meantime, he and the others were dragged individually to trees and tied to them.

"White Heart, heal my men," Krugar ordered.

"I have no mana with which to do so, sir, or I gladly would. If I could be allowed a nap and perhaps a bite to eat, I might be strong enough to heal in a little while."

She was escorted over to one of the cook fires and given a bowl of something hot and stew-like. Will's mouth watered as he watched her. But then he noticed something else. She was chatting up the cook something fierce. *Traitor.* Bitter fury coursed through him that she should be coddled like a noble while they sat, tied to trees, miserable and starving.

His rancor festered for maybe a quarter hour when, without warning, the cook from the fire strolled over to where they were tied. The fellow muttered, "It ain' much, but 'ere's some crusts soaked in stew for ye."

Will took the thick, chewy crust offered to him and wolfed it down, barely slowing down to savor the thick broth soaking it. As the worst of the pains in his stomach subsided, it dawned on him that he'd been entirely irrational just now. He should have trusted Raina's intentions. Was it just him . . . or had that been a bit of Bloodroot's malice creeping forward?

The thought chilled him. Was this what he had to look forward to? Suspicion, rage, and hatred? What had he done, keeping the disk when he could've gotten it removed? The full implication of Gawaine's insistence that this be entirely his choice struck him with force. This was why the king had been so adamant. Will had no one but himself to blame for being in this mess.

He sighed and tried to settle into a more comfortable position hugging the tree. Too bad there wasn't a dryad around to free him. But the fae wouldn't show themselves to a large force of armed soldiers if he had to guess.

If Krugar's men killed Will where he sat, he could not work up the energy to care right now. What would come, would come. Despite the ground being wet and cold, the bark rough under his cheek, his eyes closed and slumber took him.

The sun was setting when someone shook Raina's shoulder. She woke groggily, disoriented. The familiar canopy of menacing black was far overhead, but where were her friends, and who was this soldier frowning at her?

"Be ye rested, 'ealer?"

She gathered magical power to herself experimentally. The familiar tingle passed across her skin and her hands glowed in the gathering dusk. "It appears so."

"Come wit' me."

She followed the soldier, but insisted on stopping where Eben lay near death, tied to a tree. It took her several minutes to channel enough healing into her friend to clear the dire wolf's plague from his blood. But once he was clean, she nodded up at the soldier, who led her away from the clearing quickly. She spied Cicero watching her and smiled her reassurance at him, but that was all she had time for before the soldier took off running.

She dutifully jogged after him, and before long arrived at a battlefield.

"'Eal the humans. Ignore the greenskins."

"That's not how it works. I heal everyone without prejudice."

"Then start 'ere, and work thy way across the field. If'n we be lucky you'll run out o' juice afore ye reach them Boki scum."

She gave the soldier her most regal Lady Charlotte look. "You do not have jurisdiction over the White Heart. I shall heal as I see fit. Now step aside."

In point of fact, the victory appeared to have gone to the humans, and although there were many wounded, there were not many dead bodies upon the ground. She did not spare much magic for the wounded, merely easing the worst of their injuries and ensuring they were ambulatory.

In a few minutes she reached the Boki line. The slaughter was horrendous. A battle mage had been at work here, and the majority of the dead had massive holes blasted in them, burned and blackened flesh bearing testament to the power of the caster who'd attacked them.

The soldier who'd tried earlier to tell her what to do hovered nearby. Apparently, he'd been appointed her bodyguard or something.

"Why'n ye wastin' good mana on such beasts?" he finally blurted.

She snapped, "I find the Boki to be honorable in the extreme, and as I recall, these are their lands. Their home. We are the invaders, here, not them!"

Her soldier escort fell silent at that.

Most of the Boki were beyond the help of a life spell, but here and there she found a wounded or unconscious one. She ran across a conscious orc and healed the worst of his wounds for him. Another orc lay right beside him, unconscious. She was surprised as she reached for the second orc, that the first one held his companion down and then nodded to her. She cast her healing into the second orc.

The newly conscious orc lurched under his friend's fists

looing around wildly. Orc number one muttered, "Bal. Tha. Zar."

The second orc struggled for a moment and then subsided all of a sudden. "Ahh. Oh. Kay."

The first orc helped the second one to his feet. With a nod to Raina, the two jogged off the field.

Krugar's man stared at the retreating pair of orcs. He lowered his weapon slowly. She declared forcefully, "These warriors are granted safe passage from the field of battle if my colors heal them. Understood?"

When the soldier hesitated, she added, "Unless, of course, you wish me to report you to the Heart and get you censured and denied healing from any Heart healer in the future."

The fellow actually took a step back from her.

"Leave me," she ordered. "You can watch from over there." She pointed at the far side of the field well behind the human lines.

She turned to the orc warrior, who grinned up at her after a fashion. "Bal. Tha. Zar," he grunted.

She smiled broadly at the orc, pleased at the compliment. "Balthazar, indeed." And then she turned her attention back to the other orcs sprawled on the ground. It was full dark before she finished, her back aching as she straightened.

She spied a tall, lone figure watching her from across the field. *Krugar.* He had taken the place of his man watching her. What was Krugar's story? He was clearly an experienced veteran, a career soldier, an officer in a foreign legion. And yet here he was in the hinterlands, serving one such as Anton. How had that come to pass? She made her way around the corpses she had been too late to help toward Krugar.

"How does a young girl gain enough rank to wear those colors? And furthermore, how does she end up way out here in the wild lands?" Krugar asked as she drew near.

"Are you in need of healing, sir?" she asked, sidestepping his questions.

"Nay."

"Then may I inquire as to the source of the blood on your tunic? It appears to come from yon slice in your side."

"That? It is but a nick."

She rolled her eyes. Warriors were all the same. They yelled to the heaven about a cut on their finger but totally ignored the gaping wounds in their sides. Exasperated, she glared up at him. "Fast or slow?"

"Just hit me," he bit out, bracing for the burn of fast healing. She blasted the magic into his side and he absorbed it without comment or even flinching. Clearly, he'd been battle healed before.

"What will you do with me and my friends?" she ventured to ask.

"As I said I would. I shall take you back to Dupree to the governor."

She kept her face neutral, as the man was watching her entirely too closely for comfort. Caution was called for around this one.

"Come," he said harshly. "I have more men down over this way. My lions were hit hard."

She followed Krugar around in the woods for what seemed like hours. Gradually, the shape of the day's earlier battle became clear to her. Krugar, his most senior battle leaders, and a powerful battle mage appeared to have joined forces and struck at the heart of the Boki forces. It looked as if the orcs had been taken by surprise by the bold move. Once the Boki had scattered into small parties, they' been easier to pick off.

"Who was your caster?" she asked Krugar as casually as she could.

"Who else? Only Aurelius could do what you have seen this evening."

Why on Urth would the solinari help the governor's forces? Was it because of his fealty oath, or was it subterfuge? Or was it nothing more than enlightened self-interest? Gawaine's warning to be extremely careful who she trusted rang in her ears.

She was surprised when she and Krugar returned to camp to see that tents had been erected, and it appeared that the soldiers planned to stay here for a few days. "Does the governor entrench, then?" she blurted.

Krugar's face might as well have been made of stone as he answered, "The governor's already well on his way back to Dupree. I stay to mop up. To collect any stray soldiers who might have gotten separated from the main force. And then to march the wounded back to Dupree at a pace they can maintain."

Stray soldiers, huh? More like deserters attempting to flee conscripted service in the governor's army.

Will's frustration was boundless as, true to his word, Krugar stayed in the Forest of Thorns for two more days, rounding up soldiers and skirmishing here and there with Boki. But for the most part, the orcs seemed satisfied to retreat deeper within their forests until the intruders left.

Eben was beside himself at being forced to leave this area. He was sure they would lose the trail of Kendrick's kidnapper and never find it again. Will tried to reassure the jann under his breath without Krugar's men overhearing, but he had to be circumspect in what he said. Eben was not appeased in the least.

For her part, Sha'Li seemed more frantic even than Eben. Whether it was captivity that made her so panicked, or the prospect of facing Anton, Will could not tell. But he half-expected her to chew off one of her arms like a wild animal and make an escape if they were out here much longer.

The third morning dawned, and Will was almost relieved to wake to Krugar's troops efficiently breaking camp. He had to give the man credit. His personal cadre was well trained and disciplined. *A fine fighting unit, curse it.*

The long march back to Dupree was slow going. The weather had gone rainy and cold and the paths were slick with mud. Raina was able to heal most of the wounded to a state where they could walk readily enough, but she could not stop the soaking rains.

Even at their leisurely pace, it took a little less than half as long to go back to Dupree as it had taken to get there. Amazing how roads and no need for stealth sped a journey along. Will had almost forgotten what it was like to openly walk in a wagon rut without diving for cover at every approaching stranger.

They reached Dupree on the fourth day of their march a bit before midday. Krugar ordered his men to tighten the prisoners' rope bindings and lash them together to hinder any shenanigans. Will cursed under his breath. The soldier was too thorough for his own good.

They passed without challenge through the main city gate—a huge, ornate affair with massive portcullises and thick wooden doors to bar the way.

As they entered the city, Will looked around in shock. Broken barrels and ruined wagons littered the streets. Storefronts were shuttered over even though it was nearly midday, and sullen-looking locals hurried on their way, throwing dirty looks at Krugar's uniformed men. The city looked worse than it had the morning after the last riots.

"What is he up to, now?" Krugar muttered from close behind Will.

A young soldier, a boy really, ran up to them about halfway across the city toward the governor's residence. "Captain Krugar, sir. Tidings. A Black Ship has been sighted entering the harbor."

Will jolted. *A Black Ship? As in a magically enhanced, Imperial Navy juggernaut vessel designed to weather the dangers of the Abyssmal Sea?* He'd heard talk of the ships around the fire of a winter eve. But never had he expected to come close to one. If only there was a way to see it—

Krugar snapped, "To the harbor, men!"

The formation turned right at the next intersection and headed downhill. The seaweed tang of salt water became strong in Will's nose. Excitement leaped in his chest. The crowds grew thicker as they neared the port, and Krugar's men had to shout and elbow people aside to make way for their formation.

Will was shocked when the troops did not stop at the end of the pier but marched right down the broad wooden dock to the very end. From here he had an unobstructed view of the mighty ship. It was indeed inky black all over. Its black sails were furled, neatly wrapped in rope, and yet it proceeded smartly toward them.

Sha'Li muttered, "Water elementals propel them, it is said."

"Silence," Krugar ordered absently, his attention entirely on the vessel as he peered through a long metal tube with a curved glass at each end.

Will jolted as a familiar voice spoke from behind him. *Selea.* "Who comes?"

Will's head swiveled, and he was not surprised to see Guildmaster Aurelius beside the nulvari. But Will *was* surprised—and elated—to see Landsgrave Hyland with the two elves.

Will would have cried out to Hyland, told him of Kendrick's capture, but Krugar had explicitly ordered the prisoners to be silent. And talk among the man's troops was that disobedience was met with swift death. And besides, Hyland moved over to Raina's side as Will watched, and the two had a quick, murmured conversation that put a deeply worried look on the landsgrave's face. Eben fell to his knees when he spied the landsgrave until a soldier hauled him roughly to his feet.

Krugar frowned. "I see Captain Kodo at the wheel. The colors of an Imperial noble also fly on the mainmast. An avarian symbol, I think."

"Syreena Wingblade, perhaps?" Selea commented. "She is quite the celebrity at court. She rose from slave through the ranks to achieve noble officer's rank."

Will noted that Krugar flinched slightly at the reference to noble officers. Had he run amok of one in Koth and been exiled down here? It would explain why he seemed such a fish out of water in the colonies.

The ship's progress was painfully slow as it spent the next quarter hour creeping forward at a snail's pace toward the pier. Time enough for Raina to sidle over to Will and murmur, "Be at ease. Hyland promises to get you all freed. And then he and his men will take us back to find Kendrick."

"Thanks be," Will muttered back.

"After that, you and I can move on to our other pressing project. Hyland thinks he can help somewhat with that."

Excellent. Will was without ideas as to how to find Bloodroot's original tree, other than it must stand somewhere in the Forest of Thorns, one of hundreds or thousands of Bloodthorn trees growing in that sprawling region.

Raina eased away, no doubt so Krugar would not spot them whispering, and Will was left to ponder how much longer he had to live before Bloodroot's poison took him. This detour to Dupree had cost him precious time that Rosana had paid dearly for and which he could ill afford to waste.

The Black Ship finally drew up alongside the pier and a bevy of sailors leaped ashore in unison, casting the mooring lines and knotting them with precision worthy of an acrobatic circus. The sailors lined up, standing smartly at attention as the gangplank was brought forth and extended toward the pier.

A furor behind Will made him glance away from the spectacle and over his shoulder. He swore under his breath. Anton was coming. His banner bobbed drunkenly through the crowd, and a phalanx of the Haelan legion shouted and cuffed aside locals. Someone fell off the dock and there was a commotion as the unfortunate fellow was fished out of the water. But Anton never slowed. He merely barged forward until he drew up beside Krugar. Will started at the smell of strong spirits and something sickly sweet clinging to the governor. Perfume to cover the other odors, mayhap.

"Ahh, Krugar. Everything cleaned up?" Anton demanded. He looked wrung out. As if he'd not slept in a long time.

"Your orders have been executed, sir."

"Good thing you're back. Cursed peasants in this city need a lesson. Unruly whoresons one and all."

As if on cue, a brawl of some kind broke out a ways down the dock. It grew until several dozen people were involved. With a low curse, Krugar dispatched a number of his men to go break it up.

Anton noticed the line of bound prisoners and demanded, "Who have you brought me, Krugar?"

"My men caught them skulking around in the forest just after you left."

Anton turned to them and examined them more closely. When he got to Will, he commented, "You're the lad with Dragon's Roar . . . ," his voice trailed off.

"What is it, my lord?" Krugar asked.

"I know him." Anton strode over to peer directly into Will's face.

Horror flooded through Will. This could not be happening! If Anton killed him or worse, he would not finish his father's quest. The people and land would not be freed. All would be lost.

"You have the look of your father about you," Anton accused. His voice rose in growing outrage. He spit, "You're De'Vir's spawn. I will have you cut down where you stand—"

Just then the gangplank thudded to the pier, distracting Anton from his threats. Will sagged in his ropes. He had to get away from here before the governor followed through on his threat. But how? Will was well and truly caught in the Empire's net. He pulled frantically at his bindings, but to no avail.

A tall, imposing man in a crisp naval-style uniform strode down the wooden bridge. He was followed closely by a smaller figure, also in an Imperial officer's uniform. The second figure was a woman, and furthermore, her entire head was covered in soft, white feathers. Will stared. An avarian!

He'd never seen one before. The mix of human and bird was actually quite attractive. As the woman neared, he saw her neck was graceful, her eyes bright and dark. Her gaze darted about with bird-like interest, taking in the fight down the pier, which seemed to be spreading rather than winding down.

"What is going on, Governor?" the tall naval officer demanded.

Anton bowed slightly. "Greetings and welcome to Dupree,

Captain Kodo. That is nothing. Merely a bit of unrest among the locals. I shall crush it before the day is out and order shall be restored."

"Why is order lost in the first place?" Kodo demanded coldly. "Are the rumors at court true, then?"

"I'm sure I have no idea what you're talking about," Anton blustered.

Kodo looked around the pier, spying Hyland and the two elves, and nodded in their direction. "Guildmaster Aurelius. Master Selea, Landsgrave Hyland."

They all bowed courteously, and Aurelius spoke for them all, saying, "At your service, my lord."

"Report on the condition of the city," Kodo ordered him tersely.

Aurelius replied, "The riots of the past two days seem to have abated for today, at least. Forced conscriptions into the Haelan legion have commenced, along with collection of the new taxes to finance expansion of the governor's armed forces."

"What's this?" Kodo demanded. "The Emperor has not authorized an increase in your legion beyond the prescribed levels."

Anton held out his hands. "Captain, I can explain. The Boki are acting up again. I have reason to believe the cursed greenskins are about to invade Dupree. I merely look to the defense of the Empire's holdings."

Hyland snorted from behind the governor, and Kodo was quick to turn on him. "Landsgrave Hyland, have you something to say?"

"If you wish, my lord."

"What say you of the greenskins? Is the governor correct?"

"Oh, aye, he's entirely correct. They are furious that the governor invaded their territories and slaughtered as many of them as he could find. I have no doubt they plan revenge for his unprovoked incursion into their lands."

"It is not like that—" Anton started hotly.

Kodo cut him off with a deadly look that effectively silenced the governor. Will literally felt the chill rolling off the ship's captain.

"Who are these prisoners of yours, Krugar?" Kodo snapped.

"I've lately come from the Forest of Thorns with the wounded troops. I caught these miscreants roaming around in the woods up there. They claim to have lost a friend of theirs, but I do not believe their story."

Kodo looked over them and zeroed in on Raina. "Does this one impersonate a White Heart member, then? She seems far too young for the colors."

Krugar answered grimly, "Oh, no. She's definitely White Heart. I've seen her do the healing . . . and gotten the complaints over it from my men."

Kodo's expression momentarily become one of commiseration with Krugar's gripe over the White Heart's stubborn neutrality and insistence on healing enemies already felled once on the field of battle.

Hyland, Aurelius, and Selea all spoke up in unison, declaring, "She's real."

Kodo nodded in their direction. And then turned his stern gaze on Raina. "Very well. With so many upstanding citizens to vouch for you, I accept your veracity. What is your name?"

"Raina of Tyrel, my Lord Captain."

"Very well, Raina of Tyrel. Now tell me. Why were you in that forest?"

"We did indeed search for a lost friend." She paused delicately and then added in a tone of regret, "It is my sad duty to inform you, sir, that we had occasion to witness the governor consorting with the Boki he claimed to attack. From the conversation we overheard, it is clear he has an arrangement with the orcs. It sounded as though he conspires with part of the Boki leadership to engineer an invasion of the outlying holdings of Dupree."

"Hey now!" Anton shouted. "She lies!"

"Silence!" Kodo hissed. The rage and power in the man's voice physically drove Will backward, his throat muscles paralyzed. He couldn't have spoken in that moment if his life depended on it. Everyone within earshot seemed similarly affected.

Kodo turned his attention back to Raina, warning, "Think carefully on what you say, Initiate Raina. Do you have proof?"

She swallowed convulsively and then said, "I have only the evidence of my eyes and ears. Along with my companions, I witnessed the governor receiving sanguine fruits from a Boki thane. To my knowledge, such fruits are mainly used in the creation of death poisons. I cannot condone such poisons, of course. In return, the governor passed what looked like several maps to the thane. Anton verbally identified them as the defense plans for Talyn, both perimeter protections and the defenses of Talyn Keep, itself."

A gasp went up among those who were close enough to hear the accusation.

"These are serious allegations, White Heart," Kodo warned.

Raina nodded. "I am fully aware of their seriousness, my lord. But I have reason to believe that if this Boki invasion occurs, many lives will be needlessly lost and much suffering will ensue. The White Heart cannot in good conscience stand by and do nothing."

Anton tried to speak, no doubt to defend himself, but Kodo was having no part of it and waved the governor sharply to silence.

Will caught the brief, triumphant glances that passed between Aurelius and Hyland behind Selea's back. The nulvari, for his part, stepped forward and bowed formally. "Well met, Captain Kodo."

Kodo nodded back and spoke more warmly. "Selea Rouge. It has been a long time. How do you fare?"

"Very well. My thanks for asking."

An elven woman as black-skinned and white-haired as Selea stepped forward beside the assassin.

Kodo smiled openly at her, his voice thawing considerably. "First Advisor Nightshade. We meet again. How have you been?"

"Well, my lord. And you?"

Will tuned out as the threesome entered into a lengthy series of inquiries among old friends about health and well wishes for one another. He perked up, though, when he heard Selea say lightly, "If I might be so bold, my Lord Captain, you may find certain documents in the first advisor's possession . . . informative."

Kodo turned to the nulvari woman. "What documents are these?"

"I believe the esteemed gentleman speaks of my journals chronicling my tenure as First Advisor. More specifically, he speaks of my records of the governor's activities since I took office working for him." She held out several large, leather-bound books that Will thought looked somewhat like his mother's financial ledger.

"What in these do you believe I need to see?" Kodo asked as he accepted the books.

"Among other things, they include true accountings of revenue and income as opposed to those amounts reported to yourself for tax collection purposes. They also record various imperial trade deals and appropriations the governor has diverted to his personal coffers. Illegally, of course. Oh, and they chronicle evidence I have gathered that implicates the governor in a plot to arrange for the Boki insurrection that nearly destroyed the colony. It was a ploy to kill his enemies and enrich himself."

Will's eyes popped open wide. That the governor had been skimming from the Empire was no surprise. But that he would arrange a lethal attack upon his own people was beyond shocking. Even Kodo seemed taken aback.

"Indeed," the captain said even more coldly than before. He spent a few minutes browsing the pages while everyone around him watched and waited in silence tempered by varying degrees of dread and eager anticipation.

As the minutes ticked by, Kodo's jaw went tight, and at some point the muscles in it began to ripple as he clenched his teeth. When Ty's jaw had done that he'd been dangerously near losing his temper and Will had generally vacated the vicinity of his father with alacrity. But today Will was trapped by the ropes binding his wrists behind him.

Kodo slammed the book shut, making everyone within hearing jump. "I have seen enough," he declared abruptly into the thunderous silence. "Governor Anton Constantine, I place you under arrest for embezzlement, graft, gross corruption, and dereliction of duty, among other charges I shall list later in my official report to the Emperor."

"What? I'm given no chance to defend myself before you level these outrageous charges? You take the word of a bunch of . . . of conspirators and criminals . . . over a governor with many long years of faithful service behind him?"

Kodo turned to Ceridwyn Nightshade. "Do I have your word of honor that everything in these journals is accurate?"

"Absolutely, my lord. My word of honor."

"Now *that* I believe, Constantine. You will be held on the

Courageous and taken back to His Resplendent Majesty for trial. Until then, you are under arrest, Constantine. Surrender your weapons to me."

"You have no authority to arrest me! How dare you. I shall take this up with the Emperor himself. You will lose your ship. Your title—"

Kodo took an angry step closer to Anton. "Did you just threaten me and my ship? You go too far now, Anton. As for begging the Emperor, he will never give you your title back after he sees the contents of these journals. And you won't have your rakasha royalty to bail you out this time. In the meantime, you are under arrest."

"This is a travesty!" Anton shouted. Will noted he made no move to hand over the golden swords hanging on his belt. "I am governor in these lands. I rule here. Not you, Kodo—"

The naval captain and Imperial Lord continued implacably, "By the authority vested in me *directly* by His Resplendent Majesty, Maximillian the Third, Emperor of Koth, I hereby remove the title of Governor of Dupree from you."

Will was so shocked, he could hardly fathom what he was witnessing. It was as if the entire order of everything had shifted. As if the entire world had shifted upon its axis. And somehow—he was not sure exactly how—he was part of whatever had been set in motion.

Forces he did not ken swirled around him, converging upon this point in space and time to a purpose he did not yet see. But one thing he knew. A blow had been struck against the Empire this day. A brick had been knocked loose from the wall of Imperial power.

Satisfaction coursed through him. One brick at a time, he would do his part to bring the Kothite house down.

Kodo glanced around at the crowd before continuing

grimly, "First Advisor Nightshade, as you are the logical choice to take over as interim governor I hereby—"

Will started when the nulvari woman interrupted. "Before you finish that statement, Captain, I must refuse the position and title of governor. This colony needs a clean start free of any taint of Anton's corrupt regime. And while I did not condone his actions, I am nonetheless not the right person for the job. My path leads in other directions."

"You are certain?" Kodo responded.

She bowed formally in the elven fashion. "I am certain, my Lord Captain." She turned and paced down the dock toward shore with all the dignity of her kind.

Will watched her departure in shock. What kind of person turned down such an honor? Such power? The world shifted a bit more out of its normal orbit. For his part, Selea looked satisfied. As if honor had been well served. What was that about?

Kodo was speaking again. ". . . Lady Wingblade, as the ranking Imperial noble present other than myself, and the only Kothite noble in this place upon whom I can count not to be tainted or corrupted by the former governor, I hereby appoint you temporary governess of Dupree until such time as a permanent replacement shall be named by the Emperor. Do you accept?"

The avarian woman looked shell-shocked. "I suppose so." Then with more strength in her voice, "Yes, Captain. I accept."

Kodo wheeled back around to face Anton. "As for you Constantine. You will return with me to the Imperial Seat and stand trial for crimes against the Empire." He gestured to his sailors. "Take him aboard the *Courageous* and lock him up—"

Anton turned without warning and barreled into the crowd.

The nearest bystanders appeared so stunned by Kodo's declaration that they did nothing to block Anton's way.

When Kodo's men would have given chase, they charged straight into the main body of Anton's guards, who seemed not to know whether to stand and fight or to flee along with their leader. The crowd roared and surged forward as sailors from the black ship and soldiers of the Haelan legion appeared to be scuffling on the dock. Will had no idea which side the locals supported, and mayhap the peasants did not know, either. The earlier brawl, which Krugar's men had mostly suppressed, flared back up, and in moments the entire pier was engulfed in fisticuffs.

A knife slipped between Will's wrists, and the ropes holding his hands fell away. Hyland's voice murmured in his ear, "My house. As soon as you can."

Will eased away from Krugar, who was busy shouting orders at his men to form up around the new governess and protect her. He saw Sha'Li slip into the crowd and disappear from sight. Rosana was already kneeling beside someone hurt on the ground, and he grabbed her arm.

"Quickly, we must go. There will be plenty of wounded to heal elsewhere."

She nodded and followed him as he plunged into the raucous crowd. He used his height and strength to protect her from the worst of the flailing fists and improvised weapons. He spied a small opening in the crush and darted for it with her in tow, slipping through it just before the gap closed behind them.

They ran, holding hands, until the worst of the fighting fell behind them. People streamed toward the shore from all over the city, and the two of them were buffeted by the crowds heading the other direction. But eventually even that abated.

"Where to now?" she panted.

"Hyland's house."

They rounded a corner and the landsgrave's walled compound loomed ahead.

"Do you suppose anyone will join us here?" she asked as they reached the barred gates.

He knocked smartly on the postern door. "Let us find out, shall we?"

One of Hyland's retainers let them into the relative quiet of the bailey. They appeared to be the first of their party to arrive. Or perhaps they were the only members of their party who planned to continue the quest.

"Is Anton Constantine really finished?" Rosana asked in a small voice.

"It appears that way." Memory of that brief glimpse of freedom Will had experienced in Gawaine's presence surged through him. Events were moving almost too quickly to comprehend, like a boulder rolling down a hill, gathering speed as it went.

Will and Rosana conversed quietly for a time about inconsequential matters. The big unanswered questions hung between them, unspoken. Would anyone else help them find Kendrick? Would the others continue the quest to finish waking the Sleeping King now that they knew full well how dangerous it would be? What would become of the two of them?

The sun was casting long shadows upon the courtyard when Eben slipped in through the postern gate. Will had been certain the jann would go after Kendrick and his sister, but it was still a huge relief to see Eben here. "How's the arm?"

Eben flexed the new arm that had regenerated upon his resurrection. "Fine. I'm just back from the Heart. The High Matriarch declared me fully cured of the plague and was kind enough to get rid of my slave mark."

Will put a hand on the jann's shoulder and said low, "I will never forget your sacrifice, my friend."

Eben nodded shortly. "A life well spent. We know what we must do next. After we find Kendrick."

"Of course." Will smiled. "Kendrick first. And then other adventures."

"No," Rosana disagreed. "Your cure first, Will Cobb. *Then* Kendrick. Then . . . the other."

"You always were a bossy little thing," Will teased her. Besides, he'd been feeling a little better since whatever she'd done with Bloodroot to save his life.

Eben's chuckle was still fading when a quick knock upon the postern door made Will turn quickly. He glimpsed a dark, shiny form slipping through the gate and into the shadows. *Sha'Li?* Now that surprised him.

Will strode over to where she lurked, looking around suspiciously. "Well met, Sha'Li," he said warmly. She lifted her chin in gruff greeting, looking as surly as ever. "What's that upon your face?" he inquired.

Her hand reached up almost shyly to brush the white lines there. They formed a stylized moon-and-stars symbol. What had she called it? The Tribe of the Moon mark? "Nothing it is," she mumbled.

If he did not know better, he would say she was embarrassed.

Rosana exclaimed, "Congratulations upon getting your mark! And a white one, no less."

"What say you?" the lizardman girl demanded in what sounded like shock. "White it be? Not black or red?"

"Nope. It's as white as Raina's tabard," Rosana replied. "It looks nice against your, uhh, scales."

"A mirror? Where find I a mirror in this mausoleum?"

Sha'Li rushed off to have a look at her mark, and came

back looking angrier that Will would ever remember seeing her. He asked, "Didn't you say the white mark in your Tribe of the Moon is for those of pure heart and a healing bent?"

Sha'Li actually snarled at him, and he grinned unrepentantly. "I knew all along you had it in you. Congratulations."

"Not one more word, pink skin. Or die you will—"

Rosana cut off Sha'Li's threat cheerfully. "As long as your Tribe lets you travel with us, I'm delighted you got your mark, white or otherwise."

Sha'Li shot back, "The Heart, upon this quest it lets you go?"

The gypsy smiled broadly. "My superiors cannot say no to a question I do not ask. I was told to watch over Will." She shrugged. "He's not done running around chasing crazy quests, so I still have to watch over him."

Will grinned. "Flawless gypsy logic."

"You don't like having a gypsy traveling companion?" Rosana demanded.

He swept her into his arms for a quick kiss. "I like it plenty," he murmured against her neck.

Light laughter sounded across the bailey, and Will looked up to see a flash of white trimmed in blue. Will was relieved. *Raina.* "Where's Cicero?" he asked her.

Sadness crossed her face. "Now that I wear these colors, I have no need of his protection. He had reason to remove himself from so much Imperial presence and has already left."

"I will miss him," Will replied soberly.

"Me, too," she sighed.

"We are all here, then," Will said. "What say we impose upon our host for provisions and be on our way?"

"Not so fast," a deep voice said from the doorway. Will looked up to see Landsgrave Hyland standing there. "While I applaud your eagerness to be on your way, you must be prepared for what lies ahead of you. Success in your future endeavors is more important than ever. The stakes have gone up considerably now that you have taken the first step."

Will looked around at the determination on the faces of his friends and pride filled him. He didn't think they'd done too badly so far. Anton was deposed, disgraced and on the run. The first brick in the wall of Kothite power had fallen. Now to turn that one brick into a mighty avalanche . . . and Will knew just the man to do it. They'd found the Sleeping King. It remained only to wake him. Somehow, someway, they *would* rouse Gawaine. Will vowed silently to his parents' fallen spirits that he would finish the second part of their quest. Soon.

Soon the king would sleep no more and freedom would awaken at long last.

EPILOGUE

Anton cursed as the underbrush caught at his rough clothing. He hated roaming around in the woods like a fugitive. Oh, wait, he was a fugitive. He alternately cursed Kodo, Ceridwyn, Selea Rouge, Aurelius, Hyland, and especially that talkative White Heart healer. They would all rue the day they'd crossed Anton Constantine. He would rule Dupree once more, and when he did he would crush them all.

Or maybe he should not wait and just crush them all now. Yes, he liked that plan better.

Where was Ki'Raiden, anyway? The greenskin had been clear. Anton was to make his way to the Forest of Thorns and the Boki would find him. So where was the cursed whoreson? Anton had been wandering around out here for two days. He was nearly out of provisions.

As if his curses had conjured the Boki thane, a voice abruptly said from in front of him, "An-ton. Why you heah?"

He pulled up sharply, twisting his ankle in a cursed hole in the doing. "About time you showed yourself. I have a proposition for you."

"Wha' that?"

"I need supplies. Safe haven in these woods for a while."

"Why? You guvnuh."

"Not anymore!" he retorted bitterly.

If orcs were capable of surprise, that emotion flashed across the thane's face. "Why help you, if you not guvnuh?"

"Because I still have information you need."

"You tell. If good, I let you stay heah."

Anton scowled. He hated negotiating from a position of weakness, but he had no choice. He had to show his cards to the orc first. "Fine. But you have to give me supplies, too."

The orc grunted his assent. And then, "Tell."

"You may have killed the Dragon. But his son yet lives."

Ki'Raiden growled deep in his chest. "Wheah? Wheah spawn of dragon? I kill now!"

That was more like it. Anton smiled coldly. "Let us speak more, my friend. . . ."

Anton and a Boki thane walked away from Kerryl's hiding place, deep in conversation. He had no care for that which they spoke of. Today was a joyous day. His mission was to find the servants of his enemy and free them. The dryads.

His wife had been one of them, so he knew them well. They were like family to him. He'd worked long to ascertain how to set them free of their bondage to the trees, and the magic was tricky. He would, in fact, be binding them to him instead, but at least they would not be trapped in their groves and would have freedom of movement. It was an improvement, at any rate.

Normally, killing a dryad's tree killed her as well. But if he used his magical dagger to pierce the heartwood and destroy only the tree's spirit, the bond between dryad and tree should be broken before the fae female perished.

As he'd suspected, they, too, had been eavesdropping on the meeting just concluded. *Nosy wenches.* He shook his head fondly. As more dryads popped out of the trees they'd been hiding in around the Boki and Anton, Kerryl crept forward.

Now. When his quarry were clustered together and distracted, chattering animatedly among themselves.

He raced around the edges of the clearing piercing tree after tree straight to the heartwood with his rune-covered black iron dagger in the shape of an edged spike. The fae screamed as they felt their trees die and the bonds break. They ran for the trees, and he roared with laughter as they slammed into the trunks, unable to pass into the wood.

One of them turned to him, wailing, "What is wrong with the trees, Moonrunner?"

"You are free now. No longer are you bound to the wood, trapped in this grove. You are bound only to me and may travel as you wish."

The dryads stared as one at him, horror writ upon their faces. The leader declared, "You are supposed to guard nature. What have you done? What have you become?"

He answered grimly, letting the darkness that consumed his spirit come forth, "I do what I must. You have no idea what comes this way, my lovelies. No idea at all."

AUTHORS' AFTERWORD

The world of Dragon Crest is real. This book describes actual characters and events from the ongoing, live, interactive game of the same name. The problems, politics, and story lines you've just read about are active today and continue to unfold.

A very special thanks goes out to Sue Keany, one of the original authors of the Dragon Crest game and wildly creative, for all her help and support over the years.

Our warmest thanks to the Dragon Crest players who have created the marvelous characters it has been our privilege to populate this book with:

- ✤ Bill Flippin, creator and player of Guildmaster Aurelius, creator and player of Lord Justinius, and creator and player of Gawaine
- ✤ Sterling Bates, creator and player of Selea Rouge
- ✤ Mark Legere, player of Anton Constantine, player of Tyviden Starfire (and Mark's actually a really nice guy in spite of carrying Anton and Starfire around in his head)
- ✤ Kevin Keany, creator and player of Captain Krugar
- ✤ Patrick O'Neal, player of Rudath, the troll king, and Balthazar of the White Heart

- ✤ Susan Keany, player of Ceridwyn Nightshade and Syreena Wingblade
- ✤ Jeanne Flippin, player of High Matriarch Lenora
- ✤ Bill Clemons, creator and player of Kadir
- ✤ Steve Lashly, creator and player of Justin
- ✤ Clint Doyle, creator and player of Cicero
- ✤ Ken Nichols, creator and player of Moto
- ✤ Mike Neveu, creator and player of Lizmorn
- ✤ Peter Miller, creator and player of Kel
- ✤ Marti Hudson, player of Adept Denia
- ✤ And a special thanks to Bill Flippin for allowing me to create and play Raina.

If you would like to come play with us in the world of Dragon Crest, we invite you to do so! You can visit www.dragoncrest .com and create your own character, and there you will find tabletop, online, and live opportunities to participate in the world and influence the continuing events you've just been reading about. Who knows? You may find yourself in the pages of a Dragon Crest book one of these days.

You may also chat directly with your favorite book characters on the Dragon Crest chat forums, and appearance schedules are posted for major characters at both gaming conventions and Dragon Crest live events. If you would like to give your greetings to Gawaine, help Will slay a monster, or have Raina heal you afterward, that's entirely possible.

Until then, safe travels to you, brave adventurer. . . .